SEVEN SHORT NOVELS

by

CHEKHOV

ANTON CHEKHOV

SEVEN SHORT NOVELS

TRANSLATED BY
BARBARA MAKANOWITZKY
WITH AN INTRODUCTION AND PREFACES BY
GLEB STRUVE

W. W. Norton & Company
New York   London

For information about permission to reproduce selections from this
book, write to Permissions, W. W. Norton & Company, Inc.,
500 Fifth Avenue, New York, NY 10110

Manufacturing by The Courier Companies, Inc.
Production manager: Amanda Morrison

ISBN 0-393-00552-6 pbk.

W. W. Norton & Company, Inc.
500 Fifth Avenue, New York, N.Y. 10110
www.wwnorton.com

W. W. Norton & Company Ltd.
Castle House, 75/76 Wells Street, London W1T 3QT

1 2 3 4 5 6 7 8 9 0

CONTENTS

INTRODUCTION

Anton Pavlovich Chekhov, who is generally recognized today as one of the greatest short-story writers in world literature, and less generally perhaps as one of the great European playwrights of modern times, was born on January 17/29, 1860,* in Taganrog, a fairly important trading port on the Sea of Azov, in southern Russia. Chekhov's family was of peasant stock. His grandfather had been born a serf on the estate of General Chertkov, the father of Leo Tolstoy's well-known friend and follower, but managed to buy himself and his family out long before the Emancipation Act of 1861. Chekhov's father rose to be a merchant. He owned a general store in Taganrog, where the writer spent his childhood and adolescence. The family was large: Anton was the third of five sons and there was also a daughter, Mariya, who never married; she lived a long life and devoted most of it to the cult of her famous brother.

The parents were old-fashioned, very religious, and Chekhov grew up in a patriarchal, conservative atmosphere of the Russian merchant class, characterized by well-enforced parental discipline and strict observance of church practices: between the ages of seven and sixteen Anton Chekhov sang regularly, with his brothers, in a church choir organized by their father. Neither Anton nor his brothers—one of them a minor writer, one an artist without much talent, and one a schoolmaster—grew up to share their parents' unquestioning faith, and there are good reasons for regarding Anton Chekhov as an agnostic; but it is wrong to represent him, with all his alleged "scientism" and positivism, as an out-and-out materialist. One of his early stories, "Easter Night" (1886), reflects his appreciation of the aesthetic side of the Russian Orthodox service, and in at least two of the stories of his mature period—"The

---

* Henceforth all the dates are given according to the old Russian calendar, which in the nineteenth century was twelve days behind the Western, and from 1900 on, thirteen days.

Student" (1894), which Chekhov himself once described as his own favorite, and "The Bishop" (1902)—it is possible to detect religious undertones; while in "The Steppe" (1888), his first longer work, we find a very sympathetic portrayal of a village priest.

Chekhov's education began in a small private Greek school (there was a large Greek population in Taganrog), but after a year he was transferred to the local State *gimnaziya* (a regular combined elementary and secondary school based on classical education, with both Latin and Greek as part of the required curriculum). Chekhov's scholastic record was far from outstanding, but he showed an early interest in literature and especially in the theatre, and wrote his first play when still a schoolboy.

In 1876 business difficulties and debts forced Chekhov Senior to move to Moscow where his two eldest sons had gone earlier to make their living. His wife followed him a little later with the two youngest children, but Anton and Ivan remained in Taganrog to complete their schooling. On rejoining the family in 1879, Chekhov enrolled in the School of Medicine at the University of Moscow, from which he was graduated in 1884. The family lived frugally and Anton had to combine his studies with breadwinning. Following the example of his elder brother Alexander, who had become a minor journalist, and in part his own inclination, Anton Chekhov began to contribute short comic stories, sketches, captions for comic drawings and cartoons, and other similar pieces to different lowbrow humorous magazines and newspapers, first in Moscow and later also in St. Petersburg. He signed these pieces with the ludicrous-sounding pseudonym "Antosha Chekhonte," which he also used for his first collection of stories. The best-known of the magazines for which Chekhov wrote in those days, one that was of a somewhat higher quality than the others, was *Oskolki* (*Splinters*). Published in St. Petersburg, it was edited by Nikolay Leykin, himself a humorous writer with a certain literary reputation, who soon came to value his young and unknown Moscow contributor.

Upon graduation, Chekhov worked for a time in a zemstvo hospital and later set up a general practice in Moscow. He spoke in those days of medicine as his lawful wife and literature as his mistress, adding: "When I get fed up with one, I spend the night with the other. Though it is irregular, it is less boring this way, and besides, neither of them loses anything through my ınfidelity." Before long, however, the "mistress" won over the "lawful wife." In later years Chekhov was to remark that he knew of no better training for a writer than to spend some years in the medical profession, and in his own work his professional training is not infrequently reflected. Even more important for him as a writer was his literary apprenticeship as a contributor to weekly or fortnightly humorous magazines and daily newspapers. It taught him to write tersely, to prune his stories of all that was superfluous. The ability to do so he came to regard as one of the writer's chief virtues. An utmost economy in the use of artistic means and, as a concomitant to it, an artistic detachment are the hallmark of his best stories.

In 1884 Chekhov published his first small collection of stories (only six of them) under the title *The Tales of Melpomene*. After that the range of his literary activities was considerably enlarged. First, he began contributing stories to a widely read, nonparty Petersburg daily, *Peterburgskaya Gazeta*. One of his stories published there in 1885, "The Huntsman," attracted the attention of the veteran writer Dmitry Grigorovich, a contemporary and friend of Turgenev and Dostoevsky, and at that time the *doyen* of letters in St. Petersburg. Grigorovich wrote Chekhov a very flattering letter and also brought his work to the attention of the poet Alexey Pleshcheev, and the celebrated journalist and publisher Alexey Suvorin. With both of them Chekhov soon contracted an intimate personal friendship. Pleshcheev, a few years later, was to sponsor Chekhov's appearance in a monthly literary magazine of high caliber. Suvorin, as early as 1886, published Chekhov's story "The Requiem" in the Sunday Literary Supplement to his daily paper *Novoe Vremya*, and this began a long association between Chekhov and Suvorin's paper and an even longer personal friendship between the two men, which, though not quite as warm after 1897, was never broken. Suvorin, himself an ex-serf and a self-made man, had begun his literary activity as an independent journalist of progressive views, but gradually moved to the right. His *Novoe Vremya* was an influential, wealthy, and widely read conservative newspaper which supported the government and its policies and was looked upon abroad as the mouthpiece of the Russian cabinet. Chekhov was essentially a nonpolitical man, and in those days certainly had no objections to Suvorin's views. Moreover, whatever the attitudes and policies of his newspaper, Suvorin himself had a shrewd and independent mind which undoubtedly appealed to Chekhov. Chekhov's letters to Suvorin are among the longest and the most interesting in his vast epistolary legacy. Even when Chekhov adopted a more progressive outlook and came to believe in the necessity of constitutional reforms for Russia, he did not break with Suvorin. The cooling-off between them was, in part at least, due to political reasons, and especially to a sharp disagreement over the famous Dreyfus affair, in which Chekhov's sympathies were on the side of Zola and his campaign. It was Suvorin, even more than Grigorovich, who helped Chekhov to strike root in the Russian literature of his time, even though the progressive circles of the Russian intelligentsia had long looked condescendingly on Chekhov's association with *Novoe Vremya;* as a whole this group did not extend its recognition to Chekhov until he began contributing to more progressive periodicals. But it was his position in *Novoe Vremya,* and the fees he commanded there, that enabled him to drop his hack work for comic magazines and to take his literary vocation more seriously. It has been said of Chekhov, and quite rightly, that he was the first major Russian writer to win wide recognition from stories printed in newspapers, though he was by no means the only one to enter literature through the "back door" of the daily press.

Chekhov's second book of short stories—*Pëstrye rasskazy* (*Motley Stories*)—was published in 1886. It was followed in 1887 by *V sumerkakh* (*In the Twilight*) and *Nevinnye rechi* (*Innocent Discourses*), and in 1890 by *Khmurye lyudi* (*Gloomy People*). Parallel with the improvement in the quality of his work, which became markedly noticeable when he no longer had to depend on keeping to deadlines and supplying editors with hastily written stories which would bring him a scanty but quick monetary reward, went a decrease in the quantity of his output: as against 129 stories and sketches in 1885 and 112 in 1886 (the first year of his association with Suvorin, when he still continued to write for some of the humorous magazines), he wrote 66 in 1887, and only 12 in 1888.

Though he had written some excellent, and typically "Chekhovian," stories before that, it is usual to date his mature period from "Skuchnaya istoriya" ("A Dreary Story," 1889). Many of his best stories were written between 1889 and 1898. Like many of his contemporaries, including some men of letters (the most notable example being Nikolay Leskov, one of the first older writers, next to Grigorovich, to give his accolade to Chekhov), Chekhov for a time succumbed to the influence of Tolstoy's ethical teaching. It is reflected in such stories of his as "Khoroshie lyudi" ("Excellent People," 1886) and "Nishchy" ("The Beggar," 1887). But this was only a passing phase, and among his later stories there are several in which he gave vent to his inner "rebellion" against Tolstoy's ideas. They include two longer stories which the reader will find in the present volume—"Palata nomer shest'" ("Ward No. 6") and "Moya zhizn'" ("My Life"). Some anti-Tolstoyan motifs will be also found in "Bab'e tsarstvo" ("A Woman's Kingdom"), "Muzhiki" ("Peasants"), and "V ovrage" ("In the Ravine").

Soon after Chekhov's graduation from the University of Moscow, the first signs of tuberculosis, which was to be the cause of his premature death, appeared; but he did not pay much attention to them. In the winter of 1889 there was a turn for the worse in his illness. Periods of great lassitude and frustration alternated with spells of hectic restlessness when he would even talk of going to America or Australia; and the next year Chekhov surprised his relatives and friends by his decision to undertake a long hazardous trip, across Siberia, to the island of Sakhalin in order to visit and describe the Russian convict settlements there. Chekhov's biographers still argue about the reasons which induced him to conceive this hazardous project, the explanations ranging from unselfish humanitarian motives to a flight from a hopeless infatuation with a married woman. The latter explanation is, however, highly unlikely, and social-humanitarian motifs undoubtedly had a say in Chekhov's project. There was no Trans-Siberian railroad in those days; Chekhov had to use all sorts of means of locomotion, and it took him a long time to reach his destination. He spent more than three months among the convicts, studying their life and background on the spot, and returned to Russia via Hongkong, Ceylon, and the Red Sea. The literary result of this journey, apart from a few stories suggested either by his stay on Sakhalin or by the return sea voyage ("In Exile," "Gusev"), was a book about the life of the convicts, a mixture of firsthand impressions and observations and statistical data. It was Chekhov's only nonfictional book and is said to have prompted some improvements and alleviations in the convicts' lot.

Soon after his return from Sakhalin, Chekhov accompanied Suvorin on a trip to western Europe, visiting Italy and France. The next year (1892) he bought a small country place at Melikhovo, not far from Moscow, where he settled down with his parents and some other members of the family and for

five years led a peaceful life, his time divided between literature, voluntary medical practice, and social work under the
local zemstvo, with occasional visits to Moscow and St. Petersburg. This relatively quiet countryside period, during which
he wrote some of his best work, came to a close in 1897,
when, on a visit to Moscow, he had a pulmonary hemorrhage.
On doctors' advice he spent the winter of 1897–1898 in Nice
and then, selling Melikhovo, made his home in Yalta, in the
Crimea, building for himself a villa on the hills above the sea
(it now houses a museum named after him). Here he spent
the greater part of his remaining years, visiting from time to
time Moscow and St. Petersburg.

Though Chekhov continued to write stories (his last story
was written in 1903), the period between 1896 and 1903
was dominated by his dramatic work. He had tried his hand
at playwriting much earlier; not counting two juvenile essays
and several one-act comedies, he wrote in 1887 his first full-
length drama, *Ivanov,* which was produced both in Moscow
and in St. Petersburg but met with little success; and a little
later, *Leshiy (The Wood Demon),* which was never published
but was subsequently reworked into *Uncle Vanya.* In 1896, the
first of his series of well-known plays, *Chayka (The Gull,*
better known in English as *The Sea Gull*) was produced by
the Imperial Alexandrine Theater in St. Petersburg. Misunderstood by the actors, the public, and most of the critics, it was
a complete flop. Chekhov fled back to Melikhovo in disgust
and disappointment, vowing that he would never again take
up pen to write another play. Even his friend Suvorin failed
to give him the comfort and encouragement he needed. But
two years later the play was taken up by the new Moscow
Art Theater, founded and directed by Konstantin Stanislavsky
(Alekseev) and Vladimir Nemirovich-Danchenko. In their
hands the play became an instant success. The name of
Chekhov as a playwright became indissolubly bound up with
that of the new theatre which was to inscribe into the history
of the modern European theatre one of its most brilliant pages.
It was quite appropriate therefore that the Moscow Art Theater
chose Chekhov's "gull" as its emblem, and that it still figures
on its curtain. It was with an eye on Stanislavsky's theatre that
Chekhov wrote two of his three last plays—*The Three Sisters*
(1901) and *The Cherry Orchard* (1904).

Chekhov's association with the Moscow Art Theater became
still closer when he married one of its leading actresses, Olga
Knipper. She played the role of Arkadina in *The Gull,* but

Chekhov had left Moscow for Yalta before the play was put on. He had seen her, however, during a rehearsal of Alexey Tolstoy's *Tsar Feodor Ioannovich,* the first play to be produced by the Moscow Art Theater, in which she played the Tsar's wife Irina. After attending this rehearsal, Chekhov wrote to Suvorin: "Irina is best of all. Had I stayed in Moscow I would have fallen in love with Irina." Later, Mme Knipper was to create the principal feminine parts in Chekhov's plays (Masha in *The Three Sisters* and Mme Ranevskaya in *The Cherry Orchard*).

Chekhov and Olga Knipper were married on May 25, 1901, but lived together little. Chekhov stayed most of the time in Yalta, while her theatrical career kept Mme Knipper in Moscow.

On January 17, 1904, the first performance of *The Cherry Orchard* took place in Moscow. Chekhov was present and was feted. In April of that year he returned to Yalta, but soon his health showed signs of deteriorating, and on the advice of his doctor he went, accompanied by his wife, to Badenweiler in the Black Forest. Death overtook him there in about three weeks: he died in the small hours of the morning on July 2, in the presence of his wife and attended by his German doctor, Dr. Schwörer, who was married to a Russian lady by the name of Zhivago. Chekhov's body was taken to Russia and buried in the cemetery of the Novodevichy Monastery.

Chekhov's literary career fell within the period marked by the fading-out of the great Russian "realistic" novel (whose three greatest practitioners were Turgenev, Dostoevsky, and Tolstoy) and the emergence of Russian symbolism, or modernism, that is, the beginnings of the second golden age of Russian poetry (now more often referred to as the "silver age"), with which Chekhov had little in common and but few direct contacts. In the history of Russian literature Chekhov thus stands as a transitional figure, alongside Maxim Gorky and Ivan Bunin. But it is not for nothing, perhaps, that Boris Pasternak, in his novel *Doktor Zhivago,* coupled Chekhov's name with that of Pushkin, who had preceded the "great age of Russian realism," when he made Yury Zhivago write in his Varykino diary:

Of all things Russian I now like best the childlike Russian quality of Pushkin and Chekhov, their shy reticence about such high-sounding matters as the ultimate goals of mankind or their own salvation. It is not that they did not understand those things, but to venture into those domains seemed to them unnecessary and presumptuous. Gogol, Tolstoy, and Dostoevsky prepared themselves for death, were restless, looked for a meaning and tried to sum up, while these two, right up to the end of their lives, were concerned with the current, private problems of their artistic vocation, and in doing so lived their private lives, treating them as a private matter of no concern to anyone else. And now their private matters have become of concern to all, and like apples picked from the trees while they are green, have ripened of themselves and are being filled ever more with sweetness and meaning.*

Chekhov worked in two principal media—the short story and the drama. In each he was something of an innovator. His reputation as a dramatist is very high today, perhaps even higher outside Russia than in his own country. But it is not indisputable. His plays have been criticized as "undramatic," and he has had some very sharp detractors, especially in Russia where two of his great contemporaries, Tolstoy and Bunin, passed very negative judgments on his plays—though both admired his short stories. It is possible that the "undramatic" qualities of Chekhov's plays were still further accentuated by their interpretation according to Stanislavsky's methods. Chekhov did not always approve of Stanislavsky's interpretation (this is particularly true of *The Cherry Orchard,* which Chekhov conceived as a "gay comedy"), nor did Vsevolod Meyerhold, that wayward genius of the modern Russian theater. Soon after his breakaway from Stanislavsky —still in Chekhov's lifetime—Meyerhold experimented with Chekhov's plays along entirely different lines.† It is certainly possible to read Chekhov's plays, not as realistic slices of life, but as works with a powerful undercurrent of symbolism (we know that Chekhov had an interest in, and admiration for, both Ibsen and Maeterlinck among the modern European dramatists).

Be that as it may, it is as a short-story writer that Chekhov

---

* See *Doktor Zhivago* (Ann Arbor: The University of Michigan Press, 1958), pp. 294–295. To keep as closely as possible to Pasternak's text, I am offering my own translation of this passage.

† This is discussed in an interesting letter which Meyerhold wrote to Chekhov. Though previously published, it was not included in the twenty-volume edition of Chekhov's *Complete Works* (Moscow, 1944–1951) because at the time Meyerhold was regarded as an "enemy of the people."

looms big in the history of modern Russian literature. This was his principal tool, an instrument which he had chiseled to perfection. More than once he toyed with the idea of writing a novel. His early completed attempt at it—"Drama na okhote. Istinnoe proisshestvie," 1884–85 (translated as "Murder at a Shooting Party: A True Story")—is generally considered a failure, unworthy of Chekhov's genius. Besides, it has elements of a parody. Later, in Chekhov's correspondence with Suvorin, we find frequent references to a novel in progress, but this novel never materialized. Chekhov did, however, write several long works, some of which are not much shorter than some of Turgenev's novels. Some of these longer stories are collected in the present volume. They can be divided into two main groups, though the division is not as clear-cut as is sometimes made out: those which deal, in the main, with individuals and their problems, as, for example, "The Duel" and "Ward No. 6";* and the others, which are mainly concerned with describing a certain social milieu, and in which Chekhov, in the words of Edmund Wilson, presents "an anatomy of Russian society . . . at the end of the nineteenth century." † Whether these latter stories can be seen, as Mr. Wilson asserts, as parallels to the plays, is, I think, highly debatable, but it is true that in such stories as "A Woman's Kingdom," "Peasants," "Three Years," "My Life," and "In the Ravine" Chekhov portrays the social milieu on a larger scale than is usual with him. All of these stories are interesting, and some of them provoked a heated controversy just because of their social-political implications (this is particularly true of "Peasants").

GLEB STRUVE

---

* See Edmund Wilson's introduction to Anton Chekhov, *Peasants and Other Stories*. (New York: Doubleday Anchor Books, 1956), p. viii.
† *Ibid.,* p. ix.

The Duel

"The Duel" was serialized in eleven issues of Suvorin's *Novoe Vremya* between October 22 and November 27, 1891, and a month later published, also by Suvorin, as a separate book. It went through several printings. In the book edition Chekhov divided the story into twenty-one chapters, instead of the original seventeen, and made a number of changes. He made still further changes when the story was, in 1901, included in his *Collected Works*.

The first idea of the story must have come to Chekhov much earlier, soon after his trip, with Suvorin, to the Caucasus. In November 1888, he wrote to Suvorin: "What a story I have written! I shall bring it to you and ask you to read it. I am writing on the subject of love. I have chosen a fictional-journalistic form. A gentleman has absconded with another gentleman's wife and is expressing his opinion about it. He parts from her—another opinion. I speak fleetingly about the theatre, about the prejudice concerning 'difference of convictions,' about the Georgian Military Highway, about family life, about the unfitness of modern intelligentsia to that kind of life, about Pechorin, about Onegin, about Mount Kazbek. Heaven forbid, what a Russian salad! My brain flaps its wings, but whither to fly I don't know."

There is no evidence of Chekhov having read his story to Suvorin. It looks as though he had abandoned it, for there is no more mention of it until the beginning of 1891, when Chekhov wrote to the same Suvorin: "My story is advancing. Everything is smooth, even; there are practically no long-winded passages. But you know what is bad? There is no movement in my story, and this frightens me. I am afraid it will be difficult to read it to the middle, let alone to the end."

Chekhov went on working on the story throughout the summer which he was spending at Bogimovo. In another letter to Suvorin, on August 6, he complained of having expended on the story "one pound of nerves," and spoke of its "intricate composition." He said that often, becoming entangled in what he was writing, he would tear it up. On August 18 he again referred to the story: "While I was writing it in devilish haste, everything got mixed up in my head; it was not my brain, but some rusty wire that was at work." In some of the letters Chekhov spoke of the story as his "novel."

The character of von Koren, and his ideas, in which one can see a mixture of Darwin and Nietzsche, may have been suggested to Chekhov by his conversations in Bogimovo with one of his neighbors there, Vladimir Wagner, a young zoologist: there was no hint of this theme in the original plan of the story, in which the love theme was to be central. There is no evidence, however, of Chekhov's firsthand acquaintance with Nietzsche before 1895, when he twice referred to the German philosopher in his letters. On February 25, 1895, Chekhov even wrote to Suvorin that he would like to meet a philosopher like Nietzsche in a railway carriage or on board a steamer and spend a whole night in a conversation with him, adding: "I regard his philosophy, however, as ephemeral. It is ostentatious, rather than convincing."

The early conception of "The Duel" is confirmed indirectly by Chekhov's later retrospective reference to it as having been written long before his account of the trip to Sakhalin; actually, the two were written more or less simultaneously, in part at least during the summer at Bogimovo.

Like many of Chekhov's longer works, "The Duel" was, on the whole, received unfavorably by the critics, though there were some exceptions. Vladimir Nemirovich-Danchenko urged Chekhov to pay no attention to what the critics said, and described "The Duel" as the best thing Chekhov had yet written. One of the critics (I. Yasinsky) saw in the story a retort to Tolstoy's *The Kreutzer Sonata.*

<><><><><><><><><><><><><><><><><><><><><><><>

I

It was eight in the morning—the hour at which the officers, officials, and travelers usually bathed in the sea after the hot, stifling night and then went to the pavilion for coffee or tea. Ivan Andreich Laevsky, a slim, blond young man of twenty-eight wearing slippers and the official cap of the Ministry of Finance, found many acquaintances on the beach when he came down to bathe, and among them, his friend Samoilenko, an army doctor.

With his big, closely cropped head, lack of neck, ruddy face, large nose, and his shaggy black brows and gray whiskers, this fat, flabby Samoilenko, who, moreover, spoke in the raucous bass voice of a line officer, made the unpleasant impression of a soldier of fortune and a bully on every new arrival; but two or three days after the first encounter, his face would begin to appear unusually kind, pleasant, and even handsome. In spite of his awkwardness and gruff manners, he was a mild man, infinitely kind, good-natured, and obliging. He was on familiar terms with everyone in town, loaned everyone money, treated everyone, arranged matches, patched up quarrels, and organized picnics on which he broiled shashlik and produced a very tasty soup of Black Sea fish; he was always using influence for somebody and writing petitions, and was always pleased about something. It was the general opinion that he had no serious faults and was liable to only two weaknesses: first, he was ashamed of his kindness and tried to hide it behind a surly look and affected gruffness, and in the second place, he liked the medical assistants and soldiers to address him as "Your Excellency," although he only held the rank of councilor of state.

"Answer me one question, Aleksandr Davidich," Laevsky began when he and Samoilenko were shoulder-deep in water. "Let's say you fell in love with a woman and became intimate with her; you lived with her, let's say, for over two years and then, as often happens, fell out of love and began feeling she was a stranger to you. What would you do in a case like that?"

"Very simple. Tell her: go where you please, Little Mother —and that's that."

"Easily said! But if she has nowhere to go? A lone woman with no relatives, without a kopeck, unable to work . . ."

"Well then? Toss her five hundred rubles down or twenty-five a month—and that's that. Very simple."

"Let's suppose you have the five hundred or twenty-five a month, but the woman I'm talking about is educated and proud. Could you really bring yourself to offer her money? And in what guise?"

Samoilenko was about to answer, but at that instant, a huge wave engulfed them both, then struck the shore and rolled back noisily over the pebbles. The friends came out on the bank and began dressing.

"Of course, it's tough to live with a woman if you don't love her," said Samoilenko, shaking sand out of his boot. "But one must take a humane view of it, Vanya. If it were I, I wouldn't let her see I'd fallen out of love and would live with her the rest of my life."

He suddenly felt ashamed of his own words, caught himself, and said: "For all of me, women might as well not exist. The devil with them!"

The friends finished dressing and went to the pavilion. Samoilenko was at home there and even had his own plates and silver. Every morning he was served a tray with a cup of coffee, a tall crystal glass of iced water, and a small glass of cognac; he drank the cognac first, then the hot coffee, then the iced water, and this collation must have been very satisfying, because afterward his eyes became oleaginous, he smoothed his whiskers with both hands and said, gazing at the sea: "Remarkably splendid view!"

After the long night, wasted on cheerless, useless thoughts which kept him from sleeping and seemed to intensify the oppressiveness and darkness of the night, Laevsky felt shattered and languid. He was no better for his dip and coffee.

"Let's continue our conversation, Aleksandr Davidich," he said. "I won't hide it, I'll speak to you frankly as a friend: things are going badly, very badly with Nadezhda Fedorovna and me! Forgive me for taking you into my private affairs, but I have to talk to someone about it."

Samoilenko, foreseeing the gist of it, dropped his eyes and began tapping his fingers on the table.

"I've lived with her two years and stopped loving her . . ." Laevsky continued, "that is, more accurately, I've realized there never was any love at all . . . These two years were a delusion."

Laevsky had a habit of carefully inspecting his pink palms, biting his nails, or crumpling his cuffs while talking. Now, too, he was doing so.

"I know perfectly well you can't help me," he said, "but I'm telling you because the only salvation for failures and superfluous people like me is in talking. I have to generalize everything I do, have to find an explanation and justification for my foolish life in someone else's theories, in literary types, in the degeneration of our aristocrats, for example, and so forth . . . Last night, for example, I consoled myself by thinking over and over: oh, how right Tolstoy was, how pitilessly right! And I felt better for it. Indeed, my friend, he is a great writer! Whatever you may say."

Samoilenko, who kept intending to read Tolstoy every day but never had, was embarrassed and said: "Yes, all writers draw from their imagination, while he writes straight from nature."

"My God," sighed Laevsky, "how crippled we are by civilization! I fell in love with a married woman, and she with me . . . We started with kisses and quiet evenings and vows and Spencer * and ideals and mutual interests . . . What a lie! We were actually running away from the husband, but we told ourselves we were running away from the emptiness of our lives among the intelligentsia. We pictured our future like this: first, in the Caucasus, while we were getting to know the place and the people, I would don a civil servant's uniform and serve the government; then we'd get ourselves a piece of land in the open country and work with the sweat of our brows, make a vineyard, fields, and so forth. If it had been you or that zoologist of yours, von Koren, instead of me, you would probably have lived with Nadezhda Fedorovna for thirty years and left your heir a rich vineyard and twenty-five thousand acres of corn, but I felt like a failure from the first day. It's unbearably hot in town, boring, there's nobody, but when you go out in the fields, you imagine poisonous scorpions and snakes under every bush and stone, and beyond the fields are only mountains and deserts. Alien people, alien nature, a lamentable culture—all this, brother, is not as easy as walking down Nevsky Prospect in a fur coat arm in arm with Nadezhda Fedorovna and dreaming about warm climates. There you need to fight not just for life, but to the death, and what kind of fighter am I? A pitiful neurasthenic, lily-handed . . . I realized the first day that my ideas about a life of labor and a vineyard—weren't worth a damn. As for love, I can tell you that living with a woman who's read Spencer and gone to the end of the earth for you is as uninteresting as living with any Anfisa or Akulina. There's the same smell of the iron, powder, medicines; the same curl-papers every morning and the same self-deception . . ."

"You can't get along without an iron in a household," said Samoilenko, blushing at Laevsky's speaking so frankly to him about a lady he knew. "Vanya, you're out of temper today, I see. Nadezhda Fedorovna is a splendid woman, cultured; you —a man of the greatest intelligence . . . Of course, you're not married," continued Samoilenko, glancing at the neighboring tables, "but that's not your fault, and moreover . . . one should be above prejudice and keep up with contemporary ideas. I'm in favor of free love, yes . . . But in my opinion,

* Herbert Spencer (1820–1903), English philosopher.

once you've become intimate, you should live together till you die."

"Without love?"

"I'll explain it to you immediately," said Samoilenko. "Eight years ago we had an agent here, an old man of the greatest intelligence. This is what he used to say: In married life, the main thing is patience. Do you hear, Vanya? Not love, but patience. Love can't last long. You spent two years in love and now, obviously, your married life has entered the period when to keep a balance, so to speak, you have to put all your patience into practice . . ."

"You believe in your old agent; his advice is meaningless to me. Your old man could play the hypocrite, could exercise patience and look at the unloved person as an object essential for his exercise, but I haven't sunk that low; if I wanted to exercise patience, I'd buy myself dumbbells or an unruly horse, but I'd leave people in peace."

Samoilenko ordered iced white wine. When they had each had a glass, Laevsky suddenly asked: "Tell me, please, what does softening of the brain mean?"

"It's—how can I explain it to you . . . a disease in which the brain becomes softer . . . as if it were dissolving."

"Curable?"

"Yes, if the disease hasn't gone too far. Cold showers, plasters . . . Well, and some internal remedies."

"So . . . so there you see my situation. I can't live with her: it's beyond my strength. When I'm with you, I can philosophize about it and smile, but at home, my spirits completely collapse. It's become so painful for me that if I were told, let's say, that I had to live with her even a month longer, I think I'd put a bullet through my head. And, at the same time, I can't possibly leave her. She's alone, can't work, I've no money, she doesn't either . . . What would become of her? Who could she turn to? There's no answer . . . Well now, tell me: what should I do?"

"Mm-yes . . ." Samoilenko growled, not knowing what to answer. "Does she love you?"

"Yes, she does, in as much as a man's necessary at her age and with her temperament. It would be as hard for her to part with me as with her powder or curl papers. To her I'm an indispensable, integral part of her boudoir."

Samoilenko was embarrassed. "You're out of temper today, Vanya," he said. "You must not have slept."

"Yes, I slept badly . . . I feel awful in general, my friend.

My head's empty, my heart's sinking, I've a kind of faintness . . . I must get away!"

"Where to?"

"Up there, to the north. To the pines, the mushrooms, people, ideas . . . I'd give half my life to be somewhere in the Moscow province or Tula, to bathe myself in a stream, to feel chilled, you know, then to wander a few hours with even the most insignificant sort of student and talk, talk . . . And how the hay smells! Remember? And in the evenings when you walk in the garden, the sounds of a piano waft from the house, you can hear a train passing . . ."

Laevsky laughed with pleasure, tears came into his eyes, and to hide them, he leaned toward the next table for matches without moving from his chair.

"I haven't been in Russia for eighteen years now," said Samoilenko. "I've even forgotten what it's like there. In my opinion, there's no country more magnificent than the Caucasus."

"One of Vereshchagin's paintings shows condemned men languishing at the bottom of a very deep well. Your magnificent Caucasus looks just like that well to me. If I were offered my choice of being a chimney sweep in St. Petersburg or a local prince, I'd take the chimney sweep's place."

Laevsky became lost in thought. Looking at Laevsky's stooping figure, his eyes fixed on one spot, his pale perspiring face and sunken temples, his bitten nails and the slipper which dangled from his heel to disclose a badly darned sock, Samoilenko was swept by pity, and, probably because Laevsky reminded him of a helpless child, he asked: "Is your mother alive?"

"Yes, but we had a disagreement. She couldn't forgive me for this affair."

Samoilenko was fond of his friend. He saw in Laevsky the good fellow, the student, the easygoing man with whom one could drink, laugh, and talk heart-to-heart. The part of Laevsky that he understood best, he heartily disliked. Laevsky drank to excess and at the wrong times, played cards, despised his work, lived beyond his means, frequently used improper expressions in conversation, wore slippers in the street, and quarreled with Nadezhda Fedorovna in front of other people —and this Samoilenko did not like. On the other hand, that Laevsky had once studied in the philological faculty, now subscribed to two thick reviews, frequently talked so cleverly that only a few understood him, and lived with a well-educated woman—all of this Samoilenko was unable to understand, and he liked it, considered Laevsky superior, and respected him.

"There's one other detail," said Laevsky, shaking his head. "Only this is between us. I'm hiding it from Nadezhda Fedorovna for the time; don't make a slip in front of her . . . Day before yesterday I got a letter that her husband died from softening of the brain."

"May he rest in peace . . ." sighed Samoilenko. "Why are you hiding it from her?"

"Showing her the letter would mean: let's go to the church to be married. But we must clarify our relationship first. When she's convinced we can't go on living together, I'll show her the letter. It will be safe then."

"You know what, Vanya?" said Samoilenko, and his face suddenly took on a sad, pleading look as if he were about to ask for something very pleasant and was afraid of being refused. "Get married, my friend!"

"What for?"

"Do your duty toward this splendid woman! Her husband died, and that's how Providence itself is showing you what to do!"

"But, understand, you queer fellow, that it's impossible. To get married without love is just as base and unworthy of a man as to serve Mass without believing."

"But you have to!"

"Why do I have to?" Laevsky asked with irritation.

"Because you took her away from her husband and assumed the responsibility."

"But I'm telling you in plain Russian: I don't love her!"

"Well, if there's no love, honor her, indulge her . . ."

"Honor, indulge . . ." mocked Laevsky. "As if she were an abbess . . . You're a poor psychologist and physiologist if you think you can manage to live with a woman with just honor and indulgence alone. A woman needs a bedroom first of all."

"Vanya, Vanya . . ." Samoilenko said, embarrassed.

"You're an elderly child, a theoretician, and I'm a young old man and a practitioner, and we'll never be able to understand each other. We'd better drop this conversation. Mustafa!" Laevsky shouted to the waiter. "How much do we owe?"

"No, no . . ." the doctor said in dismay, seizing Laevsky by the arm. "It's for me to pay. I ordered. Charge it to me!" he shouted to Mustafa.

The friends got up and walked silently along the quay. At

the boulevard they stopped and shook each other's hands in farewell.

"You're very spoiled, you gentlemen!" sighed Samoilenko. "Fate sent you a woman who's young, beautiful, cultured—and you reject her, while if God gave me a deformed old woman, but an affectionate and good one, how satisfied I'd be! I'd live with her on my own vineyard and . . ."

Samoilenko caught himself and said: "And if she were there, the old witch, she could put on the samovar."

After taking leave of Laevsky, he walked down the boulevard. As he strolled, ponderous, majestic, with a stern expression on his face, in his snow-white tunic and superbly polished boots, thrusting out his chest, which flaunted the Vladimir Cross on a ribbon, he was very pleased with himself and felt as if the whole world were watching him with pleasure. He looked from side to side without turning his head and decided that the boulevard was entirely satisfactorily laid out; that the young cypresses, eucalypti, and ugly, sickly palms were very handsome and would give broad shade in time; that the Circassians were an honest and hospitable people. "It's strange that Laevsky doesn't like the Caucasus," he thought, "very strange." He passed five soldiers with rifles who gave him a salute. The wife of an official was walking on the right-hand sidewalk with her schoolboy son.

"Marya Konstantinovna, good morning!" Samoilenko shouted to her, smiling pleasantly. "Have you been taking a dip? Ha-ha-ha . . . My respects to Nikodim Aleksandrich!"

And he walked on, still smiling pleasantly, but on seeing a military medical assistant approaching, suddenly frowned, stopped him, and asked: "Is there anyone in the hospital?"

"No one, your excellency."

"Fine, carry on . . ."

Swaying majestically, he turned toward a lemonade stand kept by a full-bosomed old Jewess who pretended to be Georgian, and said to her as loudly as if he were commanding a regiment: "Be so kind as to give me some soda water!"

II

Laevsky's coldness toward Nadezhda Fedorovna made itself felt mainly in that everything she said and did struck him as a lie or like a lie, and everything he read against women and love seemed to him to fit to perfection himself, Nadezhda Fedorovna, and her husband. When he reached home, she was sitting at the window, already dressed and combed, drinking coffee with a preoccupied face and leafing through a thick magazine; and he thought that drinking coffee is not a sufficiently remarkable occasion to merit such a preoccupied face, and that she was wasting time on a fashionable coiffure since there was no one here to charm, and no need to charm anyone. In the magazine, too, he saw a lie. She dressed and arranged her hair, he thought, in order to seem beautiful and read in order to seem intelligent.

"Is it all right if I go to bathe today?" she asked.

"Why not! If you go or don't go, I don't suppose there'll be an earthquake because of it . . ."

"No, I was asking in case the doctor would get angry."

"Then ask the doctor. I'm no doctor."

What Laevsky disliked most about Nadezhda Fedorovna this time was her bare white neck and the curls of hair on its nape; he remembered that when Anna Karenina stopped loving her husband, she disliked his ears first of all, and he thought: "How true it is! How true!" Feeling faint and empty-headed, he went to his study, lay down on the couch, and covered his face with a handkerchief to keep the flies from bothering him. Listless, depressing thoughts, always about the same thing, trailed through his mind like a long wagon train on a murky fall evening, and he fell into a drowsy, despondent state. He felt guilty toward Nadezhda and her husband, and to blame for her husband's death. He felt guilty about his own life, which he had ruined, guilty toward the world of lofty ideas, learning, and work; and this wonderful world seemed realizable and real to him—not here, on this shore tramped by hungry Turks and lazy Abkhazians—but there, in the north, where there were theaters, an opera, newspapers, and all the facets of intellectual effort. One could only be honest, intelligent, lofty, and pure there—not here. He reproached himself for not having any ideals or guiding principles in his life although he now had a vague understanding of what it meant. When he had fallen in love with Nadezhda two years ago, it had seemed to him that he had only to start living with her and to leave for the Caucasus to be rescued from the vulgarity and emptiness of his life; now he was just as certain that he had only to throw Nadezhda aside and leave for St. Petersburg to have everything he wanted.

"To get away!" he muttered, sitting up and biting his nails. "To get away!"

He pictured himself boarding the steamer and then having breakfast, drinking cold beer, talking to the ladies on deck; then boarding a train in Sebastopol and eating. Hello, freedom! The stations flash by one after another, the air becomes colder and sharper; there come the birches and firs, there comes Kursk, Moscow . . . In the refreshment rooms there is cabbage soup, mutton with *kasha*,* sturgeon, beer, in a word— no more orientalism, but Russia, the real Russia. The passengers on the train are talking about commerce, new singers, about the Franco-Russian entente; a vital, cultural, intellectual, bold life can be felt everywhere . . . Faster, faster! Here, at last, the Nevsky Prospect, Great Morskaya Street; and here is Kovensky Lane, where he once lived as a student; the dear gray sky, the drizzling rain, the drenched hackney drivers . . .

"Ivan Andreich!" someone called from the next room. "Are you home?"

"I'm here!" Laevsky answered. "What do you want?"

"Papers!"

Laevsky arose lazily, with giddiness, and yawning, shuffling his slippers, went into the next room. One of his young colleagues was standing at the window which opened onto the street and laying out some government papers on the window sill.

"Right away, friend," Laevsky said softly and went to search for the inkstand; returning to the window, he signed the papers without reading them and said: "Hot!"

"Yes. Are you coming today?"

"I doubt it . . . Not feeling well. Tell Sheshkovsky that I'll come see him after dinner, my friend."

The official left. Laevsky lay down on the couch in his room again and began thinking: "So, I must weigh all the circumstances and consider. First of all, to leave here, I ought to pay up my debts. I owe about two thousand rubles. I have no money . . . That, of course, is unimportant; part I'll pay somehow or other now, and part I'll send later from St. Petersburg. The main thing is Nadezhda Fedorovna . . . First of all, we must clarify our relationship . . . Yes."

After a short pause he reflected: Wouldn't it be better to go consult Samoilenko? "I could," he thought, "but what use would it be? I'd say something out of place to him again about boudoirs, about women, about what's honest or dishonest.

* A porridge usually made of barley or oats.

What the devil's the use of talk about honesty or dishonesty if my life has to be saved quickly, if I'm suffocating in this accursed bondage and killing myself? . . . It must be understood, finally, that to prolong the kind of life I'm leading is a villainy and cruelty which makes all the rest petty and insignificant. To get away!" he muttered, sitting up. "To get away!"

The deserted seashore, unbroken heat, the monotony of the hazy lilac mountains, eternally identical and silent, eternally solitary, drove him to despair and seemed to lull and sap him. Perhaps he was very intelligent, talented, remarkably honest; perhaps if he were not locked in on all sides by the mountains and the sea, he would have become an excellent provincial leader, a statesman, an orator, publicist, hero. Who knows! Was it not foolish to prattle about whether it was honest or dishonest if a gifted and useful man, a musician or artist, for example, broke down a wall and deceived his jailers in order to break out of captivity? Anything is honest for a man in that situation.

At two o'clock, Laevsky and Nadezhda sat down to dinner. When the cook served the rice soup with tomatoes, Laevsky said: "The very same thing every day. Why not have cabbage?"

"There is no cabbage."

"Strange. At Samoilenko's they're making cabbage soup out of cabbage and at Marya Konstantinovna's there's cabbage soup, I alone have to eat this sugary slop for some reason. It won't do, dear."

As is the case with the great majority of couples, Laevsky and Nadezhda never used to get through a dinner without caprices and scenes, but ever since Laevsky had decided he no longer loved her, he had tried to give in to Nadezhda in everything, spoke to her softly and politely, smiled, and called her darling.

"This soup tastes like licorice," he said, smiling; he made an effort to appear affable, but unable to restrain himself, said: "No one looks after the housekeeping in our house . . . If you're so sick or so busy reading, then let it go, I'll take charge of the kitchen."

In the past she would have answered him: "Go ahead," or: "I see you want to make a cook out of me," but now she just glanced at him timidly and flushed.

"Well, how do you feel today?" he asked tenderly.

"I'm all right today. Just a little weak."

"You must be careful, dear. I'm terribly worried about you."

Nadezhda had some sort of illness. Samoilenko said she had undulant fever and fed her quinine. Another doctor however, Ustimovich—a tall, spare, unsociable man who sat at home during the day and in the evenings, hands clasped behind him and holding his cane upright against his back, used to walk along the shore and cough—had decided she had a female complaint and prescribed hot compresses. Earlier, when Laevsky was in love, Nadezhda's illness moved him to pity and fear; now he saw a lie in this illness. The yellow drowsy face, listless regard, and fits of yawning Nadezhda had after her attacks of fever, and the way she lay wrapped in a blanket and looked more like a little boy than a woman during attacks, and the fact that it was stuffy and smelled badly in her room —all this, he believed, had shattered his illusion and was an argument against love and marriage.

For the second course, he was served spinach with hard-boiled eggs, while Nadezhda, as an invalid, had pudding with milk. While she first touched the pudding with a spoon and then began languidly eating it, sipping milk with a preoccupied face, Laevsky was overcome with such acute hatred on hearing her swallow that his head literally began to tingle. He realized that his feelings would be an insult even to a dog, but he was annoyed with Nadezhda, not himself, for provoking this feeling in him, and he understood why lovers sometimes kill their mistresses. He would not have done so himself, of course, but if he had been on a jury now, he would have absolved the murder.

"*Merci,* dear," he said after dinner and kissed Nadezhda on the forehead.

Going to his study, he paced from corner to corner for five minutes, glancing sidewise at his boots, then sat down on the couch and muttered: "To get away, to get away! Clarify the relationship and get away!"

He lay down on the couch and remembered again that he might be to blame for the death of Nadezhda's husband.

"It's stupid to reproach a man for falling in or out of love," he assured himself, lying down and crooking his legs to put his boots on. "Love and hate are outside our control. So far as the husband is concerned, perhaps, in an indirect way, I was one of the causes of his death, but again, am I to blame for falling in love with his wife—or his wife with me?"

Thereupon he stood up, and after finding his cap, went to see his colleague Sheshkovsky, at whose place the officials gathered daily to play vint and drink cold beer.

III

To relieve the boredom and out of kindness toward new
arrivals and people without families who had no place to eat
in the town because of the absence of hotels, Dr. Samoilenko
maintained a sort of table d'hôte. At the time described, he
had only two boarders: a young zoologist, von Koren, who
had come to the Black Sea for the summer to study the em-
bryology of the jellyfish, and Deacon Pobedov, a recent seminary graduate sent to this small town to replace the old
deacon, who had gone away for a cure. They paid twelve
rubles a month each for dinner and supper, and Samoilenko
had made each one promise on his honor to appear for dinner
punctually at two o'clock.

Von Koren usually arrived first. He would sit down silently
in the parlor and, taking up an album on the table, would
begin looking attentively through the faded photographs of
unfamiliar men in wide trousers and top hats and ladies in
crinolines and mob caps; Samoilenko remembered only a few
by name, and of those he had forgotten, he used to say with
a sigh: "Most splendid, a man of the greatest intellect!" When
through with the album, von Koren would take a pistol from
the shelf, and squinting his left eye, aim for a long time at
the portrait of Prince Vorontsov; or else he would stand in
front of the mirror and inspect his swarthy face, big forehead, black hair, curly as a Negro's, his shirt of dull-colored
cotton printed with huge flowers like a Persian rug, and the
wide leather belt he wore instead of a vest. Self-contemplation
brought him almost more satisfaction than examining photographs or the pistol in its expensive case. He was very satisfied
with his face and handsomely trimmed beard, and with the
broad shoulders which were an evident testimonial to his good
health and strong build. He was satisfied with his dashing
outfit too, from the tie, chosen for the color of his shirt, to his
yellow shoes.

While he was looking through the album and standing in
front of the mirror, in and near the kitchen, in the pantry,
Samoilenko, coatless and vestless, bare-throated, worrying and
bathed in perspiration, fussing around the tables, was preparing a salad or a sauce or meat, or cucumbers and onion for

cold soup, and meanwhile glaring angrily at the assisting orderly and brandishing a knife or a spoon at him from time to time.

"Get the vinegar!" he ordered. "That's not vinegar, I say, but salad oil!" he shouted, stamping his feet. "What did you disappear for, you brute?"

"For butter, your excellency," said the discomfited orderly in a quavering tenor.

"Hurry up! It's in the cupboard! And tell Darya to add dill to the jar of cucumbers! Dill! Cover up the sour cream, booby, so the flies don't crawl in!"

And the whole house seemed to buzz with his shouts. At ten or fifteen minutes before two, the deacon arrived, a young man of twenty-two, thin, long-haired, with no beard and barely perceptible mustaches. Coming into the parlor, he crossed himself before the icon, smiled, and extended his hand to von Koren.

"Greetings," the zoologist said coldly. "Where were you?"

"Catching chub on the quay."

"Why, naturally . . . Obviously, deacon, you'll never get down to business."

"Why not? Business isn't a bear, it won't run off to the woods," said the deacon, smiling and thrusting his hands into the very deep pockets of his white cassock.

"There's no one to beat you!" sighed the zoologist.

Another fifteen or twenty minutes passed and the dinner was still not announced, and one could still hear the orderly running back and forth between the kitchen and the pantry, his boots pounding, and Samoilenko shouting: "Put it on the table! What are you doing there? Wipe it first!"

The famished deacon and von Koren began beating their heels on the floor to express their impatience like spectators in a theater. At last the door opened and the exhausted orderly announced: "Dinner's on!" In the dining room they were met by a purple, angry Samoilenko, parboiled in the steam of the kitchen; he looked at them furiously, raised the lid from the soup tureen and served each a plateful with a horrified expression, and only when he was convinced that they were eating with relish and that the food pleased them, he sighed and sat down in his deep armchair. His face became wearily content, sensuous . . . He leisurely poured himself a glass of vodka and said: "To the health of the young generation!"

After his conversation with Laevsky, Samoilenko, despite

an excellent frame of mind, had felt a constant weight at the bottom of his heart from morning until dinnertime; he was sorry for Laevsky and wanted to help him. Finishing his glass of vodka before the soup, he sighed and said: "I saw Vanya Laevsky today. The man's having a hard time. The material side isn't reassuring, but the worst is this psychology has overtaken him. I feel sorry for the lad."

"There's a man I don't feel sorry for!" said von Koren. "If that sweet boy were drowning, I'd push him under with a stick saying: 'Drown, brother, drown . . .' "

"That's not true. You wouldn't do that."

"What makes you think so?" the zoologist shrugged his shoulders. "I'm as capable of a good deed as you."

"Then drowning someone is a good deed?" the deacon asked and laughed.

"Laevsky? Yes."

"I think something's missing in the soup . . ." said Samoilenko, wanting to change the subject.

"Laevsky is to all intents and purposes just as dangerous and injurious to society as a cholera microbe," continued von Koren. "Drowning him is a service."

"Don't pride yourself on talking that way about someone close to you. Tell me: what do you hate him for?"

"Don't talk nonsense, Doctor. To hate and despise a microbe is foolish, while to consider anybody you meet close to you without differentiation—that, thank you very much, that means giving up judgment, rejecting an equitable relationship with people, washing one's hands of it, in sum. I consider your Laevsky foul, I don't hide it and treat him as I would something foul, with full good conscience. Well, you consider him someone close to you—embrace him then; you consider him close, which means you have the same attitude toward him as toward the deacon and me, that is, none at all. You're equally indifferent to everyone."

"Calling a person foul!" muttered Samoilenko, blinking with distaste. "I can't tell you how wrong that is!"

"People are judged by their deeds," continued von Koren. "Now you judge for yourself, Deacon . . . I'm going to tell you about it, Deacon. The activity of Laevsky will be candidly unrolled before you like a long Chinese scroll, and you can read it from beginning to end. What has he been doing the two years he's lived here? Let's add it up on our fingers. First, he taught the inhabitants of the town to play vint; two years back that game was unknown here; now everyone plays vint from morning till late at night, even women and adolescents. In the second place, he's taught the residents to drink beer, which was also unknown here; the residents are obligated to him for acquainting them with the peculiarities of various sorts of vodka, so that they can now distinguish Koshelev vodka from Smirnov number twenty-one blindfolded. In the third place, people used to live with other people's wives clandestinely here on the same impulse which makes thieves steal clandestinely instead of openly; adultery was considered something people were ashamed to put on public display; Laevsky has proven a pioneer in this respect: he lives openly with someone else's wife. In the fourth place . . ."

Von Koren quickly finished his soup and handed the plate to the orderly.

"I understood Laevsky the very first month of our acquaintance," von Koren continued, turning to the deacon. "We arrived here at the same time. People like him are very fond of friendship, intimacy, solidarity, and so forth, because they always need company for vint, drinking, and eating; furthermore, they're garrulous and need listeners. We became friends, that is, he used to saunter in every day, keep me from working, and confide in me about his mistress. I was struck at first by his unusual mendacity, which sickened me. I chided him as a friend, asking why he drank too much, why he lived beyond his means and incurred debts, why he did nothing and read nothing, why he was so little educated and so little informed—and in reply to all my questions, he would smile bitterly, sigh, and say: 'I'm a failure, a superfluous man,' or: 'What can you expect, old man, from us dregs of serfowners?' or: 'We are degenerate' . . . Or he'd start weaving a long harangue about Onegin, Pechorin, Byron's Cain, Bazarov,* and call them 'our fathers in flesh and spirit.' That way, you see, it's not he who's to blame that the government parcels lie unopened for weeks and that he drinks and gets others drunk; the ones responsible for this are Onegin, Pechorin, and Turgenev, who invented the failure and the superfluous man. The cause of his extreme dissolution and indecency, you see, lies not in himself, but somewhere outside, in space. And thereby —a clever invention—it is not he alone who is dissolute, false, and foul, but we . . . 'we of the eighties,' 'we indolent, nerv-

---

* Onegin, Pechorin, Bazarov: heroes in novels by Pushkin, Lermontov, and Turgenev, respectively.

ous offspring of serfowners,' 'civilization has crippled us' . . . In sum, we are to understand that a great man like Laevsky is great even in his fall; that his dissolution, ignorance, uncleanliness, constitute a natural, historical phenomenon, sanctified by inevitability; that its causes are world-wide and fundamental, and that a candle should be lit in front of Laevsky because he is the fated victim of the times, of intellectual currents, heredity, and so forth. All the officials and ladies used to oh and ah listening to him, while it took me a long time to figure out what I was dealing with: a cynic or a clever swindler? Individuals like him, intellectual on the surface, with a little education and a great deal of talk about their own nobility, know how to impersonate unusually complex natures."

"Shut up!" flared Samoilenko. "I will not have a very noble man spoken ill of in my presence!"

"Don't interrupt, Aleksandr Davidich," said von Koren coldly. "I'm just finishing. Laevsky is a fairly uncomplicated organism. Here is his moral skeleton: in the morning—slippers, bathing, and coffee; then till dinnertime—slippers, a walk, and conversation; and at two o'clock—slippers, dinner, and liquor; at five o'clock—bathing, tea, and liquor, followed by vint and lies; at ten o'clock—supper and liquor; and after midnight, sleep and *la femme*. His being is encased in this narrow program like an egg in a shell. Whether he walks, sits, gets angry, writes, or rejoices—everything comes down to wine, cards, slippers, and women. Women play an overwhelming, fatal role in his life. He says himself he was already in love at thirteen; when he was a first-year student, he lived with a lady who had a beneficial influence on him, and to whom he is indebted for his musical education. In his second year, he bought a prostitute from a brothel and raised her to his level, that is, took her as his mistress; after living with him half a year, she ran back to the brothelkeeper, and her flight caused him no little mental suffering. Alas, he suffered so much he had to leave the university and spend two years at home doing nothing. But this was all for the best. At home he met a certain widow who advised him to leave the faculty of law and enter the philological faculty. And that's what he did. On completing his studies, he fell passionately in love with his present . . . what's her name? . . . married woman, and had to run away with her to the Caucasus, presumably in pursuit of his ideals . . . If not today, tomorrow, he'll stop loving her and escape back to St. Petersburg, also for the sake of his ideals."

"And what do you know about it?" Samoilenko muttered, looking wrathfully at the zoologist. "You'd do better to eat."

Boiled mullet with Polish sauce was served. Samoilenko gave each of the boarders a whole fish and poured the sauce himself. A couple of minutes went by in silence.

"Woman plays an essential role in every man's life," said the deacon. "There's nothing you can do about it."

"Yes, but to what degree? For each of us, woman is mother, sister, wife, friend; to Laevsky she's everything, but at the same time, only a mistress. She—that is, cohabitation with her—is bliss and the object of his life; he is gay, sad, bored, or disillusioned because of women; if life becomes tedious, a woman is to blame; if the dawn of a new life glows or ideals are discovered—look for the woman there, too . . . The only literary works or paintings which satisfy him are those in which a woman figures. In his opinion, ours are poor times and inferior to the forties or sixties solely because we do not know how to abandon ourselves to amorous ecstasy and passion to the point of self-oblivion. These voluptuaries must have a special growth in their brains akin to a sarcoma which throttles the brain and governs all their acts. Observe Laevsky sitting anywhere in company. You will notice that when a general question of some sort is raised in his presence, for example, about cells or instinct, he sits on the side line, keeps silent, and does not listen; he looks weary, disillusioned; nothing interests him; everything is vulgar and insignificant. But as soon as you begin talking about males and females, about how the female spider eats the male after fecundation—his eyes burn with curiosity, his face brightens, and the man comes to life, in short. All his thoughts, however noble, lofty, or unconcerned they may be, always have the same general meeting point. You walk down the street with him and pass a donkey, for example . . . 'Tell me please,' he asks, 'what would happen if you crossed a donkey with a camel?' And his dreams! Has he told you his dreams? It's magnificent! First he dreams he is married to the moon, then he imagines he is summoned by the police and sentenced to cohabit with a guitar . . ."

The deacon burst into ringing laughter; Samoilenko frowned and wrinkled his face angrily in order not to laugh, but was unable to restrain himself and guffawed.

"It's all a lie!" he said, wiping away the tears. "By God, it's a lie!"

IV

The deacon laughed very readily and every trifle made him roar until he had a stitch in his side and was helpless. He seemed to enjoy being with people only because they had a ridiculous side and could be given ridiculous nicknames. Samoilenko he dubbed "the tarantula," his orderly, "the drake," and he was in ecstasy when von Koren once called Laevsky and Nadezhda "the macacos." He drank in people's faces greedily, listened unblinkingly, and one could see his eyes fill with mirth and his face strain in anticipation of the moment when he could let himself go and roll with laughter.

"This is a corrupt and perverse subject," continued the zoologist, while the deacon, expecting him to say something amusing, watched his face greedily. "It's a rare thing to encounter such insignificance. His body is flabby, weak, and old, and his intellect is no different from the fat shopkeeper's wife who just gobbles food, drinks, sleeps on a featherbed and takes her coachman as her lover."

The deacon guffawed again.

"Don't laugh, Deacon," said von Koren. "It's stupid, actually. I shouldn't pay attention to his insignificance," he continued, after waiting for the deacon to stop laughing; "I should simply walk past him if he were not so harmful and dangerous. His harmfulness lies first of all in his success with women, whereby he threatens to leave a legacy, that is, to give the world a dozen Laevskys as weak and perverse as himself. In the second place, he is highly contagious. I've already told you about the vint and the beer. Another two years or so and he'll win over the whole Caucasian coast. You know how much the mass, particularly the middle layer, believes in intellectualism, in university educations, in aristocratic manners and literary language. No matter what foul thing he does, everyone will believe it is fine and proper, because he is such an intellectual, a liberal, a university man. Furthermore, he's a failure, a superfluous man, a neurasthenic, a victim of his times, and that means that everything is permitted him. He is a nice fellow, a good sort; he's so sincerely indulgent toward human weaknesses; he's complaisant, affable, accommodating, and not proud; you can drink up with him and say obscenities and carp . . . The mass, always inclined to anthropomorphism in religion and morals, has a marked preference for those godlings who have the same weaknesses as themselves. Consider what a wide field he has for contamination! In addition, he's a fair actor and a clever hypocrite, and he knows perfectly well how to play the game. Just take his tricks and dodges—for example, his attitude toward civilization. He has hardly even sniffed at civilization, but still: 'Ah, how crippled we are by civilization! Ah, how I envy those savages, those children of nature who don't know civilization!' You are supposed to understand, you see, that once, in times of yore, he was devoted to civilization with all his soul, served it uncompromisingly, but that it has exhausted, disillusioned, and deceived him; you see, he is a Faust, a second Tolstoy . . . And he treats Schopenhauer and Spencer in an offhand manner, like little boys, and claps them paternally on the shoulder: Well, now, brother Spencer? Naturally he hasn't read Spencer, but how charming he is when he says of his lady with a light, careless irony: 'She's read Spencer!' And he is listened to, and no one wants to understand that this charlatan hasn't the right to kiss the sole of Spencer's foot, much less to refer to him in that tone. To undermine civilization, authorities, other people's altars; to sling mud and wink jocosely at these things solely in order to justify and hide one's own weakness and moral poverty—only a conceited, lowly, base creature could do that."

"I don't know what you expect of him, Kolya," said Samoilenko, now looking at the zoologist guiltily rather than wrathfully. "He's a man like the rest. Not without weaknesses, of course, but he keeps up with contemporary ideas, serves the government, is useful to his country. Ten years ago there was an old agent here, a man of the greatest intelligence . . . This is what he used to say . . ."

"Nonsense, nonsense!" interrupted the zoologist. "You say he serves the government. But how does he serve it? Can you say that procedures are the better for his coming here, or officials more accurate, more honest, or more polite? On the contrary, he has just sanctioned their licentiousness with his authority of the intellectual, university man. He's punctual only on the twentieth of the month when he collects his salary; the rest of the month he shuffles his slippers at home and tries to give himself the air of doing the Russian government a great favor by living in the Caucasus. No, Aleksandr Davidich, don't defend him. You're insincere from start to finish. If you really liked him and considered him close, you'd above all not be indifferent to his weakness, not indulge him, and you'd try to render him harmless for his own benefit."

"That is?"

"Render him harmless. Since he's incorrigible, there's only one way to render him harmless . . ."

Von Koren drew his finger across his throat.

"Or drown him, why not? . . ." he added. "In the interests of humanity and in their own interests, people like that should be exterminated. Without fail."

"What are you saying?" muttered Samoilenko, getting up and looking with amazement at the zoologist's calm, cold face. "Deacon, what is he saying? But are you in your right mind?"

"I don't insist on the death penalty," said von Koren. "If it has proven harmful, then devise something else. If it's impossible to exterminate Laevsky—well then, isolate him, nullify him, send him to do public works . . ."

"What are you saying?" Samoilenko was horrified. "With pepper, with pepper!" he shouted in a despairing voice, noticing that the deacon was eating his stuffed eggplant without peppering it. "You, a man of the greatest intellect, what are you saying? To send our friend, a proud, educated man, to do public works!"

"And if he's proud and he tries to resist—in chains!"

Samoilenko was unable to utter a word and just twiddled his fingers; the deacon glanced at his stunned and truly ridiculous face and guffawed.

"Let's stop talking about this," said the zoologist. "Just bear in mind one thing, Aleksandr Davidich: that primitive man was spared types like Laevsky by the struggle for existence and natural selection. Now that our culture has significantly diminished both the struggle and the selection process, we ought to take care of the extermination of the feeble and worthless ourselves; otherwise, when the Laevskys multiply, civilization will perish and mankind completely degenerate. And we will be guilty."

"If it means drowning and hanging people," said Samoilenko, "then to hell with your civilization, to hell with mankind! To hell with it! Here's what I have to say to you: you are a very learned man of the greatest intellect and the pride of your country, but the Germans have ruined you. Yes, the Germans! The Germans!"

Since leaving Dorpat, where he had studied medicine, Samoilenko had rarely seen Germans and had not read a single German book, but, in his opinion, everything harmful in

politics and science stemmed from the Germans. He himself
could not say where he had gotten this opinion, but he maintained it firmly.

"Yes, the Germans!" he repeated again. "Let's go have tea."

The three got up, and putting on their hats, went out into
the little garden and sat down there under the shade of the
pale maples, pear trees, and a chestnut tree. The zoologist and
the deacon sat on a bench near the little table, while Samoilenko dropped down into a wicker armchair with a broad
sloping back. The orderly served tea, jam, and a bottle of
sirup.

It was very hot, ninety degrees in the shade. The sultry air
hung motionless, stagnant, and a long spider web stretching
from the chestnut tree to the ground dangled weakly, inert.

The deacon took up the guitar which always lay on the
ground near the table, tuned it, and began singing softly in a
thin voice: "Round the tavern table were the seminary lads,"
but immediately fell silent because of the heat, mopped his
forehead, and looked up at the burning blue sky. Samoilenko
was dozing. He felt intoxicated and weak from the sultriness,
the stillness, and the delicious after-dinner drowsiness which
quickly overpowered all his limbs. His arms dangled; his eyes
grew small; his head sank on his chest. He glanced up at
von Koren and the deacon with tearful tenderness and muttered: "The younger generation . . . A star of science and a
luminary of the church . . . I'll wager this long-skirted hal-
lelujah will rise into a prelate and I don't doubt we'll have to
kiss his little hand . . . Well . . . God willing . . ."

Soon a snore was heard. Von Koren and the deacon finished
their tea and went out in the street.

"Are you off to the quay to catch chub again?" asked the
zoologist.

"No, it's a bit hot."

"Come to my place. You can wrap a parcel and copy something for me. Incidentally, we can have a chat about what you
are to be doing. You must work, Deacon. This will never do."

"Your words are just and logical," said the deacon, "but my
laziness finds its excuse in my present living conditions. As
you know, the uncertainty of a situation significantly contrib-
utes to making people apathetic. God only knows whether I
was sent here temporarily or permanently; I live in uncertainty and my deaconess is vegetating at her father's and
lonely. And, I confess, my brain has grown feeble from the
heat."

"All nonsense," said the zoologist. "You can get used to the heat, and you can get used to being without the deaconess. Indulgence won't do. You must take yourself in hand."

◇◇◇◇◇◇◇◇◇◇◇◇◇◇◇◇◇◇◇◇◇◇◇◇◇◇◇◇◇◇◇◇

V

Nadezhda went to bathe in the morning and behind her, with a pitcher, a copper washbasin, towels, and a sponge, came her cook, Olga. There were two strange steamers with dirty white funnels, evidently foreign freighters, in the bay. Some men in white with white shoes were walking along the quay and shouting loudly in French, receiving answers from the ships. The bells of the little town church were ringing briskly.

"Today is Sunday!" Nadezhda remembered with satisfaction.

She felt completely well and was in a gay holiday mood. In her new, loose dress made out of thick raw silk shirting and a big straw hat, whose broad brim was firmly tilted toward her ears so that her face appeared to be looking out of a little box, she considered herself very attractive. She was thinking that there was only one young, beautiful, well-educated woman in the whole town—and that was she; and that she alone knew how to dress inexpensively, elegantly, and with taste. For example, this dress cost only twenty-two rubles, and yet how pretty it was! In the whole town, she alone knew how to be attractive, and there were many men, who therefore must all, willy-nilly, envy Laevsky.

She was glad Laevsky had been cold to her lately, distantly polite, and at times even insolent and rude; she had previously met all his sallies and contemptuous, cold, or strange, unfathomable glances with tears, reproaches, and threats to leave him or to starve herself to death; now she just blushed, looked guiltily at him, and was glad that he was not affectionate with her. She would have found it preferable and more agreeable if he had rebuked or threatened her, because she felt infinitely guilty toward him. She felt guilty first for not sympathizing with his dreams of a life of labor, for the sake of which he had thrown aside St. Petersburg and come here to the Caucasus; and she was certain he had been angry with her recently for precisely that reason. When she had left for the Caucasus, she had thought she would find a secluded little nook on the shore here the first day, a cozy little garden with shade, birds, and rivulets, where she could plant flowers and vegetables, rear ducks and chickens, receive her neighbors, nurse poor peasants, and distribute books to them. The Caucasus had turned out to consist of bare mountains, forests, and huge valleys where one had to spend a long time searching, laboring, and building; where there were no neighbors of any kind, it was very hot, and you could be robbed. Laevsky had been in no hurry to acquire a piece of land. She was glad of that, and it was as if both of them had agreed wordlessly not to allude to the life of labor. His keeping silent, she thought, meant he was angry with her for keeping silent.

In the second place, without his knowledge, she had borrowed up to three hundred rubles for a few trifles in Achmianov's store during these two years. She borrowed a little for material, for silk, for a parasol, and the debt had accumulated imperceptibly.

"I'll tell him about it today . . ." she decided, but immediately reasoned that given Laevsky's present frame of mind, it would hardly be a good time to tell him about the debt.

In the third place, she had received the local police inspector, Kirilin, at her house twice during Laevsky's absence: once in the morning when Laevsky had gone to bathe, and the second time at midnight, when he was playing cards. Recalling this, Nadezhda flushed and glanced at the cook as if afraid the latter might have overheard her thoughts. The long, unbearably hot, boring days, the beautiful, tedious evenings, the stifling nights, and this whole life in which you don't know how to spend the useless hours from morning to evening, added to the fixed idea that she was the most beautiful young woman in town and that her youth was being frittered away; and Laevsky himself, honest, idealistic, but monotonous, constantly shuffling his slippers, biting his nails, and fatiguing her with his caprices—had led to her being little by little possessed by desire, and like a lunatic she thought about one and the same thing, day and night. In her breathing, glance, tone of voice, and gait, she was conscious only of desire; the sound of the sea told her one must love, the evening darkness—the same thing, the mountains—the same . . . And when Kirilin began paying court to her, she was not strong enough and, neither wanting nor able to resist, gave herself to him . . .

The foreign steamers and men in white now made her think for some reason of a huge reception hall; the strains of a waltz began ringing in her ears along with the French words, and her heart beat with inexplicable joy. She felt a craving to dance and talk French.

With joy she reasoned that there was nothing terrible about her infidelity. Her heart had taken no part in it; she still loved Laevsky, and this was clear in that she was jealous of him, sorry for him, and longed for him when he was not home. Kirilin had turned out to be uninteresting and rather coarse, although handsome; everything was finished with him now and there would not be anything more. What had been was past; it was no one's business, and even if Laevsky heard about it, he would not believe it.

There was only one bathhouse on the shore, for women; the men bathed under the open sky. On going into the bathhouse, Nadezhda found an older woman, Marya Konstantinovna Bityugova, the wife of an official, with her fifteen-year-old daughter, Katya, a preparatory school student; they were sitting on a bench and undressing. Marya Konstantinovna was a good, enthusiastic, and tactful individual who talked with a drawl and a touch of pathos. She had been a governess until the age of thirty-two, then had married an official, Bityugov, a rather small, bald man who brushed his hair over his temples and was very mild. His wife was still in love with him, jealous of him, still blushed at the word "love," and informed everyone that she was very happy.

"My dear!" she exclaimed enthusiastically on seeing Nadezhda, and she assumed the expression all her acquaintances referred to as sugar-coated. "Sweet, how nice that you came! We'll bathe together—it's enchanting!"

Olga swiftly threw off her own dress and chemise, and began undressing her mistress.

"It's not as hot today as yesterday, is it?" said Nadezhda, shrinking from the rough touch of the naked cook. "Yesterday I almost died from the heat."

"Oh yes, my sweet! I could hardly breathe myself. Will you believe it, I bathed three times yesterday . . . imagine, sweet, three times! Nikodim Aleksandrich was even worried."

"Is it possible to be that homely?" thought Nadezhda, looking at Olga and the official's wife; she glanced at Katya and thought: "The girl's not badly built."

"Your Nikodim Aleksandrich is very, very sweet!" she said. "I've simply fallen in love with him."

"Ha-ha-ha!" Marya Konstantinovna laughed forcibly. "That's enchanting!"

Freed of her clothes, Nadezhda felt a desire to fly. And

she felt that if she waved her arms she would certainly soar upward. When she was undressed, she noticed Olga looking at her white body with distaste. Olga, a young soldier's wife, lived with her lawful husband and therefore considered herself purer and superior. Nadezhda also felt that Marya Konstantinovna and Katya did not respect her and were afraid of her. This was disagreeable, and to raise herself in their opinions, she said: "The villa life is at its height now at home in St. Petersburg. My husband and I have so many friends. We ought to go to visit them."

"Your husband is an engineer, I believe?" Marya Konstantinovna asked timidly.

"I'm speaking of Laevsky. He has a great many friends. But unfortunately his mother, a proud aristocrat, not very bright . . ."

Without finishing the sentence, Nadezhda rushed into the water; Marya Konstantinovna and Katya crawled in after her.

"There are a great many prejudices in our world," Nadezhda continued, "and living is not as easy as it seems."

Marya Konstantinovna, who had served as a governess in aristocratic families and knew the ways of the world, said: "Oh yes! Will you believe me, my sweet, at the Garatynskys' I was obliged to dress formally for lunch and dinner both, so that like an actress, I got something extra for my wardrobe in addition to my salary."

She was standing between Nadezhda and Katya as if screening her daughter from the water washing over the former. In the open doorway, which gave directly onto the sea, they could see someone swimming a hundred paces from the bathhouse.

"Mama, it's our Kostya!" said Katya.

"Ah, ah!" cackled her mother in dismay. "Ah! Kostya," she shouted, "Turn back! Kostya, turn back!"

Kostya, a boy of fourteen, plunged and swam farther to show off his courage before his mother and sister, but grew tired and hurried back, and his serious strained face showed his lack of confidence in his own strength.

"The trouble there is with these young boys, sweet!" said Marya Konstantinovna, recovering her assurance. "You just turn around and he's breaking his neck. Ah, sweet, how pleasant and yet how hard it is to be a mother! Everything frightens you."

Nadezhda put on her straw hat and swam out toward the sea. She swam about thirty feet and turned over on her back. She could see the sea to the horizon, the steamers, the people on the shore, the town; and all this, combined with the sultriness and the gentle, transparent waves, aroused her and whispered to her that one must live, live . . . A sailboat vigorously cutting through the waves and air bore swiftly past her; the man at the helm looked at her, and she found it pleasant to be looked at . . .

After their bath, the ladies dressed and walked out together.

"I have a fever every other day, but I still don't get thin," said Nadezhda, licking the salt from her lips and answering acquaintances' bows with a smile. "I was always plump, and I'm still plumper now, I believe."

"That, my dear, comes from one's natural constitution. If a person isn't inclined to plumpness, like myself for instance, then no food helps. But you've soaked your hat, sweet."

"It doesn't matter, it'll dry."

Nadezhda caught sight again of the men in white walking along the shore and talking French; and for some reason joy surged in her heart again and she was dimly reminded of a big reception hall in which she had once danced, or which, perhaps, she had once seen in a dream.

And something in the very depths of her soul whispered dimly and vaguely to her that she was a petty, vulgar, vile, worthless woman . . .

Marya Konstantinovna stopped near her gate and invited Nadezhda to come in and sit a while.

"Come in, my dear!" she said in a pleading voice, looking at Nadezhda with mixed anguish and hope: perhaps she would refuse and not come in!

"With pleasure," Nadezhda accepted. "You know how I love to visit you!"

And she went into the house. Marya Konstantinovna seated her, served her coffee, fed her milk rolls, then showed her photographs of her former charges—the Garatynsky girls, who were married now; she also showed the examination marks of Katya and Kostya. The marks were very good, but to make them seem even better, she sighed and complained about how hard the work was in school now . . . She fussed over her guest and simultaneously pitied her and suffered from the thought that she might have a bad influence on the morals of Kostya and Katya, and was glad Nikodim Aleksandrich was not at home. Since, in her opinion, all men loved "those women," Nadezhda was capable of exerting a bad influence on Nikodim Aleksandrich too.

While talking to her guest, Marya Konstantinovna kept re-

membering there was to be a picnic that evening, and that
von Koren had urgently asked her not to mention it to the
macacos, meaning to Laevsky and Nadezhda, but she blurted
it out accidentally, flushed crimson, and said in confusion: "I
hope you're coming too!"

<hr>

VI

They had arranged to drive seven versts from town on the
road to the south, to stop near an inn at the conflux of two
streams, the Black River and the Yellow River, and cook fish
soup there. They set off just after five. In front of all of them
rode Samoilenko and Laevsky in a coach; behind them, in a
carriage harnessed to three horses, Marya Konstantinovna, Nadezhda, Katya, and Kostya; they had a basket with provisions
and dishes. In the following carriage rode the police inspector,
Kirilin, and young Achmianov, the son of the same merchant
Achmianov to whom Nadezhda owed three hundred rubles,
and opposite them, cross-legged and doubled up on the little
seat, sat Nikodim Aleksandrich, rather small, rather meticu-
lous, with hair combed over his temples. Behind them rode
von Koren and the deacon; a basket of fish lay at the deacon's
feet.

"Keep rr-r-right!" shouted Samoilenko with all his might
whenever they came across a nomad cart or an Abkhazian
riding a donkey.

"In two years, when I have the means and the people ready,
I'm going to set off on an expedition," von Koren told the
deacon. "I'll follow the coast from Vladivostok to the Bering
Straits, and then from the Straits to the mouth of the Yenisei.
We'll chart a map, study the fauna and flora and engage in
detailed geological, anthropological, and ethnographical investigations. It's up to you whether you go with me or not."

"It's impossible," said the deacon.

"Why?"

"I'm not independent; I'm married."

"The deaconess will let you go. We'll provide for her. Or
better yet, if you could convince her to enter a nunnery for
the public benefit, you'd have the possibility of entering a
monastery yourself and going on the expedition as a regular
priest. I can arrange it for you."

The deacon was silent.

"Do you know your theological repertory well?" asked the zoologist.

"Rather poorly."

"Hmm . . . I can't give you any pointers on that score because I'm not very familiar with theology myself. You give me a list of the books you need and I'll send them to you from St. Petersburg this winter. You should also read through the writings of clerical voyagers; there've been some good ethnologists and scholars of Eastern languages among them. When you've familiarized yourself with their methods, you'll find it easier to enter into the work. Now, don't waste time waiting for books; come see me, and we'll study the compass, run over meteorology. All of this is essential."

"Yes, yes . . ." the deacon muttered and laughed. "I asked for a place in central Russia for myself, and my uncle, the archpriest, promised to help me. If I go with you, I'll have bothered him for nothing."

"I don't understand your hesitation. If you remain an ordinary deacon who is obliged to serve only on holidays and to rest from work the other days, in ten years you'll still be exactly what you are now, only your mustaches and beard will have grown; while if you return from the expedition after the same ten years, you'll be another person; you'll be enriched by the consciousness of having done something."

Shrieks of fright and ecstasy were heard from the ladies' carriage. The carriages were driving along a road hollowed out of a literally overhanging, craggy bank, and it seemed to all of them if they were galloping along a shelf attached to a high wall, and as if the carriages were on the verge of rolling over into the abyss. On the right stretched the sea; on the left there was a rough brown wall with black splotches, red veins, and climbing roots; serpentine fir branches looked down from above, bending over as if in fear and curiosity. A minute later there was more shrieking and laughter: they had had to drive under a huge overhanging stone.

"I don't know why the hell I'm going with you," said Laevsky. "How stupid and vulgar! I have to go north, get away, escape, yet for some reason I'm going on this idiotic picnic."

"But look what a view!" Samoilenko said to him as the horses took a left turn, the valley of the Yellow River was revealed, and the river itself sparkled—yellow, turbid, violent . . .

"I don't see what's good about that, Sasha," answered Laevsky. "Constant enthusing over nature—that's exhibiting the

poverty of one's imagination. Compared with what my imagination can give me, these streamlets and rocks are all rubbish and nothing more."

The carriages were now driving along the river bank. The
high mountainous banks gradually converged, the valley nar-
rowed and turned into a gorge ahead; the rocky mountain
around which they were driving had been amassed by nature
out of huge rocks, crushing one another with such terrible
force that Samoilenko always involuntarily cleared his throat
when he saw them. The somber and beautiful mountain was
cleft in places by narrow defiles and gorges which breathed
dampness and mystery on the passers-by; through the gorges,
other mountains could be seen: brownish, rosy, lilac, smoky,
or bathed in brilliant light. From time to time as they passed
through the gorge, they could hear water falling from the
heights and splashing on the rocks.

"Ah, accursed mountains," sighed Laevsky, "how they bore
me!"

In the place where the Black River met the Yellow and the
ink-black water sullied and fought the yellow, stood the Tartar
Kerbalai's tavern on the side of the road with the Russian
flag on its roof and a signboard with the chalked inscription:
"Pleasant Tavern." Nearby, enclosed by a wattled fence, was
a small garden with tables and benches and pitiful, prickly
bushes in the midst of which rose a solitary cypress, beautiful
and dark.

Kerbalai, a small lively Tartar in a blue shirt and white
apron, was standing on the road, and, clasping his stomach,
he bowed low toward the oncoming carriages and displayed
his brilliant white teeth in a smile.

"Greetings, Kerbalai!" Samoilenko shouted to him. "We're
going a bit farther on; bring up a samovar and some chairs
there! Make it quick!"

Kerbalai nodded his shaven head and muttered something,
and only those sitting in the last carriage could make out the
words: "There is trout today, Your Excellency."

"Bring them up, bring them up!" von Koren said to him.

The carriages stopped five hundred paces beyond the tavern.
Samoilenko chose a small meadow strewn with stones comfortable for sitting and a tree blown down in a storm with an
upturned, shaggy root and dried, yellow needles. A rickety
wooden bridge was flung across the river there, and on the
bank immediately opposite, a little shed, a drying loft for

corn, stood on four rather low stakes, recalling the fairy-tale hut on hen's legs; a ladder led down from its doorway.

The first impression of all of them was that they would never get out of there. Mountains loomed menacingly on all sides, wherever you looked, and from the direction of the tavern and the dark cypress, the evening shadows moved in swiftly, swiftly, making the sinuous narrow valley of the Black River narrower and the mountains higher. One could hear the river rumbling and the cicadas shrilling incessantly.

"Enchanting!" said Marya Konstantinovna, breathing deeply with excitement. "Children, look how splendid it is! What silence!"

"Yes, it really is splendid," agreed Laevsky, who found the view pleasing and felt melancholy for some reason as he looked at the sky and then the blue smoke coming from the tavern chimney. "Yes, it's splendid!" he repeated.

"Ivan Andreich, make a description of this view!" Marya Konstantinovna said tearfully.

"What for?" asked Laevsky. "One's impression is better than any description. This wealth of colors and sounds which everyone receives from nature by direct impression is garbled by writers into something disfigured and unrecognizable."

"Is that so?" von Koren asked coldly, choosing the biggest stone near the water for himself and trying to climb up and sit down on it. "Is that so?" he repeated, staring Laevsky in the face. "And *Romeo and Juliet?* And, for example, Pushkin's *Ukrainian Night?* Nature should come and bow at his feet."

"If you wish . . ." agreed Laevsky, too lazy to reason and contradict. "However," he added after a pause, "what is *Romeo and Juliet* basically? A beautiful, poetic, blessed love —that's the roses under which they try to hide the rot. Romeo was the same sort of animal as everybody else."

"No matter what one starts talking to you about, you always come down to . . ."

Von Koren glanced at Katya and did not finish.

"What do I come down to?" asked Laevsky.

"If someone says to you, for example, 'What a handsome cluster of grapes!'—you say: 'Yes, but how disfigured they are when mashed and digested in stomachs.' Why say it? It's not novel . . . and generally a peculiar way to behave."

Aware that von Koren disliked him, Laevsky was afraid of him and in his presence felt as if everyone were uncomfortable and someone were breathing down his neck. He walked away without answering and regretted having come.

"Gentlemen, forward after brushwood for the fire!" commanded Samoilenko.

They scattered in all directions, leaving only Kirilin, Achmianov, and Nikodim Aleksandrich on the spot. Kerbalai brought up chairs, spread a rug on the ground, and put out several bottles of wine. Police inspector Kirilin, a tall attractive man who wore an overcoat over his tunic in all weather, resembled all provincial police chiefs in their youth with his somewhat fatuous bearing, important gait, and thick, rather hoarse voice. His expression was plaintive and sleepy, as if he had just been awakened against his will.

"What's that you brought there, you swine?" he asked Kerbalai, pronouncing each word deliberately. "I ordered you to serve *kvarel* * and what did you bring, you Tartar beast? Eh? Well?"

"We have a lot of our own wine, Yegor Alekseich," Nikodim observed timidly and politely.

"So? But I want to have my own wine too. I'm participating in the picnic, and I suppose I have the full right to contribute my share. I sup-po-ose! Bring ten bottles of *kvarel!*"

"Why so many?" wondered Nikodim, knowing that Kirilin had no money.

"Twenty bottles! Thirty!" shouted Kirilin.

"Never mind, let him," Achmianov whispered to Nikodim, "I'll pay for it."

Nadezhda was in a merry, mischievous mood. She felt like leaping, laughing, shouting, teasing, and flirting. In her inexpensive cotton dress printed with blue pansies, her red slippers, and the same straw hat, she felt tiny, simple, light and airy as a butterfly. She ran over the rickety little bridge, stared for a minute in the water to make her head whirl, then shrieked and ran laughing toward the drying loft on the other bank; and she felt that all the men were admiring her, even Kerbalai. While the trees merged with the mountains in the swiftly falling darkness and the horses merged with the carriages and a lamp glittered in the windows of the tavern, she climbed up the mountain on a path winding between the rocks and thornbushes and sat down on a rock. Down below, the fire was already burning. The deacon was attending to the fire with his sleeves tucked up, and his long black shadow moved in a radius around the flames; he added brushwood and stirred the pot with a spoon attached to a long stick. Samoilenko was fussing near the fire with a copper-red face as in the kitchen

* A Georgian wine.

at his own house and shouting fiercely: "Where's the salt, gentlemen? I suppose you forgot it? What does it mean, everyone sitting down like landowners while I do everything alone?"

Laevsky and Nikodim Aleksandrich were sitting side by side on the fallen tree and watching the fire pensively. Marya Konstantinovna, Katya, and Kostya were taking cups, saucers, and plates out of a basket. Von Koren, his arms folded and one leg propped on a stone, was standing on the edge of the bank, lost in thought. The red lights from the fire crossed the ground among the shadows of the dark human figures and trembled on the mountain, the trees, the bridge, and the loft; across the river, the abrupt, hollowed-out bank was completely illuminated and flashed and reflected in the stream, where the swiftly running, turbulent water tore its reflection into bits.

The deacon went to get the fish which Kerbalai was cleaning and washing on the bank, but stopped halfway to look around. "My God, how beautiful!" he thought. "The people, the rocks, the fire, the twilight, the misshapen tree—and nothing else, but how beautiful!"

Some strangers appeared near the loft on the other bank. Because the light flickered and the smoke from the fire blew in that direction, it was impossible to have a complete view of these people, but bits were visible: now a shaggy cap and a gray beard, now a blue shirt, now rags from shoulder to knee and a dagger across the stomach, then a young, swarthy face with black eyebrows as thick and sharp as if drawn with coal. Five of them sat down in a circle on the ground while the other five went into the loft. One, standing at the door with his back toward the fire and his hands behind him, began telling something which must have been very interesting, because when Samoilenko added brushwood and the fire flared, spattered sparks, and lit the loft brightly, two calm faces expressing deep absorption could be seen looking out of the door, and those sitting in a circle turned around and began listening to the story. After a short while, the ones in the circle began quietly singing something prolonged and melodic, like Lenten church songs . . . As he listened to them, the deacon imagined what it would be like for him in ten years on his return from the expedition—a young missionary-priest, an author with a name and a magnificent past; he would be made an archimandrite, then a bishop; he would serve Mass in a cathedral; in a golden miter, with the ensign of the Virgin and Child, he would step forward, and, blessing the crowd of people with the triple and double candelabra, would pro-

nounce: "Look down from heaven, O God, and visit this vineyard planted by Thy right hand!" And the children would
sing with angelic voices in answer: "Holy God . . ."

"Deacon, where's that fish?" Samoilenko's voice rang out.

Returning to the fire, the deacon imagined himself going on
a church procession down a dusty road on a hot July day. In
front were the peasant men carrying banners and the women
and young girls with the icons; behind them came the boys'
choir and the sexton with straw in his hair, and next, in proper
order, he, the deacon; and behind him, the priest wearing a
skullcap and carrying a cross, followed by a crowd of peasants, women, and little boys raising the dust; in the crowd
were the priest's wife and the deaconess in kerchiefs. The
choir sings, the children squall, the quail shriek, the lark
carols . . . Now they've stopped and sprinkled the herd with
holy water . . . They've gone farther on and knelt to pray for
rain. Then food, conversation . . .

"And that's nice too . . ." thought the deacon.

VII

Kirilin and Achmianov were climbing the path up the
mountain. Achmianov fell behind and stopped, while Kirilin
went up to Nadezhda.

"Good evening!" he said, giving a salute.

"Good evening."

"Yes!" said Kirilin, looking at the sky thoughtfully.

"What—yes?" asked Nadezhda after a short silence, having
noticed that Achmianov was observing them.

"So then," the officer said slowly, "it seems our love withered without having had time to flower, so to speak. How is
a man to interpret this? Inborn coquetry on your part, or perhaps you consider me a simpleton with whom one can do as
one pleases?"

"It was a mistake! Leave me alone!" Nadezhda said sharply,
looking at him with fear on this beautiful marvelous evening
and asking herself in bewilderment whether there could really
have been a moment when this man attracted her and was
intimate with her.

"So then!" said Kirilin; he stood in silence for a short
while, reflecting, and said: "Well? We'll wait until you're in
a better mood, and meanwhile I'll venture to assure you, I'm

a gentleman and don't allow anyone to doubt it. No one can play with me! *Adieu!*"

He saluted and walked off, picking his way through the bushes. A moment later, Achmianov approached hesitantly.

"What a beautiful evening!" he said with a slight Armenian accent.

He was not bad-looking, dressed fashionably, behaved unaffectedly like a well-brought up youth, but Nadezhda disliked him because she was three hundred rubles in debt to his father; she found it disagreeable, too, that a shopkeeper had been invited on the picnic, and disagreeable that he should approach her on this evening in particular, when her heart felt so pure.

"The picnic is altogether a success," he said, after a silence.

"Yes," she said and, as if just reminded of her debt, added carelessly: "Yes, tell them in your shop that some day soon, Ivan Andreich will come by and pay the three hundred . . . or I don't remember how much it is."

"I'm ready to give three hundred more just in order for you not to mention that debt every day. Why so humdrum?"

Nadezhda laughed; the amusing thought had entered her mind that if she were not so moral and wished to, she could rid herself of this debt in a minute. If she were to turn the head of this handsome young fool, for instance. How amusing, ridiculous, and wild it would be, really! And she suddenly longed to make him fall in love, to plunder him, cast him aside, then see what would come of it.

"Allow me to give you one bit of advice," Achmianov said timidly. "I beg you, beware of Kirilin. He is saying horrible things about you everywhere."

"I'm not interested in knowing what every fool says about me," Nadezhda said coldly, and she was overwhelmed by anxiety; the amusing idea of playing with this young, good-looking Achmianov suddenly lost its charm.

"We must go down," she said. "They're calling."

Down below, the fish soup was ready. It was poured into plates and eaten with the solemnity found only on picnics; and all of them agreed that the fish soup was delicious and that they had never eaten anything as delicious at home. As is customary on all picnics, losing themselves in a mass of napkins, packages, and superfluous, greasy papers, gliding in the wind, they could not tell which glass and which piece of bread was whose; they poured wine on the rug and their own knees, spilled the salt; it was all dark around them, the fire was no longer burning as brightly, but everyone was reluctant to get up and add brushwood. They all drank wine; even Kostya and Katya were given a half glass each. Nadezhda drank one glass, then another, became intoxicated, and forgot about Kirilin.

"A luxurious picnic, a bewitching evening," said Laevsky, becoming gay from the wine; "but I'd prefer a fine winter to all this. 'His beaver collar is silvered with the dust of frost.' "

"Each to his own taste," remarked von Koren.

Laevsky felt a certain uneasiness: the heat of the fire fell on his back, and on his chest and face, he felt the hatred of von Koren; this hatred on the part of a respectable, intelligent man, which probably had some basic cause, humiliated him, enfeebled him, and not having the strength to fight it, he said in a wheedling tone: "I am passionately fond of nature and regret not being a naturalist. I envy you."

"Well, I have neither regret nor envy," said Nadezhda. "I don't understand how it's possible to be seriously preoccupied with scarabs and ladybirds when people are suffering."

Laevsky shared her opinion. He was totally ignorant of the natural sciences and therefore could never reconcile himself to the authoritative tone and scholarly, meditative air of people who concerned themselves with ants' antennae and cockroach claws, and it had always annoyed him that on the basis of antennae, claws, and some protoplasm (which he for some reason pictured in the form of an oyster), they presumed to resolve questions involving the origin and life of man. But he sensed a lie in Nadezhda's words, and, solely to contradict her, said: "It's not a matter of ladybirds, but of results!"

VIII

It was late, eleven o'clock, when they began getting into the carriages to go home. Everyone had taken his place except Nadezhda and Achmianov, who were running races and laughing on the far bank.

"Hurry up there!" Samoilenko shouted to them.

"Ladies shouldn't be served wine," von Koren said softly.

Laevsky, worn out by the picnic, von Koren's hatred, and his own thoughts, went to meet Nadezhda Fedorovna. When, gay, joyful, feeling light as a feather, breathless, and laughing, she seized both his hands and put her head on his chest, he

took a step backward and said harshly: "You're behaving like
. . . a cocotte."

This came out so roughly that he immediately felt sorry for
her. In his angry, weary face she read hatred, pity, annoyance
with himself, and her spirits suddenly fell. She realized she
had overstepped, behaved too freely, and feeling saddened,
heavy, fat, coarse, and drunk, she climbed into the first empty
carriage along with Achmianov. Laevsky got in with Kirilin,
the zoologist with Samoilenko, the deacon with the ladies, and
the caravan moved off.

"That's the way they are, macacos . . ." began von Koren,
wrapping his cloak around him and closing his eyes. "You
heard: she doesn't want to concern herself with scarabs and
ladybirds because people are suffering. That's the way all macacos judge us. A servile breed, sly, terrorized by the knout
and the fist for ten generations; it quakes, is moved, and burns
incense only under force; but put the macaco in a free state
where there is no one to take it by the scruff of the neck, and
there it will reveal itself and make its true self known. Watch
her boldness at painting exhibitions, at museums, in theaters,
or watch her when she passes judgment on science: she bris-
tles, flies into a passion, abuses, criticizes . . . She invariably
criticizes—it's the mark of the slave! Just listen: people in the
liberal professions are more often abused than swindlers—
that's because three-fourths of society consists of slaves, of
just such macacos. A slave never reaches out a hand to you to
thank you sincerely for your work."

'I don't know what you expect!" Samoilenko said, yawning.
"The poor thing wanted to talk to you seriously, in all simplicity, and you start drawing a conclusion. You're angry with
him for some reason, and with her, well, by association. Yet
she's a splendid woman!"

"Eh, nonsense! She's the usual mistress, dissolute and vulgar. Listen, Aleksandr Davidich, when you meet a peasant
woman who's not living with her husband, not doing anything, and who just hee-hees and ha-has, you tell her to go to
work. Why are you timid and afraid to say the truth in this
case? Just because Nadezhda Fedorovna is the mistress of an
official instead of a sailor?"

"What am I supposed to do with her?" Samoilenko flared.
"Beat her, is that it?"

"Don't play up to vice. We curse sin only behind its back,
and that's like hiding an offensive gesture in one's pocket. I'm
a zoologist, or a sociologist, which is one and the same; you're

a physician; society believes in us; we're obligated to point out to it the terrible harm threatened it and the future generation by the existence of ladies like this Nadezhda Ivanovna."

"Fedorovna," corrected Samoilenko. "And what is society supposed to do?"

"Society? That's its affair. In my opinion, the most realistic and straightforward method is compulsion. She should be dispatched to her husband *manu militari,** and if the husband won't have her, she should be turned over to penal servitude or some corrective institution."

"Oof!" sighed Samoilenko; he was silent a while and then asked gently: "A few days ago you were saying that people like Laevsky should be exterminated . . . Tell me, if it were that . . . let's say, the state or society entrusted you with exterminating him, could you . . . bring yourself to it?"

"With a steady hand."

<hr />

IX

On reaching home, Laevsky and Nadezhda went into their dark, stuffy, dull rooms. Both were silent. Laevsky lit a candle while Nadezhda sat down, and raised mournful, guilty eyes to him without taking off her coat and hat.

He understood that she was expecting to have it out with him; but having it out would be so boring, useless, and tiresome, and his heart was heavy because he had lost control and spoken roughly to her. By chance he felt in his pocket the letter which he had been hesitating to read to her for days, and it occurred to him that showing her this letter now would turn her attention to other things.

"It's time to clarify our relationship," he thought. "Let's give it to her; what will be, will be."

He pulled out the letter and gave it to her.

"Read it. It concerns you."

After saying this, he went to his study and lay down on the couch in the dark without a pillow. Nadezhda read the letter and felt as if the ceiling had descended and the walls closed in on her. It suddenly became close, dark, and frightening. She crossed herself quickly three times and uttered: "Peace to him, Lord . . . peace to him, Lord . . ."

* By military force.

And burst into tears. "Vanya!" she called. "Ivan Andreich!"

There was no answer. Thinking that Laevsky had come in and was standing behind her chair, she began sobbing like a child: "Why didn't you tell me earlier that he had died? I wouldn't have gone on the picnic, wouldn't have laughed so horribly . . . Men were saying vulgar things to me. How sinful, how sinful! Save me, Vanya, save me . . . I've lost my senses . . . I'm ruined . . ."

Laevsky heard her sobbing. He felt unbearably stifled and his heart was beating violently. In despair he got up, stood in the middle of the room, groped in the darkness for the armchair near the table, and sat down.

"This is a prison . . ." he thought. "I have to get out . . . I can't stand it . . ."

It was too late to go play cards now and there were no restaurants in town. He lay down again and stopped up his ears so as not to hear her sobbing, then he suddenly remembered he could go to Samoilenko's. To avoid walking past Nadezhda, he went out the window into the garden, climbed over the fence, and continued down the street. It was dark. A steamer had just arrived—a big passenger ship, judging by the lights . . . the anchor chain rasped. A red light was moving swiftly from the shore in the direction of the ship: the customs boat.

"The passengers are asleep in their cabins . . ." thought Laevsky and he envied the others' peace.

The windows of Samoilenko's house were open. Laevsky peered through one after another; the rooms were dark and quiet.

"Aleksandr Davidich, are you asleep?" he called. "Aleksandr Davidich!"

A cough was heard and an anxious call: "Who's there? What the devil?"

"It's I, Aleksandr Davidich. Forgive me."

The door was open slightly; a soft light glowed from the little lamp and Samoilenko's huge figure appeared all in white, wearing a white nightcap.

"What do you want?" he asked, breathing heavily, half asleep, and scratching himself. "Wait, I'll unlatch the door right away."

"Don't bother, I'll go through the window . . ."

Laevsky climbed in the window, went up to Samoilenko, and seized him by the hand.

"Aleksandr Davidich," he said in a trembling voice, "save me! I beg you, I adjure you, understand me! My situation is a torment. If it goes on for even a day or two more, I'll smother myself like . . . like a dog!"

"Wait . . . What is it about, precisely?"

"Light a candle."

"Oh, oh . . ." sighed Samoilenko, lighting a candle. "My God, my God . . . But it's already past one o'clock, brother."

"Forgive me, but I can't stay at home," said Laevsky, feeling greatly relieved by the light and the presence of Samoilenko. "You are my only, my best friend, Aleksandr Davidich . . . All my hopes lies in you. Whether you want to or not, for God's sake, rescue me. No matter what happens, I must get away from here. Give me a loan!"

"Oh, my God, my God!" sighed Samoilenko, scratching himself. "I'm falling asleep, and I hear a whistle, a steamer arriving, and then you . . . Do you need much?"

"At least three hundred rubles. I must leave her a hundred and I need two hundred for the trip . . . I owe you about four hundred already, but I'll send all of it . . . all . . ." Samoilenko held both his whiskers in one hand, took a wide stance, and sank into thought.

"So . . ." he muttered in irresolution. "Three hundred . . . Yes . . . But I haven't that much. I'd have to borrow from someone."

"Borrow, for God's sake!" said Laevsky, seeing from Samoilenko's face that he wanted to give him the money and definitely would. "Borrow, I'll pay it back without fail. I'll send it from St. Petersburg as soon as I arrive there. You can be at ease about that. Come, Sasha," he said, becoming animated, "let's have some wine!"

"Well . . . all right."

They went into the dining room.

"And what about Nadezhda Fedorovna?" asked Samoilenko, putting three bottles and a plate of peaches on the table. "She's not staying behind, is she?"

"I'll arrange everything, arrange everything . . ." said Laevsky, feeling an unexpected wave of joy. "I'll send her money afterward, and she'll come join me . . . Then we'll clarify our relationship there. To your health, friend."

"Wait!" said Samoilenko. "Drink this first . . . it's from my vineyard. This bottle here is from Navaridze's vineyard, and this one from Akhatulov's . . . Try all three kinds and tell me frankly . . . Mine seems to have a bit of acidity. Well? Don't you think so?"

"Yes. You've consoled me, Aleksandr Davidich. Thank you . . . I've revived."

"Is there any acidity?"

"The devil knows, I don't. But you're a magnificent, marvelous man!"

Looking at his pale, troubled, kind face, Samoilenko remembered von Koren's opinion that such people should be exterminated, and Laevsky struck him as a weak, defenseless child anyone could injure and exterminate.

"And make peace with your mother when you go," he said. "It's not good."

"Yes, yes, without fail."

They were silent a while. When they had finished the first bottle, Samoilenko said: "You should make peace with von Koren too. You're both fine, very intelligent people, and you look at one another like wolves."

"Yes, he's a fine, very intelligent man," agreed Laevsky, ready to praise and forgive everyone. "He's a remarkable man, but it's impossible for me to become close to him. No! Our natures are too different! I have a slothful, weak, dependent nature; I might stretch my hand out to him, perhaps, in an auspicious moment, but he would turn away from me . . . with contempt."

Laevsky sipped his wine, paced from wall to wall, then continued, standing in the middle of the room: "I understand von Koren very well. He's a relentless, strong, despotic nature. You heard: he talks about expeditions continually and it's not a matter of empty words. He needs the wilds, the moonlit night; around him, in tents and under the open sky, sleep his hungry, sick Cossacks, exhausted by hard marches; his guides, bearers, the doctor, the priest, and he alone, like Stanley, is awake and sits on his camp stool feeling like the tsar of the desert and the master of these people. He keeps going, going, going on; his people groan and fall one after the other, but he keeps on going, going, and in the end, perishes himself, but still remains the despot and tsar of the desert because the cross over his grave is visible to caravans thirty—forty miles away and reigns over the wasteland. I regret the man isn't in the army. He would make a fine, brilliant military leader. He would have been capable of drowning his cavalry in a river and making a human bridge out of the corpses, and boldness of that sort is needed more in war than any sort of fortifications and tactics. Oh, I understand him perfectly! Tell me, why is he wasting himself here? What does he want here?"

"He's studying the marine fauna."

"No. No, brother, no!" sighed Laevsky. "A traveling scientist on the steamer told me that the Black Sea is poor in fauna and that thanks to the abundance of hydrogen sulfate on the bottom, organic life can't exist. All serious zoologists work in the biological stations in Naples or Villefranche. But von Koren is independent and stubborn: he works on the Black Sea because no one else is working here; he broke with the university, doesn't want to know other scientists and colleagues because he's a despot first and a zoologist afterward, And you'll see, he'll produce a great doctrine. He's already dreaming about how, when he comes back from the expedition, he'll smoke the mediocrity and intrigue out of our universities and bring the scientists to their knees. Despotism is just as powerful in science as in war. And he's staying in this stinking town a second summer because it's better to be first in the country than second in the city. He's a king and an eagle here; he keeps all the inhabitants under his thumb and oppresses them with his authority. He keeps a tight hand over everyone, interferes in other people's business; he has to control everything and everyone is afraid of him. I'm slipping out of his clutches and he feels it and hates me. Hasn't he told you I should be exterminated or made to do public works?"

"Yes," laughed Samoilenko.

Laevsky also laughed and finished his wine.

"His ideals are despotic too," he said, smiling and biting into a peach. "Ordinary mortals, when working for the public benefit, have people close to them in mind: me, you, mankind, in short. To von Koren, people are infants and nonentities, too trivial to be the object of his life. He'll work, go on an expedition, and break his neck there, not for love of people close to him, but in the name of such abstractions as humanity, future generations, an ideal human race. He is working for the betterment of the human race, and in this respect we are only slaves to him, cannon fodder, beasts of burden. Some he would exterminate or put away at hard labor, others he would transform by discipline, like Arakcheyev,* making them get up and go to bed by a drum; he would station eunuchs to watch over our chastity and morality, order anyone shot who left the narrow circle of conservative morals, and all this in the name of the betterment of the human race . . . And what is this human race? An illusion, a mirage . . . Despots

* Count Aleksei Andreyevich Arakcheyev (1769–1834), Russian statesman and soldier, known for his iron discipline.

have always been illusionists. I understand him very well, brother. I appreciate and do not deny his importance; the world is kept going by people like him, and if the world were left to us alone, with our kindness and good intentions, we'd do to it just what those flies are doing to that picture. Yes."

Laevsky sat down next to Samoilenko and said with sincere enthusiasm: "I'm an empty, insignificant, fallen man! The air I breathe, this wine, love, in sum, life—I've gotten until now at the cost of lies, laziness, and cowardice. Until now I've deceived myself and other people, I've suffered from it, and my suffering was cheap and common. I timorously bend my back before von Koren's hatred because I hate and despise myself, too, at times."

Laevsky paced from corner to corner again in agitation and said: "I'm glad I see my own shortcomings clearly and recognize them. This will help me to start over again and become another man. My dear friend, if you only knew how passionately, with what anguish I thirst for my own transformation. And I promise you I'll be a man! I will! I don't know whether it's the wine speaking in me or whether it is really so in fact, but it seems to me as if it's been a long time since I had such lucid, pure moments as just now with you."

"It's time to sleep, brother . . ." said Samoilenko.

"Yes, yes . . . Forgive me. I'm going right away."

Laevsky bustled around the furniture and the windows, looking for his cap.

"Thank you . . ." he muttered, sighing. "Thank you . . . Kindness and a good word are better than charity. You've given me new life."

He found his cap, stopped, and looked guiltily at Samoilenko.

"Aleksandr Davidich!" he said in a pleading voice.

"What?"

"Let me spend the night at your house, my friend!"

"You're welcome to . . . why not?"

Laevsky lay down on the couch to sleep, but continued talking to the doctor for a long time.

X

Three days after the picnic, Marya Konstantinovna unexpectedly appeared at Nadezhda's and, without taking off her hat or uttering a greeting, seized Nadezhda by both hands, pressed them to her bosom, and said in great emotion: "My dear, I'm very moved and stunned. Our sweet, understanding doctor told my Nikodim Aleksandrich yesterday that your husband is dead. Tell me, my dear . . . Tell me, is it true?"

"Yes, it's true; he's dead," answered Nadezhda.

"That's dreadful, dreadful, my dear! But there's no bad news without some good. Your husband undoubtedly was a marvelous, wonderful, saintly man, and such are needed more in heaven than on earth."

All the creases and hollows on Marya Konstantinovna's face quivered as if tiny needles were jumping under her skin; she smiled saccharinely and said with enthusiasm, breathlessly: "So then you're free, my dear. Now you can hold your head high and look people in the eyes. From now on, God and man will bless your union with Ivan Andreich. It's enchanting. I'm trembling with joy; I can't find the words. I'll be your matchmaker, my sweet . . . Nikodim Aleksandrich and I have been so fond of you; you must allow us to bless your lawful, pure union. When, when are you thinking of getting married?"

"I haven't thought of it," said Nadezhda, freeing her hands.

"That's impossible, sweet. You have, you have!"

"God's truth, I haven't," laughed Nadezhda. "Why should we get married? I don't see any necessity for it. We'll live as we've been living."

"What are you saying!" Marya Konstantinovna exclaimed, horrified. "For God's sake, what are you saying!"

"Nothing would be the better for our having married. On the contrary, it would be worse. We'd lose our freedom."

"Sweet! Sweet, what are you saying!" cried Marya Konstantinovna, stepping backward and throwing up her hands. "You're preposterous! Come to your senses! Calm yourself!"

"What do you mean, calm myself? I haven't lived yet, and you tell me to calm myself!"

Nadezhda reflected that she really had not lived yet. She had graduated from school, been married to a man she did not love, then gone off with Laevsky and spent the whole time with him on this boring, desolate shore in the expectation of something better. Was that living?

"Yet we ought to get married . . ." she thought, but remembering Kirilin and Achmianov, blushed and said: "No, it's impossible. Even if Ivan Andreich begged me to on his knees, I'd still refuse."

Marya Konstantinovna sat on the couch a moment in silence, saddened, serious, staring fixedly, then got up and said coldly: "Good-by, sweet! Forgive me for disturbing you. Although it's not easy for me, I must tell you that from this day on, everything is over between us and, despite my profound respect for Ivan Andreich, the door of my house is closed to you."

She said this solemnly and was overcome by her own solemnity; her face began quivering again, took on a tender, saccharine expression; she stretched both hands out to the frightened, mortified Nadezhda and said imploringly: "My sweet, let me be your mother or older sister for just one minute! I will be as frank with you as a mother."

Nadezhda felt warmth, joy, and self-pity in her bosom as if her mother had actually risen from the dead and were standing before her. She impetuously embraced Marya Konstantinovna and pressed her face to her shoulder. Both of them started crying. They sat down on the couch and sobbed for several minutes without looking at each other, unable to utter a word.

"My sweet, my child," Marya Konstantinovna began, "I'm going to tell you some harsh truths, without sparing you."

"Do, for God's sake, for God's sake!"

"Trust me, sweet. You remember, I was the only one of all the local ladies to receive you. I was horrified by you from the first day, but I didn't have the heart to treat you with scorn like the others. I suffered for sweet, good Ivan Andreich as if he were my son. A young man in a strange country, inexperienced, weak, without his mother; I was anguished, anguished . . . My husband was against becoming acquainted with him, but I persuaded . . . convinced him . . . We began receiving Ivan Andreich, and with him, you, of course; otherwise he would have been offended. I have a daughter, a son . . . You know what the tender mind, the pure heart of a child is . . . 'whoso offendeth one of these little ones' . . . I received you and trembled for my children. Oh, when you're a mother, you'll understand my fears. And everyone was surprised at my receiving you, forgive me, like a respectable woman; they hinted to me . . . well, of course, gossip, suppositions . . . At the bottom of my heart I condemned you, but you were so unhappy, pitiful, wayward, that I ached with pity."

"But why? Why?" Nadezhda asked, her whole body trembling. "What did I do to anyone?"

"You're a terrible sinner. You broke the vow you made your husband at the altar. You seduced a splendid young man who, if he had not met you, would probably have taken a lawful life companion from a good family in his own circle and would be like everyone else now. You ruined his youth. Don't say anything, don't say anything, my dear! I won't believe it's the man who's to blame for our sins. It's always the woman who's guilty. Men are frivolous in domestic affairs, live by their minds, not their hearts, and lack understanding, while a woman understands it all. Everything is up to her. She is given much, and much is required of her. Oh, sweet, if she were stupider and weaker than man in this respect, God would not have entrusted her with bringing up little boys and girls. And furthermore, dear, you set out on the path of sin shamelessly; another woman in your situation would have hidden from people, sat at home behind closed doors, and would have been seen only in God's temple, pale, dressed in black, weeping, and everyone would have said with sincere compassion: 'Lord, this sinning angel is returning again to Thee . . .' but you, sweet, forgot all modesty, lived openly, waywardly, as if proud of your sin. You frolicked, laughed loudly, and watching you, I used to tremble with terror and be afraid the heavenly thunder might strike our home while you were visiting us. Sweet, don't say anything, don't say anything!" cried Marya Konstantinovna, noticing that Nadezhda was about to speak. "Trust me, I won't deceive you and won't hide a single truth from your soul's eyes. Listen to me, my dear . . . God marks great sinners, and you were marked. Bear in mind that your clothes have always been frightful!"

Nadezhda, who had always had the highest opinion of her clothes, stopped crying and looked at Marya Konstantinovna in bewilderment.

"Yes, frightful!" the other continued. "Anyone could judge your behavior by the flamboyance and gaudiness of your dresses. Everybody laughed and shrugged his shoulders at the sight of you, and I suffered, suffered . . . and forgive me, sweet, you're not clean! When we met in the bathhouse, you made me shudder. Your outer clothing was still presentable, but your petticoat, your chemise . . . Sweet, it makes me blush! Also, no one ties poor Ivan Andreich's tie properly, and it's obvious from his linens and the poor man's boots that no one looks after him at home. And, darling, he's always hungry, and it's true that if there's no one to see to the samovar and coffee at home, you have to spend half your salary at the pavilion. And your house is simply awful, awful! Nobody in the whole town has flies, yet you can't get rid of them; all your plates and saucers are black with them. Just look, your window sills and tables are covered with dust, dead flies, glasses . . . Why should there be glasses there? And, sweet, your table hasn't been cleared away yet. And it's embarrassing to go into your bedroom: your linens flung all around, your various rubber things hanging on the walls, dishes and basins standing about . . . Sweet! A husband is supposed to be kept in ignorance, and his wife is supposed to appear before him pure, like a little angel! I wake up every morning when it's barely light and wet my face with cold water so my Nikodim Aleksandrich won't notice the creases of sleep."

"All this is nothing," sobbed Nadezhda. "If only I were happy, but I'm so unhappy!"

"Yes, yes, you're very unhappy!" sighed Marya Konstantinovna, barely managing not to cry. "And terrible sorrow awaits you in the future. A solitary old age, illness, and then an accounting in the Last Judgment . . . It's horrible, horrible! Fate itself is holding out a helping hand to you now, and you senselessly push it aside. Get married, get married, quickly!"

"Yes, I must, I must," said Nadezhda, "but it's impossible!"

"Why so?"

"Impossible! Oh, if you only knew!"

Nadezhda wanted to tell her about Kirilin, and how she had met handsome young Achmianov yesterday evening on the quay, and how the insane, ridiculous thought had entered her head of getting rid of her three-hundred-ruble debt; it had amused her a great deal, and afterward, she returned home late in the evening, feeling irrevocably fallen and cheapened. She did not understand how it had happened herself. And now she longed to swear to Marya Konstantinovna that she would pay back the debt without fail, but sobbing and shame kept her from speaking of it.

"I'm going away," she said. "Ivan Andreich may stay, but I'm going away."

"Where to?"

"Russia."

"But what will you live on there? Why you haven't a thing."

"I'll do translations or . . . or open a little bookstore . . ."

"Don't indulge in fantasies, my sweet. A bookstore takes money. Come, I'll leave you now, and you calm yourself and think it over, and tomorrow come to me all cheerful. It will be enchanting! Well, good-by, my little angel. Let me kiss you."

Marya Konstantinovna kissed Nadezhda on the forehead, made the sign of the cross over her, and went out quietly. It was already growing dark and Olga was lighting the lamp in the kitchen. Still crying, Nadezhda went into the bedroom and lay down on the bed. She began running a high fever. She undressed lying down, crumpled her clothes under her feet, and rolled into a ball under the blanket. She was very thirsty and there was no one to bring her something to drink.

"I'll pay it back!" she said to herself, and in her delirium imagined that she was sitting beside a sick woman whom she then recognized as herself. "I'll pay it back. It would be foolish to think that for money I . . . I'll leave and send him the money from St. Petersburg. First one hundred . . . then another hundred . . . and then a hundred . . ."

Laevsky came in late that night.

"First a hundred . . ." Nadezhda told him, "then a hundred . . ."

"You should take quinine," he said, thinking: "Tomorrow's Wednesday, the steamer will be leaving, but not I. That means I'll have to stay here till Saturday."

Nadezhda rose on her knees in bed.

"I wasn't saying anything just now, was I?" she asked, smiling and blinking in the light.

"Nothing. We'll have to send for the doctor tomorrow morning. Go to sleep."

He took a pillow and went toward the door. Ever since he had made up his mind to go away and leave Nadezhda, she had begun to inspire him with pity and a feeling of guilt; he felt rather ashamed in her presence, as in the presence of a sick or old horse one has decided to shoot. He stopped in the doorway and glanced back at her.

"I was irritated at the picnic and spoke rudely to you. Forgive me, for God's sake."

After saying this, he went to his study, lay down, and was unable to sleep for a long time.

The next morning, when Samoilenko, dressed for the holiday in full parade uniform with epaulettes and medals, left the bedroom after taking Nadezhda's pulse and looking at her tongue, Laevsky, who was standing near the threshold, asked him anxiously: "Well, what? What?"

His face showed fear, great concern, and hope.

"Calm yourself, it's nothing dangerous," said Samoilenko. "The usual fever."

"I'm not talking about that," Laevsky frowned impatiently. "Did you get the money?"

"My friend, forgive me," whispered Samoilenko, embarrassed, glancing at the door. "For heaven's sake, forgive me! No one has any money to spare, and I've only collected five or ten rubles here and there—a hundred and ten all in all. I'm going to talk to somebody else today. Be patient."

"But Saturday's the final date!" whispered Laevsky, trembling with impatience. "By all that's sacred, before Saturday! If I don't leave Saturday, nothing will be of any use to me, nothing! I don't understand how a doctor could be without money!"

"Lord, Thy will be done," Samoilenko hissed quickly and with emphasis, and there was even a catch in his voice. "They've taken everything I had, they owe me seven thousand rubles, and I'm in debt all around. Am I to blame?"

"Meaning you'll get it by Saturday? Yes?"

"I'll try."

"I beg you, my dear friend. So the money is in my hands by Friday morning."

Samoilenko sat down and wrote a prescription for quinine in a solution of *kalii bromati,* tincture of rhubarb, *tincturae gentianae aquae foeniculi*—all in one mixture, added rose sirup for sweetening, and left.

XI

"You look as if you were here to arrest me," said von Koren, when he saw Samoilenko come into his place in parade uniform.

"I was just walking past and thought: why not go in and pay my respects to zoology?" said Samoilenko, sitting down at a big table the zoologist had put together himself out of plain boards. "Greetings, Holy Father!" he bowed to the deacon who was sitting at the windows copying something. "I'll stay a moment and then run home to give instructions about dinner. It's time already . . . I'm not disturbing you?"

"Not the least," answered the zoologist, spreading papers

covered with fine handwriting on the table. "We're busy copying."

"So . . . Oh, my God, my God . . ." sighed Samoilenko; he cautiously drew a dusty book with a dried spider on it from the table and said: "Think of it! Picture a green beetle of some sort going about his business and suddenly meeting a monster like that on the road. I can imagine its terror!"

"Yes, I suppose."

"Is poison given it for defense from its enemies?"

"Yes, for defense and to attack."

"Yes, yes, yes . . . Everything in nature, my dear friends, is efficient and explicable," sighed Samoilenko. "Only here's what I don't understand. You, as a man of the greatest intellect, explain it to me, please. There are some little beasts, you know, no bigger than rats, rather pretty to look at, but, let me tell you, as vicious and immoral as can be. Let's suppose one such beast is going through the woods; he sees a bird, catches it, and eats it. He goes on and sees a little nest of eggs in the grass; he doesn't want to guzzle them now, he's full, but he nevertheless bites into one egg and sweeps the rest out of the nest with his paw. Then he meets a frog and starts playing with it. After torturing the frog, he goes on, licking himself off, and sees a beetle in front of him. He takes his paw and . . . And he ruins and destroys everything on his path . . . He crawls into others' burrows, digs up anthills at random, cracks open snails . . . if he meets a rat, he gets into a fight with it; if he sees a little snake or a little mouse—he has to strangle it. And so on the whole day. Now, tell me, what use is a beast like that? Why was he created?"

"I don't know what little beast you're talking about," said von Koren, "probably about some sort of insectivore. Well, what of it? He catches the bird because it was careless; he destroys the nest with the eggs because the bird was not skillful, built the nest badly, and was unable to camouflage it. The frog probably had an imperfection somewhere in its coloring or he would not have seen it, and so forth. Your beast destroys only the weak, the unskillful, the careless—in sum, the ones with defects Nature finds it unnecessary to hand down to posterity. Only the more clever, careful, strong, and developed remain among the living. In this way, without suspecting it, your little beast serves the great end of perfecting the species."

"Yes, yes, yes . . . By the way, brother," said Samoilenko carelessly, "let me have a hundred ruble loan."

"All right. There are some very interesting types of insectivores. The mole, for example. He is said to be useful because he destroys poisonous insects. They say a certain German sent Emperor Wilhelm I a coat made out of moleskin, and the Emperor is supposed to have ordered him reprimanded for having destroyed such a quantity of useful creatures. Yet the mole is not a bit behind your beast in cruelty and is harmful in addition because he does terrible damage to the fields."

Von Koren opened a cashbox and got out a hundred ruble note.

"A mole has a powerful thorax, like a bat," he continued, locking the cashbox: "terribly well-developed bones and muscles, and an unusually well-armed mouth. If he had the dimensions of an elephant, he would be an all-destroying, invincible creature. It is interesting that when two moles meet underground, they both begin digging out a platform as if by prior agreement; they need this platform to fight more conveniently. When it is finished, they enter into a fierce battle and struggle until the weaker falls. Take this hundred rubles," said von Koren, and lowering his voice, added: "but with the understanding that you're not taking it for Laevsky."

"And what if it were for Laevsky!" exploded Samoilenko. "What business is it of yours?"

"I can't give it to you for Laevsky. I know you love to make loans. You'd loan money to the robber Kerim if he asked you, but, forgive me, I can't assist you in this bent."

"Yes, I'm asking it for Laevsky!" said Samoilenko, standing up and waving his right hand. "Yes! For Laevsky! And nobody, devil or demon, has the right to tell me how I should dispose of my own money. You aren't willing to give it to me? No?"

The deacon burst out laughing.

"Reflect, instead of boiling over," said the zoologist. "Lavishing favors on Laevsky is just as foolish, in my opinion, as watering weeds or feeding locusts."

"While in my opinion, it's our duty to help our neighbors!" shouted Samoilenko.

"In that case, help that hungry Turk there, lying under the fence! He's a worker and more needed and more useful than your Laevsky. Give him this hundred ruble note! Or offer a hundred rubles toward my expedition!"

"Are you giving it to me or not, I ask you?"

"Tell me frankly: what does he need money for?"

"That's no secret. He has to go to St. Petersburg Saturday."

"So that's how it is!" von Koren said slowly. "Aha . . . Now we understand. And is she going with him, or what?"

"She's staying here meanwhile. He's going to settle his affairs in St. Petersburg and send her money; then she'll come."

"Clever! . . ." said the zoologist and gave a short, tenor laugh. "Clever! Intelligently contrived."

He went up to Samoilenko quickly and standing face to face, looking him in the eyes, asked: "Tell me frankly, has he stopped loving her? Yes? Tell me: has he? Yes?"

"Yes," Samoilenko muttered, perspiring.

"How disgusting it is!" said von Koren, and his face clearly showed his disgust. "It's one of the two, Aleksandr Davidich: either you're in accord with him, or, forgive me, you're a simpleton. Is it possible you don't realize he's taking you in like a child in the most unscrupulous way? But, it's clear as day that he wants to get rid of her and abandon her here. She'll be on your neck, and, clear as day, you'll have to send her to St. Petersburg at your own expense. Can your splendid friend have blinded you so with his merits that you can't see even the simplest things?"

"That's just conjecture," said Samoilenko, sitting down.

"Conjecture? Then why is he going alone instead of taking her? And ask him why she shouldn't go ahead and he follow? The sly rascal!"

Crushed by sudden doubts and suspicions about his friend, Samoilenko suddenly lost heart and lowered his tone. "But it's impossible!" he said, remembering the night Laevsky had spent at his house. "He suffers so!"

"What's the significance of that? Thieves and incendiaries suffer too!"

"Even supposing you're right . . ." Samoilenko said doubtfully. "Let's assume it . . . Still, he's a young man in a strange place . . . a scholar, we're scholars too, and aside from us, there's nobody here to come to his support."

"To help him perpetrate a villainy just because you and he attended universities in different years and both idled away some time there! What rubbish!"

"Wait, let's discuss it cooly. It would be possible, I suppose, to arrange it like this . . ." Samoilenko pondered, twitching his fingers. "I'll give him the money, you see, but request his word of honor that he'll send Nadezhda Fedorovna the money for the trip in a week."

"And he'll give you his word of honor and even shed a few tears and believe it himself, but what's his word worth? He won't keep it, and when you meet him on Nevsky Prospect in a year or so with his new love on his arm, he'll justify himself by saying that civilization crippled him and that he is the image of Rudin.* Drop him, for God's sake! Get out of the mire and stop digging both hands in it!"

After a moment's thought, Samoilenko said resolutely: "But I'll still give him the money. No matter what you expect. I'm not capable of refusing a man just on the basis of conjecture."

"Very well. Kiss him too."

"So give me the hundred rubles," Samoilenko asked timidly.

"I won't."

A silence fell. Samoilenko was completely crestfallen; his face assumed a guilty, humiliated, and obsequious look, and it was somehow strange to see this pitiful, childishly embarrassed countenance on a huge man wearing epaulettes and medals.

"The local Most Eminent travels around his bishopric on horseback instead of in a coach," said the deacon, putting down his pen. "His appearance on horseback is touching in the extreme. His simplicity and humility are filled with Biblical grandeur."

"Is he a good man?" asked von Koren, delighted to change the subject.

"How could he not be? If he weren't good, would he have been consecrated a bishop?"

"You find some very good and gifted people among bishops," said von Koren. "It's a pity, though, that many of them have one failing—imagining themselves statesmen. One busies himself with Russification, another criticizes the sciences. That's not their business. They'd do better to look into the consistory more often."

"A worldly man can't judge a bishop."

"Why not, Deacon? A bishop is a man just as I am."

"Just and not just," the deacon said, offended, taking up his pen. "If you were just the same, then you would be touched by God's grace and would be a bishop yourself; and if you aren't a bishop, it means you're not just the same."

"Don't be silly, Deacon!" Samoilenko put in with annoyance. "Listen, here's what I've thought of," he said to von Koren. "Don't give me this hundred rubles. You're going to board with me three months more before winter, so pay me for three months in advance."

"I won't."

* Hero of Turgenev's *Virgin Soil.*

Samoilenko blinked his eyes and turned purple; he mechanically drew the book with the spider on it toward him and looked at it, then stood up and went after his hat. Von Koren became sorry for him.

"That's what it's like to live and do business with such gentlemen!" said the zoologist, kicking a piece of paper into the corner in indignation. "You must understand that this is not kindness, not love, but cowardice, profligacy, venom! What the mind accomplishes, your flabby, good-for-nothing hearts will destroy! When I was sick with typhoid fever as a schoolboy, my aunt fed me pickled mushrooms out of sympathy and I almost died. Both you and my aunt must understand that love for a person must not lie in the heart or the pit of the stomach or the loins, but right here!"

Von Koren tapped himself on the forehead.

"Take it!" he said, flinging the hundred ruble note. "You don't have to lose your temper, Kolya," Samoilenko remarked mildly, putting away the bill. "I understand you perfectly, but . . . put yourself in my position."

"You're an old woman, that's what!"

The deacon burst out laughing.

"Listen, Aleksandr Davidich, one last request!" von Koren said ardently. "When you give that scamp the money, make the proviso that he either leave with his lady or send her on ahead, and otherwise don't give it to him. There's no need to stand on ceremony with him. Tell him that, and, if you don't tell him, I give you my word of honor, I'll go up to his office and throw him down the stairs, and I won't have anything further to do with you. So be forewarned!"

"Why not? It will be more convenient for him to leave with her or send her ahead," said Samoilenko. "He'll even be glad. Well, good-by."

He took leave affectionately and went out, but before closing the door behind him, glanced back at von Koren, made a terrible face, and said: "It's the Germans who ruined you, brother! Yes! The Germans!"

XII

The next day, Thursday, Marya Konstantinovna was celebrating her Kostya's birthday. Everyone was invited to eat a meat pie at noon and to have chocolate in the evening. When

Laevsky and Nadezhda arrived in the evening, the zoologist, who was already sitting in the parlor drinking chocolate, asked Samoilenko: "Did you talk to him?"

"Not yet."

"Look, don't stand on ceremony. I can't understand these people's impertinence. Of course they know perfectly well how this family looks on their cohabitation, but they worm in here just the same."

"If they paid attention to every prejudice," said Samoilenko, "they'd have to not go anywhere."

"Can you call the masses' aversion to extramarital love and depravity a prejudice?"

"Of course. Prejudice and spitefulness. When soldiers see a girl of light conduct, they laugh and whistle, but just ask them what they are themselves."

"They have reason to whistle. That unmarried girls smother their illegitimate children and go to prison, and that Anna Karenina threw herself under the train, and that in the villages they tar the gates, and that what you and I like about Katya without knowing why is her purity, and that everyone dimly feels a need for a pure love, although he knows no such love exists—can all this be prejudice? This, brother, is all that has survived of natural selection, and if this obscure force regulating the relations between the sexes did not exist, the Laevskys would be showing you what to do, and the human race would degenerate in two years."

Laevsky went into the parlor; he greeted everyone and smiled ingratiatingly as he shook von Koren's hand. After waiting for a suitable moment, he told Samoilenko: "Excuse me, Aleksandr Davidich, I must have two words with you."

Samoilenko stood up, clasped him around the waist, and they went into Nikodim Aleksandrich's study.

"Tomorrow's Friday . . ." said Laevsky, biting his nails. "Did you get what you promised?"

"I only got two hundred and ten. The rest I'll get today or tomorrow. Don't worry."

"God be praised! . . ." sighed Laevsky, and his hands trembled with joy. "You are saving me, Aleksandr Davidich, and I swear to you by God, my happiness, and whatever you like, that I'll send you this money as soon as I get there. And my old debt too."

"Here's the thing, Vanya . . ." said Samoilenko, taking him by the button and reddening. "Forgive me for interfering

in your family affairs, but . . . why don't you leave with
Nadezhda Fedorovna?"

"You're a funny fellow, how could I? One of us absolutely
has to stay or the creditors would howl. I owe the shops seven
hundred rubles if not more, you see. Have patience, I'll send
them money, pay them off, then she can leave too."

"So . . . but why don't you send her on ahead?"

"Ah, my God, how could I?" Laevsky was horrified. "She's
a woman, what would she do there alone? What does she
know about things? It would be just a delay and an unnecessary waste of money."

"Reasonable . . ." thought Samoilenko, but recalling his
conversation with von Koren, he dropped his eyes and said
gruffly: "I can't agree with you. Either you go with her or
send her on ahead or . . . or I won't give you the money.
That's my last word . . ."

He retreated backward, pushed the door open with his back,
and went into the parlor, crimson, in intense embarrassment.

"Friday . . . Friday," thought Laevsky, returning to the
parlor. "Friday . . ."

A cup of chocolate was passed to him. He burned his lips
and tongue on the hot chocolate and thought: "Friday . . .
Friday . . ."

The word "Friday" somehow never left his mind; he thought
of nothing but Friday, and only somewhere in his heart, not
in his mind, was it clear to him that he would not be leaving
Saturday. In front of him stood Nikodim Aleksandrich, metic-
ulous, with his hair combed over his temples, urging: "Do
take something to eat, please . . ."

Marya Konstantinovna showed the guests Katya's marks
and drawled: "School is terribly, terribly hard these days.
They require so much . . ."

"Mama!" groaned Katya, not knowing what to do with herself from praise and embarrassment.

Laevsky also looked at the marks and praised them. Scriptures, Russian language, conduct, grades of five and four
danceᶜ before his eyes, and all this, mixed with the persistent
thought of Friday, with Nikodim Aleksandrich's combed temples and Katya's red cheeks gave him a feeling of such vast,
insuperable tedium that he barely managed not to scream with
despair and asked himself: "Am I really, really not leaving?"

They put two card tables next to each other and sat down
to play postman. Laevsky sat down too.

"Friday . . . Friday . . ." he thought, smiling and taking a pencil out of his pocket. "Friday . . ."

He wanted to think his situation through and was afraid of thinking. It frightened him to realize that the doctor had caught him in the deceit he had so long and so carefully concealed from himself. Whenever he thought about his future, he did not allow his thoughts full liberty. He would sit down in the train compartment and travel—thereby solving his life's problems, and he did not let his thoughts go further. Like a distant, dim light in the field, the thought flickered in his mind from time to time that somewhere in one of the by-lanes of St. Petersburg, in the distant future, in order to break with Nadezhda Fedorovna and pay his debts, he would be forced to resort to a little lie; he would lie just once, and then a whole new life would begin. And this was all right: at the cost of one little lie he would gain a big truth.

Just now, when the doctor had crudely hinted at deceit to him by his refusal, Laevsky realized that he would have to lie not just in the distant future, but today and tomorrow and a month from now, and perhaps even to the end of his life. In fact, in order to get away, he had to lie to Nadezhda, his creditors, and his superior; later, in order to get money in St. Petersburg, he would have to lie to his mother, to tell her he had already broken with Nadezhda; his mother would not give him more than five hundred rubles—which meant that he had already deceived the doctor, because he would not be in a position to send him money quickly. Afterward, when Nadezhda came to St. Petersburg, it would be necessary to resort to a whole series of big and little deceptions in order to break with her; and once again there would be tears, tedium, a loathsome life, remorse, meaning no new life whatsoever. Deception and nothing more. A whole mountain of lies arose in Laevsky's imagination. To leap over it in one bound and not lie piecemeal, he would have to choose a harsh method— for example, getting up without a word, putting on his hat, and leaving immediately without money, without saying a word; but Laevsky felt incapable of doing that.

"Friday, Friday . . ." he thought. "Friday . . ."

They were writing notes, folding them in two, and putting them in an old top hat of Nikodim Aleksandrich's, and when enough letters had collected, Kostya, playing the postman, walked around the table and delivered them. The deacon, Katya, and Kostya, who had received ridiculous letters and were trying to write even more ridiculous ones, were in raptures.

"We must have a little talk," Nadezhda read in her note. She exchanged glances with Marya Konstantinovna, who smiled saccharinely and nodded her head.

"What is there to talk about?" thought Nadezhda Fedorovna. "If one can't tell everything, there's no use talking."

Before leaving for the party she had tied Laevsky's tie, and this trivial task filled her soul with tenderness and melancholy. His anxious face, distraught glances, pallor, and the incomprehensible change which had taken place in him recently; the awful, repugnant secret she was keeping from him, and the trembling of her hands as she knotted his tie—all this for some reason told her that they did not have much longer to live together. She looked at him with fear and penitence as at an icon and thought: "Forgive me, forgive me . . ." Across the table from her sat Achmianov, never taking his adoring black eyes off her; desires stirred her; she was ashamed of herself and afraid that even anguish and sorrow would not keep her from yielding to an impure passion, if not today, then tomorrow—and that like a drunken alcoholic, she no longer had the strength to stop.

In order to end this life, ignominious for her and humiliating for Laevsky, she decided to go away. She would tearfully implore him to let her go, and, if he resisted, she would leave secretly. She would not tell him what had happened; let his memory of her remain pure.

"I love, love, love," she read. That was from Achmianov.

She would live somewhere in the wilderness, work, and send Laevsky money, embroidered shirts, and tobacco "from an unknown," and come back to him only in his old age, or if he fell dangerously ill and needed a nurse. When he learned in old age the reasons for which she had refused to be his wife and had left him, he would appreciate her sacrifice and forgive her.

"You have a long nose." That must be from the deacon or Kostya.

Nadezhda pictured how, in saying farewell to Laevsky, she would embrace him warmly, kiss his hand, and swear that she would love him all, all her life; and afterward, living in the wilderness among strangers, she would think every day of how she had a friend somewhere, a beloved person, pure, noble, and lofty, who had kept a pure memory of her.

"If you don't set a meeting with me today, I'll take measures, I assure you on my word of honor. Gentlemen can't be treated like this, you must understand." That was from Kirilin.

<hr>

XIII

Laevsky received two notes. He opened one and read: "Don't leave, my darling."

"Who could have written that?" he thought. "Not Samoilenko, of course . . . And not the deacon, because he doesn't know I want to leave. Could it be von Koren?"

The zoologist bent over the table and sketched a pyramid. Laevsky felt the man's eyes were smiling.

"Samoilenko must have blabbed . . ." thought Laevsky.

In the other note, in the same broken handwriting with long tails and curlicues was written: "Somebody isn't going Saturday."

"A stupid joke," thought Laevsky. "Friday, Friday . . ."

He felt something rise in his threat. He adjusted his collar and coughed, but instead of a cough, a laugh burst from his throat.

"Ha-ha-ha!" he roared. "Ha-ha-ha!" What am I laughing at? he thought. "Ha-ha-ha!"

He made an effort to restrain himself, covered his mouth with his hand, but the laugh shook his chest and neck, and his hand was unable to hide his mouth.

"But how stupid this is!" he thought, rolling with laughter. "Have I gone out of my mind or what?"

The laughter rose higher and higher and turned into something resembling a spaniel's bark. Laevsky wanted to get up from the table, but his legs refused to obey and his right hand mysteriously sprang onto the table against his will, convulsively clutched the paper notes and crushed them. He glimpsed astonished looks, Samoilenko's serious, frightened face, and the zoologist's glance, brimming with cold mockery and distaste, and understood that he was having hysterics.

"How monstrous, how shameful," he thought, feeling the warmth of tears on his face. "Ah, ah, how disgraceful! This never happened to me . . ."

Then they grasped him under the arms and, supporting his head from behind, led him somewhere; then a glass glittered before his eyes and struck his teeth, and water spilled on his chest; then there was a small room with two beds in the middle, side by side, covered with clean snow-white spreads. He rolled onto one of the beds and sobbed.

"It's nothing, it's nothing . . ." said Samoilenko. "That happens . . . That happens . . ."

Cold with fear, trembling violently, and foreboding something terrible, Nadezhda was standing next to the bed and asking: "What's wrong with you? What? For God's sake, speak . . ."

"Could Kirilin have written him something?" she thought.

"It's nothing . . ." said Laevsky, laughing and crying. "Go away . . . darling."

His face showed neither hatred nor repugnance, meaning he knew nothing; somewhat reassured, Nadezhda went back to the parlor.

"Don't worry, sweet!" Marya Konstantinovna said, sitting down beside her and taking her hand. "It will pass. Men are as weak as we sinners. You are both going through a crisis . . . it's so understandable! Now, sweet, I'm waiting for an answer. Let's have a talk."

"No, we're not going to talk . . ." said Nadezhda, listening to Laevsky's sobbing. "I'm miserable . . . Let me leave."

"What's that, what's that, sweet?" Marya Konstantinovna replied in alarm. "Could you imagine I would let you go without supper? Let's have a bite, then Godspeed."

"I'm miserable . . ." Nadezhda whispered, seizing the arm of the chair with both hands to avoid falling.

"He has eclampsia!" von Koren said merrily as he came into the parlor, but on seeing Nadezhda, was disconcerted and went out.

When the hysterics were over, Laevsky sat on the strange bed and thought: "It's a disgrace, I was yowling like a spoiled little girl! I must have been ridiculous and disgusting. I'll leave the back way . . . yet that would mean I took my hysterics seriously. Should pretend it's a joke . . ."

He looked in the mirror, sat a while, then went into the parlor.

"Well, here I am!" he said, smiling; he was painfully embarrassed, and he imagined the others felt embarrassed in his presence. "Things like that happen," he said, sitting down. "I was sitting there and suddenly, you know, felt a terrible shooting pain in my side . . . unbearable, my nerves couldn't stand it and . . . and it turned into this foolish joke. Ours is a nervous age, there's nothing to be done about it!"

At supper he drank wine, talked, and from time to time, sighing spasmodically, rubbed his side as if to show that the pain was still there. And no one except Nadezhda believed him, and he was aware of it.

After nine, they took a walk down the boulevard. Nadezhda, afraid that Kirilin might speak to her, tried to stay close to Marya Konstantinovna and the children. She was weak with fear and misery, and anticipating a fever, felt exhausted and barely able to move her legs, but did not go home because she was sure she would be followed by Kirilin or Achmianov or both. Kirilin was walking behind, next to Nikodim Aleksandrich, and chanting softly: "I won't al-lo-ow pla-ay-ing with me! I won't al-lo-ow it!"

They turned off the boulevard toward the pavilion, walked along the shore, and watched the sea phosphoresce for a long time. Von Koren began to explain what made it phosphorescent.

<hr />

XIV

"Why it's already time for my vint . . . They're waiting for me," said Laevsky. "Good-by, ladies and gentlemen."

"I'll go with you, wait," Nadezhda said, taking his arm.

They took leave of the company and walked on. Kirilin also took leave, saying he was going in the same direction, and went with them.

"What will be, will be . . ." thought Nadezhda. "So be it . . ."

She felt as if all her bad memories had left her head and were walking beside her breathing heavily in the darkness while like a fly which has fallen into an inkwell, she herself was struggling desperately over the pavement and staining Laevsky's side and hand black. If Kirilin does something evil, she thought, she alone was to blame, not he. There once was a time when no man spoke to her as Kirilin did, and it was she who had destroyed that time, rotting it as irrevocably as a piece of string—and who was to blame for that? Drunk with her own desires, she had smiled at a complete stranger, probably just because he was tall and well-built; she had tired of him in two meetings and dropped him, and didn't he therefore have the right to treat her as he pleased? she thought now.

"I'll leave you here, darling," said Laevsky, stopping. "Ilya Mikhailich will escort you."

He bowed to Kirilin and walked quickly across the boulevard, down the street to Sheshkovsky's house, where the lights were burning. Kirilin and Nadezhda heard the bang of the gate behind him.

"Permit me to make myself clear to you," Kirilin began. "I'm no little boy, nor any Achkasov or Lachkasov, Zachkasov . . . I demand serious attention!"

Nadezhda's heart started beating violently. She did not answer.

"At first I explained the abrupt change in your behavior toward me as coquetry," continued Kirilin; "now, however, I see that you simply don't know how to treat gentlemen. You just wanted to play with me like that Armenian brat, but I'm a gentleman and demand to be treated as a gentleman. So I am at your service . . ."

"I'm miserable . . ." Nadezhda said, starting to cry, and she turned away to hide her tears.

"I'm miserable too, but what of it?"

After a moment's silence Kirilin said distinctly, separating his words: "I repeat, my lady, that if you do not give me a meeting today, I'll make a scandal this very day."

"Let me go today," Nadezhda pleaded and did not recognize her own voice, it was so thin and plaintive.

"I must teach you a lesson . . . Forgive my gruff tone, but it's necessary for me to teach you. Yes, unfortunately, I must teach you. I demand two meetings: today and tomorrow. After tomorrow, you will be completely free and can go anywhere and with anyone you please. Today and tomorrow."

Nadezhda went up to her gate and stopped.

"Let me go!" she whispered, trembling all over and seeing nothing before her eyes except this white tunic. "You're right, I'm a horrible woman . . . I'm to blame, but let me go . . . I beg you . . ." she touched his cold hand and shuddered. "I implore you . . ."

"Alas!" sighed Kirilin. "Alas! It's not in my plans to let you go, I just want to teach you, to make you understand, and furthermore, madam, I have too little faith in women."

"I'm miserable . . ."

Nadezhda listened to the even roar of the sea, glanced at the star-sprinkled sky, and longed to end everything quickly and to be rid of the cursed sensation of life with its sea, stars, men, fever . . .

"But not in my house . . ." she said coldly. "Take me somewhere else."

"Let's go to Muridov's. That's the best."

"Where is it?"

"Near the old rampart."

She walked quickly down the street and then turned into a side street which led toward the mountains. It was dark. Streaks of light from the illuminated windows lay across the pavement here and there, and she felt like a fly first falling into the inkwell, then crawling out of it again into the light. Kirilin walked behind her. He stumbled in one spot, almost fell, and burst out laughing.

"He's drunk . . ." Nadezhda thought. "It's all the same . . . all the same . . . So be it."

Achmianov had also taken leave of the company quickly and followed Nadezhda to ask her to take a boat-ride. He went to her house and looked through the fence: the windows were wide open; there were no lights.

"Nadezhda Fedorovna!" he called.

A minute passed. He called again.

"Who's there?" Olga's voice rang out.

"Is Nadezhda Fedorovna at home?"

"No. She hasn't come in yet."

"Strange . . . Very strange," thought Achmianov, beginning to feel very anxious. "She was on her way home . . ."

He walked down the boulevard, then the street, and glanced in the windows of Sheshkovsky's house. Laevsky was sitting coatless at the table and looking intently at his cards.

"Strange, strange . . ." Achmianov muttered to himself, and at the recollection of Laevsky's hysterics, he felt ashamed. "If she's not at home, then where?"

He went back to Nadezhda's apartment and looked at the dark windows.

"It's a deceit, a deceit . . ." he thought, remembering that when she had met him at midday at the Bityugovs, she had promised to take a boat-ride with him that evening.

The windows were dark in the house where Kirilin lived and a policeman was sitting asleep on a little bench at the gates. As he looked at the windows and the policeman, everything became clear to Achmianov. He decided to go home and started out, but found himself outside Nadezhda's apartment again. He sat down on a bench and took off his hat, feeling his head burn with jealousy, humiliation.

The town church struck only twice in every twenty-four

hours: at midday and at midnight. Soon after it struck midnight, there were hurried footsteps.

"That means tomorrow evening at Muridov's again," Achmianov heard, and he recognized Kirilin's voice. "At eight o'clock. Till then!"

Nadezhda appeared near the fence. Without noticing Achmianov sitting on the bench, she passed him like a shadow, opened the gate, and leaving it ajar, entered the house. She lit the candle in her room, quickly undressed, but, instead of going to bed, dropped on her knees in front of a chair, put her arms around it and leaned her forehead against it.

Laevsky came home after two o'clock.

<hr />

XV

Having decided not to lie all at once, but piecemeal, Laevsky went to Samoilenko the following day between one and two to ask for money to leave Saturday for certain. After yesterday's hysterics, which had added an acute feeling of shame to his painful situation, remaining in town was inconceivable. If Samoilenko were to insist on his conditions, he thought, it would be possible to agree to them and take the money; then tomorrow, at the very moment of departure, to say that Nadezhda refused to go. It would be easy to convince her by then that this was all for her benefit. If Samoilenko, who had fallen under the obvious influence of von Koren, absolutely refused the money or proposed new conditions of some sort, then he, Laevsky, would leave today by steamer or even by sailboat for New Athos or Novorossisk, send his mother an abject telegram from there and stay there until she sent him money to travel.

When he came to Samoilenko's, he found von Koren in the parlor. The zoologist had just arrived for dinner and, as usual, was leafing through the album and scrutinizing the men in their top hats and the ladies in mobcaps.

"How badly timed," Laevsky thought on seeing him. "He could interfere."

"Greetings!"

"Greetings," von Koren answered withoutl looking at him.

"Is Aleksandr Davidich home?"

"Yes. In the kitchen."

Laevsky went into the kitchen, but, seeing from the doorway that Samoilenko was busy with the salad, he returned to the parlor and sat down. He had always been ill at ease in the zoologist's presence and was afraid now that the conversation might turn to his hysterics. More than a minute passed in silence. Von Koren suddenly raised his eyes to Laevsky and asked: "How do you feel after yesterday?"

"Fine," answered Laevsky, flushing. "Actually, you see, it was nothing particular . . ."

"Until yesterday I had supposed only women had hysterics, and therefore I at first thought you had St. Vitus's dance."

Laevsky smiled ingratiatingly and thought: "How untactful of him. He naturally knows perfectly well it's painful for me . . ."

"Yes, it was a ridiculous thing," he said, still smiling. "I laughed all morning today. The curious thing in a hysterical fit is that you know it's absurd, and you laugh at it in your heart and sob at the same time. We're slaves of our nerves in this nervous age of ours; they are our masters and do what they will with us. Civilization has done us a disservice in this respect . . ."

Laevsky found disagreeable the way von Koren listened to him seriously and attentively as he said this and watched him intently, without blinking, as if studying him; and he was vexed with himself that in spite of his dislike for von Koren, he was unable to dismiss the ingratiating smile from his own lips.

"However, I must confess," he continued, "there were more immediate reasons for the fit and fairly fundamental ones. My health has been very shaky recently. Add to that boredom, a constant shortage of money . . . the absence of people and general interests . . . My situation is worse than a refugee's."

"Yes, your situation is insoluble," said von Koren.

These calm, cold words of either mockery or uninvited prophecy offended Laevsky. He remembered the zoologist's glance yesterday, brimming with mockery and distaste, paused a moment, and then asked, no longer smiling: "And where did you learn about my situation?"

"You just spoke of it yourself, and then your friends take such a burning interest in you that you're all one hears about all day."

"What friends? Samoilenko, is that it?"

"Yes, he too."

"I should ask Aleksandr Davidich and my friends in general to be less concerned about me."

"Here comes Samoilenko, ask him to be less concerned about you."

"I don't understand your tone of voice . . ." muttered Laevsky, seized by a sensation which was as if he had just now realized that the zoologist hated him, despised and jeered at him, and was his most malignant and irreconcilable enemy. "Save that tone for someone else," he said softly, lacking the strength to speak loudly because of the hatred which already gripped his chest and neck, just as the desire to laugh had yesterday.

In came Samoilenko without his frock coat, purple and perspiring from the stifling kitchen.

"Ah, you here?" he said. "Greetings, my dear friend. Have you had dinner? Don't stand on ceremony, answer: have you had dinner?"

"Aleksandr Davidich," said Laevsky, standing up, "if I turned to you with an intimate request of some kind, that doesn't mean that I released you from the obligation of being discreet and respecting others' secrets."

"What's that?" Samoilenko was dumfounded.

"If you don't have any money," continued Laevsky, raising his voice and shifting from one foot to the other in agitation, "then don't give it, refuse; but why proclaim in every by-lane that my situation is insoluble and so on? When there's a ruble's worth of talk about a kopeck's worth of good deeds and friendly services, I can't stand it! You may boast of your good deeds as much as you please, but no one gave you the right to reveal my secrets!"

"What secrets?" asked Samoilenko, perplexed and growing angry. "If you came to be abusive, you may leave. Come back later!"

He recalled the rule of counting mentally to a hundred and calming yourself when you grow angry with your neighbor; and he began counting rapidly.

"I beg you not to be concerned about me!" continued Laevsky. "Don't pay any attention to me. And whose business am I and the way I live? Yes, I want to leave! Yes, I make debts, drink, live with somebody else's wife, have hysterics, I'm common, not so profound as some, but whose business is it? Respect privacy!"

"Forgive me, brother," said Samoilenko, who had reached number thirty-five, "but . . ."

"Respect privacy!" Laevsky interrupted him. "This constant talk at someone else's expense, oh's and ah's, continuous surveillance, eavesdropping, this friendly sympathy . . . the hell with it! They lend me money and propose conditions to me like a little boy! They treat me like the devil knows what! I don't need a thing!" shouted Laevsky, reeling with emotion and fearing he might have hysterics again. "That means I won't leave Saturday," flashed through his thoughts. "I don't need a thing! I only ask to please be spared this guardianship. I'm not a little boy or a lunatic, and I ask you to stop supervising me!"

In came the deacon, and on seeing Laevsky pale, gesticulating, and addressing this strange speech to the portrait of Prince Vorontsov, he stopped near the door as if transfixed.

"This constant peeping in my soul," continued Laevsky, "offends my human dignity, and I ask the volunteer detectives to drop their spying! I've had enough!"

"What did you . . . what did you say, Ivan Andreich Laevsky?" Samoilenko asked after counting to a hundred, turning crimson, and going up to Laevsky.

"I've had enough!" Laevsky repeated, panting and picking up his cap.

"I'm a Russian physician, an aristocrat, and a state councilor!" Samoilenko said, separating his words. "A spy I never was and I won't tolerate anybody's insults!" he shouted in a rasping voice, emphasizing the last word. "Shut up!"

The deacon, who had never seen the doctor so majestic, inflated, crimson, and fierce, covered his mouth, ran out into the entrance, and rolled with laughter. As if in a fog, Laevsky saw von Koren get up and, with his hands in his trouser pockets, strike a pose as if waiting to see what would happen next; Laevsky found this calm pose supremely insolent and insulting.

"Kindly take back what you said!" shouted Samoilenko.

Laevsky, who no longer remembered what he had said, answered: "Leave me in peace! I don't want a thing! I only want you and the other Germans of Jewish origin to leave me in peace! Otherwise I'll take steps. I'll fight!"

"Now it's clear," said von Koren, emerging from behind the table. "Monsieur Laevsky wants to divert himself with a duel before his departure. I can give him that satisfaction. Monsieur Laevsky, I accept your challenge."

"Challenge?" Laevsky articulated softly, going up to the zoologist and looking with hatred at his swarthy forehead and curly hair. "Challenge? So be it! I hate you! Hate you!"

"I'm delighted. Tomorrow morning at the earliest hour near Kerbalai's with all details to your liking. And now, clear out."

"I hate you!" Laevsky said softly, breathing heavily. "I've hated you a long time! A duel! Yes!"

"Take him away, Aleksandr Davidich, or I'll leave myself," said von Koren. "He'll bite me."

Von Koren's calm tone cooled the doctor; he seemed to come to himself with a start, recovered, put both arms around Laevsky's waist, and, leading him away from the zoologist, muttered in an affectionate voice trembling with emotion: "My friends . . . good, kind . . . Got overheated and that's enough now . . . enough . . . My friends . . ."

At the sound of the soft, friendly voice, Laevsky felt as if something fantastic and monstrous had just happened in his life, as if he had nearly been run over by a train; he almost burst into tears, waved his hand, and ran out of the room.

"To feel someone's hatred on you, to exhibit yourself in the most pitiful, despicable, helpless state in front of a man who hates you—my God, how painful!" he was thinking shortly afterward, sitting in the pavilion and feeling as if his body were blighted by the hatred he had just felt. "How harsh it is, my God!"

Cold water and cognac gave him courage. He clearly pictured to himself von Koren's calm, supercilious face, his glance of yesterday, his carpetlike shirt, his voice, his white hands, and a weighty, passionate, hungry hatred churned in Laevsky's breast and demanded satisfaction. In his imagination he threw von Koren to the ground and trampled him underfoot. He recalled everything that had happened in the most minute detail and wondered how he could have smiled ingratiatingly at an insignificant man and, in general, valued the opinion of petty little people known to nobody, living in an insignificant town, which, it seems, wasn't even on the map and wasn't known to a single decent person in St. Petersburg. If this miserable town were to sink into the ground or burn up, the news would be read in Russia with as great disinterest as an announcement of the sale of used furniture. To kill von Koren tomorrow or to leave him among the living was all equally, identically useless and uninteresting. Shoot him in the arm or leg, wound him and then laugh at him and let him— like an insect with a torn-off leg struggling in the grass—lose himself with his obscure suffering in a crowd of people as insignificant as himself.

Laevsky went to Sheshkovsky, told him everything, and

asked him to be a second; then both went to the head of the postal-telegraph office, asked him to be a second, and stayed for dinner with him. They joked and laughed a lot during dinner; Laevsky bantered about his almost total inability to shoot and called himself a royal marksman and Wilhelm Tell.

"This gentleman needs to be taught . . ." he said.

After dinner they sat down to play cards. Laevsky played, drank wine, and thought to himself that dueling was generally foolish and pointless because it merely complicated questions without settling them, but that you sometimes could not get along without it. In the given case, for example, you could not take von Koren to court! And the coming duel was a good thing too in that afterward it would be impossible for Laevsky to remain in town. He became slightly drunk, enjoyed the card game, and felt fine.

When the sun went down and it became dark, however, anxiety overtook him. It was not fear of death, because while having dinner and playing cards, he had had a certainty for some reason that the duel would end in nothing; it was fear of something unknown which was to take place tomorrow morning for the first time in his life, and dread of the approaching night . . . He knew the night would be long, sleepless, and that he would be thinking, not just about von Koren and his hatred, but about that mountain of lies he had to go through, and which he lacked the strength and skill to avoid. He felt as if he had abruptly fallen ill; he suddenly lost all interest in cards and people, began fidgeting, and asked to be allowed to go home. He longed to lie in bed as soon as possible, to be motionless, and to prepare his thoughts for the night. Sheshkovsky and the postal official left with him and went on to von Koren's to have a talk about the duel.

Near his own apartment, Laevsky met Achmianov. The young man was breathless and excited.

"I was looking for you, Ivan Andreich!" he said. "I beg you, let's go quickly . . ."

"Where?"

"A gentleman you don't know, who has very important business with you, wants to see you. He urgently begs you to come for a minute. He has something to talk to you about . . . It's a matter of life and death for him . . ."

In his excitement, Achmianov spoke with a strong Armenian accent.

"Who is this man?" asked Laevsky.

"He asked me not to give his name."

"Tell him I'm busy. Tomorrow, if it's convenient . . ."

"That's impossible!" Achmianov said aghast. "He has something of great importance to you to tell . . . great importance! If you don't go, something terrible will happen."

"Strange . . ." muttered Laevsky, not understanding why Achmianov was so excited or what secrets there could be in a boring little town of no use to anyone. "Strange," he repeated in hesitation. "However, let's go. It doesn't matter."

Achmianov walked briskly ahead, followed by Laevsky. They went down the street, then turned down a side street.

"What a bore," said Laevsky.

"Right away, right away . . . It's close."

Near the old rampart, they went through a narrow alley between two fenced empty lots, then came into a large yard and went toward a small house . . .

"That's Muridov's house, isn't it?" asked Laevsky.

"Yes."

"But why we're going by the back yards, I don't understand. We can get there by the street. It's closer . . ."

"Never mind, never mind . . ."

Laevsky found it strange that Achmianov was taking him to the back entrance and waving his hand as if urging him to walk more softly and keep quiet.

"In here, in here . . ." said Achmianov, cautiously opening the door and going in the entrance on tiptoes. "Quieter, quieter, I beg you . . . They might hear."

He listened, took a deep breath, and said in a whisper: "Open that door and go in . . . Don't be afraid."

Laevsky, bewildered, opened the door and went into a low-ceilinged room with curtained windows. There was a candle on the table.

"Who's that?" asked someone in the next room. "You, Muridov?"

Laevsky turned into that room and saw Kirilin with Nadezhda by his side.

Not hearing what was said to him, he staggered backward and found himself in the street without knowing how he got there. His hatred for von Koren and his anxiety—all had vanished from his heart. As he went home, he kept waving his right hand awkwardly and looking attentively at his feet, trying to walk where the ground was level. At home, in his study, rubbing his hands and stiffly hunching his neck and shoulders as if he felt restricted by his shirt and jacket, he

paced from corner to corner, then lit a candle and sat down
at the table . . .

"The humanitarian sciences of which you speak will only
satisfy man's mind when they will be led to converge with the
exact sciences and continue parallel to them. Whether they
will converge under a microscope or in the monologues of a
new Hamlet or in a new religion, I don't know, but it's my
belief that the earth will be coated with ice before it happens.
The most enduring and vital of all humanitarian doctrines is,
of course, the teaching of Christ, but look how variously it is
interpreted! Some teach that we should love all our neighbors,
but make an exception for soldiers, criminals, and morons:
they allow the first to be killed in war, the second to be isolated or executed, and the third they forbid to marry. Other
interpreters teach love of one's neighbors without exception,
and without distinguishing the plusses and minuses. According
to their teaching, if a tubercular or a murderer or an epileptic
comes to you to ask for your daughter's hand—give her to
him; if cretins make war on the physically and mentally
healthy—hold out your heads. This preaching of love for
love's sake, like art for art's sake, would lead to the complete
extinction of mankind in the end if it had sufficient force and
would thereby achieve the most grandiose crime on earth. The
interpretations are numerous, and because they are so numerous, the serious mind is not satisfied with any of them and
hastens to add its own version to the mass of interpretations.
Therefore, never put a question, as you say, on philosophical
or so-called Christian grounds; you thereby only put yourself
farther away from its solution."

The deacon listened to the zoologist attentively, reflected,
and asked: "Was the moral law which is innate in everyone
invented by philosophers or did God create it along with the
body?"

"I don't know. But this law is common to all peoples and
epochs to such a degree that I feel it should be recognized as
organically related to man. It was not invented, but exists and
will exist. I shan't tell you it will be seen under a microscope
some day, but its organic relationship is already proven by

evidence; serious illnesses of the brain and all the so-called mental diseases show themselves first of all in the perversion of the moral law, so far as I know."

"Very well. Which means that just as our stomach tells us to eat, a moral sense tells us to love our neighbors. Is that it? But our physical nature fights the voice of conscience and reason out of egoism and consequently raises many brain-racking questions. Where are we supposed to turn for the solution of these problems if you forbid our putting them on philosophical grounds?"

"Turn to what little exact science we have. Have confidence in evidence and the logic of facts. True, it's inadequate, but on the other hand, not as vacillating and diffuse as philosophy. Let's say the moral law requires you to love people. Well? Love should include the removal of everything which might harm people in one way or another or which threatens them in the present and future. Our knowledge and the evidence will tell you that the morally and physically abnormal represent a threat to humanity. If so, then fight against the abnormal. If you haven't the capacity to raise them to the norm, you must have the strength and skill to render them harmless, that is, to annihilate them."

"Meaning love lies in the strong conquering the weak?"

"Absolutely."

"But look at the strong who crucified our Jesus Christ!" said the deacon heatedly.

"The fact is that he was not crucified by the strong, but by the weak. Human culture has debilitated and is trying to whittle away the struggle for existence and natural selection; whence the rapid increase of the weak and their predominance over the strong. Imagine that you succeeded in instilling bees with humanitarian ideas in an undeveloped, rudimentary form. What would the result be? The drones, who should be killed, would remain alive, eat up the honey, corrupt and strangle the bees—resulting in the predominance of the weak over the strong and the degeneration of the latter. The very same thing is happening with humanity now: the weak are squeezing out the strong. Among the savages, who haven't been affected by culture yet, the strongest, wisest, and most moral leads the way: he is the chief and master. While we cultured people crucified Christ and continue to crucify Him. Meaning there is something lacking in us . . . And we must renew this 'something' in ourselves or there will be no end to these misconceptions."

"But what kind of criteria do you have for distinguishing the strong from the weak?"

"Knowledge and evidence. The tubercular and the scrofulous are recognized by their diseases, and the immoral and the insane by their acts."

"But there can be mistakes, of course!"

"Yes, but you can't worry about getting your feet wet when threatened by a flood."

"There's a philosophy," laughed the deacon.

"Not at all. You are so perverted by your seminary philosophy that you only want to see the haziness in everything. The abstract sciences with which your young head was stuffed are called abstract because they abstract your mind from the obvious. Look the devil straight in the eye, and if he's a devil, then say: 'That's a devil,' and don't go crawling after Kant or Hegel for explanations."

The zoologist paused a moment, then continued: "Two times two is four and a stone is a stone. Tomorrow, now, we're having a duel. You and I will say it's foolish and absurd, that the duel has already outlived its time, that the aristocratic duel is basically no different from a drunken brawl in a tavern, and nevertheless we shan't hesitate, we'll go off and fight. Which means there is a force stronger than our reasoning. We cry that war is brigandage, barbarism, atrocity, fratricide; we can't look at blood without fainting; but it's enough for the French or the Germans to insult us for us to immediately feel our spirits aroused; we start crying 'Hurrah' with the greatest sincerity and rush at the enemy; you will invoke God's blessing on our weapons and our valor will arouse general, and what's more, sincere enthusiasm. Meaning once again that there is a force which, if no higher, is at least stronger than ourselves and our philosophy. We can't arrest it any more than we can that cloud moving in from the sea. Don't be hypocritical, don't hide an offensive gesture in your pocket, and don't say: 'Ah, it's foolish! ah it's obsolete! ah, it's not in accord with the Scriptures!'; but look it straight in the eye, recognize its rational validity, and when, for example, it is about to annihilate an infirm, scrofulous, dissolute race, don't interfere with your remedies and citations from a largely misunderstood Bible. Leskov's conscientious Danila finds a leper outside of town, feeds and warms him in the name of Love and Christ. If this Danila actually loved people, he would have dragged the leper as far away from town as possible, thrown him in a ditch, and gone to serve the healthy. Christ, I hope, entrusted us with a reasonable, intelligent, and practical love."

"What an odd one you are!" laughed the deacon. "You don't believe in Christ; why do you mention Him so often?"

"Yes, I do believe. Except, of course, in my way, not yours. Ah, Deacon, Deacon!" the zoologist laughed; he took the deacon by the waist and said merrily: "Well, what about it? Are we going to the duel tomorrow?"

"My position doesn't permit it, otherwise I'd go."

"What do you mean—position?"

"I'm ordained. I'm in a state of grace."

"Ah, Deacon, Deacon," repeated von Koren, laughing. "I love talking to you."

"You say you have faith," said the deacon. "What kind of faith is it? I have a priest-uncle who believes so firmly that when he goes in the fields during a drought to pray for rain, he takes his umbrella and leather coat so he won't get wet on the way back. There's a faith! When he talks about Christ, a light radiates from him and all the peasant men and women sob. He would arrest this cloud and send any force of yours running. Yes . . . Faith moves mountains."

The deacon laughed and clapped the zoologist on the shoulder.

"So . . ." he continued. "Here you are, constantly teaching, probing the depths of the sea, separating the strong from the weak, writing books, and issuing challenges for duels— and everything remains in its place; but let some feeble old man stammer out just one word with a holy spirit, or a new Mahomet gallop on horseback with his scimitar out of Arabia, and you'll all turn somersaults and there won't be a stone left unturned in Europe."

"Well, that, Deacon, is in the hands of fate!"

"Faith without deeds is lifeless, and deeds without faith— even worse, just a waste of time, nothing more."

The doctor appeared along the shore. He caught sight of the deacon and the zoologist and went up to them.

"I think everything's ready," he said breathlessly. "Govorovsky and Boiko will be seconds. They'll leave tomorrow morning at five o'clock. It's piling up, isn't it!" he added, looking at the sky. "You can't see a thing. There'll be rain in a minute."

"You're going with us, I hope?" asked von Koren.

"No, God help me, I'm anxious enough as it is. Ustimovich is going instead of me. I've already spoken with him."

Far over the sea lightning flashed and a hollow peal of thunder was heard.

"How stifling it is before a storm!" said von Koren. "I'll wager you've already been to Laevsky's and cried on his shoulder."

"Why should I go see him?" the doctor answered, disconcerted. "That's a good one!"

Before sunset he had walked up and down the boulevard and the street several times in the hope of meeting Laevsky. He was ashamed of his outburst and of the sudden surge of kindness which had followed it. He wanted to apologize to Laevsky in a joking tone, to chide him, reassure him, and tell him that duels were remnants of medieval barbarism, but that Providence itself had indicated the duel as a means of reconciliation: tomorrow the two of them, splendid people of the greatest intelligence, would appreciate each other's nobility and become friends after exchanging shots. But he had not encountered Laevsky.

"Why should I go to see him?" repeated Samoilenko. "I didn't insult him, he insulted me. Tell me, please, why did he attack me? What wrong had I done him? I go into the parlor and suddenly, without rhyme or reason: a spy! That's too much! Tell me: how did it start between you? What did you tell him?"

"I told him his position was insoluble. And I was right. Only honest people and swindlers can find a solution for every situation, and someone who wants to be honest and a swindler at the same time has no solution. However, gentlemen, it's already eleven, and we're getting up early tomorrow."

There was a sudden gust of wind; it raised the dust along the shore, twisted it into whirlwinds, began howling, and drowned out the sound of the sea.

"A squall!" said the deacon. "We'd better go or our eyes will be full of dust."

As they left, Samoilenko sighed and said, clutching his cap: "I probably won't be able to sleep now."

"Don't worry," laughed the zoologist. "You can be at ease; the duel won't end in anything. Laevsky will magnanimously shoot in the air, he can't do anything else, and I probably won't shoot at all. To be arrested for Laevsky, to lose time— the game isn't worth the candle. By the way, what's the penalty for dueling?"

"Arrest, and in the case of the adversary's death, imprisonment for up to three years."

"In the Petropavlovsky prison?"

"No, the military prison, I believe."

"Yet that fine fellow should be taught a lesson."

Lightning flashed over the sea behind them and momentarily illuminated the mountains and house roofs. The friends parted near the boulevard. When the doctor had disappeared in the shadows and his footsteps had died away, von Koren shouted after him: "If only the weather doesn't interfere with us tomorrow!"

"I think it might! God willing!"

"Good night!"

"What about night? What did you say?"

It was hard to hear over the noise of the wind and the sea and the rumbling of thunder.

"Nothing!" the zoologist shouted and hurried home.

XVII

> And in my mind so bowed by anguish,
> The painful thoughts crowd in abundance,
> And then in silence memory
> Unfurls its long, long scroll before me,
> And, horrified, I read my life,
> I shudder and I curse,
> Bitterly regret and pour forth bitter tears,
> But cannot wash those grievous lines away.
> —Pushkin *

Whether he was killed tomorrow morning or laughed at, that is, left alive, he was ruined all the same. Whether this dishonored woman killed herself from despair and shame or dragged on her pitiful existence, she was ruined all the same . . .

Thus Laevsky thought as he sat at the table late in the evening, still constantly rubbing his hands. The window suddenly opened and slammed, a strong wind rushed into the room, and papers flew off the table. Laevsky closed the window and bent over to gather the papers from the floor. He had a new sensation in his body, a kind of awkwardness which he had not felt before, and his own movements seemed unrecognizable; he walked hesitatingly, knocking his elbows against his sides and twitching his shoulders, and when he sat down at the table, he

* From A. S. Pushkin's "Recollections," written in 1828.

began rubbing his hands again. His body had lost its suppleness.

On the eve of death, people are expected to write to those close to them. Laevsky thought of this, took up his pen, and wrote in a trembling hand: "Mamasha!"

He wanted to write his mother in the name of the merciful God in whom she believed to shelter and warm with affection the unhappy woman he had dishonored, now solitary, impoverished, and weak; to forget and forgive everything, everything, everything, and to redeem her son's terrible sin, if only in part, by her sacrifice. However, he recalled his mother, a stout, hefty old woman in a lace mobcap, going out of the house into the garden in the mornings, followed by her companion with the lapdog; and his mother shouting in an imperious voice to the gardener and the servants; he recalled how proud and haughty her face was—and remembering this, he struck out the word he had written.

Lightning flashed vividly in all three windows and was followed by a deafening, prolonged rumble of thunder, dull at first, then roaring and crackling so violently that the glass in the windows tinkled. Laevsky got up, went to the window and leaned his forehead against the pane. There was an intense, beautiful storm outside. On the horizon, white stripes of lightning sped uninterruptedly from the clouds to the sea and illuminated the high black waves in the far distance. Lightning flashed on the right and left and probably over the house too.

"A storm!" whispered Laevsky; he felt a desire to pray to someone or something, even to the lightning or the clouds. "Dear storm!"

He remembered as a child running out bareheaded into the garden during a storm and two blond little girls with blue eyes chasing after him and being drenched by the rain; the little girls used to giggle with delight, but when a strong clap of thunder burst, they trustingly pressed close to the little boy while he crossed himself and hastily chanted: "Holy . . ." Oh, where have you gone, in what sea did you drown, you tender shoots of a fine, pure life? He no longer feared storms nor loved nature; he had no God, all the trusting little girls he had known once had been spoiled by him and by his contemporaries; he had never planted a single tree nor grown a single blade of grass in his native garden in all his life; living among the living, had never saved so much as a fly, but only destroyed, ruined, and lied, lied . . .

"Was there anything in my past that wasn't evil?" he asked

himself, trying to catch hold of some bright memory as a man falling into a chasm catches at bushes.

School? University? But that was all deception. He had studied poorly and forgotten what he was taught. Service to society? That was a deception too because he had never done anything in the job, had been given his salary for nothing, and his job was an abominable public swindle exempt from prosecution in court.

He had no need for the truth and did not seek it; bewitched by evil and lying, his conscience had slept or kept silent; like a stranger or someone hired from another planet, he had taken no part in the common life of men, had been indifferent to their sufferings, ideas, religions, teachings, quests, and struggles; he never said a kind word to anyone; never wrote a useful or meaningful line; never did the slightest thing for others, but just ate their bread, drank their wine, stole their wives, lived on their thoughts, and to justify his despicable, parasitic life to them and to himself, always tried to make himself appear loftier and better than they. Lies, lies, lies . . .

He remembered clearly what he had seen that evening at Muridov's, and suffered from unbearable disgust and anguish. Kirilin and Achmianov were loathsome, but, of course, they were only continuing what he had begun; they were his collaborators and disciples. This weak young woman—who trusted him more than a brother—he had deprived her of husband, circle of friends, and country, and had brought here to sultry heat, fever, and tedium. Day after day, like a mirror, she had reflected his laziness, viciousness, and lying—and her weak, listless, pitiful life was filled by this and this alone. Then he had had enough of her, grown to hate her, but lacking the courage to drop her, had kept trying to ensnare her more tightly in lies, like a spiderweb . . . These men had completed the rest.

Laevsky first sat at the table, then walked over to the window again; then he put out the candle, then relit it. He cursed himself aloud, wept, wailed, and begged forgiveness; several times he ran to the table in despair and wrote: "Mamasha!"

Aside from his mother he had no relatives or close friends; but how could his mother help him? And where was she? He wanted to run to Nadezhda, to fall at her feet, kiss her hands and feet, and beg her to forgive him; but she was his victim: he was afraid of her as if she were dead.

"My life is ruined!" he muttered, rubbing his hands. "Why am I still alive, my God! . . ."

He had knocked his dim star out of the sky and it had fallen, its trace merging with the nocturnal darkness; it would never return to the sky because life is given but once and not renewed. If it were possible to recover the last days and years, he would turn the lies in them to truth, the idleness to work, the boredom to joy; he would restore purity to those he had robbed of it, would find God and righteousness, but this was as impossible as restoring the fallen star to the sky. And because it was impossible, he fell into despair.

When the storm passed, he was sitting at the open window and thinking calmly about what lay before him. Von Koren would probably kill him. The man's clear, cold view of the world permitted the annihilation of the feeble and worthless; if it wavered at the decisive moment, von Koren would be aided by the hatred and aversion with which Laevsky inspired him. If von Koren missed, or, to laugh at a despised adversary, just wounded him or fired in the air, what could he do then? Where could he go?

"To St. Petersburg?" Laevsky asked himself. "But that would mean starting over the old life I've been cursing. And anybody who looks for salvation in a change of scene like a migrating bird won't find anything, for the whole world is the same for him. Seek salvation in people? In whom and how? There is as little salvation in the kindness and generosity of Samoilenko as in the deacon's amusement and von Koren's hate. Salvation must be sought only in one's self, and if you don't find it, why waste time? You have to kill yourself, that's all . . ."

There was the sound of a vehicle. It was already dawn. An open carriage drove past, turned, and stopped near the house, its wheels grating on the wet sand. There were two men inside.

"Wait, I'll be right there!" Laevsky told them through the window. "I'm not asleep. Can it be time already?"

"Yes. Four o'clock. By the time we get there . . ."

Laevsky put on an overcoat and cap, put cigarettes in his pocket, and stopped in hesitation: he felt there was something else to be done. The seconds were talking softly in the street, the horses were snorting, and these sounds in the early damp morning, when everyone was asleep and the sky was barely light, filled Laevsky's heart with a despondent feeling resembling a foreboding of evil. He stood in hesitation for a moment, then went into the bedroom.

Nadezhda was lying in bed, stretched out, wrapped from head to toe in the blanket; she was motionless and her head in particular reminded him of an Egyptian mummy. Looking at her in silence, Laevsky mentally asked her forgiveness and thought that if the heavens were not empty and there were, in fact, a God, He would protect her; if there were no God, then let her perish; there was no reason for her to live.

She suddenly started and sat up in bed. Raising her pale face and looking with terror at Laevsky, she asked: "Is it you? Is the storm over?"

"It's over."

She remembered, covered her head with both hands, and her whole body shuddered.

"How hard it is for me!" she uttered. "If you only knew how hard it is for me! I've been waiting," she continued, frowning, "for you to kill me or chase me out of the house into the rain and storm, but you keep delaying . . . delaying . . ."

He embraced her firmly and impulsively, covered her knees and hands with kisses; when she muttered something to him and shuddered in recollection, he stroked her hair and, looking her in the face, realized that this unhappy, sinful woman was the one person close to him, tied to him, and irreplaceable.

When he left the house and sat down in the carriage, he wanted to come home alive.

XVIII

The deacon got up, dressed, took his thick, knotty walking stick and left the house quietly. It was dark, and as he walked down the street, he could not even see his white stick at first; there was not a star in the sky and it looked as if it would rain again. There was a smell of wet sand and sea.

"I hope the Chechens don't attack," thought the deacon, listening to the knock of his stick on the pavement and to the resonance and loneliness of the sound in the nocturnal stillness.

As he left the town, he began to distinguish both the road and his stick; murky spots appeared here and there in the black sky, and soon one star looked out and timidly winked its single eye. The deacon walked along the high rocky coast without seeing the sea; it lay slumbering below, and its unseen waves broke languidly and ponderously against the coast as if sighing: Oof! And how slowly! By the time one wave had broken, the deacon had time to count eight steps; then another broke, and after six steps, a third, and still nothing was visible, and in the darkness, the lazy, drowsy sound of the sea was audible, and also that infinitely remote, inconceivable time when God overcame chaos.

The deacon felt uneasy. He was wondering whether God would punish him for keeping company with unbelievers and even going to watch their duel. The duel would be trivial, bloodless, and absurd, but a heathen spectacle nevertheless, and it was completely improper for a member of the clergy to be present. He stopped and deliberated—shouldn't he go back? But an intense, troubled curiosity overcame his doubts and he went on.

"Even though they're unbelievers, they're good people and will be saved," he reassured himself. "They're bound to be saved!" he said aloud, lighting a cigarette.

By what standard should one measure people's worth in order to judge them rightly? The deacon remembered his enemy, the inspector of the clerical institution, who believed in God, did not fight duels, and lived in abstinence, but sometimes fed the deacon bread mixed with sand and had once almost torn off his ear. If human life was so stupidly arranged that everyone respected and said prayers in the institution for the health and salvation of this cruel, dishonest inspector who stole government flour, then could it be just to shun people like von Koren and Laevsky solely because they were unbelievers? The deacon tried to resolve this question, but the recollection of how ridiculous Samoilenko had looked that day interrupted his flow of thoughts. What a good laugh they would have tomorrow! The deacon pictured how he would hide behind a bush and watch, and how when von Koren began boasting at dinner tomorrow, he, the deacon, would laughingly begin telling him all the details of the duel.

"How do you know everything?" the zoologist would ask.

"I just do. I stayed home, but I know."

It would be fine to write about the duel in an amusing vein. His father-in-law would laugh when he read it; he didn't need *kasha* to eat if he could feast on amusing stories, read or told.

The Yellow River valley opened up ahead. The rain had made the river wider and more vicious, and it no longer grumbled as before, but roared. Day was breaking. The dull gray morning and the clouds scurrying to the west to overtake the thunderheads, the mountains girded with mist, and the wet trees—all looked ugly and angry to the deacon. He washed himself in the stream, said his morning prayers, and longed for the tea and hot pastries which were served at his father-in-law's every morning. He thought of the deaconess and the piece, "Beyond Recall," which she used to play on the piano. What sort of woman was she? The deacon had been introduced, engaged, and married to her in one week; he had lived with her less than a month before being ordered here, so that he had not yet figured out what sort of person she was. And still he was rather lonely without her.

"Ought to write her a letter . . ." he thought.

The flag on the tavern was rain-soaked and drooped, and the tavern itself looked darker and lower than before with its wet roof. A nomad cart was standing near the door; Kerbalai, two Abkhazians, and a young Tartar woman in baggy trousers, probably Kerbalai's wife or daughter, were carrying sacks of something out of the tavern and putting them on corn straw in the cart. Near the cart stood a pair of donkeys with lowered heads. After putting in the sacks, the Abkhazians and the Tartar woman covered them with straw, while Kerbalai hurriedly harnessed donkeys to the cart.

"Contraband, I suppose," thought the deacon.

There was the fallen tree with the dried needles; there, the black patch from the fire. It recalled the picnic in all its detail: the fire, the singing of the Abkhazians, his sweet dreams about being a bishop and about the religious procession . . . The Black River was wider and blacker from the rain. The deacon walked cautiously across the rickety little bridge, now licked by the crests of the muddy waves, and clambered up the ladder into the drying loft.

"A splendid mind!" he thought, stretching out on the straw and thinking about von Koren. "A fine mind, God grant him health. Except there's cruelty in him . . ."

Why did he hate Laevsky and Laevsky him? Why were they fighting a duel? If they had known the poverty the deacon had since childhood, if they had been brought up in the midst of ignorant, callous souls, grasping, coarse, and boorish, who abused each other for a crust of bread, who spat on the floor and belched at dinner and during prayers—if they had not been spoiled from childhood by favorable surroundings and a cultured circle, how they would have seized upon one another, how eagerly they would have mutually forgiven each other's shortcomings and valued what each had. For there were so few even outwardly respectable people in the world! True,

Laevsky was unbalanced, dissolute, and peculiar, but he didn't steal, spit loudly on the floor, or abuse his wife, saying: "You stuff yourself to the bursting but don't want to work," nor did he beat children with harness reins or feed his servants putrid salt beef—wasn't that enough for him to be treated indulgently? In addition to which, you see, he was the first to suffer from his shortcomings, like an invalid from his sores. Instead of being led from boredom and a misconception of some sort to seek degeneration, extinction, heredity, and other incomprehensible things in each other, would it not be better for them to descend and direct their hatred and anger where there were streets on end groaning with coarse ignorance, greed, reproaches, filth, cursing, women's screams . . .

The clatter of a vehicle interrupted the deacon's thoughts. He glanced out the door and saw an open carriage with three men in it: Laevsky, Sheshkovsky, and the head of the postal-telegraph office.

"Stop!" said Sheshkovsky.

All three climbed out of the carriage and looked at one another.

"They're not here yet," said Sheshkovsky, brushing off the mud. "Well? Before things get going, let's look for a suitable spot. There isn't room to turn around here."

They went farther up the river and quickly disappeared from view. The Tartar coachman sat in the carriage, leaned his head on his shoulder, and fell asleep. After waiting ten minutes, the deacon left the drying loft, and, having removed his black hat to avoid being noticed, crouching and looking around, he began picking his way along the bank through the bushes and strips of corn; big drops splattered him from the trees and bushes; the grass and corn were wet.

"It's a shame!" he muttered, picking up his wet, muddy skirt. "If I'd known, I wouldn't have come."

Soon he heard voices and saw people. Laevsky, hunched over, with his hands in his sleeves, was walking rapidly to and fro in a small glade; his seconds were standing on the bank and rolling cigarettes.

"Strange . . ." thought the deacon, not recognizing Laevsky's gait; "like an old man."

"How rude of them!" said the postal official, looking at his watch. "Maybe it's educated and fine to be late, but in my opinion, it's swinery."

Sheshkovsky, a fat man with a black beard, listened and said: "They're coming!"

XIX

"First time in my life I've seen it! How marvelous!" said von Koren, appearing in the glade and stretching out both hands to the east. "Look: green rays!"

From behind the mountains in the east spread two green rays, and it was, in fact, beautiful. The sun was rising.

"Good morning!" continued the zoologist, bowing to Laevsky's seconds. "I'm not late?"

Behind him came his seconds, two very young officers of identical height in white tunics, Boiko and Govorovsky, and the gaunt unsociable Dr. Ustimovich, who carried a bag in one hand and held the other hand behind him; as usual a walking stick was stretched along his back. Putting the bag down on the ground and greeting no one, he placed his other hand behind his back and began pacing up and down the glade.

Laevsky felt the weariness and awkwardness of a man who may soon die and is therefore the object of general interest. He longed to either be killed quickly or be taken home. He was seeing the sunrise now for the first time in his life; this early morning, the green rays, the dampness, and the people in wet boots struck him as unnecessary and superfluous in his life and disconcerted him; none of it had any connection with the night he had gone through, with his thoughts, or his feeling of guilt, and therefore he would have left gladly without waiting for the duel.

Von Koren was noticeably agitated and trying to hide it, pretending to be more interested in the green rays than anything else. The seconds were perplexed and exchanged glances with each other as if asking why they were there and what they were supposed to do.

"I suppose there's no point in our going farther, gentlemen," said Sheshkovsky. "It's all right here."

"Yes, of course," agreed von Koren.

A silence fell. Ustimovich, pacing, suddenly turned sharply toward Laevsky and said in a low voice, breathing in his face: "They probably haven't had time to inform you of my terms. Each side pays me fifteen rubles, and in the case of the death of one of the adversaries, the survivor pays the whole thirty."

Laevsky had met this man before, but only now for the first

time saw his dull eyes, bristling mustaches, and wasted, tubercular neck distinctly: a usurer, not a doctor! His breath had a disagreeable, meaty smell.

"What people there are in the world," thought Laevsky, and he answered: "Fine."

The doctor nodded and began pacing again, and it was clear that he did not need the money at all, but asked for it simply out of animosity. Everyone felt that it was now time to begin or finish what was begun, but they neither began nor finished, but walked around, stood, and smoked. The young officers—who were present at a duel for the first time in their lives and had little conviction in this civilian and, in the opinion, unnecessary duel—scrutinized their tunics and smoothed their sleeves. Sheshkovsky went up to them and said softly: "Gentlemen, we must make every effort to keep this duel from taking place. They should be reconciled."

He reddened and continued: "Yesterday Kirilin came to see me and complained that Laevsky had found him with Nadezhda Fedorovna that evening and all that."

"Yes, we knew of it too," said Boiko.

"Well, there, you see . . . Laevsky's hands are trembling and all that . . . He can't lift a pistol now. It's as inhuman to fight with him as to fight a drunk or someone with typhus. If there's no reconciliation, gentlemen, then the duel should be postponed, eh . . . It's such a sickening business I can't watch."

"You should talk to von Koren."

"I don't know the rules of dueling, the devil take them all, and I don't care to know them; perhaps he'll think Laevsky's turned coward and sent me to him. But anyhow, as he likes, I'll still speak to him."

Hesitatingly, limping slightly as if his foot had fallen asleep, Sheshkovsky went up to von Koren and his whole figure exuded indolence as he walked and cleared his throat.

"Here's what I'm obliged to tell you, sir," he began, looking intently at the flowers on the zoologist's shirt. "This is confidential . . . I don't know the rules of dueling, the devil take them, and I don't want to know them and am speaking not as a second and all that, but as a man and so on."

"Yes. Well?"

"When seconds propose reconciliation, they're usually not listened to; it's looked on as a formality. Vanity and so on. But I humbly beg you to look carefully at Ivan Andreich. He's not in a normal condition today, so to speak, not in his right mind and to be pitied. He's had a misfortune. I can't stand gossip"—Sheshkovsky reddened and glanced around—"but in view of the duel, I find it necessary to inform you. Yesterday evening he found his lady in Muridov's house with . . . a certain gentleman."

"How revolting!" muttered the zoologist; he paled, blinked, and spat loudly. "Tfoo!"

His lower lip began to tremble; he walked away from Sheshkovsky, not wanting to hear more, and as if he had accidentally tasted something bitter, spat loudly again and for the first time that morning glanced with animosity at Laevsky. His agitation and awkwardness had passed; he shook his head and said loudly: "Gentlemen, what are we waiting for, I ask you? Why don't we begin?"

Sheshkovsky exchanged glances with the officers and shrugged his shoulders.

"Gentlemen!" he said loudly without addressing anyone in particular. "Gentlemen! We propose a reconciliation!"

"Let's end the formalities as quickly as possible," said von Koren. "Reconciliation has already been discussed. Now what other formality is there? Make it quick, gentlemen, time doesn't wait."

"But we nevertheless insist on a reconciliation," said Sheshkovsky in the guilty voice of a man forced to interfere in someone else's affairs; he flushed, put his hand on his heart, and continued: "Gentlemen, we do not see a reasonable connection between the affront and a duel. The insults we sometimes inflict on each other through human weakness have nothing to do with dueling. You are university men and educated, and you yourselves naturally regard the duel as just an outdated, empty formality and all that. We look at it the same way or we shouldn't have come, as we can't permit people to shoot one another in our presence, and so on." Sheshkovsky wiped the perspiration from his face and continued: "Put an end to your misunderstanding, gentlemen, shake hands, and let's go home to drink to peace. On my word, gentlemen!"

Von Koren was silent. Laevsky, noticing that the others were looking at him, said: "I have nothing against Nikolai Vassilievich. If he finds me guilty, I'm ready to apologize to him."

Von Koren was offended. "Obviously, gentlemen," he said, "it suits you for Monsieur Laevsky to return home magnanimous and chivalrous, but I cannot give you or him this satisfaction. And there was no need to get up early and drive ten versts out of town in order to drink to peace, have a bite, and explain to me that a duel is an outdated formality. A duel is a duel, and it should not be made more stupid and false than it actually is. I want to fight!"

A silence fell. Boiko took two pistols out of the box: one was given to von Koren, the other to Laevsky, and then ensued a confusion which diverted the zoologist and the seconds briefly. It turned out that not one of those present had ever been at a duel in his life and no one knew exactly how the parties were supposed to stand and what the seconds were to do and say. But then Boiko remembered, and smiling, began to explain.

"Gentlemen, who remembers the description in Lermontov?" asked von Koren, laughing. "In Turgenev, too, Bazarov exchanged shots with someone there . . ."

"What is there to remember?" said Ustimovich impatiently, stopping still. "Measure off the distance—that's all."

And he took three paces as if to show how the measuring should be done. Boiko counted off the paces while his companion unsheathed his saber and scratched the ground at the extremes to mark the barrier.

The opponents took their places in a general silence.

"Moles," thought the deacon from his seat in the bushes.

Sheshkovsky said something, Boiko explained something again, but Laevsky failed to hear, or, to be more exact, heard, but did not understand. When the time came, he cocked the cold, heavy pistol and raised its muzzle upward. He had forgotten to unbutton his overcoat; it bound him sharply in the shoulder and under the arm, and he lifted his arm as awkwardly as if his sleeve were made of iron. He recalled his hatred of yesterday for the swarthy forehead and curly hair, and thought that even yesterday, in a moment of intense hatred and anger, he could not have shot a man. Afraid the bullet might hit von Koren by accident, he kept lifting his pistol higher and higher, and although he felt this overobvious magnanimity was indelicate and not magnanimous, he could not do otherwise. Looking at the pale, sarcastically smiling face of von Koren, who obviously had been certain from the very beginning that his adversary would shoot in the air, Laevsky thought that now, thank God, everything would be finished and he only had to squeeze the trigger tighter . . .

There was a violent blow on his shoulder, the shot rang out, and in the mountains, the echo answered: pah-tah!

Von Koren cocked his gun too and glanced in the direction

of Ustimovich, who was pacing as before, his hands behind his back, not paying attention to anything.

"Doctor," said the zoologist, "be so kind as not to walk like a pendulum. You're distracting my vision."

The doctor stopped. Von Koren aimed at Laevsky.

"It's finished!" thought Laevsky.

The muzzle of the pistol, aimed directly in his face; the expression of hatred and contempt in von Koren's stance and entire body; this slaughter which was about to be committed by a respectable man in broad daylight in front of respectable people; this hush, and the strange force compelling Laevsky to stand still and not run away—how mysterious all this was, how incomprehensible and terrible! The time von Koren took to aim seemed longer than a night to Laevsky. He glanced imploringly at the seconds; they were immobile and pale.

"Hurry up and shoot!" thought Laevsky and felt that his pale, quivering, pitiable face must be arousing even more hatred in von Koren.

"I'll kill him now," thought von Koren, aiming at Laevsky's forehead and fingering the trigger. "Yes, of course I'll kill him . . ."

"He'll kill him!" a despairing cry was heard from somewhere very close.

Just then the shot rang out. On seeing Laevsky standing in the same spot, still upright, everyone looked in the direction of the cry and saw the deacon. Pale, with wet hair clinging to his cheeks and forehead, thoroughly drenched and muddy, he was standing on the far bank in a cornfield, smiling somewhat oddly and waving his wet hat. Sheshkovsky laughed with joy, burst into tears, and went off to one side . . .

XX

A bit later von Koren and the deacon met near the bridge. The deacon was excited, breathing heavily, and avoided looking von Koren in the eyes. He was ashamed of both his fright and his dirty, wet clothing.

"It seemed to me you wanted to kill him . . ." he muttered. "How contrary to human nature this is! How intensely unnatural!"

"But how did you get here?" asked the zoologist.

"Don't ask me!" the deacon waved his hand. "The Evil One tempted me, saying: 'Go, go' . . . So I went and I almost died of fright in the cornfield. But now, thank God, thank God . . . I'm thoroughly pleased with you," muttered the deacon. "And our Grandpa Tarantula will be pleased . . . What a good laugh, what a good laugh! But I sincerely beg you not to tell anyone I was here or I might get in trouble with the authorities. They'll say that the deacon was a second."

"Gentlemen!" said von Koren. "The deacon asks you not to tell anyone you saw him here. It could have unpleasant consequences."

"How contrary to human nature this is!" sighed the deacon. "Be kind enough to forgive me, but your expression made me think you would surely kill him."

"I was strongly tempted to put an end to that scoundrel," said von Koren, "but you shouted close by and I missed him. Nevertheless, this whole procedure is unpleasant if you're not used to it and it's worn me out, Deacon. I feel terribly exhausted. Let's go . . ."

"No, let me go on foot now. I must get dry, I'm drenched and frozen."

"Well, as you think best," the exhausted zoologist said wearily as he got into the carriage and closed his eyes. "As you think best . . ."

While the men were walking around their vehicles and taking their places, Kerbalai stood at the roadside, both hands on his stomach, bowing low and displaying his teeth; he thought the gentlemen had come to enjoy nature and drink tea and did not understand why they were getting into their carriages.

The caravan started off in general silence leaving only the deacon near the tavern.

"Came tavern, drink tea," he said to Kerbalai. "Me want eat."

Kerbalai spoke Russian well, but the deacon thought the Tartar would understand him better if adressed in broken Russian.

"Cook egg, give cheese . . ."

"Come in, come in, Father," said Kerbalai, bowing. "I'll provide everything . . . There's cheese and there's wine . . . Eat whatever you want."

"What is 'God' in Tartar?" the deacon asked, going into the tavern.

"Your God and my God are the same," answered Kerbalai, who had misunderstood. "There is one God for all, only people are different. Some are Russian, some Turkish, some English—there are many peoples of all kinds, but one God."

"Fine. If all peoples worship one God, then why should you Moslems regard Christians as your eternal enemies?"

"Why get angry?" said Kerbalai, embracing his stomach with both hands. "You're a priest, I'm a Moslem, you say 'I want to eat,' I give you food . . . Only the rich distinguish which is your God and which mine; to the poor it's all the same. Eat, if you please."

While this theological discussion was taking place in the tavern, Laevsky was driving home and remembering how hard it had been for him to leave at dawn when the road, rocks, and mountains were wet and dark and the unknown future seemed as awesome as a bottomless abyss, while now the raindrops clinging to the grass and stones sparkled like diamonds in the sun, nature smiled joyfully, and the awesome future had been left behind. He looked at Sheshkovsky's sullen, tearstained face, glanced ahead at the two carriages in which von Koren, his seconds, and the doctor were sitting, and it seemed to him as if they were all returning from the cemetery where they had just buried a tedious, unbearable man who had been a burden to everyone.

"Everything's finished." He thought of his past, cautiously stroking his neck with his fingers.

A small blister the length and breadth of his little finger was swelling on the right side of his neck, near the collar, and he felt a pain as if a hot iron had brushed his neck. It was the contusion of a bullet.

Later, when he reached home, there stretched before him a long, strange, sweet day, as misty as slumber. Like a man just released from prison or a hospital, he stared at long-familiar objects and marveled to find that the tables, windows, chairs, light, and sea aroused a keen, childish joy in him such as he had not felt since long, long ago. Pale, wan Nadezhda found his kind voice and unfamiliar bearing inexplicable; she hastily told him everything that had happened to her . . . She felt he must be listening inattentively and failing to understand her, and that if he knew everything, he would curse and kill her, but he listened to her, stroked her face and hair, looked her in the eyes, and said: "I have no one but you . . ."

Then they sat in the garden for a long time, pressed against each other, and were silent or, dreaming aloud about their future happy life, said short, broken phrases, and it seemed to

Laevsky that he had never before spoken so lengthily and eloquently.

XXI

More than three months had passed.

The day von Koren had chosen for his departure arrived. A heavy, cold rain had been falling since early morning; the northeast wind was blowing and the waves were high on the sea. It was said that in such weather the steamer could barely get into the roadstead. According to the schedule, it was to arrive at ten in the morning, but von Koren, going out on the shore before and after the midday meal, saw nothing through his binoculars except the gray waves and rain, sheathing the horizon.

Toward the end of the day, the rain stopped and the wind began dropping perceptibly. Von Koren had already become reconciled to the thought that he would not leave that day and had settled down to play chess with Samoilenko; but when twilight fell, the orderly announced that lights had appeared on the sea and the signal rockets had been sighted.

Von Koren hurried. He put his satchel over his shoulder, embraced Samoilenko and the deacon, walked around all the rooms completely uselessly, took leave of the orderly and the cook, and went out in the street with the feeling that he had forgotten something at the doctor's apartment or in his own. He walked down the street beside Samoilenko, followed by the deacon with a chest, and, last of all, the orderly with two small trunks. Only Samoilenko and the orderly were able to make out the dim lights on the sea; the rest stared into the darkness and saw nothing. The steamer had stopped far from shore.

"Faster, faster," hurried von Koren. "I'm afraid it'll leave!"

As they passed the three-windowed little house to which Laevsky had moved soon after the duel, von Koren could not resist glancing through the window. Laevsky was sitting, writing, bent over a table with his back to the window.

"I'm amazed," said the zoologist softly. "How he's sobered down!"

"Yes, it merits amazement," sighed Samoilenko. "He sits like that from morning till evening, just sits and works. He wants to pay off his debts. And, brother, he lives worse than a pauper!"

Half a minute passed in silence. The zoologist, the doctor, and the deacon stood at the window and watched Laevsky.

"So he never got away from here, the poor man," said Samoilenko. "And do you remember the efforts he made?"

"Yes, he's greatly sobered down," von Koren repeated. "His marriage, this all-day labor for a crust of bread, a new expression in his face and even his bearing—it's all so extraordinary that I don't know what to call it." The zoologist took Samoilenko by the sleeve and continued in an agitated voice: "Tell him and his wife that when I was leaving I marveled at them, wished them the best of everything . . . and beg him, if he can, not to bear me ill will. He knows me. He knows that if I could have foreseen this change back then, I might have become his best friend."

"You go see him; say farewell."

"No. It's awkward."

"Why? God knows, you may never see him again."

After a moment's reflection, the zoologist said: "That's true."

Samoilenko tapped gently on the window with his fingers. Laevsky started and looked around.

"Vanya, Nikolai Vassilievich wants to say good-by to you," said Samoilenko. "He's leaving right now."

Laevsky got up from the table and went to the entrance to open the door. Samoilenko, von Koren, and the deacon came into the house.

"I'll only stay a minute," the zoologist began, taking off his galoshes in the entrance and already regretting that he had yielded to his feelings and come in uninvited. It's as if I were intruding, he thought, and it's stupid. "Forgive me for disturbing you," he said, following Laevsky into the room, "but I'm leaving right now and I felt like seeing you. God knows whether we'll meet again."

"I'm delighted . . . Do sit down, please," said Laevsky, and he awkwardly placed chairs for his guests as if wanting to bar the way to them, then stopped in the middle of the room, rubbing his hands.

"Too bad I didn't leave my witnesses in the street," thought von Koren, and he said firmly: "Don't bear me ill will, Ivan Andreich. Of course, the past can't be forgotten, it's too painful, and I did not come here to apologize or to claim I wasn't guilty. I acted sincerely and haven't changed my convictions since . . . It's true, as I see now, to my great joy, that I was mistaken about you, but, of course, it's human fate to stumble even on a level road; it's man's lot: if you're not mistaken in the major things, you make mistakes in the details. No one knows the real truth."

"Yes, no one knows the truth . . ." said Laevsky.

"Well, good-by . . . God give you all the best."

Von Koren gave Laevsky his hand; the latter pressed it and bowed.

"Don't bear ill will," said von Koren. "My respects to your wife, and tell her I very much regret not being able to say good-by to her."

"She's home."

Laevsky went to the door and called into the next room: "Nadya, Nikolai Vassilievich wants to say good-by to you."

In came Nadezhda; she stopped near the doorway and glanced timidly at the guests. Her face looked guilty and alarmed, and she held her hands like a schoolgirl being scolded.

"I'm leaving right now, Nadezhda Fedorovna," said von Koren, "and came to say good-by."

She hesitatingly held out her hand, while Laevsky bowed.

"But how pitiful they both are!" thought von Koren. "This life of theirs isn't easy for them."

"I'll be in Moscow and St. Petersburg," he said. "Isn't there anything you want sent from there?"

"Well," said Nadezhda, and she exchanged anxious glances with her husband. "Nothing, I think . . ."

"No, nothing . . ." said Laevsky, rubbing his hands. "My best wishes."

Von Koren did not know what else could or should be said, although when he had come in, he had thought he would say a great deal that was fine, warm, and significant. He silently pressed Laevsky's hand and his wife's, and left their house with a heavy feeling.

"What people!" said the deacon in a low voice, walking behind. "My God, what people! Verily, God's right hand planted this vine. Lord, Lord! One man conquers thousands and another ten thousand. Nikolai Vassilievich," he said enthusiastically, "you know, today you conquered man's greatest enemy —pride!"

"Nonsense, Deacon! What sort of conquerors do we make? Conquerors look like eagles, while he's pitiful, timid, beaten, bowing like a Chinese idol, and I'm . . . I'm saddened."

There were footsteps behind. It was Laevsky running to see him off. On the wharf stood the orderly with two trunks, and somewhat in the distance, four oarsmen.

"Why it's blowing . . . brr!" said Samoilenko. "Must be a bit of a storm at sea now— Yes, yes! You're not leaving at a good time, Kolya."

"I'm not afraid of seasickness."

"That's not the point . . . If these fools just don't capsize you. You ought to have gone on the agent's sloop. Where's the agent's sloop?" he shouted to the oarsmen.

"It's gone, Your Excellency."

"And the customs sloop?"

"Gone, too."

"Why didn't they announce it?" Samoilenko grew angry. "Blockheads!"

"It doesn't matter, don't worry . . ." said von Koren. "Well, good-by. God keep you."

Samoilenko embraced von Koren and made the sign of the cross over him three times.

"Don't forget us, Kolya . . . Write . . . We'll expect you next spring."

"Good-by, Deacon," said von Koren, shaking the deacon's hand. "Thanks for your company and the good conversation. Think about the expedition."

"Yes, Lord, even to the end of the earth!" laughed the deacon. "I've nothing against it."

Von Koren recognized Laevsky in the darkness and silently held out his hand. The oarsmen were standing below now, holding back the boat, which was beating against the piles, although the jetty protected it from the big breakers. Von Koren descended the ladder, jumped onto the boat, and sat down at the helm.

"Write!" Samoilenko shouted to him. "Take care of yourself!"

"No one knows the real truth," thought Laevsky, raising the collar of his overcoat and thrusting his hands into his sleeves.

The boat swiftly left the harbor for the open sea. Disappearing in the waves, it would immediately glide from a deep pit onto a high crest so that the men and even the oars could be distinguished. For every three yards the boat advanced, it was hurled back two.

"Write!" shouted Samoilenko. "What the devil makes you go off in this weather!"

"Yes, no one knows the real truth . . ." thought Laevsky, looking with despair at the agitated, black sea.

"It hurls the boat back," he thought; "she takes two steps forward and one backward, but the oarsmen are stubborn, they ply the oars indefatigably and aren't afraid of the high waves. The boat keeps advancing and advancing; now it's out of sight, and in half an hour the oarsmen will see the steamer lights clearly, and in an hour they'll already be alongside the steamer ladder. It's the same in life . . . In searching for the truth, men take two steps forward and one backward. Suffering, mistakes, and the tedium of life thrust them back, but the thirst for the truth and a stubborn will drive them on and on. And who knows? Maybe they'll reach the real truth . . ."

"Good-by-y-y!" shouted Samoilenko.

"Out of sight and out of hearing," said the deacon. "Happy journey!"

Rain began sprinkling.

Ward No. 6

<<<><><><><><><><><><><><><><><><><><><><><><><><><><>>>

This story was written by Chekhov early in 1892. On March 31, he wrote to Suvorin that he was writing a story in which there was a great deal of "argument" and "no love element," which had a plot and a denouement, and was "liberal" in its orientation. About a month later, when the story was finished, he described it to Mme Avilova as "very tedious," because there was no woman in it and no love element, adding: "I cannot stand this kind of story, I wrote it somehow inadvertently, out of frivolousness." The story was to be published in *Russkoe Obozrenie* (*The Russian Review*), and Chekhov even received an advance payment of five hundred rubles. He used, however, some pretext for reclaiming his manuscript, refunded the money, and handed the story over to Vukol Lavrov, the well-known translator of Polish novelists and the joint editor of the Liberal-Populist *Russkaya Mysl* (*Russian Thought*). This marked the beginning of Chekhov's long association with this progressive journal, one of the leading Russian literary-political monthlies, which a couple of years earlier had accused him of "lack of principles." The reconciliation came about on Lavrov's initiative: in April 1892 he wrote Chekhov a letter, asking him to forget their "misunderstanding" and inviting contributions from him. Chekhov immediately agreed and sent him "An Anonymous Story," but later asked that priority be given to "Ward No. 6." The latter was published in the November 1892 issue of *Russian Thought*. When he sent the story to Lavrov, Chekhov described it—not without some false modesty perhaps—as something that needed "refurbishing," for "otherwise it smells of a hospital and a mortuary," adding again: "I am not one for this kind of story."

The story was enthusiastically received by many of Chekhov's literary and artistic friends. The celebrated artist Ilya Repin spoke of the great impression which Chekhov's "hospital story" had made on him. "It is just incomprehensible," he wrote to Chekhov, "how out of such a simple unpretentious story, so skimpy even in contents, there emerges ultimately such an irresistibly profound and colossal idea of mankind. I am amazed, fascinated." Vladimir Chertkov, Tolstoy's friend and follower, wrote Chekhov an enthusiastic letter and asked for permission to publish the story as part of the series of inexpensive editions for the people, launched by himself and another Tolstoyan, Ivan Gorbunov-Posadov. Later Chertkov mentioned Tolstoy's favorable opinion of the story. The well-known writer Alexander Ertel, in a letter to Lavrov, spoke of the story as "a masterly and profound piece, though not without defects from the point of view of Pushkinian clarity and soberness," adding that it "represented fictional meditations about life rather than life itself." The impression produced on Lenin by the story is often quoted from the reminiscences of his sister. According to her, Lenin said that the reading of "Ward No. 6" had such an oppressive effect on him that he felt like going out of his room and taking a breath of fresh air: while he was reading it, it seemed to him that he had himself been locked up in Ward No. 6.

The story was also praised by most of the critics, although not without some reservations; thus, Nikolay Mikhailovsky found the idea of the story unclear. As was usual in those days, it was the social and ideological "message" of the story, rather than its literary qualities, that received critical attention. The story was interpreted both as a symbol (Chekhov's psychiatric ward as a microcosm of contemporary Russia— something that was probably quite far from Chekhov's own intentions) and on a purely utilitarian plane. This latter approach is illustrated by the following episode. Many years later, the editor of the unofficial section of an official provincial newspaper (*The Arkhangelsk Provincial Gazette*) asked for permission to reprint the story in his paper in order to attract attention to the abuses rampant in the local hospital and especially in its psychiatric section. Chekhov passed on the request to his publisher Marks, but the latter turned it down. In modern Chekhov criticism the story is often interpreted as a rejoinder to Tolstoy's doctrine of nonresistance to evil.

The story was reprinted in 1893 in a collection bearing the same title, and there was also an almost simultaneous separate edition of it, with some cuts made by the censorship. On the whole, Chekhov was, however, surprised by the leniency shown by the censors.

—◇◇◇◇◇◇◇◇◇◇◇◇◇◇◇◇◇◇◇◇◇◇◇◇◇◇◇◇◇◇◇—

I

In the hospital courtyard stands a rather small annex, enclosed by a whole forest of burdocks, nettles, and wild hemp. Its roof is rusted, its chimney half collapsed, the porch steps are rotted and overgrown with grass, and only traces remain of the stucco. The front faces the hospital; the back overlooks a field, isolated by the gray, nail-studded hospital wall. These nails, their tips pointed upward, the wall, and the annex itself have that unique, melancholy, accursed look peculiar to our hospital and prison edifices.

If you are not afraid of being stung by the nettles, let us go up the narrow path leading to the building and see what is happening inside. Opening the first door, we walk into the entry. Here, along the walls and around the stove, are piled mounds of hospital rubbish. Mattresses, old, torn bathrobes, trousers, blue-striped shirts, utterly useless, worn-out shoes— all this trash is piled in heaps, rumpled and entangled, rotting and emitting a suffocating stench.

On top of the trash, a pipe invariably clenched in his teeth, lies the watchman, Nikita, an old, retired soldier with faded chevrons. He has a red nose and a harsh, weary face with overhanging brows which give him the expression of a steppe sheep dog; he is short in stature, lean and sinewy in appearance, but his bearing is authoritative and his fists hardy. He is one of those simple, positive, diligent, and dense people who love order above anything in the world and are therefore convinced that *they* have to be beaten. He hits faces, chests, backs—whatever he can reach—and is convinced that there would otherwise be no order at all.

Next, you walk into a large, wide room which occupies the entire building, not counting the entry. The walls are covered with dirty blue paint, the ceiling is smoke-blackened as in a chimneyless peasant's hut—it obviously becomes stifling when the stove smokes here in winter. The windows are disfigured by iron bars on the inside. The floor is gray and splintery. It stinks of sour cabbage, smoldering wicks, bugs, and ammonia, and in the first instant, this stench gives you the impression that you are entering a bear pit.

About the room stand beds, screwed to the floor. Sitting and lying on them are men in dark blue hospital bathrobes and, as in the old days, nightcaps. These are the lunatics.

There are five in all. Only one is of noble birth; the rest are commoners. The nearest to the door, a tall, spare man with shining red mustaches and tear-swollen eyes, sits holding his head and staring. He grieves day and night, shaking his head, sighing, and smiling bitterly; he rarely takes part in conversations and usually does not reply to questions. He eats and drinks mechanically whenever served. Judging from his tortured, racking cough, his emaciation, and his flushed cheeks, he is tubercular.

Next to him is a small, lively, very active old man with a pointed little beard and dark hair as curly as a Negro's. He spends the day walking around the ward from window to window or sitting on his bed, his legs folded Turkish-style, whistling indefatigably like a bullfinch, singing softly, and giggling. At night he manifests the same childish gaiety and lively character when he gets up to pray, that is, to beat his fists on his chest and dig at the doors with his fingers. This is the Jew, Moiseika, a fool, who lost his mind twenty years ago when his hat workshop burned down.

Of all the inmates of Ward No. 6, he alone is allowed to go out of the building and even out of the hospital courtyard into the street. He has probably enjoyed this privilege for a long time, as an old inmate of the hospital and a gentle, harmless fool, a town joke, long a familiar sight in the streets, surrounded by little boys and dogs. In his shabby bathrobe, ridiculous nightcap and slippers, sometimes stockingless and even trouserless, he walks through the streets, stopping at house gates and shops, begging a kopeck. In one place they give him kvass,* in another—bread, in a third—a kopeck, so that he usually returns to the annex sated and rich. Everything Moiseika brings back is confiscated by Nikita for his own use. This the soldier does roughly, ardently, turning Moiseika's pockets inside out and calling God to witness that he will never let the Jew out in the street again, and that disorder is the worst thing in the world.

Moiseika loves to be of service. He brings his companions water, covers them up while they sleep, promises to bring each a little kopeck from the street and to make each one a new hat; he even spoonfeeds his neighbor on the left, a paralytic. He does not act this way out of compassion or any con-

_____
* A thin, sour fermented beverage made from rye or barley.

cept of human fellowship, but parroting and involuntarily subordinating himself to his neighbor on the right, Gromov.

Ivan Dmitrich Gromov, a man of thirty-three, of noble birth, formerly a court process server and provincial secretary, suffers from paranoia. He either lies in bed, crumpled into a ball, or paces from corner to corner as if for the exercise; very rarely does he sit. He is always excited, agitated, and tense with some sort of troubled, undefined anticipation. The slightest rustle in the entry or cry in the courtyard is enough for him to raise his head and begin listening: is it not someone coming for him? Someone searching for him? And at this he displays intense anxiety and horror.

I like his broad face with its prominent cheekbones, perpetually pale and unhappy, reflecting like a mirror the agonizing, protracted fear in his soul. His grimaces are strange and sickly, but the sharp traits carved on his face by profound, sincere suffering are rational and intelligent, and his eyes have a warm, healthy glow. I like him, too: polite, obliging, and unusually delicate in his behavior toward everyone except Nikita. When anyone drops a button or a spoon, he quickly jumps out of bed to pick it up. Every day he greets his comrades with a good morning, and on going to bed he wishes them good night.

In addition to grimaces and constant tension, his madness shows itself in the following way. From time to time in the evening, he wraps his bathrobe tightly around himself and, his whole body trembling and his teeth chattering, begins to dart rapidly from corner to corner and between the beds. He acts as if he had a high fever. From the way he stops suddenly and glances at his companions, it is clear that he wants to say something very important, but apparently concluding that they will neither listen nor understand, he impatiently shakes his head and resumes his pacing.

Soon, however, the urge to speak dominates all other considerations, and he unleashes his feelings, talking heatedly and passionately. His speech is disorganized, feverish, broken, and not always intelligible, as in a delirium—but something exceptionally fine is nevertheless perceptible in his words and voice. When he talks, you recognize both the lunatic and the man in him. His mad harangue is hard to reproduce on paper. He talks about human villainy, about violence crushing truth, about the splendid life there will be on earth in time, about window bars, reminding him every minute of the denseness

and cruelty of the violators. It is a disorderly, disconnected
potpourri put together out of the old refrains.

❖◇◇◇◇◇◇◇◇◇◇◇◇◇◇◇◇◇◇◇◇◇◇◇◇◇◇◇◇◇◇◇◇◇◇◇◇❖

II

Twelve—or fifteen—years ago, an official named Gromov,
a solid and wealthy man, lived in his own house on the main
street of a town. He had two sons: Sergei and Ivan. When
still a fourth form student, Sergei caught galloping consump-
tion and died, and this death seemed to be the prelude to a
whole series of misfortunes which suddenly befell the Gromov
family. A week after Sergei's burial, the aged father was taken
to court for fraud and embezzlement and died soon after of
typhus in a prison hospital. The house and all the household
goods were seized and auctioned, and Ivan Dmitrich and his
mother were left without means.

During his father's lifetime, Ivan Dmitrich was allotted
sixty to seventy rubles a month while living in St. Petersburg
as a university student, and had no conception whatsoever of
need; now he was obliged to transform his life abruptly. He
had to give ill-paid lessons from morning till night and work
as a scribe and still go hungry because all his earnings went
to his mother for her subsistence. Ivan Dmitrich could not
withstand this sort of life; he lost heart, languished, and quit-
ting the university, went home. Here, in the small town, he
obtained a position as a teacher in the district school through
his connections, but failed to get along with his colleagues,
was disliked by his pupils, and soon resigned. His mother died.
For half a year he went jobless, living on bread and water
alone, then entered the court staff as a process server. He held
this job until he was cashiered because of ill health.

Even in his youthful student days he had never looked
healthy. Always pale, thin, subject to colds, he ate little; slept
badly. One glass of wine made his head whirl and gave him
hysterics. He was always drawn to people, but thanks to his
irascible character and mistrustfulness, never became close to
anyone and had no friends. The townspeople he always referred to with contempt, saying that he found their coarse
ignorance and sluggish animal life nasty and repelling. He
spoke in a tenor, loudly, heatedly, and invariably either with
exasperation and indignation or with enthusiasm and wonder

—and always sincerely. No matter what you talked to him about, he always came back to the same theme: the town is oppressive and boring to live in; the society has no elevated interests: it leads a dingy, unreflecting life which it diversifies with violence, coarse debauchery, and hypocrisy; the scoundrels are well-fed and well-dressed, while the honest sustain themselves on crumbs; there is need for schools, a local paper with an honest viewpoint, a theater, public readings, and a fraternity of intellectual forces; society needs to realize what it is and take alarm. In judging people, he laid the colors on heavily, black and white only, recognizing no shades whatsoever; for him, humanity was divided into the honest and the scoundrels; there was no middle ground. He always spoke passionately, with enthusiasm, of women and love, but he had never been in love.

In spite of the sharpness of his judgments and his restlessness, he was well liked in town and behind his back was affectionately spoken of as Vanya. His innate delicacy, complaisance, respectability, and moral purity, his worn frock coat, sickly appearance, and family misfortunes inspired a pleasant, warm, melancholy feeling; moreover, he was well-educated and well-read; in the townspeople's opinion, he knew everything, and he was a kind of local walking encyclopedia.

He read a great deal. He used to sit in the club, nervously plucking at his beard and leafing through magazines and books; it was obvious from his face that he was not reading, but gulping with barely time to digest. One must conclude that reading was one of his morbid habits because he threw himself with the same avidity on everything which fell under his hands, even last year's newspapers and calendars. At home he always read lying down.

III

One fall morning, the collar of his overcoat turned up, splashing through the mud, Ivan Dmitrich was making his way through alleys and back ways to some tradesman or other to collect a fine. He was in a gloomy mood, as always in the morning. In one of the alleys he met two convicts in chains, escorted by four guards with rifles. Ivan Dmitrich had often encountered convicts before, and they invariably aroused feelings of pity and awkwardness in him; this encounter awakened a peculiar, strange feeling. For some reason he suddenly felt that he, too, could be clapped in irons and led through the mud to prison in just the same way. As he passed the post office on his return, he met a police inspector he knew who greeted him and accompanied him a few paces down the street; for some reason this seemed suspicious to Ivan Dmitrich. The prisoners and the soldiers with their rifles stayed on his mind all day at home, and an inexplicable inner anxiety kept him from reading and concentrating. That evening he did not light the lamp and that night he did not sleep, but kept thinking about how he could be arrested, clapped in irons, and put in prison. He knew of no crime in his past and knew he would never kill, burn, or steal in the future; but was it so hard, then, to commit a crime accidentally, involuntarily, and was calumny inconceivable, or even judicial error? It is certainly not for nothing that ageless popular experience teaches that no one is immune to poverty and prison. Besides, a judicial error can easily happen under current judicial procedures, and there is nothing exceptional about it. People who have official, professional relations with someone else's suffering—judges, authorities, physicians, for example—become so inured in the course of time, from force of habit, that even should they want to be sympathetic, they are incapable of any but a formal concern for their clients. In this respect they are no different from the peasant who slaughters sheep and cattle in his backyard without noticing the blood. Having this formal, heartless relationship toward the individual, a judge needs just one thing to deprive an innocent man of all his property rights and sentence him to hard labor: time. Just time for the observation of formalities of some sort, for which the judge earns his wages, and then—it is all over. Try to find justice or protection then in this dirty little town, twenty versts from the railroad line! Yes, and is it not absurd to think of justice when society accepts every kind of violence as a rational and expedient necessity, while every act of mercy, such as an exculpatory decree, provokes an explosion of dissatisfied, vindictive feelings?

That morning Ivan Dmitrich got out of bed in terror with cold sweat on his forehead, now absolutely certain he could be arrested any moment. "If yesterday's gloomy ideas have not left me by now," he thought, "it means they have a measure of truth. They certainly could not enter my mind for no reason."

A policeman walked slowly past the window: it was not for nothing. Over there, two men stopped near the house and stood in silence. Why were they silent?

Thus the days and nights of torment began for Ivan Dmitrich. All the people passing by his window or entering the courtyard looked like spies and detectives. At noon the district police inspector usually drove down the street with his pair of horses on his way from his estate on the outskirts of town to the police administration, but each time it seemed to Ivan Dmitrich that he was driving too fast and had a singular expression; obviously he was hurrying to announce that a very important criminal had appeared in town. Ivan Dmitrich trembled at every ring and knock at the gate; he was anguished when someone new visited the landlady; on meeting policemen and gendarmes, he would smile and whistle to show his indifference. He spent night after night without sleeping, awaiting arrest, but he snored loudly and sighed to make the landlady believe he was asleep: you see, if he is awake it means the gnawing of his conscience is tormenting him—what damning evidence! Reality and common sense told him that all these fears were psychopathic nonsense; that, taking a broader view, there is really nothing frightening about arrest and imprisonment if your conscience is at peace; but the more sensibly and logically he reasoned, the stronger and more tormenting his inner anxiety became. He was like the hermit who wanted to clear a place for himself in a virgin forest; the more vigorously he wielded his ax, the thicker and stronger the forest grew. Realizing in the end that it was useless, Ivan Dmitrich completely stopped reasoning and abandoned himself entirely to fear and despair.

He began to avoid people and seek seclusion. His job, distasteful to him before, now became unbearable. He was afraid they would trick him, put a bribe in his pocket without his noticing, and then convict him; or that he himself would accidentally make an error tantamount to fraud in state fiscal papers, or would lose other people's money. Strangely, never before had his thinking been so supple and inventive as now, when he thought up a thousand different reasons for being seriously afraid of losing his freedom and honor. But in return, his interest in the outside world, and particularly in books, decreased significantly, and his memory began to fail notably.

When the snow melted in the spring, two half-rotted corpses were discovered in the ravine near the cemetery—an old

woman and a young boy, with the marks of a violent death.
These corpses and their unknown murderers were the only
topic discussed in town. So they would not think he was the
killer, Ivan Dmitrich walked through the streets and smiled,
but when he met acquaintances, he turned pale, blushed, and
vehemently asserted that there was no crime more reprehen-
sible than the murder of the weak and defenseless. But this
lie soon wearied him, and after some thought, he decided that
in his position the best thing was to hide in the landlady's cellar. He sat in the cellar the whole day, then that night and
the following day, became thoroughly chilled, and after waiting for darkness, stole secretly, like a thief, to his own room.
He stood in the middle of the room, immobile, listening, until
daybreak. The stokers came to the landlady's early in the
morning, before sunrise. Ivan Dmitrich knew perfectly well
they had come to start the fire in the kitchen, but fear whispered to him that it was the police, disguised as stokers. He
quietly left the apartment, and seized by terror, ran hatless
and coatless down the street. Barking, dogs chased after him;
a peasant shouted somewhere behind him; the wind whistled
in his ears, and it seemed to Ivan Dmitrich that all the violence of the world had gathered behind his back and was
hunting him down.

They caught him, brought him home, and sent the landlady
for a doctor. Dr. Andrei Yefimich, of whom more later, prescribed cold compresses for his head and cherry-laurel drops,
sadly shook his head and left, telling the landlady he would
not come again as it was not right to keep people from going
out of their minds. Because Ivan Dmitrich could not afford to
be treated at home, they soon sent him to the hospital and put
him in the ward for venereal diseases. He did not sleep at
night, was capricious, disturbed the other patients, and soon,
on Andrei Yefimich's orders, was transferred to Ward No. 6.

Within a year Ivan Dmitrich had already been completely
forgotten in the town, and his books, which the landlady had
piled in the storeroom under the eaves, had been pilfered by
little boys.

IV

The neighbor on Ivan Dmitrich's left, as I have already said,
is the Jew, Moiseika; on his right is a fat-swollen, almost round

peasant with a dull, completely blank face. This is an immobile, gluttonous, slovenly animal, who long ago lost the capacity to think and feel. He continuously gives off a sharp, suffocating stench.

When cleaning up after him, Nikita beats him mercilessly with all his strength, not sparing his fists; what is awful is not that this stupefied animal is beaten—one can get used to that —but that it does not respond to blows by sound, movement, or an expression of the eyes, but just rocks slightly like a heavy barrel.

The fifth and last inmate of Ward No. 6 is a former mail sorter at the post office, a small thin blond with a kindly but somewhat cunning face. Judging from his wise, peaceful eyes with their clear, merry gaze, he has a very important and agreeable secret. He keeps something under his pillow and mattress that he never shows to anyone, not from fear of its being taken away or stolen, but from modesty. Sometimes he goes up to the window and, turning his back on his comrades, puts something on his chest and crooks his head to look at it; if you approach him at that moment, he becomes flustered and snatches the object off his chest. But his secret is not hard to guess.

"Congratulate me," he often says to Ivan Dmitrich; "I was recommended for the Stanislas, second grade, with a star. The second grade with a star is only given to foreigners, but they wanted to make an exception for me for some reason," he smiles, shrugging his shoulders in bewilderment. "That, I confess, I hadn't expected!"

"I don't understand any of this," Ivan Dmitrich declares morosely.

"But you know what I'll get sooner or later?" the former mail sorter continues with a sly wink. "I'll undoubtedly receive the Swedish 'polar star.' That's a medal worth angling for. A white cross and black ribbon. It's very handsome."

There is probably no place on earth where life is as monotonous as in the annex. In the mornings, the patients, except for the paralytic and the fat peasant, wash in the entry in a big tub and dry themselves with the tails of their bathrobes; after that they drink tea brought by Nikita from the main building in tin mugs; each is entitled to one mugful. At noon they eat *kasha* * and sour cabbage soup; in the evening they sup on the *kasha* left over from dinner. In the intervals they lie, sleep, look out the window, and pace the room. And so on

* A porridge usually made of barley or oats.

every day. And the former mail sorter keeps talking about the very same medals.

New faces are rarely seen in Ward No. 6. The doctor stopped admitting new lunatics long ago, and amateurs of visits to insane asylums are few in the world. Once every two months Semon Lazarich, the barber, comes to the annex. Of how he shears the lunatics, and how Nikita helps him do it, and what pandemonium overtakes the patients every time the drunken smiling barber appears, we shall not speak.

Aside from the barber, no one casts a glance in the annex. The patients are condemned to seeing only Nikita day after day.

However, not long ago, a rather strange rumor began circulating among the hospital corps.

The rumor reported that the doctor had started to visit Ward No. 6.

<><><><><><><><><><><><><><><><><><><><><><><><>

v

A strange rumor!

Dr. Andrei Yefimich Ragin was a remarkable man in his way. They say he was religious in his early youth and prepared himself for a clerical career, and that, after graduating from preparatory school in 1863, he had intended to enter a theological academy. However, his father, a doctor of medicine and a surgeon, is supposed to have sneered and laughed at him, and declared categorically that he would disown him if he became a priest. How much is true, I do not know, but Andrei Yefimich himself confessed more than once that he had never felt any calling for medicine nor for the specialized sciences in general.

However that may be, after graduating from the medical faculty, he did not take the habit. He gave no sign of piety and looked as little like a priest at the beginning of his medical career as now.

His outward appearance is heavy, coarse, virile; his face, beard, dull hair, and strong clumsy build evoke an innkeeper on the highway: well-fattened, intemperate, and gruff. His face is harsh, covered with blue veins; his eyes small; his nose red. In relation to his height and the breadth of his shoulders, his hands and feet are huge, as if one blow would knock you out. But his conduct is gentle and his bearing cautious, ingratiating; on encountering someone in a narrow corridor, he is always the first to stop to make room and to say—not, as you would expect, in a bass voice, but in a thin, soft tenor— "My fault!" He has a small tumor on his neck which keeps him from wearing stiff, starched collars, and he therefore always goes around in a soft linen or cotton shirt. On the whole, he does not dress like a doctor. He has been wearing out the same suit for ten years, and his new clothes, which he usually buys in a Jewish shop, look as worn and rumpled on him as the old ones; he receives patients, eats dinner, and goes out in the same frock coat; not, however, from parsimony, but from a complete lack of attention to his outward appearance.

When Andrei Yefimich arrived in town to assume his responsibilities, the "charitable institution" was in a terrible state. It was hard to breathe for the stench in the wards, corridors, and hospital courtyard. The hospital attendants, the nurses, and their children slept in the wards with the patients. They complained that one could not live for the cockroaches, bugs, and mice. Erysipelas had not been eliminated in the surgical section. There were only two scalpels in the entire hospital and not one thermometer; they stored potatoes in the bathrooms. The superintendent, the housekeeper, and the assistant physician robbed the patients, and the previous doctor, Andrei Yefimich's predecessor, was said to have engaged in the clandestine sale of hospital alcohol and to have organized a whole harem for himself among the nurses and women patients. These disorders were very well known in town and even exaggerated, but were taken calmly; some justified them on the grounds that the only people confined in the hospital were commoners and peasants who could not be dissatisfied since they lived much worse at home; and in any case you could hardly feed them on woodcocks! Others said in justification that the town was unable to support a good hospital without the villagers' help, and thank God it's there, poor as it is! But the recently formed village council opened no infirmaries either in or near the town on the grounds that the town already had a hospital.

After looking the hospital over, Andrei Yefimich came to the conclusion that the institution was immoral and exceedingly harmful to the health of the patients. In his opinion, the wisest thing to do was to release the patients and close the hospital. But he reasoned that his will alone was not enough to accomplish this, and that it would be useless. Drive physical and moral uncleanliness from one spot and it will move to another; one must wait for it to clear up by itself. Moreover, people had opened the hospital and tolerated it among themselves, which meant that they needed it; prejudices and all life's filth and foulness were needed because they would be transformed into something useful with the passage of time, just as manure becomes rich soil. There is nothing on earth so fine that it has not had some filth at its origin.

After taking up his duties, Andrei Yefimich seemed to accept disorder fairly indifferently. He asked only that the hospital attendants and nurses not sleep in the wards, and he installed two cupboards of instruments; the superintendent, the housekeeper, the assistant physician, and the surgical erysipelas remained in their places.

Andrei Yefimich loves reason and honesty intensely, but has insufficient character and belief in his rights to build a reasonable and honest life around him. He is positively incapable of commanding, forbidding, insisting. It is as though he had vowed never to raise his voice or use the imperative mood. Saying "fetch" or "bring" is difficult for him; when he wants to eat, he clears his throat haltingly and says to the cook: "If I might have tea . . ." or: "If I might have dinner." To tell the superintendent to stop stealing or to turn him out, or even to abolish this unnecessary, parasitic job, is completely beyond his strength. When Andrei Yefimich is cheated or flattered or brought a deliberately falsified account to sign, he reddens like a lobster and feels guilty, but signs the account just the same; when the patients complain to him of hunger or the nurses' callousness, he is flustered and mutters guiltily: "Fine, fine, I'll look into that later . . . There's probably a misunderstanding . . ."

Andrei Yefimich worked very hard in the beginning. He received patients from morning until dinnertime daily, performed operations, and even took care of the maternity practice. The ladies said he was attentive and diagnosed illnesses exceptionally well, particularly women's and children's. But in the course of time he became visibly bored with the monotony and obvious uselessness of his work. You receive thirty patients today and tomorrow—look—thirty-five of them have crowded in, and the day after, forty, and so on, day after day, year after year, while the mortality rate of the town remains undiminished and the sick never stop coming. Rendering real assistance to forty outpatients between morning and dinnertime is a physical impossibility, inevitably resulting in a swindle. To receive twelve thousand outpatients in a year means, by simple calculation, the swindling of twelve thousand people. Putting the seriously ill in wards and taking care of them according to scientific principles is also impossible because while the principles exist, scientific means do not. To abandon philosophy and pedantically follow the rules as other doctors do, you need cleanliness and ventilation first of all, not filth; healthy nourishment, not soup made of reeking sour cabbage, and good assistants, not thieves.

Yes, and furthermore, why keep people from dying if death is the normal, legitimate end for everyone? What difference does it make if some peddler or official lives an extra five or ten years? If one sees the purpose of medicine in the alleviation of sufferings by medication, the question necessarily arises: Why alleviate them? Firstly, suffering is said to lead man to perfection, and secondly, if humanity does, in fact, learn to alleviate its sufferings with drops and pills, it will completely cast aside religion and philosophy, in which it has found until now not just a defense against all kinds of ills, but even happiness. Pushkin underwent terrible torments before his death; poor Heine lay paralyzed for several years; why should an Andrei Yefimich or a Matrona Savshina be spared illness, when their lives are null and would be utterly empty and like an amoeba's were it not for suffering?

Crushed by these arguments, Andrei Yefimich lost courage and stopped going to the hospital every day.

VI

His life goes like this. He usually gets up at eight in the morning, dresses, and has tea. Then he either sits in his study and reads or goes to the hospital. In the narrow dark little corridor of the hospital sit the ambulatory patients, waiting to be received. Past them, their shoes pounding on the brick floor, run the attendants and nurses; gaunt patients walk by in bathrobes; corpses and used dishes with their refuse are carried through; children cry; a sharp draft blows. Andrei Yefimich knows such surroundings are a torment for the fever-stricken, the tubercular, and for impressionable patients in general, but what can you do? In the receiving room he meets his assistant, Sergei Sergeich, a fat little man with a shaven, cleanly scrubbed, bloated face and mild, facile manners, wearing an amply cut new suit and looking more like a senator than a doctor. He has a large practice in town, wears a white tie, and considers himself more competent than the doctor, who has no practice at all. In one corner of the reception room is a big image in a case with a heavy incense lamp; nearby is a candle-stand on a white cloth; on the walls hang portraits of prelates, a view of the Sviatogorsky Monastery, and wreaths of dried cornflowers. Sergei Sergeich is pious and loves pomp. The image was installed at his expense; on his orders, one of the patients reads the hymns of praise aloud in the reception room on Sundays, and after the reading, Sergei Sergeich himself walks through all the wards with a censer and thurifies them with incense.

The patients are numerous, but time short, and therefore the examination is limited to a brief questioning and the handing out of some medicament or other, such as a volatile salve or castor oil. Andrei Yefimich sits, his cheek propped on his fist, lost in thought, and poses questions mechanically. Sergei Sergeich sits there too, rubbing his hands and interfering now and then.

"We are sick and endure want," he says, "because we pray badly to the All-Merciful Lord. Yes!"

Andrei Yefimich performs no operations during receiving hours; he has been out of practice for a long time, and the sight of blood affects him unpleasantly. When he has to open a child's mouth to look in his throat, if the child screams and shields himself with his little hands, Andrei Yefimich's head spins from the noise and tears start in his eyes. He hastens to prescribe some medication and gestures for the woman to take the child away as quickly as possible.

In receiving, he soon wearies of the timidity of the patients and their digressions, of the proximity of the pompous Sergei Sergeich, of the portraits on the walls, and of his own questions, which he has been asking unchanged for already more than twenty years. And he goes away after seeing five or six patients, leaving the rest to his assistant.

With the agreeable thought that, thank God, he has not had any private practice for a long time and no one will bother him, Andrei Yefimich sits down at the desk in his study and begins reading as soon as he reaches home. He reads a great deal and always with much pleasure. Half his salary is spent on purchasing books, and of the six rooms in his apartment, three are crammed with books and old magazines. He favors

works of history and philosophy; as for medicine, he sub-
scribes only to *The Physician,* which he always begins reading
from the back. His reading invariably continues without in-
terruption for several hours, and without tiring him. He does
not read as quickly nor as impetuously as Ivan Dmitrich used
to, but slowly, with absorption, often stopping at places pleasing or puzzling to him. There is always a small decanter of
vodka near the book, and a salted cucumber or a pickled apple
placed directly on the tablecloth. Every half hour, without removing his eyes from his book, he pours himself a glass of
vodka and drains it, then, without looking, gropes for the
cucumber and bites off a morsel.

At three o'clock he cautiously approaches the kitchen door,
coughs, and says: "Darushka, if I might have dinner . . ."

After a rather poor, slipshod dinner, Andrei Yefimich walks
around his rooms, arms folded on his chest, and thinks. Four
o'clock strikes, then five, and still he walks and thinks. From
time to time the kitchen door creaks and from behind it appears the red, sleepy face of Darushka.

"Andrei Yefimich, isn't it time for your beer?" she asks
anxiously.

"No, it's not time yet . . ." he answers. "I'll wait a bit . . .
a bit . . ."

Toward evening the postmaster, Mikhail Averyanich, usually calls, the only person in the entire town whose company
is not a burden to Andrei Yefimich. Mikhail Averyanich, a
former cavalry officer, had once been a very rich landowner,
but had ruined himself and been forced to enter the postal
service in his old age. He has a sound, healthy appearance,
luxuriant gray side-whiskers, good manners, and a loud, pleasant voice. He is kind and sensitive, but irascible. When anyone at the post office protests, disagrees, or simply starts to
argue, Mikhail Averyanich turns purple, trembles from head
to toe, and shouts in a thunderous voice: "Shut up!" As a result, the postal division long ago acquired the reputation of
being an awesome institution to visit. Mikhail Averyanich
esteems and likes Andrei Yefimich for his culture and nobility
of spirit; with the rest of the inhabitants he behaves haughtily,
as toward his inferiors.

"And here I am!" he says, coming into Andrei Yefimich's
apartment. "Greetings, my dear! Perhaps you're already tired
of me, ah?"

"On the contrary, I'm delighted," the doctor answered him.
"I'm always delighted to see you."

The friends sit down on the sofa in the study and smoke in silence for a while.

"Darushka, if we might have some beer!" says Andrei Yefimich.

The first bottle they drink in silence, the doctor lost in thought; Mikhail Averyanich with the merry lively look of a man with something very interesting to tell. The doctor always starts the conversation.

"What a pity," he says slowly and softly, nodding his head and not looking in his companion's eyes (he never looks anyone in the eyes); "what a great pity, honored Mikhail Averyanich, that there are simply no people in our town who could and would enjoy holding an intelligent and interesting conversation. It's a great privation for us. Even the intelligentsia doesn't rise above vulgarity; its level of development, I assure you, is not a bit higher than in the lowest class."

"Absolutely true. I agree."

"As you yourself know," the doctor continues softly, after a pause, "everything in the world is insignificant and uninteresting except the high spiritual manifestations of the human mind. The mind marks a sharp division between animal and man, suggests the divinity of the latter, and to some degree even compensates him for immortality, which does not exist. As a consequence, the mind serves as the only possible source of pleasure. We, however, neither see nor hear minds around us—meaning that we are deprived of pleasure. True, we have books, but that is not at all the same as a live conversation and exchange. If you will excuse a not completely successful comparison: books are notes, and conversation singing."

"Absolutely true."

A silence falls. Darushka comes out of the kitchen and, propping her face on her fist with an expression of dense sorrow, stays near the door to listen.

"Eh!" sighs Mikhail Averyanich. "What can you expect from today's minds!"

And he tells how healthily, merrily, and interestingly he used to live, how intelligent the intelligentsia in Russia had been, and how highly it had valued an understanding of honor and friendship. They used to lend each other money without promissory notes, and considered it disgraceful not to extend a helping hand to a companion in need. And what campaigns there were! What adventures, skirmishes; what comrades, what women! And the Caucasus—what a marvelous land! There was the wife of one of the battalion commanders, a strange woman, who used to put on an officer's uniform and drive out in the mountains at night alone, without escort. They say she had a romance with some prince or other in a native village.

"Heavenly Tsaritsa, Little Mother . . ." sighs Darushka.

"And how we used to drink! And eat! And what desperate liberals we were!"

Andrei Yefimich listens without hearing; he is lost in thought, sipping his beer.

"I often dream of intelligent people and conversation with them," he says unexpectedly, interrupting Mikhail Averyanich. "My father gave me an excellent education, but under the influence of the ideas of the sixties, forced me to become a physician. It seems to me that if I hadn't listened to him then, I'd find myself in the very center of an intellectual movement now. I'd probably have been a member of some faculty or other. Of course the intellect is transitory and not eternal, but you already know why I maintain an inclination toward it. Life is an exasperating trap. When a thoughtful person reaches manhood and arrives at a mature understanding, he involuntarily feels caught in a trap from which there is no exit. Indeed, he is brought to life from nothingness against his will, by chance . . . Why? If he tries to learn the meaning and aim of his own existence, he is either told nothing or told nonsense; he knocks—no one opens; death overtakes him—also against his will. And so, just as people in prison, linked by common misfortune, feel better in a group, in life you don't notice the trap when people inclined to analysis and deduction get together and pass the time in the exchange of proud, free ideas. In this sense, the mind is an irreplaceable source of pleasure."

"Absolutely true."

Not looking his friend in the eyes, softly, with pauses, Andrei Yefimich continues to talk about intelligent people and conversation with them, while Mikhail Averyanich listens to him attentively and agrees: "Absolutely true."

"Then you don't believe in the immortality of the soul?" the postmaster asks suddenly.

"No, respected Mikhail Averyanich, I don't believe in it and haven't any basis for believing."

"I confess I, too, have doubts. But, however, on the other hand, I have a feeling as though I would never die. Aiee, I think to myself, old fogey, it's time to die! But in my soul a kind of little voice says: 'Don't believe it, you won't die!' . . ."

A little after nine, Mikhail Averyanich leaves. Putting on his fur coat in the entry, he says with a sigh: "Still, what a desert fate brought us to! What's most annoying is that we'll have to die here. Eh! . . ."

<hr />

VII

After showing his friend out, Andrei Yefimich sits at his desk and resumes his reading. The silence of the evening and then the night is unbroken by a single sound, and time seems to stop and fade away along with the doctor over his book, as if nothing exists except this book and the lamp with the green globe. Little by little, the doctor's coarse peasant face is illuminated by a smile of emotion and excitement before the progress of the human mind. Oh, why isn't man immortal? he reflects. Why have brain centers and nerves, why have vision, speech, internal sensations, genius, if all this is condemned to disappear into the ground, and in the final end to grow cold along with the earth's crust and then hover with the earth around the sun senselessly and aimlessly for millions of years? To grow cold and then hover, it is absolutely unnecessary to draw man with his lofty, almost divine mind out of nothingness and then, like a joke, turn him into clay.

The transmutation of matter! But how cowardly to comfort oneself with this substitute immortality! The unconscious processes which take place in nature are beneath even human stupidity, for in stupidity there is still consciousness and will, while in these processes there is absolutely nothing. Only a coward who has less dignity than fear of death can comfort himself that in time his body will be reborn in grass, rock, a toad . . . Seeing his own immortality in the transmutation of matter is as strange as predicting a brilliant future for the violin case after a precious violin has been smashed and rendered worthless.

When the clock strikes, Andrei Yefimich leans back in his armchair and closes his eyes to think awhile. And unintentionally, under the influence of the fine thoughts gleaned from his book, he casts a glance over his past and present.

The past is repellent; best not to recall it. And the present is the same as the past. He knows that at the same time that his thoughts are hovering with the cooled earth around the sun, in a large building next to his apartment, people are languishing in sickness and filth. Perhaps someone is awake, waging war with the bugs; someone else is catching erysipelas or groaning because of tightly wound bandages; perhaps the patients are playing cards with the nurses and drinking vodka. Twelve thousand people are swindled a year; the whole hospital business is founded, just as it was twenty years ago, on theft, scandal, slander, nepotism, on crude charlatanism and, as before, the hospital is an immoral institution, exceedingly harmful to the health of the inmates. He knows that in Ward No. 6, Nikita thrashes the patients behind bars, and that Moiseika goes around town every day to collect alms.

On the other hand, he knows very well that medicine has undergone a fantastic transformation in the last twenty-five years. When he was studying at the university, he felt that the fate of alchemy and metaphysics would soon overtake medicine; now, when he reads at night, medicine moves him and arouses his wonder, and even enthusiasm. In truth, what unexpected brilliance, what a revolution! Thanks to antiseptics, they perform operations the great Pirogov used to consider impossible, even *in spe.** Ordinary village physicians take the decision of making a resection of the knee joint; for a hundred abdominal operations, there is only one mortality, while gallstones are considered such a trifle that nothing is even written about them. There is a complete cure for syphilis. And what of the theory of heredity, hypnotism, the discoveries of Pasteur and Koch, statistical hygenics, and our Russian village doctors? Psychiatry with its current classification of diseases, methods of diagnosis and treatment—this, in comparison with what used to be, is a whole Mount Elbrus. They don't pour cold water over the heads of the insane now or envelop them in hot plasters; they are treated humanely and, according to the newspapers, balls and spectacles are even organized for them. Andrei Yefimich knows that according to current views and tastes, an abomination such as Ward No. 6 is possible only two hundred versts away from the railroad line, in a small town where the mayor and all the councilmen are semiliterate commoners who regard the doctor as a

* In the future.

sacrificial priest to be trusted without criticism, even if he pours molten lead down people's throats; in another place, the public and the newspapers would have scattered this little Bastille to bits long ago.

"And what then?" Andrei Yefimich asked himself, opening his eyes. "What of it, then? There's antiseptics and Koch and Pasteur, but the essence of the work hasn't changed a bit. Illness and mortality exist just the same. They organize spectacles and balls for the insane, but still don't let them free. Meaning it's all rubbish and bustle, and the difference between the best Viennese clinic and my hospital is, in effect, nonexistent."

But dejection and a feeling resembling envy prevent him from being indifferent. It must be from tiredness. His heavy head sinks toward the book; he cradles his face in his hands and thinks: "I serve a pernicious business and receive a salary from people I swindle; I'm dishonest. But, of course, I'm nothing by myself, I'm only a part of an inevitable social evil: all provincial officials are harmful and receive salaries for nothing . . . Meaning it's not I who am guilty in my dishonesty, but the times . . . If I had been born two hundred years later, I would be another person."

When three o'clock struck, he put out the lamp and went to his bedroom. He had no desire to sleep.

VIII

Two years ago, in a generous mood, the village council decided to hand out three hundred rubles annually to contribute to the strengthening of the medical staff in the town hospital until the opening of a village hospital, and the district physician, Yevgeny Fedorich Khobotov, was hired by the town as Andrei Yefimich's assistant. He is still a young man —not yet thirty—tall, dark, with wide cheekbones and small eyes; his ancestors were probably of another race. He arrived in town without a kopeck, bringing only a small trunk and a homely young woman whom he called his cook. This woman had a newborn child. Yevgeny Fedorich goes around in high boots and a forage cap with a visor, and wears a short fur coat in winter. He is friendly with the assistant, Sergei Sergeich, and the paymaster, but for some reason calls the rest of the staff "aristocrats" and avoids them. There is only one book in his entire apartment—*The Latest Prescriptions of the Viennese Clinic for 1881*. He always brings this book with him when he visits a patient. In the evenings, he plays billiards in the club; cards he does not like. He is a great enthusiast of the use in conversation of expressions such as "trumpery," "flummery with sauce," "don't cloud things over," and so forth.

Twice a week he visits the hospital, goes through the wards, and receives patients. The complete absence of antiseptics and the practice of blood cupping disturb him, but he does not introduce any improvements for fear of insulting Andrei Yefimich. He considers his colleague Andrei Yefimich an old fraud, suspects him of large means, and secretly envies him. He would eagerly take his place.

◆◇◇◇◇◇◇◇◇◇◇◇◇◇◇◇◇◇◇◇◇◇◇◇◇◇◇◇◇◆

IX

On a spring evening at the end of March, when all the snow had melted on the ground and the starlings were singing in the hospital garden, the doctor came out to escort his friend the postmaster to the gates. At that moment, the Jew Moiseika walked into the courtyard with his spoils. He was hatless, wore galoshes on his bare legs, and held a small sack with alms in his hands.

"Give a little kopeck!" he said, trembling with cold and smiling, to the doctor.

Andrei Yefimich, who had never been able to refuse, gave him a ten-kopeck piece.

"How awful this is," he thought, glancing at Moiseika's bare legs with their thick red ankles. "After all, it's wet."

And moved by a feeling akin to pity and aversion, glancing from the Jew's bald pate to his ankles, the doctor followed him into the annex. At the doctor's entrance, Nikita jumped up from a pile of rubbish and drew himself to attention.

"Good day, Nikita," Andrei Yefimich said softly. "If this Jew might be issued boots, what? or he'll catch cold."

"At your orders, your honor. I'll notify the superintendent."

"Please do. Ask him in my name. Say I requested it."

The door to the ward was open. Ivan Dmitrich, who was lying in bed and had raised himself on his elbow, listened anxiously to the unfamiliar voice and suddenly recognized the doctor. Trembling with anger, he jumped up with a red, spiteful face; his eyes protruding, he ran out into the middle of the ward.

"The doctor has come!" he shouted and burst out laughing. "At last! Gentlemen, I congratulate you, the doctor is honoring us with his visit! Cursed vermin!" he shrieked and in a rage such as they had never seen in the ward, he stamped his foot. "Kill this vermin! No, killing isn't enough! Drown him in the toilet!"

Hearing this, Andrei Yefimich glanced from the entry into the ward and asked softly: "What for?"

"What for?" shouted Ivan Dmitrich, going up to him with a threatening look and feverishly wrapping himself in his bathrobe. "What for? Thief!" he pronounced with revulsion, moving his lips as though about to spit. "Charlatan! Hangman!"

"Calm yourself," said Andrei Yefimich, smiling guiltily. "I assure you I never stole anything; for the rest, you are probably greatly exaggerating. I see you are angry with me. Calm yourself, I beg you, if you can, and tell me coolly: why are you angry?"

"Why do you keep me here?"

"Because you're sick."

"Yes, I'm sick. But look, dozens, hundreds of lunatics are walking around in freedom because your ignorance is incapable of distinguishing them from the sane. Why then should I and these unfortunates be forced to sit here like scapegoats for the rest? You, the assistant, the superintendent, and all your hospital riffraff are morally immeasurably inferior to every one of us; then why should we sit here and not you? Where's the logic?"

"Morals and logic do not enter into it. Everything depends on chance. Whoever is locked up, sits there; and whoever is not, walks around; that's all. There is neither morality nor logic in the fact that I'm a doctor and you're mentally ill, but just an empty hazard."

"I don't understand this bosh . . ." Ivan Dmitrich said dully and sat down on his bed.

Moiseika, whom Nikita had hesitated to search in the doctor's presence, was laying out bits of bread, paper, and little bones on his bed and, still trembling with cold, quickly chanting something in Hebrew. He probably imagined he had opened his shop.

"Release me," said Ivan Dmitrich, and his voice quavered. "I can't."

"But why? Why?"

"Because it's not in my power. Think, what use would it be to you if I released you? You leave. The townspeople or the police will stop you and bring you back here."

"Yes, yes, it's true . . ." said Ivan Dmitrich and rubbed his forehead. "It's horrible! But what can I do then? What?"

Ivan Dmitrich's voice and his intelligent young face with its grimaces pleased Andrei Yefimich. He wanted to treat the young man kindly and soothe him. He sat down beside him on the bed, thought a moment, and said: "You're asking me what to do? The best thing in your position—run away from here. But, unfortunately, it's useless. They'll arrest you. When society fences itself off from criminals, from the mentally ill and generally disconcerting people, it is invincible. You have one thing left: to soothe yourself with the thought that your presence here is indispensable."

"No one needs it."

"Once prisons and insane asylums exist, there must be someone to sit in them. If not you—then I; if not I—then some third person. Wait a bit till, in the distant future, prisons and insane asylums will have ceased to exist; then there will be no bars on the windows, no bathrobes. Such a time will come, of course, sooner or later."

Ivan Dmitrich smiled derisively.

"You're joking," he said, squinting. "People like you and your helper Nikita have no concern with the future, but you may be sure, my dear sir, that better times will come! If I express myself vulgarly, you may laugh; but the dawn of a new life is beginning to glow, truth will triumph—it'll be our turn to celebrate! I won't last that long, I'll expire, but, on the other hand, someone's great-grandsons will last out. I greet them with all my heart and I'm glad, glad for them! Forward! May God help you, friends!"

Ivan Dmitrich arose with shining eyes, and stretching his arms toward the window, continued with emotion in his voice: "From behind these bars I bless you! Yes, long live the truth! I'm glad!"

"I find no particular reason to be glad," said Andrei Yefimich, who found Ivan Dmitrich's gesture theatrical, but at the same time very pleasing. "Prisons and insane asylums won't exist, and the truth, as you like to put it, will triumph, but you see, the essence of things will not change, the laws of nature will remain exactly the same. People will suffer, grow old, and die, just as now. Whatever magnificent dawn illuminated your life, just the same, in the final end, they'd nail you in a coffin and throw you in a pit."

"And immortality?"

"Eh, nonsense!"

"You don't believe in it; well, I do. In Dostoevsky or in Voltaire, someone says if there were no God, people would have invented him. But I deeply believe that if there is no immortality, the great human mind will contrive it, sooner or later."

"Well said," Andrei Yefimich commented, smiling with pleasure. "It's good that you believe. With such faith, one can be well off even walled in. Did you have an education somewhere, if I may ask?"

"Yes, I attended the university, but didn't finish."

"You are a reasoning and meditative man. You can find consolation in yourself in any surroundings. Free and profound thought which strives toward an understanding of life, and a complete contempt for the foolish bustle of the world —those are two blessings higher than any man has ever known. And you can possess them even if you live behind three sets of bars. Diogenes lived in a barrel, yet was happier than all the earthly tsars."

"Your Diogenes was a blockhead," Ivan Dmitrich remarked morosely. "What's this you're telling me about Diogenes and about some kind of understanding?" He suddenly became angry and jumped up. "I love life, love it passionately! I have a persecution complex, a constantly tormenting fear, but there are minutes when a thirst for life seizes me, and then I am afraid of going out of my mind. I want terribly to live, terribly!"

He walked through the ward in agitation and said, lowering his voice: "When I dream, phantoms visit me. People of some sort come toward me; I hear voices, music, and it seems to me that I am walking through a kind of woods, along the seashore, and I long passionately for the bustle, the worries . . . Tell me, well, what's new over there?" asked Ivan Dmitrich. "What's happening?"

"You want to hear about the town or things in general?"

"Well, first tell me about the town, and then things in general."

"Well? In town it's tediously boring . . . There's nobody

to exchange a word with, nobody to listen to. No new people. However, not long ago a young doctor arrived: Khobotov."

"He arrived after I was already here. An oaf, eh?"

"Yes, an uncultured man. It's strange, you know . . . Everything considered, there's no intellectual stagnation in our cities, there's movement—meaning, there must be genuine people there, but for some reason they invariably send us people the like of which you've never seen. Unfortunate town!"

"Yes, unfortunate town!" sighed Ivan Dmitrich, and he started laughing. "And how are things in general? What are they writing in the papers and magazines?"

It was already dark in the ward. The doctor rose and standing, began to describe what was being written abroad and in Russia, and what trend of thought was discernible now. Ivan Dmitrich listened attentively and posed questions, but suddenly, as if he had remembered something horrible, he seized his head and lay down on the bed with his back to the doctor.

"What's wrong with you?" asked Andrei Yefimich.

"You won't hear another word from me," Ivan Dmitrich said roughly. "Leave me alone!"

"Why?"

"I tell you: leave me! What the hell!"

Andrei Yefimich shrugged his shoulders, sighed, and went out. As he crossed the entry, he said: "If it might be cleaned up here, Nikita . . . Terribly strong odor!"

"At your orders, Your Honor."

"What a pleasant young man!" thought Andrei Yefimich as he went home to his apartment. "In all the time I've been living here, he seems to be the first one can talk to. He can reason and is interested in just the right things."

Reading, and then going to bed, he continued to think about Ivan Dmitrich, and on waking up the next morning, he remembered that he had met an intelligent and interesting person the day before, and decided to visit him again as soon as possible.

X

Ivan Dmitrich was lying in the very same position as yesterday, his head clutched in his hands and his legs folded under. His face was not visible.

"Greetings, my friend," said Andrei Yefimich. "You're not asleep?"

"First of all, I'm no friend to you," Ivan Dmitrich answered into his pillow, "and secondly, you're exerting yourself in vain: you won't get a single word out of me."

"Strange . . ." Andrei Yefimich muttered, disconcerted. "Yesterday we were chatting so peacefully, but suddenly you took offense at something and immediately broke off . . . I probably expressed something awkwardly or, perhaps, uttered a thought not in accord with your convictions . . ."

"So you want me to believe that!" said Ivan Dmitrich, raising himself slightly and looking at the doctor derisively and anxiously; his eyes were red. "You can go spy and probe somewhere else, but there's nothing for you here. I already understood yesterday what you came for."

"A strange fantasy!" smiled the doctor. "Meaning you think I'm a spy?"

"Yes, I think so . . . Spy or doctor, through whom they're testing me—it's all the same."

"Ah, truly, what a—forgive me—odd fellow you are!" The doctor sat down on a stool near the bed and shook his head reproachfully. "But let us say you're right," he said. "Let us say I treacherously trip you on a word in order to hand you over to the police. They arrest you and then try you. But would you be worse off in court and in prison than here? And if they sent you to a settlement and even to hard labor, would it be worse than being locked up in this annex? I think it's no worse . . . What are you afraid of then?"

Evidently these words had an effect on Ivan Dmitrich. He sat down peacefully.

It was after four in the afternoon—the time when Andrei Yefimich is usually pacing around his apartment and Darushka is asking him if it is not time for his beer. In the courtyard, the weather was still and clear.

"I went out for a walk after dinner, and here I came to call, as you see," said the doctor. "It's really spring."

"What month is it now? March?" asked Ivan Dmitrich.

"Yes, the end of March."

"Muddy in the courtyard?"

"No, not very. You can already walk on the paths in the garden."

"It would be nice to drive somewhere out of town now in an open carriage," said Ivan Dmitrich, rubbing his red eyes as if only half awake; "and then return home to a warm, comfortable study and . . . have one's headache treated by a decent doctor . . . It's been so long since I lived like a human being. It's foul here! Unbearably foul!"

After yesterday's excitement he was exhausted and limp and spoke unwillingly. His fingers trembled and his face showed that he was suffering from an acute headache.

"There is no difference whatsoever between a warm, cozy study and this ward," said Andrei Yefimich. "Man's peace and contentment are not outside but within himself."

"How is that?"

"The ordinary man awaits the good or the bad from the outside, that is, from a carriage and a study, while the reasoning man—from his own self."

"Go preach that philosophy in Greece where it's warm and smells of oranges; it doesn't fit the climate here. Who was it I was talking to about Diogenes? You, wasn't it?"

"Yes, yesterday, to me."

"Diogenes didn't need a study and a warm place to live; it was hot without that there. Lie down in a barrel and eat oranges and olives. But take him to Russia to live and he'd be begging for a room inside in May, not just in December. He'd probably be doubled up from the cold."

"No. It's possible to not feel the cold, as with any other discomfort in general. Marcus Aurelius said: 'Pain is the living image of pain: make an effort to change this image, thrust it away, stop complaining, and the pain will disappear.' It's true. A sage or simply a reasoning, meditative man is distinguished precisely by his contempt for suffering; he is always content and never surprised by anything."

"Meaning I am an idiot since I suffer, am discontented, and am surprised at human villainy."

"You're wrong there. If you will reflect more often, you'll understand how insignificant all the exterior things which agitate us are. One must strive for an understanding of life, for in that lies the true blessing."

"Understanding . . ." frowned Ivan Dmitrich. "External, internal . . . I'm sorry, I don't understand it. All I know," he said, standing up and looking angrily at the doctor; "all I know is that God created me out of warm blood and nerves, yes! And organic tissue, if it's viable, must react to every irritation. And I react! I answer pain with a cry and tears; villainy with displeasure; foulness with revulsion. In my opinion this is reality and what is called life. The lower the organism, the less sensitive it is, and the more feebly it responds to irritation; the higher it is, the more responsively and energetically it reacts to reality. How could one deny that? A doctor, and he doesn't know such simple things! In order to despise suffering, to be always content, and to be surprised at nothing, you must reach this state here," and Ivan Dmitrich pointed to the bloated, fat-swollen peasant, "or inure yourself through suffering until you become completely insensitive to it, that is, in other words, until you stop living. I'm sorry, I'm no sage and no philosopher," Ivan Dmitrich continued with irritation, "and I don't understand any of this. I'm not in condition to argue."

"On the contrary you are arguing splendidly."

"The Stoics, whom you parody, were remarkable people, but their teaching became inert a good two thousand years ago, hasn't moved an inch forward since, and won't move because it's not practical and not part of life. Its success was limited to the minority which spends its life in the study and savoring of every kind of learning; the majority did not understand it. A doctrine which teaches indifference to wealth and the comforts of life, contempt for suffering and death, is absolutely incomprehensible to the large majority, because this majority has never known either wealth or comfort in life; and to despise suffering would mean to despise one's own life, for man's whole existence consists of the sensations of hunger, cold, insult, deprivation, and a Hamletlike fear of death. The whole of life lies in these sensations: one may be oppressed by it, hate it, but not despise it. Yes, so, I repeat, the Stoics' teachings can never have a future, they progress, as you see, from the beginning of the century to today, the struggle, sensibility to pain, a capacity for responding to irritation . . ."

Ivan Dmitrich suddenly lost the thread of his thoughts, stopped, and rubbed his forehead with vexation.

"I was about to say something important, then lost myself," he said. "Where was I? Yes! Here's what I'm saying: one of the Stoics sold himself into slavery in order to ransom someone close to him. There you see, meaning, the Stoic reacted to irritation too, because for such a magnanimous deed as self-destruction for someone close, one must have indignation, a compassionate heart. If I hadn't forgotten everything I'd ever learned here in confinement, I could recall something else. And take Christ? Christ responded to reality by crying, smiling, grieving, growing angry; even feeling melancholy; He didn't go to meet sufferings with a smile and didn't have con-

tempt for death, but prayed in the Garden of Gethsemane
that this cup would pass Him by."

Ivan Dmitrich laughed and sat down.

"Let us assume that man's peace and contentment is not
outside him, but within himself," he continued. "Let us assume it's necessary to despise suffering and be surprised at
nothing. But what basis do you yourself have for preaching
this? Are you a sage? A philosopher?"

"No, I'm no philosopher, but everyone should preach this
because it's common sense."

"No, I want to know why you consider yourself competent
in the matter of understanding, contempt for suffering, and so
on? Have you ever suffered? Do you have a knowledge of
suffering? Allow me: were you whipped as a child?"

"No, my parents were averse to physical punishment."

"While my father flogged me cruelly. My father was a stern,
hemorrhoidal functionary with a long nose and yellow neck.
But let's talk about you. Throughout your whole life no one
laid a finger on you, no one frightened you or hit you; you're
strong as an ox. You grew up under your father's wing and
studied at his expense, and then immediately got hold of a
sinecure. For more than twenty years you've been living in a
rent-free apartment with heat, light, a maid, and having in
addition the right to work however and as much as you please,
or even to do nothing at all. By nature you're a soft, lazy man,
and you therefore tried to arrange your life so that nothing
would bother you or force you to budge. You handed the
work over to your assistant and such swine, while you yourself
sat in warmth and tranquillity, amassed money, passed the
time reading books, amusing yourself with reflections about
diverse exalted nonsense and (Ivan Dmitrich glanced at the
doctor's red nose) with drinking. In short, you haven't seen
life, you don't know it at all, and you're acquainted with reality in theory only. Yet you despise suffering and are surprised
at nothing for a very simple reason: all this hustle-bustle, external and internal, this contempt for life, suffering, and death;
understanding, true blessing—all this is the most convenient
philosophy for a Russian sluggard. For example, you see a
peasant beating his wife. Why meddle? Let him beat her,
they'll both die sooner or later just the same; and moreover,
the one who beats wrongs himself, not the person he's beating. Getting drunk is stupid, unseemly, but if you drink—you
die, and if you don't drink—you die. A woman comes with a
toothache . . . Well, so what? Pain is an image of pain and

furthermore, you can't live without sickness in this world; we all die, and therefore off with the woman, don't disturb my thinking and drinking vodka. A young man asks for advice on what to do, how to live; someone else would have reflected a bit before answering, but here there's a ready answer: strive for understanding or for the true blessing. But what is this fantastic 'true blessing'? There's no answer, naturally. We're kept behind bars, left to rot, tortured, but this is splendid and rational because between this ward and a warm, cozy study there is no difference whatsoever. A comfortable philosophy: there's nothing to be done, your conscience is clear and you feel you're a sage . . . No sir, this is no philosophy, no thought, no breadth of vision, but laziness, sham, sluggish stupefaction . . . Yes!" Ivan Dmitrich became angry again. "You despise suffering, but never fear, pinch your finger in the door and you'll start howling at the top of your voice!"

"But perhaps I wouldn't howl," said Andrei Yefimich, smiling benignly.

"Yes, I bet! Look, if paralysis hit you, or, let's say, some fool and upstart used his position and rank to insult you publicly, and you knew he would go unpunished for it—well, then you would understand what it is to send other people off to understanding and the true blessing."

"That's original," said Andrei Yefimich, smiling with pleasure and rubbing his hands. "I'm pleasantly struck by your inclination to deduction, and the character sketch you just made of me is simply brilliant. I confess that talking with you gives me great pleasure. Well, I heard you through now please hear me out . . ."

XI

This conversation continued for about an hour more and evidently made a deep impression on Andrei Yefimich. He began going to the annex every day. He went there in the mornings and after dinner, and often the evening darkness found him in conversation with Ivan Dmitrich. At first Ivan Dmitrich was wary of him, suspected him of evil intentions, and frankly expressed his hostility; then he became accustomed to him and his abrupt attitude turned into condescending irony.

Soon rumors about Dr. Andrei Yefimich's visits to Ward

No. 6 began going around the hospital. No one—not the assistant nor Nikita nor the nurses—could understand why he went there, spent hours there; what he talked about, and why he wrote no prescriptions. His conduct seemed strange. Mikhail Averyanich frequently failed to find him home, which had never happened before, and Darushka was very disturbed because the doctor no longer drank beer at the appointed time and sometimes was even late for dinner.

One day—it was already the end of June—Dr. Khobotov came to see Andrei Yefimich on some business or other; not finding him at home, he went to look for him in the courtyard; he was told that the old doctor had gone to visit the mentally ill. Entering the annex and stopping in the entry, Khobotov heard the following conversation: "We'll never be in accord and you'll never succeed in converting me to your belief," Ivan Dmitrich was saying with irritation. "You are completely unfamiliar with reality and you've never suffered, but just fed on others' sufferings like a leech; while I've suffered uninterruptedly from the day I was born till now. Therefore I tell you frankly, I consider myself above you and more competent in every respect. It's not for you to teach me."

"I haven't the slightest pretension of converting you to my belief," said Andrei Yefimich softly, regretting people's refusal to understand him. "And that's not the point, my friend. The point is not that you've suffered and I haven't. Sufferings and joys are transitory; leave them; the devil with them. The point is that you and I think; we see in each other people capable of thinking and reasoning, and this gives us solidarity, no matter how dissimilar our views may be. If you only knew, my friend, how bored I am by the general senselessness, incapability, denseness, and with what pleasure I talk to you each time! You are an intelligent man and I find you delightful."

Khobotov opened the door an inch and glanced in the ward: Ivan Dmitrich in his nightcap and Dr. Andrei Yefimich were sitting side by side. The lunatic was grimacing, shuddering and feverishly wrapping himself in his bathrobe, while the doctor sat motionless with head lowered, and his face was red, helpless, and sad. Khobotov shrugged his shoulders, grinned, and exchanged glances with Nikita, who also shrugged his shoulders.

The next day, Khobotov came to the annex with the assistant physician. Both stood eavesdropping in the entry.

"Looks like our old man's gone completely cuckoo!" said Khobotov on leaving the annex.

"Lord, have mercy on us sinners!" sighed the pompous
Sergei Sergeich, carefully walking around a puddle to avoid
spotting his brightly polished boots. "I confess, honored Yevgeny Fedorich, I've been expecting this for a long time!"

XII

Thereafter, Andrei Yefimich began to notice a kind of
secrecy around him. On meeting him, the attendants, nurses,
and patients would look at him inquiringly and then whisper
to each other. Little Masha, the superintendent's daughter,
whom he used to enjoy meeting in the hospital garden, now
inexplicably dashed away when he went up to her with a smile
to stroke her head. When listening to him, postmaster Mikhail
Averyanich no longer said: "Absolutely true," but muttered in
incomprehensible embarrassment: "Yes, yes, yes . . ." and
looked at him thoughtfully and sadly. For some reason he
began advising his friend to give up vodka and beer, but being
a delicate man, he did not talk about this directly, but through
hints, telling first about a certain battalion commander, an excellent man, then about a regimental priest, a splendid fellow,
both of whom drank and fell ill, but completely recovered
after giving up drink. Two or three times, Andrei Yefimich's
colleague Khobotov visited him; he, too, advised giving up
drinking, and for no apparent reason prescribed bromic drops.

In August Andrei Yefimich received a letter from the town
mayor requesting his presence on a very important matter.
Arriving at the town hall at the appointed time, Andrei Yefimich found the military commander, the district school superintendent, a member of the town council, Khobotov, and also
a fat, blond man who was introduced to him as a doctor. This
doctor, who had a difficult Polish name, lived thirty versts
away on a stud farm and was just passing through town.

"This concerns you, sir," the council member said to Andrei
Yefimich after everyone had exchanged greetings and sat down
at the table. "Yevgeny Fedorich here says that the dispensary
is crowded in inadequate space in the main building and
should be moved into one of the annexes. That, of course, is
no problem; it can be moved, but the main difficulty is the
annex needs repair."

"Yes, it won't do without repairs," said Andrei Yefimich
after some thought. "If, for example, the corner annex were

to be used as a dispensary, I believe a minimum of five hundred rubles would be needed for that. An unproductive expenditure."

Everyone was silent a moment.

"I already had the honor of reporting ten years ago," Andrei Yefimich continued in a gentle voice, "that in its present form this hospital represents a luxury beyond the town's means. It was built in the forties, but of course the means were not the same then. The town spends too much on unnecessary buildings and superfluous personnel. I think it would be possible, with another system, to support two model hospitals for the same money."

"Well then, please give us another system," the council member said briskly.

"I have already had the honor of reporting on this: transfer the medical section to the jurisdiction of the village council."

"Yes, give the village council money and it will steal it," laughed the fair-haired doctor.

"That's how it goes," agreed the town council member, and he also started laughing.

Andrei Yefimich looked languidly and dully at the fair-haired doctor and said: "One must be just."

Again they were silent. Tea was served. The military commander, very embarrassed for some reason, touched Andrei Yefimich's hand across the table and said: "You've completely forgotten us, Doctor. But then, you're a monk: you don't play cards, don't like women. You're bored with our kind."

Everyone began talking about how boring it was for a well-bred person to live in this town. No theater, no music, and at the last dance at the club, there were about twenty ladies and only two cavaliers. The young people don't dance, but crowd around the buffet or play cards the whole time. Slowly and gently, not looking at anyone, Andrei Yefimich began to talk about what a pity, what a great pity it was that the citizens squander their vital energy, hearts, and minds on cards and gossip, and neither can nor want to spend the time in interesting conversation and reading, and do not want to make use of the pleasures the mind offers. There was only one interesting and remarkable mind; all the rest were base and shallow. Khobotov listened to his colleague attentively and suddenly asked: "Andrei Yefimich, what date is it today?"

Having received an answer, he and the fair-haired doctor, in the tone of examiners conscious of their own incompetence, began asking Andrei Yefimich what day it was today, how many days there are in a year, and whether it was true that a remarkable prophet lived in Ward No. 6.

In response to the last question, Andrei Yefimich blushed and said: "Yes, he's sick, but an interesting young man."

They asked him no more questions.

When he was putting on his overcoat in the entry, the military commander put a hand on his shoulder and said with a sigh: "For us old men, it's time for a rest."

As he left the hall, Andrei Yefimich understood that this had been a commission appointed to examine the state of his mind. He remembered the questions put to him, blushed, and for the first time in his life, deplored medicine.

"My God," he thought, remembering how the doctors had just examined him, "but they just heard about psychiatry so recently, and they hold an examination—how can they be so utterly ignorant? They haven't the slightest understanding of psychiatry!"

And for the first time in his life, he felt insulted and infuriated.

That same day, Mikhail Averyanich came to his house in the evening. Without a greeting, the postmaster went up to him, took him by both hands and said with emotion: "My dear, my friend, show me you believe in my sincere good will and consider me your friend . . . My friend!" And preventing Andrei Yefimich from speaking, he continued in agitation: "I love you for your erudition and the nobility of your soul. Listen to me, my dear. The rules of science oblige the doctors to hide the truth from you, but like a soldier I'll tell you the plain facts boldly: you're unwell! Forgive me, my dear, but it's the truth, everyone around noticed it long ago. Just now Dr. Yevgeny Fedorich told me you must rest and have some distraction for the sake of your health. Absolutely true! Splendid! I'm taking a leave now and going away to breathe another atmosphere. Show you're my friend, let's go together! Let's go, let's recapture our youth."

"I feel completely well," said Andrei Yefimich after reflecting. "And I can't go. Let me show you my friendship in some other way."

To go somewhere, for no reason, without books, without Darushka, without beer; to abruptly break a pattern of life established for twenty years—an idea of this sort seemed wild and fantastic to him at first. Then he thought of the conversation in the town hall, and his depressed frame of mind on returning home from there, and the thought of leaving, for a short time, the town in which stupid people considered him insane pleased him very much.

"And where exactly do you intend to go?" he asked.

"To Moscow, to St. Petersburg, to Warsaw . . . I spent five of the happiest years of my life in Warsaw. What an extraordinary town! Let's go, my dear!"

XIII

A week later, Andrei Yefimich was offered a rest, that is, asked to hand in his resignation, to which he reacted with indifference, and in another week he and Mikhail Averyanich were setting off in the stagecoach for the nearest railroad station. The days were cool, clear, with a blue sky and transparent horizon. They drove the two hundred versts to the station in forty-eight hours, stopping for the night twice on the way. When they were given badly washed glasses or when it took too long to harness the horses in the posting stations, Mikhail Averyanich would turn purple and, shaking all over, shout: "Shut up! Don't argue!" Seated in the carriage, he recounted without a minute's pause his travels through the Caucasus and the Polish Kingdom. How many adventures there had been, what encounters! He spoke loudly and made such round eyes that it was easy to believe he was lying. Moreover, as he talked, he breathed in Andrei Yefimich's face and guffawed in his ear. This bothered the doctor and kept him from thinking and concentrating.

For economy's sake, they traveled third class on the train in a car for nonsmokers. Half the passengers were respectable. Mikhail Averyanich soon became acquainted with everyone and, going from bench to bench, said loudly that one should not travel on these shocking railways. A complete fraud! It isn't like being on horseback: you sweep over a hundred versts in a day and feel healthy and fresh. And we have unproductive crops because they drained the Pinsky marshes. In general, the disorder is terrible. He became heated, spoke loudly, and did not let anyone else talk. This continual chatter interspersed with loud guffaws and vigorous gestures irked Andrei Yefimich.

"Which of us is insane?" he thought with annoyance. "I, who try not to disturb the passengers in any way, or this egoist, who thinks he is more intelligent and more interesting than anyone else and therefore gives nobody any peace?"

In Moscow, Mikhail Averyanich put on a military jacket without insignia and trousers with red piping. He walked around the streets in a military forage cap and a greatcoat, and soldiers saluted him. He now appeared to Andrei Yefimich as a man who had dissipated all the good traits of his aristocracy and kept only the bad. He loved to be waited on, even when it was completely unnecessary. He would shout for the waiter to bring him matches when there were matches lying on the table in front of him in plain sight; he was unembarrassed to appear in his underwear in front of the chambermaid; he indiscriminately addressed all lackeys, even the old men, with condescension, and when irritated, dubbed them blockheads and fools. This, Andrei Yefimich thought, was lordly, but disgusting.

Mikhail Averyanich first took his friend to the Iversky Chapel. He prayed fervently, bowing to the ground and weeping, after which he sighed deeply and said: "Even though you don't believe, it's somehow more peaceful when you pray. Kiss the holy image, my dear."

Andrei Yefimich became flustered and kissed the image while Mikhail Averyanich prayed in a whisper, his lips protruding and his head nodding, and tears started again in his eyes. Then they went to the Kremlin where they saw the Tsar-cannon and the Tsar-bell and even touched them with their fingers, enjoyed the view of the river, and visited Saint Savior's and the Rumyantsev Museum.

They had dinner at Testov's. Mikhail Averyanich studied the menu for a long time, smoothing his whiskers, and said in the tone of a gourmet at home in restaurants: "We'll see what you'll feed us today, my lamb!"

XIV

The doctor walked, gawked, ate, drank, but had only one feeling: annoyance with Mikhail Averyanich. He longed to take a rest from his friend, to get away from him, to hide; but his friend considered it his duty not to let the doctor out of his sight and to provide him with as many distractions as possible. When there was nothing to look at, he entertained him with conversation. Andrei Yefimich stood it for two days, then on the third, informed his friend he was ill and wished to spend the whole day in his room. His friend said in that case he, too, would stay home. Indeed, one must rest or one's legs would never hold out. Andrei Yefimich lay down on the couch, his face to the wall, and clenching his teeth, listened while his friend heatedly assured him that France would sooner or later, inevitably, beat Germany, that there were a great many swindlers in Moscow, and that one should never judge a horse's merits by its appearance. The doctor's ears began to hum and his heart to pound, but he was unable to make up his mind to ask his friend to either leave or be silent. Fortunately, Mikhail Averyanich tired of sitting in a hotel room and went out for a walk after dinner.

Left alone, Andrei Yefimich succumbed to a feeling of relief. How pleasant to lie motionless on a couch and know you are alone in the room! True happiness is impossible without solitude. The fallen angel probably betrayed God because he wanted solitude, which is unknown to the angels. Andrei Yefimich wanted to concentrate on the things he had seen and heard in the last few days, but he could not get Mikhail Averyanich out of his mind.

"But here he took leave and went with me out of friendship, out of magnanimity," the doctor thought with irritation. "There's nothing worse than this friendly guardianship. There you are, he seems kind, magnanimous, a jolly fellow, but he's boring. Unbearably boring. There are people like that who say nothing but intelligent and good things, yet you feel that they're unbearably dense."

During the following days, Andrei Yefimich declared himself sick and did not leave the hotel room. He lay with his face to the wall and suffered while his friend distracted him with conversation, or rested when his friend was absent. He was annoyed with himself for having come, and with his friend, who became more garrulous and familiar every day; he was completely unsuccessful in organizing his thoughts on a serious, elevated plane.

"I must be experiencing the reality Ivan Dmitrich spoke of," he thought, growing angry at his own pettiness. "However, it's rubbish . . . I'll get home—and everything will go on as before . . ."

In St. Petersburg, too, it was exactly the same: he did not leave the hotel room for days, lay on the couch, and only got up to drink beer.

Mikhail Averyanich was constantly in a hurry to get to Warsaw.

"My dear, why should I go there?" said Andrei Yefimich in a pleading voice. "Go alone, but let me go home! I beg you!"

"Under no condition!" protested Mikhail Averyanich. "It's an extraordinary town. I spent five of the happiest years of my life in it! I beg you!"

Andrei Yefimich did not have enough character to insist on his way, and with a sinking heart, he went to Warsaw. There he did not leave the hotel room, lay on the couch, and raged at himself, his friend, and the lackeys, who stubbornly refused to understand Russian, while Mikhail Averyanich, as usual, was hale, hearty, and jolly, scouring the city from morning till night and looking for his old acquaintances. Several times he did not come home for the night. After one night, spent no one knows where, he returned home in the early morning in a state of violent agitation. Red and disheveled, he paced from corner to corner for a long time, muttering to himself, then stopped and said: "Honor above all!"

After pacing a bit more, he clutched his head and announced in a tragic voice: "Yes, honor above all! Curse the moment I first thought of going into that Babylon! My dear," he turned to the doctor, "despise me! I've ruined myself gambling! Give me five hundred rubles!"

Andrei Yefimich counted out five hundred rubles and silently handed them to his friend. The latter, still purple with shame and anger, incoherently uttered some superfluous oath, put on his forage cap, and went out. Returning about two hours later, he fell into an armchair, sighed loudly, and said: "My honor is saved! Let's go, my friend! I don't want to stay in this accursed town another minute. Swindlers! Austrian spies!"

When the two friends returned to their own town, it was already November and a deep snow lay on the streets. Dr. Khobotov had taken Andrei Yefimich's place; he was still living in his old lodgings, waiting for Andrei Yefimich to come and clear out the hospital apartment. The homely woman he called his cook was already living in one of the annexes.

New hospital gossip was going around town. It was said that the homely woman had quarreled with the superintendent and that he had crawled on his knees before her, begging forgiveness.

Andrei Yefimich was obliged to look for a new apartment the very day of his return.

"My friend," the postmaster said to him timidly, "forgive an indiscreet question: what means do you have at your disposal?"

Andrei Yefimich silently counted his money and said: "Eighty-six rubles."

"I didn't mean that," Mikhail Averyanich said in confusion, not understanding the doctor. "I meant: what means do you have in general?"

"That's what I'm telling you: eighty-six rubles . . . I have nothing else."

Mikhail Averyanich considered the doctor an honest and honorable man, but still suspected him of having put aside at least twenty thousand. On learning that Andrei Yefimich was a pauper and had nothing to live on, he for some reason suddenly burst into tears and embraced his friend.

XV

Andrei Yefimich was now living in the three-windowed little house of the commoner Belova. There were only three rooms in the house, not counting the kitchen. Two of them, with windows on the street, were occupied by the doctor, while Darushka and Belova with her three children lived in the third room and the kitchen. Occasionally a lover, a drunken peasant who bellowed and filled Darushka and the children with terror, came to spend the night with the mistress of the house. When he arrived, sat down in the kitchen and began demanding vodka, everyone became very uncomfortable, and the doctor used to take in the crying children out of pity and put them to bed on his floor, and this gave him great satisfaction.

The doctor arose at eight o'clock as before, and after having tea, sat down to read his old books and magazines. He no longer had money for new ones. Because the books were old or, perhaps, because of the change of circumstances, reading no longer fascinated, but tired him. To avoid spending his time idly, he organized a detailed catalogue of his books and glued labels on the backs of their covers; this mechanical, tedious work seemed more interesting to him than reading. In some incomprehensible way, monotonous, tedious work lulled his mind; he no longer thought about anything, and time passed quickly. Even sitting in the kitchen and scrubbing potatoes with Darushka or sorting over buckwheat seemed entertaining to him. On Saturdays and Sundays he went to church. Standing close to the wall and blinking his eyes, he would listen to the choir and think about his father, his mother, the university, and about religion; he was peaceful, melancholy, and later, as he left the church, he would regret that the service had ended so quickly.

Twice he went to the hospital to talk to Ivan Dmitrich. But both times, Ivan Dmitrich was unusually agitated and spiteful; he asked to be left in peace because he had tired of empty chatter long ago, and said that for all his sufferings, he asked the cursed wretched people for only one reward—solitary confinement. Could they refuse him even this? Both times, when Andrei Yefimich took leave of him and wished him good night, he snarled and said: "Go to the devil!"

And Andrei Yefimich did not know whether to go a third time or not. However, he wanted to go.

Formerly, after dinner, Andrei Yefimich used to walk around the room and think; now, from dinnertime until evening tea, he lay on the couch with his face to its back and yielded to petty thoughts which he was completely unable to subdue. He felt offended that after his more than twenty-year service they had given him neither a pension nor a bonus. True, he had served dishonestly, but then all civil employees receive pensions without exception, honest or not. Contemporary justice lies precisely in the fact that ranks, medals, and pensions are issued to reward not moral qualities and ability, but service in general, whatever it was. Why should he alone be an exception? He had absolutely no money. He was ashamed to walk past the tavern and see the owner. There were already thirty-two rubles due for beer. Money was due Belova, too. Darushka quietly sold old clothes and books and lied to the landlady, saying the doctor would soon receive a great deal of money.

He was angry with himself for having consumed on the trip the thousand rubles he had saved. How useful that thousand would be now! It annoyed him that people did not leave him in peace. Khobotov considered himself obliged to call on his sick colleague from time to time. Everything about him repelled Andrei Yefimich: the sated face and ugly, condescending voice, the word "colleague" and the high boots; what was particularly repellent was that he considered it his duty to treat Andrei Yefimich and thought he was in fact doing so. He brought a vial of bromic drops and some rhubarb pills on every visit.

Mikhail Averyanich also considered it his duty to call on his friend and entertain him. On each visit he behaved with affected familiarity, guffawed constrainedly, and assured Andrei Yefimich that he looked splendid today and that, thank God, things were getting better, and from this one could conclude that he considered his friend's condition hopeless. He had not yet paid back his Warsaw debt and was oppressed by a heavy shame; feeling constrained, he strove to laugh louder and talk more amusingly. His anecdotes and stories now seemed endless, and were agonizing for both Andrei Yefimich and himself.

In his presence, Andrei Yefimich usually lay on the couch with his face to the wall and listened, clenching his teeth; layers of seething distaste weighed on his heart, and after each of his friend's visits, he felt this seething rise higher and higher as if it were going to choke him.

To still his petty feelings, he would quickly start thinking about how he, Khobotov, and Mikhail Averyanich were to die sooner or later without leaving a dint on nature. When he tried to picture some sort of spirit flying past the earth in space after a million years, he saw only clay and naked rocks. Everything—even culture and moral law—would vanish without giving growth to so much as a bur. What did shame before the tavernkeeper matter, or the inane Khobotov, or the heavy friendship of Mikhail Averyanich? All that was trivia and nonsense.

But such arguments no longer helped. Hardly had he pictured the globe after a million years, when out from the naked rock appeared Khobotov in high boots or Mikhail Averyanich, guffawing constrainedly, and he even heard a shamefaced whisper: "And the Warsaw debt, my dear, I'll pay you back in the next few days . . . without fail."

XVI

One day Mikhail Averyanich came after dinner when Andrei Yefimich was lying on the couch. Khobotov happened to appear with bromic drops at the same time. Andrei Yefimich painfully raised himself, sat down, and braced himself on the couch with both hands.

"And today, my dear," Mikhail Averyanich began, "your face has much better color than yesterday. Yes, you're a fine fellow! A fine fellow, by God!"

"It's time now, it's time to get well, colleague," said Khobotov, yawning. "Perhaps you're getting tired of this trumpery yourself."

"We'll get well!" Mikhail Averyanich said merrily. "We'll live another hundred years! Yes, yes!"

"A hundred or not, twenty will be enough," comforted Khobotov. "Never mind, never mind, colleague, don't give up . . . Don't cloud things over."

"We'll still show what we're made of!" guffawed Mikhail Averyanich, and he slapped his friend on the knee. "We'll show them! Next summer, God willing, we'll sweep over to the Caucasus and ride all over it on horseback—clop! clop! clop! When we come back from the Caucasus, I shouldn't be surprised if we'd be going to a wedding." Mikhail Averyanich winked slyly. "We'll marry you, dear friend . . . marry . . ."

Andrei Yefimich suddenly felt the seething reach his throat; his heart was pounding frightfully.

"That's vulgar!" he said, quickly getting up and walking over to the window. "Don't you realize that you're saying vulgarities?"

He wanted to continue softly and politely, but in spite of himself, he suddenly clenched his fists and raised them above his head.

"Leave me!" he shouted in a strange voice, turning purple and trembling all over. "Out! Both of you, out, both!"

Mikhail Averyanich and Khobotov got up and stared at him, first in bewilderment and then in fear.

"Out, both of you!" Andrei Yefimich kept shouting. "Dense people! Stupid people! I don't need friendship nor your medicines, dense man! Vulgarity! Filth!"

Khobotov and Mikhail Averyanich, exchanging distraught glances, retreated to the door and went out in the entrance. Andrei Yefimich seized the vial of bromic drops and flung it after them; the vial shattered on the threshold with a crash.

"Go to the devil!" he shouted in a tearful voice, running into the entrance. "To the devil!"

After his guests' departure, shaking as if with fever, Andrei

Yefimich lay down on the couch and kept repeating for a long time: "Dense people! Stupid people!"

When he had calmed himself, the first thought that came to him was that poor Mikhail Averyanich must now be frightfully embarrassed and heavyhearted, and that all this was terrible. Nothing of the kind had ever happened before. Where was his intelligence and tact? His understanding of things and philosophical indifference?

All night the doctor was unable to sleep from shame and annoyance with himself, and in the morning, at ten o'clock, he set off for the post office to apologize to the postmaster.

"We won't recall what happened," said Mikhail Averyanich with a sigh, much moved, firmly pressing his friend's hand. "Let whoever remembers the past lose an eye. Lyubavkin!" he suddenly shouted so loudly that all the postal staff and visitors jumped. "Bring a chair. And you wait a bit!" he shouted at a peasant woman who was poking a registered letter toward him through the grill. "Don't you see I'm busy? We won't remember the past," he continued tenderly, turning to Andrei Yefimich. "Sit down, I humbly beg you, my dear."

For a minute he silently stroked his knee and then said: "It didn't even occur to me to be offended by you. Illness isn't easy to take, I understand. Your fit frightened the doctor and me yesterday and we talked about you for a long time after. My dear, why don't you want to take care of your illness seriously? Can this go on? Forgive me for my friendly frankness," Mikhail Averyanich began whispering; "you live under the most unfavorable conditions: it's crowded, dirty, there's no one to nurse you, no money for treatment . . . My dear friend, the doctor and I implore you with all our hearts to listen to our advice: go to the hospital! There there's wholesome food and nursing and treatment. Between us, although Yevgeny Fedorovich is *mauvais ton*,* he's still knowledgeable; you can fully depend on him. He gave me his word he'd take care of you."

Andrei Yefimich was moved by the frank sympathy and the tears suddenly glistening on the postmaster's cheeks.

"Honored friend, don't believe it!" he whispered, putting his hand over his heart. "Don't believe them. It's a trick! My illness is only that in twenty years I've found only one intelligent person in the whole town, and he's a lunatic. There's no illness whatsoever; I simply fell into a bewitched circle

* Bad taste.

from which there's no exit. It's all the same to me, I'm ready for anything."

"Go to the hospital, my dear."

"It's all the same to me, even into a pit."

"Give me your word, my dear, that you'll listen to Yevgeny Fedorich in everything."

"If you like, I'll give you my word. But I repeat, respected friend, I've fallen into a bewitched circle. Now everything, even the sincere sympathy of my friends, is bent to the same end—my finish. I'm finished and have the manliness to recognize it."

"You'll get well, dear friend."

"Why do you say that?" Andrei Yefimich asked with irritation. "It's a rare man who, before the end of his life, doesn't go through what I'm undergoing now. When you are told you have something on the order of bad kidneys or an enlarged heart and you begin taking treatment, or when they say you're a lunatic or a criminal, that is, in short, when people suddenly pay attention to you, then you know that you've fallen into a bewitched circle you'll never get out of. If you try to get out, you get still more lost. You'd better give up because no human efforts can save you. That's how it seems to me."

Meanwhile people were crowding around the window grill. To avoid being in the way, Andrei Yefimich stood up and began taking leave. Mikhail Averyanich once again asked for his word of honor, and escorted him to the door.

Before evening that same day, Khobotov unexpectedly appeared at Andrei Yefimich's in his short fur coat and high boots, and said as if nothing had happened the day before: "I came to see you on business, colleague. I came to ask you: wouldn't you like to come with me on a consultation, ah?"

Thinking Khobotov wanted to distract him with a stroll or actually to permit him to earn something, Andrei Yefimich put on a coat and went out in the street. He was glad to have an opportunity to smooth over yesterday's wrong and make peace, and in his heart, he thanked Khobotov, who had not even mentioned yesterday and was apparently sparing his feelings. Such delicacy was hardly to be expected from this uncouth man.

"And where is your patient?" asked Andrei Yefimich.

"In the hospital. I've been wanting to show you for a long time now . . . Most interesting case."

They went into the hospital courtyard, and skirting the main building, turned toward the annex where the insane were housed. And all this in silence, for some reason. When they came into the annex, Nikita, as usual, jumped up and drew himself to attention.

"One man here developed a complication in the lungs," Khobotov said in an undertone as he entered the ward with Andrei Yefimich. "Wait here a moment, I'll be right back. I'm just going for a stethoscope."

And he left.

XVII

It was already dusk. Ivan Dmitrich lay on his bed, his face buried in his pillow; the paralytic sat motionless, crying softly and moving his lips. The fat peasant and the former mail sorter were asleep. It was quiet.

Andrei Yefimich sat on Ivan Dmitrich's bed and waited. But half an hour went by, and instead of Khobotov, into the ward came Nikita, carrying a bathrobe, some underclothes, and slippers.

"Please get dressed, Your Honor," he said quietly. "This is your little bed, if you please, here," he added, pointing to an empty, obviously recently acquired bed. "It's nothing, God granting, you'll get well."

Andrei Yefimich understood everything. Without a word, he walked over to the bed at which Nikita was pointing and sat down; noticing that Nikita was standing and waiting, he undressed completely, feeling ashamed. Then he put on the hospital clothing; the drawers were very short, the shirt long, and the bathrobe smelled of smoked fish.

"You'll get well, God granting," repeated Nikita.

He collected Andrei Yefimich's clothing in his arms and went out, shutting the door behind him.

"It's all the same . . ." thought Andrei Yefimich, bashfully wrapping himself in his bathrobe and feeling that he looked like a convict in his new clothing. "It's all the same . . . All the same: a frock coat, a uniform, this bathrobe . . ."

But what about his watch? And the notebook which had been in his side pocket? And his cigarettes? Where had Nikita taken his clothes? Now, perhaps, he would never again put on trousers, a waistcoat, and boots for the rest of his life. All this was somehow strange and even incomprehensible at first.

Andrei Yefimich was still convinced now that there was no difference whatsoever between Belova's house and Ward No. 6, that everything in this world is nonsense and hustle and bustle; but still, his hands were trembling, his legs were growing cold, and he was uneasy at the thought that Ivan Dmitrich would soon wake up and see him in a bathrobe. He stood up, walked across the room, and sat down again.

Here he had been sitting for a half an hour, an hour, and was bored to exhaustion; was it possible to live through a day here, a week, and even years like these people? Here, now, he had sat a while, walked across the room, and sat down again; you could go look out the window and walk from corner to corner again. And then what? Sit there all the time like a Buddha and think? No, it was hardly possible.

Andrei Yefimich lay down, but immediately got up, wiped the cold sweat off his forehead with his sleeve, and felt that his whole face smelled of smoked fish. He walked across again.

"It's some kind of misunderstanding . . ." he said aloud, spreading his hands in bewilderment. "It must be cleared up, there's a misunderstanding . . ."

At that moment Ivan Dmitrich awoke. He sat up and propped his cheeks on his fists. He spat. Then he lazily glanced at the doctor and apparently understood nothing for the first moment; but soon his sleepy face became spiteful and derisive.

"Aha, they've shut you up here too, darling!" he said in a hoarse, drowsy voice, winking. "I'm very glad. First you drank other people's blood and now they'll drink yours. Splendid!"

"It's some kind of misunderstanding . . ." said Andrei Yefimich, frightened by Ivan Dmitrich's words; he shrugged his shoulders and repeated: "A misunderstanding of some kind . . ."

Ivan Dmitrich spat again and lay down. "Cursed life!" he snarled. "And what's bitter and insulting, you see, is this life won't end with a reward for suffering or an apotheosis, as in opera, but with death; peasants will come and drag the corpse by the hands and feet to the cellar. Brr! Well, never mind . . . In return, we'll have our holiday in the other world . . . I'll come back here from that world as a ghost and scare these vermin. I'll make them turn gray."

Moiseika returned home from one of his walks, and held out his hand on seeing the doctor.

"Give a little kopeck!" he said.

XVIII

Andrei Yefimich walked over to the window and looked at the fields. Darkness was already falling, and on the horizon to the right, a cold, livid moon was rising. Not far from the hospital fence, at about two hundred yards, no more, stood a tall white house surrounded by a stone wall. This was the prison.

"So this is reality!" thought Andrei Yefimich, and he became terrified.

The moon was terrifying, and the prison and the nails on the fence, the distant flames in the bone-charring factory. Andrei Yefimich heard a sigh behind him. He glanced around and saw a man with glistening stars and medals on his chest who was smiling and slyly winking. This, too, seemed terrifying.

Andrei Yefimich assured himself that there was nothing special about the moon and the prison, that sane people wear medals too, and that with time everything will rot and turn into clay; but despair suddenly overwhelmed him; he seized the window bars with both hands and shook them with all his strength. The strong bars did not yield.

Then, to calm his terror, he went over to Ivan Dmitrich's bed and sat down.

"I've lost heart, my dear," he murmured, trembling and wiping off cold sweat. "Lost heart."

"Then philosophize," Ivan Dmitrich said derisively.

"My God, my God . . . Yes, yes . . . You once said there was no philosophy in Russia, but that everyone philosophizes, even the nobodies. But you see, the philosophizing of the nobodies does no one any harm," said Andrei Yefimich in a voice as if longing to cry and complain. "Why this spiteful laugh, my friend? And how can these nobodies avoid philosophizing if they're discontented? For an intelligent, cultured, proud, freedom-loving man, in God's image, to have no alternative to becoming a doctor in a dirty, stupid little town with a whole lifetime of cupping glasses, leeches, and mustard plaster! Charlatanism, narrowness, vulgarity! Oh, my God!"

"You're babbling idiocies. If being a doctor repels you, be a minister instead."

"There's nothing, nothing to be done. We're weak, my dear

. . . I was indifferent once, reasoned boldly and soundly, but it took just one rough touch from life for me to lose heart . . . Prostration . . . We're weak, we're wretched . . . And you, too, my friend. You're intelligent, well-born, you imbibed good impulses with your mother's milk, but hardly had you stepped out into life than you were worn out and fell ill . . . Weak, weak!"

Aside from fear and a feeling of insult, something else harassed Andrei Yefimich constantly from the onset of evening. At last he realized it was a desire for beer and a smoke.

"I'm going out of here, my dear," he said. "I'll tell them to give us some light here . . . I can't . . . not up to . . ."

Andrei Yefimich went to the door and opened it, but Nikita immediately jumped up and stood in his way.

"Where're you going? Forbidden, forbidden!" said he. "It's time to sleep!"

"But, just for a minute, to walk around the courtyard!" Andrei Yefimich became panic-stricken.

"Forbidden, forbidden, not allowed. You know yourself."

Nikita slammed the door and leaned his back against it.

"But what difference will it make to anyone if I go out?" asked Andrei Yefimich, shrugging his shoulders. "I don't understand! Nikita, I must go out!" he said in a trembling voice. "I have to!"

"Don't make disorders, it's not good!" said Nikita didactically.

"The devil knows what this is!" screamed Ivan Dmitrich suddenly, and he jumped up. "What right does he have not to let us out? How dare they hold us here? It's clearly stated in the law, I think, that no one can be deprived of freedom without a trial! It's violence! Tyranny!"

"Of course it's tyranny!" said Andrei Yefimich, encouraged by Ivan Dmitrich's cry. "I must, I have to go out. He has no right. Give way, I tell you!"

"Do you hear, you dense brute?" cried Ivan Dmitrich and he rapped his fist on the door. "Open or I'll break down the door. Slaughterer!"

"Open!" cried Andrei Yefimich, his whole body trembling. "I insist!"

"Talk away!" answered Nikita behind the door. "Talk away!"

"At least go call Yevgeny Fedorich here. Tell him I ask him to come . . . for a minute!"

"Tomorrow he'll come himself."

"They'll never let us out!" Ivan Dmitrich was saying meanwhile. "They'll let us rot here! O Lord, is there really no hell in the other world and will these scoundrels be forgiven? Where is justice then? Open, scoundrel, I'm suffocating!" he cried in a hoarse voice and charged the door. "I'll beat my brains out! Murderers!"

Nikita quickly opened the door, shoved Andrei Yefimich aside roughly with both hands and his knee, then swung and struck him in the face with his fist. Andrei Yefimich felt as though a huge salt wave had covered him from his head down and was dragging him to bed; it was, in fact, salty in his mouth: probably blood flowing from his teeth. As if trying to swim out, he waved his arms and seized at someone's bed, and at that moment felt Nikita strike him twice on the back.

A loud shriek came from Ivan Dmitrich. They must be beating him too.

Then everything grew still. Watery moonlight filtered through the bars, and on the floor lay a shadow like a snare. It was terrible. Andrei Yefimich lay holding his breath; he was waiting with terror to be struck again. It was as though someone had taken a sickle, thrust it in him, and turned it a few times in his chest and bowels. He bit the pillow and clenched his teeth with pain, and suddenly amid the chaos, the terrible unendurable thought flashed clearly in his mind that these people who now looked like black shadows in the moonlight must have experienced the same pain for years, day after day. How could it happen that throughout over twenty years he had not known and had not wanted to know that? He had not known, had had no understanding of pain, meaning he was not guilty, yet his conscience, as intractable and hard as Nikita, made him grow cold from the top of his head to his heels. He jumped up, wanted to cry out with all his strength and run as fast as possible to kill Nikita, then Khobotov, the superintendent, and the orderly, then himself, but not a sound came out of his chest and his legs would not obey; panting, he tore at the bathrobe and shirt over his chest, ripped them, and fell unconscious on the bed.

XIX

The next morning his head ached, his ears hummed, and he felt unwell throughout his body. He was not ashamed to remember his weakness of yesterday. He had been fainthearted, afraid even of the moon, had frankly expressed feelings and thoughts he had not suspected in himself before. For example, his thoughts about the discontent of the philosophizing no-bodies. But now it was all the same to him.

He did not eat, did not drink, lay motionless, and kept silent.

"It's all the same to me," he thought when they questioned him. "I won't answer . . . It's all the same."

After dinner Mikhail Averyanich came bringing a quarter-pound of tea and a pound of fruit candy. Darushka also came and stood by the bed for a whole hour with an expression of dense sorrow on her face. Dr. Khobotov visited him too. He brought a vial of bromic drops and ordered Nikita to fumi-gate the ward.

Toward evening Andrei Yefimich died of an apoplectic fit. At first he felt a violent chill and nausea; something horrid seemed to penetrate his whole body, even his fingers, stretch from his stomach to his head, and flood his eyes and ears. It turned green before his eyes. Andrei Yefimich understood that his end had come and remembered that Ivan Dmitrich, Mikhail Averyanich, and millions of people believe in im-mortality. If it should suddenly exist? But he did not want immortality, and thought of it only for an instant. A herd of unusually handsome and graceful deer he had been reading about yesterday ran past him; then a woman stretched a hand toward him with a registered letter . . . Mikhail Averyanich said something. Then everything disappeared and Andrei Yefi-mich lost consciousness forever.

The peasants came, took him by the hands and feet, and carried him off to the chapel. There he lay on a table with open eyes and the moon illuminated him through the night. In the morning, Sergei Sergeich came, prayed piously before the crucifix, and closed his former superior's eyes.

A day later they buried Andrei Yefimich. The funeral was attended only by Mikhail Averyanich and Darushka.

A Woman's Kingdom

<><><><><><><><><><><><><><><><><><><><><><><><><><><><><>

This story was finished by Chekhov in November 1893 and published in the January 1894 issue of *Russian Thought*. Shortly before its publication Chekhov mentioned it to Suvorin, referring to it as "a description of a young woman." This seems to be a clear indication that for the author himself the character of Anna Akimovna, a twenty-five-year-old unmarried woman who suddenly finds herself an heiress to a fortune and the owner of a big factory, and the portrayal of her frustrations, her vague longing for a marriage and a happy family life, were the real focus of the story; while the depiction of the milieu, of the conditions of factory life (in all probability suggested to Chekhov by his dealings with the local factory at Melikhovo, especially during the cholera epidemics of 1892 and 1893), was more or less incidental.

The story had a rather cool reception from the critics. Some of them noted that Anna Akimovna was "a remarkable type of a woman from the merchant milieu," but they overlooked the wonderful portrayal of various minor characters, full of fine satirical touches, and paid little attention to the subtle composition of the story. It covers almost exactly twenty-four hours in the life of Anna Akimovna, beginning on Christmas Eve and ending on the evening of Christmas Day, and is divided into four chapters, which, contrary to Chekhov's usual practice, bear titles. The story is, essentially, another variation on Chekhov's main theme—that of human isolation and mutual incomprehensibility. Unlike "Ward No. 6," "The Duel," and "Peasants," it is not concerned with any ideological or social problems, even though it is projected against a clearcut background. It is a very good example of Chekhov's impressionist technique. One should note perhaps that into the mouth of one of the characters Chekhov puts his own admiration for Maupassant as a writer.

<><><><><><><><><><><><><><><><><><><><><><><><><><><><><><><>

I

CHRISTMAS EVE

Here was a thick bundle of money. From the timber estate, sent by the overseer. He wrote he was sending fifteen hundred rubles in damages he collected from someone after winning his case in the court of the second instance. Anna Akimovna disliked and dreaded words such as "damages" and "winning cases." She knew jurisprudence was indispensable, but for some reason, when the factory director Nazarych or the overseer of the timber estate, both of whom went to court frequently, won some case or other on her behalf, she always felt uneasy and as if ashamed. Now, too, she felt uneasy and awkward and wanted to put this fifteen hundred rubles away where she would not see it.

She thought with annoyance that other girls her age—she had turned twenty-five—were now bustling around the house wearing themselves out and would sleep soundly to wake up tomorrow morning in a holiday mood; many of them had married long ago and had children. Only she alone is for some reason obliged to sit over these letters like an old woman, make notes on them, write answers, then do nothing all evening until midnight and wait for the desire to sleep; and all day tomorrow they will come with Christmas greetings to congratulate and petition her, while the day after, some scandal will inevitably take place in the factory—someone will be beaten, or somebody will die from drinking too much vodka, and her conscience will torment her for some reason; and after the holidays, Nazarych will dismiss twenty men for truancy, and all twenty will crowd bareheaded around her porch, and she will be ashamed to go out to them and to have them driven off like dogs. And all her acquaintances will say behind her back and write her in anonymous letters that she is a millionaire, an exploiter, devouring others' lives and sucking the workers' blood.

There, apart, lies a package of letters already read and put aside. From petitioners. Here are the hungry, the drunk, the overburdened with many-membered families, the sick, the meek, the unrecognized . . . Anna Akimovna had already noted on each letter which one should get three rubles, which five; these letters would go to the office today, and tomorrow the distribution of aid would take place or, as the servants said, the feeding of the beasts.

Four hundred and seventy rubles will be distributed piece-meal—the percentage on the capital bequeathed by the late Akim Ivanich for the poor and needy. There will be an ugly mob. A long file will stretch from the gate to the office door of some sort of alien people with beastly faces, in rags, frozen, hungry, and already drunk, calling upon the Little Mother-Benefactress Anna Akimovna and her parents in quavering voices; the rearmost will shove the foremost, and the foremost will utter filthy curses. The clerk, exasperated by the noise, wrangling, and wailing, will jump out and box someone's ears to the general satisfaction. And her own men, the workers, having gotten nothing for the holiday except their own salaries and having already squandered it to the last kopeck, will stand in the middle of the courtyard, watch, and snicker—some enviously, others ironically.

"Merchants, and particularly their wives, have more love for the poor than for their own workers," thought Anna. "It's always like that."

Her glance fell on the bundle of money. It would be fine to distribute this unnecessary, offensive money to the workers tomorrow, but you can't give a worker anything for nothing or he'll demand it the next time. Yes, and what would this fifteen hundred amount to when there are a thousand eight hundred and some workers in the factory, not counting their wives and children? Or else, why not pick out one of the petitioners writing these letters, some unfortunate who long ago lost hope of a better life, and give him the fifteen hundred? The wretch would be thunderstruck by the money, and per-haps feel happy for the first time in his life. This idea seemed original and amusing to Anna and diverted her. She drew a letter from the pile at random and perused it: a certain pro-vincial secretary Chalikov, already long unemployed, ill, living in the house of Gushchin; a tubercular wife, five little daugh-ters. The four-storied Gushchin house in which Chalikov lived was very familiar to Anna. Ah, a poor, rotting, un-healthy house!

"I'll give it to this Chalikov," she decided. "I shan't send it, it's better if I go myself so there'll be no unnecessary talk. Yes," she reasoned, slipping the fifteen hundred rubles in her pocket, "I'll have a look and perhaps I can place the little girls somewhere."

She began to feel merry; she rang and ordered the horses brought.

It was seven in the evening when she settled in the sleigh. The windows in all the buildings were brightly lit and it therefore seemed very dark in the huge courtyard. Electric lanterns burned at the gates and far in the dimness of the courtyard near the warehouses and the workers' barracks.

Anna disliked and dreaded these dark, gloomy buildings, warehouses and workers' barracks. After her father's death, she had only been in the main building once. The high ceilings with the iron girders, the mass of huge, swiftly turning wheels, driving belts and levers, the shrill hissing, the screech of steel, the jarring of wagonettes, the fierce gasp of steam; the faces, pale or crimson or black with coal dust; the shirts damp with sweat; the gleam of steel, copper, and fire; the smell of oil and coal; and the draft, now very hot, now cold, gave her the impression of hell. It seemed to her that the wheels, levers, and hot, hissing cylinders were trying to tear loose from their bonds to destroy people, while the people ran and fussed near the machines with worried faces, deaf to each other, trying to arrest their terrifying movement. They were showing and respectfully explaining something to Anna. She recalled how they had pulled pieces of red-hot iron out of the furnace in the smithy, and how one old man with a small strap on his head, and another—young, in a blue blouse with a watch chain on his chest and an angry face, undoubtedly one of the foremen—were beating a piece of iron with hammers; and how golden sparks whizzed in all directions, and how, after a short pause, they rattled a huge piece of sheet iron in front of her; the old man stood at attention and smiled, while the young one wiped his wet face on his sleeve and explained something to her. And she recalled, too, how an old man with one eye was filing pieces of iron in the other shop, scattering iron dust, and how a redhead, in dark glasses with rents in his shirt, was working at a turner's lathe, making something out of a piece of steel. The lathe roared and shrieked and whistled, and Anna was nauseated by this noise and felt as though they were drilling through her ears. She looked, listened, not understanding, smiled benevolently, and was ashamed. To make a living and earn a hundred thousand from a business you don't understand and can't like— how strange!

She had never set foot in the workers' barracks. Inside, they said, was dampness, bugs, depravity, anarchy. An astonishing business: a thousand rubles went for the improvement of the barracks annually, but the workers' situation, to believe the anonymous letters, grew worse and worse each year . . .

"There was more order in Father's time," thought Anna as she drove out of the courtyard, "because he was a worker himself and knew what was needed. While I don't know anything and only make blunders."

She felt weary again, was no longer glad she had gone, and the thought of the happy one on whom the fifteen hundred rubles would drop from heaven no longer seemed original and amusing. To go to this Chalikov while a million-ruble business is gradually disintegrating and sinking at home and the workers live worse than convicts in their barracks—that's blundering and self-deception. Along the highway and across the nearby fields, heading toward the city lights, walked crowds of workers from the neighboring cotton and paper factories. Laughter and merry talk rang out in the frozen air. Anna looked at the women and little children and suddenly longed for the simple, the coarse crowds. She clearly pictured that distant time when she was called Anyutka and when, as a little child, she used to lie under the same blanket with her mother, while alongside, in the next room, the laundress scrubbed the linens, and from the adjoining rooms, cursing, children's crying, a harmonica, and the buzzing of turners' lathes and sewing machines could be heard through the thin walls, and her father, Akim Ivanich, who knew almost all trades, soldered or traced or planed something near the stove, completely oblivious to the overcrowding and noise. And she felt a longing to scrub, to iron, to run to the shop and the tavern as she had every day when she lived with her mother. She should have been a working woman, not a proprietress. Her big house with chandeliers and pictures; the lackey Mishenka in his frock coat with his velvet whiskers; the pompous Varvarushka and the sycophantic Agafyushka; and those young people of both sexes who came to her almost daily to ask for money, before whom she always felt guilty for some reason; and those officials, doctors, and ladies, philanthropizing at her expense, flattering her and secretly despising her for her humble origin—how tiresome and alien all this was to her!

Now comes the railroad crossing and the town gates; the houses alternate with vegetable gardens; then, at last, the broad street on which the well-known house of Gushchin stands. There is a great turmoil now in the usually quiet street because of the holiday tomorrow. They are raising an uproar in the inns and beer taverns. If someone from another section, someone living in the center of town, had driven through the street now, he would have noticed only filthy, drunken, squabbling people, but Anna, having lived in these parts since childhood, recognized first her late father, then her mother, then her grandfather in the crowd. Father had been a mild, maundering soul, somewhat visionary, careless, and giddy. He had no fondness for money, esteem, or power; he used to say the working man did not have time for holidays and going to church, and were it not for his wife, he probably would never have taken communion and would have eaten forbidden food during Lent. Uncle Ivan Ivanich, on the other hand, was a hard man; in everything connected with religion, politics, and morality, he was harsh and inflexible, and watched not only over himself, but all his servants and acquaintances. God grant no one go into a room where he was without crossing himself! The luxurious mansion in which Anna Akimovna now lives, he used to keep locked, opening it only on big holidays for important guests, while he himself lived in the office, in one tiny room, arrayed with icons. He was inclined to the old faith and constantly received prelates and priests of the old belief, although he was christened and married and buried his wife according to the rites of the Orthodox Church. He disliked his sole heir, brother Akim, for his giddiness, which he termed simpleness and stupidity, and for his indifference to religion. He kept him down, in a worker's job; paid him sixteen rubles a month. Akim addressed his brother in the formal second person plural and bowed to his feet on the day of forgiveness before Lent. But three years before Ivan Ivanich died, he brought his brother close to him, forgave him, and ordered a governess hired for Anna.

The gateway in front of the Gushchin house was dark, deep, and malodorous; near the walls, one could hear men's intermittent coughing. Leaving the sleigh in the street, Anna went into the courtyard and asked how to find the official Chalikov in apartment number forty-six. She was directed to the farthest door on the right, third floor. In the courtyard, near the farthest door, and even in the stairway, there was the same repellent odor as near the gates. Anna had lived in houses like that in her childhod when her father had been a plain workman, and later, when circumstances changed, she had often visited them in the role of benefactress; the narrow stone staircase with the high steps, dirty, interrupted at each floor by a landing; the sooty lantern in the aperture; the stench on the landings, near the doors, of tubs, pots, rags— all this was familiar to her from long ago . . . One door was open through which Jewish tailors were visible sitting at tables in their caps and sewing. Anna passed people on the stairs, but it never entered her head that they might insult her. She had as little fear of workers and peasants, drunk or sober, as of her intellectual acquaintances.

There was no entrance hall in apartment number forty-six, and she came directly into the kitchen. The kitchens of factory hands and artisans usually smell of varnish, resin, leather, smoke—according to the trade of the occupant; the apartments of impoverished aristocrats and officials can be recognized by a rank smell of something sour. This repellent smell enveloped Anna now when she had barely crossed the threshold. At a table in the corner sat a man in a black frock coat with his back toward the door, probably Chalikov himself, and there were five little girls with him. The oldest, broad-faced and thin, with a little comb in her hair, looked about fifteen, while the youngest, chubby, with hair like a hedgehog's, was no more than three. All six were eating. Next to the stove, an oven fork in her hand, stood a rather small, very thin, yellow-faced woman in a skirt and white jacket, big with child.

"I hadn't expected you to be so disobedient, Lizochka," the man was saying with reproach. "Ay, ay, how shameful! So you want Papochka to whip you, eh?"

Catching sight of the unfamiliar lady in the doorway, the gaunt woman started and dropped the fork.

"Vassily Nikitich!" she cried out in a dull voice, not immediately, as if disbelieving her eyes.

The man glanced around and jumped up. He was a bony, narrow-shouldered man with sunken temples and a hollow chest. His eyes were small, deep-set, with dark circles; his nose long, birdlike, and slightly twisted to the right; his mouth wide. His beard was parted; he oiled his mustaches, and this made him look more like a railroad porter than an official.

"Does a gentleman named Chalikov live here?" asked Anna Akimovna.

"Precisely," Chalikov answered gruffly, but thereupon im-

mediately recognized Anna and cried out: "Madame Glago-
leva! Anna Akimovna!" and suddenly he became breathless
and flung his hands in the air as if in panic. "The benefactress!"

With a groan he ran toward her and garbling like a paralytic—there was cabbage on his beard and he smelled of
vodka—he pressed his forehead against her muff and looked
as if transfixed.

"The little hand! The holy little hand!" he intoned, panting. "A dream! A marvelous dream! Children, wake me up!"

He turned toward the table and said in a sobbing voice,
shaking his fists: "Providence heard us! Our savior has come,
our angel! We are saved! On your knees, children! On your
knees!"

His wife and the little girls, except the very youngest, for
some reason began quickly clearing away the table.

"You wrote that your wife was very sick," said Anna, and
she became ashamed and annoyed.

"I won't give them fifteen hundred," she thought.

"There she is, my wife!" said Chailkov in a thin, womanish
voice as if the tears had gone to his head. "There she is, the
unfortunate! One foot in the grave! But, my lady, we do not
complain. Better to die than live like this. Die, unfortunate
one!"

"What is he putting on?" Anna thought with irritation.
"It's obvious now that he's used to dealing with merchants."

"Please speak to me like a human being," she said. "I
don't like farces."

"Yes, my lady, five orphaned children around their mother's
grave in the light of funeral tapers—that's a farce! Eh!" Chalikov said bitterly and he turned away.

"Shut up!" whispered his wife, plucking at his sleeve. "Our
home, my lady, is not in order," she said, turning to Anna:
"you must excuse it . . . A family, you know how it is.
Cramped but contented."

"I'm not going to give them fifteen hundred," Anna thought
again.

And in order to have done with these people and the sour
smell as quickly as possible, she had decided to leave twenty-
five rubles—no more, and had started to reach for her purse,
when suddenly she became ashamed that she had gone so
far and disturbed people for trifles.

"If you'll give me paper and ink, I shall write at once to a
doctor, a good friend of mine, to visit you," she said, blush-

ing. "He's a very good doctor. And I'll leave you something for medicine."

Chalikov's wife rushed to wipe off the table.

"It's not clean here. What are you doing?" hissed Chalikov, looking at her malevolently. "Take her to the boarder's! If you please, my lady, may I ask you to come to the boarder's room?" he said to Anna. "It's clean there."

"Osip Ilich doesn't permit us to go in his room!" one of the little girls said sternly.

But they were already leading Anna from the kitchen through a narrow connecting room, between two beds; it could be seen from the position of the beds that two slept lengthwise on one, and on the other—three across. The next room, the boarder's, was, in fact, clean. There was a tidy bed with a red wool spread, a pillow in a white case, and even a case in the form of a shoe for the watch; a table covered with a hempen cloth on which stood a milk-colored ink bottle, pens, paper, framed photographs, all in order; and another table, black, on which lay watchmaking instruments and dismantled watches, neatly arranged. The walls were hung with hammers, pincers, augers, chisels, pliers, and so forth, and three wall clocks which ticked; one of them was huge, with thick weights, such as you find in inns.

As she started her letter, Anna noticed a portrait of her father and her own portrait on the table in front of her. This surprised her.

"Who lives here with you?" she asked.

"A boarder, my lady, Pimenov. He works at your factory."

"So? But I thought he was a watchmaker."

"He works on watches in a private capacity, in his spare time. An amateur, my lady."

After a silence during which all that could be heard was the clocks ticking and the pen scratching on the paper, Chalikov sighed sarcastically and said with indignation: "It's the truth: you can't make yourself a fur coat out of noble birth or rank. A cockade on the forehead and a noble title, but nothing to eat. In my opinion, if a man of low station helps the poor, he is much nobler than any Chalikov who's sunk into poverty and vice."

To flatter Anna he said a few more phrases disparaging his aristocratic origin, and it was obvious that he was deprecating himself because he felt superior to her. She had finished and sealed the letter meanwhile. The letter would be thrown out and the money would not go for medicine—this she knew, but she nevertheless placed twenty-five rubles on the table, and after brief reflection, added two handsome bank notes. Madame Chalikova's thin yellow hand like a hen's claw flashed before her eyes and crumpled the money into a ball.

"You were kind enough to give this for medicine," said Chalikov in a trembling voice; "but reach out a helping hand to me too . . . and to the children," he added and sobbed, "—unfortunate children! I'm not afraid for myself, I'm afraid for my daughters! I'm afraid of the hydras of lechery!"

Trying to open her purse, which had a damaged clasp, Anna became flustered; she blushed. She was ashamed that people were standing in front of her, watching her hands and waiting and probably laughing at her in the depths of their souls. Just then, someone came into the kitchen and stamped his feet, shaking off the snow.

"The boarder has arrived," said Chalikov's wife.

Anna became still more flustered. She did not want one of the employees to find her in this ridiculous situation. As fate would have it, the boarder came into his room at the very moment when, having finally broken the clasp, she was handing Chalikov a few bank notes while Chalikov lowed like a mute and sought to kiss her hand. She recognized in the boarder the workman who had once rattled the sheet iron in front of her in the smithy and given her explanations. He had evidently just come from the factory: his face was dark with soot; one cheek was spattered with smut near the nose. His hands were completely black and his beltless blouse was shiny with oily scum. He was a man of about thirty, of average height, black haired, broad-shouldered, and obviously very strong. At first glance, Anna recognized him as a foreman earning no less than thirty-five rubles a month, strict, vociferous, browbeating the workmen, and this was plain from the way he stood, from the pose he unconsciously assumed on seeing a lady in his room, but mainly because he wore his trousers outside his boots, had pockets on his chest, and wore a pointed, handsomely trimmed beard. Her late father, Akim Ivanich, had been the proprietor's brother, but nevertheless feared foremen like this boarder and tried to ingratiate himself with them.

"Forgive us, we made ourselves at home here in your absence," said Anna.

The worker looked at her with astonishment, smiled bashfully, and was silent.

"A little louder, my lady . . ." Chalikov said softly.

"When he comes from the factory in the evenings, Master Pimenov has trouble with his ears."

But Anna, delighted that there was nothing more for her to do here, nodded her head and went out quickly. Pimenov accompanied her.

"Have you been with us long?" she asked loudly without turning toward him.

"Since nine years ago. I'd already signed up in your uncle's time."

"But, how long ago! Why, Uncle and Father knew all the employees, while I know almost no one. I've seen you before, but did not know your name was Pimenov."

Anna felt a desire to justify herself to him, to make it appear that she had given away money just now in fun, not seriously.

"Oh, this poverty!" she sighed. "We invent good deeds on both holidays and workdays, but there's still no point. It seems to me that helping the like of that Chalikov is useless."

"Naturally it's useless," agreed Pimenov. "No matter how much you give, he'll drink it up. And now all night husband and wife will be snatching it away from each other and fighting," he added and laughed.

"Yes, one must confess our philanthropy is useless, tiresome, and ridiculous. But, well, you must agree too, it's impossible to sit with folded hands; you have to do something. What, for example, can be done with the Chalikovs?"

She turned toward Pimenov and stopped, waiting for an answer from him; he also stopped and slowly and silently shrugged his shoulders. Obviously he knew what to do with the Chalikovs, but it was so coarse and inhumane that he could not bring himself to even say it. And the Chalikovs were so uninteresting and insignificant to him that in a moment he had forgotten them. Looking Anna in the eyes, he smiled with pleasure and looked as if he were dreaming of something very fine. It was only now, as she stood close to him, that Anna noticed from his face, particularly his eyes, how exhausted he was and how much he longed for sleep.

"What if I gave him this fifteen hundred!" she thought, but the idea for some reason struck her as unsuitable and insulting to Pimenov.

"Your whole body is probably aching from work, yet you accompany me," she said, descending the stairs. "Go back home."

But he did not catch her words. When they came out on

the street, he ran ahead, unfastened the fur cover in the sleigh, and after helping Anna in, said: "I wish you a happy holiday!"

✧✧✧✧✧✧✧✧✧✧✧✧✧✧✧✧✧✧✧✧✧✧✧✧✧✧✧✧✧

II

CHRISTMAS MORNING

"They stopped ringing long ago already! It's God's punishment, and you won't even get there by the end! Get up!"

"Two horses running, running . . ." said Anna and woke up; in front of her, a candle in her hands, stood her chambermaid, redheaded Masha. "What? What's the matter?"

"Mass is already over!" said Masha in despair. "It's the third time I called you! Sleep till evening for all I care, but you yourself told me to wake you up!"

Anna raised herself on her elbow and glanced toward the window. It was still totally dark in the courtyard and only the lower edge of the window frame reflected light from the snow. A deep, low ringing was audible, but it came, not from the parish, but from somewhere farther away. The clock on the little table showed three minutes after six.

"All right, Masha . . . In three minutes . . ." Anna said in a pleading voice and covered up her head.

She pictured the snow on the roof, the sleigh, the dark sky, the crowd in the church and the smell of junipers, and she felt uneasy, but nevertheless decided that she would get up immediately and go to early Mass. And while she warmed herself in bed and wrestled with dreams which, as if on purpose, are often remarkably sweet when one is not permitted to sleep, and while she had visions of first a huge garden on a hill, then the Gushchin house, she was continuously disturbed by the thought that she must get up this minute and go to church.

But when she got up, it was already completely light, and the clock pointed to nine-thirty. Much new snow had fallen during the night, the trees were dressed in white, and the air was unusually bright, transparent, and fresh, so that when Anna looked out the window, she first of all felt a desire to breathe deeply—deeply. And while she was washing, the remnant of a distant childhod feeling—joy that today was Christ-

mas, suddenly stirred in her bosom, and thereafter she felt
light, free, and pure in spirit, as if her soul had been washed
or plunged in the white snow. Masha came in, all dressed up
and tightly corseted, and congratulated her on the holiday;
then she spent a long time dressing her mistress' hair and
helping her dress. The smell and feel of the new, lovely,
sumptuous dress, its delicate rustle and the smell of fresh
perfume stimulated Anna.

"Christmas is here," she said merrily to Masha. "Now we'll
find out our fortunes."

"Last year it said I'd marry an old man. Three times it's
come out like that."

"Come now, God is merciful."

"Well, why not, Anna Akimovna? What I think is if there's
no other way out, then it's better to marry an old one,"
Masha said sadly and sighed. "My twenty-first year's already
gone by, it's no joke."

Everyone in the house knew that redheaded Masha was in
love with the lackey Mishenka, and that this profound, passionate, but hopeless love had already lasted three years now.

"Come, enough nonsense said," comforted Anna. "I'll soon
be thirty, but I still expect to marry a young man."

While the mistress dressed, Mishenka, in a new frock coat
and polished boots, walked through the hall and the salon
as he waited for her to come out in order to greet her on
the holiday. He always walked rather peculiarly, stepping
softly and delicately; looking at his feet, his hands, and the
angle of his head, one might think he was not just walking,
but studying the first figure of the quadrille. In spite of his
thin, velvet mustaches and handsome, even somewhat slick
exterior, he was staid, judicious, and as devout as an old
man. He always bowed to the ground when he prayed and
was fond of burning incense in his room. The rich and distinguished he respected and venerated; the poor and petitioners of all sorts he despised with the full force of his tidy
lackey's soul. Under his starched shirt he still wore flannel,
which he put on winter and summer, dearly prizing his health;
his ears were stuffed with cotton wool.

When Anna walked through the hall with Masha, he
bowed his head low and slightly to one side and said in his
pleasant, honeyed voice: "I have the honor of congratulating
you, Anna Akimovna, on the very solemn occasion of the
birth of Christ."

Anna gave him five rubles; poor Masha was overcome.

His holiday appearance, pose, voice, and what he had said struck her with its beauty and elegance; continuing to walk behind her mistress, she thought of nothing at all, saw nothing, and simply smiled, first blissfully, then bitterly.

The upper story of the house was called the proper or noble half, and the big house; the lower part, where Aunty Tatyana Ivanovna reigned, had acquired the name of service, old people's, or simply women's half. The well-born and cultured were usually received in the former, while in the second—simpler people and Aunty's personal acquaintances. Beautiful, plump, healthy, still young and fresh, conscious of the luxurious dress she wore, which seemed to her to radiate in all directions, Anna descended to the lower floor. There she was met with reproaches that she, the educated one, had forgotten God, slept through Mass, and not come below to break the fast; and they all clasped their hands and said sincerely that she was beautiful, extraordinary; and she believed it, smiled, embraced, and slipped this one a ruble, that one three or five, according to the individual. She liked it downstairs. Whenever you looked there were image cases, icons, incense lamps, portraits of ecclesiastical figures, and there was a monk-like smell; in the kitchen, feet were pattering, and the smell of something forbidden during fasts and very tasty was already wafting through all the rooms. The yellow-stained floors gleamed and from the door to the icon corner stretched strips of narrow carpet with bright-blue stripes, and the sun seemed to slice through the window.

There were some unfamiliar old ladies sitting in the dining room; there were old ladies in Varvarushka's room also, and with them a deaf-mute girl who felt ashamed about something and kept saying: "Blee, blee . . ." Two rather emaciated girls brought from the orphanage for the holiday went up to Anna to kiss her hand and stopped in front of her, dumfounded by the splendor of her dress; she noticed that one of the girls was cross-eyed, and in the midst of her carefree holiday mood, her heart suddenly twinged painfully at the thought that suitors would scorn this girl and she would never get married. In the room of the cook, Agafyushka, five huge peasants in brand-new shirts were sitting around the samovar; they were the cook's relatives, not workers from the factory. On seeing Anna, the peasants jumped up and for propriety's sake, stopped chewing, although they all had full mouths. Stepan, the chef, in a white cap with knife in hand, came to greet her; the yardmen arrived in their felt boots and also greeted her. The water carrier looked in with icicles on his beard, but did not dare enter.

Anna walked through the rooms, followed by the entire household staff: Aunty, Varvarushka, Nikandrovna, the seamstress Marfa Petrovna, the downstairs Masha. Varvarushka, gaunt, thin, tall, taller than anyone in the house, dressed all in black, smelling of cypress and coffee, crossed herself and bowed from the waist in front of the icon in each room, and looking at her, one was for some reason always reminded that she had already sewn herself a shroud for the hour of death, and that the same storage chest which held the shroud also concealed her lottery tickets.

"Anyutka, be merciful for the sake of the holiday," she said, opening the door to the kitchen. "Forgive him, God help him. That's the way they are!"

On his knees in the middle of the kitchen was the coachman Pantelei, dismissed for drunkenness in November. He was a good man, but when he was drunk, became boisterous and unable to sleep; he used to walk through the main building and shout in a threatening tone: "I know everything!" It was obvious now from his sagging mouth, puffy face, and bloodshot eyes, that he had drunk without stopping from November to the holidays.

"Forgive me, Anna Akimovna," he said in a hoarse voice, knocking his forehead on the floor and showing his oxlike nape.

"Aunty dismissed you; ask her."

"What about Aunty?" said Aunty, coming into the kitchen and breathing with difficulty; she was very fat and there was room on her bosom for a samovar and a tray of teacups. "What about Aunty now? You're the mistress here and you give the orders, but to me it wouldn't matter if they never existed, the wretches. Come, get up, you boar!" she shouted at Pantelei, out of patience. "Get out of my sight! It's the last time I'll forgive you, and just one more sin—don't come asking forgiveness!"

Thereupon they went into the dining room to have coffee. But hardly had they sat down at the table, when the downstairs Masha ran in breathlessly and uttered in terror: "The singers!"—and ran back. Nose-blowing was heard, a low bass cough, and a pounding of feet as though shoed horses were being led into the entrance near the hall. For half a minute everything was still . . . The singers shrieked suddenly and so suddenly and so loudly that everyone shuddered. While they were singing, the priest from the charity hospital arrived, and with him the deacon and the sexton. Putting on his stole, the priest told how that night, when the bells rang for matins, snow was falling and it was not cold, while toward morning the freeze began to intensify, God help it, and now it must be below zero.

"Many, however, claim winter is healthier for a man than summer," said the deacon, but immediately assumed a severe expression and began singing right after the priest: "Thy birth, Christ, our Lord . . ."

Soon the priest from the hospital for manual laborers arrived along with the deacon; then the parish nuns, the children from the orphanage, and singing rang out almost uninterruptedly. They sang, ate, and left.

Employees from the factory came to give Christmas greetings. Only the foremen were here: the mechanics, their helpers, the patternmakers, the bookkeeper, and so forth—all attractive, in new black frock coats. They were all fine fellows, like top-quality goods; each knew his worth, that is, he knew that if he lost his place today, another factory would take him with delight tomorrow. They evidently loved Aunty, because they behaved freely in front of her and even smoked, and when they went up to the buffet in a crowd, the bookkeeper took her by her broad waist. They were familiar in part, perhaps, because Varvarushka, who had wielded great power in the old men's time and used to keep watch over the employees' morals, now had no importance at all in the household; and also, perhaps, because many of them still remembered the time when Aunty Tatyana Ivanovna, kept in austerity by her brothers, used to dress like a simple peasant woman in the manner of Agafyushka, and when Anna used to run through the courtyard near the main building and was called Anyutka by everyone.

The employees ate, talked, and stared with bewilderment at Anna: how she had grown up, how pretty she had become! But this elegant girl educated by governesses and teachers was already alien to them, incomprehensible, and they unconsciously stayed closer to Aunty, who addressed them familiarly, constantly plied them with delicacies, and clinked glasses with them, even drinking down two glasses of cordial. Anna was always afraid that they would think she was proud, a usurper, or a crow in peacock's feathers; now, while the employees were crowding around the buffet, she stayed in the dining room and joined in the conversation. She asked her acquaintance of yesterday, Pimenov: "Why do you have so many watches in your room?"

"I take them for repair," he answered. "I do it in my free time, on holidays or when I can't sleep."

"Then if my watch gets out of order I can give it to you for repair?" Anna asked, laughing.

"Of course, I'd be pleased," said Pimenov, and his face showed sympathy when, without knowing why herself, she detached a magnificent little watch from her chain and gave it to him; he looked at it silently and returned it. "Of course, I'd be pleased," he repeated. "I no longer mend pocket watches. My eyesight is weak and the doctor forbids me to do fine work. But for you, I can make an exception."

"Doctors are liars," the bookkeeper said. Everyone laughed. "Don't you believe them," he continued, profiting from this laughter. "Last year at Lent a peg flew out of a drum and went smack into Kalmykov's head so you could see his brain, and the doctor said he'd die, but he's still alive and working to this day, only after that trick, he began stuttering."

"They lie, doctors lie, sure, but not that much," sighed Aunty. "The late Piotr Andreich lost his eyes. Just like you there, he worked all day in the factory near the blazing furnace and went blind. Eyes don't like the heat. But come, why chatter?" She shook herself. "Let's drink up. My best wishes for the holiday, my darlings. I don't drink with anyone, but with you, I'll drink up, sinner that I am. God help me!"

It seemed to Anna that after yesterday Pimenov despised her as a philanthropist, but was captivated by her as a woman. She watched him and thought he behaved very pleasantly and dressed suitably. True, the sleeves of his frock coat are a little short, and his waist seems high and his trousers unfashionable, not wide enough, but on the other hand, his tie is knotted with taste and care, and is not as flashy as the ones the others wore. And he is obviously a kindhearted man, because he obediently eats everything Aunty puts on his plate. She remembered how black he was yesterday and how he longed to sleep, and this recollection moved her for some reason.

When the employees were getting ready to leave, Anna gave Pimenov her hand and wanted to tell him to come visit without ceremony some time, but did not dare: somehow her tongue would not obey; and so that they would not think she particularly liked Pimenov, she gave his comrades her hand as well.

Then came the pupils of the school of which she was
trustee. They were all closely cropped and dressed in identical gray smocks. The teacher—a tall, still beardless young
man with red spots on his face—perceptibly agitated, had
arranged the pupils in rows; the little boys began singing in
harmony but in sharp unpleasant voices. The factory director
Nazarych, a bald, sharp-eyed man of the old faith, never got
along with the teachers, but this one in particular, who was
now busily waving his hand, he despised and detested without knowing why himself. He treated him haughtily and
rudely, held up his salary, and interfered in the teaching. To
drive him away for good, two weeks before the holiday, he
had appointed as guard in the school a distant relative of his
wife, a drunken peasant who did not obey the teacher and
spoke to him insolently in front of the pupils.

Anna knew all this, but was unable to help because she
was afraid of Nazarych herself. She wanted to at least treat
the teacher kindly now and tell him she was very satisfied
with him. But when he became badly flustered and began
apologizing for something after the singing, and when Aunty,
addressing him informally, dragged him familiarly to the
buffet table, Anna felt weary and awkward, ordered gifts distributed to the children, and went upstairs to her own part of
the house.

"There's much that's actually cruel in these holiday cere-
monies," she said to herself after a short pause while looking
through the window at the little boys as they went from the
house to the gates in a flock, shrinking from the cold and
putting on their fur coats and overcoats as they walked. "On
holidays one feels like resting, sitting home with one's relatives, but the poor little boys, the teacher, and the employees
are obliged for some reason to walk through the freezing cold,
to give their congratulations, express their respect, flustered . . ."

Mishenka, who had been standing in the hall right by the
door and heard this, said: "It didn't start with us and won't
be ended by us. Of course I'm an uneducated person, Anna
Akimovna, but as I understand it, the poor must always
respect the rich. They say God marks the rascal. In jails, in
night shelters, and in taverns, there are always only the poor,
while proper people, you notice, are always rich. And of the
rich they say: plenty attracts plenty."

"Misha, somehow you always express yourself tiresomely

and incomprehensibly," said Anna and she went to the other end of the hall.

It was just after eleven. The stillness of the huge rooms, broken only from time to time by the singing carried from the lower floor, was conducive to yawning. The bronzes, the albums, and the pictures on the walls depicting the sea with little ships, a meadow with little cows, and Rhine scenes, were so far from new that the eye glided over them without noticing them. The holiday mood had already begun to pall. Anna felt as before that she was beautiful, good, and extraordinary, but it now seemed to her that no one had any need for it; she felt she had put on this expensive dress without knowing for whom or for what. And as on all holidays, she had already begun to suffer from loneliness and the importunate thought that her beauty, health, and riches were merely a fraud because she was superfluous in this world; no one needed her; no one loved her. She walked through all the rooms, humming and looking out the windows. Stopping in the hall, she could not keep from speaking to Mishenka.

"I don't know what you think of yourself, Misha," she said and sighed. "Truly, God will punish you for this."

"What are you talking about, my lady?"

"You know what. Excuse my medding in your personal affairs, but it seems to me you are spoiling your own life out of obstinacy. You must agree that it's time you got married now, and she's a splendid girl, deserving. You'll never find anyone better than she. A beauty, intelligent, kind, devoted . . . And her looks! . . . If she belonged to our society or to a superior one, she would have been loved for her marvelous red hair alone. Notice how her hair goes with her complexion. Ah, my God, you don't understand anything and you yourself don't know what you need," said Anna with bitterness and tears started in her eyes. "The poor girl, I'm so sorry for her! I know you want to marry into money, but I've already told you, I'll give Masha a dowry."

Mishenka invariably pictured his future spouse in his imagination as a tall, plump, solid, and exceedingly pious woman with a gait like a peahen, always, for some reason, wearing a long shawl around her shoulders; while Masha was thin and lean, tightly laced in her corset; her gait was delicate and, principally, she was too alluring. While she sometimes greatly attracted Mishenka, in his opinion, this kind of attraction was suitable only for misconduct, not for marriage. When Anna Akimovna promised to provide the dowry, he vacillated for some time; but one day a poor student with a brown coat over his uniform who had come to Anna Akimovna with a letter was unable to restrain himself and, enraptured, embraced Masha downstairs near the coat stand, and she gave a faint shriek; Mishenka, standing at the top of the stairs, saw this, and from then on harbored a squeamish feeling toward Masha. A poor student! Who knows, had it been a rich student or an officer who embraced her, the consequences might have been otherwise . . .

"But why don't you want to?" asked Anna. "What more do you need?"

Mishenka was silent and raising her eyebrows, stared motionlessly at an armchair.

"Do you love someone else?"

Silence. In came redheaded Masha with letters and visiting cards on a tray. Guessing that the conversation was about her, she reddened to tears.

"The postmen came," she muttered. "And there came a certain official Chalikov and he's waiting below. He says you told him to come today for something or other."

"What impertinence!" Anna exploded. "I told him nothing at all. Tell him to leave, I'm not home."

The bell rang. It was the priests from her own parish; they were always received in the noble half, that is, upstairs. Following the priests came the factory director Nazarych and the plant doctor; then Mishenka announced the inspector of public schools. The reception of callers was beginning.

When free moments occurred, Anna sat in the salon in a deep armchair and closing her eyes, thought how her loneliness was entirely natural since she had never married and never would. But she was not to blame for this. Fate itself had flung her from a simple worker's setting where, to believe her memories, she had felt so comfortable and at home, into these vast rooms where she was completely unable to imagine what to do with herself, and unable to understand why so many people were flashing in front of her; what was happening now seemed to her insignificant and unnecessary since it gave her no happiness, even for a moment, and could not do so.

"If I fell in love," she thought, stretching herself, and her heart grew warm from the thought alone; "and freed myself from the factory . . ." she mused, imagining how all these heavy buildings, the barracks, and the school would roll off her conscience . . . Then she remembered her father and

thought that if he had lived longer he would surely have
married her to a common man, for example, to Pimenov. He
would have ordered her to marry him—and that would be
that. And it would be fine: the factory would fall into real
hands then.

She pictured his curly head, bold profile, thin mocking lips,
and the strength, the terrible strength in his shoulders, hands,
chest, and the tenderness with which he had examined her
little watch today.

"Well then?" she said aloud. "There would be nothing more
to it . . . I would have married."

"Anna Akimovna!" Mishenka called her, noiselessly entering the salon.

"How you frightened me!" she said, her whole body
quivering. "What is it?"

"Anna Akimovna!" he repeated, putting his hand to his
heart and raising his eyebrows. "You are my mistress and
benefactress and you alone can guide me in marrying, as you
are just like my own mother to me . . . But order them not
to snicker and tease downstairs. They won't let me alone."

"And how do they tease you?"

"They keep saying: Mashenka's Mishenka."

"Fi, what nonsense!" Anna was indignant. "How stupid
you all are! How stupid you are, Misha! How you bore me!
I don't want you in my sight!"

III

DINNER

As in the year before, the last to come to call here were
the present state councilor Krylin and the well-known lawyer
Lysevich. They drove up when it was already growing dark
in the courtyard. Krylin, an old man past sixty with a wide
mouth and gray sideburns close to his ears, with a lynxlike
face, was in uniform with the Anna ribbon and white trousers.
He held Anna Akimovna's hand in both of his for a long
time and finally said with hesitation in a single tone: "I
respected your dear uncle . . . and your dear father, and
benefited from their favor. Now I consider it my pleasant
duty, as you see, to congratulate their respected successor

. . . in spite of illness and the considerable distance . . . And I am very glad to see you in good health."

The advocate Lysevich, a tall, handsome blond man with a light sprinkling of gray at the temples and in his beard, was distinguished by unusually elegant manners. He entered with a lilting walk, bowed as if against his will, and moved his shoulders while talking, all with the indolent grace of a pampered steed which has been kept standing still too long. He was replete, extremely healthy, and rich; he even won forty thousand rubles once, but hid it from his acquaintances. He loved to eat well, particularly cheese, truffles, and horse-radish with hemp oil; while in Paris, according to his own words, he ate uncleaned tripe cooked. He spoke harmoni-ously, fluidly, without faltering, and only out of coquetry sometimes allowed himself to stutter and snap his fingers as if searching for a word. He long ago ceased to believe in what he had to say in court, or perhaps he did believe in it, but attached no importance to it; it was all already so familiar, stale, and ordinary . . . He believed only in the original and exceptional. A truism in an original form brought him to tears. His two notebooks were filled with unusual expressions he had excerpted from various authors, and when he wanted to locate some expression or other, he scrambled nervously through both notebooks, usually without finding it. The late Akim Ivanich, in a lighthearted moment, had invited him out of vanity to investigate the factory cases and allotted him a salary of twelve thousand. The factory affairs consisted of only two or three trifling debt collections, which Lysevich assigned to his assistants.

Anna knew there was nothing for him to do in the factory, but she could not refuse him: she lacked the courage, and furthermore, she was used to him. He called himself her legal adviser and his own salary, which he sent for punctually on each first of the month, "hard prose." Anna knew that when her woods had been sold for railway ties after her father's death, Lysevich had made more than fifty thousand on the sale and divided it with Nazarych. On learning of this swindle, Anna burst into bitter tears, but then she became used to the idea.

After greeting her and kissing both her hands, he measured her with a glance and frowned.

"You mustn't," he said with sincere concern. "I said, my dear, you mustn't!"

"What are you talking about, Viktor Nikolaich?"

"I said: you mustn't gain. Everyone in your family has an unfortunate tendency to plumpness. You mustn't," he repeated in a pleading voice, and he kissed her hand. "You're so good! You're so lovely! Here, Your Excellency," he turned to Krylin: "I commend to you the only woman on earth I ever seriously loved."

"That's not surprising. To know Anna Akimovna at your age and not to love her—it's impossible."

"I worship her!" the lawyer continued completely sincerely, but with his usual indolent grace. "I love her, not because I am a man and she a woman—when I'm with her, it seems as if she is of some third sex and I of a fourth, and we are swept away together to a region of the most delicate flowering hues and merge there into the spectrum. Leconte de Lisle defines such relationships better than anyone. He has one splendid spot, a wonderful spot."

Lysevich tore through one notebook, then the other, and not finding the phrase, resumed his calm. They began talking about the weather, about opera, about how Duse was arriving soon. Anna remembered that Lysevich and, it seemed, Krylin, had had dinner with her last year, and now as they were preparing to leave, she argued with them sincerely and in a pleading voice that since they had no more visits to make, they must stay to dine with her. After some hesitation, the guests agreed.

Besides the dinner, consisting of cabbage soup, suckling pig, goose with apples, etc., on big holidays, a so-called French or chef's dinner was also prepared in the kitchen in case one of the guests upstairs wanted to sample it. When the dishes began clatttering in the dining room, Lysevich displayed marked excitement; he rubbed his hands, shrugged his shoulders, blinked, and spoke with feeling about what dinners the old people used to serve, and what a marvelous *matelote* of turbot the cook here could prepare—it was not a *matelote*, but a revelation! He foretasted the dinner; mentally he was already eating it and enjoying himself. When Anna led him arm in arm to the dining room, and he at last drank a glass of vodka and put a morsel of salmon in his mouth, he even purred from pleasure. He chewed loudly, repulsively, making noises through his nose, and his eyes became oily and rapacious.

The appetizers were luxurious. There were, among other things, fresh white mushrooms in sour cream and a Provençal sauce of baked oysters and crayfish tails, strongly seasoned

with bitter pickles. The meal itself consisted of exquisite holiday dishes and the wines were excellent. Mishenka served
the table in ecstasy. When he placed some new viand on the
table and removed the lid from the gleaming saucepan or
poured the wine, he did so with the solemnity of a professor
of black magic, and looking at his face and his gait which
resembled the first figure of a quadrille, the lawyer thought
several times: "What a fool!"

After the third course, Lysevich said, turning to Anna:
"A *fin de siècle*** woman—assuming she's young and, of
course, rich—should be independent, intelligent, exquisite,
well-educated, daring, and a little depraved. Depraved in
moderation, slightly, because, as you'll agree, satiety immediately becomes wearisome. You shouldn't vegetate, my dear,
shouldn't live like everyone else, but should savor life, and
a slight depravity is the sauce of life. Swarm in flowers with
a heady aroma, smother yourself in musk, eat hashish, and,
most important, love, love, and love . . . For the first stage,
in your place, I'd provide myself with seven men for the
number of days in the week, and I'd call one Monday, the
next—Tuesday, the third—Wednesday, et cetera, so that
each would know his day."

This conversation agitated Anna. She ate nothing and just
drank a glass of wine.

"Let me speak now, at last!" she said. "For myself person-
ally, I cannot conceive of love without a family. I'm alone,
alone, like the moon in the sky, and moreover on the wane,
and no matter what you're saying there, I'm certain, I feel,
that this wane can be filled only by love in the usual sense.
It seems to me that this love will shape my obligations, my
work, illuminate my view of the world. I want the peace of
my soul and calm from love; I want what's beyond musk and
all spiritisms and *fin de siècle* . . . in a word," she became
flustered, "a husband and children."

"You want to be married? Why not? That's possible too,"
agreed Lysevich. "You must experience everything: marriage
and jealousy and the sweetness of the first infidelity, and even
children . . . But hurry to start living, hurry, my dear, time
goes by, it doesn't wait."

"So I'll go and marry!" she said, looking angrily at his
satiated, satisfied face. "I'll marry the most ordinary, the most
commonplace way, and glow with happiness. And you may

* End of the century.

be sure, I'll marry a simple working man, some mechanic or draftsman."

"That's all right too. Duchess Josiane fell in love with Gwynplaine and she is allowed to because she is a duchess; everything is allowed you, too, because you are extraordinary. If you have a desire to love a Negro or an Arab, my dear, don't restrain yourself, order yourself a Negro. Don't refuse yourself anything. You should be as bold as your desires. Don't lag behind them."

"Is it really so hard to understand me?" asked Anna with wonder, and her eyes glistened with tears. "Understand that I have a huge business on my hands, two thousand workers, for whom I must answer before God. The people who work for me are going blind and deaf. Life is terrible for me, terrible! I suffer and you have the cruelty to talk to me about some Negroes or other and . . . and you're smiling!" Anna struck her fist on the table. "To continue the life I'm leading now or to marry a person as useless and incapable as myself would be simply a crime. I can't live like this any more," she said heatedly, "I can't!"

"How good she is!" uttered Lysevich, admiring her. "My God, how good she is! But why get angry, dear? Suppose I'm not right, do you really think that the workers will be the better for it if, for the sake of an idea which I, on the other hand, deeply respect, you are bored and deny yourself life's pleasures? Hardly! No, depravity, depravity!" he said decisively. "It's essential for you, you have to be depraved! Think it over, dear, think it over."

Anna was glad she had spoken out and she became gayer. She was pleased to have expressed herself so well and thought so honestly and beautifully, and she was convinced now that if, for example, Pimenov loved her, she would be happy to become his wife.

Mishenka poured the champagne.

"You irritate me, Viktor Nikolaich," she said, clinking glasses with the lawyer. "It annoys me that you give advice when you yourself don't know life at all. In your opinion, if a man's a mechanic or a draftsman, he's inevitably a peasant and an ignoramus. But these are the most intelligent people! Extraordinary people!"

"Your father and uncle . . . I knew and respected them," Krylin pronounced with a hesitation; he had been sitting as rigidly as a statue, eating without stopping the entire time.

"They were people of remarkable intelligence and . . . of the highest spiritual qualities."

"All right, we know these qualities!" muttered the lawyer, and he asked permission to smoke.

When dinner was over, Krylin was led away to rest. Lysevich finished smoking his cigar, then, nodding from satiety, followed Anna into her study. Secluded nooks with photographs, fans on the walls, and the inevitable rose or blue lantern in the middle of the ceiling, he disliked as the expression of a limp, unoriginal character; in addition, recollections of some of his novels of which he was now ashamed were connected in his mind with this kind of lantern. Anna's study with its bare walls and characterless furniture pleased him very much. He found it soft and cozy sitting on the Turkish couch and looking at Anna, who usually sat on the rug in front of the fireplace, her arms wrapped around her knees, watching the fire and musing; and he felt the blood of peasants, of old believers, coursing in her at such moments.

After dinner, when coffee and liqueurs were served, he always became lively and told her various bits of literary news. He spoke oratorically, with inspiration, carried away by his own story, while she listened to him and thought each time that one could pay not twelve thousand, but three times as much for such pleasure, and she forgave him everything she disliked about him. He used to tell her the contents of tales or even of novels and two or three hours would go by imperceptibly, like minutes. Now he began somewhat sourly, in a weakened voice and with closed eyes.

"I haven't read anything, dear, for a long time now," he said when she asked him to tell something. "However, sometimes I read Jules Verne."

"But I thought you would tell me something new."

"Hmm . . . new," muttered Lysevich drowsily, and he sank still deeper in the corner of the couch. "All this new literature doesn't suit you and me, my dear. Of course, it should be such as it is, and not to recognize it—would mean not to recognize the natural order of things, and I do recognize it, but . . ."

Lysevich seemed to have fallen asleep. But a minute later his voice was heard again: "All new literature groans and howls like a fall wind in the chimney: 'Ah, unfortunate! Ah, your life is like a tomb! Ah, how dark and damp it is in your tomb! Ah, you're certain to die and there's no salvation for you!' That's fine, but I should prefer a literature which teaches how to escape from the tomb. Among all the contemporary writers, however, I sometimes read a certain Maupassant." Lysevich opened his eyes. "A good writer, an excellent writer!" Lysevich stirred on the couch. "A wonderful artist! A terrible, prodigious, superhuman artist!" Lysevich arose from the couch and raised his right hand. "Maupassant!" he said in ecstasy. "My dear, read Maupassant! One page of his will give you more than all the riches of the earth! There isn't a line that's not a new horizon. The mildest, tenderest movements of the soul turn into strong, stormy feelings; as if under an atmospheric pressure of forty thousand pounds, your soul changes into insignificant bits of some undetermined substance, rose-colored, which, it seems to me, would have a tart, voluptuous taste if it could be put on the tongue. What a frenzy of transitions, of motives, of melodies! You lie down on lilies of the valley and roses and suddenly a thought, a terrible, splendid, irresistible thought, unexpectedly swoops upon you like a locomotive, envelops you in hot steam, and deafens you with its whistle. Read, read Maupassant! My dear, I insist on it!"

Lysevich began waving his hands and pacing from corner to corner in strong agitation. "No, it's impossible!" he said as if in despair. "His latest thing exhausted, intoxicated me! But I'm afraid you'll remain indifferent to it. For it to carry you away, you have to savor it, slowly squeeze the juice out of each line, drink . . . you have to drink it!"

After a long preamble in which there were many words such as "demonic sensuality," "a network of the finest nerves," "simoon," "crystal," and so forth, he at last began telling the contents of the novel. He told it less rhetorically, but very minutely, quoting whole descriptions and conversations; the characters in the novel transported him, and in characterizing them, he assumed poses, changed his facial expression and voice, like a true actor. In his excitement, he sometimes laughed in a bass, sometimes in a very thin little voice, clasped his hands, or seized his head as if it were about to burst. Anna listened enraptured, although she had already read this novel, and the advocate's rendering seemed to her many times more beautiful and complex than the book. He directed her attention to various fine points and underlined fortunate expressions and profound thoughts, but she saw only life, life, life, and her own self as if she were a character

in the novel; her spirits rose, and also laughing and clasping
her hands, she thought that one must not continue to live
like this, that there is no need to live badly when one can live
well; she recalled her own words and thoughts at dinner and
was proud of them, and when Pimenov suddenly arose in her
imagination, she felt gay and wanted him to be in love
with her.

When he finished telling the story, Lysevich sat down,
exhausted, on the couch.

"How delightful you are! How good!" he began after a
short pause in a weak voice as if ill. "I'm happy near you,
dear, but just the same, why am I forty-two and not thirty?
My tastes and yours don't coincide: you should be depraved,
while I already lived through that phase long ago and want
the most delicate, immaterial love, like a sunbeam, meaning,
from the point of view of a woman of your years, I'm no
longer fit for the devil."

According to what he said, he loved Turgenev, the minstrel
of maidenly love, purity, youth, and melancholy Russian
nature, but he himself loved maidenly love from a distance,
from hearsay, as something abstract, existing outside real life.
Now he assured himself that he loved Anna Akimovna
platonically, ideally, although he himself did not know what
he meant. But he felt fine, comfortable, warm; Anna appeared
enchanting, original, and he thought the pleasant sensation
aroused in him by his surroundings was precisely what is
called platonic love.

He pressed his cheek to her hand and said in the tone in
which people usually cajole small children: "My sweet, what
did you fine me for?"

"How? When?"

"I didn't receive a bonus from you for Christmas."

Anna had not heard before that the lawyer was sent a
Christmas bonus, and she now found herself in the dilemma
of how much to give him. And it was necessary to give, for
he was waiting, although he looked at her with eyes filled with
love.

"Nazarych must have forgotten," she said. "But it's not too
late to rectify it."

Suddenly she remembered yesterday's fifteen hundred rubles
which were now lying in a little dressing table in her bedroom.
And when she fetched this distasteful money and gave it to
the advocate, and when he thrust it into his side pocket with

indolent grace, it all happened somehow pleasantly and naturally. The unexpected reminder about bonuses and these fifteen hundred rubles fitted the advocate.

"Merci," he said and kissed her finger.

In came Krylin with a sleepy, blissful face, without having put his medals back on yet.

He and Lysevich sat a while longer, drank a glass of tea, and prepared to leave. Anna was a little troubled . . . She had completely forgotten where Krylin was employed and whether it was necessary to give him money or not, and, if necessary, whether she should give it now or send it in an envelope.

"Where does he work?" she whispered to Lysevich.

"The devil knows," muttered the advocate, yawning.

She reasoned that if Krylin had been with her uncle and father and respected them, it was not for nothing: obviously, he must have done good deeds on their behalf and was an administrator in some kind of charitable institution. On saying good-by, she thrust three hundred rubles into his pocket; he seemed astonished and looked at her with leaden eyes in silence for a minute, but then seemed to understand and said: "But you won't be able to have the receipt until New Year's, most respected Anna Akimovna." Lysevich was totally exhausted and was cumbersome and unsteady when Mishenka helped him into his fur coat. And as he descended below, he looked utterly debilitated, and it was clear that he would fall asleep as soon as he sat in the sleigh.

"Your Excellency," he said to Krylin wearily, stopping in the middle of the stairway, "has it ever happened to you to have a feeling as if some invisible force were stretching you lengthwise, that you were dragged, dragged, and finally turned into the finest wire? This expresses itself subjectively in a kind of special, sensual feeling, not to be compared with anything else."

Anna, standing upstairs, saw them each give Mishenka a bank note.

"Don't forget! Till we meet again!" she cried to them and ran to her bedroom.

She quickly threw off the dress, of which she had already tired, put on a dressing gown, and ran downstairs. And as she ran down the staircase, she laughed and stamped her feet like a mischievous child. She felt a strong yearning to play pranks.

IV

EVENING

Aunty, in a loose cotton blouse, Varvarushka, and two other old women were sitting in the dining room having supper. On the table in front of them lay a large piece of salt beef, a ham, and various salty appetizers, and steam rolled to the ceiling from the salt beef, which was very fat and succulent-looking. Vineyard wines were not served downstairs, but on the other hand, there were more varied kinds of vodkas and liquors. The cook, Agafyushka, plump, white, overfed, stood at the door with arms folded and chatted with the old women, while the downstairs Masha, a brunette with a crimson ribbon in her hair, served and carried in the food. The old women had been full ever since morning and an hour before supper had had tea with sweet cakes, and they consequently were eating with an effort now, as if duty bound.

"Oh, Little Mother!" groaned Aunty when Anna suddenly ran into the dining room and sat down on a chair next to her. "You've frightened me to death!"

The household loved it when Anna was in good spirits and clowned; it was always a reminder that the old men were now dead, the old women no longer had any power in the house, and everyone could live as he pleased without fear of being sternly called to account. Only the two unfamiliar old ladies looked at Anna askance, in bewilderment: she was humming, yet it was a sin to sing at the table.

"Our Little Mother, the beauty, a real picture!" Agafyushka began enumerating mawkishly. "Our priceless jewel! . . . The people were coming now to look at our king's daughter— God's will be done! Generals and officers and gentlemen . . . I looked, looked out the window, counted, counted, but finally gave up."

"As for me, they might just as well not have come, the wretches!" said Aunty; she looked sorrowfully at her niece and added: "They just wasted my poor orphan's time."

Anna was hungry, for she had eaten nothing since morning. They poured her a very bitter liqueur; she drank it down and tried the salt beef with mustard, which she found unusually tasty. Then the downstairs Masha served turkey-hen, pickled apples, and gooseberries. And this pleased her too. But there was one unpleasant thing: steam poured from the Dutch tile stove, it was stifling, and everyone's cheeks were burning. After supper they took the cloth off the table and put on plates of mint gingerbread, nuts, and raisins.

"You sit down too . . . what are you doing there!" said Aunty to the cook.

Agafyushka sighed and sat down at the table; Masha put a liqueur glass in front of her too, and Anna Akimovna began to feel that as much steam rolled off Agafyushka's white neck as from the stove. They talked continuously about how hard it had grown to find a husband now; how in former times men were seduced by money, if not by beauty, while now you couldn't figure out what they wanted, and whereas only the hunchbacked and lame remained old maids before, now not even the beautiful and rich were taken. Aunty began explaining this by the lack of morals and fear of God, but suddenly remembered that her brother Ivan Ivanich and Varvarushka—both of whom had led pious lives and were God-fearing—had nevertheless begotten children secretly and sent them to a foundling home; she checked herself and turned the conversation to how she had once had a suitor among the factory workers, and how she had loved him, but her brothers had married her forcibly to a widower, an icon painter, who, glory be to God, died two years later. The downstairs Masha also took a place at the table and with an air of mystery told how a strange man with black mustaches in an overcoat with a sheepskin collar had appeared in the courtyard every day in the morning for a week now: he came in the courtyard, looked in the window of the big house, and went on to the factory building; a tolerable sort of man, good-looking . . .

All these conversations suddenly gave Anna a desire to be married, a strong desire, approaching anguish; she felt she would have given half her life and all her fortune just to know there was someone upstairs who was closer to her than anyone on earth, and to know he loved her deeply and yearned for her; and the thought of this closeness, delightful, inexpressible in words, stirred her heart. And the instinct of health and youth flattered her and lied to her that the true poetry of life had not yet begun, but still lay ahead; she believed it, and leaning back in the chair (at this, her hair loosened), began to laugh, and looking at her, the rest of them laughed too; and it was a long time before the reasonless laughter died down in the dining room.

They announced that the Hornet had come to spend the night. This was the devout Pasha, or Spiridonovna, a smallish, thin woman of fifty in a black dress and white kerchief, sharp-eyed, sharp-nosed, with a sharp chin; her eyes were shrewd, spiteful, and looked as if they saw through everyone. Her lips were pursed. For her spitefulness and hatefulness, she had been nicknamed the Hornet in the merchants' houses.

Coming into the dining room without looking at anyone, she went toward the icons and sang in an alto "Thy Birth," then "The Virgin This Day," followed by "Christ Is Born," whereupon she turned and pierced everyone with a glance.

"Happy holiday!" she said and kissed Anna on the shoulder. "At last, at last, I got to you, my benefactresses." She kissed Aunty on the shoulder. "I was walking to your house already this morning, but on the road visited some good people to rest. 'Stay, but stay, Spiridonovna'—and I didn't see evening come on."

Since she did not eat meat, they gave her caviar and salmon. She ate, looking at everyone from under her brows, and drank three glasses of vodka. When she finished eating, she prayed to God and bowed to Anna's feet.

Just as they had last year and the year before, they began playing Kings, and all the servants, everyone, from both floors, stood in the doorway to watch the game. Anna thought she saw Mishenka appear once or twice with a condescending smile in the crowd of peasant men and women. The first to become king was the Hornet, and Anna as a soldier paid her tribute; then Aunty became king, and Anna fell down to the peasants or "bottoms," which provoked general excitement, while Agafyushka became a prince and blushed with pleasure. Another game was formed at the other end of the table: both Mashas, Varvarushka, and the seamstress, Marfa Petrovna, who had been woken up expressly to play Kings, and whose face was sleepy; malevolent.

During the game, the conversation went on about men, about how hard it is to marry a good man now, and about which is the better fate—spinsterhood or widowhood.

"You're a beautiful, healthy, strong maiden," said the Hornet to Anna. "Only I can't understand, I say, who you're keeping yourself for."

"What can I do if no one wants to take me?"

"But, could be she made a vow to stay a spinster?" continued the Hornet as if not listening. "Why not? It's a fine thing, stay one . . . Stay one," she repeated, looking carefully and shrewdly at her cards. "Aye, brother, stay one . . . yes . . . Only spinsters, these very reverend ones, come in many kinds," she sighed and led out a king. "Oh, many kinds, I say! Some actually watch over themselves like monks and there's not the slightest blue of smoke, and if one of them sins once, she's so tormented, poor thing, it's a shame to condemn her. Yet here are other girls walking around in black dresses and sewing themselves shrouds, while themselves love old moneybags on the sly. Ye-es, my little canaries. Many an adventuress bewitches an old man and rules him, my darlings, rules, twists him around, twists, and when she's piled up enough money and lottery tickets, she bewitches him to his death."

In response to these hints, Varvarushka just sighed and glanced at the icon. Her face portrayed Christian humility.

"I know a girl like that, my fiercest enemy," continued the Hornet, looking at everyone triumphantly. "She also keeps sighing and keeps looking at icons, the devil-woman. When she ruled over a certain old man, it used to happen, you come to her and she'd give you a crust of bread while making you bow to the ground, and she'd chant: 'In conception immaculate still' . . . she'd give you a crust on holidays and cast it in your teeth on workdays. Well, and now I'm having my fun with her! I have all the fun I want, my diamond!"

Varvarushka again looked at the icon and crossed herself.

"But no one wants to take me, Spiridonovna," said Anna in order to change the subject. "What can one do?"

"You're to blame yourself, I say. You keep waiting for the aristocratic and cultured, while you should marry your own kind—a merchant."

"No need for a merchant!" said Aunty, becoming alarmed. "Save us, heavenly Tsaritsa! An aristocrat will squander your money, but on the other hand, he'll be kindly to you, a foolish woman. While a merchant will introduce such strictness you won't find a place for yourself in your own house any more. If you want to caress him, he'll be clipping coupons, and if you sit down to eat with him, he'll fling a crust of bread in your teeth, you country bumpkin! . . . Marry an aristocrat."

They all started talking at once, loudly interrupting one another, while Aunty banged on the table with a pair of nutcrackers and, red-faced, angry, repeated: "Not a merchant, no! You bring a merchant in the house, I'll go to the poorhouse!"

"Sh . . . hush!" shouted the Hornet; when everyone had become still, she squinted one eye and said: "You know what, Annushka, my swallow? There's no point in your marrying for good like everybody else. You're a rich woman, free; you're your own king. But staying an old maid doesn't fit you, child. I'll find you, you know, some sort of useless and simple-minded man; you take him for the eyes of the law and then—have fun, Malashka! Well, you slip the husband five or ten thousand and let him go back where he came from, while you're the lady of the house—you love whoever you want and no one can criticize you. And then you can love your aristocrats and cultured men. Eh, it's no life, it's a carnival!" the Hornet shook her fingers and whistled under her breath, "Have fun, Malashka!"

"It's a sin!" said Aunty.

"Ah, a sin," laughed the Hornet. "She's educated, she understands. To cut somebody's throat or bewitch an old man—that's a sin all right, but to love a nice little friend is very far from a sin. Yes, what of it, truly! It's far from a sin! That was all thought up by the devout to swindle simple people. Here I go everywhere saying—it's a sin, a sin, but myself I don't know why it's a sin." The Hornet drank a liqueur and cleared her throat. "Have fun, Malashka!" she said, this time obviously addressing herself. "Thirty years, my butterflies, I kept thinking about sins and was scared, and now I see I missed, I muffed! Eh, I'm a fool, a fool!" She sighed. "A woman's time is a short time and each little day should be treasured. You're beautiful, Annushka, and very rich, but already when thirty-five or forty years knock, you'll be writing an end to your time too. Don't listen to anyone, friend: live, have fun till you're forty, and then hurry and pray it off; there'll be time enough for beating your head to the ground and sewing shrouds. A candle to God and a fork to the devil! It's all one and the same! Well, how about it? Do you want to cover someone with riches?"

"I do," laughed Anna. "It's all the same to me now, I'd marry a common man."

"Why not? That would be fine too! Ooh, what a fine fellow you could pick yourself then!" The Hornet winked and nodded her head. "Oooh!"

"I tell her the same myself: you can't keep waiting for an aristocrat and you shouldn't marry a merchant, but someone simpler," said Aunty. "At least we'd be taking a master into the house. And are there so few good people? Take our factory men. All sober, steady . . ."

"And more!" agreed the Hornet. "Splendid fellows. Aunty, do you want me to match Annushka with Lebedinsky, Vassily?"

"Well, Vassy has such long legs," said Aunty seriously. "Very cold. No prospect."

Laughter burst out in the crowd near the door.

"Well, to Pimenov. You want to marry Pimenov?" the Hornet asked Anna.

"Fine. Match me with Pimenov."

"God's truth?"

"Match me!" Anna said decisively and struck the table. "Word of honor, I'll marry him!"

"God's truth?"

Anna suddenly felt embarrassed that her cheeks were burning and that everyone was watching her; she jumbled the cards on the table and ran out of the room, and as she ran up the stairway and arrived upstairs and sat down at the piano in the salon, a rumble like the sea roaring reached her from the lower floor; they were probably talking about her and about Pimenov, and perhaps, profiting from her absence, the Hornet had insulted Varvarushka, and was of course no longer measuring her words.

Throughout the entire upper floor only one lamp was burning in the hall, and its weak light came through the doorway into the dark salon. It was between nine and ten, no later. Anna played a waltz, then another, a third—she played without stopping. She glanced in the dark corner behind the piano, smiled, mentally called out, and the thought entered her head: why not go to town now to see someone, Lysevich, for example, and tell him what was happening in her heart now? She longed to talk incessantly, to laugh, to frolic, but the dark corner behind the piano was gloomily silent, and around her, in all the rooms of the upper floor, it was still, empty.

She loved tender ballads, but had a rough, untrained voice, and therefore just played the accompaniment and sang barely audibly in almost the same breath. She sang ballad after ballad in a whisper, more and more about love, farewells, lost hopes, and she imagined how she would stretch out her hand to him and say with entreaty, with tears: "Pimenov, take this load from me!" And then, as if her sins were forgiven, her soul would become light, joyful, and it would be the beginning of a free and maybe happy life. In the anguish of waiting, she leaned on the keyboard and longed passionately for the change in her life to take place now, immediately, and the thought that her former life would still go on for some time frightened her. Then she played again and sang barely audibly, and all around it was still. The rumble was no longer rising from downstairs: they must have gone to bed. Ten had struck long ago already. The long, lonely, boring night was approaching.

Anna walked through all the rooms, lay down on the couch, read in her study the letters received that evening. There were twelve letters of holiday greeting and three anonymous ones. In one of them, some simple workman, in terrible, barely legible handwriting, complained that the workers were sold bitter vegetable oil which smelled of kerosene in the factory store; in another—someone respectfully reported that in his latest transaction, the purchase of iron, Nazarych had taken a thousand ruble bribe from someone; in the third, she was cursed for her inhumanity.

The holiday excitement was leaving her now, and in order to maintain it, Anna again sat down at the piano and began quietly playing one of the new waltzes; then she remembered how intelligently and honestly she had thought and spoken today at dinner. She looked around at the dark windows and walls hung with pictures, at the weak light coming from the hall, and suddenly, unexpectedly, burst into tears and became annoyed that she was alone, that she had no one to talk to, to consult. To give herself courage, she tried to sketch Pimenov in her imagination, but nothing emerged.

Twelve o'clock struck. Mishenka, now wearing a jacket instead of his frock coat, came in and silently lit two candles; then he went out and returned a minute later with a tray bearing a cup of tea.

"What are you laughing at?" she asked, noticing the smile on his face.

"I was below and heard how you joked about Pimenov . . ." he said and covered his laughing mouth with his hand. "He should have been seated for dinner with Viktor Nikolaich and the general a bit ago, he'd of died of fright." Mishenka's shoulders began to shake with laughter. "He probably can't even hold a fork right."

The lackey's laughter, his words, jacket, and mustaches made an impression of uncleanliness on Anna. She closed her

eyes so as not to see him, and against her will, pictured
Pimenov having dinner with Lysevich and Krylin, and his
timid, uncultivated face seemed pitiful and helpless to her,
and she felt repelled. And only now, for the first time in the
whole day, she understood clearly that everything she had
been thinking and saying about Pimenov and about marriage
to a simple workman was rubbish, nonsense, and foolishness.
To convince herself of the contrary, to overcome her revulsion, she tried to remember the words she had said at dinner,
but she could no longer summon them; shame for her own
thoughts and deeds, the fear that she had perhaps said too
much today, and revulsion at her own cowardice, disturbed
her acutely. She took a candle and swiftly, as if pursued
by someone, went downstairs, woke up Spiridonovna, and
assured her she had been joking. Then she went to her own
bedroom. Redhaired Masha, dozing in an armchair near the
bed, jumped up and began straightening the cushions. Her
face was weary, sleepy, and the magnificent hair was heaped
to one side.

"This evening the official Chalikov came again," she said,
yawning; "but I didn't dare announce him. Already very
drunk. He says he'll come again tomorrow."

"What does he want from me?" Anna fumed and banged
a comb on the floor. "I don't want to see him! I don't
want to!"

She decided there was no one left in her life but this
Chalikov, that he would never stop pursuing her and reminding her daily how uninteresting and absurd her life was.
Look, that's all she can do: help the poor. Oh, how stupid
it was!

She lay down without undressing and sobbed from shame
and boredom. What seemed most annoying and stupid of all
to her was that today's dreams about Pimenov were honest,
lofty, noble, yet at the same time, she felt Lysevich and even
Krylin were closer to her than Pimenov and all the workmen
taken together. She thought now that if it were possible to
depict the long, lived-through day in a painting, everything
bad and vulgar, such as, for instance, the dinner, the advocate's words, the game of Kings—would be true, while the
dreams and talk about Pimenov would be entirely fabricated,
like an ambush, a chicanery. And she thought, too, that it
was too late now for her to dream of happiness; that everything was ruined for her already; and that to return to the
life in which she used to sleep with her mother under the

same blanket, or to invent a new, special life of some sort, was now impossible.

Redheaded Masha knelt in front of the bed and looked at her sadly, with bewilderment, then burst into tears herself and pressed her face to her mistress' hand; and it was clear without a word why she was so miserable.

"We're fools, you and I," said Anna Akimovna, crying and laughing. "We're fools! Ah, what fools we are!"

Three Years

◇◇◇◇◇◇◇◇◇◇◇◇◇◇◇◇◇◇◇◇◇◇◇◇◇◇◇◇◇◇◇◇◇◇◇

Chekhov first referred to "Three Years" in a sentence in a letter to Suvorin, dated December 8, 1892, in which he speaks of being engaged on a work with about a hundred characters and the action taking place in summer and autumn. In Chekhov's notebooks we find various things jotted down, obviously with an eye on "Three Years." But the first specific mention of it occurs in his correspondence much later, in September 1894. Writing to his sister, he said jokingly that, being envious of the laurels of Peter Boborykin (a very prolific author of enormously long novels dealing with various strata of contemporary Russian society), he had begun "a novel of Moscow life," in imitation of Boborykin's *The Pass*. Later, when the story was almost finished, he again mentioned the name of Boborykin in a letter to Suvorin. To another correspondent, N. Ezhov, he wrote (November 28, 1894) that the story was turning out "tedious and flabby." He was even more critical of it in a letter to a young woman writer, Elizaveta Shavrova, who often asked him for literary advice. He wrote to her on December 4, 1894: "My intention was one thing, but what has come of it is something different, rather flabby, made not of silk as I meant it to be, but of muslin. You're an expressionist, you won't like it." This piece of self-criticism was followed immediately by the well-known and often quoted passage in which Chekhov speaks of being fed up with realistic stories about ordinary people of his own time—the stuff that is demanded and expected of him: "I am fed up with always the same things, I feel like writing about devils, about terrible, volcanic women, about wizards, but alas! they demand from me well-intentioned novels and stories from the lives of Ivan Gavrilychs and their spouses."

"Three Years" had originally for its subtitle "Scenes from Family Life," but Chekhov allowed the editor of *Russian Thought* to substitute for it either "From Family Life" or simply "A Story." Goltsev, the editor, chose the latter alternative. The story was published in the January and February 1895 issues of *Russian Thought*.

Suvorin thought that Laptev Senior was modeled on Chekhov's father, but Chekhov denied this, saying that his father was a very ordinary, average man. It is doubtful whether Chekhov's primary concern in this story was with the portrayal of the merchant milieu. His reference to Boborykin was obviously facetious: the story, impressionistically written, has nothing in common with Boborykin's interminable novels about Moscow life. As usual, Chekhov was interested, above all, in human relationships, and "Three Years" is essentially a love story. It is built along the curve of Laptev's relations with Yulia: his falling in love with her; their marriage, in which there is no love on her side; their growing alienation; and the change in her attitude to him, so that their respective final positions are almost opposite to the initial ones. There is a parallel story of Laptev's and Yartsev's relationship with Polina Rasudina. All the characters in the story, both the principals and the minor ones, help to make it into a typically Chekhovian tale of futility and frustration. The critics, with one or two exceptions, were rather severe on it. When the story was included in Chekhov's *Collected Works* the author made some substantial cuts in it.

<><><><><><><><><><><><><><><><><><><><><><>

I

It was already dark, the lamps were being lit here and there in the houses, and the pale moon was rising behind the casern at the end of the street. Laptev was sitting on a bench by the gates and waiting for vespers to end in the Church of Peter and Paul. He calculated that Yulia Sergeyevna would pass by on her way back from vespers, and that he would then start a conversation with her and perhaps spend the whole evening with her.

He had been sitting there for an hour and a half, and during that time, had been picturing his Moscow apartment, Moscow friends, the footman Piotr, his writing desk; he stared with bewilderment at the dark, motionless trees, and it seemed strange to him not to be living in a summer villa at Sokolniki now, but in a provincial town, in a house past which a huge herd was driven every morning and evening, accompanied by a frightful cloud of dust and the playing of a horn. He remembered the interminable Moscow conversations he him-

self had taken part in not so long ago—conversations to the
effect that it was possible to live without love; that passionate
love is a psychosis; that, in the final analysis, there is no love
of any kind, but only a physical attraction of the sexes—and
everything on that order; as he remembered, he reflected
sadly that if he were asked now what love is, he would not
have an answer.

Vespers came to an end, a crowd appeared. Laptev strained
to see the dark figures. The archbishop had already driven
through in his coach, the bells had stopped ringing, the red
and green lights—lit for church holidays—had gone out one
by one in the belfry, while people were still coming unhurriedly, stopping under windows to talk. But now, at last,
Laptev heard the familiar voice; his heart began beating
hard, and because Yulia Sergeyevna was not alone, but with
two other women, he was overcome with despair.

"That's terrible, terrible!" he whispered, jealous. "That's
terrible!"

At the corner, before turning into a side street, she stopped
to take leave of these ladies and, at that moment, glanced at
Laptev.

"Why, I was just going to your house," he said. "I was
going to have a talk with your papa. Is he home?"

"Probably," she replied. "It's early for him to be at the
club."

The side street was entirely lined with gardens, and linden
trees grew along the fences, casting broad shadows now in the
moonlight so that the fences and gates on one side were
completely drowned in darkness; sounds came from there of
women's whispering, suppressed laughter, and someone softly,
very softly, playing a balalaika. There was a smell of lindens
and hay. The whispering of the unseen people and this smell
goaded Laptev. He suddenly, passionately, longed to embrace
his companion, to cover her face, arms, and elbows with
kisses, to burst into sobs, fall at her feet, tell her how long he
had been waiting for her. She gave off a light, barely perceptible scent of incense, and it reminded him of the time
when he, too, had believed in God and gone to vespers, and
when he had dreamed of a pure, poetic love. And because
this girl did not love him, it now seemed to him that the
possibility of the happiness he had dreamed of then was lost
to him forever.

She began talking with interest about the health of his
sister, Nina Fedorovna. Two months ago, his sister had been

operated on for cancer and now they were all expecting a relapse.

"I went to see her this morning," said Yulia Sergeyevna, "and it seemed to me that this week she had not really gotten thinner, but paler."

"Yes, yes," agreed Laptev. "There's been no relapse, yet each day I see her getting weaker and weaker all the time and melting before my eyes. I don't understand what's wrong with her."

"Lord, and yet how healthy, plump, and red-cheeked she used to be!" Yulia Sergeyevna uttered after a momentary silence. "Everyone here used to call her the Muscovite. How she used to laugh! She used to deck herself out as a simple peasant woman on holidays, and it suited her very well."

Dr. Sergei Borisich was at home; stout, red, in a frock coat reaching below his knees and making him look short-legged, he was pacing his study from corner to corner, his hands thrust in his pockets, singing softly: "Roo-roo-roo-roo." His gray whiskers were straggling; his hair was uncombed as if he had just gotten out of bed. And his study, with pillows on the couches, bundles of old papers in the corners, and a sick and dirty poodle under the table, had the same straggling, shaggy look as he himself.

"M'sieu Laptev wants to see you," his daughter said to him as she came into the study.

"Roo-roo-roo-roo," he sang more loudly, then, turning toward the parlor, shook hands with Laptev and asked: "What's the good news?"

It was dark in the parlor. Without sitting down and still holding his cap in his hands, Laptev began to apologize for his intrusion: he asked what to do to enable his sister to sleep at night and why she was growing so terribly thin, and the thought bothered him that these seemed to be the same questions he had asked the doctor that day during the latter's morning visit.

"Tell me," he asked, "shouldn't we call in some sort of specialist in internal diseases from Moscow? What do you think?"

The doctor sighed, shrugged his shoulders, and made an indeterminate gesture with both hands.

It was obvious that he was insulted. He was an extremely susceptible, apprehensive doctor, who always felt he was mistrusted, unrecognized, and insufficiently respected; that he was exploited by the public; and that his colleagues were malicious toward him. He ridiculed himself constantly, saying that fools such as he were created only for the public to ride roughshod over them.

Yulia Sergeyevna lit the lamp. She had been exhausted by the service, and it could be seen in her pale weary face, her listless gait. She longed to rest. She sat down on the couch, put her hands on her knees, and became lost in thought. Laptev knew he was homely and it seemed to him now that he could even feel his homeliness in his body. He was short, thin, with red cheeks, and his hair had already grown so much thinner that his head felt cold. There was no trace in his expression of that exquisite simplicity which makes even coarse, homely faces attractive; in the society of women, he was awkward, overtalkative, mannered. And now he almost hated himself for this. For Yulia Sergeyevna not to be bored in his company, it was necessary to talk. But about what? His sister's illness again?

And he began saying what is usually said about medicine; he extolled hygiene and said he had been wanting to build a night shelter in Moscow for a long time and already had an estimate of costs. According to his plan, for five or six kopecks, a worker coming to the night shelter in the evening would get a portion of hot cabbage soup with bread, a warm, dry bed with a blanket, and a place to dry his shoes and clothes.

Yulia Sergeyevna was usually silent in his presence, and in a mysterious way, perhaps with the sensitivity of a person in love, he used to guess her thoughts and intentions. Now he surmised that if she had not come home from vespers in order to change and have tea, it meant she was invited somewhere this evening.

"But I'm in no hurry about the night shelter," he continued with irritation and annoyance, turning to the doctor, who was watching him somewhat dimly and with uncertainty, obviously failing to understand why Laptev felt impelled to start a conversation about medicine and hygiene. "And probably I won't make use of the estimate in the near future. I'm afraid our night shelter will fall into the hands of our Muscovite bigots and lady philanthropists, who ruin every enterprise."

Yulia Sergeyevna got up and offered her hand to Laptev.

"I'm sorry," she said, "it's time for me to go. Please give your sister my best."

"Roo-roo-roo-roo," sang the doctor. "Roo-roo-roo-roo."

Yulia Sergeyevna went out, and Laptev took leave of the

doctor and went home soon thereafter. When a man is dissatisfied and feels unfortunate, how banal he finds the breath from these lindens, shadows, clouds, from all the beauties of nature, smug and indifferent! The moon was already high and clouds were racing swiftly under it. "But what a naive, provincial moon, what thin, pitiful clouds!" thought Laptev. He was ashamed of his talk about medicine and the night shelter, and was horrified to think that tomorrow, too, lacking character, he would again try to catch sight of her, talk to her, and be convinced again that he was a stranger to her. Day after tomorrow—the same thing again. Why? And when and how would all this end?

He went to see his sister on reaching home. Nina Fedorovna still looked sturdy and gave the impression of a strong, well-built woman, but her acute pallor made her appear corpse-like, particularly when, as now, she was lying on her back with her eyes closed; beside her sat her older daughter, ten-year-old Sasha, reading aloud out of her chrestomathy.

"Alesha's come," the invalid said softly to herself.

A wordless agreement had been concluded between Sasha and her uncle long ago: they alternated with each other. Sasha closed her chrestomathy now and quietly went out of the room without saying anything; Laptev took a historical novel off the dresser, hunted for the right page, sat down, and began reading aloud.

Nina Fedorovna was a native Muscovite. She and her two brothers had spent their childhood and youth on Pyatnitskaya Street with their family, who were merchants. It was an interminable, tedious childhood. Her father was strict and even birched her on three occasions; her mother had suffered a lengthy illness and died; the servants were dirty, coarse, hypocritical; the priests and monks who came to the house frequently were also coarse and hypocritical: they drank, ate, and crudely flattered her father, whom they disliked. The boys were fortunate in being sent to preparatory school, while Nina remained uneducated; she wrote in a scrawl throughout her life and read only historical novels. Seventeen years ago, when she was twenty-two, on the summer estate at Khimki, she had met her present husband, a landowner named Panaurov, fallen in love with him and married him secretly, against her father's will. Panaurov, handsome and somewhat brazen, who lit his cigarettes from icon lamps and whistled, seemed a complete nonentity to her father, and when his son-in-law later began asking for a dowry in his letters, the old man wrote his daughter that he was sending her the fur coat, silver, and various things left by her mother, and thirty thousand rubles, but without his parental blessing; later he sent twenty thousand more. This money and the dowry were spent, the estate sold, and Panaurov moved to town with his family and went to work in the provincial administration. He acquired a second family in town, and this aroused a great deal of daily gossip because his illegitimate family lived quite openly.

Nina Fedorovna worshiped her husband. Now, too, as she listened to the historical novel, she was thinking about how much she had gone through, how greatly she had suffered throughout, and that if someone were to write the story of her life, it would be very pitiful. Because her tumor was in her chest, she was convinced that she was suffering from love, from her marital life, and that it was tears and jealousy which had brought her to bed.

But just then Aleksei Fedorich closed the book and said: "The end, and God be praised. Tomorrow we'll start another."

Nina Fedorovna laughed. She had always laughed easily, but Laptev had noticed lately that at certain moments her mind seemed affected by her illness and she laughed at the slightest trifle and even without reason.

"Yulia came before dinner while you weren't here," she said. "I noticed she didn't have much faith in her papasha. Let my papa treat you, she says, but, just the same, write quietly to a holy hermit to pray for you. They've found themselves a hermit somewhere. Yulia forgot her umbrella in my room, take it to her tomorrow," she continued after a short silence. "No, when the end's already come, neither the doctor nor the hermit can help."

"Nina, why don't you sleep at night?" Laptev asked in order to change the subject.

"Just can't. I don't sleep, that's all. I lie by myself and think."

"What do you think about, dear?"

"About the children, about you . . . about my own life. You see, Alesha, I've lived through a lot. When you start remembering, when you start . . . Lord, my God!" She laughed. "It's not easy giving birth five times and burying three . . . There you are, about to give birth, and Grigory Nikolaich is sitting at the other woman's house, there's no one to send for a midwife or a peasant woman, you go in the

entrance or the kitchen for the maid, and there you find
Jews, shopkeepers, moneylenders—waiting for him to come
home. Your head swims . . . He didn't love me, although
he never said so. Now I've calmed down, settled in my heart,
but earlier, when I was younger, it was painful—painful, oh,
how painful, darling! Once—it was still in the country—I
found him in the garden with a certain lady and I walked
away . . . walked wherever my feet led me, and I don't
know how I came to be on the church porch; I fell on my
knees: 'Tsaritsa in heaven!' I say. And it's night in the courtyard, the moon is shining . . ."

She became tired, out of breath; then, after resting a
moment, she took her brother's hand and continued in a weak,
hollow voice: "How good you are, Alesha . . . How intelligent . . . What a fine man you turned into!"

At midnight Laptev left her room, taking with him the
umbrella Yulia Sergeyevna had forgotten. In spite of the late
hour, the servants, men and women, were drinking tea in the
dining room. What disorder! The children were awake and
sitting there in the dining room too. Everyone was talking
quietly, in soft voices, not noticing that the lamp was flickering and about to go out. All these people, young and old,
were upset by a whole series of unfavorable omens and in a
gloomy mood: the mirror in the antechamber had broken, the
samovar hummed every day and, as if in spite, was humming
even now; they were telling how when Nina Fedorovna got
dressed, a mouse jumped out of her boots. And the terrible
significance of all these signs was known to the children by
now: the elder daughter, Sasha, a thin brunette, was sitting
motionless at the table, and her face was frightened, grief-
stricken; young Lida, a plump blond seven-year-old, was
standing near her sister and watching the fire from under her
brows.

Laptev went downstairs to his own part of the house on the
lower floor in low-ceilinged rooms which were always stifling
and smelled of geraniums. In his parlor sat Panaurov, Nina
Fedorovna's husband, reading a paper. Laptev nodded to him
and sat down opposite. Both sat in silence. They used to
spend whole evenings without a word, and this silence did
not embarrass them.

The little girls came downstairs to say good night. Silently,
without hurrying, Panaurov made the sign of the cross over
both of them several times and gave them his hand to kiss;

they curtsied, then went up to Laptev, who also had to make the sign of the cross over them and give them his hand to kiss. This ceremony of kisses and curtsies was repeated every evening.

When the girls had gone out, Panaurov put aside his paper and said: "How dull it is in our God-blessed town! I confess, my dear friend," he continued with a sigh, "I'm very glad you've finally found a diversion for yourself."

"What are you talking about?" asked Laptev.

"I saw you coming out of Dr. Belavin's house yesterday. I hope you weren't going there for Papasha's sake."

"Naturally not," Laptev said, blushing.

"Well, naturally. And, by the way, you couldn't find another carrion like this Papasha with a lamp in broad daylight. You can't imagine what a slovenly, untalented, clumsy beast he is! Where you live, there, in the capital, they're still only interested in the provinces from the lyrical standpoint, so to speak, from the standpoint of landscapes and *Anton Goremyka,** but, take it with my compliments, my friend, there isn't any lyricism whatsoever, just savagery, vulgarity, nastiness—nothing more. Take our local sacrificial priests of science, so to speak, the intelligentsia. Can you imagine, here, in a town with twenty-eight doctors, they've all made themselves fortunes and own their own houses, while the populace is as completely uncared for as before. Here Nina had to have an operation, basically trifling, and for this, you see, a surgeon had to be sent for from Moscow—not one here could undertake it. You can't imagine. They know nothing, understand nothing, are interested in nothing. Just ask them here, for example, what cancer is? What is it? What does it come from?"

And Panaurov began to explain what cancer was. He was a specialist in all sciences and explained everything scientifically, no matter what the subject was. But he explained everything in rather his own way. He had his own theory of blood circulation, his own chemistry, his own astronomy. He spoke slowly, softly, convincingly, and the words "you can't imagine" he pronounced in a pleading voice, squinting his eyes, sighing wearily, and smiling graciously like a king, and he was obviously very pleased with himself and not giving a thought to the fact that he was already fifty.

"I feel rather hungry," said Laptev. "I could eat something salty with pleasure."

* A novel by Dmitry Vasilievich Grigorovich (1822–1900).

"Well, why not? That can be arranged right away."

Shortly thereafter, Laptev and his brother-in-law were sitting upstairs in the dining room having supper. Laptev had a glass of vodka and then began drinking wine; Panaurov did not drink anything. He never drank and did not play cards, but, in spite of this, had gone through his own and his wife's fortune and accumulated many debts. No particular passion was necessary in order to go through so much in such a short time, but something else, a special talent. Panaurov loved to eat well, loved fine tableware, dinner music, speeches, and the bows of lackeys, to whom he would carelessly toss a tip of ten or even twenty-five rubles each; he always participated in all subscriptions and lotteries, sent friends bouquets on their saints' days, bought cups, tea-glass holders, shirt studs, ties, walking sticks, perfumes, cigarette holders, pipes, dogs, parrots, Japanese bibelots, antiques; his nightshirts were silk, his bed of ebony inlaid with mother-of-pearl, his dressing gown a real Bukharian, and so on, and for all this went, as he himself put it, a "mountain" of money.

At supper he kept sighing and shaking his head.

"Yes, everything has its end in this world," he said softly, squinting his dark eyes. "You fall in love and you suffer; fall out of love and you're deceived, because there isn't a woman who won't deceive you; you suffer, fall into despair, and deceive in your turn. But the time will come when all this will be memories and you will reason clearly and consider these things utter trivialities . . ."

Laptev, tired, slightly drunk, looked at Panaurov's handsome head, at his dark trimmed beard, and felt he understood why women loved this spoiled, self-assured, and physically charming man.

After supper, Panaurov did not stay at the house, but went to his other apartment. Laptev accompanied him part way. Panaurov was the only man in the whole town who wore a top hat, and next to the gray fences, the pitiful three-windowed little houses, and the nettle bushes, his exquisite, foppish figure, top hat, and orange-colored gloves always made a strange, melancholy impression.

After leaving him, Laptev walked back leisurely. The moon was shining brightly; every blade of grass on the ground was distinct, and it seemed to Laptev as if the moonlight were caressing his uncovered head, as if someone were brushing eiderdown over his hair.

"I'm in love!" he said aloud, and he felt a sudden desire to run, overtake Panaurov, embrace him, forgive him, give him a great deal of money, then to run off across the fields, through the forest, and to keep running without looking around.

At home he saw, lying on a chair, the umbrella forgotten by Yulia Sergeyevna; he seized it and greedily kissed it. The umbrella was silk, no longer new, tied with an old rubber band; the handle was of ordinary white bone, inexpensive. Laptev opened it over himself and it seemed to him that it even gave off a smell of happiness.

He settled down more comfortably and, without letting the umbrella out of his hand, began writing to one of his friends in Moscow: "Dear, sweet Kostya, here is news for you: I'm in love again! I say *again* because six years ago I was in love with a Moscow actress whom I never even managed to meet, and during the last year and a half I lived with an 'individual' you know well, who is neither young nor beautiful. Ah, dear friend, how unlucky I am in love in general! I never had success with women, and if I say *again*, it's only because it's somehow sad and painful to admit to oneself that youth has passed completely without love, and that I am only really in love now, at the age of thirty-four. Let it be: I'm in love *again*.

"If you only knew what a girl she is! She could never be called a beauty—her face is broad, she's very thin, but what a marvelous expression of goodness when she smiles. Her voice sings and tinkles when she talks. She has never entered into conversation with me, I don't know her, but when I'm nearby, I sense in her a rare, extraordinary being, permeated with wisdom and lofty aims. She is religious, and you can imagine how this touches me and raises her in my eyes. I'm ready to dispute this point endlessly with you. You're right, let it be your way, but I still love it when she goes to church to pray. She's a provincial girl, but she studied in Moscow, loves our Moscow, dresses Moscow-style, and I love her for this too, love, love . . . I see you frowning and standing up in order to read me a long lecture about what love is and whom one can love and can't, and so on and so on. But, dear Kostya, when I was not in love myself, I also knew exactly what love is.

"My sister thanks you for your greetings. She often remembers how she once drove Kostya Kochevoi to school, and to this day still calls you *that poor boy* because she remembers you as the orphan boy. So, poor orphan, I'm in love. For the time it's a secret, don't say anything *there* to the 'individual' in question. This, I think, will be settled by itself, or, as the footman used to say in Tolstoy, *form itself . . .*"

After finishing the letter, Laptev lay down on his bed. He closed his eyes with fatigue, but for some reason did not sleep; he thought it was the street noises which kept him awake. The cattle were driven past, the horn was played, and soon after, the bells rang for early Mass. Now a cart went squeaking by, now the voice of a woman going to market called out somewhere. And the sparrows chirruped without stopping.

II

The morning was merry, festive. At ten o'clock, Nina Fedorovna, in a brown dress with her hair combed, was led, supported on both sides, to the parlor, where she stayed awhile, standing at the open window; her smile was broad, naive, and in her glance something indeed resembled a holy image, as a certain local painter used to say, an alcoholic who wanted to use her as a model to symbolize a Russian carnival. And everyone—the children, the servants, and even her brother Aleksei Fedorich and she herself—felt a sudden certainty that she would undoubtedly recover. The little girls chased after and caught their uncle, and the house was filled with noise.

Outsiders came to inquire about her health, brought bread blessed in church, and said that Te Deums were being held in almost all the churches that day. She was the benefactress of her town and was loved. She did good deeds with unusual ease, just like her brother Aleksei, who handed out money very easily without deliberating whether it was necessary to give or not. Nina Fedorovna paid fees for impoverished students, distributed tea, sugar, and jam to old people, outfitted poor brides, and whenever a newspaper fell in her hands, she looked first of all to see whether there was an appeal of some sort or a notice of someone's adverse circumstances.

She had a bundle of notes in her hand now on the strength of which various paupers, petitioners of hers, had purchased groceries, for which the merchant had sent her a bill of eighty-two rubles the day before.

"Look how much they bought, those shameless people!" she said, barely able to make out her own irregular hand-writing on the notes. "Is it a joke? Eighty-two rubles! Maybe I'll just not pay it!"

"I'll pay it today," said Laptev.

"Why should it be, why?" Nina Fedorovna worried. "It's enough that I have two hundred and fifty a month from you and my other brother, God bless you," she added softly so that the servants would not hear.

"Well, I go through two thousand five hundred in a month," he said. "I tell you again, dear: you have the same right to spend as Fedor and I. Understand that once and for all. Father had three of us and one out of every three kopecks belongs to you."

But Nina Fedorovna did not understand and looked as if she were trying to work out a very difficult problem in her head. And this lack of comprehension in money matters always disturbed and worried Laptev. Moreover, he suspected that she had debts of her own which she was embarrassed to tell him about and which tormented her.

They heard steps and heavy breathing: it was the doctor coming up the stairs, as usual disheveled and uncombed.

"Roo-roo-roo," he sang. "Roo-roo."

To avoid meeting him, Laptev went into the dining room, then down below to his own rooms. He saw clearly that to become closer to the doctor and visit him informally in his house was an impossible affair; and encountering this "carrion," as Panaurov called him, was disagreeable. And that was why he so rarely saw Yulia Sergeyevna. He reasoned now that since her father was not home, if he brought Yulia Sergeyevna her umbrella, he would find her home alone for certain, and his heart contracted with joy. Quickly, quickly!

He took the umbrella and, in great excitement, flew on the wings of love. It was hot in the street. At the doctor's, in the huge courtyard overgrown with weeds and nettles, two dozen little boys were playing ball. They were all children of lodgers, artisans housed in three ugly old annexes which the doctor planned to repair every year but always put off doing. Resonant, healthy voices rang out. Far to one side, near her own wing, stood Yulia Sergeyevna, her hands behind her back, watching the game.

"Greetings!" Laptev called.

She looked around. He usually saw her looking indifferent, cold, or, as yesterday, tired. Now her expression was lively and playful, like that of the little boys playing ball.

"Look, they never play that gaily in Moscow," she said, going to meet him. "Yet, of course there are no such big courtyards there. But Papa just went to your house," she added, glancing back at the children.

"I know, but I didn't come to see him, but to see you," said Laptev, admiring her youth, which he had not remarked before and seemed to have just discovered in her today; he felt he was seeing her slender, white neck with the gold chain around it for the first time. "I came to see you . . ." he repeated. "Sister sent your umbrella, you forgot it yesterday."

She stretched out a hand to take the umbrella, but he pressed it to his chest and uttered passionately, unrestrainedly, yielding again to the sweet excitement he had felt yesterday evening while sitting under the umbrella: "I beg you, give it to me. I'll keep it in memory of you . . . of our acquaintanceship. It's so marvelous!"

"Take it," she said and blushed. "But there is nothing remarkable about it."

He looked at her in rapture, silently, not knowing what to say.

"Why am I keeping you here in the heat?" she said after a silence and laughed. "Let's go in the house."

"But I'm not interrupting you?"

They went into the entrance. Yulia Sergeyevna ran ahead, rustling her dress, which was white with blue flowers.

"It's impossible to interrupt me," she answered, pausing on the stairs, "for I never do anything. It's a holiday for me every day, from morning till evening."

"What you're saying is incomprehensible to me," he said, approaching her. "I grew up in a milieu in which people work every day, everyone without exception, both men and women."

"But if there's nothing to be done?" she asked.

"You have to organize your life so work becomes unavoidable. There can be no pure and happy life without work."

He again pressed the umbrella to his chest and said softly, to his own surprise, not recognizing his voice: "If you would consent to be my wife, I'd sacrifice everything. I'd sacrifice everything . . . There's no price, no sacrifice to which I would not go."

She shuddered and looked at him with fear and amazement.

"What are you saying, what are you saying!" she uttered, turning pale. "It's impossible, I assure you. Forgive me."

Thereupon swiftly, with the same rustle of her dress, she went up the stairs and slipped through the door.

Laptev understood what that meant, and his mood changed immediately, abruptly, as if a light had suddenly gone out in his heart. Feeling shame, the humiliation of a man who has been spurned, who is unattractive, repugnant, perhaps even odious, from whom people run away, he walked out of the house.

"I'd sacrifice everything," he mocked himself walking home in the heat and recalling the details of his declaration of love. "I'd sacrifice everything—absolutely like a shopkeeper. Much in demand, this *everything* of yours!"

Everything he had just said seemed to him repulsively stupid. Why had he invented having grown up in a milieu in which everyone without exception worked? Why had he spoken in a preceptorial tone about a pure, happy life? It was not clever, not interesting; it was false—false Moscow talk. But then, little by little, ensued the mood of indifference criminals sink into after the pronouncement of a severe sentence; by now he was thinking that, thank God, everything was over and there was no more of this terrible uncertainty; he no longer had to wait day after day, to be in anguish, to keep thinking about the same thing; now everything was clear: all hopes of personal happiness must be left behind and one must live without desires, without hopes, not dreaming, not expecting, and to avoid this boredom one was already tired of cultivating, one could become interested in others' affairs, others' happiness, and then age would come on imperceptibly, life would come to an end—and nothing more was necessary. It was already all the same to him; there was nothing he wanted and he could reason coldly, but in his face, particularly under his eyes, there was a kind of heaviness; his forehead quivered like rubber—and the tears were about to spring. Feeling a weakness throughout his whole body, he lay down on his bed and was sound asleep in five minutes.

III

The proposal Laptev had made so unexpectedly had put Yulia Sergeyevna in despair.

She knew Laptev slightly, had met him by chance; he was a rich man, the representative of the well-known Moscow firm of Fedor Laptev and Sons, always very serious, to all appearances, intelligent; concerned about his sister's illness. It seemed to her that he had never paid the slightest attention to her, and she herself had been so completely indifferent to him—and suddenly this declaration on the stairs, this pitiful, enraptured face . . .

The proposal disconcerted her by its suddenness and because the word *wife* had been pronounced, and because she had been obliged to answer with a refusal. She no longer remembered what she had said to Laptev, but she still felt the traces of the impulsive, disagreeable feeling with which she had refused him. He did not attract her; his exterior was clerk-like; he himself was uninteresting. She could not have answered except by refusing, but she nevertheless felt uneasy as if she had done wrong.

"My God—not coming into the apartment, right on the steps," she said with despair, addressing the icon which hung above her from the head of the bed; "and never having paid court before, and somehow peculiar, unusual . . ."

In her solitude, her anxiety intensified with every hour, and she lacked the strength to come to terms with this oppressive feeling by herself; she needed someone to listen to her and tell her that she had done right. But there was no one to talk to. She had been motherless for a long time; she considered her father an odd man and was unable to talk to him seriously. He disconcerted her with his caprices, extreme apprehensiveness, and indeterminate gestures; and one had only to start a conversation with him for him to immediately begin talking about himself. When she prayed, too, she was not completely frank because she did not know for certain what she was supposed to ask of God.

The samovar was brought in. Yulia Sergeyevna, very pale, tired, with a helpless expression, went into the dining room, made tea—it was one of her duties—and poured a glass for her father. Sergei Borisich, in his long frock coat reaching below his knees, red-faced, uncombed, with his hands in his pockets, was pacing the dining room, not from corner to corner, but at random, like a wild beast in a cage. He stopped at the table, sipped from his glass with relish, and paced again, constantly absorbed in thought.

"Laptev proposed to me today," said Yulia Sergeyevna and she blushed.

The doctor looked at her as if he had not understood.

"Laptev? Panaurov's brother?"

He loved his daughter; it was probable that she would marry sooner or later and leave him, but he tried not to think about it. Solitude frightened him and for some reason it seemed to him that if he stayed alone in this big house he would have an apoplectic fit, but he did not like to speak openly about it.

"Well, I'm very glad," he said and shrugged his shoulders. "I congratulate you from my heart. Now you have a splendid opportunity to leave me, to your great satisfaction. And I fully understand you. Living with an aged father, a sick man, half-witted, must be very hard at your age. I understand you perfectly. And if I were to expire sooner, or if the devils were to come take me, everyone would be glad. I congratulate you from my heart."

"I refused him."

The doctor's heart felt lighter, but he no longer had the power to stop and continued: "I wonder, I've been wondering for a long time now: why haven't they put me in an insane asylum yet? Why am I wearing this frock coat instead of a strait jacket? I still believe in truth, in goodness, I'm a fool-idealist, and isn't that insanity in our times? And how do they respond to my truth, my honest intentions? They all but throw stones at me and ride roughshod over me. And even my next of kin are only trying to ride over my neck, devil take me, idiotic old man . . ."

"It's impossible to talk to you like a human being!" said Yulia.

She got up from the table violently and went to her own room in intense anger, remembering how often her father had been unjust to her. But in a short while she became sorry for him, and when he left for the club, she accompanied him downstairs and locked the door after him herself. The weather outside was bad, turbulent; the door trembled from the pressure of the wind and the drafts coming from all directions in the entry almost blew out the candle. In her own part of the house, upstairs, Yulia walked around all the rooms and made the sign of the cross over all the doors and windows; the wind howled and it sounded as if there were someone walking on the roof. It seemed more lonely than ever before; never had she felt so solitary.

She asked herself: had she done right to refuse a man just because his appearance did not please her? True, he was not someone she loved, and to marry him would mean to part forever with her dreams, her conceptions of happiness and married life, but would she ever meet the man she dreamed of and fall in love with him? She was already twenty-one. There were no eligible bachelors in town. She pictured all the men she knew—officials, teachers, officers—some of them were already married, and their home lives were notable for their emptiness and tedium; the others were uninteresting, colorless, unintelligent, immoral. Laptev now, whatever else he might be, was a Muscovite, had graduated from the university, and spoke French; he lived in the capital where there are many intelligent, noble, remarkable people, where you find activity, splendid theaters, musical evenings, excellent dressmakers, confectioners . . . In the Holy Writ it says that a wife should love her husband, and in novels love is given great importance, but wasn't there some exaggeration in that? Was married life inconceivable without love? You see, they say love passes by quickly and only habit is left, and that the true object of married life does not lie in love or happiness, but in obligations, for example, the education of children, household tasks, and so forth. Yes, and the Holy Writ may have in view love for one's husband like love for one's neighbor: respect for him, indulgence.

That night, Yulia read through her evening prayers attentively, then knelt, and, pressing her hands to her bosom, looking at the corner with the icon lamps, said with emotion: "Guide me, Mother-Intercessor! Guide me, Lord!"

During her lifetime, she had come across middle-aged old maids, pale and insignificant, who bitterly repented and regretted having once refused their suitors. Would not the same thing happen to her? Should she not enter a convent or become a charity nurse?

She undressed and went to bed, crossing herself and making crosses in the air around her. Suddenly the bell rang sharply and plaintively in the corridor.

"Ah, my God!" she said, feeling a sickly irritation throughout her body from this ringing. She continued lying in bed and thought how barren and uneventful this provincial life was, how monotonous, and, at the same time, how disquieting. One kept having occasion to shudder, to be on guard, to become angry or feel guilty, and one's nerves in the end were so shattered that it became frightening to look out from under the counterpane.

Half an hour later the bell rang again just as sharply. The servants must be asleep and not have heard. Yulia Sergeyevna lit a candle and trembling, annoyed with the maid, got dressed; when she finished dressing and went out into the corridor, the chambermaid was already locking the door downstairs.

"I thought it was the master, but it was someone about a patient," she said.

Yulia Sergeyevna returned to her room. She got a deck of cards out of the dresser and decided she would shuffle the cards well and cut them, and if there was a red card at the bottom, it would mean *yes,* that is, that she must accept Laptev's proposal, and if it was black, that would mean *no.* The card was the ten of spades.

That reassured her; she fell asleep, but toward morning it was again neither *yes* nor *no,* and she kept thinking that she could transform her life now if she wished. Harassed by her thoughts, she became weak and felt sick, but, nevertheless, shortly after eleven, she dressed and went to visit Nina Fedorovna. She wanted to see Laptev: perhaps he would look better to her now; perhaps she had been mistaken up to now . . .

She found it difficult walking against the wind; she barely moved forward, holding on to her hat with both hands, and could see nothing for the dust.

◇◇◇◇◇◇◇◇◇◇◇◇◇◇◇◇◇◇◇◇◇◇◇◇◇◇◇◇◇◇◇◇

IV

Going into his sister's room and unexpectedly catching sight of Yulia Sergeyevna, Laptev again felt the humiliation of a man found repugnant. He concluded that if she could visit his sister and confront him so easily after yesterday, it meant that she paid no attention to him or considered him the most complete nonentity. But when he greeted her, she looked at him with a pale face and dust under her eyes, mournfully and guiltily; he realized that she was suffering too.

She felt unwell. She stayed a short time, ten minutes, and took leave. And as she left, she said to Laptev: "Escort me home, Aleksei Fedorich."

They walked down the street in silence, holding onto their hats, and he, walking behind, tried to screen her from the wind. It was calmer in the side street, and they walked side by side.

"If I was unkind yesterday, forgive me," she began, and her voice quivered as if she were about to cry. "It's such torment! I didn't sleep all night."

"While I slept splendidly the whole night," said Laptev without looking at her, "but that doesn't mean I'm fine. My life is broken, I'm profoundly unhappy, and after your refusal yesterday, I walk about like someone who's been poisoned. The hardest part was said yesterday; today I no longer feel constrained with you and can speak frankly. I love you more than my sister, more than my late mother . . . I can live without my sister and without my mother, but to live without you—it's unthinkable for me, I can't . . ."

And now, as usual, he guessed her intentions. He understood that she wanted to continue yesterday's conversation, and that it was only for that she had asked him to accompany her and was taking him to her house now. But what could she add to her refusal? What new thing had she devised? In everything: in her glances, her smile, and even in the way she held her head and shoulders as she walked beside him— he could see that, as before, she did not love him; that he was a stranger to her. What more did she want to say then?

Dr. Sergei Borisich was at home.

"You are welcome, very glad to see you, Fedor Alekseich," he said, muddling his name. "Very glad, very glad."

He had not been so receptive previously, and Laptev concluded that the doctor already knew of his proposal, and this displeased him. He was sitting in the parlor now; this room made a peculiar impression because of its poor, common furniture, its bad pictures, and although there were armchairs and a huge lamp with a shade, it still looked like an uninhabited dwelling, a big shed, and it was obvious that only a man like the doctor could feel at home in this room. The other reception room, almost twice as big, was called the hall, and there were only chairs in it, as in dancing class. As he sat in the parlor talking to the doctor about his sister, a certain suspicion began to torment Laptev. Had Yulia Sergeyevna been to his sister Nina's and then led him here in order to announce that she accepted his proposal? Oh, how horrible that was, yet the most horrible of all was that his heart could entertain such suspicions. He pictured the father and daughter consulting at length the night before, perhaps arguing at length, and then coming to the agreement that Yulia had acted thoughtlessly in refusing a rich man. Even the words parents say in those circumstances rang in his ears: "It's true you don't love him, but on the other hand, think how much good you could do!"

The doctor got ready to visit his patients. Laptev was about to go out with him, when Yulia Sergeyevna said: "But you stay, please."

She was exhausted, depressed, and kept assuring herself now that to refuse a respectable, kind, devoted man solely because he was not attractive, particularly when this marriage offered her the opportunity of transforming her life, her cheerless, monotonous, idle life, when youth was passing and there was nothing brighter to foresee in the future—to refuse under such circumstances was madness, caprice, and vagary, for which God might even punish her.

Her father left. When his footsteps had faded way, she suddenly paused in front of Laptev and said decisively, turning terribly pale as she did so: "I thought for a long time yesterday, Aleksei Fedorich . . . I accept your proposal."

He stooped and kissed her hand; she awkwardly kissed him on the head with cold lips. He felt that in this declaration of love the most important thing was lacking—her love, and that there was much that was superfluous. He longed to cry out, to run away, to leave immediately for Moscow; but she stood close by looking so beautiful to him that passion suddenly overwhelmed him; he realized that it was too late to deliberate now, embraced her passionately, clasped her to his chest, and muttering a few words, addressed her affectionately, kissed her on the neck, then on the cheek, on the head . . .

She walked over to the window, afraid of these caresses, and they both regretted now that the question was settled, and each was asking himself in agitation: "Why did this happen?"

"If you only knew how unhappy I am!" she said, clasping her hands together.

"What troubles you?" he asked, going up to her and also clasping his hands together. "My dear, for God's sake, tell me—what? But only the truth, I beg you, only the truth!"

"Don't pay any attention," she said and smiled with an effort. "I promise you, I'll be a true, devoted wife . . . Come tomorrow evening."

Sitting in his sister's room afterward and reading a historical novel, he recalled all this and felt offended that his magnificent, pure, expansive feeling should be responded to so pettily; he was not loved, but his proposal was accepted, probably only because he was rich, that is, because they respected in him what he himself valued least. It could be presumed that Yulia, pure and fervently pious, had never given a thought to money, but of course she did not love him, did not love, and obviously had some sort of motive, although perhaps confused and not fully conscious, but nevertheless a motive. The doctor's house was repugnant with its common furniture; the doctor himself was a pitiable, squabby skinflint, a sort of operetta Gaspard straight out of *Les Cloches de Corneville;* * the very name Yulia had a common sound. He imagined how he and his Yulia would go to the wedding ceremony, basically complete strangers to each other, without a drop of feeling on her part, as if a matchmaker had betrothed them; and he was left only one consolation, as banal as this wedding itself: the consolation that he would not be the first nor the last to marry in that way and that thousands of men and women did so, and that with time, when she knew him better, Yulia might, perhaps, grow to love him.

"Romeo and Yulia!" he said, closing the book and giving a laugh. "I, Nina, am Romeo. You may congratulate me, I proposed to Yulia Belavina today."

Nina Fedorovna thought he was joking, but then realized it was true and burst into tears. The news did not please her.

"Well then, I congratulate you," she said. "But why so suddenly?"

"No, it isn't sudden. It's been dragging since March, you just don't notice anything . . . I was already in love in March when I met her right here in your room."

"And I always thought you'd marry one of our Muscovites," Nina Fedorovna said after a silence. "The girls in our circle are simpler. But the important thing, Alesha, is for you to be happy, that's the most important. My Grigory Nikolaich never loved me, and there's no hiding it, you can see how we live. Of course, any woman could love you for your goodness and intelligence, but, you see, Yulichka—educated in a young ladies' institute, an aristocrat—intellect and goodness aren't

* *The Bells of Corneville,* an operetta by the French composer Robert Planquette (1848–1903).

much to her. She's young, while you, Alesha, are not young any more and not handsome."

To soften her last words, she stroked his cheek and said: "You're not handsome, but you're charming."

She became so agitated that a light flush appeared on her cheeks, and she spoke ecstatically about how appropriate it would be for her to bless Alesha with the image—you see, she was the older sister and replaced his mother; and she kept trying to convince her woebegone brother that the wedding should take place properly, ceremoniously and merrily, so that no one could criticize.

Thereafter he began going to the Belavins' as an accepted suitor three and four times a day, and he no longer had time to relieve Sasha and read historical novels. Yulia received him in her own two rooms, far from the parlor and her father's study, and they pleased him very much. Here the walls were dark; in the corner stood the case with holy images; there was a smell of fine perfume and icon lamp oil. She lived in the most remote rooms; her bed and dressing table were blocked off by screens, the glass doors of the bookcase were covered with a green curtain inside, and she walked across her carpeted rooms in such a way that her footsteps were completely inaudible—and from this he concluded that she had a secretive character and liked a quiet, peaceful, secluded life. At home she was still in the position of a nonadult; she had no money of her own and sometimes became embarrassed on outings that she did not have a kopeck with her. Her father did not give her much for dresses and books, no more than a hundred rubles a year. And the doctor himself hardly had any money in spite of his good practice. Every evening he played cards at the club and always lost. In addition, he bought houses in a mutual credit society by transferring the mortgages, and would then turn over the rent to the society; although the lodgers paid him irregularly, the doctor was convinced that these operations with houses were highly profitable. He had mortgaged his own house, the one in which he lived with his daughter, and used the money to buy a plot of land on which he had already begun building a big, two-story house in order to mortgage it.

Laptev now lived as if in a cloud, as if he were not himself but his double, and he did many things he never would have before. He went to the club with the doctor three times, had supper with him, and volunteered money for his building; he even visited Panaurov in his other apartment. One day,

Panaurov invited Laptev to dinner, and Laptev accepted without thinking. He was met by a lady of thirty-five, tall and thin, with black eyebrows and a sprinkling of gray, obviously not Russian. She had white patches of powder on her face, smiled insipidly, and shook hands briskly, making the bracelets on her white arms jangle. Laptev felt she smiled that way to hide from others that she was unhappy. He also saw her two little girls, five and three years old, resembling Sasha. The dinner consisted of milk soup, cold veal with carrots, and chocolate—it was sugary and tasteless, yet gold forks gleamed on the table, there were flagons with soya and cayenne pepper, an unusually elaborate cruet, and a gold pepper shaker.

Only after eating the milk soup, Laptev realized how inappropriate his coming there for supper was, in fact. The lady was disconcerted, smiled all the time, displaying her teeth; Panaurov explained scientifically what being in love is and what produces it.

"Here we are dealing with one aspect of electricity," he said in French, addressing the lady. "Microscopic glands which contain a current are planted inside the skin of every person. If you meet an individual whose current parallels yours, then you have love."

When Laptev returned home and his sister asked him where he had been, he felt awkward and did not answer.

The whole time up to the wedding, he felt he was in a false position. His love grew stronger and stronger every day, and Yulia seemed poetic and elevated to him, but still there was no mutual love, and the essence of it was that he was buying and she was selling. Sometimes, after thinking about it, he simply became desperate and asked himself if he shouldn't run away. He now spent whole nights without sleeping and thought constantly about the lady he called the "individual" in letters to his friends, and how he would meet her in Moscow after the wedding, and about how his father and brother, ponderous men, would react to his marriage and to Yulia. He was afraid his father might say something rude to Yulia at the first meeting. And something strange had been happening to his brother Fedor. Fedor wrote in his long letters about the importance of health, about the influence of illnesses on the state of the mind, about the nature of religion, but not a word about Moscow or business. These letters irritated Laptev and it seemed to him that his brother's character was changing for the worse.

The wedding was in September. The ceremony took place

in the Church of Peter and Paul after a Mass, and the young couple left for Moscow the same day. When Laptev and his wife, wearing a black dress with a train and no longer looking like a young girl, but a true woman, said farewell to Nina Fedorovna, the invalid's whole face became twisted, but not one tear flowed from her dry eyes. She said: "If I should die, God forbid, take in my little girls."

"Oh, I promise you!" answered Yulia, and her lips and eyelids began to twitch nervously too.

"I'll come visit you in October," said Laptev, moved. "Get well, my dear."

They traveled in a private railway compartment. Both felt sad and awkward. She sat in the corner without taking off her hat and pretended she was dozing, while he lay on the couch opposite her and was troubled by various thoughts: about his father, about the "individual," about whether Yulia would like his Moscow apartment. And looking at his wife, who did not love him, he thought dejectedly: "Why did this happen?"

V

In Moscow the Laptevs directed a wholesale trade in haberdashery: fringes, braids, ornaments, crocheting cotton, buttons, and so forth. The gross proceeds reached two million a year; how much of it was pure profit, no one knew except the old man. His sons and clerks estimated this profit at approximately three hundred thousand and said it would be a hundred thousand more if the old man "weren't so expansive," that is, did not give credit indiscriminately; in the last ten years alone, hopeless promissory notes amounted to almost a million, and the elder clerk, when the subject turned to this, used to wink slyly and say something, the meaning of which was not clear to all: "The psychological consequences of the century."

Most of the buying and selling took place in the commercial area of town in premises called the warehouse. The entrance to the warehouse was from the courtyard, where it was always murky, smelled of mats, and the cart horses clattered their hoofs on the asphalt. The door, very modest in appearance, trimmed with iron, led from the courtyard to a room with walls gray-brown from dampness, scribbled with charcoal, and lit by a narrow window with an iron grating; next on the left was another room, larger and cleaner, with a cast-iron stove and two tables, but also with a prison window: this was the office, and from here a narrow stone staircase led to the second floor, which was the main part of the establishment. This was a fairly large room, but because of the constant half-light, the low ceiling, and the space taken up by the cases, bales, and bustling people, it made the same impression of disorder on a newcomer as the floor below. Upstairs, and also in the office, merchandise lay on the floor in bales, bundles, and cardboard boxes; no order or care was discernible in its disposition, and if there had not been crimson buttons looking out of the holes in the paper parcels here and there, and a tassel and the end of a fringe, it would have been impossible to guess what was traded here. And from a glance at these crumpled paper parcels and boxes, one would not have believed that millions were earned with such trifles, and that fifty people were kept busy here in the warehouse every day, not counting the buyers.

When Laptev came into the warehouse at noon the day after his arrival in Moscow, the errand boy, packing up goods, was pounding the cases so loudly that no one heard Laptev come into the first room and the office; the familiar postman, coming down the stairs with a bundle of letters in his hand and blinking from the din, also failed to notice him. The first person he met upstairs was his brother Fedor Fedorich, so similar to him that they were considered twins. This similarity was a constant reminder to Laptev of his own appearance, and now, on seeing before him a shortish man with red cheeks, sparse hair on his head, thin, plebeian thighs, so uninteresting and unintellectual in appearance, he asked himself: "Can I really be like that too?"

"How glad I am to see you!" said Fedor, embracing his brother and pressing his hand firmly. "I've been waiting for you impatiently every day, my dear. When you wrote you were getting married, curiosity began tormenting me, and also I missed you, Brother. Judge for yourself—we haven't seen each other for half a year. Well, what? How is it? Is Nina bad? Very?"

"Very bad."

"It's God's will," sighed Fedor. "Well, and your wife? A beauty, I suppose? I already love her; of course, she's coming to me as a little sister. We'll spoil her together."

Then Laptev caught sight of the long-familiar, broad,

stooped paternal back of Fedor Stepanich. The old man was sitting near the counter on a stool and talking with a buyer.

"Papasha, God sent us joy!" shouted Fedor. "Brother's come."

Fedor Stepanich was tall and extremely sturdily built so that in spite of his eighty years and wrinkles, he still looked like a strong, healthy man. He spoke in a ponderous, deep "droning" bass which emerged from his broad chest as if from a barrel. He shaved his beard, wore mustaches clipped in military style, and smoked cigars. As he always felt hot, he went about in a simple canvas jacket in the warehouse and at home at all times of the year. He had had a cataract removed not long ago, had poor eyesight, and no longer took care of business, but just talked and drank tea with jam.

Laptev bowed and kissed him on the hand, then on the lips.

"It's been a time since we saw each other, dear sir," said the old man. "A time. Well then, are you asking us to congratulate you on your lawful marriage? Well, all right, I congratulate you."

And he offered his lips for a kiss. Laptev bowed and kissed him.

"Well then, and did you bring your lady?" asked the old man, and, without waiting for an answer, said, turning to the buyer: "I hereby inform you, Papasha, I'm getting married to such and such a girl. Yes. And asking Papasha for his blessing and advice is nowhere in the rules. Now they make up their own minds. When I was married, I was over forty, but I threw myself at my father's feet and asked his advice. Now there's no more of that."

The old man was delighted to see his son, but considered it improper to be tender with him or to display his delight in any way. His voice and way of saying "lady" plunged Laptev into the bad mood he always had in the warehouse. Every trifle there reminded him of the past when he was whipped and kept on fasting food; he knew that apprentices are whipped and given bloody noses now, too, and that when these boys grow up, they will administer beatings themselves. But he had only to be in the warehouse five minutes to feel that he would be abused or struck on the nose any moment.

Fedor clapped a buyer on the shoulder and said to his brother: "Here, Alesha, I recommend to you our Tambov benefactor, Grigory Timofeich. He can serve as an example for today's youth: already entered his sixth decade and he has nursing children."

The clerks started laughing, and the buyer, a fat old man with a pale face, also laughed.

"A nature superior to the usual events," remarked the senior clerk, who was standing right behind the counter. "What goes in, comes out."

The senior clerk, a tall man of fifty with a dark beard, in spectacles, with a pencil behind his ear, usually expressed his thoughts unclearly, by remote allusions, and it was obvious from his sly smile that he attributed a special, fine meaning of some sort to his words. He was fond of obscuring his speech with literary words, which he understood in his own fashion, and many ordinary words, he often used in a distorted sense. For example, the word "besides." When he expressed a thought categorically and did not want to be contradicted, he stretched out his right arm and pronounced: "Besides!"

The most surprising thing was that the other clerks and the buyers understood him perfectly. His name was Ivan Vassilich Pochatkin and he was a native of Kashira. Now, congratulating Laptev, he expressed himself as follows: "On your part it's an act of courage, for a woman's heart is a Shamil." *

The other important personage in the warehouse was the clerk Makichev, a plump solid blond man with an entirely bald crown and whiskers. He went up to Laptev and congratulated him respectfully, in a low voice: "It is my privilege, sir . . . The Lord heard the prayers of your father, sir. God be praised, sir."

Thereupon the other clerks began coming up and congratulating him on his lawful marriage. They were all dressed fashionably and had the appearance of fully respectable, educated people. They stressed the *o*, pronounced the hard *g* sound softly like a Latin *g*, and because they inserted the deferential *s* sound representing the word *sir* after almost every two words, their congratulations, uttered rapidly—for example, the phrase: "Wish you every sort of happiness"—sounded like a whip flourished in the air: *"Shvisss."*

All this quickly bored Laptev and he wanted to go home, but it was awkward to leave. Propriety demanded spending at least two hours in the warehouse. He walked away from the counter and asked Makichev whether the summer had passed well and whether there was anything new, and Makichev answered him respectfully without looking him in the eyes. A young boy with close-cropped hair, in a gray blouse, brought Laptev a glass of tea without a saucer; a short while

* A hero of Caucasian resistance to the Russians between 1830 and 1859.

later, another apprentice tripped over a packing case as he went by and almost fell, and Makichev suddenly made a terrible, evil face, the face of a monster, and shouted at him: "Walk on your feet!"

The clerks were glad the young master had gotten married, and, at last, had arrived; they looked at him with curiosity and welcome, and each one felt obliged to say something pleasant to him respectfully as he passed by. But Laptev was convinced that all this was insincere and that they flattered him because they feared him. He was totally unable to forget how fifteen years ago, one of the clerks, mentally ill, had run out into the street in just his underclothes, barefooted, and threatening the masters' windows with his fists, shouted that they had tormented him to death; and they had laughed at the poor creature for a long time after his recovery, and kept reminding him of the way he had shouted at the masters: "Planters!" instead of "exploiters." In general, the employees lived very badly at the Laptevs', and the whole merchants' row had been talking about it for a long time. The worst of all was that Fedor Stepanich practiced a kind of Oriental despotism toward them. Thus, no one knew how much his favorites, Pochatkin and Makichev, were paid; they received three thousand a year each including bonuses, no more, but it was thought that he paid them seven each; bonuses were distributed every year to all of the clerks, but secretly, so that someone receiving little was obliged by vanity to say he received a lot; not one of the apprentices knew when he would be made a clerk; not one of the employees knew whether or not the master was satisfied with him. Nothing was explicitly forbidden the clerks, and they consequently did not know what was permitted and what was not. They were not forbidden to marry, but did not do so from fear of displeasing the master. They were allowed to have friends and accept invitations, but the gate was locked at nine in the evening, and the master inspected all the employees suspiciously every morning to determine whether any of them smelled of vodka: "Come now there, breathe!"

Every holiday the employees were obliged to go to early Mass and to arrange themselves in church so that the master could see them all. Fasts were strictly supervised. On days of celebration, for example, the name day of the master or members of his family, the clerks were obliged to subscribe to the presentation of a sweet pie from Fley's or an album. They lived on the lower floor of the house on Pyatnitskaya Street and in the annex, three and four in one room, and at dinner, they ate from a common tureen, although each had a plate in front of him. If one of the masters came in at dinnertime, they all stood up.

Laptev realized that only those who were corrupted by the old man's teachings could seriously consider him a benefactor; the rest already saw in him the enemy and the "planter." Now, after a half year's absence, he saw no change for the better, and there was even something new which boded no good. Brother Fedor, previously quiet, pensive, and extremely soft-spoken, now ran through the warehouse with a pencil behind his ear and the look of a very active, busy man, slapped buyers on the shoulder, and shouted to the clerks: "Friends!" He was obviously playing a role of some kind and Laptev did not recognize him in this new role.

The old man's voice droned uninterruptedly. Because he had nothing to do, the old man spent his time telling the buyers how to live and how to conduct their affairs, and in doing so, always presented himself as an example. This boasting, this authoritative, dominating tone, Laptev had heard ten, fifteen, twenty years back. The old man worshiped himself; it always appeared from what he said that he was responsible for the happiness of his late wife and her family, had rewarded his children, covered his clerks and employees with benefits, and given all his acquaintances and the whole street reason to pray for him perpetually; whatever he did was all very fine, and if other people's businesses went badly, it was only because they were not willing to take his advice; without his advice, no business could succeed. In church, he always stood in front of everyone and even made observations to the priests when, in his opinion, they did not serve Mass correctly, and he thought this pleased God because God loved him.

By two o'clock, everyone was already back at work in the warehouse, except for the master, who was still droning. Laptev, to avoid standing around idly, took an ornament from one of the skilled women workers and let her go about her work, then listened to a buyer, a merchant from Vologda, and ordered one of the clerks to take care of him.

"*T, V, A!*" was heard on all sides (in the warehouse, letters designated the prices and numbers of the wares). "*R, I, T!*"

As he went out, Laptev took leave only of Fedor.

"I'll come to Pyatnitskaya Street tomorrow with my wife,"

he said, "but I warn you, if Father says even one coarse word to her, I won't stay a minute there."

"Well, you're just the same," sighed Fedor. "Married, but unchanged. You have to indulge the old man, Brother. So then, that's tomorrow about eleven. We'll be waiting impatiently. So come straight from Mass."

"I don't go to Mass."

"Well, it doesn't matter. The main thing is no later than eleven so that there'll be time to pray to God and to have lunch together. I have the feeling I'll love her," Fedor added with complete sincerity. "I envy you, Brother!" he cried when Laptev was already going down the stairs.

"And why does he always shrink bashfully like that as if he felt naked?" Laptev thought, walking down Nikolskaya Street and trying to understand the change which had taken place in Fedor. "And he talks in some new way: Brother, dear Brother, God sent us joy, we'll pray to God—just like Shchedrin's Little Judas." *

—◇—◇—◇—◇—◇—◇—◇—◇—◇—◇—◇—◇—◇—◇—◇—◇—

VI

The next day, Sunday, he drove down Pyatnitskaya Street with his wife at eleven o'clock in a light calash with one horse. He was dreading a sally on the part of Fedor Stepanich and felt uncomfortable in anticipation. After two nights in her husband's house, Yulia already considered her marriage a mistake, a misfortune, and she felt that if she had happened to live with her husband in some city other than Moscow, she would be unable to bear this disaster. Moscow distracted her; the streets, the houses, and the churches she found very attractive, and if she had been able to drive through Moscow in one of those splendid sleighs with superb horses, to drive all day from morning till evening, breathing in the chilly fall air in a very fast ride, she might then not have felt so unfortunate.

Near a white, recently stuccoed, two-story house, the coachman reined the horse and pulled over to the right. They were all waiting there. Near the gate, beside two policemen, stood the porter in a new caftan, high boots, and galoshes; the entire area from the middle of the street to the gate and throughout

* "Little Judas," hero of a novel by Shchedrin.

the courtyard up to the steps was sprinkled with fresh sand. The porter took off his cap, the policemen saluted.

"I'm very glad to meet you, Little Sister," Fedor said, kissing Yulia's hand. "You are welcome here."

He led her upstairs by the arm, then down the corridor through a multitude of men and women. The antechamber was crowded and smelled of incense.

"I'll present you to our Little Father now," Fedor whispered in the sepulchral ceremonious silence. "The respected old man, paterfamilias."

In the big hall near the table prepared for the Te Deum stood, obviously waiting, Fedor Stepanich, the priest in his skullcap, and the deacon. The old man gave Yulia his hand without saying a word. Everyone was silent. Yulia was disconcerted.

The priest and the deacon began putting on their priestly vestments. The censer was brought in, scattering sparks and giving off a smell of incense and coal. The candles were lit. The clerks came into the hall on tiptoe and stood next to the wall in two rows. It was still; no one even coughed.

"Bless us, Lord," began the deacon.

The Te Deum was served ceremoniously, with nothing omitted, and two songs of praise were read: "To Jesus the Sweet" and "To The Most Holy Virgin Mary." The singers sang entirely with music and at great length. Laptev had noticed his wife's discomposure shortly before; while the songs of praise were being read and the singers sang the triad "Lord have mercy" in various harmonies, he kept waiting with tension in his heart for the old man to glance around and make some remark on the order of: "You don't know how to cross yourself"; he was annoyed, too, thinking: What is the point of this crowd, what is the point of all this ceremony with priests and singers? It was too merchantlike. But when she stretched out her head over the Gospel along with the old man and then dropped to her knees several times, he understood that she liked all this and he felt reassured.

At the end of the Te Deum, when the prayers for longevity were being said, the priest gave the old man and Aleksei the cross to kiss, but when Yulia Sergeyevna came, he covered the cross with his hand and indicated that he wished to speak. They waved to the choir to be quiet.

"The prophet Samuel," began the priest, "came to Bethlehem on the Lord's command, and there the town's most ancient men asked him in anxiety: 'Art thou come on peace, O

Seer?' And the reply of the prophet was: 'Peace, serve ye the Lord, be sanctified, and celebrate this day with me.' Should we, too, ask you, God's slave, Yulia, if you bear peace to this house? . . ."

Yulia flushed with emotion. On finishing, the priest gave her the cross to kiss and said in quite a different tone: "Now Fedor Fedorich must marry. It's time."

The choir began singing again, the people began to stir, and it became noisy. The old man, moved, with tear-filled eyes, kissed Yulia three times, made the sign of the cross over her face, and said: "This is your home. I'm an old man and don't need anything."

The clerks made their congratulations and remarks, but the choir sang so loudly that none of it could be understood. Then they had lunch and drank champagne. She sat next to the old man, who talked to her about how bad it was to live apart—they should live together in the same house—and how divisions and discord led to ruin.

"I earned money, but the children just spend it," he said. "Now, you should live with me in the same house and earn. It's time for an old man like me to rest."

Yulia kept noticing Fedor, who was very like her husband, but more lively and more bashful; he fidgeted nearby and frequently kissed her hand.

"We're simple people, Little Sister," he said, and at this, patches of red appeared on his face. "We live simply, like Russians, like Christians, Little Sister."

When they returned home, Laptev, very pleased that everything had gone well and that despite his apprehensions nothing particular had happened, remarked to his wife: "You're surprised that a sturdy, broad-shouldered father should have such small, weak-chested children as myself and Fedor. But it's so understandable! My father married my mother when he was forty-five and she, only seventeen. She used to turn pale and tremble in his presence. Nina was born first, born by a comparatively healthy mother, and therefore she turned out sturdier and better than we; Fedor and I were conceived and born when Mother was already exhausted by constant fear. I can remember my father beginning to teach me, or, to put it more simply, to beat me, when I was not yet five years old. He whipped me with birch rods, pulled my ears, hit me on the head, and when I woke up each morning, the first thing I thought of was: Will I be beaten today? Fedor and I were forbidden to play and frolic; we had to go to matins and early

Mass, kiss the priests' and monks' hands, read the songs of praise at home. Now, you love religion and all that, while I'm afraid of religion, and when I pass a church, it reminds me of my childhood and makes me miserable. I was already going to the warehouse at the age of eight. I worked as an ordinary apprentice, and this was unhealthy because I was given a beating there almost every day. Then, when I was sent to preparatory school, I used to study until dinner, and from dinner-time until evening was made to sit in the warehouse, and so on, until the age of twenty-two, when I met Yartsev in the university and he persuaded me to leave my father's house. This Yartsev did me a great deal of good. You know what," said Laptev, and he laughed with pleasure: "Let's go visit Yartsev now. He's the noblest person! How touched he'll be!"

VII

One November Saturday, Anton Rubinstein was conducting the symphony orchestra. It was very hot and stuffy. Laptev was standing behind the pillars; his wife and Kostya Kochevoi were sitting far in front, in the third or fourth row. At the very beginning of the intermission, completely unexpectedly, past him walked the "individual," Polina Nikolayevna Razsudina. After his wedding, he had often anxiously pictured the possibility of meeting her. When she glanced at him frankly and directly now, he remembered that, as if he had been hiding from her, he still had not brought himself to give her an explanation or even write her two or three friendly lines; he felt ashamed and blushed. She shook his hand briskly and firmly and asked: "Have you seen Yartsev?"

And without waiting for an answer, she walked on hastily, taking broad strides as if she were being pushed by someone behind her.

She was very thin and homely with a long nose, and her face was always tired, harassed, and she looked as if it cost her a great effort to hold her eyes open and remain upright. She had magnificent dark eyes and an intelligent, kind, frank expression, but angular, sharp movements. She was not easy to talk to because she was incapable of listening or talking calmly. Making love to her was depressing. When she stayed with Laptev, she used to laugh at length, cover her face with her hands, and assert that love was not the main thing in life for her, mince like a seventeen-year-old girl, and before she would allow herself to be kissed, all the candles had to be put out. She was already thirty. She was married to a teacher, but had not lived with her husband for a long time now. She earned her living by giving music lessons and participating in quartets.

She walked past again as if by accident just in time for the Ninth Symphony, but the crowd of men standing like a thick wall around the pillars kept her from going farther, and she stopped. Laptev noticed she was wearing the same velvet jacket she had worn to concerts last year and the year before. Her gloves were new; her fan also new, but inexpensive. She was fond of clothes, but lacked taste and regretted spending money for them, and she dressed so badly and negligently that when she walked to her lessons with hasty, broad strides, she could easily be taken for a young novice.

The public was applauding and shouting for encores.

"You spend the evening with me," said Polina Nikolayevna, going up to Laptev and looking at him sternly. "From here, we'll go have tea together. You hear? I demand it. You're much indebted to me and have no moral right to refuse me such a trifle."

"Fine, let's go," agreed Laptev.

After the symphony ended, began endless curtain calls. The public got up and went out extremely slowly, but Laptev was unable to leave without telling his wife. They had to stand at the door and wait.

"I'm desperate for some tea," complained Razsudina. "Burning with thirst."

"We could have tea here," said Laptev. "Let's go to the counter."

"No, I've no money to throw away at the counter. I'm no tradesman."

He offered her his arm; she refused, uttering a long, tiresome phrase he had heard from her many times, namely, that she did not consider herself part of the beautiful weaker sex and did not need any favors from gentlemen.

While talking to him, she kept glancing at the audience and frequently exchanging greetings with acquaintances; these were her former companions in school and at the conservatory, and her pupils. She shook their hands firmly and briskly, as though tugging at them. But then she began twitching her shoulders as if she had a fever and started trembling, and, at last, said quietly, looking at Laptev with horror: "Whom did you marry? Where were your eyes, you insane man? What did you find in that stupid, insignificant hussy? You see, I loved you for your intelligence, for your soul, and that china doll only wanted your money!"

"Let's leave that aside, Polina," he said in an imploring voice. "Everything you can say to me on the subject of my marriage, I've already said to myself many times . . . Don't cause me extra pain."

Yulia Sergeyevna appeared in a black dress with the big diamond brooch sent her by her father-in-law after the Te Deum; behind her came her retinue: Kochevoi, two doctors she knew, an officer, and a plump young man in a student's uniform called Kish.

"Go with Kostya," Laptev said to his wife. "I'll come later on foot."

Yulia nodded her head and went on. Polina Nikolayevna followed her with a glance, her whole body trembling and shrinking nervously, and this glance of hers was full of revulsion, hate, and pain.

Laptev was afraid to go with her, foreseeing an unpleasant scene, bitterness, and tears, and he proposed having tea in a restaurant. But she said: "No, no, let's go to my place. Don't you dare talk to me of restaurants."

She did not like going to restaurants because she felt the air was poisoned by tobacco and men's breath. She had a peculiar prejudice against all strange men, considered them all rakes, capable of throwing themselves at her at any minute. Moreover, the music in restaurants irritated her so much that it gave her a headache.

On leaving the Noble Assembly Hall, they hired a hackney to Ostozhenka, to Savelovsky Lane, where Razsudina lived. Laptev thought about her the whole way. He was much obligated to her, in fact. He had met her at the apartment of his friend Yartsev, to whom she was teaching music theory. She had fallen intensely in love with him, completely unselfishly, and after going to live with him, had continued to give lessons and work to exhaustion as before. Thanks to her, he had begun to understand and love music, to which he had been previously almost indifferent.

"Half a kingdom for a glass of tea!" she uttered in a hollow voice, covering her mouth with her muff to avoid catching cold. "I went to five lessons, the devil take them! The pupils are such dolts, such keyboard pounders, I nearly died with rage. And I don't know when this penal servitude will end.

I'm exhausted. As soon as I save three hundred rubles, I'll drop everything and go to the Crimea. I'll lie on the shore and gulp oxygen. How I love the sea, ah, how I love the sea!"

"You won't go anywhere," said Laptev. "In the first place, you'll never save anything, and in the second, you're a miser. Forgive me, I'll say it once again: is it less degrading to collect this three hundred rubles bit by bit from idle people—who study music with you because they have nothing to do—rather than taking them in a loan from your friends?"

"I have no friends!" she said crossly. "And I beg you not to say idiocies. The working class, to which I belong, has one privilege: the consciousness of its own incorruptibility, the right not to be indebted to tradesmen and to have contempt. No, sir, you don't buy me! I'm not Yulichka!"

Laptev did not try to pay the coachman, knowing that this would bring forth a whole flood of words heard many times before. It was she who paid.

She rented a small furnished room with board in the apartment of a solitary lady. She kept her big Bekker piano at Yartsev's on Bolshaya Nikitskaya Street and went there daily to play. In her room there were armchairs in slipcovers, flowers belonging to the landlady, a bed with a white summer counterpane, oleographs on the walls, and nothing to indicate that a woman and former student lived here. She had no dresser, no books, not even a writing desk. It was obvious that she went to bed as soon as she reached home, and on getting up in the morning, immediately left the house.

The cook brought in the samovar. Polina Nikolayevna made tea, and still trembling constantly—it was cold in the room—began to abuse the singers who had performed in the Ninth Symphony. Her eyes closed with weariness. She drank one glass, then another, then a third.

"So, you're married," she said. "But don't worry, I won't turn sour, I can tear you out of my heart. It's just irritating and embittering that you're the same trash as everyone else; that you don't want a mind or intellect in a woman, but a body, beauty, youth . . . Youth!" she pronounced through her nose as if in imitation of someone, and she laughed. "Youth! You need purity, *Reinheit! Reinheit!*" * she laughed louder, throwing herself back in her chair, *"Reinheit!"*

When she stopped laughing, her eyes were filled with tears.

"You're happy, at least?" she asked.

"No."

* Purity.

"She loves you?"

"No."

Laptev, perturbed, feeling unhappy, got up and began walking about the room.

"No," he repeated. "Polina, if you want to know, I am very unhappy. What can one do? I did a stupid thing, it can't be righted now. Have to take it philosophically. She got married without love, stupidly, perhaps also with a motive, but without deliberating, and now, obviously, she recognizes her own mistake and suffers from it. I can see it. We sleep together at night, but during the day she's afraid to stay alone with me even five minutes and seeks distractions, company. She feels ashamed and frightened with me."

"But she accepts money from you nevertheless?"

"That's stupid, Polina!" cried Laptev. "She accepts money from me because it's positively exactly the same to her whether I have any or not. She's an honest, pure person. She married me simply because she wanted to get away from her father, and that's all."

"But are you sure she would have married you if you weren't rich?" asked Razsudina.

"I'm not sure of anything," Laptev said with anguish. "Not of anything. I don't understanding anything. For God's sake, Polina, let's not talk about it."

"Do you love her?"

"Insanely."

Thereupon a silence fell. She drank her fourth glass of tea while he continued pacing and thinking that his wife probably was now having supper at the doctors' club.

"But can one love without knowing why?" asked Razsudina and she shrugged her shoulders. "No, it's the animal passion speaking in you! You're intoxicated! You're poisoned by that beautiful body, that *Reinheit!* Get away from me, you're dirty. Go to her!"

She waved a hand at him, then seized his hat and flung it at him. He silently put on his fur coat and went out, but she ran into the entrance and convulsively clutched his shoulder in her hand and burst into sobs.

"Stop, Polina! Enough!" he said, but was absolutely unable to force her fingers open. "Calm yourself, I beg you!"

She closed her eyes, turned pale, and her long nose became an unpleasant waxen color like a corpse's; Laptev was still unable to unclasp her fingers. She had fainted. He carefully lifted her, placed her on the bed, and sat beside her for ten minutes until she regained consciousness. Her hands were cold, her pulse weak and irregular.

"Go home," she said, opening her eyes. "Go home or I'll start howling again. Must get myself in hand."

After leaving her, he went home instead of to the doctors' club where his party was waiting for him. All the way he kept asking himself with reproach: why had he not established his family with this woman who loved him so and was already in fact his wife and companion? She was the only person who was attached to him, and in addition to that, would it not be a gratifying, worthy task to give happiness, shelter, and peace to this intelligent, proud creature, exhausted by work? Was it for him—he asked himself—these aspirations for beauty, youth, for that very happiness which was impossible and which, as if in punishment or mockery, had kept him in a gloomy oppressed state for three months now? The honeymoon was long past and, strange to say, he still did not know what his wife was like. She wrote long, five-page letters to her school friends and her father and found something to write about, while with him, she spoke only about the weather and about how it was time for dinner or supper. When she prayed lengthily before going to sleep and then kissed her little crosses and icons, he thought bitterly as he watched her: "She's praying, but what does she pray about? What?" He abused both her and himself in his thoughts, saying that in going to bed with her and taking her in his embrace, he was taking what he had paid for, but that proved to be horrifying; had she been a healthy, bold, sinful woman, but, you see, here was youth, piety, gentleness, innocent pure eyes . . . When she had been his fiancée, he had been touched by her piety; now this same predetermined precision of attitudes and convictions presented a barrier to him which kept the real truth from sight. Everything about his conjugal life was painful now. When his wife sighed or laughed out frankly while sitting beside him at the theater, he felt bitter at her enjoying herself alone without wanting to share her enthusiasm with him. And it was remarkable that she had become close to all his friends, and that they all now knew what she was like, while he alone knew nothing and was just melancholy and silently jealous.

When he reached home, Laptev put on a dressing gown and slippers and sat in his study to read a novel. His wife was not home. But no more than half an hour had gone by when there was a ring at the entrance and the hollow echo of

Piotr's footsteps as he ran to open. It was Yulia. She came into the study in a fur coat with cheeks red from the cold.

"There's a big fire at Presnya," she said breathlessly. "A huge red glare in the sky. I'm going there with Konstantin Ivanich."

"God go with you!"

The sight of her health, freshness, and the childish fear in her eyes soothed Laptev. He read another half hour and went to bed.

The following day, Polina Nikolayevna sent two books she had once borrowed, all his letters, and his photograph to him at the warehouse; with this was a note consisting of only one word: "Enough!"

VIII

At the end of October, Nina Fedorovna definitely had a relapse. She grew thin rapidly and altered before their eyes. Despite intense pain, she imagined that she was recovering now and got dressed every morning as if she were well, and then lay in bed dressed the whole day. And toward the end, she became very talkative. She lay on her back, continually recounting something softly, with an effort, breathing heavily. She died suddenly, in the following way: It was a clear moonlit evening; in the street, they were sleighing on the fresh snow, and the noise drifted to her room from outside. Nina Fedorovna lay on her back in bed while Sasha, who no longer had anyone to relieve her, sat nearby and dozed.

"I don't remember his patronymic," Nina Fedorovna was saying softly, "but they called him Ivan, surnamed Kochevoi, a needy official. He was a terrible drunk, may he rest in peace. He used to come around to our house, and every month we gave him a pound of sugar and an eighth of tea. Well, and money sometimes, too, of course. Yes . . . Then what happened was our Kochevoi drank a lot rapidly and died, burned up with vodka. He left a little son, a lad of seven. A little orphan . . . We took him and hid him in the clerks' quarters, and he lived like that a whole year without Papasha knowing it. And when Papasha caught sight of him, he just waved his hand and said nothing. When Kostya, an orphan, became eight—and I was then already old enough to be married—I took him to all the schools. Here, there, they accept him nowhere. And he starts crying . . . 'What are you crying for, little fool?' I say. I took him to the second school in Razgulyai and there, by the grace of God, they took him . . . And the little boy began going on foot every day from Pyatnitskaya to Razgulyai, and from Razgulyai to Pyatnitskaya . . . Alesha paid for him . . . Merciful Lord, the boy began to study well, to absorb and get the sense from it . . . He's a lawyer now in Moscow, a friend of Alesha with the same high learning. That time we didn't turn someone away, we took him in the house and now I suppose he prays God for us . . . Yes . . ."

Nina Fedorovna kept speaking more and more softly, with long pauses, then, after a short silence, suddenly raised herself and sat up.

"But I'm not . . . not well, it seems," she said. "Merciful Lord. Aiee, I can't breathe!"

Sasha knew her mother was to die soon; now, on seeing how suddenly her face had become sunken, she guessed it was the end and became frightened.

"Mamochka, you mustn't!" she sobbed. "You mustn't!"

"Run to the kitchen, let them send for Father. I'm very bad."

Sasha ran through all the rooms and called, but there was not a single servant in the whole house, and all she found was Lida, sleeping on a trunk in her clothes without a pillow in the dining room. As she was, without galoshes, Sasha ran out in the courtyard, then into the street. Their nurse was sitting on a bench outside the gates and watching the sleighing. The sounds of military music came from the river where people were skating.

"Nurse, Mother's dying!" said Sasha, sobbing. "Have to send for Papa! . . ."

The nurse went upstairs in the bedroom and, after a glance at the invalid, thrust a lighted wax candle in her hands. Sasha fidgeted about in terror, beseeching she did not know whom herself, to send for Papa; then she put on her overcoat and kerchief and ran out into the street. From the servants, she knew that Father had another wife and two little girls with whom he lived on Bazarnaya Street. She ran to the left of the gates, crying and feeling afraid of strangers, and she soon began to sink in the snow and be numbed by the cold.

She met a driver with an empty vehicle, but did not take him: he might carry her off outside the town, rob her, and throw her in the cemetery (the servants had told of such a case at tea). She kept walking and walking, breathless with weariness and sobbing. When she reached Bazarnaya Street, she asked where Panaurov lived. A strange woman explained it to her at length, and on seeing that she understood nothing, led her by the hand to the single-storied house with a porch. The door was open. Sasha ran through the entrance, then the corridor, and finally found herself in a light, warm room where her father was sitting behind a samovar beside a lady with two little girls. But she was unable to utter a word and just sobbed. Panaurov understood.

"Probably Mama's unwell?" he asked. "Speak, child: Mama's unwell?"

He became alarmed and sent for a hackney.

When they reached home, Nina Fedorovna was sitting surrounded by cushions with the candle in her hand. Her face had grown dark and her eyes were closed. In the bedroom, crowding in the doorway, stood the nurse, the cook, the chambermaid, the helper Prokofy, and other unfamiliar, simple people. Nurse was giving orders in a whisper which they failed to understand. At the other end of the room, at the window, stood Lida, pale, sleep-drugged, staring sternly at her mother.

Panaurov took the candle out of Nina Fedorovna's hand and, frowning squeamishly, flung it onto the dresser.

"It's horrible!" he uttered and his shoulders twitched. "Nina, you must lie down," he said tenderly. "Lie down, my dear."

She looked at him without recognition . . . They placed her on her back.

When the priest and Dr. Sergei Borisich arrived, the servants were already piously crossing themselves and praying for her soul.

"What a thing!" said the doctor in reflection as he went out into the parlor. "Why, she's still young, she wasn't even forty."

The little girls were sobbing loudly. Panaurov, pale, with moist eyes, went up to the doctor and said in a weak, faint voice: "My dear friend, do me a favor and send a telegram to Moscow. I'm decidedly not up to it."

The doctor got out ink and wrote his daughter the following telegram: "Panaurov's wife died at eight this evening. Tell your husband: house being sold Dvoryanskaya Street with assumption of mortgage plus nine to pay down. Auction the But what were they called? Come now, remember!"

Laptev lived in one of the side streets of Little Dmitrovka, not far from the old Church of Pimen. In addition to the big house on the street, he also rented a two-story annex in the courtyard for his friend Kochevoi, an advocate's assistant, whom all the Laptevs called simply Kostya because he had grown up under their eyes. Opposite this annex stood another building, also two-storied, occupied by a French family consisting of husband, wife, and five daughters.

It was below zero. The windows were covered with hoarfrost. On waking up in the morning, Kostya took fifteen drops of medicine with a preoccupied face, then, after getting two weights out of the bookcase, began doing gymnastics. He was tall, very thin, with big, reddish mustaches; but the most remarkable part of his appearance was his unusually long nose.

Piotr, a middle-aged man wearing a jacket and cotton trousers thrust into high boots, brought the samovar and made tea.

"It's very fine weather today, Konstantin Ivanich," he said.

"Yes, it's fine, except, you see, brother, it's too bad your life and mine aren't jollier."

Piotr sighed politely.

"How are the little girls?" asked Kochevoi.

"The priest didn't come. Aleksei Fedorich is taking charge of them himself."

Kostya found a small unfrosted spot on the windowpane and looked through his binoculars, directing them at the windows of the French family's dwelling.

"Can't see," he said.

Downstairs, meanwhile, Aleksei Fedorich was teaching the law of God to Sasha and Lida. They had already been living in Moscow for two weeks in the lower floor of the annex along with their own governess, and they were visited three times a week by a teacher from the city institute and a priest. Sasha had gone through the New Testament, while Lida had recently begun the Old Testament. Last time, Lida had been assigned to recite up to Abraham.

"So, Adam and Eve had two sons," said Laptev. "Splendid. But what were they called? Come now, remember!"

Lida, stern as before, was silent, looking at the table, and just moved her lips, while the elder Sasha watched her face and suffered.

"You know perfectly well, just don't be nervous," said Laptev. "Now what were Adam's sons called?"

"Abel and Kabel," whispered Lida.

"Cain and Abel," corrected Laptev.

Two huge tears crept down Lida's cheeks and fell onto the book. Sasha also lowered her eyes and flushed, about to cry. Laptev was unable to speak from pity, tears rose in his throat; he got up from the table and lit a cigarette. Just then, Kostya came down from upstairs with the newspaper in his hands. The little girls got up and curtsied without looking at him.

"For God's sake, Kostya, you take charge of them," Laptev said, turning to him. "I'm afraid I'll start crying myself, and I have to go to the warehouse and back before dinner."

"All right."

Aleksei Fedorich went out. With a very serious face, frowning, Kostya sat down at the table and drew the book of sacred history toward himself.

"Well then?" he asked. "Where were you?"

"She knows about the flood," said Sasha.

"About the flood? All right, we'll give the flood a look. Let's skim over the flood." Kostya ran through a short description in the book and said: "I must point out to you that a flood like the one described here never really happened. And there was no Noah. Several thousand years before the birth of Christ, there was an extraordinary inundation on the earth, and it's mentioned, not only in the Hebrew Bible, but in the books of other ancient peoples, such as the Greeks, the Chaldeans, the Hindus. But whatever the inundation was like, it couldn't submerge everything on earth. Well, the plains were flooded, but the mountains were left, I suppose. You can read this book if you want, but don't put much faith in it."

Tears flowed from Lida again, she turned away, and suddenly sobbed so loudly that Kostya started and got up from his chair in intense confusion.

"I want to go home," she got out. "To Papa and Nanny."

Sasha burst out crying too. Kostya went to his own apartment upstairs and told Yulia on the telephone: "Darling, both little girls are crying again. It's absolutely impossible."

Yulia ran over from the big house in just a dress and a

kerchief, pierced by the cold, and began comforting the little girls.

"Believe me, believe me," she said in a pleading voice, hugging first one, then the other to her bosom, "your papa is coming today; he sent a telegram. You miss Mama and I miss her, my heart aches, but what can one do? You can't go against God, you see!"

When they stopped crying, she bundled them up and took them sleighing. They drove first through Little Dmitrovka, then past Our Savior on Tverskaya Street; near the Iversky Chapel, they stopped and lit a candle each and prayed on their knees. On the way back, they went to Filipov's for lenten cracknels with poppyseed.

The Laptevs had dinner toward three o'clock. Piotr served the table. During the day, Piotr ran first to the post office, then to the warehouse, then to the circuit court for Kostya, then served the table; in the evenings, he rolled cigarettes; at night, he ran to open the door; at five in the morning, he was already lighting the stove, and no one knew when he slept. He was very fond of uncorking seltzer water and did it easily, noiselessly, without spilling a drop.

"Praise God!" said Kostya, drinking a glass of vodka before the soup.

Yulia had not liked Kostya at first; his bass voice, his use of little expressions on the order of "throw out the door," "smack in the mug," "lousiness," "turn into a samovar," and his habit of clinking glasses and lamenting over his drink, seemed trivial to her. But when she grew to know him better, she began to feel very much at ease in his presence. He was frank with her, loved to spend evenings talking to her in a soft voice, and even let her read novels he had written himself and which, until then, had been kept secret from friends of his such as Laptev and Yartsev. She read these novels and praised them in order not to offend him, and he was delighted because he hoped to become a famous writer sooner or later. His novels were exclusively about the country and country gentlemen's estates, although he had hardly ever seen the country, only when at friends' summer villas, and had been on a real country estate just once in his life, when he went to Volokamsk on judicial business. He avoided the love element as if ashamed, wrote frequent descriptions of nature, and in doing so, was fond of using expressions such as "the whimsical contours of the mountains," "fantastic forms of the clouds," or "the chord of mysterious harmonies" . . . His novels had never been published anywhere, and this he attributed to the rules of censorship.

He liked jurisprudence, yet considered his main occupation not law, but these novels. He believed he had a fine, artistic nature, and he had always been drawn to art. He did not sing or play an instrument himself, had no musical ear whatsoever, but attended all the symphonic and philharmonic concerts, organized performances for charity, and made friends with singers . . .

They were at the dinner table, talking.

"It's an amazing thing," said Laptev; "my Fedor nonplused me again. 'We must find out when our firm will have completed its hundred years,' he said, 'to start soliciting for our ennoblement,' and he says this in the most serious possible way. What's happened to him? Frankly speaking, I'm beginning to worry."

They talked about Fedor, about how it was the fashion now to adopt a style. For example, Fedor tried to look like a simple merchant, although he was no longer a merchant, and when the teacher from the school of which old man Laptev was trustee came to him for his salary, Fedor changed his voice and gait and treated the teacher like an inferior.

After dinner, having nothing to do, they went to the study. They discussed the decadents,* *The Maid of Orléans,* and Kostya read a whole monologue; he felt his imitation of Madame Yermolova was very successful. Then they sat down to play vint. Instead of going to their rooms in the annex, the little girls sat, pale and mournful, both in one armchair, listening to the noises in the street; wasn't that Father coming? In the evenings, in darkness and candlelight, they felt an anguished longing. The conversation after vint, Piotr's footsteps, and the crackle in the fireplace irritated them, and they avoided looking at the fire; in the evenings, they no longer felt like crying, but were miserable and heavyhearted. And they found it incomprehensible that there could be talk and laughter, now that their mother was dead.

"What did you see through the binoculars today?" Yulia asked Kostya.

"Nothing today, but yesterday the old Frenchman himself took a bath."

At seven Yulia and Kostya left for the Maly Theater. Laptev stayed with the little girls.

* A school of nineteenth-century writers now known as the symbolists.

"Well, your papa should have come by now," he said, looking at his watch. "The train must have been late."

The little girls sat silently in the armchair, huddled against one another like little wild animals in the cold, while Laptev kept walking through the rooms and looking at his watch with impatience. It was quiet in the house. But then, just before nine, someone rang. Piotr went to open.

On hearing the familiar voice, the little girls shrieked, burst into sobs and rushed into the antechamber. Panaurov was wearing a luxurious fur coat and his beard and mustaches were white with frost.

"In a moment, in a moment," he muttered, while Sasha and Lida, sobbing and laughing, kissed his cold hands, his hat, his fur coat. Handsome, slender, basking in affection, he caressed the little girls unhurriedly, then went into the study and said, rubbing his hands: "I won't stay long with you, my friends. Tomorrow I leave for St. Petersburg. They promised me a transfer to another city."

He was staying in the Dresden.

X

The Laptevs were frequently visited by Yartsev, Ivan Gavrilich. He was a healthy, sturdy man, black-haired, with an intelligent, pleasant face; he was considered handsome, but had recently started growing fat, which spoiled both his face and his figure; his appearance was spoiled, too, by his closely cropped, almost bald head. At the university, thanks to his height and strength, the students used to call him "the bouncer."

He had graduated from the philological faculty along with the Laptev brothers, then gone into the natural science faculty, and now had a degree as master of chemistry. He was not planning for a university chair and was not even a laboratory assistant anywhere, but taught physics and natural history in a modern school and in two women's preparatory schools. He was enthusiastic about his students, particularly his women students, and said that a remarkable generation was now growing up. In addition to chemistry, he busied himself at home with sociology and Russian history, and sometimes printed his brief essays in newspapers and magazines, signed with the letter Y. When he spoke about something pertaining to botany or zoology, he sounded like a historian; and when he considered some historical question, he sounded like a scientist.

Among the other people constantly at the Laptevs' was Kish, known as the eternal student. He had spent three years studying in the medical faculty, then transferred to the mathematical, where he spent two years on each course. His father, a provincial apothecary, sent him forty rubles a month, and his mother sent him ten more, unknown to his father, and this money was enough for his living expenses and even for such luxuries as a Polish beaver coat, gloves, perfume, and photographs (he frequently had his picture taken and distributed it to acquaintances). Tidy, somewhat bald, with golden side whiskers close to his ears, modest, he always had the look of a man ready to oblige. He was constantly being active on other people's behalf: now he was carrying around a subscription list, now freezing from early morning on in front of a box office window to buy a ticket for a lady; now ordering a wreath or a bouquet on someone's request. All that was said about him was: Kish is fetching, Kish is doing, Kish is buying. He carried out orders badly for the most part. Reproaches rained on him, people often forgot to pay him back for purchases, but he never said anything, and in difficult cases, simply sighed. He was never either particularly delighted or insulted, always told stories lengthily and boringly, and his witticisms invariably produced a laugh solely because they were not funny. For instance, with the intention of joking, he once said to Piotr: "Piotr, you're not an otter," and this brought general laughter, and he himself laughed at length, pleased with the success of his wit. When there was a funeral for one of the professors, it was Kish who walked in front with the torchbearers.

Yartsev and Kish usually came for tea in the evening. If their hosts were not going to the theater or a concert, evening tea would stretch on until supper. On one February evening, the following conversation took place in the dining room: "An artistic creation is only significant and useful when its concept comprises some serious social problem," said Kostya, looking angrily at Yartsev. "If there's a protest in a creative work against serfholding rights, or if the author expresses himself against high society and its vulgarities, then the work is significant and useful. Those novels and tales where there is *ahing* and *ohing*, yes she loves him, but he no longer loves her—

works like that, I say, are insignificant and to the devil with them."

"I agree with you, Konstantin Ivanich," said Yulia. "One describes a lovers' meeting, the next—a betrayal, the third—a reunion. Aren't there any other subjects? Naturally, for a great many people—sick, unhappy, suffering from want—this must be unbearable to read."

Laptev found it unpleasant that his wife, a young woman not yet twenty-two, should discuss love so seriously and coldly. He guessed why she did so.

"If poesy does not answer the questions you think important," said Yartsev, "then turn to technical works on political and financial law; read scientific brochures. Why should the subject of *Romeo and Juliet* have to be, instead of love, let's say, pedagogical freedom or the disinfection of prisons, if you can find this in specialized articles and manuals?"

"Uncle, that's an exaggeration!" interrupted Kostya. "We're not talking about giants like Shakespeare and Goethe; we're talking about the hundred talented and mediocre writers who would contribute more if they dropped love and concerned themselves with spreading knowledge and humanistic ideas among the masses."

Kish, burring and speaking somewhat through his nose, began telling the contents of a story he had read long ago. He told it in detail, without hurrying; three minutes went by, then five, ten, but he still continued; no one could understand what he was talking about and his face became more and more indifferent and his eyes grew dim.

"Kish, tell it quicker," Yulia was unable to keep from saying. "Otherwise it's agonizing!"

"Stop, Kish!" Kostya shouted at him.

They all laughed, including Kish himself.

Fedor came in. With red blotches on his face, hurrying, he exchanged greetings and led his brother into the study. Recently he had avoided gatherings of many people and preferred the company of one person.

"Let the young people laugh in there while we have a heart to heart talk here," he said, sitting down in a deep armchair farthest from the lamp. "It's been a time since we saw each other, Little Brother. How long has it been since you were in the warehouse? A week, I think."

"Yes. There's nothing for me to do at your place there. And also the old man annoyed me, I confess."

"Naturally they could get along without you and me in the warehouse, but one must have some kind of occupation. In the sweat of thy face shalt thou eat thy bread, as it says. God loves labor."

Piotr brought a glass of tea on a tray. Fedor drank it without sugar and asked for more. He drank great quantities of tea and could consume ten glasses in an evening.

"You know what, Brother?" he said, getting up and approaching his brother. "Not beating around the bush, you put yourself up for office, and little by little, by easy stages, we'll get you to be a member of the board and then assistant chairman. Farther and furthermore, you're an intelligent man, cultured, they'll notice you and call you to St. Petersburg— town and country administrators are in fashion there now, and you'll see, before you're fifty, you'll be a privy councilor with a ribbon over your shoulder."

Laptev did not answer; he understood that all this—the privy councilorship and the ribbon, was what Fedor wanted himself, and he did not know what to answer.

The brothers sat in silence. Fedor opened his watch and looked at it for a long, very long time with strained attention as if trying to observe the movements of the needle, and his expression seemed strange to Laptev.

Supper was announced. Laptev went to the dining room while Fedor stayed in the study. The argument was now over, but Yartsev was speaking in the tone of a professor reading a lecture: "By the consequences of the variety of climates, energies, tastes, ages—equality among people is physically impossible. But the cultured man can render this inequality harmless just as he already has swamps and bears. One scholar got his cat, mouse, merlin, and sparrow to eat out of the same dish, and education, it must be hoped, will do the same with people. Life keeps going forward and forward, culture makes enormous strides before our eyes, and obviously, the time will come when, for example, we'll find the current condition of factory workers as absurd as we now find serfholding rights, under which a little girl used to be exchanged for a dog."

"It won't come soon, not soon at all," said Kostya and he smiled; "not soon at all, the day Rothschild finds his cellars of gold absurd, and, until then, the worker can break his back and waste away with hunger. Well, no, Uncle. One must not wait, but fight. If a cat eats out of the same dish as a

mouse, do you think it's because it was instilled with conscience? Far from it. It was made to by force."

"Fedor and I are rich, our father is a capitalist, a millionaire; we should be fought!" uttered Laptev, wiping his
forehead with his palm. "Fight me—how incongruous that
seems to my mind. I'm rich, but what has money done for
me up to now, what has this power given me? In what way
am I happier than you? My childhood was penal servitude
and money didn't spare me the rod. When Nina fell ill and
died, my money didn't help her. When I'm not loved, I can't
make myself loved, even if I spend a hundred million."

"But you can do a great deal of good," said Kish.

"What sort of good! Yesterday you asked me for a favor
for some sort of mathematician who's looking for work. Believe me, I can do as little for him as you. I can give him
money, but, you see, that's not what he wants. Once I asked
a famous musician for a place for some impoverished violin-
ist, and he answered: 'You're asking me because you're not
a musician.' I answer you the same way: 'You're turning to
me for help so confidently because you've never been in the
position of a rich man yourself.' "

"Why this comparison with the famous musician, I don't
understand!" Yulia said and she blushed. "What does the
famous musician have to do with it!"

Her face quivered with hatred, and she dropped her eyes
to hide her feelings, but her expression was understood not
only by her husband, but by everyone at the table.

"What does the famous musician have to do with it!" she
repeated softly. "There's nothing easier than helping a poor
man."

A silence fell. Piotr served the woodcocks, but no one
touched them; everyone ate just salad. Laptev no longer
remembered what he had said, but it was clear to him that
the hatred was not for his words but his interference in the
conversation.

After supper he went to his study; straining, with pounding heart, expecting new humiliations, he listened to what was
happening in the hall. An argument was beginning there
again; then Yartsev sat at the piano and sang a sentimental
romance. He was proficient in everything: he sang and
played and even did sleights of hand.

"Do as you like, gentlemen, but I don't want to sit at
home," said Yulia. "I have to go somewhere."

They decided to take a tour outside of town and sent Kish

to the merchants' club for a troika. Laptev was not invited
to go with them because he usually did not go on excursions
into the suburbs, and because his brother was waiting for
him, but he understood it to mean that his society bored
them, that he was quite superfluous in this merry young group.
And his chagrin, his feelings of bitterness, were so strong that
he was close to tears; he even felt pleased that they treated
him so unkindly, that he was a stupid, boring husband, the
bag of gold, and it seemed to him that he would be even
more pleased if his wife were to be unfaithful to him that
night with his best friend and then confess it, looking at him
with hatred . . . He was jealous of students she knew, actors, singers, Yartsev, even people she passed, and now he
longed passionately for her to be actually untrue to him,
longed to discover her with someone, then to poison himself
and be rid of this nightmare once and for all. Fedor drank
some tea, swallowing loudly. But now he was getting ready
to leave.

"Our old man must have amaurosis," he said as he put on
his fur coat. "He's begun seeing very poorly."

Laptev also put on his coat and went out. After accompanying his brother up to Our Saviour's, he took a hackney and
drove to the Yar.

"And this is called marital happiness!" he mocked himself.
"This is love!"

His teeth chattered and he did not know whether it was
from jealousy or something else. At the Yar, he walked around
the tables and listened to a rhymester in the hall: he did not
have a single phrase ready in case he met his party, and he
was certain beforehand that in front of his wife, he would
just smile pitifully and foolishly, and everyone would understand the feeling that had driven him here. He was irritated by
the electric lights, the loud music, the smell of powder, and
the glances of women he passed. He stopped by the door,
tried to see and overhear what was going on in the private
rooms, and it seemed to him that he was playing a low, contemptible role in concert with the rhymester and these women.
Then he went to Strelna's, but there, too, he failed to find
any of his party, and it was only afterward, when he drove up
to the Yar again on the way back, that a troika passed him
noisily, the drunken driver shouted, and Yartsev's laugh rang
out: "Ha-ha-ha!"

Laptev returned home between three and four o'clock. Yulia
was in bed. On seeing that she was not asleep, he went up to

her and said sharply: "I understand your disgust, your hatred, but you might spare me in front of other people, might hide your feelings."

She sat up in bed, letting her legs dangle. Her eyes looked huge, black, in the light of the lamp.

"I beg your pardon," she said.

His emotion and the trembling of his whole body kept him from uttering a single word, and he stood in front of her in silence. She also shuddered and sat with the look of a criminal awaiting indictment.

"How I suffer!" he said, at last, and clutched his head. "It's as if I were in hell, I've been going out of my mind!"

"And is it easy for me?" she asked in a trembling voice. "Only God knows what it's like for me."

"You've been my wife for half a year now, but there's not even the spark of love in your heart, there's no hope of any kind, no bright spot! Why did you marry me?" Laptev continued with despair. "Why? What demon propelled you into my arms? What did you hope for? What did you want?"

She was looking at him in terror as if afraid he would kill her.

"Did I attract you? Did you love me?" he continued, suffocating. "No! Then what? What? I say: what?" he shouted. "Oh, cursed money! Cursed money!"

"I swear to God, no!" she shrieked and crossed herself; her whole body shrank from the insult, and, for the first time, he heard her cry. "I swear to God, no!" she repeated. "I didn't think of money, I don't need it, it simply seemed to me that I would be acting badly if I refused you. I was afraid of spoiling your life and my own. And now I'm suffering for my mistake, suffering unbearably!"

She burst into bitter sobs; he realized how miserable she was, and, not knowing what to say, he dropped down before her on the carpet.

"Enough, enough," he muttered. "I insulted you because I love you insanely." He suddenly kissed her foot and embraced it passionately. "For only a spark of love!" he muttered. "Come, lie to me! Lie! Don't say it was a mistake! . . ."

But she continued to cry, and he felt that she endured his caresses only as the inevitable consequences of her mistake. And she folded the foot he had kissed under herself like a bird. He became sorry for her.

She lay down and covered up her head; he undressed and also lay down. In the morning, they both felt embarrassed and did not know what to say, and it seemed to him that she avoided putting weight on the foot he had kissed.

Before dinner, Panaurov came to take leave. Yulia had an irresistible longing to go home; it would be good to get away, she thought, to take a rest from marital life and the troubling and ever-present consciousness that she had done the wrong thing. It was decided at dinner that she would leave with Panaurov and stay with her father two or three weeks, until she became bored.

XI

Yulia and Panaurov traveled in a private compartment; he wore a rather oddly shaped sheepskin cap on his head.

"Yes, St. Petersburg did not give me satisfaction," he said with pauses and sighs. "They promised a great deal, but nothing was fixed. Yes, my dear. I've been on the town court, been a permanent member, the representative of the town union, and, lastly, adviser to the provincial administration; it would seem that I had served the fatherland and had the right to some attention, but there you are: there was no way I could get a transfer to another town."

Panaurov closed his eyes and nodded his head. "They don't appreciate me," he continued as if falling asleep. "Of course I'm not a gifted administrator, but, on the other hand, I'm a respectable, honest man, and in these times, that's a rarity. I regret to say I sometimes deceived women a little, but in relation to the Russian government, I was always a gentleman. But enough about that," he said, opening his eyes; "let's talk about you. What made you suddenly think of going home to Papasha?"

"Well, I had a slight disagreement with my husband," said Yulia, looking at his cap.

"Yes, he must be rather strange to you. All the Laptevs are strange. Your husband is still all right, more or less, but his brother Fedor is a complete fool."

Panaurov sighed and asked gravely: "And do you have a lover yet?"

Yulia looked at him in astonishment and smiled. "Lord, what are you saying!"

At a principal stop, some time after ten o'clock, they got

out to have supper. When the train went on, Panaurov took off his overcoat and cap and sat down next to Yulia.

"You're very sweet, I must tell you," he began. "Forgive me for a restaurantlike comparison: you remind me of a freshly pickled cucumber; it still smells of its counterpart, but has already absorbed a little salt and the smell of dill. Little by little you're turning into a magnificent woman, a marvelous, elegant woman. If this trip of ours had taken place five years back," he sighed, "I would have considered it my pleasant duty to enter the ranks of your worshipers, but now—alas!—I'm an invalid."

He smiled sadly and at the same time graciously, and took her around the waist.

"You've gone out of your mind!" she said, blushing and so frightened that her hands and feet grew cold. "Stop, Grigory Nikolaich!"

"What are you afraid of, sweet?" he asked softly. "What's terrifying about that? You're just not used to it."

When a woman protested, all it signified to him was that he had made an impression and was found attractive. Holding Yulia by the waist, he kissed her firmly on the cheek, then the lips, in the full certainty that he was giving her great pleasure. Yulia recovered from her fear and embarrassment and began laughing. He kissed her once again and said, putting on his ridiculous cap: "That's all an invalid can give you. A certain Turkish pasha, a kind old man, received a whole harem as a gift from someone, or, I think it was, as an inheritance. When his beautiful young wives drew themselves up in a line in front of him, he kissed each one and said: 'That's all I'm in a position to give you now.' And I say the same thing."

All this seemed foolish and unusual to her and amused her. She felt playful. Standing on the couch and humming, she reached for a box of candy on the shelf and called out, throwing a piece of chocolate: "Catch!"

He caught it; she threw him another piece with a peal of laughter, then a third, and he caught them all and put them in his mouth while looking at her with pleading eyes; and it seemed to her that there was much that was feminine and childlike in his traits and his expression. When she sat down breathlessly on the couch and continued to laugh as she looked at him, he touched her cheek with two fingers and said as if annoyed: "Wretched little girl!"

"Take them," she said, giving him the box. "I don't like sweets."

He ate up all the candy, to the last piece, and locked the empty box in his trunk; he was fond of boxes with pictures.

"However, enough playing," he said. "It's time for the invalid to go by-by."

He got his Bukharian dressing gown and a pillow out of his bag, lay down, and covered himself with the gown.

"Good night, darling!" he said softly and sighed as if his whole body ached.

And snoring was soon to be heard. Feeling no embarrassment whatsoever, she also lay down and soon fell asleep.

As she drove from the station to her house the next morning in her native town, the streets looked barren and empty to her, the snow gray, and the houses small, as if someone had flattened them. She met a procession: a corpse was being carried in an open coffin with church banners.

"It's lucky to pass a corpse, they say," she thought.

The windows of the house Nina Fedorovna had once lived in were pasted with white notices now.

With a sinking heart, she drove into her own courtyard and rang at the door. She was let in by an unfamiliar maid, plump, sleepy, in a warm, padded jacket. As she went up the stairs, Yulia remembered how Laptev had made his declaration of love there, but the stairway was dirty now, covered with streaks. Upstairs, in the cold corridor, patients were waiting in fur coats. And for some reason her heart beat strongly and she was barely able to walk from agitation.

The doctor, even fatter, red as a brick, with disheveled hair, was having his tea. He was delighted and even shed tears at seeing his daughter; she thought to herself that she was the only joy in this old man's life, and feeling moved, hugged him firmly and said she would stay with him a long time, until Easter. After changing clothes in her own room, she went to the dining room to have tea with him; he was pacing from corner to corner, his hands in his pockets, singing: "Roo-roo-roo"—which meant he was dissatisfied with something.

"You lead a very gay life in Moscow," he said. "I'm very glad for you . . . An old man like me doesn't need anything. I'll breathe my last soon and free you all. And one must marvel that I've such a sturdy hide I'm still alive! It's astonishing!"

He said he was a tenacious old jackass over whom everyone

rode roughshod. They had burdened him not only with Nina Fedorovna's treatment, but with troubles over her children and her funeral; and that fop Panaurov didn't want to even hear about it and had borrowed a hundred rubles which he hadn't returned yet.

"Take me to Moscow and put me in an insane asylum there!" said the doctor. "I'm insane, I'm a naive child because I keep on believing in truth and justice!"

Then he reproached her husband with lack of foresight: he was not buying houses which were being sold so advantageously. And it now appeared to Yulia that she was not the only joy in this old man's life. While he was receiving his patients and after he left to make his rounds, she walked through all the rooms, not knowing what to do or what to think. She no longer felt at home in her native town and her own house; she was no longer tempted to go out or to see people she knew; she felt no sadness at remembrances of former friends and her girlhood and had no regret for the past.

In the evening, she dressed more elegantly and went to vespers. But there were only simple people in church and her magnificent fur coat and hat made no impression whatsoever. It seemed to her that a change of some kind had taken place in both the church and herself. She had enjoyed it in the old days when the canon was read during vespers and the choir sang the first verses of humns, for example, "I raise my voice"; she had enjoyed moving slowly through the crowd to the priest, standing in the middle of the church, and then feeling the holy oil on her forehead; now she was only anxious for the service to end. And on leaving the church, she was afraid that beggars might ask her for alms; it would be annoying to stop and search her pockets, and, furthermore, she had no copper coins, only rubles.

She went to bed early, but fell asleep late. She kept dreaming of some sort of portraits and of the funeral procession she had seen that morning; the open coffin with the corpse was brought into the courtyard and stopped at the door; then the coffin was rocked slowly onto strips of cloth and, with a full swing, flung against the door. Yulia awoke and jumped up in terror. In fact, there was a knocking on the door downstairs and the doorbell wire was scraping against the wall, although the bell was not audible.

The doctor coughed; then the chambermaid went downstairs and came back.

"My lady," the maid said, knocking on the door. "My lady!"

"What is it?" asked Yulia.

"A telegram for you!"

Yulia went out to the door with a candle. Behind the chambermaid stood the doctor in his nightshirt and overcoat, also carrying a candle.

"Our bell is broken," he said, yawning, half asleep. "Should have been repaired long ago."

Yulia opened the telegram and read: "We're drinking to your health. Yartsev, Kochevoi."

"Ah, what fools!" she said and laughed loudly; her heart became light and merry.

Returning to her room, she quietly washed, dressed, then spent a long time packing her things, until dawn came, and at noon she left for Moscow.

XII

During Holy Week, the Laptevs drove to the painting school to see an exhibit. In Moscow style, they took the whole household with them, both little girls, the governess, and Kostya.

Laptev knew all the famous artists by name and never missed an exhibit. He sometimes painted landscapes at the villa in the summertime, and he felt he had a great deal of taste and would probably have become a good artist by applying himself. He sometimes visited antique shops abroad and examined the antiques with the air of an expert, expressed his opinion, and bought something or other for which the dealer charged as much as he wanted, and the purchase then lay forgotten in a chest in the carriage house until it disappeared no one knew where. Or, going into a print shop, he would examine the pictures and plates at length and attentively, make various observations, and suddenly buy a woodcut frame or a box of worthless paper. The paintings in his house were all of large dimensions and poor; the better ones were badly hung. It happened to him more than once to pay dearly for things which turned out to be crude fakes. And it was remarkable that, generally timid in life, he was extremely bold and self-assured at picture exhibitions. Why?

Yulia looked at pictures the way her husband did, through a cupped hand or binoculars, and marveled that the people in the pictures were like live ones and the trees like real ones; but she did not understand them, and it seemed to her that many of the pictures at the exhibition were identical and that the whole aim of art was for the people and objects in the pictures to look like real ones when squinted at through a cupped hand.

"This is Shishkin here," her husband explained to her. "He always paints the very same thing . . . And here, notice: there never was any lilac snow like that . . . And this little boy's left hand is shorter than his right."

When they were all exhausted and Laptev had gone to find Kostya in order to go home, Yulia stopped in front of a rather small landscape and examined it with indifference. In the foreground was a little stream; across it, a little log bridge; on the far bank, a little path, disappearing in the dark grass; a field; then, on the right, a patch of woods; near it, a campfire: probably the night cattle watch. And in the distance, the fading glow of the sunset.

Yulia imagined herself walking over the little bridge, then the little path, farther and farther, with stillness all around, the sleepy crakes calling, the fire twinkling in the distance. And for some reason, she suddenly felt she had already seen these same clouds which stretched across the red glow in the sky, and the woods, and the field long ago and many times; she felt alone and longed to keep walking, walking, and walking down the path; and there, in the glow of the sunset, lay the calm reflection of something unearthly, eternal.

"How well that's painted!" she uttered, surprised that the picture had suddenly become comprehensible to her. "Look, Alesha! Do you see how still it is there?"

She tried to explain why she liked this landscape so much, but neither her husband nor Kostya understood her. She kept looking at the landscape with a melancholy smile, and it bothered her that the others found nothing special in it; then she began walking through the rooms again, looking at the pictures; she wanted to understand them and no longer felt that there were many identical pictures at the exhibition. When, on returning home, she noticed, for the first time in all these months, the big painting hanging in the hall, she felt animosity toward it and said: "To want to have paintings like that!"

And thereafter, the gold cornices, the Venetian mirrors

with flowers, and paintings on the order of the one hanging over the piano, and also the reflections of her husband and Kostya about art, aroused a feeling of weariness and irritation in her and, at times, even hatred.

Life flowed ordinarily from day to day, not promising anything in particular. The theatrical season was now over; the warm spell had come. The weather remained splendid all the time. One morning, the Laptevs were getting ready to go to the circuit court to hear Kostya, who was defending a man on the court's appointment. They tarried at home and arrived at the court when the cross-examination of witnesses had already begun. A soldier in the reserve was accused of theft and housebreaking. There were many laundresses present as witnesses; they testified that the accused frequently visited their employer's house; the evening before the Exaltation of the Cross, he had come late in the evening and asked for money in order to get drunk, but no one had given him any; then he left, but returned an hour later with beer and mint gingerbread for the girls. They drank and sang songs until almost dawn, but in the morning, they became aware that the lock was broken on the entrance to the loft, and the laundry was short three men's shirts, a skirt, and two sheets. Kostya asked each witness mockingly whether she had not drunk the beer brought by the accused on the evening before the holiday. He was obviously leading up to the conclusion that the laundresses were guilty of robbery themselves. He delivered his speech without the slightest emotion, looking angrily at the jurors.

He explained the nature of simple theft and of theft with housebreaking. He spoke in great detail, convincingly, displaying an unusual talent for speaking at length and in a serious tone about something long familiar to everyone. And it was hard to understand precisely what his aim was. A juror could come to only one conclusion from his long speech: "There was housebreaking but no theft because the laundresses themselves drank the proceeds, or there was theft without housebreaking." But, obviously, he said precisely what was needed to impress the jurors and the public, and his speech was very much appreciated. When a verdict of not guilty was returned, Yulia nodded to Kostya and shook his hand firmly afterward.

In May, the Laptevs went to the summer villa in Sokolniki. Yulia was already with child.

❖⟡❖⟡❖⟡❖⟡❖⟡❖⟡❖⟡❖⟡❖⟡❖⟡❖⟡❖⟡❖⟡❖⟡❖⟡❖⟡❖⟡❖

XIII

More than a year had passed. Yulia and Yartsev were sitting on the grass in Sokolniki, not far from the Yaroslav raliroad; Kochevoi lay slightly removed, his hands under his head, looking at the sky. The three of them had taken a long walk and were waiting for the passage of the six o'clock summer local to go home and have tea.

"Mothers see something unusual in their own children, that's the way nature arranged it," said Yulia. "A mother stands for hours on end by the little bed, looking at the kind of ears, eyes, and little nose her child has, enraptured. If an outsider kisses her child, she, poor woman, thinks it gives him great pleasure. And the mother doesn't talk about anything except her child. I know this weakness of mothers and keep watch over myself, but it's true, my Olya is unusual. The way she looks when she suckles! The way she laughs! She's only eight months old, but, it's God's truth, I never saw such intelligent eyes even on a three-year-old."

"Tell me, by the way," asked Yartsev; "whom do you love more: your husband or your child?"

Yulia shrugged her shoulders.

"I don't know," she said. "I never loved my husband very much, and Olya—she's actually my first love. You know, I didn't marry Aleksei for love. At first I was foolish, suffered, kept thinking I had ruined his life and my own, but now I see no love is necessary, it's all rubbish."

"But if there's no love, what feeling ties you to your husband? Why do you live with him?"

"I don't know . . . Just habit, probably. I respect him, I'm lonely when he's not here for long, but that's not love. He's an intelligent, honest man, and that's enough for my happiness. He's very kind, sincere . . ."

"Alesha's intelligent, Alesha's kind," said Kostya, lazily raising his head; "but, my dear, to learn that he's intelligent and kind, you have to have consumed three pounds of salt at his table . . . And what point is there in his kindness or intelligence? He'll hand over as much money as you want, that he can do, but when it's necessary to use character, to rebuff some upstart or malapert, he's disconcerted and loses heart. People like your beloved Aleksei are fine people, but no good at all in a fight. Yes, and generally they're no good for anything."

At last the train appeared. Completely pink smoke poured from the smokestack and rose above the grove, and two windows in the last car suddenly flashed so brightly in the sunlight that it hurt to look at them.

"Teatime!" said Yulia, getting up.

She had grown plump recently and her gait was now womanly, somewhat indolent.

"But it's not good, nevertheless, to live without love," said Yartsev, walking behind her. "We talk and read about love alone all the time, but we have little love ourselves, and that, it's true, is not good."

"That's all nonsense, Ivan Gavrilich," said Yulia. "That's not where happiness lies."

They had tea in the little garden where mignonette, stock, and tobacco were blooming, and where the early gladioli were already budding. Yartsev and Kochevoi saw from Yulia's face that she was living through a happy time of inner peace, that she needed nothing besides what she had, and their own hearts became thoroughly peaceful. Whatever anyone said seemed appropriate and intelligent. The pines were beautiful, there was a marvelous smell of resin as never before, and the cream was very tasty, and Sasha was a well-behaved, good little girl . . .

After tea, Yartsev sang romances, accompanying himself on the piano, while Yulia and Kochevoi sat listening in silence, except that Yulia got up from time to time and went out quietly to look at the baby and Lida, who had had a fever for two days now and refused to eat.

" 'My friend, my tender friend,' " sang Yartsev; then he said, shaking his head: "No, gentlemen, no matter how you slice it, I don't understand what you have against love! If I weren't busy fifteen hours out of twenty-four, I'd certainly have fallen in love."

Supper was set on the terrace; it was warm and quiet, but Yulia wrapped herself in a scarf and complained of the dampness. When it grew dark, she did not feel like herself for some reason, kept shivering and begged the guests to stay a while longer; she served wine and ordered cognac brought after supper so that they would not leave. She did not feel like being left alone with the children and servants.

"We summer people are organizing a spectacle for the children here," she said. "We already have everything—the theater, the actors; the only obstacle is the play. We were sent two dozen various plays, but not one is suitable. Here, you're fond of the theater and know history well," she said to Yartsev; "you write us a historical play."

"Why not? It's possible."

The guests finished all the cognac and got ready to leave. It was ten o'clock now, and for summer people, that was late.

"How dark it is, pitch black," said Yulia, accompanying them outside the gate. "I don't know how you'll get there, gentlemen. But it's cold out!"

She wrapped herself up more tightly and went back to the porch.

"My Aleksei is probably playing cards somewhere!" she called. "Good night!"

After the bright rooms, they could see nothing. Yartsev and Kostya found their way to the railroad by feeling, like blind men, and crossed it.

"Can't see the devil," said Kostya in a bass voice, stopping to look at the sky. "But the stars there, the stars are like new little fifteen-kopeck pieces! Gavrilich!"

"What?" called Yartsev from somewhere.

"I said I can't see a thing! Where are you?"

Yartsev, whistling, went up to him and took him by the arm.

"Hey, summer people!" Kostya suddenly shouted at the top of his voice. "They've caught a socialist!"

When tipsy, he was always very troublesome, shouted, picked quarrels with policemen and cab drivers, sang, and laughed violently.

"To hell with you, nature!" he shouted.

"Come, come," Yartsev restrained him. "That's unnecessary. I beg you."

The friends soon became used to the darkness and began to distinguish the silhouettes of tall pines and telegraph poles. Whistles came from the Moscow stations from time to time and the telegraph wires hummed plaintively. Not a single sound came from the grove itself, and in this silence there was a feeling of something proud, powerful, and mysterious, and now, in the night, the tops of the pines seemed to almost touch the sky. The friends at last found the gap in the trees and followed it. It was completely dark there, and they could only tell by the long strip of sky sown with stars and the beaten ground under their feet that they were still going down the alley of trees. They walked side by side in silence and had the feeling that people of some sort were coming toward them. Their tipsiness passed. It occurred to Yartsev that perhaps the souls of Moscow tsars, boyars, and patriarchs haunted this grove, and he wanted to say so to Kostya, but restrained himself.

When they reached the city gates, there was still barely any daylight in the sky. Keeping their silence, Yartsev and Kochevoi walked down the pavement past cheap summer houses, inns, lumber depots; the interlacing branches over the road scattered a pleasant dampness on them with a smell of linden trees, and then the long wide street opened up with not a soul, not a light on it . . . When they reached the Red Pond, it was already daybreak.

"Moscow—there's a city which still has a great deal to suffer," said Yartsev, looking at the Alexeyevsky Monastery.

"What's that that just came into your head?"

"Nothing special. I love Moscow."

Both Yartsev and Kostya had been born in Moscow, worshiped it, and regarded other cities with some hostility; they were convinced that Moscow was a remarkable city and Russia a remarkable country. In the Crimea, in the Caucasus, and abroad, they felt bored, uncomfortable, disgruntled, and they found their gray Moscow weather the most pleasant and healthy. The days when the cold rain beats on the windows and twilight comes early and the walls of the houses and churches take on a melancholy gray-brown color, and when you don't know what to put on to go out in the street—days like that stirred them pleasantly.

At last, near the station, they hired a hackney.

"In fact, it would be a good idea to write a historical play," said Yartsev; "but you know, without putting in any Lyapunovs and Godunovs,* and from the times of Yaroslav and Monomach † . . . I detest Russian historical plays, all except Pimen's monologue. When you come across a historical source of some kind and when you read even a textbook of Russian history, you feel that everyone in Russia is unusually talented, gifted, and interesting, but when I see a historical play in the theater, it strikes me as ungifted, unwholesome, and unoriginal."

* Aristocratic Russian families.
† Princes of Kiev and Novgorod in the eleventh and twelfth centuries.

Near Dmitrovka, the friends parted and Yartsev drove on to his home on Nikitskaya Street. He dozed, rocked, and kept thinking about the play. He imagined suddenly a terrible noise, clattering, shouting, incomprehensible, as if in Kalmuck; and a village of some kind, completely enveloped in flames, and the neighboring woods, covered with rime and delicately pink from the glare, which could be seen far around and so clearly that every fir was distinct; some sort of savages were sweeping through the villages on horseback and on foot, both they and their horses as crimson as the glare in the sky.

"That's the Polovtsy,"* thought Yartsev.

One of them—old, terrifying, with a blood-covered face, scorched from head to toe—is tying to his saddle a young girl with a pale Russian face. The old man shouts something furiously, while the girl watches sadly, wisely . . . Yartsev shook his head and woke up.

" 'My friend, my tender friend . . .' " he sang.

After paying the driver and climbing up his stairs, he was still unable to wake up completely, and he saw flames cross to the woods, the trees beginning to crackle and smoke, and a huge wild boar, driven insane by terror, rushing through the woods . . . while the young girl tied to the saddle continued to watch.

It was already light when he reached his own apartment. Two candles were burning out on the piano near the open music. On the couch lay Razsudina, wearing a black dress and belt, sound asleep with a newspaper in her hands. She must have played a long time while waiting for Yartsev's return, and unable to wait it out, fallen asleep.

"How exhausted she was!" he thought.

Carefully taking the newspaper out of her hands, he covered her with a blanket, put out the candles, and went to his bedroom. As he lay down, he was still thinking about the historical play and still hearing the theme, "My friend, my tender friend . . ."

Two days later, Laptev came by for a moment to say that Lida had been stricken with diphtheria and that Yulia and the baby had caught it from her; and five days later, the news came that Lida and Yulia were recovering, but the baby had died, and the Laptevs were fleeing their Sokolniki villa for town.

---

* A primitive people who invaded Hungary and the Byzantine Empire and warred against Kiev in the eleventh and twelfth centuries.

XIV

It had become unpleasant for Laptev to stay at home for long. His wife frequently went to the annex, saying that she had to take care of the little girls, but he knew that she did not go there to take care of anything, but to cry at Kostya's. It was the ninth day, then the twentieth, then the fortieth, and it was still necessary to drive to the Alekseyevsky Cemetery to hear a requiem and then grieve day and night, to think exclusively about that unfortunate child, and to say various trivialities in consolation to his wife. He seldom went to the warehouse now, occupying himself exclusively with charitable deeds, inventing various tasks and cares for himself, and delighted when he had to drive around all day over some trifle. He had recently been making preparations to go abroad to acquaint himself with the study of night shelters there, and this idea distracted him now.

It was a fall day. Yulia had just gone to the annex to cry and Laptev was lying on the couch in the study and thinking up some place to go. Just then, Piotr announced Razsudina's arrival. Laptev was overjoyed, jumped up, and went to meet the unexpected caller, his former companion, whom he had almost begun to forget. She was exactly the same, not a bit changed since he had seen her last.

"Polina!" he said, stretching both hands out to her. "So many winters, so many years! If you only knew how glad I am to see you! You are very welcome here!"

Razsudina, greeting him, twitched his hand and, without taking off her hat or coat, went into the study and sat down.

"I came to see you for just one minute," she said. "I've no time to discuss trifles. Please sit down and listen. Whether you're glad to see me or not is absolutely the same to me because I don't put any value on favorable attention paid me by gentlemen. If I came to you, it's because I was already in five places today and was refused everywhere, and the matter can't be put off. Listen," she continued, looking him in the eyes; "five students I know, limited and stupid people, but indisputably poor, haven't paid their fees and are about to be expelled. Your wealth imposes the obligation on you of going to the university right now and paying for them."

"With pleasure, Polina."

"Here are their names for you," said Razsudina, giving Laptev a memorandum. "Go this minute, you'll have time to enjoy your marital happiness afterward."

Just then there was a rustle behind the door leading into the parlor, probably the dog scratching itself. Razsudina flushed and jumped up: "Your sweetheart is eavesdropping!" she said. "That's contemptible!"

Laptev felt offended for Yulia.

"She's not here, she's in the annex," he said. "And don't talk about her like that. Our child died and she is in terrible sorrow now."

"You can console her," Razsudina laughed, sitting down again; "there'll be a whole dozen more. Who's ever had too little intelligence to bear children?"

Laptev remembered having heard the same thing or something similar many times long ago, and it gave him a whiff of the poesy of the past, free solitary bachelor life, when he had felt he was young and could do everything he wanted to, and when love for his wife and memories of his child had not existed.

"Let's go together," he said, stretching himself.

When they reached the university, Razsudina waited by the gate while Laptev went to the office; he returned shortly and handed Razsudina five receipts.

"Where are you going now?"

"To Yartsev's."

"I'll go with you."

"But see here, you'll interfere with his work."

"No, I assure you!" he said and looked at her pleadingly.

She was wearing a black hat with crepe trimming, almost like a mourning hat, and a very short, worn coat with gaping pockets. Her nose looked longer than ever and there was not a drop of blood in her face in spite of the cold. Laptev found it pleasant to walk behind her, to apologize to her and listen to her grumbling. He thought about her as he walked: what inner force this woman must have if, being so homely, awkward, harassed, unable to dress properly, always sloppily combed and always somehow disjointed, she nevertheless was attractive.

They went into Yartsev's by the back way, through the kitchen, where they were met by the cook, a tidy old woman with gray curls; she was very disconcerted, gave a sweet smile which made her tiny face look like a meat patty, and said: "If you please."

Yartsev was not home; Razsudina sat down at the piano and began doing boring, difficult exercises after ordering Laptev not to bother her. And he did not distract her with conversation, but sat to one side, leafing through *The European Messenger*. After playing two hours—that was her daily stint—she ate something in the lunchroom and went off to give her lessons. Laptev read an installment of a novel, then sat for a long time, not reading, not feeling bored, and pleased that he was late for dinner at home by now.

"Ha-ha-ha!" Yartsev's laugh rang out and in he came himself, healthy, sound, red-cheeked, in a new frock coat with shiny buttons. "Ha-ha-ha!"

The friends had dinner together. Then Laptev lay down on the couch while Yartsev sat nearby and lit a cigar. Twilight fell.

"I must be beginning to grow old," said Laptev. "Since my sister Nina died, I've started thinking about death often for some reason."

They began talking about death, about the immortal soul, about how fine it would be to actually rise from the dead and fly off somewhere to Mars, to be idle and happy eternally, and, above all, to reason in a special, unearthly way.

"But I don't want to die," Yartsev said softly. "No philosophy of any kind can reconcile me with death, and I look at it simply as perdition. I want to live."

"You love life, Gavrilich?"

"Yes, I love it."

"You know, I can't understand myself in that respect. I'm either in a gloomy mood or an indifferent one. I'm timid, unsure of myself, I have a cowardly conscience, I simply can't adjust to life, master it. Another person can say idiocies and cheat, joyously, while I, it happens, consciously do good and in doing so only feel uneasy or totally indifferent. I explain all this, Gavrilich, by my being a slave, the grandson of a serf. Before we dregs work our way onto the right road, many of us will leave our bones behind!"

"That's all fine, darling," Yartsev said and he sighed. "It merely shows once and again how rich and varied Russian life is. Ah, how rich! You know, every day I'm more and more convinced that we live on the eve of a great triumph, and I'd like to live to see it, to take part myself. Whether you want to believe it or not, in my opinion, there's a remarkable generation growing up now. When I work with children, particularly little girls, I am extremely pleased. Marvelous children!"

Yartsev went over to the piano and struck a chord.

"I'm a chemist, I think like a chemist and I'll die a chemist," he continued. "But I'm greedy, I'm afraid I'll die without having had my fill, and chemistry alone isn't enough for me. I turn my hand to Russian history, art history, teaching, music . . . Your wife said once this summer that I should write a historical play, and now I feel I'd like to write and write, to sit for three days and nights without getting up and write all the time. Images have exhausted me, my head is stuffed, and I feel as if there were a pulse beating in my brain. I don't even want to produce something special, to create something great; I simply want to live, dream, hope, get everywhere . . . Life is short, dear friend, and one must live it as well as possible."

After this amiable conversation, which ended only at midnight, Laptev began visiting Yartsev almost every day. He was drawn to him. Usually he came toward evening, lay down, and awaited Yartsev's arrival patiently, without feeling the slightest boredom. Yartsev, after returning from his teaching and having dinner, used to sit down to work, but Laptev would present him with a question of some kind; a conversation would start; soon there would be no more question of work; and at midnight, the friends would part, very pleased with one another.

But this did not continue for long. One day when he came to Yartsev's, Laptev found Razsudina alone, sitting at the piano and playing her exercises. She looked at him coldly, almost hostilely, and asked without offering him her hand: "Tell me, please, when is this going to end?"

"This what?" asked Laptev, not understanding.

"You come here every day and interfere with Yartsev's work. Yartsev is a scholar, not a merchant; every minute of his life is valuable. You should understand and have at least a little delicacy!"

"If you find I'm interfering," Laptev said mildly, disconcerted, "I'll stop my visits."

"Fine. Go away then, or he might come in now and find you here."

The tone in which this was said and Razsudina's indifferent eyes disconcerted him. She no longer had any feeling toward him except the desire for him to leave as quickly as possible—how unlike her former love this was! He left without shaking her hand and imagined she had called him to come back, but he heard scales again, and as he went slowly down the stairs, he realized he was a stranger to her now.

Three days later Yartsev came to see him to spend the evening together.

"Well, I've some news," he said and laughed. "Polina Nikolayevna moved to my place altogether." He was somewhat embarrassed and continued in a soft voice. "Why not? Of course, we're not in love with each other, but I think that . . . that doesn't matter. I'm glad I can give her asylum and peace and the possibility of not working if she falls ill, and she feels that her moving in with me will lead to more order in my life, and that under her influence, I'll become a great scientist. That's what she thinks. And let her think it. The southerners have a saying: 'The simpleton gets rich on illusions.' Ha-ha-ha!"

Laptev was silent. Yartsev walked across the study, looked at the pictures he had already seen many times, and said, sighing: "Yes, my friend. I'm three years older than you and it's too late now for me to think about real love, and, in reality, a woman like Polina Nikolayevna is a godsend for me, and I'll naturally live happily with her until old age, but the devil knows why, there's still something sad, something wanting, and I still feel as if I were lying in the Daghestan Valley dreaming of a ball. In a word, a man's never satisfied with what he has."

He went into the parlor and, as if nothing had happened, sang romances, while Laptev sat in his study with eyes closed, trying to understand why Razsudina had gone to live with Yartsev. And then he became very sad that there are no lasting, permanent attachments, and he was annoyed that Polina Nikolayevna had gone to live with Yartsev, and annoyed with himself that his feeling for his wife was no longer what it had been before.

XV

Laptev was sitting in an armchair, rocking and reading; Yulia was in the study too, also reading. It seemed as if there was nothing to talk about and both had been silent since morning. From time to time he looked at her over his book and thought: whether you marry for passionate love or completely without love—isn't it all the same? And the days when he had been jealous, agitated, and suffered, seemed remote to him now. He had taken his trip abroad already and was now resting from the journey and making plans to return when spring came, to England, which he liked very much.

In the meantime, Yulia had become reconciled to her grief and stopped going to the annex to cry. This winter she no longer went shopping or attended theaters or concerts, but stayed home. She disliked large rooms and was always either in her husband's study or in her own room, where she kept the image cases which had been part of her dowry and the landscape she had liked so much at the exhibition. She spent almost no money on herself and expended as little now as she once had in her father's house.

The winter flowed by cheerlessly. Everywhere in Moscow, everyone was playing cards, but if some other diversion was introduced instead, for example, singing, reading, or sketching, it turned out to be still more boring. Because there were few talented people in Moscow, and the very same singers and readers therefore took part in all the parties, the enjoyment of the art gradually palled and became for many a boring, monotonous obligation.

In addition, not a day went by without trouble at the Laptevs'. Old man Fedor Stepanich's sight was very bad; he no longer went to the warehouse, and the eye specialists said he would soon go blind. Fedor had also stopped going to the warehouse for some reason and sat at home all day writing something. Panaurov had received a transfer with a promotion to active councilor of state, and he now lived at the Dresden and came to Laptev almost daily to ask for money. Kish had graduated from the university at last and, while waiting for the Laptevs to find him some sort of occupation, spent day after day at their house telling long, boring stories. All this was irritating and tiring and made daily life unpleasant.

Piotr came into the study and announced the arrival of a strange lady. On the card he produced was: "Josefina Josifovna Milan."

Yulia got up lazily and went out, limping slightly as if her foot had gone to sleep. In the doorway appeared a thin, very pale lady with dark eyebrows, dressed entirely in black. She pressed her hands to her bosom and uttered entreatingly: "M'sieu Laptev, save my children!"

The jangle of bracelets and the face with patches of powder were familiar to Laptev; he recognized the lady at whose house he had so inappropriately had supper once before his marriage. She was Panaurov's second wife.

"Save my children!" she repeated, and her face began to tremble, suddenly grew old and pitiful, and her eyes reddened. "Only you alone can save us, and I spent my last ruble to come to you in Moscow! My children will starve to death!"

She made a movement as if she were about to fall on her knees. Alarmed, Laptev seized her by the arm above the elbow.

"Sit down, sit down . . ." he muttered, seating her. "I beg you, sit down."

"We have no money to buy bread now," she said. "Grigory Nikolaich is leaving for a new post but does not want to take me and the children with him, and the money you generously sent us, he spends on himself alone. What are we to do? What? Poor, unhappy children!"

"Calm yourself, I beg you. I'll order the office to send the money in your name."

She began sobbing, then calmed herself, and he noticed that the tears made little paths on her powdered cheeks and that she was growing mustaches.

"You are infinitely generous, M'sieu Laptev. But be our angel, our good fairy, persuade Grigory Nikolaich not to leave me, but to take me with him. You see, I love him, love him insanely, he's my consolation."

Laptev gave her a hundred rubles and promised to have a talk with Panaurov, and as he accompanied her to the entrance, he kept fearing she would burst into sobs or fall on her knees.

After her, came Kish. Then Kostya came with his camera. He had become enthusiastic about photography recently and took pictures of everyone in the house several times a day; this new occupation had been the source of many vexations for him and was even making him lose weight.

Before evening tea, Fedor came. Sitting down in a corner in the study, he opened a book and kept looking at the same page for a long time, obviously not reading. Then he drank tea at length, his face red. In his presence, Laptev felt a weight on his heart; even his brother's silence was disagreeable to him.

"You may congratulate Russia on a new publicist," said Fedor. "However, joking aside, I've brought forth one little article, a trial of the pen, so to speak, and brought it to show you. Read it, my dear, and give me your opinion. Only frankly."

He pulled a notebook out of his pocket and handed it to his brother. The article was called: "The Russian Soul"; it was tediously written with the colorless words ungifted, secretly vain people commonly use, and the main idea of it was as follows: The well-educated man has the right not to believe in the supernatural, but it is his duty to hide his disbelief to avoid being a temptation or shaking people's faith; without faith there is no idealism, and idealism is predestined to save Europe and show mankind the true road.

"But you don't say what Europe has to be saved from," said Laptev.

"That's clear by itself."

"Nothing is clear," Laptev said and took a turn around the room in agitation. "It's not clear why you wrote this. However, that's your business."

"I want to publish a brochure."

"That's your business."

They were silent a moment. Fedor sighed and said: "It's profoundly, infinitely sad that you and I think differently. Ah, Alesha, Alesha, my dear brother! You and I are Russians, Orthodox people of vision; are all these little German and Jewish ideas for us? You see, you and I aren't swindlers of some sort, but representatives of eminent merchant stock."

"What sort of stock?" uttered Laptev, restraining his irritation. "Eminent stock! Our grandfather was flogged by the landowners and every last little clerk slapped his face. Grandfather flogged father, father flogged you and me. What has this eminent stock of yours given us? What kind of nerves and blood did we inherit? Here you've been reflecting for three years like a deacon now, you say all sorts of nonsense, and now you've written—why, it's a sniveling delirium! And I, and I? Look at me . . . No suppleness, no courage, no strength of will; I'm frightened after every step I take as if I were to be thrashed; I quail in front of nobodies, idiots, cattle, immeasurably inferior to me mentally and morally; I'm afraid of the yardmen, the doorkeepers, policemen, gendarmes; I'm afraid of everyone because I was born of a persecuted mother; I was beaten and terrorized from childhood on! . . . You and I would do well not to have children. Oh, if God would only let this eminent merchant stock end with us!"

Yulia came into the study and sat down at the table.

"You were arguing about something?" she said. "I'm not interrupting?"

"No, Little Sister," Fedor answered; "we're discussing a matter of principles. Now, you say: what stock!" he added, turning to his brother. "Nevertheless, this stock created a million-ruble business. And that's worth something!"

"Very important—a million-ruble business! A man of no particular intelligence, with no talent, becomes a hawker by chance, then a rich man, trades day after day without any system, any purpose, not even being greedy for money, trades mechanically, and money comes to him of itself, not he to it. He sits at his business his whole life and loves it only because he can rule over the clerks, make fun of the buyers. He's an elder in the church because there he can rule over the singers and bend them to the yoke; he's the trustee of the school because he likes the feeling that he is the teacher's superior and can play the ruler in front of him. The merchant enjoys ruling, not trading, and your warehouse is not a trading establishment, but a torture chamber! Yes, for a trade like yours, you need clerks stripped of their personalities, of their due, and you create them for yourself by making them bow to your feet for a crust of bread from childhood; and from childhood you train them to the idea that you are their benefactor. I don't suppose you'd take a university man in the warehouse!"

"University men don't fit in our business."

"That's not true!" shouted Laptev. "A lie!"

"Excuse me, it seems to me you're spitting in the well you drink from," Fedor said and got up. "Our business is hateful to you, but you use its gains."

"Aha, now we agree!" Laptev said and laughed, looking angrily at his brother. "Yes, if I didn't belong to your eminent stock, if I had even a grain of will power and courage, I'd have flung these gains away long ago and gone to earn my own bread. But you stamped out my personality from childhood in your warehouse! I'm yours!"

Fedor glanced at his watch and hastily took leave. He kissed Yulia's hand and went out, but instead of going into the antechamber, he walked through the parlor, then the bedroom.

"I'd forgotten the order of the rooms," he said in great bewilderment. "It's a strange house. Isn't it true, it's a strange house?"

When he put on his coat, he seemed stunned and his face showed suffering. Laptev no longer felt anger; he had both fear and pity for Fedor, and that warm, good love for his brother, which had seemed to be extinguished in him during these three years, was awakened now in his heart, and he had a strong desire to express this love.

"Come have dinner with us tomorrow, Fedya," he said and patted him on the shoulder. "Will you come?"

"Fine, fine. But give me some water."

Laptev ran to the dining room himself, took the first thing which fell under his hands—a tall beer jug—poured water and brought it to his brother. Fedor began drinking greedily, but suddenly bit the jug and there was a grating sound, then sobbing. Laptev, who had never seen a man cry before, stood in embarrassment and fright, not knowing what to do. He watched distractedly while Yulia and the maid took off Fedor's coat and led him back to the room; Laptev followed them, feeling guilty.

Yulia helped Fedor to lie down and dropped on her knees in front of him.

"It's nothing," she comforted. "It's your nerves . . ."

"Darling, I'm so miserable!" he said. "I'm unhappy, unhappy . . . but all the time I've hid it, hid it!"

He embraced her around the neck and whispered in her ear: "Every night I see my sister Nina. She comes and sits in the armchair near my bed . . ."

When, an hour later, he again put on his fur coat in the antechamber, he was smiling and felt ashamed in front of the chambermaid. Laptev drove with him to Pyatnitskaya Street.

"You come to us for dinner tomorrow," he said on the way, holding his brother by the arm; "and at Easter, we'll go abroad together. You must breathe some fresh air or you'll go completely stale."

"Yes, yes. I'll go, I'll go . . . And we'll take the little sister with us."

When he returned home, Laptev found his wife in a state of intense nervous agitation. The incident with Fedor had shaken her, and she was quite unable to calm herself. She did not cry, but was very pale, tossed restlessly in bed, and clutched tenaciously at the blanket, the pillow, and her husband's hands. Her eyes were huge, frightened.

"Don't leave me, don't leave," she said to her husband. "Tell me, Alesha, why have I stopped praying to God? Where is my faith? Ah, why did you talk about religion in front of me? You've confused me, you and your friends. I can't pray any more."

He put compresses on her forehead, warmed her hands, poured her tea, while she clung to him in fear . . .

Toward morning she became exhausted and fell asleep, while Laptev sat beside her and held her hand. Thus he, too, missed his sleep. The whole next day he felt spent, dull, thought about nothing, and wandered listlessly through the house.

XVI

The doctor said Fedor was mentally ill. Laptev no longer knew what was happening on Pyatnitskaya Street, and the dark warehouse, in which neither the old man nor Fedor appeared any more, seemed like a tomb to him. When his wife told him it was essential for him to visit the warehouse and Pyatnitskaya Street every day, he either was silent or began talking with irritation about his childhood, about how it was beyond his strength to forgive his father for the past, how he hated Pyatnitskaya Street and the warehouse, and so forth.

One Sunday morning, Yulia drove to Pyatnitskaya Street herself. She found old man Fedor Stepanich in the same large room in which the Te Deum had been held on the occasion of her arrival. Tieless, wearing slippers and his canvas jacket, he was sitting immobile in an armchair and blinking his blind eyes.

"It's I, your daughter-in-law," she said, going up to him. "I came to visit you."

He began breathing heavily with emotion. Moved by his misfortune and his loneliness, she kissed his hand, while he felt her face and head; then, as if satisfied that it was she, he made the sign of the cross over her.

"Thank you, thank you," he said. "Now I've lost my eyes and can't see anything . . . I just barely see the window and the light, but I don't notice people and objects. Yes, I'm going blind, Fedor's fallen ill, and things are bad now without the master's eyes. If there's some kind of disorder, there's no one to take charge; the employees will become slack. And what did Fedor get sick from? A cold, wasn't it? And here

I've never been ill and never taken treatment. I've never known any doctors."

And the old man began boasting as usual. The servants were hastily setting the table in the meantime, and putting out appetizers and bottles of liquor. Ten bottles were brought, one of which was shaped like the Eiffel Tower. A whole plate of hot little pies which smelled of rice and fish was served.

"I beg my dear guest to eat," said the old man.

She took him by the arm, led him to the table, and poured him vodka.

"I'll come to see you tomorrow, too," she said, "and bring your nieces, Sasha and Lida, with me. They'll be nice and affectionate to you."

"No need, don't bring them. They're illegitimate."

"Why illegitimate? But their father and mother were married."

"Without my permission. I didn't bless them and don't want to know them. I don't want anything to do with them."

"That's strange talk, Fedor Stepanich," Yulia said and sighed.

"It says in the Bible: children must respect and fear their parents."

"Nothing of the kind. It says in the Bible that we should forgive even our enemies."

"You can't forgive in our business. If you forgive everyone, in three years you'll be escaping by the chimney."

"But to forgive, to say a kind, welcoming word to a person, even a guilty one—that's above business, above wealth!"

Yulia longed to mellow the old man, to instill a feeling of pity in him, to awaken repentance in him, but everything she said he merely listened to indulgently, in the way adults listen to children.

"Fedor Stepanich," said Yulia determinedly; "you are old now, and God will soon call you to Himself; He won't ask you how you managed your business and if it went well, but whether you were benevolent to people, whether you weren't severe with those weaker than you, for example, the servants, the clerks."

"I was always a benefactor to my employees and they can pray eternally for me," the old man said with conviction; but touched by Yulia's sincere tone and wanting to give her pleasure, he said: "Fine, bring the nieces tomorrow. I'll have some little presents bought for them."

The old man was carelessly dressed, he had cigar ashes on

his chest and knees, and it was obvious that no one cleaned his boots or his clothes. The rice in the pies was not cooked through, the tablecloth smelled of soap, the maids walked noisily. The old man and the whole house on Pyatnitskaya Street had a rejected look, and Yulia, conscious of it, became ashamed of herself and her husband.

"I'll come see you tomorrow without fail," she said.

She walked through the house and ordered the old man's bedroom put in order and his lamp lit. Fedor was sitting in his own room, staring at a closed book, not reading; Yulia talked to him for a while and ordered his room put in order too, then went downstairs to the clerks' part of the house. In the middle of the room in which the clerks had dinner was an unpainted wooden column supporting the ceiling to keep it from falling in; the ceilings here were low, the walls covered with cheap wallpaper; it was smoky and smelled of cooking. Because of the holiday, the clerks were all at home, sitting on their beds, waiting for supper. When Yulia came in, they jumped up and answered her questions timidly, looking up at her from under their brows like prisoners.

"Gentlemen, what poor lodgings you have!" she said, clasping her hands. "And aren't you crowded here?"

"Crowded but content," said Makichev. "We're very satisfied with you and offer our prayers to the merciful Lord."

"The conformities of life are according to personal ambition," said Pochatkin.

When he saw that Yulia did not understand Pochatkin, Makichev hastened to explain: "We're little people and must live in conformance with our calling."

She inspected the premises for the apprentices and the kitchen, met the housekeeper, and remained very dissatisfied.

When she returned home, she said to her husband: "We should move to Pyatnitskaya Street as soon as possible to live. And you will go to the warehouse every day."

Then they both sat side by side in the study in silence. He was heavyhearted and had no wish to go either to Pyatnitskaya Street or to the warehouse, but he guessed his wife's thoughts and could not bring himself to contradict her. He stroked her cheek and said: "I feel as if our life were already over and the gray half-life were beginning for us now. When I learned that brother Fedor was incurably ill, I burst into tears; we spent our childhood and youth together; once I loved him with all my heart, and now here's this catastrophe, and I feel that in losing him, I'm making a final break with my past. And when you said just now that we had to move to Pyatnitskaya Street, to that prison, I began feeling I have no future either."

He got up and walked over to the window.

"However that may be, we have to say good-by to thoughts of happiness," he said, looking at the street. "There is none. There never was any for me, and it probably doesn't even exist. However, I was happy once in my life when I sat under your umbrella one night. Remember how you forgot your umbrella at sister Nina's once?" he asked, turning to his wife. "I was in love with you then, and I remember sitting under that umbrella the whole night in a state of bliss."

Near the bookcase in the study stood a mahogany chest of drawers trimmed with bronze in which Laptev kept various unnecessary items, among which was the umbrella. He got it and handed it to his wife.

"Here it is."

Yulia looked at the umbrella for a minute, recognized it, and smiled ruefully.

"I remember." she said. "When you declared your love to me, you were holding it in your arms"; and noticing that he was about to leave, she added: "If you can, please come back earlier. I'm lonely without you."

Then she went to her own room and stared at the umbrella for a long time.

XVII

In spite of the complexity of the business and the large volume of trade, there was no bookkeeper in the warehouse, and it was impossible to make anything out of the books kept by the clerk. Purchasing agents, German and English, with whom the clerks discussed politics and religion, came to the warehouse daily; an alcoholic aristocrat came, a sick, pitiful man, who translated the foreign correspondence in the office; the clerks called him the jellyfish and put salt in his tea. In general, all this traffic seemed like a vast aberration to Laptav.

He visited the warehouse daily and tried to introduce a new order; he forbid whipping the apprentices and making fun of the buyers; he lost his temper when the clerks, chuckling merrily, sent worthless, rejected goods to the provinces with the claim that it was the newest and most fashionable. He was now the main personage in the warehouse, but, just as before, he had no idea of the size of his fortune, whether his business was going well, how much the senior clerks were paid, and so forth. Pochatkin and Makichev considered him young and inexperienced, concealed a great deal from him, and whispered mysteriously with the blind old man every evening.

Once, in the beginning of June, Laptev and Pochatkin went to the Bubnov Inn to have lunch and, incidentally, talk about business. Pochatkin had worked for the Laptevs for a long time, having started with them when he was only eight. He was a man of his word, was fully trusted, and when, on leaving the warehouse, he collected all the proceeds from the cashbox and stuffed his pockets with them, it aroused no suspicion of any kind. He was the superior in the warehouse and the house, and also in the church, where he performed the duties of elder in the old man's place. For his cruel treatment of junior clerks and apprentices, he was nicknamed the Child Skuratov. *

As they entered the inn, he nodded to the waiter and said: "Give us here a half wild and twenty-four disagreeables, brother."

The waiter, after a short delay, brought a tray with a half bottle of vodka and several dishes with various appetizers.

"Here now, sweetheart," Pochatkin said to him; "give us a portion of the chief master of scandal and slander with a purée of potatoes."

The waiter was embarrassed, failing to understand; he was about to speak, but Pochatkin looked at him sternly and said: "Besides!"

The waiter thought hard, went to consult his fellow waiters, and at last managed to guess and brought a portion of tongue. When they had had two glasses each and eaten, Laptev asked: "Tell me, Ivan Vassilich, is it true that our business started going down these last years?"

"By no means."

"Tell me frankly, so that it's clear, how much did we used to make, how much do we make, and how large is our fortune? It's impossible to go on walking in the dark, you see. We had an accounting at the warehouse not long ago but, forgive me, I don't believe in that accounting; you find it necessary to hide something from me and tell the truth only to Father. You've been accustomed to playing politics from your early days and can't get along without it now. But what's the

* Skuratov was one of Tsar Ivan's favorites and executor of his wishes.

point of it? So, now, I beg you, be frank. What state is our business in?"

"Everything depends on the fluctuation of credit," Pochatkin answered after reflecting.

"What do you mean by the fluctuation of credit?"

Pochatkin began explaining, but Laptev understood nothing and sent for Makichev. The latter appeared immediately, ate, said his prayers, and in his ponderous, full baritone, began speaking first about how it was the clerks' duty to pray day and night for their benefactors.

"Splendid, but allow me not to consider myself your benefactor," said Laptev.

"Every person ought to remember what he is and be conscious of his station. You, by the grace of God, are our father and benefactor and we are your slaves."

"I am tired of all this for once and for all!" Laptev became angry. "Please, you be my benefactor now and explain what state our business is in. Don't treat me like a little boy, or I'll close down the warehouse tomorrow. Father's gone blind, Brother's in an insane asylum, my nieces are still young; I detest this business, I'd gladly leave, but there's no one to replace me, you know that yourselves. Drop this playing of politics, for God's sake!"

They went to the warehouse to make calculations. Then they continued at home in the evenings with the help of the old man himself; as he initiated his son into his commercial secrets, his tone of voice was as if he were talking about witchcraft, not commerce. It turned out that their income had been increasing yearly by approximately 10 percent, and that the Laptevs' fortune, counting only cash and bonds, amounted to six million rubles.

When Laptev went out into the fresh air after midnight when the accounting was finished, he felt still under the spell of these figures. The night was still, moonlit, sultry; the white walls of the houses beyond the Moskva River, the sight of the heavy, locked gates, the stillness and dark shadows, gave a general impression of some sort of fortress, and all that was missing was a sentry with a rifle. Laptev went to the little garden and sat down on a bench near the fence separating it from the neighboring courtyard where there was also a little garden. The black alder was in flower. Laptev recalled that this black alder had had the same curvature and the same height in his childhood and had not changed a bit since then. Every corner of the garden and the courtyard reminded him of the distant past. And in childhood, just as now, through the sparse trees, the whole courtyard was visible, flooded with moonlight; as now, the shadows were severe and mysterious; as now, there was a black dog lying in the middle of the courtyard and the clerks' windows were wide open. And all of these memories were gloomy.

Beyond the fence, he heard light footsteps in the other courtyard.

"My dear, my sweet . . ." a male voice whispered, so close to the fence that Laptev heard even his breathing. Then they kissed.

Laptev was certain that the millions and the business for which he had no attachment would spoil his life and eventually turn him into a slave; he pictured to himself how he would little by little become accustomed to his position, little by little enter into the role of the head of a commercial firm, grow stupid, grow old, and in the end, die as mediocrities usually die; miserably, sourly, agonizing everyone around him. But what then kept him from throwing aside the millions, the business, and leaving this little garden and courtyard he had hated since childhood?

The whispering and kissing behind the fence disturbed him. He went out to the middle of the courtyard, and unbuttoning his shirt over his chest, looked at the moon, and he felt like ordering the gates opened, going out, and never coming back here; his heart contracted pleasantly with the foretaste of freedom, he laughed joyously and imagined what a marvelous, poetic, perhaps even blessed life . . .

But he still stood, not leaving, asking himself: "What holds me here?" And he was annoyed with himself and with the black dog which was lying on the stones instead of going into the fields or the woods where she would be independent, joyful. And obviously both he and this dog were kept from leaving the courtyard by the very same things: the habit of captivity, of a servile state . . .

At noon the next day, he drove to visit his wife, taking Yartsev with him so that it would not be boring. Yulia was living in a summer villa at Butovo, and he had not been to see her for five days now. On their arrival at the station, the friends got into the carriage, and Yartsev sang the whole way and exclaimed over the magnificent weather. The villa was on a big estate not far from the station. At the beginning of the principal alley, twenty paces from the gates, Yulia was sitting, awaiting her guests, under a broad old poplar. She was wearing an exquisite light dress, trimmed with lace, a clear, cream-colored dress, and had the same old familiar umbrella in her hands. Yartsev greeted her and went to the house from where the voices of Sasha and Lida could be heard, while Laptev sat down beside her to talk things over.

"Why haven't you come in so long?" she asked, holding onto his hand. "I spend whole days sitting here, watching for you. I'm lonely without you!"

She stood up, ran her hand through his hair, and scanned his face, shoulders, and hat with curiosity.

"You know, I love you," she said and blushed. "You're precious to me. Now you've come, I see you and am happy, I don't know just how. Well, let's talk. Tell me something."

She had told him she loved him, while he only felt as if he had been married to her for ten years, and he was hungry for lunch. She embraced him around the neck, tickling his cheek with the silk of her dress; he gently pushed her hand aside, got up, and without a word, went to the house. The little girls ran to meet him.

"How they've grown!" he thought. "And how many changes in these three years . . . But then, perhaps I'll have to live another thirteen, thirty years . . . other things await us in the future! Live—and see."

He embraced Sasha and Lida, who hung on his neck, and told them: "Grandpa sends greetings . . . Uncle Fedya is going to die soon. Uncle Kostya sent a letter from America with greetings for you. He's bored at the exhibition and coming back soon. And Uncle Alesha is hungry."

Then he sat on the terrace and watched his wife going quietly down the alley toward the house. She was thinking about something, her face had a charming, melancholy expression, and tears glistened in her eyes. She was no longer a thin, frail, pallid young girl, but a mature, beautiful, strong woman. Laptev noticed, too, Yartsev's emotion as he walked to meet her, and the way her lovely new expression was reflected on his face, equally melancholy and enraptured. It was as if he were seeing her for the first time in his life. And when they had lunch on the terrace, Yartsev smiled in a somewhat joyful, timid way and kept looking at Yulia, at her beautiful neck. Laptev observed him without wanting to and kept thinking how he might have to live another thirteen, thirty years . . . And what would he have to go through in that time? What awaits us in the future?

And he thought: "Live—and see."

My Life

"My Life" is another story which Chekhov described as "a novel" when he began working on it. Chekhov began writing it in the spring of 1896 and worked on it through July of that year. It was originally to be called "My Marriage." Chekhov wrote it for the monthly literary supplement to the popular weekly magazine *Niva*, published by Marks and edited at that time by Vladimir Tikhonov-Lugovoy. Later, Chekhov changed the title to "My Life," but he did not like this either—especially the word "my" in it. He even suggested to Tikhonov changing it to "In the Nineties," but the idea did not appeal to Tikhonov. Chekhov complained that for the first time he was having real trouble with the title (he had always attached great importance to the naming of his stories). In the end the story was published as "My Life" in Nos. 10, 11, and 12 of the literary supplement to *Niva* for 1896.

Just like some other works by Chekhov at this time, especially the longer ones, "My Life" was hardly noticed by the critics, but some of Chekhov's literary and artistic friends praised it highly. Chekhov was horrified by the cuts made by the censorship. In a letter to Tolstoy's daughter Tatyana he spoke of his "aversion" for the story because of the cuts which had made some passages "unrecognizable." To Suvorin he wrote that the last part of the story had been turned by the censor "into a desert," and that some passages had become meaningless.

"My Life" is one of Chekhov's few stories written in the first person; it is this perhaps which imparts to it more unity and a greater clarity of outline than is the case with most of Chekhov's other longer works. Although, as Chekhov himself said while working on the story, "My Life" is supposed to describe provincial intelligentsia, it seems to me a mistake to regard this story as primarily a picture of a certain social milieu. Chekhov's main characters are not particularly typical

279

of the intelligentsia; nor does he confine himself to showing the latter (there is Radish, there are the nurse and her adopted son, none of whom belong to the intelligentsia). Nor is the story, in the first place, a social problem story, even though the narrator is portrayed as a Tolstoyan of sorts who preaches and practices simple life, manual labor, etc. (the story was written when Chekhov himself had no longer any use for such ideas, but he studiously avoids engaging in open polemics or drawing conclusions). Tolstoy said that the narrator of the story had been modeled by Chekhov on Prince V. Vyazemsky, whose practice of "simple living" had attracted considerable attention.

Once again the central theme of the story seems to be the relationship between Missail and Marya Viktorovna: their love for one another, their marriage, their growing mutual alienation, and their final parting. The principal subtheme is the story of the love affair between Missail's sister and Dr. Blagovo. As a kind of an echo of these two love stories we have Anyuta Blagovo's unspoken but clearly felt love for the hero. Anyuta herself flits by like a shadow in the background of the main incidents of the story, but is nevertheless a memorable creation. In the final analysis, "My Life" is neither a picture of mores of provincial intelligentsia, nor a story of a disillusioned Tolstoyan, but another Chekhovian love story, a sort of *triple* love story, as well as another variation on the theme of mutual unintelligibility and frustration.

When "My Life" was published together with "Peasants" in book form some critics noted that Chekhov's picture of provincial urban life, of its falsehood and corruption, was hardly less harsh than that of the backward Russian village.

I

The director told me: "I only keep you out of respect for your esteemed father, otherwise you would have been sent flying out of here long ago." I answered him: "You flatter me, Your Excellency, assuming I know how to fly." And then I heard him say: "Take this gentleman away, he gets on my nerves."

Two days later I was discharged. Thus, since the time I was

considered grown, I had changed jobs nine times, to the great sorrow of my father, the town architect.

I had served in various governmental departments, but all nine jobs were as alike as drops of water: I had to sit, write, listen to stupid or coarse remarks, and wait to be discharged.

When I approached Father, he was sitting deep in an armchair with his eyes closed. His face, gaunt, dry, with a dark blue cast on the shaven parts, expressed humility and resignation (facially he resembled an old Catholic organist). Without answering my greeting or opening his eyes, he said: "If my dear wife, your mother, were alive, your life would be a source of constant grief for her. In her premature death, I see the provident hand of God. I ask you to tell me, you wretch," he continued, opening his eyes, "what am I to do with you?"

Previously, when I was younger, my friends and relatives had known what to do with me: some advised me to go into the army, others to go into the pharmaceutical business, still others, into the telegraph service. Now that I had turned twenty-five and gray was appearing at my temples, and I had already been in the army, in a pharmacy, and in the telegraph office, everything on earth seemed to have been exhausted and people no longer gave me advice, but just sighed and shook their heads.

"What do you think of yourself?" Father continued. "At your age, other young men already have stable social positions, but just look at yourself: a proletarian, a beggar, living on your father's neck!"

And as usual, he began talking about how today's young people were going to ruin, to ruin from lack of faith, materialism, and inordinate conceit, and how amateur theatricals should be forbidden because they distracted young people from religion and duty.

"Tomorrow we'll go together, and you apologize to the director and promise to work for him conscientiously," he concluded. "You must not remain a single day without a position in society."

"I beg you to listen to me," I said gloomily, expecting nothing good from this conversation. "What you call a position in society is made up of the privileges of capital and education. Poor and uneducated people earn their crust of bread by manual labor, and I see no reason for my being an exception."

"When you start talking about manual labor, what comes out is stupid and vulgar!" said Father with irritation. "Understand, you dense person, understand, blockhead, that in addition to crude physical force, you have a divine spirit, a sacred fire, which distinguishes you to the ultimate degree from a jackass or a reptile, and brings you closer to divinity. This fire is the fruit of the best of mankind throughout thousands of years. Your great-grandfather Poloznev, the general, fought at Borodino; your grandfather was a poet, an orator, and a marshal of the nobility; your uncle—a pedagogue; lastly I, your father—an architect! All the Poloznevs guarded the sacred fire only for you to extinguish it!"

"One must be just," I said. "Many people perform manual labor."

"Let them! They don't know how to do anything else! The most abject fool or criminal can do manual labor; such labor is the hallmark of the slave and the barbarian, while fate gives the sacred fire to only a few!"

Continuing this conversation was useless; Father worshiped himself, and was convinced only by what he himself said. Furthermore, I knew very well that the disdain with which he spoke of manual labor was based not so much on a notion about the sacred fire as the secret fear that I would become a laborer and start the whole town talking; but the most important thing was that all my contemporaries had graduated from the university long ago and were well on the road: the son of the director of the state bank was already a collegiate assessor, while I, an only son, was nothing! Continuing this conversation was useless and unpleasant, but I sat there, replying feebly, hoping that at last I might be understood. For the whole question was clear and simple and merely concerned the way for me to earn a living, but they always failed to see the simplicity and spoke to me in mawkishly turned phrases about Borodino, about the sacred fire, about my grandfather, the forgotten poet, who used to write rotten, artificial verses, and they rudely called me a blockhead and a dense individual. Yet how I longed for them to understand me! In spite of everything, I love my father and sister, and the habit of consulting them has been rooted in me since childhood, so deeply rooted that I barely manage to get away from it at times. Whether right or wrong, I am constantly afraid of offending them; afraid that Father's thin neck will turn red with agitation at any minute, afraid that he might have a stroke.

"Sitting in a stuffy room," I continued, "copying, competing with a typewriter, is shameful and insulting for a person of my age. How can talk of the sacred fire enter into that!"

"It's intellectual work, nevertheless," said Father. "But that's enough, let us put an end to this conversation, and in any case, let me tell you: if you don't go back to work now, but follow your despicable inclinations, my daughter and I will deprive you of our love. I'll deprive you of your inheritance —by the true God!"

Quite sincerely, in order to demonstrate the complete purity of the dictates by which I wanted to conduct myself throughout my life, I said: "The question of inheritance is of no importance to me. I renounce it in advance."

For some reason, quite unexpectedly for me, these words deeply insulted Father. He turned purple all over.

"Don't you dare talk to me like that, stupid!" he shouted in a thin, shrill voice. "Good-for-nothing!" And quickly and adroitly, with a habitual movement, he hit me twice on the cheek. "You're forgetting yourself."

In my childhood, when Father beat me, I was made to stand straight, arms to my sides, and look him in the face. And when he beat me now, I completely forgot myself, and as if still in my childhood, drew myself up and tried to look him straight in the eyes. My father was old and very thin, but his slender muscles must have been as sturdy as thongs, because his blows were very painful.

I retreated to the entrance hall, where he seized his umbrella and struck me on the head and shoulders several times; at that moment, my sister opened the parlor door to find out what the noise was, but immediately turned back with a look of horror and pity, without a word in my defense.

My determination not to return to the government office, and to begin a new life as a workman, was unshakable. All that remained was to choose a specific occupation—and this did not present any special difficulty because I felt I was very strong, persevering, and capable of the heaviest labor. Before me lay a monotonous worker's life with hunger, smells, and coarse surroundings, and continuous preoccupation with wages and bread. And—who knows?—returning from work along the Bolshoi Dvoryansky, I might more than once envy Engineer Dolzhikov, earning his living by intellectual work; but at present, the thought of these future hardships of mine was a joy to me. I had once dreamed of intellectual activity, picturing myself first as a teacher, then a doctor, then a writer; but these dreams had remained dreams. The taste for intellectual pleasures—for books and the theater, for example—was developed to a passionate degree in me, but whether I had a capacity for intellectual work—I do not know. In preparatory school, I had such an insurmountable aversion to Greek, that I had to be taken out of the fourth class. For a long time, tutors came to prepare me for the fifth class; then I served in various government departments, spending the greater part of the day in complete idleness, and they told me this was intellectual work. My activity in the realms of study and work demanded no application of the mind, no talent, no personal capabilities or creative spirit: it was mechanical, and I rank this kind of intellectual work below manual labor. I despise it and do not think it can justify an idle, carefree life for one minute, because it is merely a fraud and one aspect of that very idleness. In all probability, I have never known any genuine intellectual work.

Evening came. We lived on the Bolshoi Dvoryansky—the principal street of the town, down which our beau monde * strolled in the evenings for lack of a decent city park. This pleasant street was a partial substitute for a park, for both sides were lined with poplars which smelled sweet, particularly after a rain, and acacia, tall bushes of lilac, black alders, and apple trees overhung the fences and palisades, enclosing them. The May twilight, the tender young greenery with its shadows, the smell of lilacs, the droning of insects, the stillness and warmth—all this seemed new and in some way unusual, even though spring repeated itself every year. I stood at the gates and watched the strollers. I had grown up with most of them and once played games with them, but now my proximity might be embarrassing to them because I was poorly and unfashionably dressed; they used to say my very narrow trousers and large, clumsy shoes looked like macaroni sticking out of tugboats. Moreover, I had a poor reputation in town because I had no social position and often played billiards in cheap taverns, and furthermore, perhaps, because for no reason on my part, I had been brought before an officer of the gendarmery twice.

Someone was playing the piano in the big house opposite, Engineer Dolzhikov's. Darkness was falling and stars glittered in the sky. Here, slowly returning bows of greeting, came Father in his old top hat with its wide turned-up brim, with my sister on his arm.

"Look!" he was saying to Sister, pointing to the sky with the same umbrella he had used to beat me a short time before. "Look at the sky! The stars, even the very smallest—are all worlds! How insignificant man is in relation to the universe!"

* Fashionable society.

And his tone in saying this was as if he found it extremely
flattering and agreeable to be so insignificant. What an ungifted man! Unfortunately, he was our only architect, and for
the last fifteen or twenty years that I could remember, not one
decent house had been built in the town. When he had an
order for a plan, he usually sketched the reception hall and
drawing room first; just as schoolgirls used to be able to start
a dance only from the vicinity of the stove, his artistic inspiration could only spring and evolve from the hall and the drawing room. He sketched a dining room, nursery, and study onto them, joining the rooms by doors, and consequently all the
rooms inevitably turned into passageways, and each had two,
or even three, superfluous doors. His concept was probably
unclear, extremely confused, and stunted. Invariably, as if
sensing that something was lacking, he would resort to various
sorts of annexes, planting one next to the other, and I can see
as if it were today the narrow entrance ways, the narrow corridors, the crooked little staircases leading to landings where
one could only stand doubled up and which would have three
huge steps like benches in a bathhouse instead of a level floor.
The kitchen with its arches and brick floor was invariably
located under the house. The façade had an unbending, insensitive look; its lines were dry and timid; the roof was low,
flattened; while the thick, doughy chimneys were inevitably
topped by conical wire lids with black, squeaking weather-
vanes. And for some reason all these houses Father built, all
of them identical, reminded me uncomfortably of his top hat
and the nape of his neck: dry and unbending. In the course of
time, the townspeople became indifferent through habit to
Father's ineptitude; it took root and became our style.

Father also introduced this style into my sister's life. To
begin with, he named her Cleopatra (similarly, I was named
Missail). When she was still a little girl, he frightened her with
references to the stars, the ancient wisemen, and our fore-
fathers; he explained to her at length what life was and what
duty was. And now, when she was already twenty-six, he continued in the very same vein, allowing her to walk arm in arm
with no one but himself, and imagining for some reason that
sooner or later a suitable young man would appear who would
want to marry her out of respect for her father's personal
qualities. For her part, she worshiped Father and feared and
believed in his unusual intelligence.

It was completely dark and the streets emptied little by
little. The music stopped in the house opposite; the gates

swung wide open, and down our street, frolicking, with bells playing softly, trotted a troika. It was the engineer and his daughter going for a drive. Time, for bed!

I had my own room in the house, but I lived in the yard in a shanty which shared the roof of the brick shed and had probably been built at some time for keeping harnesses— there were huge hooks driven into the walls; the shanty was no longer needed, and for the last thirty years, Father had used it to store his newspaper, which he for some reason bound by the half year and forbade anyone to touch. Living here, I rarely came in sight of Father and his guests, and it seemed to me that if I did not live in a real room and did not go to the house for dinner every day, my father's saying that I lived on his neck would sound less insulting.

Sister was waiting for me. She had brought me supper without Father's knowledge: a rather small piece of veal and a slice of bread. It was often reiterated in our house that "money thrives on accounting," "enough kopecks will take care of the rubles," and other similar sayings, and crushed by this vulgarity, my sister's sole concern was to cut down expenses, and we were consequently badly fed. Putting the plate on the table, she sat down on my bed and burst into tears.

"Missail," she said, "what are you doing to us?"

She did not cover her face; her tears rolled down her bosom and onto her hands, and she looked unconsolable. She fell on the pillow and gave way to her tears, her whole body shuddering and sobbing.

"You've left your job again . . ." she uttered. "Oh, how horrible it is!"

"But try to understand, Sister, try to understand . . ." I said, and I was overcome with despair because of her tears.

As if from spite, all the kerosene in my lamp was burned up and the lamp was smoke-blackened, about to go out, while the old hooks in the walls watched sternly and their shadows flickered.

"Have mercy on us!" said my sister, getting up. "Father is in terrible sorrow, and I'm sick, I'm going out of my mind. What will become of you?" she asked, crying and stretching her hands toward me. "I beg you, I implore you, in the name of our late mother, I beg you: go back to work!"

"I can't, Cleopatra!" said I, feeling that just a little more— and I should give in. "I can't!"

"Why?" Sister continued. "Why? Come, if you didn't get along with the director, find yourself another place. For instance, why don't you go into service on the railroad? I was just talking to Anyuta Blagovo; she assured me they'd take you on the railroad and even promised to solicit for you. For God's sake, Missail, think about it! Think about it, I implore you!"

We talked a while longer and I gave in. I said that the thought of working on the railroad then under construction had never once entered my head and that, if she liked, I was ready to try.

She smiled joyfully through her tears, pressed my hand, and unable to stop, continued crying while I went to the kitchen for kerosene.

II

Among the town's devotees of amateur theatricals, concerts, and *tableaux vivants* for charitable ends, the Azhogins, who had their own house on the Bolshoi Dvoryansky, were the leaders. It was they who always provided the place and assumed all the trouble and expense. This rich landowning family had about eight thousand acres and a luxurious estate, but disliked the country and lived in town, winter and summer. The family consisted of the mother, a tall, thin, delicate lady who wore short hair, a short jacket, and a plain, English-style skirt, and three daughters, who were never referred to by their names, but simply called the Oldest, the Middle, and the Youngest. They all had ugly, sharp chins, were shortsighted, stooped, dressed just like their mother, lisped unpleasantly, and in spite of this, invariably participated in every performance and were always doing something for a charitable purpose—they played, read, and sang. They were very serious, never smiled, and performed even musicals without a trace of gaiety, with as businesslike a manner as if they were doing bookkeeping.

I loved our theatricals, particularly the frequent, somewhat pointless and noisy rehearsals, after which we were all given supper. In the choice of plays and the distribution of roles, I took no part at all. My responsibilities lay backstage. I painted the scenery, copied the parts, did the makeup, and was also in charge of the arrangement of various sound effects such as thunder, nightingales singing, etc. Because I had no social position or decent clothes, I kept to myself in the backstage darkness during rehearsals and was timidly silent.

I painted the scenery in the shed or the courtyard at the Azhogins'. I was assisted by a house painter, or, as he called himself, contractor for house-painting work, Andrei Ivanov, a tall, very thin and pale man of fifty with a sunken chest, sunken temples, and blue under his eyes, who was even a little frightening in appearance. He had an exhausting illness of some sort; every fall and spring he was said to be passing away, but after a period in bed, he would get up and say with astonishment: "Once again I lived through it!"

The townspeople called him Radish and claimed that was his real name. He was as fond of the theater as I was, and as soon as the rumor that we were planning a performance reached him, he would throw aside all his work and go to the Azhogins' to paint scenery.

The day following my talk with my sister, I worked at the Azhogins' from morning till evening. The rehearsal was scheduled for seven in the evening, and an hour before it began, all the amateurs had already assembled and the Oldest, the Middle, and the Youngest were walking around the stage reading from scripts. Radish, in a long carrot-red overcoat with a scarf wound around his neck, was standing, leaning his temple against the wall and watching the scene with a reverent expression. Mother Azhogina was walking up to her guests one after the other and saying something pleasant to each. She had a way of looking fixedly in one's face and speaking softly, as if in conspiracy.

"It must be difficult to paint scenery," she said softly as she came up to me. "Why, I was just talking to Madame Mufke about prejudices when I saw you come in. My God, all, all my life I've been struggling against prejudices! To convince the servants what nonsense all these fears of theirs are, I always light three candles for myself and start all important affairs on the thirteenth."

Engineer Dolzhikov's daughter arrived, a beautiful, plump blonde, dressed in what we called an entirely Parisian style. She did not take a part, but a chair was put on the stage for her at rehearsals, and performances never began until she had appeared in the first row, glowing and dazzling everyone with her finery. As a belle from the capital, she was allowed to make observations during rehearsals; she did so with a kind, indulgent smile, and it was evident that she regarded our spectacles as a childish pastime. She was said to have studied singing in the St. Petersburg Conservatory, and to have sung an entire winter in a private opera. I found her very charming and usually did not take my eyes off her during rehearsals and performances.

I had just picked up the script to begin prompting when my sister suddenly appeared. Without taking off her cloak or hat, she came up to me and said: "I beg you, let's go."

I went. At the door backstage stood Anyuta Blagovo, also in a hat, with a dark veil. She was the daughter of the assistant president of the court, who had held office in our town for a long time, almost since the very foundation of the district court. Because she was tall and well-proportioned, her participation in *tableaux vivants* was considered indispensable, and her face used to burn with shame when she played the part of a fairy or something like Glory. However, she took no part in dramatic performances and only stopped in at rehearsals for a moment on business of some sort, not going into the hall. Now, too, it was obvious that she had only dropped by for a moment.

"My father spoke about you," she said dryly, blushing and not looking at me. "Dolzhikov promised you a place on the railroad. Go see him tomorrow, he'll be home."

I bowed and expressed thanks for the intercession.

"And you can give this up," she added, indicating the script.

My sister and she went up to Madame Azhogina and whispered with her for a few minutes, looking at me. They seemed to be consulting about something.

"Indeed," said Madame Azhogina softly, coming up to me and looking me fixedly in the face, "indeed, if this distracts you from serious occupations," she drew the script out of my fingers, "then you can turn it over to someone else. Don't worry, my friend, God be with you."

I took leave of her and went out, feeling embarrassed. As I walked downstairs, I saw my sister and Anyuta Blagovo leaving; they were hurrying, discussing something animatedly, probably my going into the railway service. My sister had never been to a rehearsal before, and she was probably conscience-stricken now and afraid Father might find out she had been to the Azhogins' without his permission.

I went to the Dolzhikovs' house between twelve and one the next day. A footman ushered me into a very beautiful room which served as both the engineer's drawing room and his study. Everything here was soft and elegant, and to someone as unaccustomed to it as I, even seemed odd. There were costly carpets, huge armchairs, bronzes, pictures, gold and plush frames; the photographs distributed about the walls portrayed very beautiful women with splendid, intelligent faces and relaxed attitudes. The drawing-room door led directly into the garden, onto a veranda; lilacs were visible, a table set for lunch, many bottles, a bouquet of roses; it smelled of spring and an expensive cigar; it smelled of happiness—and everything seemed to be saying that here was a man who had lived, toiled, and, at last, attained whatever happiness is possible on earth. The engineer's daughter was sitting at the desk and reading a newspaper.

"You came to see Father?" she asked. "He's taking a shower. He'll be here right away. Sit down meanwhile, if you please."

I sat down.

"You live opposite us, I believe?" she asked after a silence.
"Yes."

"I look out the window every day out of boredom, you must forgive me," she continued, looking at the newspaper; "and I often see you and your sister. She always has such a kind, concentrated look."

In came Dolzhikov. He was wiping his neck with a towel.

"Papa, Monsieur Poloznev," said his daughter.

"Yes, yes, Blagovo spoke to me," he said, turning to me briskly without offering his hand. "But look here, what can I give you? What openings do I have? You're an odd lot, you gentlemen!" he continued loudly in a voice of reprimand. "You come to me at the rate of twenty a day, imagining I have a department! I have a railway line, gentlemen. I have hard, manual jobs. I need mechanics, locksmiths, excavators, carpenters, well-borers, and here all of you only know how to sit and write, nothing else! You're all writers!"

I felt the same breath of happiness emanate from him as from his carpets and armchairs. Plump, healthy, with red cheeks and a broad chest, well-scrubbed, in a printed cotton shirt and wide breeches, he looked just like a toy porcelain coachman. He had a round, curly little beard—and not one gray hair, a nose with a little hump, and dark, clear, guileless eyes.

"What do you know how to do?" he continued. "You don't know how to do anything! I'm an engineer, I'm a successful man, but before I was given the railway line, I had my nose to the grindstone for a long time; I was a machinist, I worked two years in Belgium as a plain greaser. You judge for your-self, my dear fellow: what kind of work can I offer you?"

"It's true, of course . . ." I muttered in intense embarrass-ment, unable to endure his clear, guileless eyes.

"Can you at least handle a telegraph apparatus?" he asked after reflection.

"Yes, I used to work in the telegraph office."

"Hmm . . . Well, we'll see then. Go to Dubechnya now. I already have somebody there, but he's a terrible idiot."

"And what will my duties include?" I asked.

"We'll see there. Go, and I'll make arrangements mean-while. Just please don't get drunk on me and don't bother me with any requests or I'll throw you out."

He walked away from me without a nod. I bowed to him and to his daughter, who was reading her newspaper, and went out. My spirits were so low that when Sister began asking how the engineer had received me, I was unable to utter a word.

I got up early in the morning, with the sunrise, to go to Dubechnya. There was not a soul yet on our Bolshoi Dvoryan-sky; everyone was still asleep, and my footsteps sounded lonely and muffled. The dew-covered poplars filled the air with a tender aroma. I felt sad and did not want to leave the town; I loved my native town. It seemed so beautiful and warm to me! I loved this greenery, the still, sunny mornings, the sound of our bells; but the people I lived with in this town I found bor-ing, alien, and at times even repugnant. I neither liked nor understood them.

I did not understand for what or by what all these sixty-five thousand people lived. I knew that Kimry earns its bread by shoes, that Tula makes samovars and rifles, that Odessa is a port town, but what our town was and what it did—I did not know. The Bolshoi Dvoryansky and the other two most re-spectable streets lived on invested capital and official salaries paid by the Treasury; but what supported the remaining eight streets, which stretched parallel for three versts and disap-peared over the hill—that had always been an enigma to me. And the way these people lived was shameful to describe! No park, no theater, no decent orchestra; the town and club li-braries were only visited by the Jewish youth, so that maga-zines and new books lay around uncut for months; the rich and educated slept in stuffy, close bedrooms on bug-ridden, wooden beds; they kept their children in disgustingly dirty premises known as nurseries, while the servants, even the old

and respected ones, slept on the floor in the kitchen and covered themselves with rags. On ordinary days the house smelled
of borscht and on fast days, of sturgeon baked in sunflower
oil. They ate tastelessly; drank polluted water. They had been
talking for years in the town council, at the governor's, at the
prelate's, in all the houses everywhere, about the fact that our
town had no good cheap water, and that it was essential to get
a two hundred thousand ruble loan from the Treasury for a
water supply system. The very rich in our town could be estimated at about thirty, and they sometimes lost their entire
fortunes at cards; yet they, too, drank polluted water and
ardently discussed the loan all their lives—and I was unable
to understand this; it seemed to me simpler for them to take
the two hundred thousand rubles out of their own pockets and
invest it.

I did not know one honest person in the entire town. My
father took bribes and thought they were given him out of
respect for his spiritual qualities. In order to be promoted
from one class to another, students went to board with their
teachers, who grossly overcharged them for it. The wife of the
military commander accepted money from the recruits at en-
listment time and even allowed them to entertain her; she was
once so drunk in church that she was totally unable to get up
from her knees. Doctors accepted money too, at recruitment
time, and the town doctor and the veterinarian levied a tax on
butcher shops and inns. At the district college there was a
brisk trade in certificates granting military exemptions for the
third school year. The higher clergy accepted money from
their subordinates and the church elders. At the town council,
the citizen's council, the medical board, and all similar boards,
the cry: "You have to give thanks!" followed every petitioner,
and the petitioner would return to give thirty or forty kopecks.
And those who did not take bribes, dignitaries of the Department of Justice, for example, were haughty, extended two
fingers for a handshake, distinguished themselves by their
coldness and narrowness of judgment, played cards a great
deal, drank copiously, married rich women, and undoubtedly
had a harmful, corrupting influence on society. Only from
some of the younger girls was there a breath of moral purity.
The majority of them had lofty aspirations and honest, pure
souls, but they had no knowledge of life and believed bribes
were given out of respect for spiritual qualities; on marrying,
they aged rapidly, let themselves go, and sank hopelessly into
the mire of a vulgar plebeian existence.

~~~~~~

III

A railroad was being built in our area. On the eve of holidays, crowds of tatterdemalions who were called "railers" and feared used to go through the town. I occasionally saw a capless tatterdemalion with a blood-stained face being led to the police, followed by someone carrying a samovar or some recently washed, still wet linen as a material witness. The "railers" usually crowded around the taverns and bazars; they drank, ate, cursed, and followed every passing woman of light character with a shrill whistle. To divert this hungry rabble, our shopkeepers used to feed dogs and cats vodka, or tie a tin kerosene can to a dog's tail and start yelling and whistling; the dog would twist down the street, rattling the can, howling with terror; feeling himself hotly pursued by some sort of monster, he would run far beyond the town and exhaust his strength there in the open fields. There were a few dogs in our town who were always slunken-tailed and trembling; they were said to have been driven out of their minds, unable to endure this diversion.

The station was being built five versts from town. It was said that the engineers had demanded a bribe of fifty thousand rubles to make the line reach the town itself, while the town administration would only agree to forty. They had parted company over the ten thousand, and now the citizens were regretting it because the road they had to build to the station was estimated at more. Ties and rails were in place throughout the line; service trains were going through carting building material and workers, and the only delay was for the bridges Dolzhikov was building, and for stations which were not yet ready here and there.

Dubechnya—as our first station was called—was located seventeen versts from the town. I went on foot. The spring and summer corn gleamed green in the embrace of the morning sun. The country was flat, cheerful, and in the distance lay the clear outlines of the station, the mounds, the far-off farms . . . How splendid it was here in the open! And how I longed to steep myself in the feeling of freedom, even for this one morning, in order not to think of what was happening in town, not to think about my own needs, not to want to eat! Nothing has marred my life so much as the sharp feeling of hunger at which my finest thoughts become stangely confused with thoughts of barley *kasha,** cutlets, and baked fish. Here I am standing alone in the fields and looking up at a swallow hovering in the air and warbling as if hysterical, and I find myself thinking: "It would be nice to have some bread and butter now!" Or here I am sitting by the side of the road and closing my eyes to rest and listen attentively to some marvelous May sound, and I'm reminded of the smell of a hot potato. For my height and sturdy build, I generally had too little to eat, and consequently my principal sensation throughout the day was hunger, and it was perhaps because of that that I understood perfectly why such a mass of people work just for a crust of bread and can talk only about food.

In Dubechnya they were plastering the inside of the railroad station and building the wooden upper story for the water pump house. It was hot, there was a smell of lime, and the workmen were wandering idly around heaps of chips and rubble; the switchman was asleep near his signal box with the sun burning directly on his face. There was not a single tree. The telegraph wire hummed faintly and hawks rested on it here and there. Also wandering through the rubbish heaps and not knowing what to do, I remembered the engineer's reply to my question about what my duties would be: "We'll see there." But what was there to see in this wilderness? The plasterers mentioned a foreman and a certain Fedot Vassiliev—I did not understand and was gradually overcome by a malaise, the physical malaise in which you are conscious of your arms, legs, and your whole huge body and do not know what to do with them, where to put them.

After walking around for at least two hours, I noticed telegraph poles leading from the station to somewhere right of the rail line and ending after one and a half or two versts at a white stone wall; the workmen said the office was located there, and I at last decided that that was where I should go.

It was a very old, long-deserted little estate. The white, porous stone wall was weatherworn and crumbling in places, and the roof of the annex, whose blind wall gave onto a field, was rusted; patches of tin gleamed on it here and there. Through the gates I could see a spacious courtyard, overgrown with field grass, and the old manor house with jalousies on the windows and a high roof, carrot-red with rust. On either side of the house stood two identical annexes. The

* A porridge usually made of barley or oats.

windows of one were boarded up; washing was hanging on a line and cattle were wandering near the other, whose windows were open. The last telegraph pole stood in this courtyard; the wire went from it to the window of the building whose blind wall faced the field. The door was open; I went in. Behind the table near the telegraph apparatus sat a dark, curly-haired man in a canvas jacket. He looked at me sternly from under his eyebrows, then immediately smiled and said: "Greetings, Small Pickings!"

It was Ivan Cheprakov, one of my former schoolmates, who had been expelled from the second class for smoking. We used to catch goldfinches, greenfinches, and hawfinches in the fall and sell them at the market early in the morning while our parents were still asleep. We would lie in wait for flocks of migratory starlings and fire small shot at them, then collect the wounded. Some died on us in terrible agony (I can still remember how they used to moan in the cage at night); those which recovered, we sold, insolently swearing they were all males. Sometimes at the market I would be left with just one starling, and after offering it for sale for a long time, I would finally get rid of it for one kopeck. "Small pickings, but still something!" I would console myself as I pocketed the kopeck, and from that time on, the street urchins and schoolboys nicknamed me "Small Pickings"; even now, the urchins and shopkeepers make fun of me with this nickname, although no one remembers its origin but me.

Cheprakov did not have a strong constitution; he was narrow-chested, round-shouldered, and long-legged. He wore a tie made of cord, no waistcoat, and his boots with their crooked heels were worse than mine. He rarely blinked his eyes and had a strained expression as if he were about to clutch something, and he was always fussing.

"Now you hold on," he used to say, fussily. "Now you listen! . . . What was I just saying now?"

We began talking. I learned that the estate on which I now found myself had belonged to the Cheprakovs until recently and had just last fall passed to Engineer Dolzhikov, who thought it more profitable to have money in land than in notes and had already bought three fair-sized estates in our area by taking on the mortgages. At the time of the sale, Mother Cheprakova had reserved herself the right to live in one of the side buildings for two years longer and had obtained a post for her son in the office.

"Why shouldn't he buy it!" Cheprakov said of the engineer.

"He fleeces so much out of the contractors alone! He fleeces everybody!"

Then, having decided with a certain amount of fussing that I should live with him in the annex and take meals at his mother's, he took me home for dinner.

"She's a frugal one," he said, "but she won't charge you much."

The little rooms in which his mother lived were very cramped. All of them, even the entrance and the antechamber, were obstructed by the furniture moved here from the big house after the sale of the estate; all of it was old-fashioned and mahogany. Madame Cheprakova, a very stout, middle-aged woman with slanting Chinese eyes, was sitting by the window in a big armchair and knitting a sock. She received me ceremoniously.

"This is Poloznev, Mama," Cheprakov said, presenting me. "He's going to work here."

"You're an aristocrat?" she asked in a strange, disagreeable voice; it sounded to me as if there were lard boiling in her throat.

"Yes," I answered.

"Sit down."

The dinner was very bad. They served only pies stuffed with sour curds and milk soup. Elena Nikiforovna, the hostess, winked rather oddly all the time with first one eye, then the other. She talked, ate, but there was something mortuary about her person and she even seemed to emanate the odor of a corpse. There was a glimmer of life in her and a glimmer of consciousness that she was a noblewoman and a landowner who had once had her own serfs; that she was a general's widow, whom servants had to address as "Your Excellency"; and when these pitiable remnants of life flickered in her for a moment, she would say to her son: "Zhan, that's not the way to hold your knife!"

Or, painfully drawing her breath, she would talk to me with the affectation of a hostess trying to entertain a guest: "Well, you know, we've sold our estate. Of course, it's a pity, we were used to it here, but Dolzhikov promised to make Zhan the director of the Dubechnya station, so we wouldn't have to leave. We'll live there at the station, and it's just the same as being on the estate. The engineer is so kind! Don't you find him very handsome?"

Until not long ago, the Cheprakovs had lived well, but everything had changed after the general's death. Elena Nikiforovna started quarreling with her neighbors, going to court, and not paying her overseers and workers; she lived in constant fear of being robbed—and in about ten years, Dubechnya became unrecognizable.

Behind the big house was an old garden, now gone wild and overgrown with field grass and bushes. I walked around the terrace, still solid and handsome; through the glass door, I could see a room with a parquet floor, probably the drawing room; there was an old-fashioned piano and engravings in wide mahogany frames on the walls—and nothing else. In the former flowerbeds, the only survivors were peonies and poppies, raising their white and brilliant red heads above the grass; along the paths, reaching out, entangling each other, were maples and elms, already stripped by cows. The garden was dense and looked impassable, but that was only close to the house where the old poplars, pines, and lindens, all of the same age, still stood, relics of the former alleys. Beyond them the garden had been cleared for mowing, and there it was no longer sultry, cobwebs no longer slipped into your mouth and eyes, and a light breeze blew. The farther you went, the more open it became, and there were cherries, plums, and spreading apple trees, disfigured by props and canker, growing in the open space; and the pear trees were so tall that it was impossible to believe they were pear trees. This part of the grounds was farmed by merchants from our town, and a moronic peasant living in a shack guarded it from thieves and starlings.

The garden, continuously thinning out, changing into a real meadow, dropped down to a river, overgrown with green reeds and willows. Near the milldam there was a pond, deep and full of fish; a rather small mill with a straw roof rumbled angrily; the frogs croaked frenetically. Circles floated by from time to time on the mirror-smooth water, and the water lilies trembled, disturbed by the playful fish. On the other side of the stream was the little village of Dubechnya. The quiet, blue stretch of water was enticing, promising coolness and peace. And now all this—the pond and the mill and the comfortable banks—belonged to the engineer!

And thus my new job began. I received and forwarded telegrams, wrote various accounts, and made clean copies of the notes of requests, the claims, and the reports sent to our office by illiterate foremen and skilled workers. But the greater part of the day, I just walked around the room, waiting for telegrams, or had a boy sit in the annex while I

went out and walked in the garden until the boy came running
to tell me the apparatus was clicking. I had my dinner with
Madame Cheprakova. Meat was very seldom served; all the
food was milky. Wednesdays and Saturdays were fast days,
and on those days pink dishes known as fasting plates were
used. Madame Cheprakova winked constantly—it was an
obtrusive mannerism, and I always began to feel uneasy in
her presence.

As there was not enough work in the annex for one person,
Cheprakov did nothing but sleep or go off with his rifle to
the pond to shoot ducks. In the evenings he got drunk in the
village or at the station, and before going to bed, would look
in the mirror and shout: "Greetings, Ivan Cheprakov!"

When drunk he was very pale and constantly rubbed his
hands and laughed as if he were whinnying: "Hee-hee-hee!"
From bravado, he used to undress completely and run naked
through the field. He also ate flies and said they were rather
sour.

IV

After dinner one day, he came running breathlessly to the
annex and said: "Come, your sister's arrived!"

I went out. And in fact, a city hackney was standing by
the porch of the big house. My sister had come, and with
her Anyuta Blagovo, and also a gentleman in a military
tunic. On coming closer, I recognized the officer; it was
Anyuta's brother, a doctor.

"We came to your place for a picnic," he said. "All right?"

My sister and Anyuta wanted to ask how I was getting
along here, but both kept silent and just looked at me. I was
silent too. They understood I did not like it here, and tears
started in my sister's eyes, while Anyuta Blagovo turned red.
We went into the garden. The doctor walked in front of
everyone and kept saying enthusiastically: "What air here!
Holy Mother, what air here!"

He still looked like a student. He spoke and walked like a
student, and the glance of his gray eyes was as lively, frank,
and open as a good student's. Next to his tall, beautiful sister,
he appeared weak and puny; his beard was puny, and his
voice, too, was a puny tenor—fairly pleasant, however. He

was serving in a regiment somewhere, had just come on leave
to visit his parents, and said he was going to St. Petersburg
in the fall for his examination as doctor of medicine. He
already had a family of his own—a wife and three children.
He had married young, while still in his second year at the
university, and the town said he was unhappily married and
no longer lived with his wife.

"What time is it now?" my sister worried. "We must get
back early enough; Papa gave me permission to visit my
brother only till six o'clock."

"Oh, your papa again!" sighed the doctor.

I put on the samovar. We had tea on a carpet in front of
the terrace of the big house, and the doctor, kneeling, drank
from a saucer and said he was in bliss. Then Cheprakov
fetched the key and unlocked the glass door, and we all
went into the house. It was dusky there and mysterious; it
smelled of fungus, and our footsteps echoed resonantly as if
there were a cellar under the floor. Standing, the doctor
touched the piano keyboard, and it answered him weakly
with a trembling, hoarse, but still harmonious chord. He tried
his voice and began singing a song, frowning and impatiently
tapping his foot when one of the keys proved mute. My
sister had stopped getting ready to go home and walked
around the room in agitation saying: "I feel so gay! I feel
very, very gay!"

Her voice had a note of astonishment as if she found it
unbelievable that she, too, could be in good spirits. It was
the first time in my life that I had seen her so gay. She even
grew prettier. She had an unattractive profile: her nose and
mouth jutted forward somehow, and she looked as if she
were blowing air, but she had lovely dark eyes, a pale, very
delicate complexion, a touching expression of kindness and
melancholy, and when she spoke, she seemed attractive and
even beautiful. Both she and I took after our mother, broad-
shouldered, strong, tenacious; but my sister had a morbid
pallor, coughed frequently, and I sometimes caught in her
eyes the expression people have who are seriously ill but hide
it for some reason. In her present gaiety there was something
childish and naive, as if the joy which was crushed and
stifled during our childhood by strict discipline was suddenly
being awakened now in her soul and was breaking forth to
freedom.

But when evening came and the horses were brought, Sister

grew quiet, drooped, and took her place in the hackney as if it were the prisoners' dock.

Now they all left, the noise died down . . . I remembered that throughout the whole visit, Anyuta Blagovo had not exchanged a word with me.

"Wonderful girl!" I thought. "Wonderful girl!"

The fast of St. Peter began, and we were served a fasting diet every day. A physical anguish weighed on me because of idleness and my indefinite position, and dissatisfied with myself, listless, and hungry, I strolled around the garden only waiting for a suitable frame of mind to leave.

Toward evening one day, when Radish was sitting with us in the annex, Dolzhikov arrived unexpectedly, sunburned and gray with dust. He was spending three days in our section, had just come to Dubechnya by train, and had walked to our place from the station. While awaiting the carriage which was supposed to come from town, he walked around the estate with his overseer, giving orders in a loud voice; then sat in our annex for a whole hour writing letters of some sort. While he was there, some telegrams arrived in his name to which he sent the answers himself. We three stood silently at attention.

"What disorder!" he said after looking over the office report with disdain. "I'm moving the office to the station in two weeks and I don't know yet what to do with you, gentlemen."

"I'm trying, Your Excellency," Cheprakov uttered.

"I can see how you're trying. Drawing your salary's all you know how to do," continued the engineer, looking at me. "You all count on patronage to *faire la carrière* * the quickest and easiest way. Well, I don't recognize patronage. Nobody used influence for me. Before they gave me the railway line, I worked as a machinist; labored in Belgium as an ordinary greaser. And you, Pantelei, what do you do here?" he asked, turning to Radish. "Get drunk with them?"

For some reason he called all common people Pantelei, and those like Cheprakov and myself, he despised and called drunks, cattle, and swine to their faces. He was cruel to minor employees in general and used to fine them and throw them out of the service coldly, without explanation.

At last the horses came for him. In farewell, he promised to dismiss us all in two weeks, called the overseer a blockhead, and then, lolling in his carriage, galloped off to town.

* Make a career.

"Andrei Ivanich," I said to Radish, "take me on as a workman."

"Well, why not?"

And we set off for town together. When the station and the estate were far behind us, I asked: "Andrei Ivanich, why did you come to Dubechnya just now?"

"First, my fellows are working on the line, and secondly—I came to pay interest to the general's widow. I borrowed fifty rubles from her last year, and now I pay her a ruble a month."

The housepainter stopped and took me by the button.

"Missail Alekseich, angel of ours," he continued, "the way I understand it, if a common man or a gentleman takes even the very smallest interest, he's a villain. Truth can't live in a man like that."

Thin, pale, frightening-looking, Radish closed his eyes, shook his head, and intoned with the air of a philosopher: "Lice eat grass, rust eats iron, and a lie, the soul. Lord, deliver us sinners!"

V

Radish was impractical and very poor at visualizing; he used to take on more work than he could finish, and when doing the accounts, would become alarmed, lose his head, and therefore almost always be out of pocket. He painted, put in window panes, pasted wallpaper, and even undertook roof work, and I remember how he used to run around for three days looking for roofers for some insignificant order. He was an excellent craftsman; he sometimes earned up to ten rubles a day, and had it not been for his desire, come what may, to be the chief and be called a contractor, he probably would have made good money.

He himself was paid by the job, but paid me and the other fellows by the day, from seventy kopecks to a ruble daily. When the weather was hot and dry, we did various outdoor tasks, generally roof painting. From lack of training, my feet felt as hot as if I were walking on red-hot bricks and sweltered when I put on my felt boots. But this happened only the first few times; then I became habituated and everything went as if on wheels. I now lived among people for whom

work was compulsory and inevitable and who worked like
draft horses, often without recognizing the moral significance
of work and never even using the word "labor" in conversation; among them I felt like a draft horse too, more and
more filled with the compulsoriness and inevitability of what
I was doing, and this feeling lightened my life, ridding it of
all doubts.

Everything interested me at first; everything was new, as if
I had been born anew. I could sleep on the ground, could
walk barefoot—and this was extremely pleasant. I could stand
in a crowd of common people without inhibiting anyone,
and when a hackney horse fell down in the street, I could
run to help lift it without being afraid of dirtying my clothes.
But the most important thing was that I lived on my own
money and was a burden to no one!

Roof painting, particularly with our own drying oil and
paint, was considered a very profitable job, and therefore,
even good master workers such as Radish did not disdain
this crude, tedious work. With his thin, lilac legs in short
breeches, he used to work about the roof like a stork, and I
could hear him sigh heavily and say as he plied his brush:
"Woe, woe on us sinners!"

He walked on roofs just as freely as on the ground.
Although he was ill and pale as a corpse, he was extraordi-
narily nimble: he painted the cupolas and domes of churches
without scaffolding, with only the aid of ladders and ropes,
just like the young men, and it was rather frightening to see
him stand there on a pinnacle far above the earth, draw
himself to his full height, and pronounce, no one knows for
whose benefit: "Lice eat grass, rust eats iron, and a lie, the
soul!"

Or, thinking about something, he would answer his thoughts
aloud: "Anything can happen! Anything can happen!"

When I went home from work, all the people sitting on
benches by their gates, all the shopkeepers, boys, and their
masters, used to shout various mocking and malicious remarks
after me, and the first few times, this upset me and struck
me as monstrous.

"Small Pickings!" I heard on all sides. "Painter! Yellow
Ocher!"

And no one was as unkind to me as those who had recently
been humble people and earned their bread by manual labor
themselves. When I walked by the hardware shop in the
merchants' row, they used to splatter water on me as if by

accident, and once someone even whacked me with a stick.
And a certain fish merchant, a gray-haired old man, barred
the road to me and said, looking at me with spite: "It's not
you I'm sorry for, you idiot! I'm sorry for your father!"

For some reason, my acquaintances became embarrassed
on meeting me. Some looked on me as an odd fellow and a
buffoon; others were sorry for me; still others did not know
how to treat me, and I found them hard to understand. One
day I met Anyuta Blagovo on a side street near our Bolshoi
Dvoryansky as I was walking to work carrying two long
brushes and a pail of paint. When she recognized me, Anyuta
flared in anger.

"I beg you not to bow to me on the street . . ." she said
nervously, sternly, in a trembling voice, without offering me
her hand, and tears suddenly glistened in her eyes. "If you
think all this is so necessary, then go ahead . . . go ahead,
but I beg you not to greet me!"

I was no longer living on the Bolshoi Dvoryansky, but in
the suburb of Makarikhe, at the house of our former nurse,
Karpovna, a kind but gloomy old woman who was always
anticipating misfortune, was frightened by all dreams on
principle, and even saw bad omens in the bees and wasps
which flew into her room. And my becoming a worker pre-
saged nothing good in her opinion.

"You're done for!" she said sadly, shaking her head. "Done
for!"

Her adopted son, Prokofy, lived with her in the little
house—a butcher, a huge, awkward man of thirty, red-haired,
with stiff mustaches. When he met me in the entrance, he
kept silent and respectfully made way for me, and when he
was drunk, he would give me a five-fingered salute. When he
had supper in the evenings I could hear him through the
board partition clearing his throat, sighing, and drinking
glass after glass.

"Mamasha!" he would call in an undertone.

"Well?" Karpovna, who loved her adopted child beyond
reason, would answer. "What, my little son?"

"I can make an indulgence for you, Mamasha. During this
earthly life, I'll support you in your old age in this vale of
tears, and when you die, I'll bury you at my own expense.
I've said it—and it's true."

I got up before sunrise every day and went to bed early.
We painters ate a great deal and slept soundly, except that
our hearts beat violently at night for some reason. I did not

quarrel with my comrades. Cursing, desperate oaths, and remarks such as "Blast your eyes" or "Cholera take you" went on all day, but we got along well with each other nevertheless. The fellows suspected me of being a religious dissenter and good-naturedly made fun of me, saying that even my own father had renounced me; and thereupon they would add that they themselves rarely glanced in God's house and that many of them had not been to confession in ten years, and they justified their laxness by saying that a painter was among men like a jackdaw among birds.

The fellows respected me and treated me with consideration; they obviously approved my not drinking, not smoking, and leading a quiet, sedate life. All that shocked them was that I did not take part in stealing drying oil and did not go up to clients with them to ask for tips. Stealing the master's oil and paint was customary among painters and not considered theft, and it was striking that a man as upright as Radish would always take a little whiting and drying oil with him on leaving work. Even the respected seniors who had houses of their own in Makarikhe were not ashamed to ask for tips, and it was irritating and embarrassing to see the fellows go in a body to congratulate some nonentity on the beginning or completion of a job and thank him humbly on being given ten kopecks.

They behaved like wily courtiers with the clients, and I was reminded almost daily of Shakespeare's Polonius.

"Ah, it'll probably rain!" a client would say, looking at the sky.

"It will, it undoubtedly will!" the painters would agree.

"On the other hand, those aren't rain clouds. Perhaps it won't rain."

"It won't, Your Excellency! Indeed, it won't."

They treated clients ironically behind their backs as a rule, and when they saw a gentleman sitting on a balcony with a newspaper, for example, they would remark: "He has a newspaper to read and nothing to eat, I bet."

I never went home to my family. On returning from work, I often found letters at my place, short and anxious notes in which my sister would write me about Father: how he had been so particularly pensive at dinner and had eaten nothing; how he had been dizzy or locked himself in his room and not come out for a long time. This sort of news disturbed me and kept me from sleeping. I even used to walk past our house on the Bolshoi Dvoryansky at night, glancing in the dark windows and trying to guess whether things were going well at home. My sister visited me on Sundays, but in secret, pretending she came to see our nurse, not me. And if she came into my room, she would be very pale, with tear-stained eyes, and begin crying immediately.

"Our father will never live through this!" she would say. "If something happens to him, God forbid, your conscience will torment you the rest of your life. This is terrible, Missail! In our mother's name, I beg you—reform!"

"Sister dear," I said, "how can I reform if I'm convinced I'm following my conscience? Try to understand!"

"I know you're following your conscience, but perhaps it could be managed some other way, so no one is hurt."

"Oh, holy saints!" sighed the old woman from behind the door. "You're done for! There's a calamity coming, my dears, there's a calamity coming!"

VI

One Sunday Dr. Blagovo appeared unexpectedly at my place. He wore a military tunic over a silk shirt and high patent leather boots.

"Well, I came by to see you!" he began, shaking my hand vigorously as students do. "I keep hearing about you every day and meaning to come have a talk with you, heart to heart, as they say. It's dreadfully boring in town; there isn't one lively soul, no one to say a word to. It's hot, Holy Mother!" he continued, taking off his tunic, leaving just his silk shirt. "My dear friend, let me talk to you!"

I was bored myself and had been longing for the company of someone beside the painters for a long time. I was sincerely delighted to see him.

"I'll begin with this," he said, sitting down on my bed; "that I sympathize with you with my whole heart and profoundly admire this life of yours. They don't understand you here in town, and who is there to understand, since, as you know yourself, with very few exceptions they're all Gogolesque pig-snouts. But I already saw what you were at the time of the picnic. You are a noble spirit, a sincere, elevated person! I respect you and consider it a great honor to shake your hand!" he continued enthusiastically. "To change your life as sharply and severely as you did must mean going through a complicated spiritual process, and to continue this life now and constantly keep yourself at the height of your convictions, you must have to exert your heart and mind day after day. Now, to start our conversation, tell me, don't you find that if you had devoted this will power, exertion, and all this potentiality on something else, for example, on eventually becoming a great scholar or artist, that your life would have become broader and deeper and be more productive in every respect?"

We talked, and when our conversation turned to manual labor, I expressed the following thought: that the strong must not enslave the weak, and the minority must not be a parasite or a pump, chronically sucking out the vital sap of the majority; in other words, that everyone without exception—strong and weak, rich and poor—must participate equally in the struggle for existence, each for himself, and that there is no better leveler for this than manual labor in the form of a general, universally compulsory obligation.

"Then in your opinion everyone without exception should do manual labor?" asked the doctor.

"Yes."

"But don't you find that if everyone, including the best people, the thinkers and great scholars, each participating in the struggle for existence for himself, should spend his time breaking stones or painting roofs, might this not present a grave danger to progress?"

"Where's the danger?" I asked. "Look: progress is to be found in matters of love, in the fulfillment of the moral law. If you don't enslave anyone, are a burden to no one, what more progress do you need?"

"But allow me!" Blagovo suddenly exploded, standing up. "But allow me! When a snail in its shell busies itself with personal self-realization and dabbles in moral law, do you call that progress?"

"Why 'dabbles'?" I felt offended. "If you don't make your neighbors feed you, clothe you, carry you around and defend you from your enemies, isn't that progress in a life based completely on slavery? In my opinion, that is the most genuine progress, and perhaps the only one possible and necessary for man."

"The limits of universal, world progress lie in infinity, and to speak of some 'possible' progress, limited by our needs or current convictions, forgive my saying so, but I find that quite strange."

"If the limits of progress lie in infinity as you say, that means its aims are indefinite," I said. "Living and not knowing definitely what you're living for!"

"So be it! But this 'not knowing' isn't as dull as your 'knowing.' I'm climbing up a ladder called progress, civilization, culture; climbing. and climbing, not knowing definitely where I'm climbing to, but, truly, life's worth living just for the sake of this marvelous ladder. You, meanwhile, know what you live for—for some people not to enslave others, for the artist and the one who grinds colors for him to have equally good dinners. But you see, that's the ordinary, kitchen, gray side of life, and to live for that alone—isn't it repellent? If some insects enslave others, the devil with them, let them eat each other up! We shouldn't be thinking about them— you see, they'll all die and rot just the same, no matter what you do to save them from slavery—we should be thinking about that great x which awaits all humanity in the distant future."

Blagovo argued with me heatedly, but I could see that he was simultaneously preoccupied by another consideration.

"I suppose your sister isn't coming," he said, looking at his watch. "She was at our house yesterday and said she would be at your place. You keep harping on slavery, slavery . . ." he resumed. "But you see, that's a special question, and all such questions are resolved by humanity gradually."

We began discussing gradualness. I said the question of doing good or evil was decided by everyone for himself without waiting for humanity to reach a decision on this question by gradual evolution. In addition, gradualness is a two-ended stick. Along with the gradual development of humanistic ideas, one sees the gradual growth of ideas of another kind. The right to have serfs no longer exists, but capitalism is growing. And in the very thick of emancipating ideas, just as in the time of Batu Khan, the majority feeds, clothes, and defends the minority while remaining hungry, unclothed, and defenseless itself. This sort of arrangement adapts itself splendidly to whatever tendencies or currents of opinion you like, because the art of enslavement is also being developed gradually. We no longer flog our lackeys in the stable: we give slavery more refined forms; at least, we are able to find justification for it in each individual case. We have ideas and ideas, but if it were possible now, at the end of the nineteenth century, to burden the workers with our most unpleasant physiological functions as well, we should do so, and then, of course, say in justification that if, pray, the better people, the thinkers and great scholars, were to waste their golden time on these functions, progress might be confronted by a grave danger.

But then my sister arrived. When she saw the doctor, she became uneasy, alarmed, and immediately began saying it was time for her to go home to Father.

"Cleopatra Alekseyevna," said Blagovo persuasively, pressing both hands to his heart, "what will happen to your papa if you spend a little half hour with me and your brother?"

He was candid and able to communicate his own animation to others. After a moment's reflection, my sister laughed and suddenly became gay, just as she had before, at the picnic. We went out in the field, settled on the grass, and continued our conversation, gazing at the town where all the windows facing west looked bright gold because the sun was setting.

Thereafter, every time my sister visited me, Blagovo also appeared, and they would greet each other as if their meeting at my place were accidental. My sister used to listen while the doctor and I argued; her expression throughout was joyfully excited, moved, and curious, and it seemed to me as if another world were opening before her eyes little by little, a world she had never even dreamed of before, and which she was now trying to fathom. When the doctor was not there, she was quiet and sad, and if she sometimes cried now while sitting on my bed, it was for reasons of which she did not speak.

In August Radish told us to get ready to go work on the railway line. A few days before we were "exiled" from town, Father came to see me. He sat down and unhurriedly wiped his red face without looking at me, then got our town *Messenger* out of his pocket and slowly, emphasizing every word, read how one of my contemporaries, the son of the director of the office of the State Bank, had been appointed a division chief in the Treasury.

"And now look at yourself," he said, folding the newspaper; "a beggar, a ragamuffin, a good-for-nothing! Even commoners and peasants are educated to become men, while you, a Poloznev, with famous, aristocratic ancestors, are aiming for the gutter! But I didn't come here to talk to you. I've already washed my hands of you," he continued in a strangled voice, standing up. "I came here to find out—where is your sister, you good-for-nothing? She left the house after dinner this afternoon, and here it's already after seven, but she's not there. She's begun leaving frequently without telling me; she's even less respectful—and I see there your evil, sneaking influence. Where is she?"

He held in his hands the umbrella I knew so well; I involuntarily started coming to attention like a schoolboy, waiting for Father to hit me, but he noticed my glance at the umbrella and this probably restrained him.

"Live as you please!" he said. "I deprive you of my blessing!"

"Holy saints," muttered Nurse from behind the door. "You poor, unlucky child! Oh, my heart feels trouble, trouble coming!"

I was working on the line. All August it rained without stopping; it was damp and cold. The grain was not carted from the fields, and on the big estates where they had mowed with machines, the wheat lay in heaps, not sheaves, and I remember seeing those miserable heaps turning darker every day and the grain sprouting in them. Working was difficult; the heavy rains spoiled everything we managed to get done. We were not permitted to live or sleep in the station buildings, and took refuge in dirty, dank mud huts the "railers" used in the summer, and I was unable to sleep at night for the cold and the wood lice crawling over my face and arms. When we worked near the bridges, the tough "railers" used to come in a gang in the evenings just to beat up the painters—it was a kind of sport for them. They beat us, pilfered our brushes, and to provoke us and incite us to fight, they used to spoil our work, smearing the signal boxes with green paint, for example. To complete our troubles, Radish became very irregular in paying us. All the painting work on the section was assigned to a contractor; he handed it over to someone else, who handed it over to Radish after reserving 20 percent for himself. The job was an unprofitable one, and in addition there were the rains. Time was lost, we were unable to work, yet Radish was obliged to pay the workmen by the day. The hungry painters almost beat him up, called him a cheat, a bloodsucker, a Judas Christ-seller, while the poor man sighed, raised his hands to heaven in despair, and constantly went to Madame Cheprakova for money.

VII

Then came a rainy, muddy, dark fall. And unemployment: I used to sit at home for three days at a time without work, or used to do various nonpainting jobs. For example, I hauled earth for ballast for about twenty kopecks a day. Dr. Blagovo had left for St. Petersburg. Sister did not visit me. Radish lay at home sick, awaiting death from day to day.

My frame of mind was autumnal too. Perhaps because, now that I had become a worker, I saw our town's life solely wrong side out, I happened to make discoveries almost every day which drove me to desperation. Fellow citizens of mine, of whom I had had no opinion at all before and who seemed perfectly proper from the outside, now proved to be base, cruel people, capable of every sort of nastiness. We common people were defrauded, cheated in accounts, kept waiting for hours at a time in cold entrances or kitchens; we were insulted and treated extremely roughly. During the fall, I papered the walls of the reading room and two other rooms in our club; they paid me seven kopecks per piece, but ordered me to give a receipt for twelve, and when I refused to do so, a benevolent-looking gentleman in gold spectacles, probably one of the elders of the club, told me: "If you argue any more about this, I'll smash your face in."

And when the lackey whispered to him that I was the son of the architect Poloznev, he became flustered, reddened, then instantly recovering himself, said: "The devil with him!"

In the shops, the tradesmen used to unload their rotten meat, musty flour, and left-over tea on us workers; in the churches, the police shoved us around; in the hospitals, the doctors' assistants and nurses fleeced us, and if we were too poor to bribe them, they would feed us from dirty dishes in revenge; in the post office, the pettiest clerk felt he had the right to treat us like animals and to shout rudely and insolently: "Hold on there. Where are you crawling to?" Even the yard dogs—they, too, treated us with hostility, rushing at us with a special malevolence. But what struck me most of all in my new position was the total absence of justice, the very thing popularly expressed by the words: "They've forgotten God." A day rarely went by without swindling. We were swindled by the merchants who sold us drying oil, by the contractors, our own workmen, and the clients themselves. It goes without saying that there was no question of our having any rights, and we always had to ask for the money we had earned as if it were charity—standing cap in hand by the back stairs.

I was papering one of the club rooms which adjoined the reading room. One evening as I was getting ready to leave, the daughter of Engineer Dolzhikov came into the room with a bundle of books in her arms.

I bowed to her.

"Ah, how are you!" she said, immediately recognizing me and extending her hand. "Very glad to see you."

She smiled and looked with curiosity and wonder at my smock, the pail of paste, and the wallpaper spread out on the floor; I became embarrassed, and she also felt awkward.

"You must excuse my looking at you like that," she said. "I've been hearing a lot about you. Particularly from Dr. Blagovo—he's simply in love with you. And I've met your sister; a sweet, agreeable girl, but I am quite unable to convince her there is nothing terrible in your choosing the simple life. On the contrary, you are now the most interesting person in town."

She glanced again at the pail of paste and the wallpaper, and continued: "I asked Dr. Blagovo to help me get to know you better, but he evidently forgot or couldn't. However that may be, we are acquainted nevertheless, and I should be very obliged to you if you would call on me informally sometime. I long so to talk! I'm a simple person," she said, extending her hand to me, "and I hope you will not feel constrained with me. Father's not home, he's in St. Petersburg."

She went off to the reading room, her dress rustling; when I arrived home, I was unable to sleep for a long time.

Throughout this cheerless fall, some good soul who apparently wanted to lighten my existence sent me tea and lemons, or baked goods and roast woodcocks from time to time. Karpovna said they were always brought by a soldier, from someone unknown, and that the soldier would ask whether I was well, whether I ate dinner every day, and whether I had warm clothing. When the frosts came, in the same way, the same soldier came during my absence to bring a soft knitted scarf, which gave off a delicate, fugitive scent of perfume, and I guessed who my good fairy was. The scarf smelled of lilies of the valley, Anyuta Blagovo's favorite perfume.

Toward winter there was more work; life became jollier. Radish recovered again, and we worked together in the cemetery chapel where the iconostasis was being prepared for gilding. It was clean, peaceful work, and, as we used to say, it paid. It was possible to accomplish a lot in a day, and time raced by swiftly, imperceptibly. There was no cursing, no laughing, no loud talk. The place imposed silence and decorum and disposed one to quiet, serious thoughts. Immersed in work, we would stand or sit as motionlessly as statues; there was a deadly silence, befitting a cemetery, so that if a tool fell or the flame crackled in an icon lamp, the sounds echoed resoundingly and sharply, making us turn to look. A long silence would be broken by a humming like bees flying: the soft, slow chanting at the church entrance of a little boy's requiem; or else the artist painting a dove with stars around it on the cupola would begin to whistle softly, and correcting himself, immediately fall silent; or Radish, answering his own thoughts, would say with a sigh: "Anything can happen! Anything can happen!"; or a slow doleful tolling would ring out above our heads, and the painters would remark that it must be a rich man's corpse being carried by . . .

I spent the days in this stillness, in the dimness of the church, and during the long evenings, I played billiards or sat in the gallery of the theater in the new serge suit I had bought with my wages. The performances and concerts had already begun at the Azhogins'; Radish painted the scenery alone now. He described the contents of the plays and *tableaux vivants* he had occasion to see there, and I listened to him with envy. I felt a strong urge to attend the rehearsals, but could not bring myself to go to the Azhogins'.

A week before Christmas, Dr. Blagovo arrived. And again we argued and played billiards in the evening. He used to take off his jacket and unbutton his shirt over his chest when he played, and for some reason generally tried to give himself the air of a desperate rake. He drank sparingly, but noisily, and managed to spend twenty rubles in an evening at a bad, cheap inn like the Volga.

Sister began to visit me again. Each time, they would act surprised on seeing each other, but it was clear from her joyful, guilty face that these meetings were not accidental. Once, when we were playing billiards in the evening, the doctor said to me: "Listen, why don't you go to see Dolzhikov's daughter? You don't know Marya Viktorovna; she's a clever girl, delightful, a simple, good soul."

I told him how the engineer had received me that spring.

"Nonsense!" laughed the doctor. "The engineer is one thing and she's another. Truly, my friend, don't hurt her feelings. Go see her some time. Let's go see her tomorrow evening, for instance. Want to?"

He persuaded me. The following evening, after putting on my new serge suit, I set off for the Dolzhikovs' in a state of agitation. The footman no longer seemed as arrogant and frightening nor the furniture as luxurious as that morning when I had appeared here as a petitioner. Marya Viktorovna was expecting me, greeted me as an old acquaintance, and shook my hand firmly, in a friendly way. She was wearing a gray broadcloth dress with wide sleeves and the coiffure we used to call "dog ears" when it came into style in our town a year ago; her hair was combed from the temples over the ears, which made her face seem broader, and this time she looked to me very much like her father, who had a broad, ruddy face with an expression somewhat like a coachman's. She was beautiful and elegant, but not youthful; she looked thirty, although, in fact, she was no more than twenty-five.

"Dear Doctor, how grateful I am to him!" she said, asking me to sit down. "If it weren't for him, you wouldn't have come to see me. I'm bored to death! Father went away and left me alone, and I don't know what to do with myself in this town."

Then she began asking me where I worked now, how much I earned, and where I lived.

"You spend only what you earn on yourself?" she asked. "Yes."

"Happy man!" she sighed. "All the evil in life, it seems to me, comes from idleness, from boredom, from spiritual emptiness, and all this is inevitable when you are used to living at others' expense. Don't think I'm showing off. I tell you sincerely: it's uninteresting and disagreeable to be rich. Unjust wealth makes friends—so it is said, because in general there isn't and can't be any just wealth."

She glanced at the furniture with a serious, cold expression as if adding up its cost, and continued: "Comfort and ease take possession with magical power; little by little they draw in even strong-willed people. Father and I once lived modestly, simply, and you see how we live now. It's inadmissible," she said, shrugging her shoulders, "we go through up to twenty thousand a year! In the provinces!"

"We've come to look on comfort and ease as the inevitable

privilege of capital and culture," I said, "and it seems to me
that the comforts of life could be combined with labor, even
the hardest and dirtiest. Your father is rich, yet, as he says,
he had occasion to be a machinist and an ordinary greaser."

She smiled and shook her head in doubt.

"Father sometimes eats bread dipped in kvass," * she said.
"A joke, a whim!"

At that moment the bell rang and she got up.

"The cultured and rich should work like everyone else,"
she continued, "and if comfort exists, it should be the same
for all. There should be no privileges of any kind. Well,
enough philosophy. Tell me something jollier. Tell me about
the painters. What are they like? Amusing?"

The doctor came in. I began telling about the painters,
but from lack of habit, felt strained and talked like an eth-
nographer, seriously and tediously. The doctor recounted
several anecdotes from the life of workmen too. He staggered,
cried, knelt, and even lay down on the floor to imitate a
drunk. It was real acting, and Marya Viktorovna laughed till
the tears came watching him. Then he played the piano and
sang in his pleasant, rather thin tenor, while Marya Viktorovna stood near by, selected what she should sing, and corrected him when he made a mistake.

"I heard you sing also?" I asked.

"Also!" the doctor said, horrified. "She's a marvelous
singer, an artist, and you say 'also'!"

"I studied it seriously at one time," she replied to my
question; "but I've dropped it now."

Sitting on a low stool, she told us about her life in St.
Petersburg and imitated famous singers, mimicking their
voices and manner of singing; she sketched the doctor in her
album, then me; she drew poorly, but both sketches were
likenesses. She laughed, frolicked, and made wry faces charm-
ingly—all of which suited her better than talk of unjust
wealth, and it seemed to me that when she had spoken to me
shortly before about wealth and comfort, it was not from
conviction, but in imitation of someone. She was a superb
comedienne. I mentally compared her to our aristocratic
ladies, and even the beautiful, sedate Anyuta Blagovo could
not withstand the comparison; the difference was vast, like
that between a fine, cultured rose and a wild one.

The three of us had supper together. The doctor and Marya
Viktorovna drank red wine, champagne, and coffee with

* A thin, sour, fermented beverage made from rye or barley.

cognac; they clinked glasses and drank to friendship, to
intelligence, to progress, to freedom, and did not get drunk,
but became flushed and frequently laughed for no reason until
the tears came. To avoid seeming dull, I drank some red
wine too.

"Talented, richly endowed natures," said Marya Viktorovna, "know how to live and follow their own path. Average
people, like me, for instance, don't know anything and can't
do anything themselves. There is nothing left for them except
to pick out some profound social movement and to float wherever it goes."

"How can one pick out something that's not there?" asked
the doctor.

"It's just that we don't see it."

"So? Social movements—they were invented by the new
literature. We don't have any."

An argument started.

"We don't have any profound social movements and never
did," the doctor said loudly. "There's little the new literature
hasn't invented! It's also invented some sort of intellectual
toilers in the country, but search our whole countryside and
you'll find at best one Snotty-Pot in a jacket or black frock
coat who'll make four mistakes in the word 'yet.' Our cultural
life hasn't begun. There's the same wildness, the same thick
coarseness, the same emptiness there was five hundred years
back. Movements and tendencies exist, but you see, they're
all petty, miserable, bent on cheap, vulgar little interests—
can one find anything serious in them? If you feel you have
picked out a profound social movement, and to follow it,
devote your life to missions in contemporary favor such as
the liberation of insects from slavery or abstinence from meat
cutlets—then you have my congratulations, my lady. We must
study, study, and study, but let us wait a while for the profound social movements: we haven't grown up to them yet,
and in good conscience, we understand nothing about them."

"You don't understand, but I do," retorted Marya Viktorovna. "God knows how tiresome you are today!"

"Our business is to study and study, to try to accumulate
as much knowledge as possible because serious social movements exist where there is knowledge, and the happiness of
future mankind lies in knowledge too. I drink to science!"

"One thing is certain: one must arrange one's life differently somehow," said Marya Viktorovna after silence and

reflection. "Life as it has been up to now is not worth anything. Let's not even talk about it."

When we left her, the cathedral clock was already striking two.

"Did you like her?" asked the doctor. "Isn't she splendid?"

We had dinner at Marya Viktorovna's the first day of the Christmas season, and then went to her house almost every day throughout the holidays. We were the only guests, and she had been truthful when she said she knew no one in town besides ourselves. We spent the time in conversation for the most part; sometimes the doctor brought a book of some kind or a magazine with him and read aloud to us. In reality, he was the first cultivated man I had met in my life. I can't judge whether he knew much, but he displayed his knowledge continuously as if he wanted others to share it. When he spoke of anything related to medicine, he was not like any of our town doctors, but made a rather novel, special impression, and I felt that if he wanted to, he would become a true scientist. And he was probably the only person who had a serious influence on me at that time. Seeing him and reading the books he gave me, I gradually began to feel a need for knowledge to inspire my cheerless work. It seemed strange to me now that I had not previously known, for example, that the whole world is composed of sixty basic elements; had not known what drying oil is, what paints are, and had somehow gotten along without this knowledge. Friendship with the doctor elevated me morally too. I often argued with him, and although I usually kept my own view, still, thanks to him, I began to observe little by little that everything was not clear to me, and I now started trying to elaborate as precise convictions as possible so that the dictates of my conscience would be precise and unconfused. Still, this man, the finest and most cultured in town, was far from perfect. In his manners, in his habit of leading every conversation to an argument, in his pleasant tenor, and even in his friendliness, there was something coarse, something seminarylike; and when he took off his frock coat, leaving just his silk shirt, or flung a tip to a waiter in an inn, it always seemed to me that culture or not, the Tartar was still alive in him.

At Epiphany he went back to St. Petersburg. He left in the morning, and after dinner, my sister came to see me. Without removing her fur coat and hat, she sat down in silence, very pale, and stared at one spot. She was frozen and obviously overwrought.

"You've probably caught cold," I said.

Her eyes filled with tears; she stood up and went to Karpovna without a word to me as if I had offended her. And after a short pause, I heard her say in a tone of bitter reproach: "Nurse, what have I been living for until now? What for? Tell me: I've wasted my own youth, haven't I? Through the best years of my life to know only writing down expenditures, pouring tea, counting kopecks, entertaining guests, and to think there's nothing higher than that in the world! Nurse, you must understand me; you see, I have human desires and I want to live, and they've made a sort of housekeeper out of me. Don't you see, it's horrible, horrible!"

She flung the keys at the door and they landed in my room with a ring. They were the keys to the sideboard, the kitchen cupboard, the cellar, and the tea caddy—the same keys my mother once carried.

"Ah, oh, Little Fathers!" The old woman was horrified. "Heavenly saints!"

When she left for home, Sister came to my room to pick up the keys and said: "Forgive me. Something strange has been happening to me lately."

<><><><><><><><><><><><><><><><><><><><><><><>

VIII

Returning from Marya Viktorovna's late one evening, I found a young district inspector in a new uniform in my room; he was sitting at my table and leafing through one of my books.

"At last!" he said getting up and stretching. "This is the third time I've come to see you. The governor orders you to appear before him tomorrow promptly at nine in the morning. Without fail."

He took a signed statement from me saying I would fulfill His Excellency's order scrupulously, and he left. This late visit from the police inspector and the unexpected invitation to the governor's had an extremely depressing effect on me. I had kept a fear of gendarmes, policemen, and officers of the law from early childhood, and I was racked by worry now as if I were actually guilty of something. I was totally unable to sleep. Nurse and Prokofy were also upset and could not sleep. Nurse, moreover, had an earache; she groaned and began crying from pain several times. Hearing that I was awake, Prokofy came in to me cautiously with a little lamp and sat down at the table.

"You ought to drink some *pertsovka* * . . ." he said after reflection. "In this vale of tears, things stop counting if you just take a drink. And if Mamasha would pour some *pertsovka* in her ear, it'd be a big help."

Before three, he got ready to go to the slaughterhouse for meat. I knew I would not fall asleep before morning, and to shorten the time until nine o'clock somehow, I set off with him. We walked carrying a lantern, while Nikolka, his thirteen-year-old helper, whose face was splotched with blue from frostbite—a complete ruffian judging from his expression—drove after us in the sleigh, urging the horses on in a hoarse voice.

"At the governor's, they'll probably punish you," Prokofy said to me on the way. "There's a governor's science, there's a bishop's science, there's an officer's science, and for every station, there's its own science. But you haven't stuck to your own science, and they'll never let you do that."

The slaughterhouse was behind the cemetery, and I had only seen it from a distance before. There were three murky sheds, surrounded by a gray fence, and a hot stifling stench came from them when the wind blew from that side on hot summer days. On entering the courtyard now, I could not see the sheds in the darkness. I kept coming across horses and sleighs, some empty, some already loaded with meat. People were walking about with lanterns and cursing repulsively. Prokofy and Nikolka swore too, equally nastily, and an incessant din hung in the air from the cursing, coughing, and neighing.

There was an odor of corpses and manure. It was thawing, the snow was already mixed with mud, and in the darkness I felt that I was walking in pools of blood.

After collecting a sleighful of meat, we set off for the butcher shop in the market. Dawn was breaking. Cooks with baskets and middle-aged women in cloaks passed one after the other. Prokofy, in a white blood-spattered apron with an ax in his hand, swearing frightfully, crossed himself in the direction of the church and shouted loudly to the whole market that he was giving his meat away at cost and even to his own loss. He cheated in weighing and giving change;

* Pepper vodka.

the cooks saw it, but deafened by his shouts, did not protest and just called him a hangman. Raising and dropping his terrifying ax, he assumed picturesque poses and uttered the sound "Gek!" with a ferocious expression each time; and I was afraid that he might actually cut off someone's head or hand.

I spent the whole morning in the butcher shop and when I went to the governor's at last, my fur coat smelled of meat and blood. My mental state was precisely as if someone had ordered me to go after a bear with a hunting pole. I remember the tall staircase with the striped carpet, and the young official in his shiny-buttoned frock coat who showed me the door silently, with both hands, and ran to announce me. I came into a reception hall luxuriously but coldly and tastelessly furnished, and the tall, narrow mirrors between the windows and the bright yellow curtains struck my eyes particularly disagreeably. It was obvious that although the governors changed, the furniture remained the same. The young official again indicated the door to me with both hands, and I walked toward a big green table behind which sat an army general with the Order of Vladimir around his neck.

"Monsieur Poloznev, I asked you to appear," he began, holding a note of some sort in his hand and opening his mouth wide and round like the letter o; "I asked you to appear to communicate the following to you. Your honored father turned to the marshal of the nobility orally and in writing, begging him to summon you and confront you with the total unsuitability of your conduct to the aristocratic status you have the honor to uphold. His Excellency Aleksandr Pavlovich, justly supposing that your conduct might serve as a temptation, and believing that persuasion on his part would be insufficient alone, and that a serious administrative intervention was essential, set before me in this letter his reflections concerning you, which I share."

He said this softly, respectfully, standing erect as if I were his superior, and looking at me not at all severely. His face was flabby, worn, and all wrinkled; bags hung under his eyes, he dyed his hair, and it was impossible to tell from his appearance how old he was—forty or sixty.

"I trust," he continued, "that you appreciate the delicacy of the respected Aleksandr Pavlovich, who turned to me in a private capacity, not officially. I also asked you to come unofficially, and am speaking to you not as a governor, but as a sincere admirer of your father. Thus, I ask you—either change

your conduct and return to the responsibilities proper to your
station, or, to avoid being a temptation, move to another place
where you are not known and where you can do whatever you
please. In case of the contrary, I shall be obliged to take extreme measures."

He stood in silence, open-mouthed, for half a minute, looking at me.

"Are you a vegetarian?" he asked.

"No, Your Excellency, I eat meat."

He sat down and drew a paper of some sort toward himself;
I bowed and left.

It was not worth while going to work before dinner. I went
home to sleep, but was unable to because of the disagreeable,
sickly feeling brought on by the slaughterhouse and my talk
with the governor, and after waiting for evening, upset and
gloomy, I went to see Marya Viktorovna. When I told how I
had been to the governor's, she looked at me in bewilderment
as if she did not believe it, then suddenly laughed merrily,
loudly, and passionately, as only goodhearted, laughter-loving
people can.

"If that were to be told in St. Petersburg!" she said, almost
falling with laughter and leaning over her table. "If that were
to be told in St. Petersburg!"

IX

We saw each other frequently now, once or twice a day.
She came to the cemetery almost daily after dinner and read
the epitaphs on the crosses and monuments while waiting for
me. Sometimes she went into the church and stood beside me
to watch me work. The silence, the naive work of the artists
and gilders, Radish's sober judgment, and the fact that I did
not look different from the other skilled workmen in any way
and, like them, worked in a vest and worn-out shoes, and that
they addressed me familiarly—all this was new to her and
touched her. Once, while she was there, the artist painting the
dove on the ceiling shouted to me: "Missail, hand up the
whiting!"

I brought him the whiting, and as I climbed down the
rickety scaffolding, she watched me, moved to tears, and
smiled.

"How nice you are!" she said.

I had a childhood recollection of how a green parrot belonging to one of our rich citizens had flown out of its cage, and how this beautiful bird had wandered throughout the town for a whole month, idly flying from garden to garden, lonely and homeless. Marya Viktorovna reminded me of this bird.

"Aside from the cemetery, I have absolutely no place to go now," she told me with a laugh. "The town bores me to the point of disgust. They are still reading, singing, and lisping at the Azhogins' house; I can't bear them lately. Your sister's unsociable, Mademoiselle Blagovo hates me for some reason or other, and I don't like the theater. Where would you have me go?"

When I called on her, I smelled of paint and turpentine, my hands were black—and this pleased her. She also wanted me to come to her house in just my usual working clothes, but these clothes embarrassed me in her drawing room; I became as flustered as if I had been in uniform, and therefore, when I dressed to visit her, I always put on my new serge suit. And this she did not like.

"You must confess you aren't completely at home in your new role," she said to me once. "Workmen's clothes embarrass you, you feel awkward in them. Tell me, isn't it because you have no conviction and aren't satisfied? The very kind of work you chose, this painting of yours—can it satisfy you?" she asked, laughing. "I know painting makes objects more beautiful and more durable, but you see, these objects belong to the townspeople, the rich, and in the final analysis, constitute a luxury. Moreover, you've said more than once yourself that everyone should earn his own bread with his own hands, yet you earn money, not bread. Why not stick literally to your words? One must earn bread itself, that is: plow, sow, reap, thresh, or do something that is directly connected with agriculture—herding cows, for instance, digging earth, building huts . . ."

She opened a pretty cupboard near her desk and said: "I'm saying all this to you because I want to let you in on my own secret. *Voilà!* This is my agricultural library. There's the field, the vegetable garden, the orchard, the cattle yard, and the apiary. I read greedily and I've learned everything to the last bit in theory. My dream, my sweet reverie, is to leave for our Dubechnya as soon as March comes. It's marvelous there, wonderful! Isn't it true? The first year, I'll look into the business and get used to it, and the next year, I'll start really working myself, not sparing the animal, as they say. Father promised to give me Dubechnya, and I'm going to do everything I want to in it."

Blushing, excited to tears and laughing, she dreamed aloud about the way she would live in Dubechnya and what an interesting life it would be. And I envied her. March was already near, the days were growing longer and longer, and on bright sunny noons, the roofs dripped and it smelled of spring; I longed for the country myself.

And when she said she was moving to Dubechnya to live, I vividly pictured myself staying in town alone, and I felt jealous of her with her cupboard of books and her agriculture. I neither knew about nor liked agriculture and was about to tell her that farming was a slavish occupation, when I remembered that my father had said something similar more than once, and I kept silent.

Lent started. Enginer Viktor Ivanich, whose existence I had almost forgotten, arrived from St. Petersburg. He came unexpectedly, without even forewarning by telegram. When I came as usual in the evening, he was there, shaved, washed, younger by ten years, walking around the drawing room and telling a story; his daughter was on her knees, removing boxes, flagons, and books from trunks and handing them all to the footman, Pavel. I involuntarily took a step backward on seeing the engineer, but he reached both hands out to me and said, smiling, showing his strong, white coachman's teeth: "Here he is, here he is! Very glad to see you, Master Painter! Masha has told me everything, she sang a whole panegyric to you. I fully understand you and approve!" he continued, taking me by the arm. "To be a good workman is vastly more intelligent and honest than using up the Treasury's paper and wearing a cockade on your forehead. I myself worked in Belgium with these very hands, then spent two years as a machinist . . ."

He was wearing a short jacket and house slippers; he walked like a man with gout, rolling slightly and rubbing his hands. Humming something, he purred softly, contracting with pleasure that he had at last returned home and been able to take his beloved shower.

"Indisputably," he said to me at supper, "indisputably you're all sweet, agreeable people, but for some reason, gentlemen, as soon as you take up physical labor or begin saving the peasant, it all comes down to sectarianism in the end. You're a sectar-

ian, aren't you? Look, you don't drink vodka. What's that if it
isn't sectarianism?"

To please him, I drank some vodka. I also drank some wine.
We tasted the cheese, sausages, pâtés, pickles, and the delicacies of every conceivable sort brought back by the engineer,
and the wines received from abroad during his absence. The
wines were superb. For some reason, the engineer received
wine and cigars from abroad duty-free; caviar and dried sturgeon were also sent him free by someone; he paid no rent
because the owner of the house supplied kerosene to the railway; and in general, he and his daughter gave me the impression of having the best of everything in the world at their
service and given to them completely free.

I continued to visit them, but no longer as eagerly. The engineer inhibited me and I felt as if tied hand and foot in his
presence. I could not bear his clear, innocent eyes; his reflections irritated and repelled me, and I was also irritated by the
recollection that I had been subordinate to this well-fed, ruddy
man so recently, and that he had been unmercifully rude to
me. True, he used to take me by the waist, clap me affectionately on the shoulder, and praise my way of life, but I felt he
despised my insignificance as before and tolerated me only to
oblige his daughter. I could no longer laugh and say what I
wanted to, and I kept aloof, always expecting him to turn
around and call me Pantalei as he did his footman, Pavel. How
my provincial, workman's pride rebelled. I, a proletarian, a
house painter, called daily on rich people, alien to me, whom
the whole town regarded as foreigners, and drank expensive
wines and ate extraordinary things at their house daily—my
conscience refused to be reconciled with this! When I was on
my way to their house, I would sullenly avoid meeting people
and glance around me from under my brows as if I actually
were a sectarian, and when I left the engineer's for home, I
would feel ashamed of my own satiety.

But above all I was afraid of being carried away. Whether I
was walking along the street, working, or talking with the
fellows, I thought only about how I would go to see Marya
Viktorovna in the evening, and I kept picturing her voice,
laugh, and bearing to myself. When I was getting ready to
visit her, I would always stand in front of the warped mirror
at Nurse's for a long time, knotting my tie; my serge suit
looked repulsive to me, and I suffered and simultaneously despised myself for being so petty. When she used to call to me

from the next room that she was not dressed and ask me to wait, I would hear her dressing; this agitated me; I felt as if the ground were giving way under me. And whenever I saw the figure of a woman in the street, even at a distance, I inevitably made a comparison. I felt then that all of our women and girls were vulgar, absurdly dressed, and did not know how to behave; and these comparisons aroused a feeling of pride in me: Marya Viktorovna was the best of them all! And at night I dreamed of her and myself.

At supper we once consumed a whole lobster with the engineer. Returning home afterward, I remembered that the engineer had called me "my dear friend" twice at dinner, and I reasoned that they treated me affectionately in that house like a big unhappy dog rejected by his own master; that they were amusing themselves with me, and when I became tiresome, would chase me out like a dog. I became ashamed and hurt, hurt to tears, as if I had been insulted, and looking at the sky, I swore to put an end to all this.

The following day I did not go to the Dolzhikovs'. Late in the evening, when it was quite dark and pouring rain, I walked down the Bolshoi Dvoryansky, looking at the windows. At the Azhogins' they were already asleep, except for a light burning in one of the far windows: that was old woman Azhogina embroidering by three candles in her room and imagining that she was fighting prejudice. Our house was dark, while in the Dolzhikovs' house across the street, the windows were lighted, but it was impossible to see through the flowers and curtains. I kept walking along the street; the cold March rain poured over me. I heard my father returning from the club; he knocked at the gates; a moment later, a light appeared in the window and I saw Sister, walking hurriedly with a lamp and straightening her thick hair with one hand as she went. Then Father paced from one end of the parlor to the other and talked about something, rubbing his hands, while Sister sat motionless in an armchair, thinking about something, not listening to him.

But now they left, the light went out . . . I glanced at the engineer's house—it was all dark too. In the darkness, in the rain, I felt hopelessly alone, tossed to the mercy of fate. I felt that compared to this loneliness of mine, compared to my present suffering and to what still lay before me in life, all my concerns were petty, all my desires, and everything I had thought and said up to then. Alas, the concerns and thoughts of living creatures are far from as significant as their sufferings! And without realizing clearly what I was doing, I pulled with all my strength on the bell of the Dolzhikovs' gate, tore it off, and ran down the street like a naughty boy, feeling terror and thinking that they would certainly come out any moment and recognize me. When I stopped at the end of the street to catch my breath, I could hear only the noise of the rain and the watchman banging on a piece of sheet iron far off somewhere.

I had not been to the Dolzhikovs' for a whole week. The serge suit was sold. There were no painting jobs and I was again half-starving, earning ten to twenty kopecks a day where I could, by heavy, disagreeable work. Wallowing up to my knees in cold mud, straining my chest, I wanted to stifle my memories and punish myself as it were for all the cheese and conserves to which I had been treated at the engineer's; but all the same, hardly had I lain down in bed, hungry and wet, when my sinful imagination would begin depicting marvelous, alluring pictures for me, and I would confess to myself with wonder that I was in love, passionately in love, and would sleep firmly and soundly, feeling that my body was growing stronger and younger every day from this convict's life.

One of those evenings, snow fell unseasonably and the north wind blew as if winter were beginning again. Returning from work that evening, I found Marya Viktorovna in my room. She was sitting in a fur coat, holding both hands in a muff.

"Why don't you visit me?" she asked, raising her intelligent, clear eyes, and I was intensely shaken by joy and stood at attention before her as I used to before my father when he was about to beat me. She looked me in the face, and I could see in her eyes that she understood why I was shaken.

"Why don't you visit me?" she repeated. "If you don't want to call, you see, I've come myself."

She stood up and came close to me.

"Don't abandon me," she said, and her eyes filled with tears. "I'm alone, I'm utterly alone!"

She began crying and continued, covering her face with her muff: "Alone! Life is hard for me, very hard, and I have no one in the whole world but you. Don't abandon me!"

Searching for her handkerchief to wipe away the tears, she smiled; we were silent for a time, then I embraced and kissed her, scratching my cheek on her hat pin till it bled as I did so.

And we began talking as if we had been close to one another since long, long ago . . .

X

Two days later she sent me to Dubechnya, and I was unutterably delighted by this. As I went to the station and afterward as I sat in the train, I laughed for no reason and people
looked at me as if I were drunk. Snow still fell and there was
frost in the mornings, but the roads had already turned darker
and rooks flew cawing above them.

I first intended to arrange a dwelling for us, for Masha and
me, in the side annex, opposite the annex of Madame Cheprakova, but it turned out that pigeons and ducks had inhabited it
for a long time, and it was impossible to clean without destroy-
ing a multitude of nests. Like it or not, we had to go to the
comfortless rooms of the big house with the jalousies. The
peasants called this the palace. It had over twenty rooms, but
the only furniture was a piano and a child's armchair, lying in
the attic, and if Masha had brought all her own furniture
from town, we still should not have been able to eliminate the
impression of gloomy emptiness and cold. I selected three
rather small rooms with windows on the garden and worked
on them from early morning till night, putting in new window
panes, pasting wallpaper, stopping up holes and crevices in
the floor. It was easy, pleasant work. I ran to the river constantly to see whether the ice was moving; I kept imagining
that the starlings were arriving. At night, thinking about
Masha, I listened with an ineffably sweet feeling, with an en-
veloping joy, to the noise of the rats and the droning and
knocking of the wind above the ceiling; it sounded like an old
house-demon coughing in the attic.

The snow was deep; much fell even at the end of March,
but it thawed quickly, as if by magic. The spring floods ran
furiously, so that by the beginning of April, the starlings were
already noisy and yellow butterflies were flying in the garden.
The weather was marvelous. I walked to town to meet Masha
every day toward evening, and what a pleasure it was to go
barefoot over the drying but still soft road!

Halfway, I used to sit down and look at the town, unable to
bring myself to go close to it. The sight of it disturbed me. I
kept thinking: How will my acquaintances treat me after learning about my love? What would Father say? I was particularly

disturbed by the thought that my life had become more complicated, and that I had completely lost the power to right it; that it was carrying me away God knows where like a balloon. I stopped thinking about how to earn my subsistence, how to live, and thought about—in truth, I don't remember what.

Masha used to arrive by carriage; I would get in with her and we would drive together to Dubechnya, gay and free. Or sometimes, after waiting till sunset, I would return home despondent, weary, wondering why Masha had not come, and at the yard gate or in the garden, I would be unexpectedly met by a sweet apparition—it was she! It would turn out that she had come by train and walked from the station. What a feast that was! In a simple wool dress, a little kerchief, with a modest umbrella, but laced, slender, in expensive, imported boots—she was a gifted actress playing a little shopgirl. We would look over our estate and decide which room would be which, and where we would have our alley, our vegetable garden, and our apiary. We already had hens, ducks, and geese, which we loved because they were ours. Everything was ready for the sowing of oats, clover, timothy, buckwheat, and vegetables, and we inspected it all each time and discussed at length what the harvest might be like, and everything Masha said to me struck me as exceptionally intelligent and fine. This was the happiest time of my life.

A little over a week after Easter, we were married in our parish church, in the village of Kurilovka, three versts from Dubechnya. Masha wanted everything to be done modestly; at her wish, our ushers were peasant lads, the deacon sang alone, and we returned from the church in a small, jolting buggy which she drove herself. Our only guest from town was my sister Cleopatra, whom Masha had invited by letter three days before the wedding. Sister wore a white dress and gloves. During the wedding, she cried quietly from emotion and joy; her expression was maternal and infinitely good. She was intoxicated by our happiness and smiled as if inhaling sweet odors, and as I watched her during the wedding, I realized that for her there was nothing on earth higher than love, earthly love, and that she dreamed of it secretly, timidly, but constantly and passionately. She embraced and kissed Masha, and not knowing how to express her ecstasy, said to her: "He's kind! He's very kind!"

Before leaving us, she changed into her everyday clothes and led me into the garden to talk privately.

"Father is very hurt that you didn't write him anything,"

she said; "you should have asked for his blessing. But, in reality, he's very satisfied. He says this marriage will raise you in the eyes of all society and that under Marya Viktorovna's influence, you will take life more seriously. We talk of nothing but you in the evenings now, and yesterday he even used the words: 'Our Missail.' That delighted me. He seems to be planning something, and I think he wants to show you a magnanimous example and be the first to speak of reconciliation. It's entirely possible that he'll come here to see you one of these days."

She made the sign of the cross over me hastily several times and said: "Well, God be with you; be happy. Anyuta Blagovo is a very clever girl; she says of your marriage that God is sending you a new trial. Why not? There aren't just joys in married life, but suffering too. Bound to be."

Masha and I escorted her three versts on foot; returning afterward, we walked slowly and silently, as if resting. Masha held my hand, my heart was light, and the desire to talk about love no longer existed. The wedding had made us closer and more akin to one another, and we felt that nothing could separate us now.

"Your sister is a sweet creature," said Masha, "but it's as if she had been tormented for a long time. Your father must be a terrible person."

I began telling her how my sister and I had been educated, and how tormented and senseless our childhood had, in fact, been. When she learned that Father had beaten me so recently, she shuddered and pressed close to me.

"Don't tell me any more," she said. "It's horrible."

Now she never left my side. We lived in the big house, in three rooms, and in the evenings, tightly bolted the door leading into the empty part of the house as if someone we did not know and feared lived there. I got up early, at dawn, and immediately started to work. I repaired the carts, made paths in the garden, dug flower beds, painted the roof of the house. When the time came to sow oats, I tried doing the second plowing, the harrowing, and the sowing, and did it all conscientiously, never falling behind the hired man; the rain and cutting, cold wind exhausted me and made my face and legs burn for a long time; I used to dream of plowed land at night. But work on the land did not attract me. I neither understood nor liked farming, perhaps because my ancestors were not farmers and pure city blood flowed in my veins. Nature I loved tenderly; I loved the fields, the meadows, the vegetable gardens, but the peasant, turning the soil with his plow, driving on his pitiful, broken-down, wet horse with its outstretched neck, was to me a manifestation of a crude, wild, ugly force, and watching his clumsy movements involuntarily made me think of the remote, legendary life before men knew the use of fire. The fierce bull in the peasants' herd, and the horses, when they rushed through the village with stamping hoofs, frightened me, and everything somewhat big, strong, and fierce, whether a horned ram, a gander, or a watchdog, was to me a manifestation of this same crude, savage force. This prejudice affected me particularly strongly in bad weather when heavy clouds hung over the black plowed fields. Most important of all, when I was plowing or sowing with two or three people standing by to watch how I did it, I had no consciousness of the compulsoriness and inevitability of this work, and I felt as if I were merely playing. I preferred doing something in the yard and liked nothing so much as painting the roof.

I used to walk through the garden and the field to our mill. It was rented by Stepan, a peasant from Kurilovka: handsome, swarthy, and robust-looking, with a thick black beard. He disliked miller's work, which he considered tiresome and unprofitable, and lived at the mill solely to avoid living at home. He was a harnessmaker, and there was always a pleasant smell of resin and leather around him. He did not like to talk, was listless and inert, and constantly chanted "U-lyu-lyu-lyu" as he sat on the riverbank or the threshold of the mill. Sometimes his wife and mother-in-law, both pale, languid, and meek, visited him from Kurilovka. They bowed deeply to him and called him "Stepan Petrovich," addressing him formally. And he would sit apart on the bank without answering their bows by word or movement and softly chant: "U-lyu-lyu-lyu." An hour or two would pass in silence. His mother-in-law and wife, after exchanging whispers, would stand up and gaze at him for a while, waiting for him to look around, then bow low and say in sweet, singsong voices: "Good-by, Stepan Petrovich!"

And they would leave. Afterward, having put away the bundle containing biscuits or a shirt they had left him, Stepan would sigh and say, winking in their direction: "The feminine sex!"

The mill worked day and night with two millstones. I used to help Stepan; I enjoyed it, and when he went off somewhere, I was delighted to take his place.

XI

After the bright warm weather came the season of bad roads; rain fell throughout May; it was cold. The sound of the mill wheels and the rain induced laziness and sleepiness. The floor trembled, there was a smell of flour, and this also brought on drowsiness. My wife appeared twice a day in a short fur coat and high peasant galoshes and always said the very same thing: "And this is called summer! It's worse than October!"

We drank tea together, cooked *kasha,* or sat for hours at a time in silence, waiting for the rain to stop. Once, when Stepan went off somewhere to market, Masha spent the whole night at the mill. When we got up, it was impossible to tell what time it was, the whole sky was so overcast with rain clouds, but the sleepy roosters were crowing in Dubechnya and the crakes were calling in the meadow; it was still very, very early . . . My wife and I went down to the pond and drew up the creel Stepan had cast for us the day before. There was a big bass struggling in it and a crayfish bristling, waving his claws overhead.

"Let them go," said Masha. "Let them be happy too."

Because we had gotten up very early and then done nothing, the day seemed very long, the longest in my life. Toward evening Stepan came back and I went home to the estate.

"Your father came today," Masha told me.

"Where is he?" I asked.

"He left. I didn't receive him."

When she saw me standing in silence, saw that I was sorry for my father, she said: "One must be consistent. I didn't receive him and had him told not to bother us again and not to come to see us."

A minute later I was already beyond the gates and on my way to town on foot to explain to Father. It was muddy, slippery, cold. For the first time since our wedding, I felt depressed; the thought entered my mind, wearied by the long gray day, that perhaps I was not living as I should. I was exhausted; faintheartedness and laziness gradually overpowered me. I did not feel like moving or thinking, and after continuing for a while, I threw up my hands and turned back.

The engineer, wearing a hooded leather overcoat, was standing in the middle of the courtyard and saying loudly: "Where's the furniture? There was fine furniture, Empire style, there were pictures, there were vases, and now you could play ball in there. I bought the place with furniture, devil take her!"

Beside him, mashing his hat in his hands, stood the general's widow's hired man, Moisei, a lad of twenty-five, thin, pock-marked, with tiny, impudent eyes; one of his cheeks was larger than the other as if he had overslept on it.

"Your honor was pleased to buy the place without furniture," he said hesitantly. "I remember, sir."

"Shut up!" shouted the engineer. He turned purple, quivered, and the echo in the garden loudly repeated his shout.

XII

Whenever I did anything in the garden or the yard, Moisei would stand nearby, his hands behind his back, watching me lazily and impudently with his tiny eyes. And this used to irritate me so much that I would throw the work aside and leave.

We learned from Stepan that Moisei was Madame Cheprakova's lover. I noticed that when people came to her to borrow money, they addressed Moisei first, and once I saw one peasant, black from head to foot—probably a charcoal burner—bow to Moisei's feet. Sometimes, after a whispered exchange, he would hand out the money himself without telling his mistress, from which I concluded that he occasionally did business independently, on his own account.

He used to shoot near our windows in our garden, take food out of our cellar, and use our horses without asking. We were indignant. We stopped feeling that Dubechnya was ours, and Masha used to say, pale-faced: "Must we live with this rabble for a year and a half more?"

Madame Cheprakova's son, Ivan, worked as a conductor on our railroad. He had grown much thinner and weaker during the winter and now got drunk on a single glass and shivered in the shade. He wore his conductor's uniform with loathing and was ashamed of it, but considered his post profitable because he was able to steal candles and sell them. My new position aroused in him a mixed feeling of astonishment, envy, and a vague hope that something similar might happen to him, too. He followed Masha with enraptured eyes, asked me what

I had for supper now; a sweet melancholy expression would appear on his gaunt, homely face, and he would move his fingers as if he were touching my happiness.

"Listen, Small Pickings," he said fussily, relighting his cigarette every minute; there was always a litter wherever he stood because he used to use a dozen matches on one cigarette. "Listen, my life couldn't be fouler now. The worst is that any underling can shout: 'Hey, conductor! Hey you!' I've overheard a hodgepodge of things in the train and you know, I've realized it's a filthy life! My mother ruined me! A doctor on the train told me that if parents are dissolute, their children turn out drunks or criminals. There's something for you!"

One day he came staggering into the courtyard. His eyes wandered senselessly, his breathing was belabored; he laughed, cried, and babbled as if in a delirium, and in his muddled talk all I could understand were the words: "My mother! Where's my mother?" which he uttered with the wail of a child who has lost his mother in a crowd. I led him into our garden and laid him down under a tree, and Masha and I took turns sitting with him all that day and night. He was miserable, but Masha looked with distaste at his pale, wet face and said: "Is this rabble going to go on living in our courtyard a year and a half more? It's horrible! It's horrible!"

And how many mortifications the peasants caused us! How many painful disappointments in the beginning, in the spring months, when there was such longing to be happy! My wife was having a school built. I drew the plan of a school for sixty little boys and the local administration approved it, but recommended building the school in Kurilovka, the big village three versts from us. It happened that the Kurilovka school, in which children from four villages including our Dubechnya studied, was old and crowded, and the rotted floor had to be walked on with caution. At the end of March, Masha was appointed the trustee of the Kurilovka school at her own wish, and in the beginning of April we called three meetings to try to persuade the peasants that their present school was crowded and old, and that building a new one was necessary. A member of the local administration and the inspector of public schools also came to persuade them. After every meeting, we were surrounded and asked to give a bucket of vodka; it was hot in the crowd and we were quickly exhausted, and used to return home dissatisfied and somewhat disconcerted. In the end, the peasants allotted land for the school and pledged themselves to fetch all the building material from town with their own horses. And as soon as they had taken care of the spring corn, on the first Sunday, carts set off from Kurilovka and Dubechnya after bricks for the foundation. They left when it was barely light and returned late in the evening; the peasants were drunk and said they were exhausted.

As if to spite us, the rain and cold continued throughout May. The road was impaired and turned into mud. The carts usually turned into our courtyard on their way from town—and what a horror that was! A horse would appear at the gates with spreading forelegs, potbellied; it would stumble as if bowing as it came into the yard; in would crawl a thirty-foot beam, wet and slimy-looking, on a wagon; alongside it, wrapped up against the rain, not watching his feet, not avoiding puddles, would come a peasant with his coat tails tucked in his belt. Another wagon would appear with boards, then a third with a beam, a fourth . . . and the space in front of the house was gradually jammed with horses, beams, and planks. The peasant men and women, with muffled voices and tucked-up clothes, glared malevolently at our windows, noisily demanding that the mistress come out to them; coarse cursing could be heard. Moisei used to stand on the sidelines and it seemed to us that he enjoyed our degradation.

"We're not carting any more!" the men used to cry. "We're worn out! Let her go cart herself!"

Masha, pale, cowed, thinking they would break into the house any minute, would send out half a pail of vodka; after that, the noise would diminish, and the long beams would crawl back out of the yard one by one.

When I was about to visit the construction site, my wife became anxious and said: "The peasants are furious. If only they don't do something to you. No, wait, I'll go with you."

We drove together to Kurilovka, where the carpenters asked us for a tip. The framework was already completed and was ready for the laying of the foundation, but the masons had not come; a delay had resulted and the carpenters were grumbling. But when the masons came at last, it turned out that there was no sand. The need for it had somehow been overlooked. Taking advantage of our helpless position, the peasants demanded thirty kopecks a load, although it was not four versts from the building site to the river where they collected sand, and a total of over five hundred wagonloads were required. There was no end to the misunderstandings, the cursing and begging; my wife became indignant and the head mason, Tit Petrov, an old man of seventy, took her by the arm and said:

"You look here! You look here! You just bring me sand; I'll bring in ten men immediately and it'll be ready in two days! You look here!"

But after the sand was brought, two, then four days, then a week went by, and a pit still gaped on the site of the future foundation.

"You could go out of your mind!" my wife said heatedly. "What people! What people!"

In the midst of this chaos, Engineer Viktor Ivanich came to visit us. He brought sacks of wine and delicacies with him, ate lengthily, then lay down to sleep on the terrace and snored so loudly that the workers nodded their heads and said: "Upon my soul!"

Masha was not pleased at his coming. She did not have confidence in him, but listened to his advice nevertheless. When he woke up in a bad mood after sleeping too long after dinner, and made unpleasant remarks about our management or expressed regret at having bought Dubechnya, which was only bringing him losses, poor Masha's face would look anguished. When she complained to him, he would yawn and say peasants had to be flogged.

He called our marriage and our life a farce; he used to say it was a caprice, an indulgence.

"Something similar already happened to her once," he told me of Masha. "She once fancied herself an opera singer and left me; I looked for her for two months and, my dear friend, spent a thousand rubles on telegrams alone."

He no longer called me a sectarian or Master Painter, nor spoke of my worker's life with approval as before, but would say: "You're a strange person! You're an abnormal person! I won't venture a prediction, but you'll end badly, sir!"

Masha, meanwhile, slept poorly at night and used to sit at our bedroom window lost in thought. There was no more laughter or charming grimaces at supper. I suffered, and when the rain fell, every drop cut into my heart like small shot and I was ready to fall on my knees before Masha and apologize for the weather. I felt guilty, too, when the peasants made an uproar in the courtyard. I used to sit in one spot for hours at a time, thinking only about what a magnificent person Masha was, what a marvelous person. I loved her passionately, and was captivated by everything she did, everything she said. She had a penchant for quiet, studious occupations; she loved to read for hours, to study something. Although she only knew agriculture from books, she amazed us all with her information, and all the advice she gave was useful; none of it was wasted. And in everything there was such nobility, taste, and serenity, that serenity found only among very well-educated people!

For this woman with her healthy, positive mind, the disorderly surroundings filled with petty worries and ugliness in which we now lived were painful. I could see this and was unable to sleep at night myself; my mind churned and tears came into my throat. I used to rush about without knowing what to do.

I galloped to town to bring Masha books, papers, sweets, and flowers. Along with Stepan, I fished, wandering for hours on end up to my neck in cold water in the rain to catch a turbot and vary our fare. I humbly begged the peasants not to make noise, gave them vodka, bribed them, made them all sorts of promises. And how many other foolish things I did!

At last the rain stopped; the ground dried. You would get up in the morning around four o'clock and go out in the garden—the dew glittered on the flowers, there was a buzzing of birds and insects and not a cloud in the sky; and the garden, the meadow, and the river were so beautiful—but there were those recollections of the peasants, of the carts, of the engineer! Masha and I drove to the fields together in the racing droshky to look at the oats. She drove while I sat in back; her shoulders were raised and the wind played with her hair.

"Keep right!" she would shout to someone passing by.

"You're like a coachman!" I told her once.

"Well, perhaps! You see, my grandfather, the engineer's father, was a coachman. Didn't you know that?" she asked, turning to me, and thereupon she imitated the way coachmen shout and sing.

"Glory to God!" I thought, listening to her. "Glory to God!"

And again came the recollections of the peasants, of the carts, of the engineer . . .

XIII

Dr. Blagovo arrived on his cycle. Sister began visiting often. Again there were discussions about manual labor, about progress, about the mysterious x awaiting humanity in the remote future. The doctor disliked our farming because it interfered with our discussions, and he said that plowing, reaping, and grazing cattle were unworthy of a free man, and that in time people would relegate all these coarse aspects of the struggle for existence to animals and machines, while they concerned themselves solely with scientific investigations. My sister was always begging to be allowed to go home earlier, and if she stayed till a late hour or spent the night, there was no end to the agitation.

"My God, what a child you still are!" Masha said with reproach. "It's positively ridiculous."

"Yes, it's ridiculous!" Sister agreed. "I realize it's ridiculous, but what can I do if I haven't the strength to master myself? I always feel I'm behaving badly."

At haymaking time, my whole body ached from the unaccustomed work; while sitting, talking on the terrace in the evenings with my guests, I used to suddenly fall asleep, and they would laugh loudly at me. They would wake me up and sit me at the table to have supper; drowsiness would overcome me, and I would see lights, faces, and plates, and hear voices without understanding them, as if half-dozing. But when I got up early in the morning, I would immediately start reaping or walk out to the construction site and work the whole day.

When I stayed home on holidays, I noticed that my wife and sister were hiding something from me and even seemed to be avoiding me. My wife was tender with me as before, but she had private thoughts of some kind which she did not tell me. It was certain that her irritation with the peasants was growing, that life was becoming harder and harder for her, yet she no longer complained to me. She talked more readily to the doctor than to me, and I had no idea why this was so.

It was the custom in our province for the farmhands to come to the manor house at haymaking and harvest time to be treated to vodka; even the young girls had a glass each. We did not keep up the practice, and the reapers and peasant women used to stand in our courtyard until late in the evening waiting for vodka, and then walk away cursing. Meanwhile Masha would frown grimly in silence or say softly to the doctor with exasperation: "Savages! Pechenegs!"

Newcomers were rudely received in the village, almost belligerently, like new arrivals at school. We were received the same way. At first they regarded us as stupid and simpleminded people who had bought themselves an estate simply because they had nothing to do with their money. They laughed at us. The peasants pastured their cattle in our woods and even in our garden; they drove our cows and horses onto their own land in the village and then came to demand damages. Whole communities came into our courtyard and noisily claimed that we had mowed hay somewhere or other on land belonging to the village of Bysheevka or the village of Semonikha, and since we did not know the precise boundaries of our property, we used to take them at their word and pay the fine; later we would learn that we had been mowing on our own property. They stripped the bark off the linden trees in our woods. One peasant from Dubechnya, a sharper who sold vodka without a license, bribed our hired men and swindled us with their aid in the most underhanded ways: they used to exchange the new wheels on our carts for old ones, take our plowing harnesses and sell them back to us, and so forth. But what hurt most was what went on in the construction at Kurilovka. The peasant women used to steal scantling, bricks, tiles, and scraps of iron nightly; the elder searched their huts with witnesses, the town meeting fined each one two rubles, and then the penalty money was drunk up by the whole community.

When Masha learned of this, she remarked to the doctor or to my sister with indignation: "What animals! It's a horror! A horror!"

And more than once I heard her express regret that she had thought of building a school.

"Understand," the doctor said in an effort to convince her; "understand that if you build this school and do good generally, it isn't for the peasants, but in the name of culture, in the name of the future. And the worse the peasants are, the more reason for building the school. Try to understand!"

There was uncertainty in his voice, however, and it seemed to me that both he and Masha detested the peasants.

Masha often walked over to the mill and took my sister along; the two used to say laughingly that they went to watch Stepan because he was so handsome. Stepan, it turned out, was sluggish and untalkative only with men; in feminine society he was relaxed and talked without stopping. Once, coming to the river to bathe, I accidentally overheard one of their conversations. Masha and Cleopatra, both in white dresses, were sitting on the bank in the broad shade of the willow while Stepan stood nearby with his hands behind his back, saying: "Can peasants be people? They're not people but, forgive me, beasts, charlatans. What's a peasant's life? Just eating and drinking, wishing victuals'd be cheaper, and bawling in the tavern; and you don't have any good conversation or manners or formality, but just ignorance! He lives in filth and his wife lives in filth and his children live in filth, and he'll lie down in whatever he has on, pick potatoes out of his cabbage soup right with his fingers, drink kvass with a cockroach in it—not even blowing it away!"

"It's the poverty, of course!" Sister put in.

"What do you mean, poverty! There's need, sure, but you see not all needs are the same, my lady. Here if a man's sitting in irons, or, let's say, is blind, or legless, well, God spare anybody that, really! But if he's free, in his right mind, has his eyes and hands and his strength, by God, what more does he need? It's coddling, my lady, it's ignorance, not poverty. If you good people here, let's say, because of your upbringing, want to do something useful for him out of kindness, he'll drink up your money out of spite or, what's worse, open up a tavern and start robbing people on your money. You were pleased to say it's poverty. But does the rich peasant live any better? Also like swine, if you'll excuse me. Clodhopper, brawler, blockhead, wider than he is long, swollen-mugged, red-faced—makes you want to pull back and swat him, the wretch. Take Larion of Dubechnya, he's rich, too, but probably as good at stripping the linden in your woods as the poor man; and he's a brawler, and his children are brawlers, and when he drinks too much, he falls nose down in a puddle and sleeps. All worthless, my lady. Living with them in the village is just like living in hell. It's stuck in my throat, that village, and I thank the Lord, the heavenly Tsar, that I can feed and clothe myself, and that I've served my time in the dragoons, spent three years as village elder, and I'm a free Cossack now: I live where I want to. I don't want to live in the village and no one has the right to make me. What do they say about my wife: they say, you've got to live in a hut with your wife. And why so? I'm not hired to her."

"Tell me, Stepan, did you marry for love?" asked Masha.

"What's love in our village?" Stepan answered and snickered. "If you really want to know, my lady, I was married twice. I'm not from Kurilovka, but Zalegoshcho, and they took me as a son-in-law in Kurilovka later. That is, my father didn't want to divide up among us—we were five brothers in all, and I said good-by and was the one to move to a strange village, to my wife's family. But my first wife died young."

"What from?"

"From stupidity. She used to cry, cry all the time and she

cried without stopping, so she pined away. She kept drinking some kind of grass teas to grow prettier, and she must have hurt her insides. And my second wife, the Kurilovka one— what's there to her? She's a village woman, a peasant, and nothing more. When I got engaged to her, I was attracted: I'm thinking, she's young, fair, lives a clean life. Her mother's some kind of Khlystovian * and drinks coffee, but the important thing, that is, is they live clean. So I got married and sat down the next day to have dinner. I order my mother-in-law to give me a spoon and she gives me a spoon and I see her wipe it on her finger. There you have it, I think: fine cleanliness in your house. I lived with them a year and left. Maybe I should have married a town woman," he continued after a silence. "They say a wife's a husband's helper. What do I need a helper for? I can help myself, and it's better to have someone to talk to, not like that, always tee-tee-tee-tee, but specifically, with feeling. What's life without good conversation!"

Stepan suddenly fell silent, and I immediately heard his tiresome, monotonous "U-lyu-lyu-lyu." That meant he had caught sight of me.

Masha visited the mill frequently and obviously enjoyed talking to Stepan; Stepan cursed the peasants so sincerely and decisively—and this attracted her to him. When she returned from the mill, the idiot-peasant who watched over the garden always shouted after her: "Miss Palashka! Well done, Miss Palashka!" and would bark like a dog after her: "Gav! Gav!"

And she would stop and look at him attentively as if she found a response to her thoughts in this idiot's bark, and he probably attracted her in the same way that Stepan did. At home there would be some news awaiting her such as, for example, that the village geese had rifled the cabbage in our vegetable garden, or that Larion had stolen the reins, and she would say with a grin, shrugging her shoulders: "What can you expect from these people!"

She was exasperated, distaste was mounting in her, while I was becoming used to the peasants and more and more drawn to them. For the most part they were nervous, irritated, abused people; they were people of stifled imagination, ignorant, with a poor, dim field of vision, whose thoughts were always the same: about the gray earth, the gray days, black bread; people who were wily but, like birds, hid only their heads behind the tree—who were incapable of calculating. They wouldn't go to

* Member of a Russian religious sect that repudiates the established church and the priesthood.

harvest your hay for twenty rubles, but for a half pail of vodka, although they could have bought four pails for twenty rubles. There was, in fact, filth and drunkenness and stupidity and deceit, but still, along with all this, you had the feeling that, on the whole, the peasants' life kept a kind of solid, healthy core. No matter how crude a beast the peasant might seem as he walked behind his plow, and no matter how he stupefied himself with vodka, still, when you took a closer look at him, you felt there was something essential and very important in him—which was not to be found, for example, in Masha and in the doctor—and that was his belief that truth is the most important thing on earth, that his salvation and that of all people lies in truth alone; and his consequent love of justice above anything else on earth. I used to tell my wife that she saw the spots on the glass, but not the glass itself; she would be silent in response, or sing, like Stepan: "U-lyu-lyu-lyu" . . . When this kind, intelligent woman turned pale with indignation and spoke to the doctor with a tremor in her voice about drunkenness and swindling, it puzzled me, and her forgetfulness struck me. How could she forget that her father the engineer also drank, drank heavily, and that the money with which Dubechnya had been bought was acquired through a whole series of bold, unscrupulous frauds? How could she forget?

XIV

My sister was also living a life of her own which she carefully hid from me. She frequently exchanged whispers with Masha. When I came near her, she would shrink, and her eyes would become guilty, imploring; something obviously was happening in her heart of which she was afraid or ashamed. To avoid meeting me in the garden or being left alone with me, she stayed close to Masha at all times, and I rarely had a chance to talk to her except at dinner.

One evening I was walking quietly through the garden on my way back from the building site. It was already growing dark. Without noticing me or hearing my footsteps, my sister was walking near the broad old apple tree utterly noiselessly, as if she were a phantom. She was dressed in black and walked swiftly back and forth, always in the same line, looking at the ground. An apple fell from the tree; she shuddered at the sound, stopped, and pressed her hands to her temples. At that moment I went up to her.

In the burst of tender love which suddenly poured into my heart, reminded for some reason of our mother and our childhood, I put my arm around her shoulders and kissed her.

"What's wrong with you?" I asked. "You're suffering, I saw it long ago. Tell me, what's wrong with you?"

"I'm afraid . . ." she said, trembling.

"What is wrong with you?" I tried again. "For God's sake, be frank!"

"I will, I will be frank, I'll tell you the whole truth. Hiding from you—it's so painful, so agonizing! Missail, I'm in love . . ." she continued in a whisper. "I'm in love, I'm in love . . . I'm happy, but why am I so afraid!"

There were footsteps; Dr. Blagovo appeared between the trees in a silk shirt and high boots. Obviously, here near the apple tree was their chosen meeting place. On seeing him, she rushed impetuously toward him, with a sickly cry as if he were being taken away from her: "Vladimir! Vladimir!"

She pressed close to him and looked eagerly into his face, and it was only then that I noticed how much thinner and paler she had grown recently. This change was particularly marked by her lace collar, long familiar to me, which now hung more loosely than before around her long thin neck. The doctor was flustered, but immediately recovered himself and said, stroking her hair: "Come, enough, enough . . . Why so nervous? You see, I came."

We were silent, looking at one another bashfully. Then the three of us walked on together, and I heard the doctor say to me: "Cultured life hasn't yet begun for us. The old men console themselves that if there is nothing now, at least there was something in the forties or sixties; but that's the old men. You and I are young, our brains haven't been touched by *marasmus senilis* * yet, we can't console ourselves with such illusions. Russia's beginning was in 862, but the beginning of cultural Russia, as I understand it, hasn't come yet."

But I was not participating in these reflections. It was somehow strange—it was hard to believe—that my sister was in love, that here she was, walking, holding a stranger's hand and looking tenderly at him. My sister, this nervous, frightened, downtrodden, captive creature, loved someone who was already married and had children! I felt pity for something,

* Senility.

but for just what—I do not know; the doctor's presence was disagreeable now for some reason, and I was completely unable to conceive what could come of this love of theirs.

◇◇◇◇◇◇◇◇◇◇◇◇◇◇◇◇◇◇◇◇◇◇◇◇◇◇◇◇◇◇◇◇◇◇

XV

Masha and I drove to the dedication of the school in Kurilovka.

"Fall, fall, fall . . ." Masha said softly, looking around. "Summer's past. No birds now, and the only green is the willows."

Yes, summer was already past. The days were bright, warm, but fresh in the mornings; the shepherds were already wearing sheepskin coats, and the dew on the asters in our garden was not dry by the end of the day. Plaintive sounds were heard continuously, and you couldn't figure out whether it was the shutters creaking on their rusty hinges or cranes flying—and you felt good in your soul and so eager for life!

"Summer's passed . . ." said Masha. "Now you and I can balance our accounts. We've worked a lot, thought a lot, we're the better for it—honor and glory to us—we've succeeded in improving ourselves, but have these successes of ours had a perceptible influence on life around us? Have they benefited anyone whatsoever? No. Ignorance, physical filth, drunkenness, an astonishingly high infantile mortality rate—everything has remained as it was, and no one is the better for your having plowed and sowed and my having spent money and read books. Obviously we were working only for ourselves, and thought only for ourselves."

This sort of reasoning wearied me and left me not knowing what to think.

"We were sincere from beginning to end," I said, "and anyone who's sincere is right."

"Who's arguing? We were right, but we were wrong in the way we realized what we were right about. First of all, take our outward behavior—isn't that wrong? You want to be useful to people, but by just buying an estate, you bar any possibility of doing something useful for them from the outset. However, if you work, dress, and eat like a peasant, you sort of sanction the heavy, awkward clothing, horrible huts, and those stupid beards with your own authority . . . On the other hand, let us assume you work a long time, a very long time, your whole life, and that in the end you have some kind of practical results, but these results of yours— what can they do against such elemental forces as wholesale ignorance, hunger, cold, degeneration? It's a drop in the ocean! Other methods of fighting are needed here: strong, bold, quick! If you really want to be useful, you have to get out of this narrow circle of the usual activities and try to have an immediate effect on the mass. First of all you need a loud, rousing sermon. Why are art and music, for instance, so vital, so popular, and actually so powerful? Why, because the musician or singer has an immediate effect on thousands. Sweet, sweet art!" she continued, looking dreamily at the sky. "Art gives wings and carries one far off, far off! Anyone who is tired of filth, of cheap, petty interests, who is revolted, hurt, and indignant, can find peace and satisfaction only in the beautiful."

When we drove up to Kurilovka, the weather was bright and joyous. They were threshing in the courtyard; there was a smell of rye straw. Behind the wattle fences, the sorbs were turning crimson, and wherever you looked, all the trees were golden or red. They were ringing bells in the tower, carrying images to the school, and one could hear them singing: "Ardent intercessor." And what transparent air; how high the doves were flying!

Mass was held in the classroom. Then the peasants from Kurilovka brought Masha an icon, and those from Dubechnya brought a big twisted loaf of bread and a gilded salt cellar. And Masha burst into sobs.

"And if anything unnecessary was said, or there was anything unsatisfactory, forgive it," said one old man as he bowed to her and to me.

As we drove home, Masha glanced around at the school; we could see the green roof I had painted glistening in the sun for a long time. And I felt that Masha's backward glances were in farewell.

<hr />

XVI

That evening she got ready to go to town.

She had driven to town often lately and spent the night there. I was unable to work in her absence; my hands slackened and weakened; our big courtyard seemed dreary, a loathsome emptiness; the garden clamored angrily, and without her, the house, the trees, and the horses were no longer "ours" for me.

I did not leave the house and sat at her table, near her cupboard with the agricultural books, those former favorites now no longer needed, which looked at me so perplexedly. For hour after hour, until it was seven, eight, nine o'clock, until the autumn night fell beyond the windows, black as soot, I would examine her old glove or the pen with which she always wrote or her tiny scissors. I did nothing and realized clearly that anything I had done before—plowing, mowing, chopping—was only because she wanted it. If she had sent me to clean a deep well in which I stood up to my waist in water, I would have crawled into the well without considering whether it was necessary or not. And now that she was away, Dubechnya with its debris and disorder, with its flapping shutters, its thieves day and night, seemed to me a chaos in which all work was useless. Yes, and why should I work there, why should I worry and think of the future when I felt the ground going from under me—felt that my role here in Dubechnya was played out; that, in sum, the very same fate awaited me that had overtaken the books on agriculture? Oh, what anguish the hours of solitude were at night, when I listened anxiously every minute as if waiting for someone to cry out that it was time I left. I did not regret Dubechnya; I regretted my love whose own autumn had evidently begun. What supreme happiness it is to love and be loved, and how horrible to feel that you are beginning to slip off that pinnacle!

Masha came back from town the next day toward evening. She was annoyed about something, but hid it and merely said why were all the storm windows put up—it was enough to suffocate one. I took out two of the storm windows. We did not feel like eating, but sat down to supper.

"Go wash your hands," said my wife. "You smell of putty."

She had brought some new illustrated magazines from town and we looked through them together after supper. There were supplements with fashion pictures and patterns. Masha glanced at them briefly and put them aside to be examined in detail, properly; but one dress with a wide smooth skirt like a bell and big sleeves interested her, and she looked at it seriously and attentively for a minute.

"That's not bad," she said.

"Yes, that dress would suit you very well!" I said. "Very!"

And looking at the dress with emotion, admiring this gray patch only because she liked it, I went on tenderly: "A wonderful, delightful dress! Splendid, magnificent Masha! My darling Masha!"

And tears dropped onto the illustration.

"Magnificent Masha . . ." I muttered. "Sweet, darling Masha . . ."

She went to bed while I sat and looked at the illustrations for another hour.

"Too bad you took the storm windows off," she said from the bedroom. "I'm afraid it's going to be cold. Listen to it starting to blow!"

I read something in the "miscellany"—about the preparation of cheap ink and the largest diamond in the world. I again came across the fashion illustration with the dress she had liked, and I imagined her at a ball with a fan, bare-shouldered, dazzling, elegant, well-informed about music, painting, and literature; and how small and dwarfed my role seemed to me.

Our meeting, and this marriage of ours, was only an episode, of which there would be quite a few more in the life of this vital, richly endowed woman. All the best in the world, as I have already said, was at her service and given her completely free, and even ideas and fashionable intellectual movements served her pleasure, varying her life, while I was only the coachman who had transported her from one distraction to another. Now she no longer needed me; she would flit away, and I should be left alone.

As if in response to my thoughts, a despairing cry rang out in the courtyard: "He-e-elp!"

It was a thin, womanish voice and, in mockery, the wind blew in the chimney in a thin voice too. Half a minute went by, and again, through the noise of the wind, but now as if it came from the other end of the courtyard, I heard: "He-e-elp!"

"Missail, do you hear that?" my wife asked softly. "Do you hear that?"

She came out of the bedroom to me in just her nightgown with her hair down and listened, looking out the dark window.

"Someone's being choked!" she said. "That's all we needed!"

I took my rifle and went out. It was very dark in the courtyard; such a strong wind was blowing that it was hard to stand up. I walked over to the gate and listened: the trees roared, the wind whistled, and in the garden, a dog, probably belonging to the idiot-peasant, was howling lazily. There was total darkness beyond the gate; not one light on the rail line. Near the annex which had housed the office the year before, a smothered cry suddenly rang out: "He-e-elp!"

"Who's there?" I called.

Two men were struggling, one pushing while the other resisted, and both were panting heavily.

"Let go!" said one, and I recognized Ivan Cheprakov; he was the one shouting in a thin, womanish voice. "Let go, wretch, or I'll bite off your hand!"

In the other, I recognized Moisei. I separated them, and unable to restrain myself, hit Moisei in the face twice. He fell down, got up, and I hit him once again.

"He wanted to kill me," he muttered. "He was stealing from Mamasha's chest of drawers . . . I want to lock him up in the annex for security."

Cheprakov was drunk, did not recognize me, and kept inhaling deeply, as if gathering wind to shout for help again.

I left them and went back to the house; my wife was lying on the bed, already dressed. I told her what had happened in the courtyard, and did not hide that I had beaten Moisei.

"It's frightful living in the country," she said. "And what a long night, heaven take it."

"He-e-elp!" was heard again after a short pause.

"I'll go catch them," I said.

"No, let them chew each other into bits," she said with a disgusted expression.

She stared at the ceiling and listened, while I sat nearby, not daring to speak to her and feeling as if I were to blame for their shouting "Help" in the courtyard, and for the night being so long.

We remained silent, and I waited with impatience for the light to dawn in the window. Masha, meanwhile, kept looking as if she were coming out of a coma and was now wondering how she, who was so intelligent, cultured, and so fastidious, could have fallen into this pitiful provincial hole among a band of petty, worthless people, and how she could have forgotten herself to the extent of being captivated by one of these people and being his wife for over half a year. It seemed to me that it made no difference to her now whether it was I or Moisei or Cheprakov; for her, everything merged into this drunken, savage "Help"—me, our marriage, our household, and the fall mud; and when she sighed or shifted to a more comfortable position, I could read on her face: "Oh, for morning to come sooner!"

In the morning she drove away.

I lived at Dubechnya three days longer, waiting for her, then collected all our things in one room, locked it, and walked to town. When I rang at the engineer's it was already evening, and the street lights were burning on our Bolshoi Dvoryansky. Pavel told me there was no one at home: Viktor Ivanich had gone to St. Petersburg and Marya Viktorovna was probably attending the rehearsal at the Azhogins'. I remember with what agitation I walked to the Azhogins' house then; how my heart beat and felt faint as I climbed up the stairs and stood on the landing for a long time, not daring to enter this temple of the muses! In the big reception hall, there were lighted candles on the table, on the piano, on the stage, always in threes; the first performance was set for the thirteenth, and the first rehearsal was now, on Monday—an unlucky day. The fight against prejudice! All the devotees of the dramatic art were already assembled; the Elder, the Middle, and the Younger were walking about on the stage reading their roles from scripts. On one side, apart from everyone, stood Radish, motionless, leaning his temple against the scenery, watching the stage with adoration as he waited for the rehearsal to begin. Everything was as it used to be.

I went toward the hostess—I had to pay my respects—but suddenly everyone began hissing and motioning to me not to make noise walking. A hush fell. The piano lid was raised, a woman sat down, squinting her nearsighted eyes at the music, and toward the piano came my Masha, elegantly dressed and beautiful, but beautiful in a rather special way, a new way, not at all like the Masha who used to come to me at the mill in the spring. She began singing: "Why do I love you, shining night?"

It was the first time I had heard her sing in all the time I had known her. She had a fine, succulent, powerful voice, and when she sang, I felt as if I were eating a ripe, sweet, fragrant melon. Now she finished; they applauded her and she smiled, very pleased, her eyes glancing about, her hands leafing through the music and smoothing her dress, like a bird that has at last burst out of its cage and is preening its wings in freedom. Her hair was combed over her ears, and her face had a bad, defiant expression as if she wanted to

challenge us all, or shout at us, as one shouts to horses:
"Hey there, my beauties!"

And at that moment, she probably greatly resembled her
coachman grandfather.

"You here too?" she asked, giving me her hand. "Did you
hear me sing? Well, how did you find it?" and without waiting
for my answer, she continued: "You came at a very good
time. I'm leaving for St. Petersburg for a short while tonight.
You'll let me go?"

I accompanied her to the station at midnight. She embraced
me tenderly, probably in gratitude that I had not posed
unnecessary questions, and she promised to write me. I
pressed her hands for a long time and kissed them, barely
holding back my tears and not saying a word to her.

When she left, I stood and watched the disappearing
lights, caressed her in my imagination, and said softly: "My
sweet Masha, magnificent Masha . . ."

I spent the night at Karpovna's in Makarikhe, and by
morning was already at work with Radish, covering furniture
at the house of a rich merchant who was marrying his daughter to a doctor.

XVII

Sunday my sister came after dinner and had tea with me.

"I read a lot now," she said, showing me the books she
had taken from the town library on her way to me. "Thanks
to your wife and Vladimir; they aroused my self-awareness.
They saved me, transformed me so I now feel like a human
being. I didn't use to sleep at nights because of all sorts of
worries: 'Ah, this week we went through so much sugar! Ah,
how can I avoid oversalting the cucumbers!' And now I don't
sleep either, but I have other thoughts. I am tormented that
half my life went by so stupidly, so timorously. I despise my
past, am ashamed of it, and I now regard Father as our
enemy. Oh, how grateful I am to your wife! And Vladimir?
He's such a wonderful person. They opened my eyes."

"It's not good that you don't sleep at night," I said.

"You're thinking that I'm sick? Not at all. Vladimir
sounded me and said I'm completely healthy. But health isn't
the question, that's not so important . . . Tell me: am I
right?"

She needed moral support—that was obvious. Masha had left, Dr. Blagovo was in St. Petersburg, and there was no one left in town to tell her she was right except me. She looked me fixedly in the face, trying to read my hidden thoughts, and if I became pensive or silent in her presence, she would think it was on her account and grow sad. I had to become more and more careful, and when she asked me whether she was right, I would hasten to answer that she was, and that I deeply respected her.

"Did you know? They gave me a role at the Azhogins'," she continued. "I want to act on the stage. I want to live; in a word, want to drink from a full cup. I have no talent whatsoever, and the role is ten lines in all, but just the same, it's immeasurably higher and nobler than pouring tea five times a day and watching to see that the cook doesn't eat a bit extra. But the important thing, let's say, is that Father will finally see I'm capable of protest too."

After tea she stretched out on my bed and lay motionless for a while with closed eyes, very pale.

"What weakness!" she said, getting up. "Vladimir said all city women and girls are anemic from idleness. What an intelligent person Vladimir is! He's right, eternally right. One must work!"

Two days later she came to the Azhogins' for rehearsal with her script. She wore a black dress with a coral necklace, a brooch which looked like a little puff pastry from a distance, and big, glittering diamond earrings. I became uncomfortable when I looked at her: I was struck by her lack of taste. Others also noticed that she had put on earrings and diamonds inappropriately and was strangely dressed; I saw smiles on their faces and heard someone say with a laugh: "Cleopatra the Egyptian."

She was trying to be worldly, uninhibited, and calm, and therefore seemed mannered and strange. Her simplicity and charm were gone.

"I just announced to Father that I was going to rehearsal," she began, coming up to me, "and he shouted that he would deprive me of his blessing, and even almost hit me. Imagine, I don't know my own role," she said, looking at the script. "I'm sure to bungle it. Well, the die is cast," she continued in intense excitement. "The die is cast . . ."

It seemed to her that everyone was watching her, that everyone was astonished by this important step she had resolved upon, and that everyone was expecting something special from her; to convince her that no one paid any attention to such unimportant and uninteresting people as herself and me was impossible.

She had nothing to do until the third act, and her role of a guest, a provincial gossip, consisted only in standing at the door as if overhearing, then delivering a short monologue. It was at least an hour and a half until her appearance, and meanwhile they were walking about on the stage, reading, drinking tea, and arguing. She did not leave my side for a moment and kept muttering her role, nervously crumpling her script; imagining that everyone was watching her and waiting for her appearance, she straightened her hair with a trembling hand and said to me: "I'm sure to bungle . . . How heavy my heart is, if you only knew! I'm as scared as if I were being taken away to the scaffold right now."

At last her turn came.

"Cleopatra Alekseyevna—you're on!" said the director.

She emerged in the middle of the stage with an expression of horror on her face, looking ugly and angular, and stood for half a minute as if dazed, completely motionless, except for the big earrings bobbing under her ears.

"You can use a script the first time," someone said.

It was clear to me that she was trembling and unable to speak or open the script from trembling, and that she was not at all up to the role. I was just about to go to her and say something to her, when she suddenly dropped onto her knees in the middle of the stage and burst into loud sobs.

Everyone stirred, everyone made noise; I alone stood leaning against the scenery, dumfounded by what was happening, uncomprehending, not knowing what I should do. I saw them lift her and lead her away. I saw Anyuta Blagovo come up to me; I had not noticed her in the hall earlier, and now she seemed to have sprung out of the ground. She was wearing a hat under a veil, and, as always, looked as if she had just dropped in for a moment.

"I told her she shouldn't play," she said angrily, articulating each word abruptly and blushing. "It's insanity. You should have stopped her!"

Madame Azhogina came swiftly up wearing a short jacket with short sleeves, with tobacco ashes on her thin, flat chest.

"My friend, this is terrible," she said, wringing her hands and as usual, looking me fixedly in the face. "It's terrible. Your sister is in a condition . . . she's pregnant! Take her away, I beg you . . ."

She was breathing heavily with emotion. And to one side stood the three daughters, just as thin and flat-chested as she, huddled together timorously. They were alarmed and stunned, as if a criminal had just been caught in their house. What a scandal, how dreadful! Yet this respected family had spent its whole life fighting prejudice; evidently it presumed that the prejudices and vagaries of humanity are to be found only in three candles, the thirteenth of the month, and the unlucky day—Monday!

"I do beg you . . . I do beg you . . ." Madame Azhogina repeated, making her lips heartshaped and pronouncing "do" like "dyu." "I *dyu* beg you, take her home."

<hr />

XVIII

Shortly thereafter, Sister and I were going down the stairs. I covered her with the tails of my coat; we hurried, choosing the alley where there were no lights, hiding from passers-by, and it was like a flight. She had stopped crying and looked at me with dry eyes. To Makarikhe, where I was taking her, was only a twenty minute walk, and the strange thing was that during this short period we had time to recall our whole life; we talked over everything together, thought out our position, reflected . . .

We decided it was impossible for us to stay in this town, and that when I had earned a little money, we should move to some other place. In some of the houses they were already sleeping, in others they were playing cards; we hated these houses, were afraid of them, and spoke about the zealousness, the hearty coarseness, the pettiness of these respected families, of these amateurs of dramatic art whom we had frightened so. I kept asking in what way these stupid, cruel, lazy, dishonest people were better than the drunken, superstitious peasants of Kurilovka, or in what way they were better than animals who also go into an uproar when some event or other breaks the monotony of their lives, circumscribed by instinct. What would have happened to Sister now if she had gone on living at home? What moral torture would she have gone through, talking to Father, meeting acquaintances daily? As I pictured this, people immediately came into my mind, all people I had known, who had been slowly driven to the grave by their near and dear; I remembered the tormented dogs, going out of their minds, the live sparrows, plucked bare by little boys and then thrown in the water—and the long series of obscure, protracted sufferings which I had observed in this town uninterruptedly since my childhood; and it was incomprehensible to me what these sixty thousand people lived by, what they read the Bible for, what they prayed for, what they read books and magazines for. What benefit did they derive from all that was said and written until now if they still had the same spiritual darkness and the same distaste for freedom that existed a hundred or three hundred years back? The master carpenter builds houses in town all his life and says "galdery" for "gallery" till the day of his death, and in the same way, these sixty thousand inhabitants read and listen with reverent genuflections to words about truth, mercy, and freedom, and still, until their very deaths, lie from morning till night, torment one another, and fear and hate freedom as an enemy.

"So, my fate is decided," said my sister when we reached home. "After everything that's happened, I can't go back *there* now. Lord, how good that is! My spirits feel lighter."

She immediately lay down in bed. Tears glistened on her eyelashes, but her expression was happy, she slept soundly and sweetly, and one could see that she was truly light in spirit and was resting well. It had been a long, long time since she had slept like this!

And so we began living together. She sang all the time and said she was fine, and I would carry back unread the books we borrowed from the library, for she was no longer able to read; all she wanted was to dream and talk about the future. Mending my linens or helping Karpovna around the stove, she would sing or talk about her Vladimir, about his mind, elegant manners, goodness; about his unusual erudition, and I used to agree with her although I no longer liked her doctor. She wanted to work, to live independently, on her own earnings, and said she would become a teacher or a nurse as soon as her health permitted, and would wash floors herself and do laundry. She already loved her child passionately; although he was not yet in this world, she already knew what his eyes and hands were like and how he laughed. She was fond of talking about education, or about how Vladimir was the best person in the world, and all her reflections on education could be summed up by saying that the boy should be as charming as his father. It was an endless subject of conversation and everything she said aroused an intense joy in her. Sometimes I felt joyful too, without knowing why myself.

She must have infected me with her dreaminess. I also read nothing and just dreamed; in the evenings, in spite of my fatigue, I would pace the room from corner to corner, my hands in my pockets, and talk about Masha.

"What do you think?" I would ask Sister. "When will she come back? I think she'll come back for Christmas, no later. What's there for her to do there?"

"If she doesn't write you, then she's evidently coming back very soon."

"That's true," I would agree, although I knew very well that Masha would not come back to our town for anything.

I missed her intensely, was no longer able to delude myself, and sought delusion from others. My sister was waiting for her doctor, and I for Masha, and both of us talked incessantly, laughed, and did not notice that we were making sleep impossible for Karpovna, who lay in her place next to the stove and kept muttering: "That samovar there was humming this morning, hum-ming! Oh, it's not for the good, my dears, not for the good."

No one came to see us except the postman, bringing Sister letters from the doctor, and Prokofy, who sometimes dropped by in the evenings, looked silently at Sister, and left; he used to say to himself in the kitchen: "Every class should know its science, and anyone who refuses to understand through pride will find the vale of tears."

He loved his "vale of tears." One day—it was already the Christmas season—as I went past the market, he called me to his butcher shop, and without offering his hand, announced that he had to speak to me on a very important matter. He was red with cold and vodka; near him, behind the counter, stood Nikolka with his ruffian's face, holding a bloody knife in his hand.

"I want to say my say to you," Prokofy began. "This incident can't go on because, as you understand yourself, people won't be praising us nor you for this vale of tears. Mamasha, of course, can't say unpleasant things to you out of pity, that your sister should move to another place because of her condition, but I don't want any more, because I can't approve her behavior."

I understood him and left the shop. That same day, Sister and I moved to Radish's place. We had no money for a hackney and went on foot; I carried a bundle with our belongings on my back, and although my sister had nothing in her hands, she gasped, coughed, and kept asking whether we would soon arrive.

XIX

At last a letter came from Masha.

"Dear, good M.A.," she wrote, "good, kind 'angel of ours,' as the old painter calls you, farewell, I'm going to America with Father for an exhibition. In a few days I'll see the ocean—so far from Dubechnya, it's frightening to think of it! It's far and immeasurable, like the sky, and I long to go there in freedom. I'm celebrating, I'm crazy, and you see how disconnected my letter is. Dear, kind one, give me freedom, break the thread which still binds you and me as quickly as possible. That I met and knew you was a ray from heaven, illuminating my existence; but that I became your wife was a mistake, you understand that, and the consciousness of this mistake weighs on me now, and I beg you on my knees, my magnanimous friend, telegraph, soonest, soonest, before I leave for the ocean, that you agree to right our mutual mistake, to take this sole stone off my wings, and my father, who will take all the trouble on himself, promises me not to overburden you with formalities. So, free in all directions? All right?

"Be happy, and God bless you, forgive me, a sinner.

"I'm alive and well. I squander money, do many foolish things, and thank God every minute that such a bad woman as I has no children. I sing and have some success, but it's not a passion; no, that's—my harbor, my cell, to which I go for peace. King David had a ring with the inscription: 'All things pass.' When I'm sad, these words make me merry, and when I'm merry, I become sad. And I ordered myself a ring like that with Hebrew letters, and this talisman keeps me from becoming impassioned. All things pass, life passes too, and that means that nothing is essential. Or the only thing which is essential is consciousness of freedom, because when a man is free, he needs nothing, nothing, nothing. Break the thread. I embrace you and your sister warmly. Forgive and forget your M."

Sister used to lie down in one room; Radish, who had been sick again and was now getting better, in another. Just at the moment I received this letter, Sister went quietly into the painter's room, sat down beside him, and began reading. Every day she read him Ostrovsky or Gogol, and he used to listen, staring at one spot, never laughing, nodding his head, and muttering to himself from time to time: "Anything can happen! Anything can happen!"

If something ugly or monstrous was depicted in the work, he would say almost spitefully, poking his finger in the book: "There it is, the lie! That's what it does, the lie!"

The works delighted him for their contents, their moral, and for their complex, artistic construction, and he would marvel at *him,* never referring to *him* by name: "How cleverly *he* fits everything in place!"

Sister read just one page softly now, then did not have enough voice to continue. Radish took her hand, and moving his parched lips, said in a barely audible, hoarse voice: "The soul of the righteous is white and smooth as chalk, while the sinner's is like pumice. The soul of the righteous is a clear oil, and the sinner's, coal tar. One must labor, grieve, and be ill," he continued, "and anyone who hasn't labored or grieved will not be in the heavenly kingdom. Woe, woe to the well-fed, woe to the strong, woe to the rich, woe to the money-lenders! They won't be seeing the heavenly kingdom. Lice eat grass, rust eats iron . . ."

"And a lie—the soul," Sister continued and laughed.

I read the letter through again. At that moment, into the kitchen came the soldier who had been coming twice a week to bring us tea, French bread, and woodcocks which smelled of perfume from the anonymous donor. I was out of work and used to sit at home for days at a time, and whoever sent us this bread probably knew we were in need.

I heard Sister talking to the soldier and laughing merrily. Then, lying down, she ate some bread and told me: "When you did not want to be in government service and went off to be a painter, Anyuta Blagovo and I knew from the very beginning that you were right, but we were afraid to say so aloud. Tell me, what is this power which keeps you from acknowledging what you think? Take Anyuta Blagovo, for instance. She loves, she worships you, she knows you're right; she loves me too, like a sister, and knows I'm right, and maybe envies me in her soul, but a power of some sort keeps her from coming to see us; she avoids us, is afraid."

Sister crossed her arms on her breast and said with passion: "How she loves you, if you only knew! She's confessed her love only to me, and then secretly, in the dark. She used to lead me into a dark alley in the garden and begin whispering how dear you were to her. You'll see, she'll never marry because she loves you. Are you sorry for her?"

"Yes."

"It's she who sent the bread. She's ridiculous, it's true, why hide oneself? I was ridiculous and foolish too, and now I've gotten away from that and am no longer afraid of anyone; I think and say out loud what I want to—and I've become happy. When I lived at home, I had no conception of happiness, but now I wouldn't change places with a queen."

Dr. Blagovo arrived. He had received his doctor's degree and was now living in our town, resting at his father's house; he said he would soon leave for St. Petersburg again. He wanted to work on typhus vaccines, and, I believe, cholera; he wanted to go abroad to perfect himself and then to have a chair at a university. He was no longer in military service and wore an ample serge jacket, very wide trousers, and magnificent ties. Sister was in raptures over his tie pin, studs, and the red silk handkerchief which he kept in his front jacket pocket, from coquetry, I suppose. Once, having nothing to do, we tried to count up all his suits from memory and decided there were at least ten. It was obvious that he loved my sister as before, but he never said even in joke that he would take her with him to St. Petersburg or abroad, and I could not picture clearly what would become of her if she lived; what would become of her child. However, she simply dreamed endlessly and did not consider the future seriously; she used to say he should go where he wanted to and even throw her aside, as long as he himself was happy; she was content with what had been.

When he came to see us, he usually sounded her very carefully and insisted that she drink milk with drops in it in front of him. This time it was the same too. He sounded her and made her drink down a glass of milk, and our apartment smelled of creosote afterward.

"There's a good girl," he said, taking the glass from her. "You shouldn't talk much, and lately you chatter like a magpie. Please keep quiet."

She laughed. Then he went into Radish's room where I was sitting and clapped me affectionately on the shoulder.

"Well, old man?" he asked, leaning over the invalid.

"Your honor . . ." Radish uttered, moving his lips slowly, "your honor, I'm bold enough to proclaim . . . we all walk in God's sight, all of us have to die . . . Allow me to tell you the truth . . . Your honor, there'll be no heavenly kingdom for you!"

"What can one do?" joked the doctor. "There has to be somebody in hell."

And suddenly something happened to my consciousness; I had a vision of myself in winter, at night, standing in the courtyard of the slaughterhouse, and next to me was Prokofy, smelling of *pertsovka;* I made an effort and rubbed my eyes, and immediately imagined that I was on the way to the interview with the governor. Nothing of the kind had ever happened to me before or since, and I attribute these strange, dreamlike recollections to exhausted nerves. I experienced both the slaughterhouse and the interview with the governor, and at the same time, dimly realized that this was not really taking place.

When I came to, I saw that I was no longer at home, but standing with the doctor in the street near a lamppost.

"It's so sad, so sad," he said, and tears rolled down his cheeks. "She's merry, laughs all the time, keeps hoping, and her position is hopeless, my dear fellow. Your Radish hates me and keeps trying to make me understand that I've treated her badly. He's right from his standpoint, but I have my own point of view too, and I don't regret what happened in the slightest. One must love; we all should love—isn't it true? Without love there would be no life; anyone who fears and avoids love is not free."

Little by little he switched to other subjects, began speaking of science, of his dissertation, which had been well received in St. Petersburg; he spoke with enthusiasm, no longer thinking of my sister, his own grief, or me. Life impassioned him. She has America and the ring with its inscription, I thought, and he his doctor's degree and scientific career, and only my sister and I are left as before.

After taking leave of him, I moved close to the street light and read through the letter once again. And I remembered, remembered vividly, how that spring morning, she had come to me in the mill, lain down, and covered herself with her coat—she wanted to look like a simple peasant woman; and another time—it was also in the morning—when we had fished the net out of the water, huge raindrops sprinkled us from the bordering willows, and we laughed . . .

It was dark in our house on the Bolshoi Dvoryansky. I crawled over the fence and went into the kitchen by the back door to get a lamp as I used to do in the old days. There was no one in the kitchen. Near the stove, the samovar was hissing, awaiting my father. "Who pours Father tea now?" I wondered. Taking a lamp, I went to the shanty and made myself a bed out of newspapers. The hooks on the wall stared sternly as before and their shadows flickered. It was cold. I imagined my sister coming in now to bring me supper, but immediately remembered that she was lying sick in Radish's house, and it seemed strange to me that I had climbed over the fence and was lying in an unheated shanty. My mind wandered and I imagined all sorts of nonsense.

A bell rang: sounds familiar from childhood: first a wire rustled on the wall, then a brief, plaintive sound rang out in the kitchen. It was Father returning from the club. I got up and went to the kitchen. On seeing me, the cook, Aksinya, clasped her hands and for some reason burst into tears.

"My child!" she said softly. "Dear one! Oh, Lord!"

And she began crumpling her apron in her hands with emotion. In the window stood four jars of berries and vodka. I poured myself a teacupful and drank it down greedily because I was extremely thirsty. Aksinya had washed the table and benches not long ago, and the kitchen had the smell found in bright, cozy kitchens kept by orderly cooks. This smell and the chirp of the cricket used to lure us here to the kitchen in childhood and put us in the mood for storytelling and playing Kings . . .

"But where is Cleopatra?" Aksinya asked softly, hastily, holding her breath. "And where's your cap, Little Father? And your wife, they say, left for Petersburg?"

She had been in our service in our mother's time and sometimes used to bathe Cleopatra and me in the laundry tub, and to her we were still children who needed guidance. In about a quarter of an hour, she put before me all the reflections she had stored up with the sagacity of an old servant in the stillness of this kitchen since we had seen each other. She said the doctor should be forced to marry Cleopatra—one only had to frighten him, and if the petition were well written, the prelate would annul his first marriage; that it would be good to sell Dubechnya without my wife's knowledge, and to put the money in a bank in my name; that if sister and I bowed to Father's feet and begged him nicely, he might forgive us; that we should have a Te Deum said to the heavenly Tsaritsa . . .

"Come, go, Little Father, talk to him," she said on hearing Father's cough. "Go on, talk, bow, your head won't roll off."

I went. Father was already seated at the table and drafting the plan of a summer villa with Gothic windows and a fat tower like a fire watchtower—somewhat unusually unbending and untalented. Going into the study, I stopped where I could see this draft. I did not know why I had come to see Father, but I remember that when I caught sight of his thin face, red neck, and his shadow on the wall, I longed to throw myself on his neck and bow to his feet as Aksinya had told me to; but the sight of the summer villa with the Gothic windows and fat tower restrained me.

"Good evening," I said.

He glanced at me and immediately dropped his eyes to his draft.

"What do you want?" he asked after a short pause.

"I came to tell you—Sister is very ill. She'll die soon," I added dully.

"Well?" sighed Father, taking off his spectacles and putting them on the table. "What thou sowest, thou shalt reap. What thou sowest," he repeated, getting up from the table, "thou shalt reap. I beg you to remember how you came to me two years back, and here on this very spot I begged you, implored you to drop your erring ways; I reminded you of duty, honor, and of your obligations toward your ancestors, whose tradition we must piously uphold. Did you listen to me? You scorned my words and obstinately continued to maintain your erroneous views; not only that, but you involved your sister in your erring ways too, and made her lose her morals and sense of shame. Now you're both badly off. Well? What thou sowest, thou shalt reap!"

After saying this, he paced around the study. He probably thought I had come to acknowledge my error and was probably waiting for me to begin pleading for myself and my sister. I felt cold; I shuddered as if feverish, and spoke with difficulty in a hoarse voice: "And I also beg you to remember," I said, "that on this very spot, I implored you to understand me, to reflect, to decide along with me how we should live and what for, and in reply, you began talking about ancestors, about my grandfather who wrote poetry. Now you're told your only daughter is beyond hope, and you start in again about ancestors, traditions . . . what giddiness in your old age, when death is not far beyond the horizon, when you only have some five or ten years left to live!"

"What did you come here for?" Father asked severely, evidently offended that I had accused him of giddiness.

"I don't know. I love you, I'm unutterably sorry that we're so far apart—so I came. I still love you, but Sister has broken with you forever. She hasn't forgiven you and can't now. Your name alone arouses her revulsion toward the past, toward life."

"And who's to blame?" shouted Father. "It's you who's to blame, you good-for-nothing!"

"Well, suppose I'm to blame," I said. "I confess I'm to blame for many things, but why is this life of yours, which you consider obligatory for us too—why is it so dreary, so untalented, why isn't there anyone in one of these houses you've been building for thirty years now from whom I might have learned how to live so as not to be guilty? There isn't one honest person in the whole town! These houses of yours are accursed nests in which mothers and daughters are killed by inches, children are tormented . . . My poor mother!" I continued in despair. "Poor Sister! You have to stupefy yourself with vodka, cards, scandal, you have to cringe, be hypocritical, or draw plans and plans for dozens of years in order not to notice all the horror hidden in these houses. Our town has existed for hundreds of years, and during all that time it hasn't given the country one useful man—not one! You've nipped everything vital and bright in the bud, little by little! It's a town of shopkeepers, innkeepers, clerks, hypocrites, an unnecessary, useless town, which not one soul would regret if it suddenly sank underground."

"I don't want to listen to you, you good-for-nothing!" Father said and picked his ruler off the table. "You're drunk! Don't you dare appear in such a state before your father! I'm telling you for the last time, and you can transmit this to your immoral sister, that you shall get nothing from me. I've torn my disobedient children out of my heart, and if they suffer from their disobedience and obstinacy, I'm not sorry for them. You can go back where you came from! God was pleased to punish me with you, but I'll bear this trial with resignation and, like Job, find comfort in suffering and constant work. You must not cross my threshold until you have reformed. I'm just, everything I say is for your benefit, and if you wish yourself well, you ought to remember what I've told you and am telling you now all your life."

I flung up my hands and left. I don't remember what happened afterward, that night and the next day.

They say I walked bareheaded through the streets, staggering and singing loudly, followed by a crowd of little boys
shouting: "Small Pickings! Small Pickings!"

XX

If I had wanted to order a ring for myself, I should have
chosen the following inscription: "Nothing passes." I believe
nothing passes without leaving a trace, and that the slightest
step we take is of significance in our present and future life.

What I had lived through did not pass by for nothing. My
great misfortunes and my endurance touched the hearts of the
inhabitants and they no longer call me "Small Pickings"; they
don't laugh at me, and when I walk through the shopkeepers'
row, they no longer splash water on me. They are used to my
having become a worker now, and see nothing strange in that
I, an aristocrat, carry a pail of paint and put in windowpanes.
On the contrary, they are glad to give me orders, and I am
now considered a good workman and the best contractor after
Radish who, although he has recovered and paints cupolas
on belfries without scaffolding as before, no longer has the
strength to manage the fellows. I run through town and look
for orders in his place; I hire and pay the fellows; I borrow
money at high interest rates. And now that I've become a
contractor, I understand why one has to run around town for
a couple of days to find roofers for a petty order. People are
polite to me, address me formally, and in the houses in which
I work, they serve me tea and send someone to ask whether I
wouldn't like dinner. Children and young girls often come to
watch me with curiosity and sorrow.

I was working in the governor's garden one day, painting
an arbor there to look like marble. The governor, taking a
walk, came up to the arbor, and because he had nothing to do,
began talking to me; I reminded him of how he had summoned
me once for an explanation. He looked me in the face for a
minute, then made a mouth like an *o*, flung up his hands, and
said: "I don't remember!"

I have aged, grown silent, harsh, stern, and rarely laugh,

and they say I've become like Radish, and like him, irk the fellows with my useless instructions.

Marya Viktorovna, my former wife, is living abroad now, and her father, the engineer, is building a road somewhere in the eastern provinces and buying an estate there. Dr. Blagovo is also abroad. Dubechnya has gone back to Madame Cheprakova, who bought it after squeezing a 20 percent reduction out of the engineer. Moisei now goes around in a bowler hat; he often drives to town in a racing carriage on business of some sort and stops near the bank. They say he has bought himself a mortgaged estate and is constantly consulting the bank about Dubechnya, which he is planning to buy, too. Poor Ivan Cheprakov has been staggering through town for a long time, drinking and doing nothing. I tried to get him into our business, and he painted roofs and put in windowpanes with us for a time; he even acquired a taste for it, and stole oil, begged for tips, and got drunk like a regular painter. But the work soon bored him, he tired of it and returned to Dubechnya, and the fellows confessed to me later that he had tried to persuade them to go with him some night to kill Moisei and rob Madame Cheprakova.

Father has aged a great deal, become stooped, and takes walks close to his house in the evenings. I never visit him.

Prokofy treated the shopkeepers with *pertsovka* and tar during cholera time and took money for it, and I learned in our newspaper that he had been flogged for maligning doctors while sitting in his butcher shop. His helper, Nikolka, died of cholera. Karpovna is still alive and loves and fears her Prokofy as before. On seeing me, she always shakes her head sadly and says with a sigh: "You're done for!"

On weekdays I'm busy from early morning until evening. And on holidays, in good weather, I take my tiny niece (my sister expected a boy, but gave birth to a girl) and walk leisurely to the cemetery. There I stand or sit and look for a long time at the grave dear to me, and tell the little girl that is where her mother lies.

Sometimes I find Anyuta Blagovo at the grave. We greet each other and stand in silence or talk about Cleopatra, about her little girl, about how sad life is in this world. Then leaving the cemetery, we walk silently, and she slows down her steps on purpose in order to walk beside me longer. The child, gay, happy, blinking in the bright daylight, laughing, stretches out her little hands to her and we stop and caress the sweet little girl together.

But when we come into town, Anyuta Blagovo, agitated and blushing, takes leave of me and walks on alone, sedate and austere. And no one she meets then could think on seeing her that she has just been walking beside me and even caressing the child.

Peasants

The story was written in the spring of 1897. On March 1, 1897, Chekhov wrote to Suvorin: ". . . I have written a story from peasant life, but they say it will not pass the censorship and will have to be shortened by half."

On April 2, Chekhov wrote to his brother Alexander that the story contained a description of a fire which occurred in Melikhovo—"on the occasion of your arrival." Actually, Chekhov may have used in Chapter V of "Peasants" a much earlier description of such a fire, for as early as November 1888 he wrote to Suvorin: "For my future novel I have written some three hundred lines about a village fire: in the manor house they wake up at night and see the glow; impressions of conversations, of the clatter of bare feet on an iron roof, of bustling around . . ."

The story was published in *Russian Thought* in April 1897. The censorship passed the story, but demanded the replacement of one page when the whole thing had already been set. In a report submitted and dated April 2, 1897, the censor Sokolov wrote that Chekhov's story deserved particular attention because it described the plight of the peasants in much too somber colors. Pages 193-194 were cut from the magazine and one of them replaced by a new text (in the last chapter of the story). When the story was published, the same year, in book form, together with "My Life," the original text was restored. Small changes were made in the text by Chekhov when the story was included in his *Collected Works*. The story was almost immediately translated into French. When a new French translation was made, in 1900, by Denis Roche (this translation was published with a drawing by Repin on the cover), Chekhov wrote to Professor Batyushkov in connection with the translator's request to send him the passages that had been cut out by the censors: "But there were no such passages. There was one chapter which was not included either in the magazine or in the book; it dealt with a conversation among the peasants about religion and the authorities. But there is no need to send this chapter to Paris, as there was no need altogether to translate 'Peasants' into French." The manuscript of this chapter has not been preserved. On the other hand, there were found, among Chekhov's papers, draft fragments of Chapters X and XI in which the Moscow life of some of the characters (Olga, Sasha, Kiryak) is described, and some of the characters, barely mentioned in the story, are further developed (Olga's sister, a prostitute; the waiter Makarychev; etc.). Chekhov must have planned to continue the story, with the action back in Moscow.

"Peasants" made a great impression on the public and was discussed more in the press than any other of Chekhov's works of this period. The magazine *The Northern Messenger* even said that these discussions reminded one of the times when a new novel by Turgenev or Dostoevsky made its appearance. The interest was aroused not so much by the story's purely literary qualities as by the ruthless depiction of the backwardness and poverty of the Russian peasants. Its theme was quite topical, for it appeared at the height of the controversy between the Russian Marxists and the Populists about the village community and other problems of Russia's social development. Thus the story itself became the object of a heated Marxist-Populist debate. In the Marxist magazine *Novoe Slovo* (*The New Word*), one of the leaders of the so-called "legal" Marxists, Peter Struve, published a very favorable review of the story (it was signed "Novus"). In the Populist *Russkoe Bogatstvo* (*The Russian Wealth*), its *de facto* editor and the most influential literary critic of those days, Nikolay Mikhailovsky, made an attack on both Chekhov and Struve.

The well-known playwright and actor Yuzhin-Sumbatov, in a letter to Chekhov, described "Peasants" as "the greatest work in the whole world for many, many years, at least for a Russian." He found in it "a matchless tragedy of the truth," which he compared to Shakespeare's. "It is as though you were not a writer, but nature itself," he wrote. The episode with Nikolai and his waiter's tailcoat seemed to Yuzhin a stroke of genius: "I never cry. When he [Nikolai] put on and then repacked his tailcoat I could not read on for a long time," he wrote to Chekhov.

There were, of course, also adverse opinions, besides Mikhailovsky's, voiced in the press and expressed privately. Tolstoy was reported to have described the story as "a sin with regard to the people," and to have said that Chekhov did not know the people. This opinion is not, however, documented in Tolstoy's own writings.

The story was greatly admired by Maxim Gorky, just as he was later to admire Bunin's equally somber picture of peasant life in *The Village*.

✧✧✧✧✧✧✧✧✧✧✧✧✧✧✧✧✧✧✧✧✧✧✧✧✧✧✧✧✧

I

A waiter at the Moscow hotel Slavonic Bazaar, Nikolai Chikildeyev, fell ill. His legs became numb and his gait so altered that as he was walking down the corridor one day he stumbled and fell with a tray of ham and green peas. He was forced to leave his job. Whatever money he and his wife had saved, he spent on treatment; there was nothing left to live on, it became tedious being without work, and he decided that, probably, he should go home to his village. It is easier to be at home when you are sick, and it is cheaper to live there. How truly is it said that the walls of home are a help.

He arrived at his native Zhukovo toward evening. In his childhood memories, the parental nest appeared to him as bright, cozy, and comfortable; now, on entering the wooden hut, he even felt frightened, it was so dark, close, and dirty. His wife Olga and daughter Sasha accompanying him looked with bewilderment at the big, squalid stove occupying almost half the hut and black with soot and flies. So many flies! The stove pitched, the log walls sloped, and the hut seemed about to collapse that instant. In the shrine corner, near the icon, bottle labels and bits of newspaper were pasted in place of pictures. Poverty, poverty! None of the adults were at home, all were harvesting. On a bunk over the stove sat a little girl of eight, towheaded, unwashed, impassive; she did not even glance at the new arrivals. On the floor, a white cat was rubbing against the oven fork.

"Puss, Puss!" Sasha enticed her. "Puss!"

"She's not hearing us," said the little girl. "Gone deaf."

"What from?"

"Just like that. Got hit."

From the first glance, Nikolai and Olga understod what life was like here, but they said nothing to each other; they silently unloaded their bundles and silently went out in the street. Their hut was the third from the end and looked the poorest and oldest; the second was little better, but the farthest had an iron roof and curtains at the windows. This hut, unfenced, stood by itself; it was the tavern. The huts proceeded in a single row, and the whole hamlet, quiet and pensive, with willows, elders, and sorbs glancing out of the yards, had a pleasing appearance.

Beyond the peasants' farmyards began the drop to the river, so steep and abrupt that huge rocks were bared here and there in the clay soil. Paths meandered over the slope near these boulders and the pits dug by potters; fragments of broken pottery, some brown, some red, were piled in heaps; below stretched the broad, level, bright green meadow, already mowed, over which the peasants' herd now wandered. The river was a verst from the village, twisting with splendid bushy banks; beyond it there was another broad meadow, a herd, long files of white geese, and then, just as on this side, an abrupt ascent to the top, and on a ridge above, a village with a five-domed church and, slightly removed, a manor house.

"How nice it is here!" said Olga, crossing herself facing the church. "What space, Lord!"

Just at that moment the call to vespers struck. Tomorrow was Sunday. Two little girls who were dragging a barrel of water down below looked back at the church to listen to the ringing.

"It's about dinnertime now in the Slavonic Bazaar . . ." Nikolai said dreamily.

Sitting on the edge of the bluff, Nikolai and Olga watched the sun go down; watched the sky, crimson and gold, reflected in the river, in the church windows, and throughout the atmosphere, soft, peaceful, ineffably pure, as it never is in Moscow. And when the sun had set, the herd went by with bleating and lowing, the geese flew in from the far bank—and everything grew quiet; the gentle light faded from the air and the evening darkness descended swiftly.

Meanwhile the old people had come back: Nikolai's father and mother, gaunt, bent, toothless, and of identical height. The women had arrived too—the daughters-in-law, Marya and Fekla, who had been working for the landowner across the river. Marya, the wife of brother Kiryak, had six children; Fekla, the wife of brother Denis, who had gone into the army, had two; and when Nikolai entered the hut and saw the whole family, all the big and little bodies stirring on the plank-beds, in the cradles, and in every corner, and when he saw how greedily the old man and the women were eating black bread, dunking it in water, he realized it had been senseless for him to come here sick, with no money, and, moreover, with a family—senseless!

"And where's brother Kiryak?" he asked after they had greeted each other.

"He stays in the woods with a merchant as a watchman," answered the father. "He's not a bad worker, but he can pour it down fast."

"He's no breadwinner!" the old woman added tearfully. "Our men are a sad lot. They bring nothing to the house but take plenty out of it. Kiryak drinks, and the old man, there's no hiding the sin, knows the way to the tavern, too. It's the wrath of the heavenly Tsaritsa on us."

Because of the guests, they put the samovar on. The tea smelled of fish, the sugar was nibbled and gray, cockroaches scurried across the bread and dishes; it was repellent to drink and the conversation was also repellent—entirely about poverty and disease. But they had hardly had time for a cup each, when a loud, drawn-out, drunken shout came from the courtyard: "Ma-arya!"

"Sounds like Kiryak," said the old man; "speak of the devil."

Everyone was still. After a short pause, the same shout came again, coarse and drawn-out, as if from underground: "Ma-arya!"

Marya, the elder daughter-in-law, turning pale, huddled against the stove, and it was somehow strange to see the look of terror on the face of this broad-shouldered, strong, homely woman. Her daughter, the same little girl who had been sitting on the stove and appeared impassive, suddenly started crying noisily.

"What's wrong with you, pest?" Fekla, a handsome woman, also strong and broad-shouldered, shouted at her. "Never fear, he won't kill anybody!"

From the old man, Nikolai learned that Marya was afraid to live in the woods with Kiryak, and that when drunk, he always came for her and blustered and beat her without mercy.

"Ma-arya!" rang the shout from the very door.

"Defend me, for the love of Christ, kinfolk," stammered Marya, breathing as though being plunged into very cold water, "defend me, kinfolk . . ."

All the children in the hut started crying, and at the sight of them, Sasha also burst into tears. A drunken cough was heard and into the hut came a tall, black-bearded peasant in a winter cap, and because his face was invisible in the dim light of the little lamp, he was terrifying. This was Kiryak. Going up to his wife, he swung and struck her in the face with his fist; stunned by the blow, she did not utter a sound, but just sank down, and her nose instantly started to bleed.

"What a shame, a shame," muttered the old man, climbing onto the shelf over the stove; "and in front of guests! Such a sin!"

The old woman sat silently, hunched over, pondering; Fekla was rocking the cradle . . . Apparently aware he was terrifying and pleased by it, Kiryak seized Marya by the hand, dragged her toward the door and roared like a wild beast to appear even more terrifying, but just then, he suddenly caught sight of the guests and stopped.

"Oh, they came . . ." he said, releasing his wife. "My own brother and his family . . ."

He said a prayer in front of the icon, reeling and opening his drunken, red eyes wide, then continued: "Brother and his family came to the paternal home . . . from Moscow, that is. The ancient capital, that is, the city of Moscow, the mother of cities . . . Forgive me . . ."

He dropped onto the bench near the samovar and started drinking tea, loudly sipping out of a saucer in the general silence . . . He drank a dozen cups, then slumped down on the bench and snored.

They got ready for bed. Nikolai, being sick, was put on the shelf over the stove with the old man; Sasha lay down on the floor, while Olga went with the women to the shed.

"Now, now, my dove," she said as she lay down on the hay beside Marya, "you won't help grief by crying! Bear with it, that's all. It says in the Scriptures: 'Whosoever shall smite thee on thy right cheek, turn to him the other also' . . . Now, now, my dove!"

Then in a whispered singsong, she told about Moscow, her life, and her work as a chambermaid in furnished rooms.

"And in Moscow the houses are big and stone," she said; "and so many, many churches, forty times forty, my dove, and in the houses they're all gentlefolk, and so pretty, so proper!"

Marya said she had not only never been to Moscow, but not even to their own district town; she was illiterate and knew no prayers, not even "Our Father." She and the other daughter-in-law, Fekla, who was now sitting slightly apart and listening, were both extremely backward and unable to understand anything. Neither liked her husband; Marya was afraid of Kiryak, trembled with fear when he stayed with her, and got a headache when near him from the fumes of vodka and tobacco. While Fekla, when asked whether she was not bored without her husband, used to answer with irritation: "That one!"

They talked a while, then became silent . . .

It was chilly and a cock was crowing near the shed at the top of its voice, disturbing sleep. When the bluish morning light had already pierced through all the chinks, Fekla got up, went out quietly, and could be heard running off somewhere, her bare feet thudding.

II

Olga went to church and took Marya with her. They both felt merry as they descended the path to the meadow. Olga enjoyed the open country, and Marya began to feel very close to her sister-in-law. The sun was rising. A drowsy hawk hovered low over the meadow, the river was murky, fog drifted here and there, but on the far bank, a strip of light was already spreading over the hill, the church glittered, and the rooks were screeching furiously in the manor-house garden.

"The old man's all right," said Marya, "but Granny's strict; always slapping. Our grain lasted till Shrovetide only, so we buy flour in the tavern—well, she gets angry; you eat a lot, she says."

"Now, now, my dove! Bear with it, that's all. It's said: 'Come unto me all ye that labor and are heavy laden.' "

Olga spoke gravely in a singsong, and her gait was rapid and bustling like a pilgrim's. She read the Gospel daily, reading aloud like a deacon; much of it she did not understand, but the holy words moved her, and she pronounced words such as "whensoever" and "henchforth" with a sweet sinking of the heart. She believed in God, in the Virgin Mother, and in the saints; she believed that one must never harm anyone in this world—not common people, nor Germans, nor gypsies, nor

Jews, and that woe would befall even people who were not
kind to animals; she believed that was what was written in the
Holy Scripture, and therefore, when she pronounced the words
of the Bible, even the incomprehensible ones, her face became
compassionate, tender, and blissful.

"Where do you come from?" asked Marya.

"I'm a Vladimirian. Only I was taken to Moscow a long
time ago already, when I was eight."

They came to the river. On the far side, at the very edge of
the water, stood a woman, undressing.

"That's our Fekla," Marya recognized; "she's been across
the river to the manor house. To the hired men! She's a hussy
and foulmouthed—dreadful!"

Fekla, black-browed, with disheveled hair, still young and
strong as a girl, leaped off the bank and began thrashing the
water with her legs, sending waves in all directions.

"A hussy—dreadful!" repeated Marya.

A shaky little log footbridge had been placed across the
river, and directly under it, in the clear translucent water,
swam schools of broadbrowed chub. The dew sparkled on the
green bushes which gazed at themselves in the water. The air
grew warmer and became pleasant. What a glorious morning!
And how glorious life probably would be in this world if
there were no want, terrible, inescapable want, from which
there is no refuge. One had only to look back at the village
now to remember all yesterday's happenings vividly—and the
spell of happiness which seemed to ring them instantly dis-
solved.

They went into the church. Marya stopped in the entrance,
not daring to go farther. Nor did she dare sit down, although
the bells only began ringing for Mass at eight o'clock. She
stood throughout.

While the Gospel was being read, the people suddenly moved
to make way for the landowner's family; in came two girls
in white dresses and wide-brimmed hats, and with them, a
chubby, rosy little boy in a sailor suit. Their appearance excited Olga. She decided at first glance that they were decent,
cultivated, and elegant people. Marya looked at them from
under her brows, sullenly, sadly, as if it were not people who
had come in, but monsters who might squash her if she did
not move aside.

And every time the deacon intoned something in his bass
voice, the cry came to her: "Ma-arya!"—and she shuddered.

III

The guests' arrival had become known in the village, and after Mass, many people were already gathering in the hut. The Leonychevs, the Matveichevs, and the Ilyichovs came to hear about their relatives in service in Moscow. All the literate children of Zhukovo were taken off to Moscow and apprenticed as waiters and roomboys (just as from the village on the other side of the river, they were apprenticed exclusively as bakers). And this had been the rule for a long time, ever since, in the days of serfdom, a certain Luka Ivanich, a peasant from Zhukovo who was now already legendary, a bartender in one of the Moscow clubs, had accepted only his countrymen in his service, and the latter, on coming into power, had written for their own relatives and placed them in taverns and restaurants. From that time on, the village of Zhukovo was never referred to by the surrounding inhabitants as anything but Churlburg or Flunkeytown. Nikolai had been taken to Moscow at the age of eleven and appointed to his post by Ivan Makarich of the Matveichev family, who was then serving as an attendant in the Hermitage garden restaurant. And now, turning to the Matveichevs, Nikolai said didactically: "Ivan Makarich is my benefactor, and I am bound to pray God for him night and day, as it was through him I became a good man."

"Little Father," a tall old woman, Ivan Makarich's sister, uttered tearfully, "and there's been nothing heard about him, the darling."

"He was serving at Omon's last winter, and there was a rumor he was somewhere out of town this season, in a garden restaurant . . . He's aged! Before, in summer service, it used to happen he'd bring home up to ten rubles a day, but now things are quiet everywhere. It's hard on the old fellow."

The old men and women looked at Nikolai's legs clothed in felt boots and at his pale face, and said sadly: "You're no breadwinner, Nikolai Osipich, no breadwinner! No indeed!"

And they all caressed Sasha. She had just turned ten, but was small, very thin, and from her appearance one might give her about seven years, no more. Next to the other little girls, sunburned, badly sheared, dressed in long, faded smocks, Sasha, who was rather pale, with big dark eyes, and a red ribbon in her hair, looked comical, like a little wild animal caught in the field and brought into the hut.

"And just think, she can read, too!" boasted Olga, looking tenderly at her daughter. "Read a bit, child!" she said, getting the Gospel from the corner. "You read and the good Orthodox folk will listen."

The Gospel was old, heavy, dog-eared, and leather-covered, and the smell it gave off was as though monks had just come into the hut. Sasha raised her eyebrows and began loudly in a singsong: " 'And when they were departed, behold, the angel of the Lord appeareth to Joseph in a dream, saying, Arise, and take the young child and his mother . . .' "

"The young child and his mother," Olga repeated, and she blushed all over with emotion.

" 'And flee into Egypt, and be thou there until I bring thee word: for Herod will seek the young child to destroy him . . .' "

At these words, Olga was unable to control herself and burst into tears. On seeing her, Marya sobbed, followed by Ivan Makarich's sister. The old man hemmed and bustled about for a gift for his granddaughter, but found nothing and simply waved his hands. And when the reading was over, the neighbors dispersed to their homes, moved and very pleased with Olga and Sasha.

Because of the holiday, the family stayed home all day. The old woman, whom everyone—her husband and the daughters-in-law and the grandsons—all called Granny, tried to do everything herself. She used to stoke the stove and put on the samovar herself, and even take the noon meal to the fields herself, and then complain that she was worn out with work. And she worried constantly for fear someone might eat an extra bite or the old man and the daughters-in-law might sit idly. Now she heard the tavern geese getting into her vegetable garden from the rear, and she ran out of the hut with a long stick and shrieked piercingly for half an hour beside the cabbages, withered and meager as herself; now she thought a crow was sneaking up on the chickens, and she rushed, cursing, at the crow. She raged and grumbled from morning till night, and often raised such a clamor that passers-by stopped in the street.

She treated her old man unkindly, calling him a lazybones and a pest. He was a vacillating, irresponsible peasant, and perhaps if she had not prodded him constantly, he would not have worked at all, but just sat on his bunk over the stove and talked. He told his son at length about some of his enemies, complained of affronts he apparently suffered daily from the neighbors, and it was tiresome listening to him.

"Yes," he would say, with arms akimbo. "Yes . . . After the Exaltation of the Cross, a week later, I sold some hay for thirty kopecks a pood,* on my own . . . Yes . . . Fine . . . Except this, that is, I'm carting the hay in the morning on my own, not hurting nobody; at an unlucky moment I look—out of the tavern comes the elder Antip Sedelnikov. 'Where are you taking that, you so-and-so?' and he cuffs me one on the ear."

Kiryak had an acute headache from drinking and was ashamed in front of his brother.

"What vodka will do! Ah, my God!" he muttered, shaking his throbbing head. "You there, brothers and sisters, forgive me for the sake of Christ; I'm not pleased myself."

Because of the holiday, they bought a herring at the tavern and made soup out of the head. At noon they all sat down to have tea and drank it for a long time, until they perspired and seemed swollen with tea; only after that did they start eating the soup, all from the same pot. The herring Granny hid.

That evening, a potter was firing pots in the ravine. On the meadow below, young girls were doing a round dance and singing. A harmonica was playing. And on the far side of the river, too, a kiln was burning and girls were singing, and from a distance this singing sounded harmonious and delicate. In and around the tavern, the peasant men were raising an uproar; some were singing in drunken voices, each separately, and they swore so that Olga just shuddered and kept saying: "Ah, holy saints! . . ."

It surprised her that the cursing rang out uninterruptedly, and that those cursing longest and loudest of all were the old men, whose time had already come. The children and young girls listened to this cursing without the slightest embarrassment, and it was obvious they were used to it from the cradle.

Midnight passed, the kilns were already extinguished here and on the other side, but on the meadow below and in the inn, they were still making merry. The old man and Kiryak, drunk, arm in arm, bumping each other's shoulders, went to the shed where Olga and Marya were lying.

"Leave her be," the old man urged, "leave her be . . . She's a harmless woman . . . It's a sin . . ."

"Ma-arya!" shouted Kiryak.

* A Russian weight, equivalent to 36.113 pounds.

"Leave her be . . . It's a sin . . . She's all right."

The two stood near the shed for a moment, then left.

"I lo-ove the flowers of the fi-ield!" the old man suddenly sang in a high, penetrating tenor. "I lo-ove to pick them in the meadows!"

Then he spat, swore filthily, and went into the hut.

IV

Granny stationed Sasha near the vegetable garden and ordered her to keep the geese out. It was a hot August day. The tavern geese could slip through to the garden from the rear, but they were busy with their own affairs now, picking oats near the tavern, peacefully chattering, and only the gander raised his head high as if to see whether the old woman was coming with her stick; other geese could have slipped in from down below, but they were now far beyond the river, feeding, stretching over the meadow in a long white garland. Sasha stood watch for a while, became bored, and observing that the geese were not coming, went over to the edge of the bluff.

There she saw Marya's oldest daughter, Motka, standing motionless on a huge rock and looking at the church. Marya had given birth thirteen times, but had only half a dozen children left, all girls, not one boy, and the oldest was eight. Motka, barefoot, in a long smock, stood in the direct sunlight, the sun burning the crown of her head, but she did not notice and seemed turned to stone. Sasha came up beside her and said, looking at the church: "God lives in the church. People burn lamps and candles, but God's little icon lamps are red, green, and blue like tiny eyes. God walks around the church at night, and with Him go the Holy Virgin Mary and Saint Nikolai—tup, tup, tup . . . and the watchman is scared, scared! Now, now, my dove," she added in imitation of her mother. "And when doomsday comes, all the churches will be carried off to heaven."

"And the bell to-wers too?" asked Motka in a bass voice, drawing out each syllable.

"And the bell towers too. And when doomsday comes, the good will go to paradise and the wicked'll burn in eternal and everlasting flames, my dove. God'll say to my Mama and to Marya too: 'You never hurt anyone so you go to the right, to paradise'; but to Kiryak and Granny, He'll say: 'And you go to the left, into the fire.' And anyone who's eaten forbidden food in fasts goes in the fire too."

She looked up at the sky, opening her eyes wide, and said: "Look at the sky, don't blink—you'll see angels."

Motka began looking at the sky too, and a minute passed in silence.

"D'you see?" Sasha asked.

"Not a thing," said Motka in her bass voice.

"Well, I do. Tiny little angels are flying through the sky with their wings going twinkle, twinkle, like little gnats."

Motka thought a while, looking at the ground, and asked: "Granny's going to burn?"

"She'll burn, my dove."

From the boulder to the very bottom of the ravine there was an even, gradual descent, covered with soft green grass one wanted to touch with one's hand or lie down on. Sasha lay down and rolled to the bottom. Motka, with a serious, stern face, puffing, also lay down and rolled, and at this her smock wriggled up to her shoulders.

"What fun that was!" Sasha exclaimed in excitement.

They both went to the top to roll down once more, but just then, a familiar, piercing voice rang out. Oh, how frightful it was! Granny, toothless, bony, hunchbacked, with short gray hair blowing in the wind, was chasing the geese from the vegetable plot with a long stick and shouting: "They've torn up all the cabbage, wretches. You should croak, you thrice-accursed scourges. Why aren't you in hell yet!"

She caught sight of the little girls, threw her stick aside, picked up a switch, and seizing Sasha by the neck with fingers hard and dry as prongs, began to whip her. Sasha cried with pain and fear, while the gander, rolling from one foot to the other and craning his neck, came up to the old woman, hissed something, and on his return to his flock, was greeted by all the geese approvingly: Ga-ga-ga! Then Granny began whipping Motka, and at this Motka's smock wriggled up again. In despair and crying loudly, Sasha went to the hut to complain; she was followed by Motka, crying too, but in a bass voice, without wiping her tears, and her face was as wet as if it had been dipped in water.

"Holy saints!" Olga exclaimed as the two came in the hut. "Heavenly Tsaritsa!"

Sasha began to tell what happened, when Granny came in with a penetrating shriek and a curse; Fekla became angry, and the hut was filled with noise.

"Never mind, never mind!" comforted Olga, pale, distressed, stroking Sasha's head. "She's your grandmother, it's a sin to be angry at her. Never mind, child."

Nikolai, who was exhausted by now from this perpetual shrieking, the hunger, fumes, and stench; who already hated and despised poverty; who was ashamed of his father and mother before his wife and daughter, swung his legs down from the stove and addressed his mother in an irritated, tearful voice: "You can't beat her! You've no right whatsoever to beat her!"

"You're half dead there on the stove, puny!" Fekla shouted at him with spite. "The devil brought you here, you spongers!"

And Sasha and Motka and the little girls, all of them, huddled in the corner over the stove, behind Nikolai's back, and listened to everything from there silently, with fear, and one could hear their little hearts beating. When there is someone sick in a family who has been ill for a long time, and hopelessly ill, those oppressive moments occur when all those close to him long for his death, timidly, secretly, in the bottom of their hearts; and only the children dread the death of a relative and are horrified at the thought of it. And now the little girls, holding their breaths, looked at Nikolai with sad faces and thought about how he would soon die, and they wanted to cry and say something affectionate, compassionate, to him.

He pressed close to Olga as if seeking her protection, and told her softly in a trembling voice: "Olga dear, I can't stand it here any longer. I haven't the strength. For God's sake, for the sake of the heavenly Christ, write your sister Klavdia Abramovna, let her sell and pawn everything she has, but let her send money; we'll get away from here. Oh, Lord," he continued in anguish, "for just one peep at Moscow! To just dream about Moscow, the little mother."

When evening came and the hut grew dark, it became so dismal that it was hard to get out a word. The angry grandmother soaked rye crusts in her cup and sucked them for a long time, a whole hour. Marya milked the cow and brought a pail of milk which she put on the bench. Granny then poured from the pail into pitchers, also lengthily, without hurry, obviously content that now, during the Fast of the Assumption, no one would drink milk and it would all remain intact. And she poured only a little, barely any, into a saucer for Fekla's child. While she and Marya were carrying the pitchers to the cellar, Motka suddenly shook herself, climbed down from the stove, and going to the bench where the wooden cup with the crusts stood, splashed milk into it from the saucer.

On returning to the hut, Granny went back to her crusts, while Sasha and Motka watched her from the shelf above the stove and were pleased that she was breaking the fast and was now already on the way to hell. Consoled, they lay down to sleep, and as she dozed off, Sasha pictured the Last Judgment: there was a huge stove burning, a sort of kiln, and the Evil One, all black, with horns like a cow, was chasing Granny into the fire with a long stick, just as she had chased the geese shortly before.

v

Some time after ten in the evening on Assumption Day, the girls and boys making merry down in the meadow suddenly started shouting and shrieking and ran in the direction of the village; and those sitting up above, on the edge of the bluff, could not at first understand the reason.

"Fire! Fire!" the despairing cry rang out below. "We're burning up!"

Those sitting above glanced around and were confronted by a terrifying and extraordinary picture. On top of the thatched roof of one of the farthest huts stood a fiery column seven feet high, whirling and showering sparks in all directions like a fountain playing. And just then the entire roof ignited in a bright blaze and the crackle of fire resounded.

The moonlight paled and the whole village was enveloped in a tremulous red light; black shadows crossed the ground; there was a scorched smell; and those who ran up from below, all breathless, unable to speak for trembling, bumped into one another, fell down, and unaccustomed to the bright light, saw poorly and failed to recognize one another. It was terrifying. It was particularly terrifying that doves were flying through the smoke above the fire and that in the tavern, where they did not know about the fire yet, they were still singing and playing the harmonica as if nothing were wrong.

"Uncle Semon is burning up!" someone shouted in a loud, coarse voice.

Marya was running distractedly around her hut, crying, her teeth chattering, wringing her hands, although the fire was far away, at the opposite end of the village; out came Nikolai in his felt boots; out ran the children in their little smocks. Near the village policeman's hut, they were beating on a piece of sheet iron. Boom, boom, boom . . . rose in the air, and this rapid relentless sound made hearts grow heavy, and a chill fell. Old women stood around holding icons. Sheep, calves, and cows were driven out of the courtyards into the street; tubs, coffers, and sheepskins were carried out. The black stallion, who was not allowed in the herd because he kicked and injured the other horses, was let loose and ran stamping, neighing through the village once or twice, then suddenly stopped near a cart and began kicking it with his hind feet.

The bells started to ring in the church across the river.

It was hot near the burning hut and so bright that every blade of grass on the ground was distinctly visible. On one of the coffers they had managed to drag out sat Semon, a red-haired, large-nosed peasant wearing a jacket and a peaked cap pulled far over his head, down to his ears; his wife lay on the ground face down, unconscious, and groaning. A short old man of about eighty with a huge beard who looked like a gnome and was not from the village, although apparently connected with the fire, walked close by bareheaded, with a white parcel in his arms, the fire reflecting in his bald pate. The elder, Antip Sedelnikov, swarthy and dark-haired as a gipsy, went up to the hut with an ax, smashed the windows, one after the other—no one knows why, then began hacking at the porch steps.

"Water, women!" he shouted. "Bring up the eng-ine! Get moving!"

The same peasants who had just been carousing in the tavern were dragging up the fire engine. They were all drunk, stumbling and falling, and all had the same helpless expression and tears in their eyes.

"Girls, water!" shouted the elder, who was also drunk. "Get moving, girls!"

The women and girls ran to the spring below, hauled full pails and buckets up the hill, and ran back again after emptying them into the fire engine. Olga, Marya, and Sasha and Motka hauled water too. The women and boys pumped water, the hose sizzled, and the elder, directing it now on the door, now on the windows, restrained the jet with his finger, which made it sizzle still more sharply.

"Good man, Antip!" approving voices rang out. "Don't give up!"

Antip crawled into the shed, into the fire, and shouted from there: "Pump! Orthodox Christians, on such an unhappy occasion!"

A flock of peasants stood near by doing nothing and watched the fire. No one knew where to begin; no one knew how to do anything, yet all around stood stacks of wheat and hay, sheds, and heaps of dry brushwood. There stood Kiryak and his father, old man Osip, both in high spirits. As if wanting to vindicate his idleness, the old man said to the woman lying on the ground: "Why carry on so, neighbor? The hut's insured—why fret!"

Semon, addressing first one then the other, told how the fire had started.

"That same little old man with the package there, General Zhukov's house serf . . . He was a cook for our general, may he rest in peace. He comes this evening: Let me spend the night, he says . . . Well, we had a little glass each, of course . . . The woman got busy with the samovar—to get the old man tea, yes, and at an unlucky hour she sat the samovar in the entry, the fire from the stovepipe, that is, went straight to the roof, the thatch, and that was it. Almost burned up ourselves. And the old man's cap burned up, what a shame."

They kept beating the sheet iron indefatigably and the church bells across the river rang frequently. Olga, bathed in light, panting, looking with horror at the rosy doves flying in the smoke and at the red sheep, ran up and down. She felt this ringing had pierced her heart like a sharp thorn, that the fire would never be over, that Sasha was lost . . . And when the ceiling collapsed resoundingly in the hut, she grew faint from the thought that now the whole village would certainly burn up. Unable to haul water any more, she simply sat down on the edge of the bluff with her pails beside her; next to and below her sat the peasant women, wailing as at a wake.

But then, from the other side of the river, from the gentleman's estate, hired men and laborers were coming in two carts, bringing a fire engine with them. A student in a white, unbuttoned summer uniform arrived on horseback; he was very young. They began hacking with axes and propped a ladder against the burning framework, which was immediately climbed by five men, led by the student, who was red-faced and kept shouting orders in a sharp, hoarse voice as if extinguishing fires was his usual occupation. They tore the hut apart beam by beam; they pulled to pieces the cattle shed, the wattle, and the closest haystack.

"Don't let them smash things!" stern voices burst out in the crowd. "Don't let them!"

Kiryak went toward the hut with a determined air as if to keep the new arrivals from smashing it, but one of the workers turned him around and struck him on the neck. Laughter was heard, the worker struck once again; Kiryak fell and crawled back into the crowd on all fours.

From the other bank came two pretty girls in hats—undoubtedly the student's sisters. They stood at a slight distance and watched the fire. The scattered beams were no longer burning, but smoked heavily; the student, working the hose, directed the stream first on these beams, then on the peasants, then on the women hauling water.

"George!" the girls shouted to him reproachfully and anxiously. "George!"

The fire was over. Only when they began to disperse did they notice that it was already dawn, that everyone looked pale and somewhat dark—as people always do in the early morning when the last stars are fading in the sky. As they separated, the peasants laughed and bantered about General Zhukov's cook and about his burned cap; they already wanted to treat the fire as a joke and seemed to regret it had been over so quickly.

"You put it out well, My Lord," Olga said to the student. "You should come to us in Moscow: imagine it, there's a fire there every day."

"Then you're from Moscow?" asked one of the young ladies.

"Exactly. My husband was employed in the Slavonic Bazaar, ma'am. And this is my daughter," she pointed to Sasha, who was chilled and clung to her. "Also a Muscovite."

The two young ladies said something to the student in French, and he gave Sasha a twenty-kopeck piece. Old man Osip saw this, and hope suddenly lighted his face.

"Thank God there was no wind, Your Honor," he said, turning to the student, "or else we'd have burned up in no time. Your honor, good gentlefolk," he added bashfully, in a lower voice, "the dawn is cold, if one could warm up . . . by your kindness, with a little pint."

They gave him nothing, and clearing his throat, he shuffled home. Olga stood on the edge of the bluff and watched the two carts cross the river at the ford and the gentlefolk walk across the meadow; a carriage was waiting for them on the other bank. Arriving at the hut, she told her husband ecstatically: "Yes, such good people! And so handsome! The young ladies are like little cherubs."

"Let them burst!" the drowsy Fekla said spitefully.

<hr />

VI

Marya considered herself unhappy and used to say she wanted to die; Fekla, on the other hand, found this life entirely to her taste: the poverty and the filth and the incessant cursing. She ate what was given, without question, slept anywhere and on anything handy; she emptied the slops from the very porch, splashing them from the doorway and then walking barefoot through the puddle. And she detested Olga and Nikolai from the very first, precisely because they disliked this life.

"We'll see what you'll eat here, Moscow gentlefolk!" she used to say maliciously. "We'll see-ee!"

One morning, it was already the beginning of September, Fekla, rosy with cold, healthy, and handsome, brought up two pails of water just as Marya and Olga were sitting at the table and drinking tea.

"Tea and even sugar!" said Fekla derisively. "Such ladies," she added, setting down the pails. "They've took up the fashion of drinking tea every day. Look out you don't puff up with your tea there!" she continued, looking at Olga with hatred. "Fattened her swollen muzzle in Moscow, the ball of fat!"

She brandished her yoke, striking Olga on the shoulder, so that the two sisters-in-law just threw up their hands and said: "Ah, Holy Saints!"

Then Fekla went to the river to wash the linen and cursed the whole way so loudly it was audible in the hut.

The day passed. The long autumn evening began. They were winding silk in the hut, everyone except Fekla, who had gone across the river. They got the silk from a nearby factory and the whole family earned a bit from it—twenty kopecks a week.

"In the master's time it was better," the old man said, winding silk. "You work and you eat and you sleep, all in its turn. For dinner there's cabbage soup and *kasha* * for you, for

* A porridge usually made of barley or oats.

supper, also cabbage soup and *kasha*. All the cucumbers and cabbages you want: you eat on your own to your heart's content. And there used to be more strictness. Everybody kept his place."

The light came from a single lamp which burned dimly and smoked. Whenever anyone obscured the lamp, a huge shadow fell on the window and the bright moonlight became visible. Old man Osip talked unhurriedly about how they used to live before the Emancipation, how in these very places where it was now so dull and miserable to live, they hunted with bird dogs, greyhounds, and retrievers; how the peasants were given vodka during the beat; how whole wagon trains of slain birds were taken to Moscow for the young gentlemen; and how evildoers used to be punished by flogging or exile to the Tver estate, while the good were rewarded. And Granny had something to tell, too. She remembered everything, absolutely everything. She told about her former mistress, a kind, God-fearing woman whose husband was a rake and a spendthrift, all of whose daughters finally got married, God knows how: one married a drunk, another—a commoner, a third eloped secretly (with the aid of Granny herself, who was then a girl), and all of them soon died of sorrow, as their mother did, too. And remembering this, Granny even shed a tear.

Suddenly someone knocked at the door and everyone shivered.

"Uncle Osip, let me spend the night!"

In came the bald little old man, General Zhukov's cook, the one whose cap had burned up. He sat down, listened a while, and also began reminiscing and recounting various stories. Nikolai, sitting on the stove, his legs dangling, listened and kept asking questions about the food that used to be prepared for the gentry. They talked about meat balls, cutlets, various soups and sauces, and the cook, who also remembered everything very clearly, named dishes which were no longer made: there was, for example, a dish prepared from bulls' eyes which was known as "Waking up in the Morning."

"And did they make cutlets *maréchal* then?" asked Nikolai.

"No."

Nikolai shook his head reproachfully and said: "Eh, you're wretched cooks!"

The little girls sitting and lying over the stove stared down unblinkingly; there seemed to be a great mass of them—like cherubs in the clouds. The stories pleased them; they sighed, trembled, and paled, now from rapture, then from fear, and they listened to Granny—who narrated more entertainingly than the others—with bated breath, afraid to move.

They lay down to sleep in silence. The old people, aroused by the stories, agitated, thought about what a splendid thing youth was which, once gone, no matter what it had been like, left only the vivid, joyous, and touching in one's memory; and how terrifyingly cold that death was that lay on the horizon now—better not to think about it! The lamp went out. And the darkness, the two little windows, sharply lit by the moon, the silence, and the creak of the cradle for some reason called to mind only that life had already slipped by, that you can't turn it back . . . You doze, lose consciousness, then suddenly someone touches your shoulder, breathes on your cheek—and there's no sleep. Your body seems numbed as if circulation had stopped, and all the thoughts of death creep into your head; you turn on the other side—death already forgotten, but through your head drift the old, tiresome, tedious thoughts about want, about food, about flour becoming dearer, and shortly thereafter, you remember again that life has already slipped by, that you can't turn it back . . .

"Oh, Lord!" sighed the cook.

Someone gently, gently, knocked on the window. Probably Fekla, returned. Olga got up and yawning, whispering a prayer, opened the door, then drew back the bolt in the entry. But no one came in; there was only a cold wind from the street and a sudden brightening from the moonlight. Through the open door the street was visible, quiet, deserted, and the moon itself, floating through the sky.

"Who's there?" Olga called out.

"Me," came the answer. "It's me."

Near the door, pressed to the wall, stood Fekla, completely naked. She was trembling with cold, her teeth were chattering, and in the brilliant moonlight she looked very pale, beautiful, and strange. The shadows and the luster of the moon on her skin were somehow strikingly distinct, and her dark brows and firm young bosom were particularly sharply accentuated.

"Those upstarts across the river stripped me and left me . . ." she said. "I came home without clothes . . . as my mother bore me. Bring something to put on."

"But come in the hut!" said Olga softly, beginning to tremble too.

"The old folks mustn't see."

In fact, Granny was already disturbed and grumbling, and the old man was asking: "Who's there?" Olga brought her own shirt and skirt, dressed Fekla, and they came quietly into the hut, trying not to rattle the doors.

"That you, sleek one?" Grany muttered angrily, guessing who it was. "Curse you, you night-owl . . . Why aren't you in hell!"

"Never mind, never mind," whispered Olga, covering up Fekla; "never mind, my dove."

It became quiet again. They always slept badly in the hut; each was kept from sleeping by something tiresome, importunate: the old man by a pain in his back; Granny by worry and malice; Marya by fear; the children by itching and hunger. And their slumber was restless now, too: they tossed from side to side, talked in their sleep, got up to drink water.

Fekla suddenly began howling in a loud, coarse voice, but immediately restrained herself and sobbed occasionally, more and more dully, until she became still. From time to time, from the other bank beyond the river, came the striking of the clock; but it struck oddly somehow, ringing five, then three.

"Oh, Lord!" sighed the cook.

Looking out the window it was difficult to determine whether it was still moonlight or already daybreak. Marya arose and went out, and one could hear her milking the cow in the courtyard and saying "Wo-oa!" Granny went out too. It was still dark in the hut, but all the objects were distinct.

Nikolai, who had not slept the whole night, climbed down from the stove. He got his frock coat out of the green storage chest, put it on, and going to the window, smoothed the sleeves, held out the tails, and smiled. Then he carefully took the coat off, put it away in the trunk, and lay down again.

Marya returned and began stoking the stove. She was obviously still half asleep and waking up as she went. She had probably had a dream or else was recalling yesterday's stories as she stretched herself with pleasure in front of the stove and said: "No, emancipation is better!"

❖◇◇◇◇◇◇◇◇◇◇◇◇◇◇◇◇◇◇◇◇◇◇◇◇◇❖

VII

The master arrived—as the rural police chief was called. For what, when, and why he was coming had been known for a week. There were only forty farms in Zhukovo, but the arrears, state and village, had piled up to over two thousand.

The police chief stopped at the tavern, where he gobbled down two glasses of tea, and then proceeded on foot to the elder's hut, near which a crowd of tax defaulters was waiting. Elder Antip Sedelnikov, in spite of his youth—he was only a little past thirty—was strict and always took the side of authority, although he himself was poor and remiss in paying his taxes. It obviously amused him to be the elder, and he enjoyed the feeling of power, which he was only able to display through strictness. He was feared and obeyed in meetings; he had been known to suddenly pounce on a drunk on the street or near a tavern, tie his hands behind his back, and put him in jail. Once he had even put Granny in jail because she had started cursing while attending a meeting in Osip's place; and he had kept her there a whole twenty-four hours. He had never lived in the city and never read books, but had collected various erudite words somewhere which he loved to use in conversation, and for this he was respected, although not always understood.

When Osip came into the elder's hut with his textbook, the police chief, an emaciated old man with long gray sideburns wearing a grayish jacket, was seated at the table in the icon corner and noting down something. The hut was clean, all the walls were multicolored with pictures clipped from magazines, and in the most prominent place, near the icons, hung a portrait of Battenberg, the former Bulgarian prince. Near the table, arms folded, stood Antip Sedelnikov.

"He's behind, Your Honor, a hundred and nineteen rubles," he said, when Osip's turn came. "He paid one ruble before Easter, and not a kopeck since."

The police chief raised his eyes to Osip and asked: "Why is that, brother?"

"Show heavenly mercy, Your Honor," Osip began in agitation; "allow me to say how last year the Lyutoretsky master says, Osip, he says, sell me hay . . . You sell it to me, says he. Why not? I had a hundred poods for sale, the women had mowed it on the water-meadow. Well, we struck a bargain, all right, on our own . . ."

He complained about the elder and kept turning again and again to the peasants as if inviting them to bear witness. His face reddened and perspired, and his eyes became sharp, malignant.

"I don't understand why you're saying all this," said the police chief. "I'm asking you . . . I'm asking you why you don't pay your debt? None of you pay, am I to answer for you?"

"I can't!"

"These words are of no consequence, Your Honor," said the elder. "In truth, the Chikildeyevs are of the needy class, but if you will ask the others, the whole reason for it is vodka, and they're terrible hooligans. Without the slightest understanding."

The police chief wrote something down and said to Osip calmly, in an even tone, as though asking for a drink of water: "Get out."

Soon he drove away, and as he sat down in his own cheap carriage and coughed, it was obvious even from his long thin back that he had already forgotten Osip and the elder and Zhukov's arrears, and was thinking about his own affairs. Before he was one verst away, Antip Sedelnikov was carrying the Chikildeyev's samovar out of the hut, pursued by Granny, shrieking piercingly and straining her lungs: "I won't give it up! I won't give it up to you, wretch!"

He walked quickly, taking long strides, while she chased after him, panting, almost falling, hunchbacked, raging; her kerchief had slipped onto her shoulders; her gray hair with its greenish cast tossed in the wind. Suddenly she stopped, and like a real rebel, began beating herself on the chest with her fists and shouting even louder, in a singing voice, and as if sobbing: "Orthodox believers in God! Little fathers, they've wronged me, kindred, they've strangled me! Oh, oh, darlings, defend me!"

"Granny, Granny," said the elder sternly, "get some sense in your head!"

It became utterly dreary in the Chikildeyev's hut without the samovar. There was something degrading in this deprivation, something insulting, as if the honor of the hut had suddenly been taken away. It would have been better even had the elder removed the table, all the benches, and all the pots—it would not have seemed as bare. Granny screamed, Marya cried, and the little girls also cried on seeing her. The old man, feeling guilty, sat downcast in a corner and kept silent. Nikolai was silent too. The grandmother loved and pitied him, but she forgot her pity now, rushing at him suddenly with curses and reproaches, thrusting her fists right under his face. She screamed that he was to blame for everything; in fact, why had he sent so little money when he himself used to brag in his letters that he earned fifty rubles a month at the Slavonic Bazaar? And why had he come here, with his family to boot? If he died, whose money would bury him? . . . And Nikolai, Olga, and Sasha were pitiful to see.

The old man hemmed, took his cap, and went to the elder's. It was already dusk. Antip Sedelnikov was soldering something near the stove with distended cheeks; it was stifling. His children, thin, unwashed, and no better off than the Chikildeyev's, were scrambling over the floor. His wife, homely, freckled, and big-bellied, was winding silk. It was an unhappy, impoverished family, and Antip alone looked sturdy and handsome. On the bench stood five samovars in a row. The old man said a prayer to Battenberg and began: "Antip, show heavenly mercy. Give back the samovar! For the sake of Christ!"

"Bring three rubles, then you'll get it."

"I can't!"

Antip puffed his cheeks; the fire droned and crackled, reflecting in the samovars. The old man kneaded his cap and said after some thought: "Give it back!"

The swarthy elder now looked completely black and like a sorcerer; he turned to Osip and intoned sternly and quickly: "Everything depends on the district magistrate. In the administrative meeting of the twenty-sixth instant you can present the cause of your dissatisfaction orally or in writing."

Osip understood nothing, but was satisfied by this and went home.

Ten days later the police chief came again, stayed about an hour, and left. The weather was continuously windy and cold at that time; the river had frozen over long ago, but there was still no snow, and people were exhausted from struggling with impassable roads. One holiday eve, the neighbors visited Osip to sit and chat. They talked in the dark because it was a sin to work, and they had therefore not lit the lamps. There was news of sorts, all fairly disagreeable. Such as that in two or three houses the hens had been confiscated for arrears and been sent to the district administration, where they had died because no one fed them; sheep had been confiscated too, and while being carted away tied together and transferred into a new cart at each village, one of them had died. And now they were trying to decide who was guilty.

"The zemstvo!"* said Osip. "Who else!"

* The local rural governing council.

"The zemstvo, of course."

They blamed the zemstvo for everything—for arrears and confiscatory exactions and crop failures, although not one of them knew what the zemstvo really was. And this had been going on since rich peasants, who had their own factories, shops, and post-inns, had served as zemstvo members themselves, been dissatisfied, and had begun cursing the zemstvo in their factories and inns.

They discussed the fact that God had not sent them snow: wood had to be hauled, but it was impossible to drive or walk over the frozen ruts. Previously, fifteen or twenty years ago and earlier, conversations in Zhukovo had been considerably more interesting. In those days every old man looked as if he were keeping a secret, as if he knew something and were waiting for something. They used to talk about a charter with a gold seal, about land partitioning, about the new lands, about treasure-troves; they used to hint at something. Now the villagers had no secrets of any kind. Their whole life was as clear to see as if it lay on the palm of your hand, and all they could talk about was poverty and food and how there was no snow . . .

They were silent a while. Then they recalled the hens and the sheep, and began discussing who was guilty again.

"The zemstvo!" said Osip gloomily. "Who else!"

VIII

The parish church was six versts away in Kosogorovo, and they visited it only when necessary: for christenings, marriages, and funerals. To pray, they went across the river. On holidays, the girls used to dress up and go to Mass in a flock in good weather, and they were a cheerful sight crossing the meadow in their red, yellow, and green dresses; in bad weather, they all stayed home. Communion was taken in the parish church, and when the priest made the rounds of the huts with the cross at Easter, he collected fifty kopecks each from those who had been unable to take the sacrament during Lent.

The old man did not believe in God because he had almost never given Him a thought; he acknowledged the supernatural but considered it of concern only to women, and when religion or miracles were discussed in front of him and he was asked a question of some sort, he would reply reluctantly, scratching himself: "Ah, who knows!"

Granny believed, but somewhat dimly; everything got mixed up in her mind, and hardly had she begun thinking about sin, about death, and about the salvation of the soul, than want and worry took over her reflections, and she immediately forgot what she had started thinking about. She did not remember prayers, and when it was time to sleep in the evening, she usually stood in front of the icons and whispered: "Holy Mother of Kazan, Holy Mother of Smolensk, Holy Mother of the Three Arms . . ."

Marya and Fekla crossed themselves, took communion every year, but understood nothing. The children were not taught how to pray, nothing was told them about God, no precepts of any sort were instilled in them; they were simply forbidden to eat certain food during fasts. In the other families, it was about the same: there were few who believed and few who understood. Yet everyone loved the Holy Scriptures, loved them tenderly, reverently, but there were no books, there was no one to read and explain, and because Olga sometimes read the Gospel, everyone respected her, and all addressed both Olga and Sasha in the formal second person plural.

Olga frequently went to the neighboring villages and the district town, in which there were two monastaries and twenty-seven churches, for special services and Te Deums. She was absent-minded, and when making a pilgrimage, completely forgot about her family; only when returning home would she suddenly make the joyful discovery that she had a husband and a daughter; then she would say, smiling and beaming: "God was bountiful!"

What went on in the village seemed disgusting to her and tormented her. On St. Elijah's Day they drank; at Assumption, they drank; at the Exaltation of the Cross, they drank. The Feast of the Intercession was a parish holiday in Zhukovo, and on this occasion the peasants drank for three days straight; they consumed the fifty rubles in the community fund and then collected more for vodka from every house. The first day, the Chikildeyevs slaughtered a sheep and ate it in the morning, at noon, and in the evening; they ate copiously, and the children, in addition, got up in the night to eat more. Kiryak was terribly drunk the whole three days, squandered everything he owned on alcohol, even his hat and boots, and beat Marya so that they had to pour water over her. Afterward, everyone felt ashamed and revolted.

However, in Zhukovo, in this "Flunkeytown," there was one genuine religious celebration. It was in August, when throughout the entire region, they carried the icon of the Life-bearing Mother of God from village to village. On the day it was expected in Zhukovo, the weather was calm and overcast. The girls had set out to meet the icon in the morning in their bright, trim dresses and brought it back toward evening, singing, in procession, and at that moment the chimes rang across the river. A huge crowd of locals and strangers choked the street; noise, dust, mob . . . The old man and Granny and Kiryak—all stretched their hands toward the icon, looked at it greedily and said, crying: "Intercede for us, Little Mother! Intercede!"

Everyone seemed to suddenly perceive that there is no void between heaven and earth, that the rich and strong have not seized everything yet, that there still is protection against injury, against bondage, against oppressive, unbearable want, against the frightful vodka.

"Intercede, Little Mother!" sobbed Marya. "Little Mother!"

But when they finished the Te Deum and took away the icon, everything was as before, and coarse, drunken voices rang out again from the inn.

Death was only feared by the rich peasants, who believed less in God and in the salvation of the soul the richer they became, and lit candles and had Masses said only from fear of their earthly end, just in case. The poorer peasants were not afraid of death. They used to tell the old man and Granny to their faces that they had outlived their span, that it was time for them to die, and this meant nothing to them. They did not hesitate to tell Fekla in front of Nikolai that when Nikolai died, her husband, Denis, would be discharged and come home from the army. Marya not only was unafraid of death, but even regretted that it was so long in coming, and was glad whenever one of her children died.

They were not afraid of death, but regarded all illnesses with an exaggerated dread. A trifle sufficed—an indigestion, a light chill, for Granny to be lying down on the bunk over the stove, wrapping herself up, and groaning loudly and incessantly: "I'm dy-y-y-ing!" The old man would hurry for the priest and Granny would receive the sacrament and take Extreme Unction. There was frequent talk of colds, intestinal worms, and tumors which moved about in the stomach and shifted up to the heart. They feared colds most of all, and therefore even in summer dressed warmly and warmed themselves at the stove. Granny loved doctoring herself and frequently traveled to the clinic where she used to say she was fifty-eight, not seventy; she assumed that if the doctor knew her true age, he would refuse to treat her and would say it was time for her to die, not to doctor herself. She usually went to the clinic early in the morning, taking two or three of the little girls with her, and she would return, hungry and cross, in the evening, with drops for herself and salves for the girls. Once she took Nikolai, too, who took drops for two weeks afterward and said he felt better.

Granny knew all the doctors, medical assistants, and witch doctors for thirty versts around, and did not like a single one of them. At the Feast of the Intercession, when the priest went around the huts with the cross, the deacon advised her to turn to a little old man, a former military corpsman who was very good at cures and lived in town near the prison. Granny obeyed. When the first snow fell, she went to town and brought back a bearded old man, a long-coated converted Jew, whose entire face was crisscrossed with blue veins. There were journeymen working in the hut at the time; an old man, a tailor, in terrifying spectacles, was cutting a jacket out of rags, and two young lads were making felt boots out of wool. Kiryak, who had been dismissed for drunkenness and was now living at home, sat repairing a yoke next to the tailor. The hut was crowded, stifling, and fetid. The convert examined Nikolai and said he had to be cupped.

While he applied the cups, the old tailor, Kiryak, and the little girls stood looking on, and it seemed to them that they could see the illness leaving Nikolai. Nikolai also watched the cups sucking at his chest and gradually filling with dark blood, and he felt as if something really were leaving him, and he smiled with contentment.

"That's good," said the tailor. "God grant it's helpful."

The convert placed twelve cups, then twelve more, drank some tea, and left. Nikolai began to shiver; his face became drawn, and as the women put it, squeezed into a fist; his fingers turned blue. He wrapped himself up in a blanket and a sheepskin coat, but kept feeling colder. Toward evening, he became miserable; he asked to be placed on the floor, asked the tailor not to smoke, then grew still under the sheepskin, and toward morning, he died.

IX

Oh, what a hard, what a long winter!

They had had no grain of their own ever since Christmas, and had been obliged to buy flour. Kiryak, who was now living at home, raised an uproar in the evenings, horrifying everyone, and suffered from headaches and shame and was pitiful to see in the mornings. The cattle shed resounded day and night with the lowing of the hungry cow, breaking the hearts of Granny and Marya. And as if on purpose, the frosts continued to be bitter, the snowdrifts piled high, and winter dragged on: at Annunciation, a real winter blizzard blew, and snow fell at Eastertime.

But however that may be, winter did come to an end. In early April, the warm days and frosty nights began; winter had not yet given in, but one warm day won out at last—and the rivulets flowed; the birds began to sing. The whole meadow and the bushes bordering the river wallowed in spring floods, and the entire expanse between Zhukovo and the far bank was a continuous, huge pond from which flocks of wild ducks took wing here and there. The spring sunset, fiery, with magnificent clouds, invented something unusual, new, and unbelievable every morning, the sort of thing one does not believe afterward on seeing the same colors and clouds in a picture.

The cranes flew swiftly, swiftly, and called plaintively as though inviting company. Standing on the edge of the bluff, Olga gazed for a long time at the flood, at the sun, at the bright, seemingly rejuvenated church, and the tears flowed, and she was breathless with a passionate longing to go away, to follow her gaze, even to the edge of the world. And it had already been decided that she would go to Moscow again as a chambermaid, and that Kiryak would be sent with her to be placed as a porter or something. Oh, to get away quickly!

When it became dry and warm, they got ready for the journey. Olga and Sasha, with knapsacks on their backs, both in bark shoes, left when it was barely light; Marya also came out to escort them. Kiryak was unwell and was being kept at home another week. Olga prayed toward the church for the last time, thinking of her husband, and did not shed a tear; her face merely wrinkled up and became ugly, like an old woman's. During the winter she had grown thinner, homelier, turned a little gray, and already, instead of her previous prettiness and pleasant smile, her face had the resigned, melancholy expression of grief endured, and there was something dull and immobile about her glance as though she could not hear. She regretted leaving the village and the peasants. She remembered how they had carried Nikolai and said a requiem near each hut, and how everyone had cried in sympathy with her sorrow. In the course of the winter and summer there had been hours and days when these people seemed to live worse than cattle; when living with them seemed frightful. They were coarse, dishonest, filthy, drunken; they did not get along and cursed each other continuously because they despised, feared, and suspected one another. Who keeps the tavern and inebriates the people? The peasant. Who pockets and drinks up the community, school, and church money? The peasant. Who steals from his neighbors, sets them on fire, gives false testimony in court for a bottle of vodka? The peasant. In the zemstvo and other meetings, who is the first to attack the peasantry? The peasant. Yes, living with them was frightful, but still, they are human beings; they suffer and cry like human beings, and there is nothing in their lives for which justification could not be found: the oppressive labor, from which the whole body aches at night, the cruel winters, the meager harvests, the overcrowding, and the lack of help or any place from which to expect it. The richer and stronger are unable to help because they themselves are coarse, dishonest, drunken, and curse each other just as disgustingly; the pettiest official or clerk treats the peasants like tramps, addresses even the church and village elders familiarly, and thinks he has the right to do so. Yes, and could any sort of help or good example come from people who are grasping, greedy, dissolute, lazy—who travel to the country only to insult, despoil, and terrorize? Olga remembered the old people's pitiful, humiliated expressions when Kiryak was led off to be flogged last winter . . . And now she felt sorry for all these people, painfully sorry, and kept looking back at the huts as she walked.

After accompanying them for three versts, Marya took leave, then knelt and began to wail, pressing her face to the ground: "Again I'm left alone, my poor little head, poor unlucky . . ."

And for a long time she wailed, and for a long time Olga and Sasha could still see her kneeling and bowing to someone on the side, her head clutched in her hands, while ravens flew above her.

The sun had risen high; it had grown hot. Zhukovo was far behind. Walking with pleasure, Olga and Sasha quickly forgot both the village and Marya; they felt merry and everything diverted them. Now there was a burial mound, now a row of telegraph poles which followed one another, no one knows where, disappearing in the horizon, the wires humming mysteriously. Then, in the distance, a little farmhouse was visible, all enclosed in greenery, smelling of dampness and linseed oil, and for some reason looking as if happy people lived there; then a horse's skeleton glowed, white and solitary in a field. And the skylarks sang indefatigably at the top of their voices, the quails called to each other, and a crake shrieked like someone dragging an old iron grapple.

At noon, Olga and Sasha arrived in a large settlement. There, on the main street, they passed General Zhukov's cook, the little old man. He was hot and his perspiring, red bald spot glistened in the sun. He and Olga failed to recognize one another, then glanced back at the same time, and without a word, each continued on his way. Stopping near a hut which looked newer and richer than the rest, Olga bowed before the open windows and said loudly in a thin, singsong voice: "Orthodox Christians, give charity for the sake of Christ, that your charity bring eternal peace to your kin in the heavenly kingdom."

"Orthodox Christians," Sasha began singing, "give for the sake of Christ, that your charity, the heavenly kingdom . . ."

In the Ravine

The publication of Chekhov's story "Peasants" had attracted the attention of the Russian Marxists to him. The controversy between Peter Struve and Nikolay Mikhailovsky about the story has been mentioned above. Chekhov was not a Marxist, of course, but his negative view of the Russian village community (see his letter to Suvorin, dated January 17, 1899) and his refusal to idealize the peasants were welcome to the Marxists. In January 1899, Peter Struve invited Chekhov to contribute to the newly founded Marxist monthly *Nachalo* (*The Beginning*), which had replaced the suppressed *Novoe Slovo*. Almost simultaneously, Gorky asked Chekhov to give a story to another Marxist periodical, *Zhizn* (*Life*), edited by Vladimir Posse. Chekhov wrote back to say that he had already promised his collaboration to Struve. Actually, it was in *Life*, and not in *The Beginning*, which had in the meantime been closed down by the government, that Chekhov's next story, "In the Ravine," saw the light of day.

Chekhov began writing "In the Ravine" in November 1899. On November 19 he wrote to Posse: "I am writing a story [*povest'*] for *Life*, and it will soon be ready, probably by the second half of December. It has only about three signatures [i.e., forty-eight printed pages], but a host of characters, full of bustling and crowding, and I have to take a lot of trouble to avoid this bustling being felt too sharply." At the same time Chekhov expressed a fear that the censors might "pick at the story."

The story was completed early in December and mailed to Posse on December 20. Chekhov warned him that he might change the title if he came upon something "more expressive and eyecatching." He stuck, however, to his original title. Posse was greatly impressed by the story: "How merciless, how ominously truthful!" he wrote. "Not a hint at a calculated effect, but the impression is enormous; it penetrates the soul and gradually grows, after the story has already been read." Informing Olga Knipper of the forthcoming publication of the story, Chekhov characterized it as "very odd," adding: "There are many characters; there is also a landscape. There is a crescent of the moon, there is a bird called the bittern, which cries, somewhere far, far away, 'boo-oo, boo-oo,' like a cow locked in a barn. Everything is in there." To one of his friends (Rossolimo) Chekhov wrote that this was to be his last story "from people's life," and this turned out to be true: Chekhov was to write only two more stories: "The Bishop" and "The Betrothed."

"In the Ravine" was published in the January 1900 issue of *Life* and was an immediate and great success. Gorky praised it in a long article, in which he wrote, among other things: "As a stylist, Chekhov is unmatchable, and the future historian of literature, in speaking of the growth of the Russian language, will say that this language was created by Pushkin, Turgenev, and Chekhov." Tolstoy, in a letter to Gorky, wrote: "How good is Chekhov's story in *Life*. I am exceedingly glad." Alexander Koni, well known both as a writer and as a lawyer of distinction, a friend of Tolstoy and Dostoevsky, wrote to Chekhov that he had read and reread the story "with delight," and went on to say: "I think it is the best thing you ever wrote and one of the profoundest works of Russian literature." Bunin regarded "In the Ravine" as one of the greatest works in contemporary literature. It is undoubtedly one of Chekhov's best and most powerful stories.

With minor changes the story was included in the last, posthumous volume of Chekhov's *Collected Works*. Chekhov's brother Michael said that for the story of Anisim, Chekhov had made use of a case he had heard about during his visit to Sakhalin, while the setting of "In the Ravine" was provided by Melikhovo (earlier Chekhov had written to Suvorin that after he had finished "Peasants" Melikhovo was no longer of interest to him as a source of literary inspiration, and that was one of the reasons for selling it).

I

The village of Ukleyevo lay in a ravine, so that from the highway and the railroad station, only the church steeple and the chimneys of the cotton mills were visible. When passers-by asked what the village was, they were told: "That's the one where the deacon ate up all the caviar at the funeral."

Once, at a funeral feast given by the mill owner, Kostyukov, an elderly deacon spotted black caviar on the buffet and
began eating it greedily; they jostled him, plucked at his
sleeves, but it was as if he were numbed by pleasure: he felt
nothing and just kept on eating. He ate up all the caviar,
and there had been four pounds in the jar. Much time had
gone by since, the deacon was long dead, but everyone
remembered the caviar. Whether because life was so meager
here, or because people were incapable of noticing anything
outside of this unimportant incident of ten years ago, it
was the only thing ever told about the village of Ukleyevo.

Fever was ever present here and the mud was deep even
in summer, particularly near the fences, overhung by old
willows giving broad shade. There was always a smell of
factory refuse and the acetic acid used for processing cotton.
The factories—three cotton and one leather—were not in
the village itself, but on the outskirts and at a distance. They
were not large and employed about four hundred workers
in all, no more. The water in the stream was often putrid
from the tannery; its refuse corrupted the fields, the peasants'
cattle suffered from anthrax, and the factory had been ordered
to close. Officially it was considered closed, but it worked in
secret with the knowledge of the rural police chief and the
district physician, who were paid ten rubles a month each
by the owner. There were only two decent houses, stone
roofed with tin, in the entire village; one housed the district
administration; in the other, a two-story building just opposite
the church, lived Tsybukin, Grigory Petrov, a tradesman
from Yepifan.

Grigory ran a small grocery store, but that was only for
appearances. In reality, he traded vodka, cattle, leather, grain,
and hogs; he traded whatever fell into his hands. When, for
example, magpies were ordered from abroad for women's
hats, he made thirty kopecks a pair; he bought timber rights,
lent money on interest, and in general was a shrewd old man.

He had two sons. The elder, Anisim, served in the police,
in the detective division, and was rarely at home. The
younger, Stepan, had gone into the trade and helped his
father, but he was not counted on for any real assistance
because he was of feeble health and deaf. Stepan's wife,
Aksinya, was a beautiful, well-proportioned woman who
promenaded with a parasol and a hat on holidays, got up
early, went to bed late, and was on the run all day, now to
the storehouse, now to the cellar, now to the shop, gathering

up her skirts and rattling her keys. Old man Tsybukin used
to watch her merrily; his eyes would take fire, and he would
regret she was not married to his older son, but to the
younger, the deaf one, who obviously had little appreciation
of feminine beauty.

The old man had always enjoyed family life and loved
his family, particularly his older, detective son and his
daughter-in-law, more than anything on earth. As soon as
she was married to the deaf son, Aksinya revealed unusual
business acumen and knew at once who could be given credit
and who could not; she kept the keys herself, not entrusting
them even to her husband; she rattled the abacus, examined
the horses' teeth like a peasant, and laughed and shouted
constantly. And no matter what she did or said, the old man
was touched and muttered: "Eh, there, daughter-in-law! Eh,
there, my beauty, Little Mother . . ."

He was a widower, but a year after his son's wedding
could stand it no longer and got married himself. Thirty
versts from Ukleyevo they found him a bride, Varvara Nikolayevna, of good family, already middle-aged, but beautiful
and shapely. Hardly had she moved into the little room on
the top floor when everything in the house brightened as
if new glass had been put in all the windows. The little icon
lamps were lit, the tables were covered with snow-white
cloths; tiny red-blossomed flowers appeared at the windows
and in the little garden, and at dinner they no longer ate out
of the same bowl, but had a plate for each. Varvara Nikolayevna smiled pleasantly and tenderly, and it seemed as if
everything in the house were smiling. In the courtyard too,
beggars, travelers, and pilgrims began to gather—something
which had never happened before; and the doleful, singsong
voices of the Ukleyevo women and the guilty coughing of
the weak, gaunt men dismissed from the factory for drunkenness could be heard under the windows. Varvara gave away
money, bread, and old clothes, and after she felt at home,
began to take things from the store too. The deaf man saw
her take a quarter pound of tea once and was disturbed.

"Look, Mamasha took a quarter pound of tea," he told
his father. "Where should I enter it?"

The old man did not reply, but stood a while in thought,
twitching his eyebrows, and then went upstairs to his wife.

"Varvarushka, Little Mother," he said tenderly, "if you
need anything in the store, just take it. Take it and welcome
to it; don't hesitate."

And the next day the deaf man shouted to her as he ran through the courtyard: "Mamasha, if you need something— take it!"

Her almsgiving was something new, something gay and light, like the little icon lamps and the red flowers. Before a fast or during a three-day parish holiday, when they sold the peasants rotten salt beef—which had such a strong odor that it was hard to stand next to the barrel—and accepted scythes, caps, and women's clothing as pledges from drunks; when the factory hands rolled in the mud, stupefied by bad vodka, and sin seemed to have condensed in the air like a fog—they felt better at the thought that there, in the house, was a neat, gentle woman who had nothing to do with the salt beef or the vodka. Her charity acted like the safety valve in a machine on these oppressive, gloomy days.

The days were spent on chores in the Tsybukin house. The sun was not yet up when Aksinya was already snorting, washing herself in the entry, and the samovar was boiling in the kitchen and droning predictions of misfortune. Old man Grigory Petrov, dressed in a long black frock coat, cotton trousers, and shiny high boots, so clean and tiny, bustled about the rooms and tapped his heels like the old father-in-law in the well-known song. They would unlock the store, and when it began getting light, bring a racing droshky up to the steps; the old man would hop in dashingly, pulling his big cap down to his ears, and no one would have said to see him that he was already fifty-six. His wife and daughter-in-law would see him off, and at times like these, when he was wearing a good, clean frock coat and the huge raven-black stallion which had cost three hundred rubles was harnessed to the droshky, the old man did not like to have the peasants come up to him with their requests and griev- ances. He despised and was repelled by the peasants, and when he saw some peasant or other waiting at the gate, he would shout angrily: "What are you standing there for? Move on!"

Or if it was a beggar, he would shout: "God will provide!"

He traveled on business frequently; his wife, dressed in dark colors, in a black apron, would straighten the rooms or help in the kitchen. Aksinya worked in the store, and from the courtyard you could hear the bottles and money ringing, Aksinya laughing or shouting, and the customers she had insulted becoming angry. You could tell, too, that the clandes- tine sale of vodka was already underway in the store. The deaf man either sat in the store or walked bareheaded along the street with his hands in his pockets and looked distractedly first at the huts, then up at the sky. They had tea at home six times a day and sat down at the table to eat four times. In the evening they calculated and entered the proceeds, then slept soundly.

In Ukleyevo, all three cotton mills and the homes of the manufacturers, the Khrymin Seniors, the Khrymin Sons, and Kostyukov, were connected by telephone. A telephone had been installed in the district administration too, but it had soon ceased to work because of the bugs and cockroaches breeding in it. The district administrative chief was poorly educated and capitalized every word in his letters, and when the telephone was ruined, he said: "Yes, it'll be a bit hard for us now without a telephone."

The Khrymin Seniors were always going to court with the Sons, and sometimes the Khrymin Sons quarreled among themselves and went to court, and then their factory would stop work for a month or two before they made peace; and this provided diversion for the inhabitants of Ukleyevo because there was much talk and gossip about the causes of each quarrel. On holidays, Kostyukov and the Khrymin Sons organized outings, swept through Ukleyevo, and slaughtered calves. Aksinya, all decked out, her starched skirts rustling, used to stroll down the street near her own store; the Sons would seize her and playfully carry her off. Then old man Tsybukin would drive out too, to display his new horse, and he would take Varvara along.

In the evening, when they went to bed after the drive, the expensive harmonica would still be playing in the Sons' courtyard, and if there was a moon, these sounds would make spirits excited and gay, and Ukleyevo would no longer seem like a hole.

II

The older son, Anisim, came home very seldom, only on important holidays, but frequently sent via countrymen gifts and letters written in a very handsome, unfamiliar handwriting, always on a sheet of writing paper and following the form of a petition. The letters were full of expressions Anisim never used in conversation: "Dearest Papasha and

Mamasha, I am sending you a pound of tea blossoms for the satisfaction of your physical demands."

At the bottom of every letter, scrawled as if with a broken pen point, was: "Anisim Tsybukin," and under this, in the same excellent handwriting: "Agent."

The letters were read aloud several times, and the old man, moved, red with emotion, would say: "So he didn't want to live at home and went into a scientific unit. Well then, let him. Each to his own bent."

One day before Shrovetide, there was a driving rain and hail; the old man and Varvara went to the window to look, and behold—there was Anisim driving from the station in a sleigh. He was not expected at all. He came into the room disturbed and agitated about something and stayed that way the whole time; he also behaved rather impertinently, was in no hurry to leave, and it was as if he had been dismissed from the service. Varvara was pleased by his coming; she kept looking at him somewhat slyly, sighing and nodding her head.

"What is this, little saints?" she said. "Here-here, a lad of already twenty-eight years walking about and still playing around as a bachelor, oh-tch-tch . . ."

From the next room her quiet even voice sounded like that: "Oh-tch-tch." She began whispering with the old man and Aksinya, and their faces also acquired the sly and mysterious expressions of conspirators.

They had decided to marry Anisim.

"Oh-tch-tch! . . . Your younger brother was married long ago," said Varvara, "while you're still without a mate like a rooster in the market. What kind of doings is that? There now, you'll be married, God willing, to your liking, and go off to the service while your wife stays home as a helper. You live in disorder, lad, and I can see you've completely forgotten about order. Oh-tch-tch, that's the trouble with you, you city folk."

When the Tsybukins got married, the most beautiful brides were chosen for them, just as for rich people. For Anisim, too, they sought a beauty. He was uninteresting and unremarkable in appearance himself; in addition to a weak, sickly build and shortish stature, he had full puffy cheeks which looked distended; his eyes were unblinking, his gaze piercing, his beard red, scanty, and when he thought, he always sucked his whiskers into his mouth and chewed them. Moreover, it was detectable in his face and his walk that he frequently overdrank. But when he was told a bride had been found for him, a very beautiful one, he said: "Well, of course, I'm no hunchback either. We Tsybukins, I must say, are all handsome."

Right next to the town was the village of Torguyevo. Half of it had been joined to the town not long ago; the other half remained a village. In the first half, a certain widow lived in her own little house; with her lived a totally destitute sister who did day work and had a daughter, Lipa, a young girl, who also did day work. Lipa's beauty was already the talk of Torguyevo, but her terrible poverty disheartened everyone; people concluded that some older man or widower would marry her, overlooking her poverty, or would take her to his house "as is," whereafter she and her mother would be in clover. Varvara heard about Lipa from the matchmakers and made a visit to Torguyevo.

Then an inspection visit of the prospective bridegroom to the bride was arranged in the aunt's house, properly, with a buffet and wine; Lipa wore a new rose-colored dress made expressly for the occasion, and a crimson ribbon gleamed like a flame in her hair. She was rather thin, frail, and wan, with fine, delicate features darkened from outdoor work; a sad, timid smile never left her lips, and her eyes looked as children's do—trustingly and with curiosity.

She was young, still a girl, with a barely perceptible bosom, but already of marriageable age. She was, in fact, beautiful, and the only thing one might find displeasing about her was her big masculine hands, which now dangled idly like two huge claws.

"There's no dowry, and we don't care," said the old man to the aunt; "we chose from a poor family for our son Stepan too, and we can't praise ourselves enough for it now. In the house as in the business, she has a golden touch."

Lipa was standing near the door and looked as if she were about to say: "Do what you want with me, I trust you," while her mother, Praskovya, the charwoman, hid in the kitchen, faint with timidity. When she was young, a merchant for whom she washed floors had become very angry and stamped his feet at her once, and she had been severely frightened, fainted, and kept the fear in her soul her whole life. This fear made her hands and legs tremble continuously; her cheeks trembled, too. As she sat in the kitchen, she tried to overhear what the guests were saying and kept crossing herself, pressing her fingers to her lips and glancing at the icon. Anisim, slightly drunk, opened the door into the kitchen and said familiarly: "What are you sitting here for, precious Mamasha? We miss you."

But Praskovya, shrinking, pressing her hands to her thin, sunken bosom, answered: "What, please, sir . . . We're very pleased with you, sir."

After the inspection, the day of the wedding was set. Anisim kept pacing the rooms at home and whistling, or, suddenly remembering something, would become pensive and look motionlessly, piercingly at the floor as if wanting to penetrate the earth deeply with his look. He expressed neither satisfaction that he was being married, married soon, the Monday after Quasimodo Sunday, nor a desire to visit his bride, but just whistled. And it was obvious that he was getting married only because his father and stepmother wished it, and because it is the custom in the country for the son to marry to provide a helper in the house. When he left, he was in no hurry and generally behaved quite differently than he had on previous visits—he was somehow particularly forward, and kept saying the wrong things.

<hr/>

III

In the village of Shikalov lived two seamstresses, two sisters belonging to the Khlystov sect.* New clothes were ordered from them for the wedding, and they frequently came for fittings and drank tea for hours. They made Varvara a brown dress with black lace and imitation jet beads, and for Aksinya—a light green one with a yellow corsage and a train. When the seamstresses had finished, Tsybukin paid them not in money but in goods from his own store, and they went away from him sad, holding in their arms bundles of stearin candles and sardines, of which they had absolutely no need, and on emerging from the village into the open field, they sat down on a hillock and started to cry.

Anisim arrived three days before the wedding in all new clothes. He wore dazzling rubber galoshes and a red cord with knots instead of a necktie, and an overcoat, also new, was slung over his shoulders with its sleeves hanging free.

* A Russian religious sect which repudiates the established church and the priesthood.

After a grave prayer, he greeted his father and gave him ten silver rubles and ten half-ruble pieces; he gave Varvara the same, too, and to Aksinya, twenty quarter rubles. The major attraction of this gift was that all the coins were new and sparkled in the sun as if they were a choice selection. Trying to look grave and serious, Anisim lengthened his face and puffed out his cheeks, and a smell of liquor wafted from him; he had probably run out to the counter at every railroad station. And again there was a kind of impertinence, something excessive about the man. Anisim and the old man then had tea and appetizers while Varvara sorted the new rubles in her hands and asked about countrymen living in town.

"They're all right, thank God, they live well," said Anisim. "Except Ivan Egorov here had an event in his family life; his old woman Sofya Nikiforovna died. Of cholera. The funeral dinner for the repose of her soul was ordered from the caterer at two and a half rubles per person. And there was vineyard wine. There were some peasants there—countrymen of ours— and it cost two and a half apiece for them, too. They didn't eat a thing. How could a peasant appreciate a sauce!"

"Two and a half rubles!" said the old man, shaking his head.

"Well, why not? It's no village there. You go in a restaurant to have a bite, you ask for this and that, a group collects, you drink up—eh, you turn around and it's already dawn and three or four rubles apiece, if you please. And with Samorodov, now, what that one likes is to top it off with a coffee and cognac, and cognac is sixty kopecks a glass."

"It can't be true," muttered the old man in ecstasy. "Can't be true!"

"I'm with Samorodov all the time now. It's the same Samorodov who writes you my letters. He writes magnificently. And if I were to tell you, Mamasha," Anisim continued gaily, turning to Varvara, "what kind of person this Samorodov is, you wouldn't believe it. We all call him Mukhtar—because he's a kind of Armenian—all black. I see right through him, I know all his tricks like my own five fingers, Mamasha, and he feels it and always follows me everywhere, never leaves my side, and you couldn't tear us apart now. He seems to be having a hard time, but he can't live without me. Wherever I am, there he is. I have true, accurate eyes, Mamasha. Take at a flea market: a peasant is selling a shirt—'Halt, the shirt's stolen!'—And it's true, that's how it comes out: the shirt is stolen goods."

"How can you tell?" asked Varvara.

"No special way, my eyes are just like that. I don't know what kind of shirt it is there, but it just for some reason draws me; it's stolen, that's all. In our detective unit, they already say: 'Well, Anisim's gone snipe-shooting!' That means to look for stolen goods. Yes . . . Anybody can steal, but then how do you keep it! The world is huge, but there's no place to hide stolen goods."

"Well, they stole a ram and two yearling ewes from the Guntorevs in our village last week," Varvara said and sighed. "And there's no one to hunt them down . . . Oh-tch-tch . . ."

"Well? They can be hunted down. That's nothing, they can."

The day of the wedding came. It was a cold but clear bright April day. People had already been driving around Ukleyevo since early morning with jingling bells and multicolored ribbons on the yokes and in the manes of the teams of horses in threes and twos. The rooks, alarmed by the driving, were making a racket in the willows, and the starlings, outdoing themselves, sang incessantly as if rejoicing that the Tsybukins were having a wedding.

Already arranged on tables in the house were long fish, hams, stuffed birds, boxes of sprats, various salted and pickled foods, and scores of bottles of vodka and wine; there was a smell of smoked sausage and pickled lobster. And around the tables walked the old man, tapping his heels and sharpening one knife against another. Varvara was being summoned constantly; something was always needed, and she would run with a distraught face, breathing heavily, to the kitchen where Kostyukov's chef and Khrymin Sons' head cook had been working since daybreak. Aksinya, in curl papers, without her dress, wearing a corset and new, squeaking boots, whirled through the courtyard like a tornado with flashes of bare knees and bosom. It was noisy; cursing and oaths rang out; passers-by stopped in front of the wide-open gates, and everything indicated that something out of the ordinary was under preparation.

"They're off to fetch the bride!"

The carriage bells pealed and died far beyond the village . . . At three o'clock a crowd came running again; again bells were audible: they were bringing the bride! The church was full, the church luster was burning, the singers were singing from music as old man Tsybukin had wanted it. The glitter of the lights and the bright dresses blinded Lipa, and she felt as if the singers were beating on her head with their loud voices like hammers; her boots and the corset which she had put on for the first time in her life were pinching her, and her expression was that of someone just coming to from a faint—she stared without comprehension. Anisim, in a black frock coat with a red cord instead of a tie, stared at one spot, lost in thought, quickly crossing himself whenever the singers screeched loudly. His soul was filled with emotion; he felt like crying. This church had been familiar to him from early childhood; his late mother once brought him here to take Communion; once he had sung in the young boys choir; every nook, every icon held memories for him. Now he was being married; he had to take a wife for the sake of order, but he was no longer thinking about that; he somehow no longer remembered, completely forgot about the wedding. Tears kept him from seeing the icons and weighed on his heart; he prayed and begged God that the inevitable misfortune which was about to burst over him, not today—tomorrow, would somehow circumvent him, as threatening clouds circumvent a village in a drought without giving a single drop of rain. And so many sins had already accumulated in the past, so many sins, insuperable, irremediable, that it was even absurd, somehow, to beg for forgiveness. But he begged, and even sobbed loudly, and all the people overlooked it because they thought he was drunk.

An anxious child's wail rang out: "Mama dear, take me away from here, my dove!"

"Quiet there!" shouted the priest.

When they came back from the church, people ran after them; there was a crowd around the shop, too, around the gates, and in the courtyard under the windows. The women came to chant praises. The young people had barely stepped across the threshold when the singers, who were already standing in the entrance with their music, shrieked loudly with all their might; the orchestra specially ordered from town began playing. Sparkling drinks were served in tall beakers, and the master carpenter, a tall, emaciated old man with eyebrows so thick that his eyes were barely visible, said, turning to the young couple: "Anisim and you, child, love one another, live in godliness, children, and the heavenly Tsaritsa will never forsake you." He fell on the old man's shoulder and sobbed. "Grigory Petrov, we're crying, crying with joy!" he uttered in a thin little voice, then immediately began chuckling and continued loudly, in a bass: "Ho-ho-ho! And that's a fine daughter-in-law you have! That is, everything about her is in its place, everything smooth, no rattles, all the mechanism in order, plenty of bolts in it."

He was from the Yegorevsky district by birth, but had worked in the factories in Ukleyevo since his youth and had become at home in the district here. He had been a familiar figure for years as an old man, just as gaunt and long as now, and had been nicknamed Crutch a long time ago. Perhaps because he had had to concern himself exclusively with repairs in the factories for more than forty years, he judged every person or thing solely from the standpoint of solidity: whether or not it needed repair. Before sitting down at the table, he tried out several chairs to see whether they were solid, and also fingered the trout.

After the sparkling drinks, they all began seating themselves at the table. The guests were talking, moving the chairs. The singers were singing in the entry, the music was playing, and the women in the courtyard were chanting praises at the same time, all in one voice—and it was a kind of horrible, savage mixture of sounds that made the head whirl.

Crutch twisted about on his chair, poked his neighbors with his elbows, and kept them from talking, first crying, then laughing.

"Children, children, children . . ." he mumbled quickly. "Aksinyushka, Little Mother, Varvarushka, we'll all live in peace and agreement, my beloved little pegs . . ."

He seldom drank and became drunk now from one glass of English bitters. This repulsive bitters, made out of no one knows what, had the effect of a concussion on everyone who drank it. Tongues became twisted.

There were the clergy, the clerks from the factories with their wives, the merchants and innkeepers from other villages. The district elder and the district clerk, who had worked together for fourteen years and during all that time never signed a single paper without defrauding nor let a single person leave the district administration office without bilking him, sat side by side, surfeited and fat, and they seemed to be impregnated with injustice to such a degree that even the skin of their faces was somehow distinctive, fraudulent. The clerk's gaunt, squint-eyed wife had brought all her children along, and scanning the plates like a bird of prey, she seized everything within arm's reach and slipped it into her own and the children's pockets.

Lipa was sitting frozen with the very same expression she had had in church. Because Anisim had not exchanged a word with her since meeting her, he did not know what her voice sounded like yet. And now, sitting side by side with her, he drank English bitters in silence, and when intoxicated, turned to his aunt, who was sitting opposite him, and said: "I've got a friend called Samorodov. A special person. A particular respectable citizen, and does he know how to talk. But, Aunty, I see right through him and he feels it. Let me drink to Samorodov's health with you, Aunty!"

Varvara walked around the table serving the guests, weary, distraught, and obviously satisfied that there were so many things to eat and that everything was so rich—no one could criticize now. The sun went down, but the dinner continued; they no longer realized what they were eating or drinking; it was impossible to hear what was said, and only from time to time, when the music died down, one woman or another in the courtyard could be clearly heard crying: "They're drunk on our blood, the monsters! Why aren't you in hell!"

In the evening there was dancing to music. The Khrymin Sons came with their own wine, and while dancing the quadrille, one of them held a bottle in each hand and a glass in his mouth, to the amusement of everyone. In the middle of the quadrille they suddenly went into the Russian leg dance; green Aksinya flashed by and her train raised a wind. Someone stepped on her flounce, tearing it, and Crutch shouted: "Hey, they ripped off the plinth down there! Children!"

Aksinya had gray, naive eyes which rarely blinked and a naive smile constantly played on her face. And in these unblinking eyes, in the little head on the long neck, in her shapeliness, there was something serpentine; green, with a yellow bosom, a smile, she looked around her the way a little snake looks, stretching and raising its neck, peering at passers-by from a young rye field in the spring. The Khrymins behaved freely with her, and it was quite obvious that she had had close relations with the oldest of them for a long time. However, the deaf man understood nothing and did not watch her; he sat, one leg over the other, eating nuts and cracking them with his teeth so loudly that it sounded like pistol shots.

But now old man Tsybukin himself went out into the middle of the floor and waved a handkerchief to signal that he too wanted to do the leg dance, and throughout the entire house and the courtyard, a rumble of approval ran through the crowd:

"He's come out! *Himself!*"

Varvara did the dance while the old man just waved his handkerchief and drummed his heels, but the people in the courtyard, hanging on one another, peering through the windows, became excited and in a moment forgave him everything—his wealth and his wrongdoing.

"Good man, Grigory Petrov!" was heard in the crowd. "Go to it! Shows you can still take care of things! Ha-ha!"

All this ended late, at two in the morning. Anisim, staggering, went around to say good-by to the singers and musicians and gave each a new half ruble. And the old man, unwavering, but constantly stepping on the same foot somehow, showed the guests out and told each one: "The wedding cost two thousand rubles."

While the guests were leaving, someone exchanged the Shikalov innkeeper's good undercoat for an old one, and Anisim suddenly flared and began shouting: "Halt! I'll investigate at once! I know who stole it! Halt!"

He ran out into the street in pursuit, but they caught him, led him home, and pushed him, drunk, red with anger and wet, into the room where his aunt was already undressing Lipa, and they locked the door.

IV

Five days went by. Anisim, about to leave, went upstairs to say good-by to Varvara. Little icon lamps were burning in her room, it smelled of incense, and she was sitting at the window and knitting a red wool stocking.

"You didn't spend much time with us," she said. "Got bored, I'm afraid? Oh-tch-tch . . . We live all right, got plenty of everything, and your wedding went off in proper order, correctly; the old man was saying two thousand rubles went on it. In a word, we live like merchants, only it's boring at our house. And we hurt people a lot. Makes my heart ache, my friend, the way we hurt them—my God! If we trade a horse or buy something or hire a man—there's cheating in all of it. Cheating and cheating. The hempseed oil in the shop is bitter, rotten; birchwood tar'd be better for people. Now tell me for goodness' sake, is it impossible to sell decent oil?"

"Each to his own bent, Mamasha."

"But everybody's got to die, don't you see? Aiee, aiee, it's the truth, you should talk to Father! . . ."

"You should talk to him yourself."

"Now-now! I've said my say to him and he says to me, like you, in a word: 'Each to his own bent.' In the next world that's how you'll be sorted out—each to his own bent. God's judgment is just."

"No one's going to be sorting," said Anisim and sighed. "There isn't any God anyhow, Mamasha. And what's there to sort, anyway!"

Varvara looked at him with amazement, burst out laughing, and clasped her hands. Because she was so frankly amazed at his words and looked at him as an oddity, he became embarrassed.

"Maybe there is a God, but only there's no faith," he said. "When I got married I was out of spirits. Like when you take an egg from under a hen and a little chicken chirps in it, it suddenly chirped like that in my conscience, and while I was being married, I kept thinking: there is a God! But when I went out of the church—there was nothing. Yes and how would I know if there's a God or not? That isn't the way we learned since childhood and while the baby's still suckling his mother, he's told only one thing: each to his own bent. Papasha, naturally, doesn't believe in God neither. You said one day Guntorev's sheep were stolen . . . I found out: a peasant from Shikalov stole 'em; he stole 'em, but Papasha has the hides . . . There's faith for you!"

Anisim winked an eye and nodded his head.

"And the elder doesn't believe in God neither," he continued, "and the clerk neither and the deacon neither. And if they go to church and keep fasts, that's so people won't say bad things about 'em and in case maybe there really is going to be a last judgment. Now they talk as if it's the end of the world come because people are going to the dogs and don't respect their parents and so on. That's rubbish. As I see it, Mamasha, all trouble comes from people's having too little conscience. I see right through things, Mamasha, and understand 'em. If a man's shirt is stolen goods, I see it. A man sits in a tavern and looks to you like he's drinking tea and nothing more, but tea or no tea, I can also see he has no conscience. You can go around like that the whole day—and not see one person with a conscience. And the whole reason's because they don't know if there's a God or not . . . Well, Mamasha, good-by. Stay alive and well, don't bear me a grudge."

Anisim bowed to Varvara's feet.

"We thank you for everything, Mamasha," he said. "You're

a great benefit to our family. You're a very decent woman, and I'm pleased with you."

Moved, Anisim went out, but came back again and said: "Samorodov got me involved in a certain affair: I'll be rich or lost. If that happens, then, Mamasha, you console my father."

"Come now, what's this! Oh-tch-tch . . . God is merciful. And you, Anisim, ought to be nice to this wife of yours here. Instead of sulking at each other, you could smile at least, really."

"Yes, what a wonder she is . . ." Anisim said and sighed. "Doesn't understand a thing, quiet all the time. She's young, let her grow up."

At the steps, a tall, well-fed white stallion was already standing, harnessed to a coach.

Old man Tsybukin took a run and jumped in adroitly, taking the reins. Anisim exchanged kisses with Varvara, Aksinya, and his brother. Lipa stood on the steps too, motionless and looking off to the side as if she had come out for no special reason and not to see anyone off. Anisim went up to her and touched his lips lightly to her cheek, just barely.

"Good-by," he said.

And she smiled rather strangely without looking at him; her face quivered, and everyone for some reason started feeling sorry for her. Anisim also installed himself with a leap and put his arms akimbo as if he considered himself a handsome fellow.

As they drove up out of the ravine, Anisim kept glancing back at the village. It was a warm, bright day. The cattle were being driven out for the first time, and women and girls, dressed for a holiday, were walking near the herd. A brown bull bellowed, rejoicing in his freedom, and pawed the ground with his forelegs. Larks were singing everywhere, above and below. Anisim looked back at the church, graceful, white— it had been recently whitewashed—and remembered how he had prayed in it five days before; he looked back at the green-roofed school, at the stream in which he had once swum and caught fish, and joy surged in his breast and he longed for a wall to suddenly spring from the ground, preventing him from going on, so that he would be left with just the past.

In the station they went to the counter and drank a glass of sherry. The old man reached in his pocket for his wallet to pay.

"My treat!" said Anisim.

The old man clapped him on the shoulder with emotion and winked at the barman: See, that's the way my son is.

"If you'd stay home, Anisim, in the business," he said, "you'd have no price! I'd gild you from head to foot, my son."

"Can't possibly, Papasha."

The sherry was sourish and smelled of sealing wax, but they had another glass each.

When the old man returned from the station, he did not recognize his young daughter-in-law at first. As soon as her husband had driven out of the courtyard, Lipa had changed, suddenly becoming merry. Barefoot, in an old worn skirt, sleeves rolled up to her shoulders, she was washing the stairway in the entrance and singing in a thin, silvery little voice, and when she carried out a big tub of dirty water and looked at the sun with her childish smile, she seemed like a lark, too.

An old laborer passing by the steps nodded his head and cleared his throat.

"Yes, and your daughters-in-law there, Grigory Petrov, were sent you by God!" he said. "They're not women, but pure treasure!"

V

On Friday the eighth of July, Elizarov—Crutch, by nickname—and Lipa were returning on foot from the village of Kazansky where they had gone on a pilgrimage for the day of the patron saint—the Holy Mother of Kazan. Far behind came Lipa's mother, Praskovya, who continuously lagged behind because she was unwell and short of breath. It was near evening.

"A-aa!" marveled Crutch, listening to Lipa. "A-aa! . . . Well?"

"I'm a great lover of jam, Ilya Makarich," said Lipa. "I set myself in a little corner and drink tea with jam all the time. Or I drink together with Varvara Nikolayevna while they tell something exciting. They've a lot of jam—four jars. 'Eat, Lipa,' they say, 'don't hesitate.' "

"A-aa! . . . Four jars!"

"They live rich. Tea with white bread; and beef, too, as much as you want. They live rich, but it's scary in their house, Ilya Makarich. Aiee, how scary it is."

"What scares you, child?" asked Crutch, and he looked around to see whether Praskovya had fallen far behind.

"First, when the wedding was through, I was scared of Anisim Grigorich. He's all right, doesn't hurt me, only, when he comes close to me, it's like a frost all over me, in all my bones. And I didn't sleep a night and kept trembling and praying to God. And now I'm scared of Aksinya, Ilya Makarich. She acts all right, always smiling, but sometimes she looks in the window and her eyes are so angry and glow green like sheep's eyes in the stall. The Khrymin Sons keep after her: 'Your old man,' they say, 'has a little place, Butyokino, some hundred acres, a little place,' they say, 'with sand and there's water, and so, Aksinya dear,' they say, 'you build yourself a brick factory and we'll go shares.' Bricks are twenty rubles a thousand now. A good business. Last night, at dinner, Aksinya tells the old man: 'I,' says she, 'wanta put a brick factory in Butyokino. I'm gonna be a merchant myself,' says she, and smiles. But Grigory Petrovich gets black in the face, it's clear he doesn't like it. 'As long as I'm alive,' says he, 'nothing'll be separate, everything's gonna be joint.' And her eyes are flashing and her teeth beginning to gnash . . . The pancakes are served but she don't eat!"

"A-aa!" marveled Crutch. "She don't eat!"

"And you please tell me when she sleeps!" continued Lipa. "Sleeps half an hour and then jumps up, walks around, keeps walking, looking to see if the peasants have set something on fire or stolen something . . . It's scary around her, Ilya Makarich! And the Khrymin Sons didn't go to bed after the wedding, but went in town to start a suit and people gossip as if it's all because of Aksinya. The two brothers promised to build her a factory and the third got angry and the factory's been standing still for a month and my Uncle Prokhor is out of work and begging crusts from door to door. 'You should go plow or saw wood meanwhile, Little Uncle,' I say, 'instead of shaming yourself.' 'I got away from Christian work,' he says. 'Nothing I can do, Lipa dear!' he says."

Near a young aspen grove, they stopped to rest and wait for Praskovya. Elizarov had been a contractor for a long time, but did not keep a horse and took every trip on foot with a single sack containing bread and onion; he took broad strides, swinging his arms, and keeping pace with him was difficult.

At the entrance to the grove stood a boundary stone. Elizarov touched it: was it solid? Up came Praskovya, panting. Her wrinkled, perpetually alarmed face radiated happiness: she

had been in church today like other people, then walked to
the bazar and drunk pear kvass * there! This was very unusual for her and it even seemed to her that she had enjoyed
herself for the first time in her life today. After resting, the
three went on side by side. The sun was setting and its rays
pierced through the grove, glistening on the trunks. Ahead,
voices resounded. The young girls from Ukleyevo had gone
on long ago, but now were lingering there in the grove, probably gathering mushrooms.

"Eh, girls!" shouted Elizarov. "Eh, my beauties!"

There was answering laughter.

"Here comes Crutch! Crutch! The old fogy!"

The echo also laughed. Now the grove was left behind. The
tops of the factory chimneys were already in sight, the cross
glittered on the belfry: it was the village, "the one where the
deacon ate up all the caviar at the funeral." They were almost
home now; all that remained was the descent into the deep
ravine. Lipa and Praskovya, who had been walking barefoot,
sat down on the grass to put on their shoes and stockings;
the contractor sat down beside them too. Seen from above,
Ukleyevo with its willows, white church, and stream looked
beautiful, tranquil, and the only detraction was the factory
roofs, painted a murky gray color for economy's sake. Rye
could be seen on the far slope—grainstacks and sheaves here
and there, some looking as if scattered by a hurricane, and
others just cut in neat rows; the oats were already ripe, too,
and gleamed in the sun like mother-of-pearl. It was harvest
time. Today was a holiday; tomorrow, Saturday, the rye was
to be gathered in, the hay carted, and then would come Sunday, another holiday. Distant thunder rumbled every day; it
was sultry as if about to rain, and looking at the fields now,
the peasants all wondered whether God would allow them to
gather the grain in time, and their hearts were merry and
joyful and anxious.

"Reapers are high now," said Praskovya. "A ruble forty a
day!"

The people kept coming and coming from the bazar in
Kazansky: women, factory workers in new caps, beggars,
children . . . Now a cart drove past, raising dust, with the
unsold horse prancing behind as if glad not to have been sold;
now an obstinate cow, led by the horn; now another cart with
drunken peasants, their legs dangling. One old woman led past
a little boy in a huge hat and huge boots; the boy was faint

* A thin, sour, fermented beverage.

from the heat and the heavy boots which did not allow his legs to bend at the knees, but he nevertheless kept blowing a toy pipe incessantly with all his might. When they had already reached the bottom and turned into the street, the pipe could still be heard uninterruptedly.

"But our manufacturers are somehow out of sorts," said Elizarov. "It's a misery. Kostyukov got mad at me. 'A lot of boards went into the cornice,' he says. What does he mean, a lot? 'There was as much as needed, Vassily Danilich,' I say, 'that's how much. I don't eat them with my *kasha*.' * 'How can you talk to me like that?' he says. 'Blockhead, so-and-so! Don't forget yourself! I made you a contractor!' he shouts—'That's a fine one!' I say. 'When I wasn't in contracting,' I say, 'I had tea every day just the same.' 'You're all cheats,' he says . . . I keep silent. We're the cheats in this world, I'm thinking, but you'll be cheated in the next. Ho-ho-ho! The next day he softened. 'Don't get mad at me,' he says, 'for what I said,' says he. 'If I went too far, then it must be said too, I'm a first guild merchant, superior to you—and you should keep quiet.' 'You're a first guild merchant while I'm a carpenter, that's right. And Saint Joseph was a carpenter too,' say I. 'Our work is upright, godly, and if,' I say, 'it pleases you to be superior, then do me the favor, Vassily Danilich.' And then, afterward, that is, after the conversation, I start thinking: who is superior? A first guild merchant or a carpenter? Must be the carpenter, children!"

Crutch thought a moment and added: "That's it, children. The one who works, the one who suffers, he's superior."

The sun had already set, and over the river, in the church-yard and on the meadows near the factories, a thick fog was rising, milk-white. As the darkness swiftly descended now, lights were flashing below and it looked as if the fog were covering a bottomless abyss. Lipa and her mother, who were born paupers and were prepared to live like that to the end, surrendering to others everything except their frightened, gentle souls—may have had a vision at that moment that in this huge, mysterious world, among the endless series of lives, they, too, were strong and superior to somebody; they felt fine sitting up here above; they smiled happily and forgot that it was nevertheless necessary to return below.

At last they went back home. Reapers were sitting on the ground near the store and at the gates. The people from Ukleyevo usually refused to work for Tsybukin and he had

* A porridge usually made of barley or oats.

to hire outsiders; in the darkness it looked as if people with long dark beards were sitting here. The store was open and through the door one could see the deaf man playing checkers with a little boy. The reapers were singing softly, barely audibly, or else loudly reclaiming yesterday's pay, but to ensure their not leaving before the next day, they were given nothing. Old man Tsybukin, wearing a vest and no frock coat, was drinking tea with Aksinya under a birch tree near the front steps, and a lamp was burning on the table.

"Gra-anpa!" one of the reapers behind the gates said as if mocking. "Pay us even half! Gra-anpa!"

And immediately a laugh was heard and then they were singing again barely audibly . . . Crutch sat down to have tea, too.

"We were there, that is, at the bazar," he began telling them. "We had a good time, children, a very good time, glory to Thee, Lord. And there was something happened, something no good: Sashka the blacksmith bought tobacco and gave a half ruble, that is, to the merchant. But the half ruble was false," Crutch continued and glanced around; he had intended to whisper, but spoke in a wheezing, hoarse voice, audible to everyone. "But the half ruble turned out false. They asked: 'Where'd you get it?' 'But,' says he, 'Anisim Tsybukin gave me this. When I was making merry at his wedding,' says he . . . They called the village policeman, led him away . . . Watch out, Petrovich, that something doesn't come of this, some talk . . ."

"Gra-anpa!" that same voice was still mocking from behind the gates. "Gra-anpa!"

Silence fell.

"Ah, children, children, children . . ." Crutch muttered quickly and got up, overcome by drowsiness. "Well, thanks for the tea, for the sugar, little children. It's time for sleep. I've already begun falling apart, my beams are rotted through. Ho-ho-ho!"

And on leaving, he said, "Must be time to die!" and he sobbed.

Old man Tsybukin did not finish his tea; he sat and thought and looked as if he were listening to Crutch's footsteps, already far down the street.

"But Sashka the blacksmith lied, probably," said Aksinya, guessing his thoughts.

He went into the house and returned shortly with a parcel; he undid it—and the rubles glittered, absolutely new. He took one, tried it in his teeth, threw it on the tray; then he threw down another . . .

"The rubles are really false," he said as if in doubt, looking at Aksinya. "These are the ones . . . Anisim brought them, they're his gift. Take them, little daughter," he whispered as he thrust the parcel into her hand; "take this and throw it in the well . . . Away with them! And see there's no talk. That nothing comes of it . . . Take away the samovar, put out the light . . ."

Lipa and Praskovya, sitting in the shed, saw all the lights put out one by one except upstairs in Varvara's room where little blue and red lamps were burning; and there was a breath of peace, contentment, and unawareness from there. Praskovya was totally unable to become used to the fact that her daughter had been given away to a rich man; when she came to the house, she would wait timidly in the entrance, smiling beseechingly, and they would send out tea and sugar for her. And Lipa, too, was unable to get used to it, and after her husband left, did not sleep in her own bed, but wherever she happened to be—in the kitchen or the shed; she washed the floors or the laundry every day and felt as if she were doing day work. Now too, on their return from the pilgrimage, they had tea in the kitchen with the cook, then went to the shed and lay down on the floor between the sleigh and the wall. It was dark and smelled of harnesses there. The lights were put out outside the house; then they heard the deaf man locking the store and the reapers settling themselves in the courtyard to sleep. Far off, at the Khrymin Sons', an expensive harmonica was being played . . . Praskovya and Lipa drifted off to sleep.

When footsteps awoke them, it was already light from the moon; at the entrance to the shed stood Aksinya, carrying bedding in her arms.

"Here, maybe it's cooler . . ." she said, then came in and lay down in the very threshold, and the moon shone full on her.

She did not sleep and kept sighing heavily, tossing with the heat, tossing almost everything off herself—and in the flickering moonlight what a beautiful, what a proud creature she was! A little time passed, and footsteps were heard again: the old man, all white, appeared at the door.

"Aksinya!" he called. "You here, are you?"

"Well!" she answered angrily.

"I told you a while ago to throw the money out in the well. Did you?"

"That's a fine one, throwing good stuff in water! I gave it to the reapers . . ."

"Oh, my God!" the old man said in stupor and fear. "What a hussy you are . . . Oh, my God!"

He clasped his hands and walked away, continuing to mutter something as he went. Soon afterward, Aksinya sat up, sighed heavily with irritation, then got up, and gathering the bedding in her arms, went out.

"And why did you give me away here, Mama!" said Lipa.

"One's got to get married, Little Daughter. It's not for us to decide."

And a feeling of inconsolable sorrow was about to overpower them. But they felt someone watching from the heights of heaven, from the deep blue where the stars are, seeing everything that happened in Ukleyevo and keeping guard. And however great the evil, the night was calm and splendid, and in God's world there still was and would be truth, just as calm and splendid, and everything on earth was poised to merge with the truth as the moonlight merges with the night.

And the two, soothed, huddled close to one another and fell asleep.

VI

Word had come long ago that Anisim was in prison for making and circulating false money. Months went by, more than half a year; a long winter passed, spring came, and in the house and the village, they grew used to Anisim's being in prison. And when someone passed the house or the store at night, he would remember that Anisim was in prison; and when the bells tolled in the cemetery, it was also for some reason remembered that he was in prison and awaiting trial.

It was as if a shadow lay over the home. The house had darkened, the roof had rusted, the door to the shop, bound with ironwork, heavy, and painted green, had yellowed, or as the deaf man said, "shaddened"; old man Tsybukin himself seemed to have gotten darker. It had been a long time since he had trimmed his overgrown hair and beard; he now got into his coach without springing and no longer shouted "God will provide!" to beggars. It was perceptible in everything that his strength was waning. People were already less afraid of

him, and the village policeman, although continuing to collect
his due as before, had served him a summons. Three times
Tsybukin had been ordered to town for trial for the clandestine
sale of liquor; the case was continually put off for lack of
witnesses, and the old man was in torment. He often went to
visit his son, hired assistance, delivered a petition to somebody,
or donated a church banner to some place. He presented the
watchman of Anisim's prison with a long spoon and a silver
tea-glass holder bearing the enameled inscription: "The soul
knows its capacity."

"Use influence, use influence, or there's no way out," said
Varvara. "Oh-tch-tch . . . You should ask one of the gentry,
write to the head man . . . So they'd let him free till the
trial . . . Why should the lad suffer!"

She was also saddened, but grew plumper, fairer, and as
before, lit her little icon lamps, saw that everything was clean
in the house, and served guests jam and apple candy. The deaf
man and Aksinya kept the shop. They had set a new business
on foot—the brick factory in Butyokino, and Aksinya went
there almost every day by carriage; she drove herself, and on
meeting acquaintances, stretched out her neck like a snake in
a young rye field and smiled naively and enigmatically. Lipa,
meanwhile, spent all her time playing with the child born to
her before Lent. He was a smallish, thin, pitiful child, and it
seemed strange that he cried, looked, and was considered an
individual and even given the name Nikifor. While he lay in
the cradle, Lipa used to step over to the door and say, bowing:
"Greetings, Nikifor Anisimich!"

And she would fly back and kiss him. Then she would step
over to the door again, bow, and repeat: "Greetings, Nikifor
Anisimich!"

He would kick up his red little legs, and his crying would be
mixed with laughter like that of Elizarov the carpenter.

At last the trial was set. The old man left for five days.
Then the peasants called as witnesses could be heard being
routed out of the village, and along with them went an old
hired man who had received a summons too.

The trial was on Thursday. But Sunday went by and the
old man had still not returned, and there was no news at all.
On Tuesday, toward evening, Varvara was sitting at the open
window and listening: wasn't the old man coming? Lipa was
playing with her child in the next room. She was tossing him
in her arms and saying in ecstasy: "You'll grow up bi-ig, bi-ig!
You'll be a big strong man and we'll go out to work together!"

"Come, come." Varvara took offense. "Why should he work? What a silly idea. He'll be a merchant . . ."

Lipa began singing softly, but shortly forgot herself and repeated: "You'll grow up bi-ig, big, be a big man, and we'll go to work together! To day work!"

"Come, come! At it again!"

Lipa stopped at the door with Nikiforov in her arms and asked: "Mamenka, why do I love him so? . . . Why do I feel so for him?" she continued in a trembling voice, and her eyes brightened with tears. "Who is he? What's he made out of? Light like a feather, like a crumb, but I love him, love him like a real person. Here he can't do a thing, doesn't talk, and yet I understand from his little eyes what he wants."

Varvara was still listening: there came the sound of the evening train arriving at the station. Hadn't the old man arrived? She neither understood nor even heard what Lipa was talking about, did not notice the passing of time, and just kept trembling all over, not with fear, but with intense curiosity. She saw a cart galloping swiftly, rattling, filled with peasants. They were the witnesses passing, returning from the station. The old hired man sprang from the cart as it galloped past and went into the courtyard. She could hear him being greeted in the courtyard, questioned . . .

"Deprivation of rights and all his fortune," he said loudly, "and to Siberia for hard labor for six years."

Aksinya could be seen coming out of the store by the back entrance; she had just poured kerosene and held a bottle in one hand, a funnel in the other, and silver coins in her mouth.

"But where's Papasha?" she asked, speaking thickly.

"At the station," answered the hired man. " 'By and by, when it's dark, I'll come,' says he."

And when it became known in the house that Anisim was sentenced to hard labor, the cook in the kitchen, thinking decency demanded it, suddenly began lamenting as over a corpse: "For whom have you left us, Anisim Grigorich, bright falcon . . ."

The excited dogs began barking. Varvara ran to the little window, and tossing in anguish, shouted to the cook at the top of her voice: "Enough, Stepanida, enough! Don't plague us for the sake of Christ!"

They forgot to put the samovar on; they no longer thought about anything. Lipa alone was unable to understand what it was about and kept on playing with her child.

When the old man arrived from the station, they did not

even ask him about anything. He exchanged greetings, then walked through all the rooms silently. He ate no supper.

"Should have tried influence . . ." Varvara began when they were alone. "I said you should ask that gentleman—you wouldn't listen then . . . A pardon might . . ."

"I tried!" the old man said and waved his hand. "When they sentenced Anisim, I went to the gentleman who defended him. 'Never mind,' he says, 'impossible now, too late.' And Anisim himself said the same: too late. But still, when I left the court, I hired a certain lawyer, gave him earnest money . . . I'll wait another week, then go again. It's in God's hands."

The old man walked silently through all the rooms again and when he came back to Varvara, he said: "I must be sick. In my head . . . it's clouding up. My thoughts are muddy."

He closed the door so Lipa would not hear and continued softly: "I'm uneasy about money. You remember, before his wedding at Easter, Anisim brought me some new rubles and half rubles? I hid a little sackful then, but the rest I mixed with my own . . . Once upon a time, when my Uncle Dmitri Filatich was alive, may the heavenly kingdom be his, he used to travel all the time first to Moscow, then to the Crimea for goods. He had a wife, and while he, that is, was going after goods, this wife played around with other men. There were six children. Well then, it used to happen that when he drank, my Uncle would laugh: 'I can't figure out nohow,' says he, 'which children belong to me and which to others.' A light woman, that is. Just like that, I can't figure out now which of my money's real and which is false. And it seems as if it's all false."

"Come now, God be with you!"

"I buy a ticket at the station, pay three rubles, and it starts me thinking, maybe they're false. And I'm scared. Sick, probably."

"What are you saying, we all walk in the sight of God . . . Oh-tch-tch . . ." uttered Varvara and she nodded her head. "We've got to think about this, Petrovich . . . At some unlucky moment, what will happen? You're not a young man. You'll die, and look, without you they might harm your grandson. Ai-ee, I'm scared they'll hurt Nikiforov, hurt him! A father, you might say he hasn't any, the mother's young and stupid . . . You ought to will him something, to the little one there, maybe land, that Butyokino, Petrovich, really! Think about it!" Varvara continued urging. "A pretty little boy, it's a shame! Here, go tomorrow and draw up the paper. Why wait?"

"But I'd forgotten about the little grandson," said Tsybukin. "Must say hello to him. So you say the boy's not bad? Well, then, let him grow up. God willing!"

He opened the door and beckoned Lipa with a crooked finger. She came up to him with the child in her arms.

"Lipa dear, if you need anything, ask," he said. "And eat whatever you want to, we won't grudge it so long as you stay well . . ." He made the sign of the cross over the child. "And look after my grandson. I have no son, but I've a grandson left."

Tears flowed over his cheeks; he sobbed and walked away. Later he went to bed and slept soundly after his seven sleepless nights.

VII

The old man made a rather short visit to town. Someone told Aksinya that he had been to the notary to write a will, and that he had willed Butyokino, the very place where she was baking bricks, to his grandson, Nikifor. She was told of this in the morning while the old man and Varvara were sitting near the front steps under the birch tree and having tea. She locked the store from the street side and the courtyard, gathered up all the keys she had, and flung that at the old man's feet.

"I'm not working for you folks any more!" she shouted loudly and suddenly started sobbing. "It comes out I'm no daughter-in-law of yours, but a hired girl! Everybody's laughing: 'Look,' they say, 'what a hired girl Tsybukin found himself!' I didn't hire myself to you. I'm no beggar, no serf of some kind. I've got a mother and father."

Not wiping away her tears, she stared at the old man with tear-filled eyes, rancorous, squinting with rage; her face and neck were red and strained as if she were shouting with all her might.

"I'm through being a servant!" she continued. "I'm worn out! When it comes to work, sitting in the shop day after day, sneaking out for vodka at night—that's for me, but when it comes to giving away land—that's for the convict's wife and her little devil! She's the mistress here, the lady, and I'm her servant! Give her everything, the criminal's wife, let her choke on it, I'm going home! Hire yourself another fool, you damned monsters!"

The old man had never once in his life reprimanded or punished his children and never even allowed himself the thought that someone in his family might speak roughly to him or act disrespectfully, and now he was very frightened, ran into the house, and hid behind the cupboard. Varvara was also so stunned that she was unable to get up and just waved both hands as if warding off bees.

"Aiee, what is this, holy saints?" she muttered in terror. "What is this she's shouting? Oh-tch-tch . . . People will hear! Not so loud . . . Aiee, not so loud!"

"They gave Butyokino away to the convict's wife," Aksinya continued shouting. "Give her everything now—I don't need anything from you! Devil take you! You're all one gang here! I'm fed up, I've had enough! You've robbed everybody going by, walking or riding, you cutthroats, you robbed young and old! Who's been selling vodka without a license? And what about false money? Crammed yourself sackfuls of false money —and now I'm no longer needed!"

A crowd had gathered near the wide-open gates by now and was looking in the courtyard.

"Let people look!" shouted Aksinya. "I'll shame you! You'll burn with shame for me! You'll wallow at my feet! Eh, Stepan!" She called to the deaf man. "Let's go home this minute! We'll go to my father and mother, I don't want to live with criminals! Get your things!"

The washing was hanging on lines stretched across the courtyard; Aksinya tore down her skirts and jackets, still wet, and threw them into the deaf man's arms. Then she whirled through the courtyard around the washing in a rage, tore off everything, trampled on the ground whatever did not belong to her.

"Ai-ee, holy saints, take her away!" moaned Varvara. "What is she? Give her Butyokino, give it to her for the sake of the heavenly Christ!"

"Come on, Gra-a-ma!" they were saying at the gates. "That's a Gra-a-ma for you! She really let fly—a real fury!"

Aksinya ran into the kitchen where the washing was being done. Lipa was laundering alone while the cook had gone to the river to rinse the linen. Steam rose from the tub and the kettle near the hearth, and it was stifling and dim in the kitchen from the vapor. There was still a pile of unwashed linen on the floor, and on a bench near by, kicking his red little legs, lay Nikifor, placed so that if he fell off, he would not hurt himself. Just as Aksinya came in, Lipa pulled a blouse of hers out of the pile and put it in the tub; she was already stretching her hand toward the big ladle for boiling water which stood on the table . . .

"Give it here!" said Aksinya, looking at her with hatred, and she snatched the blouse from the tub. "It's none of your business touching my linen! You're a convict's wife and should know your place and who you are!"

Lipa looked at her, dumfounded, uncomprehending, then suddenly caught the look the other threw at the baby, suddenly understood, and turned deathly pale . . .

"Taking my land, here's something for you!"

Saying this, Aksinya seized the kettle of boiling water and splashed it over Nikifor.

At this a shriek was heard such as had never been heard in Ukleyevo; it was unbelievable that a small, weak creature like Lipa could shriek like that. And it suddenly became quiet in the courtyard. Aksinya went silently to the house with her former naive smile . . . The deaf man kept walking around the courtyard holding linen in his arms, then started to hang it out again silently, without hurrying. And until the cook returned from the river, no one took the decision of going into the kitchen to see what had happened there.

◇───◇───◇───◇───◇───◇───◇───◇───◇───◇───◇

VIII

Nikifor was taken to the hospital, and toward evening he died there. Lipa did not wait for anyone to come for her, but wrapped the body in a blanket and started carrying it home.

The hospital, new, recently built, with huge windows, stood high on a hill; it was all lit by the setting sun and looked as if it were ablaze inside. A little settlement lay below. Lipa went down the road and before reaching the settlement, sat down near a small pond. A woman led a horse to drink and the horse refused.

"What more do you want?" the woman said gently, in bewilderment. "What more?"

A little boy in a red shirt sitting near the water was washing his father's boots. And there was not another soul to be seen either in the village or on the hill.

"Won't drink . . ." said Lipa, looking at the horse.

But now the woman and the little boy with the boots left, and there was no longer anyone in sight. The sun went to bed and covered itself with purple and gold brocade, and the long red and lilac clouds, spreading themselves across the sky, watched over its repose. From somewhere far away, no one knows where, a bittern called like a cow locked in a shed, a muffled, doleful sound. The cry of the mysterious bird was heard every evening, but no one knew what it was or where it lived. At the top of the hill, by the hospital, in the bushes by the pond itself, beyond the village and all around the field, the nightingales poured forth. The cuckoo counted out someone's remaining years, became completely tangled in the account, and started over again. In the pond, angrily straining themselves, the frogs called to one another, and one could even make out the words: "You're a this! You're a that!" What a din there was! All these creatures seemed to be shouting and singing purposely so that no one would sleep this spring evening, so that all, even the angry frogs, would cherish and enjoy every minute: for life is only given once! The silver half moon glowed in the sky; there were many stars. Lipa did not realize how long she had been sitting by the pond, but when she got up and went on, people were already sleeping in the village and there were no lights. It was probably twenty versts to home, but she lacked the strength and had no idea of which way to go; the moon shone first ahead, then on the right, and the same cuckoo kept crying, in a hoarsened voice now, with a laugh, as if mocking: "Ai-ee, look, you've gone off the road!" Lipa walked rapidly, the kerchief slipped from her head . . . She looked at the sky and wondered where her little boy's soul was now: was it following behind her or was it being carried up above near the stars, and was it already no longer thinking of its mother? Oh, how lonely it is in the fields at night in the midst of this singing when you yourself are unable to sing, in the midst of these continuous cries of joy, when you yourself cannot rejoice, when from the heavens, the moon is watching, lonely too, indifferent to everything: whether it's spring or winter now, whether people are alive or dead . . . When there is grief in the soul, it is hard to be alone. If only her mother, Praskovya, were with her; or Crutch, or the cook, or some peasant or other!

"Boo-oo!" cried the bittern. "Boo-oo!"

And suddenly a human voice was clearly audible: "Harness up, Vavila!"

Ahead, right on the road, a campfire was burning; there were no flames left, only red embers glowing. The horses could be heard munching. In the darkness, two carts stood out—one with a barrel, the other, lower, with sacks and two men: one leading the horse to be harnessed, the other standing motionless near the fire, hands behind his back. Near the carts, two dogs had begun snarling. The man leading the horse stopped and said: "Sounds like someone coming down the road."

"Quiet, Sharik!" the other shouted to the dog.

And from his voice one could tell he was an old man. Lipa stopped and said: "Help, in God's name!"

The old man went up to her and answered after a hesitation: "Greetings!"

"Your dog don't snap, Granpa?"

"It's all right, go ahead. He won't touch you."

"I was at the hospital," said Lipa after a pause. "My little boy died there. Now I'm bringing him home."

The old man must have found this unpleasant to hear because he stepped away and said hurriedly: "It's all right, dear. It's God's will. You're dawdling, lad!" he said turning to his companion. "Hurry up!"

"Your yoke isn't here," said the lad. "Nowhere to be seen."

"Oh you, Vavila . . ."

The old man picked up a coal and blew—it lighted only his eyes and nose. While they were looking for the yoke, he came up to Lipa with the light and looked at her, and his look expressed compassion and tenderness.

"You're a mother," he said. "Every mother feels for her child."

And at this he sighed and nodded his head. Vavila threw something on the fire, trampled on it—and everything immediately became very dark; visibility vanished, and as before there was only the field, the sky with the stars, and the birds making noise, keeping one another from sleeping. And a corn crake was crying in what seemed to be the very place where the fire had been.

But in a minute, the carts were visible again, and the old man, and lanky Vavila. The wagons creaked as they drove onto the road.

"You're holy men?" Lipa asked the old man.

"No, we're from Firsanov."

"You looked at me a bit ago, and my heart melted. And the lad's gentle. And I thought: 'They're holy men, probably.' "

"You got far to go?"

"To Ukleyevo."

"Get in. We're driving to Kuzmenko. There you go straight, we go left."

Vavila got in the cart with the barrel; the old man and Lipa got in the other. They went at a walk, Vavila in front.

"My little boy suffered the whole day," said Lipa. "Looks with his little eyes and is quiet and wants to talk and can't. Lord our Father, heavenly Tsaritsa! I was so took with grief I fell on the floor. I'm standing up and fall near the bed. And tell me, Granpa, why does a little boy suffer before he dies? When a grownup suffers, a man or woman, his sins are forgiven, but why a little boy when he hasn't any sins? Why?"

"Ah, who knows!" answered the old man.

They went on a half hour in silence.

"One can't know everything, why and how," said the old man. "A bird's given two wings, not four, because it can fly on two; so a man's not given to know everything, but just a half or a quarter. As much as he has to know to live—that's as much as he knows."

"I'm easier walking, Granpa. My heart's quaking so now."

"Never mind. Sit down."

The old man yawned and made the sign of the cross over his mouth.

"Never mind . . ." he repeated. "Your grief is half a grief. Life is long—something good will still happen, too, and bad—everything. Great Mother Russia!" he said, glancing to both sides. "I've been all over Russia and seen everything in it, and you can believe my words, dear. There'll be good, there'll be bad. I went to Siberia as a pioneer on foot, was on the Amur, in the Altas, and I emigrated to Siberia; I worked the land there, then got homesick for Mother Russia and came back to my native village. Back to Russia on foot; and I remember, we were crossing on a ferry and I was skinny, skinny, all in rags, lame, frozen, sucking a crust of bread, and a traveling gentleman of some sort there on the ferry—if he's dead may the heavenly kingdom be his—looks at me with pity and his tears fall. 'Eh,' he says, 'your bread's black, your days are black . . .' And I came home, as they say, to neither house nor home; I had a wife, but she was left in Siberia, buried. So, I work as a farmhand. Well then? I tell you, afterward there was bad and there was better. Look, I don't want to die, dear, I'd still live another twenty years; which means there was more good than bad. Great

Mother Russia!" he said and again looked to the side and glanced around.

"Granpa," asked Lipa, "when a person dies, how many days does his soul walk on earth afterward?"

"Ah, who knows! Here, ask Vavila—he went to school. They teach everything now. Vavila!" called the old man.

"Ah!"

"Vavila, when a person dies, how many days does his soul walk on earth?"

Vavila stopped the horse and then answered: "Nine days. My Uncle Kiril died and then his soul lived in our hut for thirteen days."

"How do you know?"

"It tapped inside the stove for thirteen days."

"Well, all right. Move on," said the old man, and it was obvious that he believed none of this.

Near Kuzmenko the carts turned onto the highroad while Lipa continued on foot. It was already light. When she descended into the ravine, the huts of Ukleyevo and the church were hidden in fog. It was cold, and it seemed to her as if the very same cuckoo were crying continuously.

When Lipa returned home, the cattle had not yet been driven out; everyone was asleep. She sat down on the steps and waited. The old man was the first to come out; immediately, at the first glance, he understood what had happened; for a long time he was unable to utter a word and just smacked his lips.

"Eh, Lipa," he pronounced, "you didn't look after my grandson . . ."

They woke up Varvara. She clasped her hands and sobbed, and immediately began dressing the child.

"And the little boy was a pretty little one . . ." she added. "Oh-tch-tch . . . He was a little boy and she didn't look after him, foolish girl . . ."

They held a Requiem Mass in the morning and in the evening. The next day he was buried, and after the burial, the guests and the clergy ate a lot and as greedily as if they had not eaten for a long time. Lipa served the table, and the priest, raising a fork with a salted mushroom on it, told her: "Don't grieve about the child. The heavenly kingdom is for the likes of him."

And it was only when they were leaving that Lipa really understood that Nikifor no longer existed and would not; understood and began sobbing. And she did not know what

room to go to to cry, for she felt she no longer had a place
in this house after the boy's death, that she had no reason to
be there, and was superfluous; and the others felt this too.

"Well, what are you wailing about there?" Aksinya suddenly
shouted, appearing at the door; she was entirely dressed in
new clothes for the funeral and was powdering herself. "Shut
up!"

Lipa wanted to stop but could not, and sobbed still louder.

"D'you hear?" Aksinya shouted and stamped her foot in
intense rage. "Who'm I talking to? Get out of the house and
don't you put a foot here again, you convict's wife! Get out!"

"Come, come, come! . . ." fussed the old man. "Aksinya
dear, calm yourself, Little Mother . . . She's crying, it's
understandable . . . her child died . . ."

"Understandable . . ." Aksinya mocked him. "Let her
spend the night, but tomorrow don't let a shadow of her be
here! Understandable! . . ." she mocked him again and,
starting to laugh, went toward the store.

Early the following morning, Lipa walked to her mother's
in Torguyevo.

IX

The roof of the store and the door are painted and gleam
like new now; gay little geraniums bloom at the windows as
before, and what happened in the house and courtyard of
the Tsybukins three years ago is almost forgotten now.

Old man Grigory Petrovich is the master in name as before;
in reality, everything has shifted into Aksinya's hands; she
does the selling and buying, and nothing can be done without
her agreement. The brick factory is going well; because
bricks are in demand for the railroad, their price has gone
up to twenty-four rubles a thousand; women and girls cart
bricks to the station and load the cars, and are paid a quarter
of a ruble each day for this work.

Aksinya has gone into partnership with the Khrymins and
their factory is now called "Khrymin Sons and Co." They
opened a tavern near the station, and the expensive harmonica
is no longer played in the factory, but in this tavern; the chief
of the postal division, who also started a business of some

sort, often goes here, and the station chief, too. The Khrymin Sons gave deaf Stepan a gold watch which he takes out of his pocket and puts to his ear constantly.

In the village they say Aksinya has acquired great power; and it is true that when she drives to her factory in the morning with a naive smile, beautiful, happy, and later, when she issues orders in the factory, a great power can be felt in her. Everyone is afraid of her at home, in the village, and in the factory. When she goes to the post office, the head of the postal division jumps up and says to her: "I humbly beg you to sit down, Kseniya Abramovna!"

One landowner, a dandy in an undercoat of fine broadcloth and high, patent leather boots, already middle-aged, was so carried away by his talk with her while selling her a horse once, that he brought the price down as low as she wanted. He held her hand for a long time, and looking at her merry, sly, naive eyes, he said: "I'm ready to do anything to please a woman like you, Kseniya Abramovna. Just tell me, when can we see each other without anyone's disturbing us?"

"But whenever you like!"

And after this, the middle-aged dandy drove to the tavern almost every day to drink beer. The beer was terrible, bitter as wormwood. The landowner shook his head, but drank it.

Old man Tsybukin no longer interferes in the business. He carries no money with him because he is totally unable to distinguish genuine from counterfeit, but he says nothing, telling no one about this weakness of his. He has become rather forgetful, and if he is not given food, does not ask for it himself; the family is used to having dinner without him now, and Varvara often remarks: "Father went to bed without eating again last night."

And she speaks with indifference because she is used to it. For some reason, he goes around in his fur coat winter and summer alike, and only on very hot days does not go out and sits at home. Usually, after putting on his fur coat and turning up the collar, wrapping himself up, he walks through the village along the road to the station or sits from morning to evening at the little shop near the church gates. Sits without moving. Passers-by bow to him, but he does not respond, for he dislikes peasants as before. When asked something, he answers completely rationally and politely, but briefly.

There is a rumor in the village that his daughter-in-law

has chased him out of his own house and gives him nothing to eat, and that he feeds himself on charity; some are glad, others sorry.

Varvara has become still plumper and fairer and does good deeds as before, and Aksinya does not bother her. She has so much jam now that they are unable to eat it up before the new berries are ripe; it turns to sugar, and Varvara almost cries, not knowing what to do with it.

They have begun to forget about Anisim. Once a letter came from him, written in stanzas on a large sheet of paper in the form of a petition, still in the same magnificent handwriting. Evidently his friend Samorodov was serving his sentence along with him. Below the stanzas, in unsightly, barely legible handwriting, was a single line: "I'm always sick here, I'm miserable, help for the sake of Christ."

Once—it was on a clear fall day toward evening—old man Tsybukin was sitting near the church gates with the collar of his fur coat turned up and only his nose and the peak of his cap visible. At the other end of the long bench sat Elizarov, the master carpenter, and next to him, the school watchman, Yakov, an old man of seventy with no teeth. Crutch and the watchman were talking.

"Children should give their old folks food and drink . . . honor thy father and mother," said Yakov with annoyance, "while she, his son's wife, has chased her father-in-law out of his own house. The old man's given nothing to eat and drink—where can he go? It's his third day without eating."

"His third day!" marveled Crutch.

"There he sits like that, always silent. Weakened. But why keep silent? Take it to court—she won't get praise in court."

"Who was praised in court?" asked Crutch, not having heard distinctly.

"What?"

"The woman's not bad, hard-working. In their business you can't get along without it . . . without sin, that is . . ."

"From his own house," continued Yakov with annoyance. "You earn your own house and then out you go. Look-a-here, she's a fine one, think of it! A pla-a-ague!"

Tsybukin listened without moving.

"Your own house or someone else's, it's all the same as long as it's warm and the women don't fight . . ." said Crutch and laughed. "In my young days, I often felt sorry for my own Nastasiya. She was a quiet little woman. And it was always: 'Buy a house, Makarich! Buy a house, Makarich! Buy a horse, Makarich!' She was dying, but kept saying, 'Buy yourself a racing droshky so you don't have to walk.' And all I ever bought her was gingerbread, nothing else."

"The husband's deaf, stupid," continued Yakov, not listening to Crutch; "a downright blockhead, just like a goose. How could he understand anything! You have to hit a goose on the head with a stick—otherwise he doesn't understand."

Crutch stood up to go home to the factory. Yakov stood up too, and the two walked off together, still talking. When they had gone fifty paces away, old man Tsybukin also stood up and dragged himself after them, stepping with hesitation as if on slippery ice.

The village was already sinking into evening twilight, and the sun was shining only at the top of the road which ran like a snake along the slope from top to bottom. The old women were returning from the woods with the children, carrying baskets of yellow and brown mushrooms. The women and girls were coming in a flock from the station where they had been loading railroad cars with bricks, and their cheeks and noses were covered with red brick dust up to their eyes. They were singing. In front of them all walked Lipa singing in a shrill voice and trilling, looking up at the sky as if glorying and giving praise that the day, thank God, had ended and one could rest. Her mother, Praskovya, the charwoman, was in the crowd, walking with a bundle in her hand and breathing heavily, as always.

"Greetings, Makarich!" said Lipa on seeing Crutch. "Greetings, dear friend!"

"Greetings, Lipa dear!" Crutch rejoiced. "Women, girls, won't you fall in love with the rich carpenter! Ho! Ho! My little children, little children." (Crutch sobbed.) "My beloved little pegs."

Crutch and Yakov walked farther on and could be heard talking. After them, the crowd came upon old man Tsybukin and suddenly became very quiet. Lipa and Praskovya fell behind a little, and when the old man came even with them, Lipa bowed low and said: "Greetings, Grigory Petrovich!"

And the mother also bowed. The old man stopped, and saying nothing, looked at them both; his lips trembled and his eyes were full of tears. Lipa fetched a piece of meat pie with *kasha* out of her mother's bundle and gave it to him. He took it and began eating.

The sun had gone down now; the ray of light went out at the top of the road. It grew dark and chilly. Lipa and Praskovya walked on and kept crossing themselves for a long time after.

CHRONOLOGY

1860   January 17/29: * Anton Chekhov born in Taganrog.

1876   The Chekhov family moves to Moscow, but Anton is left behind.

1879   Graduates from the Taganrog high school, and later goes to Moscow and enrols in the School of Medicine of the University there.

1880   First appearance in print: a short comic story in the magazine *The Dragonfly*.

1884   Graduates from the University, takes up medical practice, and publishes his first small collection of stories, *The Tales of Melpomene*.

1885   December: Visits St. Petersburg and meets Grigorovich and Suvorin.

1886   January: *Motley Stories,* a volume of short stories.
February: Begins contributing to *Novoe Vremya.*

1887   Two more collections of stories published: *In the Twilight* and *Innocent Discourses.*
November 19/December 1: First performance of *Ivanov* in Moscow.

1888   March: "The Steppe" published in *Severny Vestnik* (*The Northern Messenger*)—Chekhov's first appearance in a respectable literary monthly.
May-June: *Stories,* Chekhov's fifth volume of stories, published by Suvorin.
July: Travels with Suvorin in the Caucasus.
October: Awarded one-half of the Pushkin Prize by the Russian Academy of Sciences for his collection of stories *In the Twilight.*

1890   Leaves Moscow for Sakhalin on April 21/May 3 and returns to Moscow on December 8/20.

1891   March-April: Travels with Suvorin in Austria, Italy, and France.

1892   January-February: Goes to Nizhny-Novgorod and Voronezh to organize famine relief work.

* All the exact dates are given according to both calendars, Russian and Western.

February: Acquires a small estate near the village of Melikhovo, in the Serpukhov District, and moves there with his parents and sister.

Summer: Takes an active part in fighting a cholera epidemic in Melikhovo and around it.

Begins contributing to *Russkaya Mysl* (*Russian Thought*), one of the leading progressive monthlies, which had earlier censured him for his "lack of ideas." "Ward No. 6" published in the November issue of *Russian Thought*.

1894 September-October: Visits Suvorin in Crimea, and later travels to Austria (Vienna, Abbazia), Italy (Venice, Milan), and France (Nice, Paris).

1895 June: *The Island of Sakhalin,* previously serialized in *Russian Thought,* published in book form.

December 14/26: Makes the acquaintance of Ivan Bunin.

1896 October 17/29: The première of *The Gull* in St. Petersburg is a complete fiasco.

1897 March: Has a severe pulmonary hemorrhage and spends several weeks in a Moscow clinic.

September: Goes to Nice and remains there until next April.

1898 April: Stops in Paris on the way back to Russia.

September: First meeting with Olga Knipper at a rehearsal of *The Gull.* Leaves for the Crimea and settles in Yalta.

October 12/24: Chekhov's father dies.

November: First exchange of letters with Maxim Gorky.

December 17/29: First performance of *The Gull* by the Moscow Art Theater.

1899 January 26/February 7: Sells the copyright of all his works to the St. Petersburg publisher A. Marks for 75,000 rubles. (Ten volumes of *Collected Works* were published in 1899–1901.)

March 19/31: First meeting with Maxim Gorky in Yalta.

August: The Melikhovo estate sold.

October 26/November 7: *Uncle Vanya* performed by the Moscow Art Theater.

1900 January: Elected Honorary Fellow of the Imperial Russian Academy of Sciences.

1901 January 31/February 13: *The Three Sisters* produced by the Moscow Art Theater.

May 25/June 7: Marries Olga Knipper.

1902 Resigns his fellowship in the Academy of Sciences in protest against the cancellation of Gorky's election to it.

1903 December: "Betrothed," the last story to be written by

Chekhov, published in *Zhurnal dlya Vsekh* (*Everybody's Magazine*).

1904   January 17/30: Present at the first performance of *The Cherry Orchard* by the Moscow Art Theater.

June 3/16: Leaves for Badenweiler.

July 2/15: At 3 A.M. dies in the Hotel Sommer at Badenweiler.

BIBLIOGRAPHY

~~~~~~

Most of Chekhov's works—the exceptions are some early stories, sketches, and articles, and the book on Sakhalin—have been translated into English and published either separately or in collections, or in his *Works,* translated by Constance Garnett. There are also various selections from his letters (of which there are now eight volumes in Russian). A guide to such translations through 1949 will be found in the Heifetz bibliography listed below, but there have been many additions since then. The list of biographical and critical works given here has no claim to completeness.

BIBLIOGRAPHICAL

HEIFETZ, ANNA. *Chekhov in English: A List of Works by and About Him.* Edited and with a Foreword by Avrahm Yarmolinsky. New York, 1947.

REMINISCENCES

AVILOV, LYDIA. *Chekhov in My Life.* Translated and with an Introduction by D. Magarshack. London, 1950.

GORKY, MAXIM. *Reminiscences of Anton Chekhov.* Contains Gorky's reminiscences, the Gorky-Chekhov correspondence, and entries on Chekhov in Gorky's diary, pp. 69–127. New York, 1946.

GORKY, MAXIM, KUPRIN, ALEXANDER, and BUNIN, IVAN. *Reminiscences of Anton Chekhov.* Translated by S. S. Koteliansky and L. Woolf. New York, 1921.

KOTELIANSKY, S. S. (ed.). *Anton Tchekhov: Literary and Theatrical Reminiscences.* London, 1927.

BIOGRAPHICAL AND CRITICAL

BAKSHY, A. *The Path of the Modern Russian Stage and Other Essays.* London, [1916].

BRUFORD, W. H. *Anton Chekhov.* New Haven, 1957.

———. *Chekhov and His Russia: A Sociological Study.* London, 1947.

CHUKOVSKY, K. *Chekhov the Man*. Translated by Pauline Rose. London, 1945.

EEKMAN, T. (ed.). *Anton Čechov: 1860–1960. Some Essays.* Essays in English, French, German, and Russian. Leiden, 1960.

EHRENBURG, I. *Chekhov, Stendhal and Other Essays*. Translated by A. Bostock and Y. Kapp. London, 1962.

ELTON, O. *Chekhov*. The Taylorian Lecture. Oxford, 1929.

ERMILOV, V. *Anton Pavlovich Chekhov: 1860–1904*. Moscow, n.d. [1954?].

FARRELL, J. T. "On the Letters of Anton Chekhov," in *The League of Frightened Philistines and Other Papers*. New York, [1945].

GARNETT, E. "Tchehov and His Art," *The Quarterly Review*, CCXXXVI (1921), 257–269.

GERHARDI, W. *Anton Chekhov: A Critical Study*. London, 1923.

HINGLEY, R. *Chekhov: A Biographical and Critical Study*. London, 1950.

LAVRIN, J. "Chekhov and Maupassant," in *Studies in European Literature*. London, 1929, pp. 156–192.

MAGARSHACK, D. *Chekhov: A Life*. London and New York, 1952.
———. *Chekhov as a Dramatist*. New York, 1952.

MAUGHAM, W. SOMERSET. Introduction to *Tellers of Tales*. New York, 1939, pp. xxi–xxix.

MEISTER, CHARLES W. "Chekhov's Reception in England and America," *American Slavic and East European Review*, XII (1953), 109–121.

MIRSKY, D. S. *A History of Russian Literature*. New York, 1949.
———. "Chekhov and the English," *Monthly Criterion*, VI, 292–309.

MURRY, J. MIDDLETON. "Thoughts on Tchehov," in *Aspects of Literature*. London and New York, 1920, pp. 76–80.

NEMIROVICH-DANCHENKO, V. *My Life in the Russian Theatre*. Translated by John Cournos, Boston, 1936.

NÉMIROVSKY, I. *A Life of Chekhov*. Translated by E. de Mauny. London, 1950.

SCHNEIDER, E. "Katherine Mansfield and Chekhov," *Modern Language Notes*, L (1935), 394–397.

SHAW, BERNARD. Preface to *Heartbreak House*. In various editions of *Collected Works*.

SHESTOV, L. *Anton Chekhov and Other Essays*. Translated by S. S. Koteliansky and J. M. Murry. Dublin & London, 1916. (Also: *Penultimate Words and Other Essays*. Boston, 1916.)

STANISLAVSKY, K. *My Life in Art*. Translated by J. J. Robbins. Boston, 1924.

STRUVE, G. "Chekhov in Communist Censorship," *Slavonic and East European Review*, XXXII (1955), 327–341.

———. "On Chekhov's Craftsmanship: The Anatomy of a Story," *Slavic Review*, XX (1961), 465–476.

THOMS, H. *Anton Chekhov—Physician and Literary Artist.* New Haven, 1922.

TOUMANOVA-ANDRONIKOVA, N. *Anton Chekhov: The Voice of Twilight Russia.* New York, 1937.

WOOLF, VIRGINIA. "The Russian Point of View," in *The Common Reader.* London, 1925; New York, 1948.

RUSSIAN LITERATURE
IN NORTON PAPERBOUND EDITIONS